Fifty Years

OF THE AMERICAN
SHORT STORY

IN TWO VOLUMES

VOLUME II

Fifty Years

OF THE AMERICAN

SHORT STORY

From the O. Henry Awards

1919—1970

Edited and with an introduction by
WILLIAM ABRAHAMS

DOUBLEDAY & COMPANY, INC.
Garden City, New York
1970

Contents

Everything That Rises
Must Converge

Her doctor had told Julian's mother that she must lose twenty pounds on account of her blood pressure, so on Wednesday nights Julian had to take her downtown on the bus for a reducing class at the Y. The reducing class was designed for working girls over fifty, who weighed from 165 to 200 pounds. His mother was one of the slimmer ones, but she said ladies did not tell their age or weight. She would not ride on the buses by herself at night since they had been integrated, and because the reducing class was one of her few pleasures, necessary for her health, and *free,* she said Julian could at least put himself out to take her, considering all she did for him. Julian did not like to consider all she did for him, but every Wednesday night he braced himself and took her.

She was almost ready to go, standing before the hall mirror, putting on her hat, while he, his hands behind him, appeared pinned to the door frame, waiting like Saint Sebastian for the arrows to begin piercing him. The hat was new and had cost her seven dollars and a half. She kept saying, "Maybe I shouldn't have paid that for it. No, I shouldn't have. I'll take it off and return it tomorrow. I shouldn't have bought it."

Julian raised his eyes to heaven. "Yes, you should have bought it," he said. "Put it on and let's go." It was a hideous hat. A purple velvet flap came down on one side of it and stood up on the other; the rest of it was green and looked like a cushion with the stuffing out. He decided it was less comical than jaunty and pathetic. Everything that gave her pleasure was small and depressed him.

She lifted the hat one more time and set it down slowly on top of her head. Two wings of gray hair protruded on either side of her florid face, but her eyes, sky-blue, were as innocent and untouched by experience as they must have been when she was ten. Were it not that she was a widow who had struggled fiercely to feed and clothe and put him through school and who was supporting him still, "until he got on his feet," she might have been a little girl that he had to take to town.

"It's all right, it's all right," he said. "Let's go." He opened the door himself and started down the walk to get her going. The sky was a dying violet and the houses stood out darkly against it, bulbous liver-colored monstrosities of a uniform ugliness though no two were alike. Since this had been a fashionable neighborhood forty years ago, his mother persisted in thinking they did well to have an apartment in it. Each house had a narrow collar of dirt around it in which sat, usually, a grubby child. Julian walked with his hands in his pockets, his head down and thrust forward and his eyes glazed with the determination to make himself completely numb during the time he would be sacrificed to her pleasure.

The door closed and he turned to find the dumpy figure, surmounted by the atrocious hat, coming toward him. "Well," she said, "you only live once and paying a little more for it, I at least won't meet myself coming and going."

"Some day I'll start making money," Julian said gloomily—he knew he never would—"and you can have one of those jokes whenever you take the fit." But first they would move. He visualized a place where the nearest neighbors would be three miles away on either side.

"I think you're doing fine," she said, drawing on her gloves. "You've only been out of school a year. Rome wasn't built in a day."

She was one of the few members of the Y reducing class who arrived in hat and gloves and who had a son who had been to college. "It takes time," she said, "and the world is in such a mess. This hat looked better on me than any of the others, though when she brought it out I said, 'Take that thing back. I wouldn't have it on my head,' and she said, 'Now wait till you see it on,' and when she put it on me, I said, 'We-ull,' and she said, 'If you ask me, that hat does something for you and you do something for the hat, and besides,' she said, 'with that hat, you won't meet yourself coming and going.'"

Julian thought he could have stood his lot better if she had been selfish, if she had been an old hag who drank and screamed at him. He walked along, saturated in depression, as if in the midst of his martyrdom he had lost his faith. Catching sight of his long, hopeless, irritated face, she stopped suddenly with a grief-stricken look, and pulled back on his arm. "Wait on me," she said. "I'm going back to the house and take this thing off and tomorrow I'm going to return it. I was out of my head. I can pay the gas bill with that seven-fifty."

He caught her arm in a vicious grip. "You are not going to take it back," he said. "I like it."

"Well," she said, "I don't think I ought . . ."

"Shut up and enjoy it," he muttered, more depressed than ever.

"With the world in the mess it's in," she said, "it's a wonder we can enjoy anything. I tell you, the bottom rail is on the top."

Julian sighed.

"Of course," she said, "if you know who you are, you can go anywhere." She said this every time he took her to the reducing class. "Most of them in it are not our kind of people," she said, "but I can be gracious to anybody. I know who I am."

"They don't give a damn for your graciousness," Julian said savagely. "Knowing who you are is good for one generation only. You haven't the foggiest idea where you stand now or who you are."

She stopped and allowed her eyes to flash at him. "I most certainly do know who I am," she said, "and if you don't know who you are, I'm ashamed of you."

"Oh hell," Julian said.

"Your great-grandfather was a former governor of this state," she said. "Your grandfather was a prosperous landowner. Your grandmother was a Godhigh."

"Will you look around you," he said tensely, "and see where you are now?" and he swept his arm jerkily out to indicate the neighborhood, which the growing darkness at least made less dingy.

"You remain what you are," she said. "Your great-grandfather had a plantation and two hundred slaves."

"There are no more slaves," he said irritably.

"They were better off when they were," she said. He groaned to see that she was off on that topic. She rolled onto it every few days like a train on an open track. He knew every stop, every junction, every swamp along the way, and knew the exact point at which her conclusion would roll majestically into the station: "It's ridiculous. It's simply not realistic. They should rise, yes, but on their own side of the fence."

"Let's skip it," Julian said.

"The ones I feel sorry for," she said, "are the ones that are half white. They're tragic."

"Will you skip it?"

"Suppose we were half white. We would certainly have mixed feelings."

"I have mixed feelings now," he groaned.

"Well let's talk about something pleasant," she said. "I remember going to Grandpa's when I was a little girl. Then the house had double stairways that went up to what was really the second floor —all the cooking was done on the first. I used to like to stay down in the kitchen on account of the way the walls smelled. I would sit with my nose pressed against the plaster and take deep breaths. Actually the place belonged to the Godhighs but your grandfather Chestny paid the mortgage and saved it for them. They were in reduced circumstances," she said, "but reduced or not, they never forgot who they were."

"Doubtless that decayed mansion reminded them," Julian muttered. He never spoke of it without contempt or thought of it without longing. He had seen it once when he was a child before it had been sold. The double stairways had rotted and been torn down. Negroes were living in it. But it remained in his mind as his mother had known it. It appeared in his dreams regularly. He would stand on the wide porch, listening to the rustle of oak leaves, then wander through the high-ceilinged hall into the parlor that opened onto it and gaze at the worn rugs and faded draperies. It occurred to him that it was he, not she, who could have appreciated it. He preferred its threadbare elegance to anything he could name and it was because of it that all the neighborhoods they had lived in had been a torment to him—whereas she had hardly known the difference. She called her insensitivity "being adjustable."

"And I remember the old darky who was my nurse, Caroline. There was no better person in the world. I've always had a great respect for my colored friends," she said. "I'd do anything in the world for them and they'd . . ."

"Will you for God's sake get off that subject?" Julian said. When he got on a bus by himself, he made it a point to sit down beside a Negro, in reparation as it were for his mother's sins.

"You're mighty touchy tonight," she said. "Do you feel all right?"

"Yes I feel all right," he said. "Now lay off."

She pursed her lips. "Well, you certainly are in a vile humor," she observed. "I just won't speak to you at all."

They had reached the bus stop. There was no bus in sight and Julian, his hands still jammed in his pockets and his head thrust forward, scowled down the empty street. The frustration of having to wait on the bus as well as ride on it began to creep up his neck like a hot hand. The presence of his mother was borne in upon him as she gave a pained sigh. He looked at her bleakly. She was holding herself very erect under the preposterous hat, wearing it like a banner of her imaginary dignity. There was in him an evil urge to break her spirit. He suddenly unloosened his tie and pulled it off and put it in his pocket.

She stiffened. "Why must you look like *that* when you take me to town?" she said. "Why must you deliberately embarrass me?"

"If you'll never learn where you are," he said, "you can at least learn where I am."

"You look like a—thug," she said.

"Then I must be one," he murmured.

"I'll just go home," she said. "I will not bother you. If you can't do a little thing like that for me . . ."

Rolling his eyes upward, he put his tie back on. "Restored to my class," he muttered. He thrust his face toward her and hissed, "True culture is in the mind, the *mind*," he said, and tapped his head, "the mind."

"It's in the heart," she said, "and in how you do things and how you do things is because of who you *are*."

"Nobody in the damn bus cares who you are."

"I care who I am," she said icily.

The lighted bus appeared on top of the next hill and as it approached, they moved out into the street to meet it. He put his hand under her elbow and hoisted her up on the creaking step. She entered with a little smile, as if she were going into a drawing room where everyone had been waiting for her. While he put in the tokens, she sat down on one of the broad front seats for three which faced the aisle. A thin woman with protruding teeth and long yellow hair was sitting on the end of it. His mother moved up beside her and left room for Julian beside herself. He sat down and looked at the floor across the aisle where a pair of thin feet in red and white canvas sandals were planted.

His mother immediately began a general conversation meant to attract anyone who felt like talking. "Can it get any hotter?" she said and removed from her purse a folding fan, black with a Japanese scene on it, which she began to flutter before her.

"I reckon it might could," the woman with the protruding teeth said, "but I know for a fact my apartment couldn't get no hotter."

"It must get the afternoon sun," his mother said. She sat forward and looked up and down the bus. It was half filled. Everybody was white. "I see we have the bus to ourselves," she said. Julian cringed.

"For a change," said the woman across the aisle, the owner of the red and white canvas sandals. "I come on one the other day and they were thick as fleas—up front and all through."

"The world is in a mess everywhere," his mother said. "I don't know how we've let it get in this fix."

"What gets my goat is all those boys from good families stealing automobile tires," the woman with the protruding teeth said. "I told my boy, I said you may not be rich but you been raised right and if I ever catch you in any such mess, they can send you on to the reformatory. Be exactly where you belong."

"Training tells," his mother said. "Is your boy in high school?"

"Ninth grade," the woman said.

"My son just finished college last year. He wants to write but he's selling typewriters until he gets started," his mother said.

The woman leaned forward and peered at Julian. He threw her such a malevolent look that she subsided against the seat. On the floor across the aisle there was an abandoned newspaper. He got up and got it and opened it out in front of him. His mother discreetly continued the conversation in a lower tone but the woman across the aisle said in a loud voice, "Well that's nice. Selling typewriters is close to writing. He can go right from one to the other."

"I tell him," his mother said, "that Rome wasn't built in a day."

Behind the newspaper Julian was withdrawing into the inner compartment of his mind where he spent most of his time. This was a kind of mental bubble in which he established himself when he could not bear to be a part of what was going on around him. From it he could see out and judge but in it he was safe from any kind of penetration from without. It was the only place where he felt free of the general idiocy of his fellows. His mother had never entered it but from it he could see her with absolute clarity.

The old lady was clever enough and he thought that if she had started from any of the right premises, more might have been expected of her. She lived according to the laws of her own fantasy world, outside of which he had never seen her set foot. The law of it was to sacrifice herself for him after she had first created the necessity to do so by making a mess of things. If he had permitted her sacrifices, it was only because her lack of foresight had made them necessary. All of her life had been a struggle to act like a Chestny without the Chestny goods, and to give him everything she thought a Chestny ought to have; but since, said she, it was fun to struggle, why complain? And when you had won, as she had won, what fun to look back on the hard times! He could not forgive her that she had enjoyed the struggle and that she thought *she* had won.

What she meant when she said she had won was that she had brought him up successfully and had sent him to college and that he had turned out so well—good looking (her teeth had gone un-filled so that his could be straightened), intelligent (he realized he was too intelligent to be a success), and with a future ahead of him (there was of course no future ahead of him). She excused his gloominess on the grounds that he was still growing up and his radical ideas on his lack of practical experience. She said he didn't yet know a thing about "life," that he hadn't even entered the real world —when already he was as disenchanted with it as a man of fifty.

The further irony of all this was that in spite of her, he had turned out so well. In spite of going to only a third-rate college, he had, on his own initiative, come out with a first-rate education; in spite of growing up dominated by a small mind, he had ended up with a large one; in spite of all her foolish views, he was free of prejudice and unafraid to face facts. Most miraculous of all, in-stead of being blinded by love for her as she was for him, he had cut himself emotionally free of her and could see her with com-plete objectivity. He was not dominated by mother.

The bus stopped with a sudden jerk and shook him from his medi-tation. A woman from the back lurched forward with little steps and barely escaped falling in his newspaper as she righted herself. She got off and a large Negro got on. Julian kept his paper lowered to watch. It gave him a certain satisfaction to see injustice in daily op-eration. It confirmed his view that with a few exceptions there was no one worth knowing within a radius of three hundred miles. The Negro was well dressed and carried a briefcase. He looked around and then sat down on the other end of the seat where the woman with the red and white canvas sandals was sitting. He immediately unfolded a newspaper and obscured himself behind it. Julian's mother's elbow at once prodded insistently into his ribs. "Now you see why I won't ride on these buses by myself," she whispered.

The woman with the red and white canvas sandals had risen at the same time the Negro sat down and had gone further back in the bus and taken the seat of the woman who had got off. His mother leaned forward and cast her an approving look.

Julian rose, crossed the aisle, and sat down in the place of the woman with the canvas sandals. From this position, he looked se-renely across at his mother. Her face had turned an angry red. He stared at her, making his eyes the eyes of a stranger. He felt his ten-sion suddenly lift as if he had openly declared war on her.

He would have liked to get in conversation with the Negro and to talk with him about art or politics or any subject that would be above the comprehension of those around them, but the man remained entrenched behind his paper. He was either ignoring the change of seating or had never noticed it. There was no way for Julian to convey his sympathy.

His mother kept her eyes fixed reproachfully on his face. The woman with the protruding teeth was looking at him avidly as if he were a type of monster new to her.

"Do you have a light?" he asked the Negro.

Without looking away from his paper, the man reached in his pocket and handed him a packet of matches.

"Thanks," Julian said. For a moment he held the matches foolishly. A No SMOKING sign looked down upon him from over the door. This alone would not have deterred him; he had no cigarettes. He had quit smoking some months before because he could not afford it. "Sorry," he muttered and handed back the matches. The Negro lowered the paper and gave him an annoyed look. He took the matches and raised the paper again.

His mother continued to gaze at him but she did not take advantage of his momentary discomfort. Her eyes retained their battered look. Her face seemed to be unnaturally red, as if her blood pressure had risen. Julian allowed no glimmer of sympathy to show on his face. Having got the advantage, he wanted desperately to keep it and carry it through. He would have liked to teach her a lesson that would last her a while, but there seemed no way to continue the point. The Negro refused to come out from behind his paper.

Julian folded his arms and looked stolidly before him, facing her but as if he did not see her, as if he had ceased to recognize her existence. He visualized a scene in which, the bus having reached their stop, he would remain in his seat and when she said, "Aren't you going to get off?" he would look at her as at a stranger who had rashly addressed him. The corner they got off on was usually deserted, but it was well lighted and it would not hurt her to walk by herself the four blocks to the Y. He decided to wait until the time came and then decide whether or not he would let her get off by herself. He would have to be at the Y at ten to bring her back, but he could leave her wondering if he was going to show up. There was no reason for her to think she could always depend on him.

He retired again into the high-ceilinged room sparsely settled with large pieces of antique furniture. His soul expanded momentarily but then he became aware of his mother across from him and the vision shriveled. He studied her coldly. Her feet in little pumps dangled like a child's and did not quite reach the floor. She was training on him an exaggerated look of reproach. He felt completely detached from her. At that moment he could with pleasure have slapped her as he would have slapped a particularly obnoxious child in his charge.

He began to imagine various unlikely ways by which he could teach her a lesson. He might make friends with some distinguished Negro professor or lawyer and bring him home to spend the evening. He would be entirely justified but her blood pressure would rise to 300. He could not push her to the extent of making her have a stroke, and moreover, he had never been successful at making any Negro friends. He had tried to strike up an acquaintance on the bus with some of the better types, with ones that looked like professors or ministers or lawyers. One morning he had sat down next to a distinguished-looking dark brown man who had answered his questions with a sonorous solemnity but who had turned out to be an undertaker. Another day he had sat down beside a cigar-smoking Negro with a diamond ring on his finger, but after a few stilted pleasantries, the Negro had rung the buzzer and risen, slipping two lottery tickets into Julian's hand as he climbed over him to leave.

He imagined his mother lying desperately ill and his being able to secure only a Negro doctor for her. He toyed with that idea for a few minutes and then dropped it for a momentary vision of himself participating as a sympathizer in a sit-in demonstration. This was possible but he did not linger with it. Instead, he approached the ultimate horror. He brought home a beautiful suspiciously Negroid woman. Prepare yourself, he said. There is nothing you can do about it. This is the woman I've chosen. She's intelligent, dignified, even good, and she's suffered and she hasn't thought it *fun*. Now persecute us, go ahead and persecute us. Drive her out of here, but remember, you're driving me too. His eyes were narrowed and through the indignation he had generated, he saw his mother across the aisle, purple-faced, shrunken to the dwarflike proportions of her moral nature, sitting like a mummy beneath the ridiculous banner of her hat.

He was tilted out of his fantasy again as the bus stopped. The door opened with a sucking hiss and out of the dark a large, gaily dressed, sullen-looking colored woman got on with a little boy. The child, who might have been four, had on a short plaid suit and a Tyrolean hat with a blue feather in it. Julian hoped that he would sit down beside him and that the woman would push in beside his mother. He could think of no better arrangement.

As she waited for her tokens, the woman was surveying the seating possibilities—he hoped with the idea of sitting where she was least wanted. There was something familiar-looking about her but Julian could not place what it was. She was a giant of a woman. Her face was set not only to meet opposition but to seek it out. The downward tilt of her large lower lip was like a warning sign: DON'T TAMPER WITH ME. Her bulging figure was encased in a green crepe dress and her feet overflowed in red shoes. She had on a hideous hat. A purple velvet flap came down on one side of it and stood up on the other; the rest of it was green and looked like a cushion with the stuffing out. She carried a mammoth red pocketbook that bulged throughout as if it were stuffed with rocks.

To Julian's disappointment, the little boy climbed up on the empty seat beside his mother. His mother lumped all children, black and white, into the common category, "cute," and she thought little Negroes were on the whole cuter than little white children. She smiled at the little boy as he climbed on the seat.

Meanwhile the woman was bearing down upon the empty seat beside Julian. To his annoyance, she squeezed herself into it. He saw his mother's face change as the woman settled herself next to him and he realized with satisfaction that this was more objectionable to her than it was to him. Her face seemed almost gray and there was a look of dull recognition in her eyes, as if suddenly she had sickened at some awful confrontation. Julian saw that it was because she and the woman had, in a sense, swapped sons. Though his mother would not realize the symbolic significance of this, she would feel it. His amusement showed plainly on his face.

The woman next to him muttered something unintelligible to herself. He was conscious of a kind of bristling next to him, a muted growling like that of an angry cat. He could not see anything but the red pocketbook upright on the bulging green thighs. He visualized the woman as she had stood waiting for her tokens—the ponderous figure, rising from the red shoes upward over the solid hips, the mammoth bosom, the haughty face, to the green and purple hat.

His eyes widened.

The vision of the two hats, identical, broke upon him with the radiance of a brilliant sunrise. His face was suddenly lit with joy. He could not believe that Fate had thrust upon his mother such a lesson. He gave a loud chuckle so that she would look at him and see that he saw. She turned her eyes on him slowly. The blue in them seemed to have turned a bruised purple. For a moment he had an uncomfortable sense of her innocence, but it lasted only a second before principle rescued him. Justice entitled him to laugh. His grin hardened until it said to her as plainly as if he were saying aloud: Your punishment exactly fits your pettiness. This should teach you a permanent lesson.

Her eyes shifted to the woman. She seemed unable to bear looking at him and to find the woman preferable. He became conscious again of the bristling presence at his side. The woman was rumbling like a volcano about to become active. His mother's mouth began to twitch slightly at one corner. With a sinking heart, he saw incipient signs of recovery on her face and realized that this was going to strike her suddenly as funny and was going to be no lesson at all. She kept her eyes on the woman and an amused smile came over her face as if the woman were a monkey that had stolen her hat. The little Negro was looking up at her with large fascinated eyes. He had been trying to attract her attention for some time.

"Carver!" the woman said suddenly. "Come heah!"

When he saw that the spotlight was on him at last, Carver drew his feet up and turned himself toward Julian's mother and giggled.

"Carver!" the woman said. "You heah me? Come heah!"

Carver slid down from the seat but remained squatting with his back against the base of it, his head turned slyly around toward Julian's mother, who was smiling at him. The woman reached a hand across the aisle and snatched him to her. He righted himself and hung backwards on her knees, grinning at Julian's mother. "Isn't he cute?" Julian's mother said to the woman with the protruding teeth.

"I reckon he is," the woman said without conviction.

The Negress yanked him upright but he eased out of her grip and shot across the aisle and scrambled, giggling wildly, onto the seat beside his love.

"I think he likes me," Julian's mother said, and smiled at the woman. It was the smile she used when she was being particularly gracious to an inferior. Julian saw everything lost. The lesson had rolled off her like rain on a roof.

The woman stood up and yanked the little boy off the seat as if she were snatching him from contagion. Julian could feel the rage in her at having no weapon like his mother's smile. She gave the child a sharp slap across his leg. He howled once and then thrust his head into her stomach and kicked his feet against her shins. "Behave," she said vehemently.

The bus stopped and the Negro who had been reading the newspaper got off. The woman moved over and set the little boy down with a thump between herself and Julian. She held him firmly by the knee. In a moment he put his hands in front of his face and peeped at Julian's mother through his fingers.

"I see yoooooooo!" she said and put her hand in front of her face and peeped at him.

The woman slapped his hand down. "Quit yo' foolishness," she said, "before I knock the living Jesus out of you!"

Julian was thankful that the next stop was theirs. He reached up and pulled the cord. The woman reached up and pulled it at the same time. Oh my God, he thought. He had the terrible intuition that when they got off the bus together, his mother would open her purse and give the little boy a nickel. The gesture would be as natural to her as breathing. The bus stopped and the woman got up and lunged to the front, dragging the child, who wished to stay on, after her. Julian and his mother got up and followed. As they neared the door, Julian tried to relieve her of her pocketbook.

"No," she murmured, "I want to give the little boy a nickel."

"No!" Julian hissed. "No!"

She smiled down at the child and opened her bag. The bus door opened and the woman picked him up by the arm and descended with him, hanging at her hip. Once in the street she set him down and shook him.

Julian's mother had to close her purse while she got down the bus step but as soon as her feet were on the ground, she opened it again and began to rummage inside. "I can't find but a penny," she whispered, "but it looks like a new one."

"Don't do it!" Julian said fiercely between his teeth. There was a streetlight on the corner and she hurried to get under it so that she could better see into her pocketbook. The woman was heading off rapidly down the street with the child still hanging backward on her hand.

"Oh little boy!" Julian's mother called and took a few quick steps and caught up with them just beyond the lamppost. "Here's a bright new penny for you," and she held out the coin, which shone bronze in the dim light.

The huge woman turned and for a moment stood, her shoulders lifted and her face frozen with frustrated rage, and stared at Julian's mother. Then all at once she seemed to explode like a piece of machinery that had been given one ounce of pressure too much. Julian saw the black fist swing out with the red pocketbook. He shut his eyes and cringed as he heard the woman shout, "He don't take nobody's pennies!" When he opened his eyes, the woman was disappearing down the street with the little boy staring wide-eyed over her shoulder. Julian's mother was sitting on the sidewalk.

"I told you not to do that," Julian said angrily. "I told you not to do that!"

He stood over her for a minute, gritting his teeth. Her legs were stretched out in front of her and her hat was on her lap. He squatted down and looked her in the face. It was totally expressionless. "You got exactly what you deserved," he said. "Now get up."

He picked up her pocketbook and put what had fallen out back in it. He picked the hat up off her lap. The penny caught his eye on the sidewalk and he picked that up and let it drop before her eyes into the purse. Then he stood up and leaned over and held his hand out to pull her up. She remained immobile. He sighed. Rising above them on either side were black apartment buildings, marked with irregular rectangles of light. At the end of the block a man came out of a door and walked off in the opposite direction. "All right," he said, "suppose somebody happens by and wants to know why you're sitting on the sidewalk?"

She took the hand and, breathing hard, pulled heavily up on it and then stood for a moment, swaying slightly as if the spots of light in the darkness were circling around her. Her eyes, shadowed and confused, finally settled on his face. He did not try to conceal his irritation. "I hope this teaches you a lesson," he said. She leaned forward and her eyes raked his face. She seemed trying to determine his identity. Then, as if she found nothing familiar about him, she started off with a headlong movement in the wrong direction.

"Aren't you going on to the Y?" he asked.

"Home," she muttered.

"Well, are we walking?"

For answer she kept going. Julian followed along, his hands behind him. He saw no reason to let the lesson she had had go without backing it up with an explanation of its meaning. She might as well be made to understand what had happened to her. "Don't think that was just an uppity Negro woman," he said. "That was the whole colored race which will no longer take your condescending pennies. That was your black double. She can wear the same hat as you, and to be sure," he added gratuitously (because he thought it was funny), "it looked better on her than it did on you. What all this means," he said, "is that the old world is gone. The old manners are obsolete and your graciousness is not worth a damn." He thought bitterly of the house that had been lost for him. "You aren't who you think you are," he said.

She continued to plow ahead, paying no attention to him. Her hair had come undone on one side. She dropped her pocketbook and took no notice. He stooped and picked it up and handed it to her but she did not take it.

"You needn't act as if the world has come to an end," he said, "because it hasn't. From now on you've got to live in a new world and face a few realities for a change. Buck up," he said, "it won't kill you."

She was breathing fast.

"Let's wait on the bus," he said.

"Home," she said thickly.

"I hate to see you behave like this," he said. "Just like a child. I should be able to expect more of you." He decided to stop where he was and make her stop and wait for a bus. "I'm not going any farther," he said, stopping. "We're going on the bus."

She continued to go on as if she had not heard him. He took a few steps and caught her arm and stopped her. He looked into her face and caught his breath. He was looking into a face he had never seen before. "Tell Grandpapa to come get me," she said.

He stared, stricken.

"Tell Caroline to come get me," she said.

Stunned, he let her go and she lurched forward again, walking as if one leg were shorter than the other. A tide of darkness seemed to be sweeping her from him. "Mother!" he cried. "Darling, sweetheart, wait!" Crumpling, she fell to the pavement. He dashed forward and fell at her side, crying, "Mamma, Mamma!" He turned her over. Her face was fiercely distorted. One eye, large and staring, moved slightly to the left as if it had become unmoored. The other remained fixed on him, raked his face again, found nothing and closed.

"Wait here, wait here!" he cried and jumped up and began to run for help toward a cluster of lights he saw in the distance ahead of him. "Help, help!" he shouted, but his voice was thin, scarcely a thread of sound. The lights drifted farther away the faster he ran and his feet moved numbly as if they carried him nowhere. The tide of darkness seemed to sweep him back to her, postponing from moment to moment his entry into the world of guilt and sorrow.

Revelation

The doctor's waiting room, which was very small, was almost full when the Turpins entered and Mrs. Turpin, who was very large, made it look even smaller by her presence. She stood looming at the head of the magazine table set in the center of it, a living demonstration that the room was inadequate and ridiculous. Her little bright black eyes took in all the patients as she sized up the seating situation. There was one vacant chair and a place on the sofa occupied by a blond child in a dirty blue romper who should have been told to move over and make room for the lady. He was five or six, but Mrs. Turpin saw at once that no one was going to tell him to move over. He was slumped down in the seat, his arms idle at his sides and his eyes idle in his head; his nose ran unchecked.

Mrs. Turpin put a firm hand on Claud's shoulder and said in a voice that included anyone who wanted to listen, "Claud, you sit in that chair there," and gave him a push down into the vacant one. Claud was florid and bald and sturdy, somewhat shorter than Mrs. Turpin, but he sat down as if he were accustomed to doing what she told him to.

Mrs. Turpin remained standing. The only man in the room besides Claud was a lean stringy old fellow with a rusty hand spread out on each knee, whose eyes were closed as if he were asleep or dead or pretending to be so as not to get up and offer her his seat. Her gaze settled agreeably on a well-dressed grey-haired lady whose eyes met hers and whose expression said: if that child belonged to me, he would have some manners and move over—there's plenty of room there for you and him too.

Claud looked up with a sigh and made as if to rise.

"Sit down," Mrs. Turpin said. "You know you're not supposed to stand on that leg. He has an ulcer on his leg," she explained.

Claud lifted his foot onto the magazine table and rolled his trouser leg up to reveal a purple swelling on a plump marble-white calf.

"My!" the pleasant lady said. "How did you do that?"

"A cow kicked him," Mrs. Turpin said.

"Goodness!" said the lady.

Claud rolled his trouser leg down.

"Maybe the little boy would move over," the lady suggested, but the child did not stir.

"Somebody will be leaving in a minute," Mrs. Turpin said. She could not understand why a doctor—with as much money as they made charging five dollars a day to just stick their head in the hospital door and look at you—couldn't afford a decent-sized waiting room. This one was hardly bigger than a garage. The table was cluttered with limp-looking magazines and at one end of it there was a big green glass ash tray full of cigaret butts and cotton wads with little blood spots on them. If she had had anything to do with the running of the place, that would have been emptied every so often. There were no chairs against the wall at the head of the room. It had a rectangular-shaped panel in it that permitted a view of the office where the nurse came and went and the secretary listened to the radio. A plastic fern in a gold pot sat in the opening and trailed its fronds down almost to the floor. The radio was softly playing gospel music.

Just then the inner door opened and a nurse with the highest stack of yellow hair Mrs. Turpin had ever seen put her face in the crack and called for the next patient. The woman sitting beside Claud grasped the two arms of her chair and hoisted herself up; she pulled her dress free from her legs and lumbered through the door where the nurse had disappeared.

Mrs. Turpin eased into the vacant chair, which held her tight as a corset. "I wish I could reduce," she said, and rolled her eyes and gave a comic sigh.

"Oh, *you* aren't fat," the stylish lady said.

"Ooooo I am too," Mrs. Turpin said. "Claud he eats all he wants to and never weighs over one hundred and seventy-five pounds, but me I just look at something good to eat and I gain some weight," and her stomach and shoulders shook with laughter. "You can eat all you want to, can't you, Claud?" she asked, turning to him.

Claud only grinned.

"Well, as long as you have such a good disposition," the stylish lady said, "I don't think it makes a bit of difference what size you are. You just can't beat a good disposition."

Next to her was a fat girl of eighteen or nineteen, scowling into a thick blue book which Mrs. Turpin saw was entitled *Human Development*. The girl raised her head and directed her scowl at Mrs. Turpin as if she did not like her looks. She appeared annoyed that anyone should speak while she tried to read. The poor girl's face was blue with acne and Mrs. Turpin thought how pitiful it was to have a face like that at that age. She gave the girl a friendly smile but the girl only scowled the harder. Mrs. Turpin herself was fat but she had always had good skin, and, though she was forty-seven years old, there was not a wrinkle in her face except around her eyes from laughing too much.

Next to the ugly girl was the child, still in exactly the same position, and next to him was a thin leathery old woman in a cotton print dress. She and Claud had three sacks of chicken feed in their pump house that was in the same print. She had seen from the first that the child belonged with the old woman. She could tell by the way they sat—kind of vacant and white-trashy, as if they would sit there until Doomsday if nobody called and told them to get up. And at right angles but next to the well-dressed pleasant lady was a lank-faced woman who was certainly the child's mother. She had on a yellow sweat shirt and wine-colored slacks, both gritty-looking, and the rims of her lips were stained with snuff. Her dirty yellow hair was tied behind with a little piece of red paper ribbon. Worse than niggers any day, Mrs. Turpin thought.

The gospel hymn playing was, "When I looked up and He looked down," and Mrs. Turpin, who knew it, supplied the last line mentally, "And wona these days I know I'll we-eara crown."

Without appearing to, Mrs. Turpin always noticed people's feet. The well-dressed lady had on red and grey suede shoes to match her dress. Mrs. Turpin had on her good black patent leather pumps. The ugly girl had on Girl Scout shoes and heavy socks. The old woman had on tennis shoes and the white-trashy mother had on what appeared to be bedroom slippers, black straw with gold braid threaded through them—exactly what you would have expected her to have on.

Sometimes at night when she couldn't go to sleep, Mrs. Turpin would occupy herself with the question of who she would have chosen to be if she couldn't have been herself. If Jesus had said to her before he made her, "There's only two places available for you. You can either be a nigger or white-trash," what would she have said? "Please, Jesus, please," she would have said, "just let me wait until there's another place available," and he would have said, "No, you have to go right now and I have only those two places so make up your mind." She would have wiggled and squirmed and begged and pleaded but it would have been no use and finally she would have said, "All right, make me a nigger then—but that don't mean a trashy one." And he would have made her a neat clean respectable Negro woman, herself but black.

Next to the child's mother was a red-headed youngish woman, reading one of the magazines and working on a piece of chewing gum, hell for leather, as Claud would say. Mrs. Turpin could not see the woman's feet. She was not white-trash, just common. Sometimes Mrs. Turpin occupied herself at night naming the classes of people. On the bottom of the heap were most colored people, not the kind she would have been if she had been one, but most of them; then next to them—not above, just away from—were the white-trash; then above them were the home-owners, and above them the home-and-land owners, to which she and Claud belonged. Above she and Claud were people with a lot of money and much bigger houses and much more land. But here the complexity of it would begin to bear in on her, for some of the people with a lot of money were common and ought to be below she and Claud and some of the people who had good blood had lost their money and had to rent and then there were colored people who owned their homes and land as well. There was a colored dentist in town who had two red Lincolns and a swimming pool and a farm with registered white-face cattle on it. Usually by the time she had fallen asleep all the classes of people were moiling and roiling around in her head, and she would dream they were all crammed in together in a box car, being ridden off to be put in a gas oven.

"That's a beautiful clock," she said and nodded to her right. It was a big wall clock, the face encased in a brass sunburst.

"Yes, it's very pretty," the stylish lady said agreeably. "And right on the dot too," she added, glancing at her watch.

The ugly girl beside her cast an eye upward at the clock, smirked, then looked directly at Mrs. Turpin and smirked again. Then she returned her eyes to her book. She was obviously the lady's daughter because, although they didn't look anything alike as to disposition, they both had the same shape of face and the same blue eyes. On the lady they sparkled pleasantly but in the girl's seared face they appeared alternately to smolder and to blaze.

What if Jesus had said, "All right, you can be white-trash or a nigger or ugly"!

Mrs. Turpin felt an awful pity for the girl, though she thought it was one thing to be ugly and another to act ugly.

The woman with the snuff-stained lips turned around in her chair and looked up at the clock. Then she turned back and appeared to look a little to the side of Mrs. Turpin. There was a cast in one of her eyes. "You want to know wher you can get you one of themther clocks?" she asked in a loud voice.

"No, I already have a nice clock," Mrs. Turpin said. Once somebody like her got a leg in the conversation, she would be all over it.

"You can get you one with green stamps," the woman said. "That's most likely wher he got hisn. Save you up enough, you can get you most anythang. I got me some joo'ry."

Ought to have got you a wash rag and some soap, Mrs. Turpin thought.

"I get contour sheets with mine," the pleasant lady said.

The daughter slammed her book shut. She looked straight in front of her, directly through Mrs. Turpin and on through the yellow curtain and the plate glass window which made the wall behind her. The girl's eyes seemed lit all of a sudden with a peculiar light, an unnatural light like night road signs give. Mrs. Turpin turned her head to see if there was anything going on outside that she should see, but she could not see anything. Figures passing cast only a pale shadow through the curtain. There was no reason the girl should single her out for her ugly looks.

"Miss Finley," the nurse said, cracking the door. The gum-chewing woman got up and passed in front of her and Claud and went into the office. She had on red high-heeled shoes.

Directly across the table, the ugly girl's eyes were fixed on Mrs. Turpin as if she had some very special reason for disliking her.

"This is wonderful weather, isn't it?" the girl's mother said.

"It's good weather for cotton if you can get the niggers to pick it," Mrs. Turpin said, "but niggers don't want to pick cotton any more. You can't get the white folks to pick it and now you can't get the niggers—because they got to be right up there with the white folks."

"They gonna *try* anyways," the white-trash woman said, leaning forward.

"Do you have one of those cotton-picking machines?" the pleasant lady asked.

"No," Mrs. Turpin said, "they leave half the cotton in the field. We don't have much cotton anyway. If you want to make it farming now, you have to have a little of everything. We got a couple of acres of cotton and a few hogs and chickens and just enough white-face that Claud can look after them himself."

"One thang I don't want," the white-trash woman said, wiping her mouth with the back of her hand. "Hogs. Nasty stinking things, a-gruntin and a-rootin all over the place."

Mrs. Turpin gave her the merest edge of her attention. "Our hogs are not dirty and they don't stink," she said. "They're cleaner than some children I've seen. Their feet never touch the ground. We have a pig-parlor—that's where you raise them on concrete," she explained to the pleasant lady, "and Claud scoots them down with the hose every afternoon and washes off the floor." Cleaner by far than that child right there, she thought. Poor nasty little thing. He had not moved except to put the thumb of his dirty hand into his mouth.

The woman turned her face away from Mrs. Turpin. "I know I wouldn't scoot down no hog with no hose," she said to the wall.

You wouldn't have no hog to scoot down, Mrs. Turpin said to herself.

"A-gruntin and a-rootin and a-groanin," the woman muttered.

"We got a little of everything," Mrs. Turpin said to the pleasant lady. "It's no use in having more than you can handle yourself with help like it is. We found enough niggers to pick our cotton this year but Claud he has to go after them and take them home again in the evening. They can't walk that half a mile. No they can't. I tell you," she said and laughed merrily, "I sure am tired of buttering up niggers, but you got to love em if you want em to work for you. When they come in the morning, I run out and I say, 'Hi yawl this morning?' and when Claud drives them off to the field I just wave to beat the band and they just wave back." And she waved her hand rapidly to illustrate.

"Like you read out of the same book," the lady said, showing she understood perfectly.

"Child, yes," Mrs. Turpin said. "And when they come in from the field, I run out with a bucket of icewater. That's the way it's going to be from now on," she said. "You may as well face it."

"One thang I know," the white-trash woman said. "Two thangs I ain't going to do: love no niggers or scoot down no hog with no hose." And she let out a bark of contempt.

The look that Mrs. Turpin and the pleasant lady exchanged indicated they both understood that you had to *have* certain things before you could *know* certain things. But every time Mrs. Turpin exchanged a look with the lady, she was aware that the ugly girl's peculiar eyes were still on her, and she had trouble bringing her attention back to the conversation.

"When you got something," she said, "you got to look after it." And when you ain't got a thing but breath and britches, she added to herself, you can afford to come to town every morning and just sit on the Court House coping and spit.

A grotesque revolving shadow passed across the curtain behind her and was thrown palely on the opposite wall. Then a bicycle clattered down against the outside of the building. The door opened and a colored boy glided in with a tray from the drug store. It had two large red and white paper cups on it with tops on them. He was a tall, very black boy in discolored white pants and a green nylon shirt. He was chewing gum slowly, as if to music. He set the tray down in the office opening next to the fern and stuck his head through to look for the secretary. She was not in there. He rested his arms on the ledge and waited, his narrow bottom stuck out, swaying slowly to the left and right. He raised a hand over his head and scratched the base of his skull.

"You see that button there, boy?" Mrs. Turpin said. "You can punch that and she'll come. She's probably in the back somewhere."

"Is thas right?" the boy said agreeably, as if he had never seen the button before. He leaned to the right and put his finger on it. "She sometime out," he said and twisted around to face his audience, his elbows behind him on the counter. The nurse appeared and he twisted back again. She handed him a dollar and he rooted in his pocket and made the change and counted it out to her. She gave him fifteen cents for a tip and he went out with the empty tray. The heavy door swung to slowly and closed at length with the sound of suction. For a moment no one spoke.

"They ought to send all them niggers back to Africa," the white-trash woman said. "That's wher they come from in the first place."

"Oh, I couldn't do without my good colored friends," the pleasant lady said.

"There's a heap of things worse than a nigger," Mrs. Turpin agreed. "It's all kinds of them just like it's all kinds of us."

"Yes, and it takes all kinds to make the world go round," the lady said in her musical voice.

As she said it, the raw-complexioned girl snapped her teeth together. Her lower lip turned downwards and inside out, revealing the pale pink inside of her mouth. After a second it rolled back up. It was the ugliest face Mrs. Turpin had ever seen anyone make and for a moment she was certain that the girl had made it at her. She was looking at her as if she had known and disliked her all her life —all of Mrs. Turpin's life, it seemed too, not just all the girl's life. Why, girl, I don't even know you, Mrs. Turpin said silently.

She forced her attention back to the discussion. "It wouldn't be practical to send them back to Africa," she said. "They wouldn't want to go. They got it too good here."

"Wouldn't be what they wanted—if I had anythang to do with it," the woman said.

"It wouldn't be a way in the world you could get all the niggers back over there," Mrs. Turpin said. "They'd be hiding out and lying down and turning sick on you and wailing and hollering and raring and pitching. It wouldn't be a way in the world to get them over there."

"They got over here," the trashy woman said. "Get back like they got over."

"It wasn't so many of them then," Mrs. Turpin explained.

The woman looked at Mrs. Turpin as if here was an idiot indeed but Mrs. Turpin was not bothered by the look, considering where it came from.

"Nooo," she said, "they're going to stay here where they can go to New York and marry white folks and improve their color. That's what they all want to do, every one of them, improve their color."

"You know what comes of that, don't you?" Claud asked.

"No, Claud, what?" Mrs. Turpin said.

Claud's eyes twinkled. "White-faced niggers," he said with never a smile.

Everybody in the office laughed except the white-trash and the ugly girl. The girl gripped the book in her lap with white fingers. The trashy woman looked around her from face to face as if she thought they were all idiots. The old woman in the feed sack dress continued to gaze expressionless across the floor at the high-top shoes of the man opposite her, the one who had been pretending to be asleep when the Turpins came in. He was laughing heartily, his hands still spread out on his knees. The child had fallen to the side and was lying now almost face down in the old woman's lap.

While they recovered from their laughter, the nasal chorus on the radio kept the room from silence.

> "You go to blank blank
> And I'll go to mine
> But we'll all blank along
> To-geth-ther,

And all along the blank
We'll hep eachother out
Smile-ling in any kind of
Weath-ther!"

Mrs. Turpin didn't catch every word but she caught enough to agree with the spirit of the song and it turned her thoughts sober. To help anybody out that needed it was her philosophy of life. She never spared herself when she found somebody in need, whether they were white or black, trash or decent. And of all she had to be thankful for, she was most thankful that this was so. If Jesus had said, "You can be high society and have all the money you want and be thin and svelte-like, but you can't be a good woman with it," she would have had to say, "Well don't make me that then. Make me a good woman and it don't matter what else, how fat or how ugly or how poor!" Her heart rose. He had not made her a nigger or white-trash or ugly! He had made her herself and given her a little of everything. Jesus, thank you! she said. Thank you thank you thank you! Whenever she counted her blessings she felt as buoyant as if she weighed one hundred and twenty-five pounds instead of one hundred and eighty.

"What's wrong with your little boy?" the pleasant lady asked the white-trashy woman.

"He has a ulcer," the woman said proudly. "He ain't give me a minute's peace since he was born. Him and her are just alike," she said, nodding at the old woman, who was running her leathery fingers through the child's pale hair. "Look like I can't get nothing down them two but Co' Cola and candy."

That's all you try to get down em, Mrs. Turpin said to herself. Too lazy to light the fire. There was nothing you could tell her about people like them that she didn't know already. And it was not just that they didn't have anything. Because if you gave them everything, in two weeks it would all be broken or filthy or they would have chopped it up for lightwood. She knew all this from her own experience. Help them you must, but help them you couldn't.

All at once the ugly girl turned her lips inside out again. Her eyes were fixed like two drills on Mrs. Turpin. This time there was no mistaking that there was something urgent behind them.

Girl, Mrs. Turpin exclaimed silently, I haven't done a thing to you! The girl might be confusing her with somebody else. There was no need to sit by and let herself be intimidated. "You must be in

college," she said boldly, looking directly at the girl. "I see you reading a book there."

The girl continued to stare and pointedly did not answer.

Her mother blushed at this rudeness. "The lady asked you a question, Mary Grace," she said under her breath.

"I have ears," Mary Grace said.

The poor mother blushed again. "Mary Grace goes to Wellesley
College," she explained. She twisted one of the buttons on her dress.
"In Massachusetts," she added with a grimace. "And in the summer
she just keeps right on studying. Just reads all the time, a real book
worm. She's done real well at Wellesley; she's taking English and
Math and History and Psychology and Social Studies," she rattled
on, "and I think it's too much. I think she ought to get out and have
fun."

The girl looked as if she would like to hurl them all through the
plate glass window.

"Way up north," Mrs. Turpin murmured and thought, well, it
hasn't done much for her manners.

"I'd almost rather to have him sick," the white-trash woman said,
wrenching the attention back to herself. "He's so mean when he
ain't. Look like some children just take natural to meanness. It's some
gets bad when they get sick but he was the opposite. Took sick and
turned good. He don't give me no trouble now. It's me waitin to see
the doctor," she said.

If I was going to send anybody back to Africa, Mrs. Turpin
thought, it would be your kind, woman. "Yes, indeed," she said aloud,
but looking up at the ceiling, "it's a heap of things worse than a
nigger." And dirtier than a hog, she added to herself.

"I think people with bad dispositions are more to be pitied than
anyone on earth," the pleasant lady said in a voice that was decidedly
thin.

"I thank the Lord he has blessed me with a good one," Mrs.
Turpin said. "The day has never dawned that I couldn't find something to laugh at."

"Not since she married me anyways," Claud said with a comical
straight face.

Everybody laughed except the girl and the white-trash.

Mrs. Turpin's stomach shook. "He's such a caution," she said, "that
I can't help but laugh at him."

The girl made a loud ugly noise through her teeth.

Her mother's mouth grew thin and tight. "I think the worst thing
in the world," she said, "is an ungrateful person. To have everything

and not appreciate it. I know a girl," she said, "who has parents who would give her anything, a little brother who loves her dearly, who is getting a good education, who wears the best clothes, but who can never say a kind word to anyone, who never smiles, who just criticises and complains all day long."

"Is she too old to paddle?" Claud asked.

The girl's face was almost purple.

"Yes," the lady said, "I'm afraid there's nothing to do but leave her to her folly. Some day she'll wake up and it'll be too late."

"It never hurt anyone to smile," Mrs. Turpin said. "It just makes you feel better all over."

"Of course," the lady said sadly, "but there are just some people you can't tell anything to. They can't take criticism."

"If it's one thing I am," Mrs. Turpin said with feeling, "it's grateful. When I think who all I could have been besides myself and what all I got, a little of everything, and a good disposition besides, I just feel like shouting, 'Thank you, Jesus, for making everything the way it is!' It could have been different!" For one thing, somebody else could have got Claud. At the thought of this, she was flooded with gratitude and a terrible pang of joy ran through her. "Oh thank you, Jesus, thank you!" she cried aloud.

The book struck her directly over her left eye. It struck almost at the same instant that she realized the girl was about to hurl it. Before she could utter a sound, the raw face came crashing across the table toward her, howling. The girl's fingers sank like clamps into the soft flesh of her neck. She heard the mother cry out and Claud shout, "Whoa!" There was an instant when she was certain that she was about to be in an earthquake.

All at once her vision narrowed and she saw everything as if it were happening in a small room far away, or as if she were looking at it through the wrong end of a telescope. Claud's face crumpled and fell out of sight. The nurse ran in, then out, then in again. Then the gangling figure of the doctor rushed out of the inner door. Magazines flew this way and that as the table turned over. The girl fell with a thud and Mrs. Turpin's vision suddenly reversed itself and she saw everything large instead of small. The eyes of the white-trashy woman were staring hugely at the floor. There the girl, held down on one side by the nurse and on the other by her mother, was wrenching and turning in their grasp. The doctor was kneeling astride her, trying to hold her arm down. He managed after a second to sink a long needle into it.

Mrs. Turpin felt entirely hollow except for her heart which swung from side to side as if it were agitated in a great empty drum of flesh.

"Somebody that's not busy call for the ambulance," the doctor said in the off-hand voice young doctors adopt for terrible occasions.

Mrs. Turpin could not have moved a finger. The old man who had been sitting next to her skipped nimbly into the office and made the call, for the secretary still seemed to be gone.

"Claud!" Mrs. Turpin called.

He was not in his chair. She knew she must jump up and find him but she felt like some one trying to catch a train in a dream, when everything moves in slow motion and the faster you try to run the slower you go.

"Here I am," a suffocated voice, very unlike Claud's, said.

He was doubled up in the corner on the floor, pale as paper, holding his leg. She wanted to get up and go to him but she could not move. Instead, her gaze was drawn slowly downward to the churning face on the floor, which she could see over the doctor's shoulder.

The girl's eyes stopped rolling and focussed on her. They seemed a much lighter blue than before, as if a door that had been tightly closed behind them was now open to admit light and air.

Mrs. Turpin's head cleared and her power of motion returned. She leaned forward until she was looking directly into the fierce brilliant eyes. There was no doubt in her mind that the girl did know her, knew her in some intense and personal way, beyond time and place and condition. "What you got to say to me?" she asked hoarsely and held her breath, waiting, as for a revelation.

The girl raised her head. Her gaze locked with Mrs. Turpin's. "Go back to hell where you came from, you old wart hog," she whispered. Her voice was low but clear. Her eyes burned for a moment as if she saw with pleasure that her message had struck its target.

Mrs. Turpin sank back in her chair.

After a moment the girl's eyes closed and she turned her head wearily to the side.

The doctor rose and handed the nurse the empty syringe. He leaned over and put both hands for a moment on the mother's shoulders, which were shaking. She was sitting on the floor, her lips pressed together, holding Mary Grace's hand in her lap. The girl's fingers were gripped like a baby's around her thumb. "Go on to the hospital," he said. "I'll call and make the arrangements.

"Now let's see that neck," he said in a jovial voice to Mrs. Turpin. He began to inspect her neck with his first two fingers. Two little moon-shaped lines like pink fish bones were indented over her windpipe. There was the beginning of an angry red swelling above her eye. His fingers passed over this also.

"Lea' me be," she said thickly and shook him off. "See about Claud. She kicked him."

"I'll see about him in a minute," he said and felt her pulse. He was a thin grey-haired young man, given to pleasantries. "Go home and have yourself a vacation the rest of the day," he said and patted her on the shoulder.

Quit your pattin me, Mrs. Turpin growled to herself.

"And put an ice pack over that eye," he said. Then he went and squatted down beside Claud and looked at his leg. After a moment he pulled him up and Claud limped after him into the office.

Until the ambulance came, the only sounds in the room were the tremulous moans of the girl's mother, who continued to sit on the floor. The white-trash woman did not take her eyes off the girl. Mrs. Turpin looked straight ahead at nothing. Presently the ambulance drew up, a long dark shadow, behind the curtain. The attendants came in and set the stretcher down beside the girl and lifted her expertly onto it and carried her out. The nurse helped the mother gather up her things. The shadow of the ambulance moved silently away and the nurse came back in the office.

"That ther girl is going to be a lunatic, ain't she?" the white-trash woman asked the nurse, but the nurse kept on to the back and never answered her.

"Yes, she's going to be a lunatic," the white-trash woman said to the rest of them.

"Po' critter," the old woman murmured. The child's face was still in her lap. His eyes looked idly out over her knees. He had not moved during the disturbance except to draw one leg up under him.

"I thank Gawd," the white-trash woman said fervently, "I ain't a lunatic."

Claud came limping out and the Turpins went home.

As their pick-up truck turned into their own dirt road and made the crest of the hill, Mrs. Turpin gripped the window ledge and looked out suspiciously. The land sloped gracefully down through a field dotted with lavender weeds and at the start of the rise their small yellow frame house, with its little flower beds spread out around it like a fancy apron, sat primly in its accustomed place between two giant hickory trees. She would not have been startled to see a burnt wound between two blackened chimneys.

Neither of them felt like eating so they put on their house clothes and lowered the shade in the bedroom and lay down, Claud with his leg on a pillow and herself with a damp washcloth over her eye. The instant she was flat on her back, the image of a razor-backed hog with warts on its face and horns coming out behind its ears snorted into her head. She moaned, a low quiet moan.

"I am not," she said tearfully, "a wart hog. From hell." But the denial had no force. The girl's eyes and her words, even the tone of her voice, low but clear, directed only to her, brooked no repudiation. She had been singled out for the message, though there was trash in the room to whom it might justly have been applied. The full force of this fact struck her only now. There was a woman there who was neglecting her own child but she had been overlooked. The message had been given to Ruby Turpin, a respectable, hard-working, church-going woman. The tears dried. Her eyes began to burn instead with wrath.

She rose on her elbow and the washcloth fell into her hand. Claud was lying on his back, snoring. She wanted to tell him what the girl had said. At the same time, she did not wish to put the image of herself as a wart hog from hell into his mind.

"Hey, Claud," she muttered and pushed his shoulder.

Claud opened one pale baby blue eye.

She looked into it warily. He did not think about anything. He just went his way.

"Wha, whasit?" he said and closed the eye again.

"Nothing," she said. "Does your leg pain you?"

"Hurts like hell," Claud said.

"It'll quit terreckly," she said and lay back down. In a moment Claud was snoring again. For the rest of the afternoon they lay there. Claud slept. She scowled at the ceiling. Occasionally she raised her fist and made a small stabbing motion over her chest as if she were defending her innocence to invisible guests who were like the comforters of Job, reasonable-seeming but wrong.

About five-thirty Claud stirred. "Got to go after those niggers," he sighed, not moving.

She was looking straight up as if there were unintelligible handwriting on the ceiling. The protuberance over her eye had turned a greenish-blue. "Listen here," she said.

"What?"

"Kiss me."

Claud leaned over and kissed her loudly on the mouth. He pinched her side and their hands interlocked. Her expression of ferocious concentration did not change. Claud got up, groaning and growling, and limped off. She continued to study the ceiling.

She did not get up until she heard the pick-up truck coming back with the Negroes. Then she rose and thrust her feet in her brown oxfords, which she did not bother to lace, and stumped out onto the back porch and got her red plastic bucket. She emptied a tray of ice cubes into it and filled it half full of water and went out into the back yard. Every afternoon after Claud brought the hands in, one of the boys helped him put out hay and the rest waited in the back of the truck until he was ready to take them home. The truck was parked in the shade under one of the hickory trees.

"Hi yawl this evening?" Mrs. Turpin asked grimly, appearing with the bucket and the dipper. There were three women and a boy in the truck.

"Us doin nicely," the oldest woman said. "Hi you doin?" and her gaze stuck immediately on the dark lump on Mrs. Turpin's forehead. "You done fell down, ain't you?" she asked in a solicitous voice. The old woman was dark and almost toothless. She had on an old felt hat of Claud's set back on her head. The other two women were younger and lighter and they both had new bright green sun hats. One of them had hers on her head; the other had taken hers off and the boy was grinning beneath it.

Mrs. Turpin set the bucket down on the floor of the truck. "Yawl hep yourselves," she said. She looked around to make sure Claud had gone. "No. I didn't fall down," she said, folding her arms. "It was something worse than that."

"Ain't nothing bad happen to you!" the old woman said. She said it as if they all knew that Mrs. Turpin was protected in some special way by Divine Providence. "You just had you a little fall."

"We were in town at the doctor's office for where the cow kicked Mr. Turpin," Mrs. Turpin said in a flat tone that indicated they could leave off their foolishness. "And there was this girl there. A big fat girl with her face all broke out. I could look at that girl and tell she was peculiar but I couldn't tell how. And me and her mama were just talking and going along and all of a sudden WHAM! She throws this big book she was reading at me and . . ."

"Naw!" the old woman cried out.

"And then she jumps over the table and commences to choke me."

"Naw!" they all exclaimed, "naw!"

"Hi come she do that?" the old woman asked. "What ail her?"

Mrs. Turpin only glared in front of her.

"Somethin ail her," the old woman said.

"They carried her off in an ambulance," Mrs. Turpin continued, "but before she went she was rolling on the floor and they were try-

ing to hold her down to give her a shot and she said something to
me." She paused. "You know what she said to me?"

"What she say?" they asked.

"She said," Mrs. Turpin began, and stopped, her face very dark
and heavy. The sun was getting whiter and whiter, blanching the
sky overhead so that the leaves of the hickory tree were black in
the face of it. She could not bring forth the words. "Something real
ugly," she muttered.

"She sho shouldn't said nothin ugly to you," the old woman said.
"You so sweet. You the sweetest lady I know."

"She pretty too," the one with the hat on said.

"And stout," the other one said. "I never knowed no sweeter white
lady."

"That's the truth befo' Jesus," the old woman said. "Amen! You des
as sweet and pretty as you can be."

Mrs. Turpin knew just exactly how much Negro flattery was worth
and it added to her rage. "She said," she began again and finished
this time with a fierce rush of breath, "that I was an old wart hog
from hell."

There was an astounded silence.

"Where she at!" the youngest woman cried in a piercing voice.
"Lemme see her. I'll kill her!"

"I'll kill her with you!" the other one cried.

"She b'long in the sylum," the old woman said emphatically. "You
the sweetest white lady I know."

"She pretty too," the other two said. "Stout as she can be and sweet.
Jesus satisfied with her!"

"Deed he is," the old woman declared.

Idiots! Mrs. Turpin growled to herself. You could never say anything intelligent to a nigger. You could talk at them but not with
them. "Yawl ain't drunk your water," she said shortly. "Leave the
bucket in the truck when you're finished with it. I got more to do
than just stand around and pass the time of day," and she moved off
and into the house.

She stood for a moment in the middle of the kitchen. The dark
protuberance over her eye looked like a miniature tornado cloud
which might any moment sweep across the horizon of her brow. Her
lower lip protruded dangerously. She squared her massive shoulders.
Then she marched into the front of the house and out the side door
and started down the road to the pig parlor. She had the look of a
woman going single-handed, weaponless, into battle.

The sun was a deep yellow now like a harvest moon and was riding westward very fast over the far tree line as if it meant to reach the hogs before she did. The road was rutted and she kicked several good-sized stones out of her path as she strode along. The pig parlor was on a little knoll at the end of a lane that ran off from the side of the barn. It was a square of concrete as large as a small room, with a board fence about four feet high around it. The concrete floor sloped slightly so that the hog wash could drain off into a trench where it was carried to the field for fertilizer. Claud was standing on the outside, on the edge of the concrete, hanging onto the top board, hosing down the floor inside. The hose was connected to the faucet of a water trough nearby.

Mrs. Turpin climbed up beside him and glowered down at the hogs inside. There were seven long-snouted bristly shoats in it—tan with liver-colored spots—and an old sow a few weeks off from farrowing. She was lying on her side grunting. The shoats were running about shaking themselves like idiot children, their little slit pig eyes searching the floor for anything left. She had read that pigs were the most intelligent animal. She doubted it. They were supposed to be smarter than dogs. There had even been a pig astronaut. He had performed his assignment perfectly but died of a heart attack afterwards because they left him in his electric suit, sitting upright throughout his examination when naturally a hog should be on all fours.

A-gruntin and a-rootin and a-groanin.

"Gimme that hose," she said, yanking it away from Claud. "Go on and carry them niggers home and then get off that leg."

"You look like you might have swallowed a mad dog," Claud observed, but he got down and limped off. He paid no attention to her humors.

Until he was out of earshot, Mrs. Turpin stood on the side of the pen, holding the hose and pointing the stream of water at the hind quarters of any shoat that looked as if it might try to lie down. When he had had time to get over the hill, she turned her head slightly and wrathful eyes scanned the path. He was nowhere in sight. She turned back again and seemed to gather herself up. Her shoulders rose and she drew in her breath.

"What do you send me a message like that for?" she said in a low fierce voice, barely above a whisper but with the force of a shout in its concentrated fury. "How am I a hog and me both? How am I saved and from hell too?" Her free fist was knotted and with the other she gripped the hose, blindly pointing the stream of water in and out of the eye of the old sow whose outraged squeal she did not hear.

The pig parlor commanded a view of the back pasture where their twenty beef cows were gathered around the hay-bales Claud and the boy had put out. The freshly cut pasture sloped down to the highway. Across it was their cotton field and beyond that a dark green dusty wood which they owned as well. The sun was behind the wood, very red, looking over the paling of trees like a farmer inspecting his own hogs.

"Why me?" she rumbled. "It's no trash around here, black or white, that I haven't given to. And break my back to the bone every day working. And do for the church."

She appeared to be the right size woman to command the arena before her. "How am I a hog?" she demanded. "Exactly how am I like them?" and she jabbed the stream of water at the shoats. "There was plenty of trash there. It didn't have to be me.

"If you like trash better, go get yourself some trash then," she railed. "You could have made me trash. Or a nigger. If trash is what you wanted why didn't you make me trash?" She shook her fist with the hose in it and a watery snake appeared momentarily in the air. "I could quit working and take it easy and be filthy," she growled. "Lounge about the sidewalks all day drinking root beer. Dip snuff and spit in every puddle and have it all over my face. I could be nasty.

"Or you could have made me a nigger. It's too late for me to be a nigger," she said with deep sarcasm, "but I could act like one. Lay down in the middle of the road and stop traffic. Roll on the ground."

In the deepening light everything was taking on a mysterious hue. The pasture was growing a peculiar glassy green and the streak of highway had turned lavender. She braced herself for a final assault and this time her voice rolled out over the pasture. "Go on," she yelled, "call me a hog! Call me a hog again. From hell. Call me a wart hog from hell. Put the bottom rail on top. There'll still be a top and bottom!"

A garbled echo returned to her.

A final surge of fury shook her and she roared, "Who do you think you are?"

The color of everything, field and crimson sky, burned for a moment with a transparent intensity. The question carried over the pasture and across the highway and the cotton field and returned to her clearly like an answer from beyond the wood.

She opened her mouth but no sound came out of it.

A tiny truck, Claud's, appeared on the highway, heading rapidly out of sight. Its gears scraped thinly. It looked like a child's toy. At any moment a bigger truck might smash into it and scatter Claud's and the niggers' brains all over the road.

Mrs. Turpin stood there, her gaze fixed on the highway, all her muscles rigid, until in five or six minutes the truck reappeared, returning. She waited until it had had time to turn into their own road. Then like a monumental statue coming to life, she bent her head slowly and gazed, as if through the very heart of mystery, down into the pig parlor at the hogs. They had settled all in one corner around the old sow who was grunting softly. A red glow suffused them. They appeared to pant with a secret life.

Until the sun slipped finally behind the tree line, Mrs. Turpin remained there with her gaze bent to them as if she were absorbing some abysmal life-giving knowledge. At last she lifted her head. There was only a purple streak in the sky, cutting through a field of crimson and leading, like an extension of the highway, into the descending dusk. She raised her hands from the side of the pen in a gesture hieratic and profound. A visionary light settled in her eyes. She saw the streak as a vast swinging bridge extending upward from the earth through a field of living fire. Upon it a vast horde of souls were rumbling toward heaven. There were whole companies of whitetrash, clean for the first time in their lives, and bands of black niggers in white robes, and battalions of freaks and lunatics shouting and clapping and leaping like frogs. And bringing up the end of the procession was a tribe of people whom she recognized at once as those who, like herself and Claud, had always had a little of everything and the God-given wit to use it right. She leaned forward to observe them closer. They were marching behind the others with great dignity, accountable as they had always been for good order and common sense and respectable behavior. They alone were on key. Yet she could see by their shocked and altered faces that even their virtues were being burned away. She lowered her hands and gripped the rail of the hog pen, her eyes small but fixed unblinkingly on what lay ahead. In a moment the vision faded but she remained where she was, immobile.

At length she got down and turned off the faucet and made her slow way on the darkening path to the house. In the woods around her the invisible cricket choruses had struck up, but what she heard were the voices of the souls climbing upward into the starry field and shouting hallelujah.

Tell Me a Riddle

For forty-seven years they had been married. How deep back the stubborn, gnarled roots of the quarrel reached, no one could say— but only now, when tending to the needs of others no longer shackled them together, the roots swelled up visible, split the earth between them, and the tearing shook even to the children, long since grown.

Why now, why now? wailed Hannah.

As if when we grew up weren't enough, said Paul.

Poor Ma. Poor Dad. It hurts so for both of them, said Vivi. They never had very much, at least in old age they should be happy.

Knock their heads together, insisted Sammy, tell 'em: you're too old for this kind of thing; no reason not to get along now.

Lenny wrote to Clara: They've lived over so much together; what could possibly tear them apart?

Something tangible enough.

Arthritic hands, and such work as he got, occasional. Poverty all his life, and there was little breath left for the running. He could not, could not turn away from this desire: to have the troubling of responsibility, the fretting with money, over and done with; to be free, to be carefree where success was not measured by accumulation, and there was use for the vitality still in him.

There was a way. They could sell the house, and with the money join his lodge's Haven, cooperative for the aged. Happy communal life, and was he not already an official; had he not helped organize it, raise funds, served as a trustee?

But she—would not consider it.

"What do we need all this for?" he would ask loudly, for her hearing aid was turned down and the vacuum was shrilling. "Five rooms" (pushing the sofa so she could get into the corner) "furniture" (smoothing down the rug) "floors and surfaces to make work. Tell me, why do we need it?" And he was glad he could ask in a scream.

"Because I'm use't."

"Because you're use't. This is a reason, Mrs. Word Miser? Used to can get unused!"

"Enough unused I have to get used to already . . . Not enough words?" turning off the vacuum a moment to hear herself answer. "Because soon enough we'll need only a little closet, no windows, no furniture, no rooms, nothing to make work but for worms. Screech and blow like you're doing, you'll need that closet even sooner . . . Ha, again!" for the vacuum bag wailed, puffed half up, hung stubbornly limp. "This time fix it so it stays; quick before the phone rings and you get too important-busy."

But while he struggled with the motor, it seethed in him. Why fix it? Why have to bother? And if it can't be fixed, have to wring the mind with how to pay the repair? At the Haven they come in with their own machines to clean your room or your cottage; you fish, or play cards, or make jokes in the sun, not with knotty fingers fight to mend vacuums.

Over the dishes, coaxingly: "For once in your life, to be free, to have everything done for you, like a queen."

"I never liked queens."

"No dishes, no garbage, no towel to sop, no worry what to buy, what to eat."

"And what else would I do with my empty hands? Better to eat at my own table when I want, and to cook and eat how I want."

"In the cottages they buy what you ask, and cook it how you like. *You* are the one who always used to say: better mankind born without mouths and stomachs than always to worry for money to buy, to shop, to fix, to cook, to wash, to clean."

"How cleverly you hid that you heard. I said it then because eighteen hours a day I ran. And you never scraped a carrot or knew a dish towel sops. Now—for you and me—who cares? A herring out of a jar is enough. But when *I* want, and nobody to bother." And she turned off her ear button, so she would not have to hear.

But as *he* had no peace, juggling and re-juggling the money to figure: how will I pay for this now?; prying out the storm windows (there they take care of this); jolting in the streetcar on errands (there I would not have to ride to take care of this or that); fending the patronizing of relatives just back from Florida (there it matters what one is, not what one can afford), he gave *her* no peace.

"Look! In their bulletin. A reading circle. Twice a week it meets."

"Haumm," her answer of not listening.

"A reading circle. Chekhov they read that you like, and Peretz. Cultured people at the Haven that you would enjoy."

"Enjoy!" She tasted the word. "Now, when it pleases you, you find a reading circle for me. And forty years ago when the children were morsels and there was a Circle, did you stay home with them once so I could go? Even once? You trained me well. I do not need others to enjoy. Others!" Her voice trembled. "Because *you* want to be there with others. Already it makes me sick to think of you always around others. Clown, grimacer, floormat, yesman, entertainer, whatever they want of you." And now it was he who turned on the television loud so he need not hear.

Old scar tissue ruptured and the wounds festered anew. Chekhov indeed. She thought without softness of that young wife, who in the deep night hours while she nursed the current baby, and perhaps held another in her lap, would try to stay awake for the only time there was to read. She would feel again the weather of the outside on his cheek when, coming late from a meeting, he would find her so, and stimulated and ardent, sniffing her skin, coax: "I'll put the baby to bed, and you—put the book away, don't read, don't read."

That had been the most beguiling of all the "don't read, put your book away" her life had been. Chekhov indeed!

"Money?" She shrugged him off. "Could we get poorer than once we were? And in America, who starves?"

But as still he pressed:

"Let me alone about money. Was there ever enough? Seven little ones—for every penny I had to ask—and sometimes, remember, there was nothing. But always *I* had to manage. Now *you* manage. Rub your nose in it good."

But from those years she had had to manage, old humiliations and terrors rose up, lived again, and forced her to relive them. The children's needings; that grocer's face or this merchant's wife she had had to beg credit from when credit was a disgrace, the scenery of the long blocks she had walked around when she could not pay them; school coming, and the desperate going over the old to see what could yet be re-made; the soups of meat bones begged "for-the-dog" one winter . . .

Enough. Now they had no children. Let *him* wrack his head for how they would live. She would not exchange her solitude for anything. *Never again to be forced to move to the rhythms of others.*

For in this solitude she had won to a reconciled peace.

Tranquillity from having the empty house no longer an enemy, for it stayed clean—not as in the days when (by the perverse logic of exhausted housewifery) it was her family, the life in it, that had seemed the enemy: tracking, smudging, littering, dirtying, engaging her in endless defeating battle—and on whom her endless defeat had been spewed.

The few old books, memorized from re-reading; the pictures to ponder (the magnifying glass superimposed on her heavy eyeglasses). Or if she wishes, when he is gone, the phonograph, that if she turns up very loud and strains, she can hear: the ordered sounds, and the struggling.

Out in the garden, growing things to nurture. Birds to be kept out of the pear tree, and when the pears are heavy and ripe, the old fury of work, for all must be canned, nothing wasted.

And her one social duty (for she will not go to luncheons or meetings) the boxes of old clothes left with her, as with a life-practiced eye for finding what is still wearable within the worn (again the magnifying glass superimposed on the heavy glasses) she scans and sorts—this for rag or rummage, that for mending and cleaning, and this for sending abroad.

Being able at last to live within, and not move to the rhythms of others, as life had helped her to: denying; estranging; isolating; taking the children one by one; then deafening, half blinding—and at last, presenting her solitude.

And in it she had won to a reconciled peace.

Now he was violating it with his constant campaigning: *Sell the house and move to the Haven.* (You sit, you sit—there too you could sit like a stone.) He was making of her a battleground where old grievances tore. (Turn on your ear button—I am talking.) And stubbornly she resisted—so that from wheedling, reasoning, manipulation, it was bitterness he now started with.

And it came to where every happening lashed up a quarrel.

"I will sell the house anyway," he flung at her one night. "I am putting it up for sale. There will be a way to make you sign."

The television blared, as always it did on the evenings he stayed home, and as always it reached her only as noise. She did not know if the tumult was in her or outside. Snap! she turned the sound off. "Shadows," she whispered to him, pointing to the screen, "look, it is only shadows." And in a scream: "Did you say you will see the house? Look at me, not at that. I am no shadow. You cannot sell without me."

"Leave on the television. I am watching."

"Like Paulie, like Jenny, a four-year-old. Staring at shadows. *You cannot sell the house.*"

"I will. We are going to the Haven. There you would not have the television when you do not want it. I could sit in the social room and watch. You could lock yourself up to smell your unpleasantness in a room by yourself—for who would want to come near you?"

"No, no selling." A whisper now.

"The television is shadows. Mrs. Enlightened! Mrs. Cultured! A world comes into your house—and it is shadows. People you would never meet in a thousand lifetimes. Wonders. When you were four years old, yes, like Paulie, like Jenny, did you know of Indian dances, alligators, how they used bamboo in Malaya? No, you scratched in your dirt with the chickens and thought Olshana was the world. Yes, Mrs. Unpleasant, I will sell the house, for there better can we be rid of each other than here."

She did not know if the tumult was outside, or in her. Always a ravening inside, a pull to the bed, to lie down, to succumb.

"Have you thought maybe Ma should let a doctor have a look at her?" asked their son Paul after Sunday dinner, regarding his mother crumpled on the couch, instead of, as was her custom, busying herself in Nancy's kitchen.

"Why not the President too?"

"Seriously, Dad. This is the third Sunday she's lain down like that after dinner. Is she that way at home?"

"A regular love affair with the bed. Every time I start to talk to her."

Good protective reaction, observed Nancy to herself. The workings of hos-ti-lity.

"Nancy could take her. I don't like how she looks. Let's have Nancy arrange an appointment."

"You think she'll go?" regarding his wife gloomily. "All right, we have to have doctor bills, we have to have doctor bills." Loudly: "Something hurts you?"

She startled, looked to his lips. He repeated: "Mrs. Take It Easy, something hurts?"

"Nothing . . . Only you."

"A woman of honey. That's why you're lying down?"

"Soon I'll get up to do the dishes, Nancy."

"Leave them, Mother, I like it better this way."

"Mrs. Take It Easy, Paul says you should start ballet. You should go see a doctor and ask: how soon can you start ballet?"

"A doctor?" she begged. "Ballet?"

"We were talking, Ma," explained Paul, "you don't seem any too well. It would be a good idea for you to see a doctor for a checkup."

"I get up now to do the kitchen. Doctors are bills and foolishness, my son. I need no doctors."

"At the Haven," he could not resist pointing out, "a doctor is *not* bills. He lives beside you. You start to sneeze, he is there before you open up a kleenex. You can be sick there for free, all you want."

"Diarrhea of the mouth, is there a doctor to make you dumb?"

"Ma. Promise me you'll go. Nancy will arrange it."

"It's all of a piece when you think of it," said Nancy, "the way she attacks my kitchen, scrubbing under every cup hook, doing the inside of the oven so I can't enjoy Sunday dinner, knowing half blind or not, she's going to find every speck of dirt . . ."

"Don't, Nancy, I've told you—it's the only way she knows to be useful. What did the *doctor* say?"

"A real fatherly lecture. Sixty-nine is young these days. Go out, enjoy life, find interests. Get a new hearing aid, this one is antiquated. Old age is sickness only if one makes it so. Geriatrics, Inc."

"So there was nothing physical."

"Of course there was. How can you live to yourself the way she does without there being? Evidence of a kidney disorder, and her blood count is low. He gave her a diet, and she's to come back for follow-up and lab work . . . But he was clear enough: Number One prescription—start living like a human being. When I think of your dad who could really play the invalid with that arthritis of his, as active as a teen-ager, and twice as much fun . . ."

"You didn't tell me the doctor says your sickness is in you, how you live." He pushed his advantage. "Life and enjoyments you need better than medicine. And this diet, how can you keep it? To weigh each morsel and scrape away the bits of fat, to make this soup, that pudding. There, at the Haven, they have a dietician, they would do it for you."

She is silent.

"You would feel better there, I know it," he says gently. "There there is life and enjoyments all around."

"What is the matter, Mr. Importantbusy, you have no card game or meeting you can go to?"—turning her face to the pillow.

For a while he cut his meetings and going out, fussed over her diet, tried to wheedle her into leaving the house, brought in visitors:

"I should come to a fashion tea. I should sit and look at pretty babies in clothes I cannot buy. This is pleasure?"

"Always you are better than everyone else. The doctor said you should go out. Mrs. Brem comes to you with goodness and you turn her away."

"Because *you* asked her to, she asked me."

"They won't come back. People you need, the doctor said. Your own cousins I asked; they were willing to come and make peace as if nothing had happened . . ."

"No more crushers of people, pushers, hypocrites, around me. No more in *my* house. You go to them if you like."

"Kind he is to visit. And you, like ice."

"A babbler. All my life around babblers. Enough!"

"She's even worse, Dad? Then let her stew awhile," advised Nancy. "You can't let it destroy you; it's a psychological thing, maybe too far gone for any of us to help."

So he let her stew. More and more she lay silent in bed, and sometimes did not even get up to make the meals. No longer was the tongue-lashing inevitable if he left the coffee cup where it did not belong, or forgot to take out the garbage or mislaid the broom. The birds grew bold that summer and for once, pocked the pears, undisturbed.

A bellyful of bitterness, and every day the same quarrel in a new way and a different old grievance the quarrel forced her to enter and re-live. And the new torment: I am not really sick, the doctor said it, then why do I feel so sick?

One night she asked him: "You have a meeting tonight? Do not go. Stay . . . with me."

He had planned to watch "This Is Your Life" anyway, but half sick himself from the heavy heat, and sickening therefore the more after the brooks and woods of the Haven, with satisfaction he grated:

"Hah, Mrs. Live Alone And Like It wants company all of a sudden. It doesn't seem so good the time of solitary when she was a girl exile in Siberia. 'Do not go. Stay with me.' A new song for Mrs. Free As A Bird. Yes, I am going out, and while I am gone chew this aloneness good, and think how you keep us both from where if you want people you do not need to be alone."

"Go, go. All your life you have gone without me."

After him she sobbed curses he had not heard in years, old country curses from their childhood: Grow, oh shall you grow like an onion, with your head in the ground. Like the hide of a drum shall you be, beaten in life, beaten in death. Oh shall you be like a chandelier, to hang, and to burn . . .

She was not in their bed when he came back. She lay on the cot on the sun porch. All week she did not speak or come near him; nor did he try to make peace or care for her.

He slept badly, so used to her next to him. After all the years, old harmonies and dependencies deep in their bodies; she curled to him, or he coiled to her, each warmed, warming, turning as the other turned, the nights a long embrace.

It was not the empty bed or the storm that woke him, but a faint singing. *She* was singing. Shaking off the drops of rain, the lightning riving her lifted face, he saw her so; the cot covers on the floor.

"This is a private concert?" he asked. "Come in, you are wet."

"I can breathe now," she answered, "my lungs are rich." Though indeed the sound was hardly a breath.

"Come in, come in." Loosing the bamboo shades. "Look how wet you are." Half helping, half carrying her, still faint-breathing her song.

A Russian love song of fifty years ago.

He had found a buyer, but before he told her, he called together those children who were close enough to come. Paul, of course, Sammy from New Jersey, Hannah from Connecticut, Vivi from Ohio.

With a kindling of energy for her beloved visitors, she arrayed the house, cooked and baked. She was not prepared for the solemn after-dinner conclave, they too probing in and tearing. Her frightened eyes watched from mouth to mouth as each spoke.

His stories were eloquent and funny of her refusal to go back to the doctor; of the scorned invitations; of her stubborn silences or the bile "like a Niagara"; of her contrariness: "If I clean it's no good how I cleaned; if I don't clean, I'm still a master who thinks he has a slave."

("Vinegar, vinegar he poured on me all his life; I am well marinated; how can I be honey now?")

Deftly he marched in the rightness for moving to the Haven; their

money from social security free for visiting the children, not sucked
into daily needs and into the house; the activities in the Haven for
him; but mostly the Haven for *her*: her health, her need of care,
distraction, amusement, friends who shared her interests.

"This does offer an outlet for Dad," said Paul; "he's always been an
active person. And economic peace of mind isn't to be sneezed at,
either, I could use a little of that myself."

But when they asked: "And you, Ma, how do you feel about it?"
she could only whisper:

"For him it is good. It is not for me. I can no longer live between
people."

"You lived all your life *for* people," Vivi cried.

"Not with." Suffering doubly for the unhappiness on her children's faces.

"You have to find some compromise," Sammy insisted. "Maybe sell
the house and buy a trailer. After forty-seven years there's surely some
way you can find to live in peace."

"There is no help. Different things we need."

"Then live alone!" He could control himself no longer. "I have a
buyer for the house. Half the money for you, half for me. Either
alone or with me to the Haven. You think I can live any longer as
we are doing now?"

"Ma doesn't have to make a decision this minute, however you
feel, Dad," Paul said quickly, "and you wouldn't want her to. Let's
let it lay a few months, and then talk some more."

"I think I can work it out to take Mother home with me for a
while," Hannah said. "You both look terrible, but especially you,
Mother. I'm going to ask Phil to have a look at you."

"Sure," cracked Sammy. "What's the use of a doctor husband if
you can't get free service out of him once in a while for the family.
And absence might make the heart . . . you know."

"There was something after all," Paul told Nancy in a colorless
voice. "That was Hannah's Phil calling. Her gall bladder . . .
Surgery."

"Her *gall* bladder. If that isn't classic. 'Bitter as gall'—talk about
psychosom——"

He stepped closer, put his hand over her mouth and said in the
same colorless, plodding voice. "We have to get Dad. They operated
at once. The cancer was everywhere, surrounding the liver, everywhere. They did what they could . . . at best she has a year. Dad
. . . we have to tell him."

II

Honest in his weakness when they told him, and that she was
not to know. "I'm not an actor. She'll know right away by how I
am. O that poor woman. I am old too, it will break me into pieces.
O that poor woman. She will spit on me: 'So my sickness was how I
live.' O Paulie, how she will be, that poor woman. Only she should
not suffer . . . I can't stand sickness, Paulie, I can't go with you."

But went. And play-acted.

"A grand opening and you did not even wait for me . . . A good
thing Hannah took you with her."

"Fashion teas I needed. They cut out what tore in me; just in my
throat something hurts yet . . . Look! so many flowers, like a funeral.
Vivi called, did Hannah tell you? And Lenny from San Francisco,
and Clara; and Sammy is coming." Her gnome's face pressed happily
into the flowers.

It is impossible to predict in these cases, but once over the immediate effects of the operation, she should have several months of
comparative well-being.

The money, where will come the money?

Travel with her, Dad, the next few months. Don't take her home
to the old associations. The other children will want to see her.

The money, where will I wring the money?

Whatever happens, she is not to know. No, you can't ask her to
sign papers to sell the house; nothing to upset her. Borrow instead, then after . . .

*I had wanted to leave you each a few dollars to make life easier,
as other fathers do. There will be nothing left now. (Failure! you
and your "business is exploitation." Why didn't you make it when
it could be made?—Is that what you're thinking Sammy?)*

Sure she's unreasonable, Dad—but you have to stay with her; if
there's to be any happiness in what's left of her life, it depends on
you.

*Prop me up children, think of me, too. Shuffled, chained with her,
bitter woman. No Haven, and the little money going . . . How
happy she looks, poor creature.*

The look of excitement. The straining to hear everything (the new
hearing aid turned full). Why are you so happy, dying woman?

How the petals are, fold on fold, and the gladioli color. The autumn air.

Stranger grandsons, tall above the little gnome grandmother, the little spry grandfather. Paul in a frenzy of picture-taking before going.

She, wandering the great house. Feeling the books; laughing at the maple shoemaker's bench of a hundred years ago used as a table. The ear turned to music.

"Let us go home. See how good I walk now." "One step from the hospital," he answers, "and she wants to fly. Wait till Doctor Phil says."

"Look—the birds too are flying home. Very good Phil is and will not show it, but he is sick of sickness by the time he comes home." "Mrs. Telepathy, to read minds," he answers, "read mine what it says: when the trunks of medicines become a suitcase, then we will go."

The grandboys, they do not know what to say to us . . . Hannah, she runs around here, there, when is there time for herself?

Let us go home. Let us go home.

Musing; gentleness—*but for the incidents of the rabbi in the hospital, and of the candles of benediction.*

Of the rabbi in the hospital:

Now tell me what happened, Mother.

From the sleep I awoke, Hannah's Phil, and he stands there like a devil in a dream and calls me by name. I cannot hear. I think he prays. Go away please, I tell him, I am not a believer. Still he stands, while my heart knocks with fright.

You scared *him,* Mother. He thought you were delirious.

Who sent him? Why did he come to me?

It is a custom. The men of God come to visit those of their religion they might help. The hospital makes up the list for them—race, religion—and you are on the Jewish list. Not for rabbis. At once go and make them change. Tell them to write: Race, human; Religion, none.

And of the candles of benediction:

Look how you have upset yourself, Mrs. Excited Over Nothing. Pleasant memories you should leave.

Go in, go back to Hannah and the lights. Two weeks I saw and said nothing. But she asked me.

So what was so terrible? She forgets you never did, she asks you to light the Friday candles and say the benediction like Phil's mother when she visits. If the candles give her pleasure, why shouldn't she have the pleasure?

Not for pleasure she does it. For emptiness. Because his family
does. Because all around her do.

That is not a good reason to? But you did not hear her. For heritage, she told you. For the boys, from the past they should have
tradition.

Superstition! From the savages, afraid of the dark, of themselves:
mumbo words and magic lights to scare away ghosts.

She told you: how it started does not take away the goodness. For
Centuries, peace in the house it means.

Swindler! does she look back on the centuries? Candles bought
instead of bread and stuck into a potato for a candlestick? Religion
that stifled and said: in Paradise, woman, you will be the footstool
of your husband, and in life—poor chosen Jew—ground under,
despised, trembling in cellars. And cremated. And cremated.

This is religion's fault? You think you are still an orator of the
1905 revolution? Where are the pills for quieting? Which are they?
Heritage. How have we gone from the savages, how no longer to
be savages, this to teach. To look back and learn what ennobled
man, this to teach. To smash all ghettos that divide man, this to
teach. Books in the house, will man live or die, and she gives to her
boys—superstition.

Hannah that is so good to you. Take your pill, Mrs. Excited For
Nothing, swallow.

Heritage! But when did I have time to teach? Of Hannah I asked
only hands to help.

Swallow.

Otherwise—musing; gentleness.

Not to travel. To go home.

The children want to see you. We have to show them you are as
thorny a flower as ever.

Not to travel.

Vivi wants you should see her new baby. She sent the tickets—
airplane tickets—a Mrs. Roosevelt she wants to make of you. To
Vivi's we have to go.

A new baby. How many warm, seductive babies. She holds him
stiffly, *away* from her, so that he wails. And a long shudder begins,
and the sweat beads on her forehead.

"Hush, shush," croons the grandfather, lifting him back. "You
should forgive your grandmamma, little prince, she has never held
a baby before, only seen them in glass cases. Hush, shush."

"You're tired, Ma," says Vivi. "The travel and the noisy dinner. I'll take you to lie down."

(*A long travel from, to, what the feel of a baby evokes.*)

In the airplane, cunningly designed to encase from motion (no wind, no feel of flight), she had sat severely and still, her face turned to the sky through which they cleaved and left no scar.

So this was how it looked, the determining, the crucial sky, and this was how man moved through it, remote above the dwindled earth, the concealed human life. Vulnerable life, that could scar.

A steerage ship in memory shook across a great, circular sea: clustered, ill human beings, and through the thick-stained air, tiny fretting waters in a window round like the airplane's—sun round, moon round. (The round thatched roofs of Olshana.) Eye round —like the smaller window that framed distance the solitary year of exile when only her eyes could travel, and no voice spoke. And the polar winds hurled themselves across snow trackless and endless and white—like the clouds which had closed together below and hidden the earth.

Now they put a baby in her lap. Do not ask me, she would have liked to beg. Enough the worn face of Vivi, the remembered grandchildren. I cannot, cannot . . .

Cannot what? Unnatural grandmother, not able to make herself embrace a baby.

She lay there in the bed of the two little girls, her new hearing aid turned full, listening to the sound of the children going to sleep, the baby's fretful crying and hushing, the clatter of dishes being washed and put away. They thought she slept. Still she rode on.

It was not that she had not loved her babies, her children. The love—the passion of tending—had risen with the need like a torrent; and like a torrent drowned and immolated all else. But when the need was done—o the power that was lost in the painful damming back and drying up of what still surged, but had nowhere to go. Only the thin pulsing left that could not quiet, suffering over lives one felt, but could no longer hold nor help.

On that torrent she had borne them to their lives, and the riverbed was desert long years now. Not there would she dwell, a memoried wraith. Surely that was not all, surely there was more. Still the springs, the springs were in her seeking. Somewhere an older power that beat for life. Somewhere coherence, transport, meaning. If they would but leave her in the air now stilled of clamor, in the reconciled solitude, to journey to her life.

And they put a baby in her lap. Immediacy to embrace, and the breath of *that* past: warm flesh like this that had claims and nuzzled away all else and with lovely mouths devoured; hot living like an animal—intensely and now; the turning maze; the long drunkenness; the drowning into needing and being needed. Severely she looked back—and the shudder seized her again, and the sweat. Not that way. Not there, not now could she, not yet . . .

And all that visit, she could not touch the baby.

"Daddy, is it the . . . sickness she's like that?" asked Vivi. "I was so glad to be having the baby—for her. I told Tim, it'll give her more happiness than anything, being around a baby again. And she hasn't played with him once."

He was not listening. "Aahh little seed of life, little charmer," he crooned, "Hollywood should see you. A heart of ice you would melt. Kick, kick. The future you'll have for a ball. In 2050 still kick. Kick for your granddaddy then."

Attentive with the older children; sat through their performances (command performance; we command you to be the audience); helped Ann sort autumn leaves to find the best for a school program; listened gravely to Richard tell about his rock collection, while her lips mutely formed the words to remember: *igneous, sedimentary, metamorphic;* looked for missing socks, books and bus tickets; watched the children whoop after their grandfather who knew how to tickle, chuck, lift, toss, do tricks, tell secrets, make jokes, match riddle for riddle. (Tell me a riddle, Grammy. I know no riddles, child.) Scrubbed sills and woodwork and furniture in every room; folded the laundry; straightened drawers; emptied the heaped baskets waiting for ironing (while he or Vivi or Tim nagged: You're supposed to rest here, you've been sick) but to none tended or gave food—and could not touch the baby.

After a week she said: "Let us go home. Today call about the tickets."

"You have important business, Mrs. Inahurry? The President waits to consult with you?" He shouted, for the fear of the future raced in him. "The clothes are still warm from the suitcase, your children cannot show enough how glad they are to see you, and you want home. There is plenty of time for home. We cannot be with the children at home."

"Blind to around you as always: the little ones sleep four in a room because we take their bed. We are two more people in a house with a new baby, and no help."

"Vivi is happy so. The children should have their grandparents a
while, she told to me. I should have my mommy and daddy . . ."

"Babbler and blind. Do you look at her so tired? How she starts
to talk and she cries? I am not strong enough yet to help. Let us
go home."

(To reconciled solitude.)

*For it seemed to her the crowded noisy house was listening to her,
listening for her. She could feel it like a great ear pressed under her
heart. And everything knocked: quick constant raps: let me in, let
me in.*

*How was it that soft reaching tendrils also became blows that
knocked?*

Cmon Grandma, I want to show you . . .

Tell me a riddle, Grandma. *(I know no riddles)*

Look Grammy, he's so dumb he can't even find his hands. (Dody
and the baby on a blanket over the fermenting autumn mound)
I made them—for you. (Flat paper dolls with aprons that lifted on
scalloped skirts that lifted on flowered pants; hair of yarn and
great ringed questioning eyes) (Ann)

Watch me, Grandma. Richard snaking up the tree, hanging exult-
ant, free, with one hand at the top. Below Dody hunches over in
pretend-cooking. (Climb too, Dody, climb and look) Be my nap
bed, Grammy. (The "No!" too late.) Morty's abandoned heaviness,
while his fingers ladder up and down her hearing-aid cord to his
drowsy chant: eentsiebeentsiespider. *(Children trust)*

It's to start off your own rock collection. Grandma. That's a trilobite fossil, 200 million years old (millions of years on a boy's
mouth) and that one's obsidian, black glass.

Knocked and knocked.

Mother, I *told* you the teacher said we had to bring it back all
filled out this morning. Didn't you even ask Daddy? Then tell *me*
which plan and I'll check it: evacuate or stay in the city or wait
for you to come and take me away. (Seeing the look of straining
to hear) It's for Disaster, Grandma. *(Children trust)*

Vivi in the maze of the long, the lovely drunkenness. The old old
noises: baby sounds, screaming of a mother flayed to exasperation;
children quarreling; children playing; singing; laughter.

And Vivi's tears and memories, spilling so fast, half the words not
understood.

She had started remembering out loud deliberately, so her mother would know the past was cherished, still lived in her.

Nursing the baby: My friends marvel, and I tell them, oh it's easy to be such a cow. I remember how beautiful my mother seemed nursing my brother, and the milk just flows . . . Was that Davy? It must have been Davy . . .

Lowering a hem: How did you ever . . . when I think how you made everything we wore . . . Tim, just think, seven kids and Mommy sewed everything . . . do I remember you sang while you sewed? That white dress with the red apples on the skirt you fixed over for me, was it Hannah's or Clara's before it was mine?

Washing sweaters: Ma, I'll never forget, one of those days so nice you washed clothes outside; one of the first spring days it must have been. The bubbles just danced up and down while you scrubbed, and we chased after, and you stopped to show us how to blow our own bubbles with green onion stalks . . . you always . . .

"Strong onion, to still make you cry after so many years," her father said, to turn the tears into laughter.

While Richard bent over his homework: where is it now, do we still have it, the Book of the Martyrs? It always seemed so, well—exalted, when you'd put it on the round table and we'd all look at it together; there was even a halo from the lamp. The lamp with the beaded fringe you could move up and down; they're in style again, pulley lamps like that, but without the fringe. You know the book I'm talking about, Daddy, the Book of the Martyrs, the first picture was a bust of Socrates? I wish there was something like that for the children, Mommy, to give them what you . . . (And the tears splashed again)

(What I intended and did not? Stop it, daughter, stop it, leave that time. And he, the hypocrite, sitting there with tears in his eyes too— it was nothing to you then, nothing.)

. . . The time you came to school and I almost died of shame because of your accent and because I knew you knew I was ashamed; how could I? . . . Sammy's harmonica and you danced to it once yes you did you and Davy squealing in your arms . . . That time you bundled us up and walked us down to the railroad station to stay the night 'cause it was heated and we didn't have any coal, that winter of the strike, you didn't think I remembered that, did you, Mommy? . . . How you'd call us out to see the sunsets . . .

Day after day, the spilling memories. Worse now, questions, too. Even the grandchildren: Grandma, in the olden days, when you were little . . .

It was the afternoons that saved.

While they thought she napped, she would leave the mosaic on the wall (of children's drawings, maps, calendars, pictures, Ann's cardboard dolls with their great ringed questioning eyes) and hunch in the girls' closet, on the low shelf where the shoes stood, and the girls' dresses covered.

For that while she would painfully sheathe against the listening house, the tendrils and noises that knocked, and Vivi's spilling memories. Sometimes it helped to braid and unbraid the sashes that dangled, or to trace the pattern on the hoop slips.

Today she had jacks and children under jet trails to forget. Last night, Ann and Dody silhouetted in the window against a sunset of flaming man-made clouds of jet trail, their jacks' ball accenting the peaceful noise of dinner being made. Had she told them, yes she had told them of how they played jacks in her village though there was no ball, no jacks. Six stones, round and flat, toss them out, the seventh on the back of the hand, toss, catch and swoop up as many as possible, toss again . . .

Of stones (repeating Richard) there are three kinds (*igneous, sedimentary, metamorphic*): earth's fire jetting; rock of layered centuries; crucibled new out of the old. But there was that other—frozen to black glass, never to transform or hold the fossil memory . . . (let not my seed fall on stone). There was an ancient man who fought to heights a great rock that crashed back down eternally—eternal labor, freedom, labor . . . (stone will perish, but the word remain) And you, David, who with a stone slew, screaming: Lord, take my heart of stone and give me flesh.

Who was screaming? Why was she back in the common room of the prison, the sun motes dancing in the shafts of light, and the informer being brought in, a prisoner now, like themselves. And Lisa leaping, yes, Lisa, the gentle and tender, biting at the betrayer's jugular. Screaming and screaming.

No, it is the children screaming. Another of Paul and Sammy's terrible fights?

In Vivi's house. Severely: you are in Vivi's house.

Blows, screams, a call: "Grandma!" For her? O please not for her. Hide, hunch behind the dresses deeper. But a trembling little body hurls itself beside her—surprised, smothered laughter—arms surround her neck, tears rub dry on her cheek, and words too soft to understand whisper into her ear (Is this where you hide too, Grammy? It's my secret place, we have a secret now)

And the sweat beads, and the long shudder seizes.

It seemed the great ear pressed inside now, and the knocking. "We have to go home," she told him, "I grow ill here."

"It is your own fault, Mrs. Bodybusy, you do not rest, you do too much." He raged, but the fear was in his eyes. "It was a serious operation, they told you to take care . . . All right, we will go to where you can rest."

But where? Not home to death, not yet. He had thought to Lenny's yet, to Clara's; beautiful visits with each of the children. She would have to rest first, be stronger. If they could but go to Florida—it glittered before him the never-realized promise of Florida —California: of course. (The money, the money dwindling!) Los Angeles first for sun and rest, then to Lenny's in San Francisco.

He told her the next day. "You saw what Nancy wrote: snow and wind back home, a terrible winter. And look at you—all bones and a swollen belly. I called Phil: he said: 'A prescription, Los Angeles sun and rest.'"

"You have sold the house," she cried, "that is why we do not go home. That is why you talk no more of the Haven, that is why there is money for travel. After the children you will drag me to the Haven."

"The Haven! Who thinks of the Haven any more? Tell her, Vivi, tell Mrs. Suspicious: a prescription, sun and rest, to make you healthy . . . And how could I sell the house without *you?*"

At the place of farewells and greetings, of winds of coming and winds of going, they say their good-bys.

They look back at her with the eyes of others before them: Richard with her own blue blaze; Ann with the nordic eyes of Tim; Morty's dreaming brown of a great grandmother he will never know; Dody with the laughing eyes of him who had been her springtide love (who stands beside her now); Vivi's, all tears.

The baby's eyes are closed in sleep.

Good-by, my children.

III

It is to the back of the great city he brought her, to the dwelling places of the cast-off old. Bounded by two lines of amusement piers to the north and to the south, and between a long straight paving rimmed with black benches facing the sands—sands so wide the ocean is only a far fluting edge.

In the brief vacation season, some of the boarded stores fronting the sands open, and families, young people and children may be seen. A little tasseled tram shuttles between the piers, and the lights of roller coasters prink and tweak over those who come to have sensation made in them.

The rest of the year it is abandoned to the old, all else boarded up and still; seemingly empty, except the occasional days and hours when the sun, like a tide, sucks them out of the low rooming houses, casts them onto the benches and sandy rim of the walk—and sweeps them into decaying enclosures back again.

A few newer apartments glint among the low bleached squares. It is in one of these Lenny's Jeannie has arranged their rooms. "Only a few miles north and south people pay hundreds of dollars a month for just this gorgeous air, Granddaddy, just this ocean closeness."

She had been ill on the plane, lay ill for days in the unfamiliar room. Several times the doctor came by—left medicine she would not take. Several times Jeannie drove in the twenty miles from work, still in her Visiting Nurse uniform, the lightness and brightness of her like a healing.

"Who can believe it is winter?" he said one morning. "Beautiful it is outside like an ad. Come, Mrs. Invalid, come to taste it. You are well enough to sit in here, you are well enough to sit outside. The doctor said it too."

But the benches were encrusted with people, and the sands at the sidewalk's edge. Besides, she had seen the far ruffle of the sea: "there take me," and though she leaned against him, it was she who led.

Plodding and plodding, sitting often to rest, he grumbling. Patting the sand so warm. Once she scooped up a handful, cradling it close to her better eye; peered, and flung it back. And as they came almost to the brink and she could see the glistening wet, she sat down, pulled off her shoes and stockings, left him and began to run. "You'll catch cold," he screamed, but the sand in his shoes weighed him down—he who had always been the agile one—and already the white spray creamed her feet.

He pulled her back, took a handkerchief to wipe off the wet and the sand. "O no," she said, "the sun will dry," seized the square and smoothed it flat, dropped on it a mound of sand, knotted the kerchief corners and tied it to a bag—"to look at with the strong glass" (for the first time in years she explained an action of hers)—and lay down with the little bag against her cheek, looking toward the shore that nurtured life as it first crawled toward consciousness the millions years ago.

He took her one Sunday in the evil-smelling bus, past flat miles
of blister houses, to the home of relatives. O what is this? she cried
as the light began to smoke and the houses to dim and recede. Smog,
he said, everyone knows but you . . . Outside he kept his arms about
her, but she walked with hands pushing the heavy air as if to open
it, whispered: who has done this?, sat down suddenly to vomit at the
curb and for a long while refused to rise.

One's age as seen on the altered face of those known in youth.
Is this they he has come to visit? This Max and Rose, smooth and
pleasant, introducing them to polite children, disinterested grandchildren, "the whole family, once a month on Sundays. And why
not? We have the room, the help, the food."

Talk of cars, of houses, of success: this son that, that daughter
this. And *your* children? Hastily skimped over, the intermarriages,
the obscure work—"my doctor son-in-law, Phil"—all he has to offer.
She silent in a corner. (Carsick like a baby, he explains.) Years since
he has taken her to visit anyone but the children, and old appre-
hensions prickle: "no incidents," he silently begs, "no incidents." He
itched to tell them: "A very sick woman," significantly, indicating
her with his eyes, "a very sick woman." Their restricted faces did
not react. "Have you thought maybe she'd do better at Palm
Springs?" Rose asked. "Or at least a nicer section of the beach, nicer
people, a pool." Not to have to say "money" he said instead: "would
she have sand to look at through a magnifying glass?" and went on,
detail after detail, the old habit betraying of parading the queerness
of her for laughter.

After dinner—the others into the living room in men- or women-
clusters, or into the den to watch TV—the four of them alone. She
sat close to him, and did not speak. Jokes, stories, people they had
known, beginning of reminiscence, Russia fifty—sixty years ago.
Strange words across the Duncan Phyfe table: *hunger; human
rights; secret meetings; spies; betrayals; prison; escape*—interrupted by
one of the grandchildren: "Commercial's on; any coke left? Gee,
you're missing a real hair-raiser." And then a granddaughter (Max
proudly: "look at her, an American queen") drove them back. No
incident—except that there had been no incidents.

The first few mornings she had taken with her the magnifying
glass, but he would sit only on the benches, so she rested at the foot,
where slatted bench shadows fell, and unless she turned her hearing
aid down, other voices invaded.

Now on the days when the sun shone and she felt well enough,

he took her on the tram to where the benches ranged in oblongs,
some with tables for checkers or cards. Again the blanket on the
sand in the striped shadows, but she no longer brought the magnifying glass. He played cards, and she lay in the sun and looked
toward the waters; or they walked—two blocks down to the scaling
hotel, two blocks back—past chili-hamburger stands, open-doored
bars, Next to New and Perpetual Rummage Sale stores.

Once, out of the aimless walkers, slow and shuffling like themselves, someone ran unevenly toward them, embraced, kissed, wept:
"dear friends, old friends." A friend of *hers*, not his: Mrs. Mays who
had lived next door to them in Denver when the children were small.

Thirty years are compressed into a dozen sentences; and the present, not even in three. All is told: the children scattered; the husband dead; she lives in a room two blocks up from the sing hall—
and points to the domed auditorium jutting before the pier. The
leg? phlebitis; the heavy breathing? that one does not ask. She too
comes to the benches each nice day to sit. And tomorrow, tomorrow, are they going to the community sing? Of course he would
have heard of it, everybody goes—the big doings they wait for all
week. They have never been? She will come to them for dinner tomorrow and they will all go together.

So it is that she sits in the wind of the singing, among the thou-
sand various faces of age.

She had turned off her hearing aid at once they came into the
auditorium—as she would have wished to turn off sight.

One by one they streamed by and imprinted on her—and though
the savage zest of their singing came voicelessly soft and distant,
the faces roared—the faces densened the air—chorded

children-chants, mother-croons, singing of the chained;
love serenades, Beethoven storms, mad Lucia's scream;
drunken joy-songs, keens for the dead, work singing

> *while from floor to balcony to dome a barefooted sore-covered*
> *little girl threaded the sound-thronged tumult, danced her ec-*
> *stasy of grimace to flutes that scratched at a crossroads village*
> *wedding*

Yes, faces became sound, and the sound became faces; and faces
and sound became weight—pushed, pressed

"Air"—her hand claws his.

"Whenever I enjoy myself . . ." Then he saw the gray sweat on

her face. "Here. Up. Help me, Mrs. Mays," and they support her
out to where she can gulp the air in sob after sob.

"A doctor, we should get for her a doctor."

"Tch, it's nothing," says Ellen Mays, "I get it all the time . . .
You've missed the tram; come to my place . . . close . . . tea. My
view. See, she *wants* to come. Steady now, that's how." Adding
mysteriously: "Remember your advice, easy to keep your head above
water, empty things float. Float."

The singing a fading march for them, tall woman with a swollen
leg, weaving little man, and the swollen thinness they help between.

The stench in the hall: mildew? decay? "We sit and rest then
climb. My gorgeous view. We help each other and here we are."

The stench along into the slab of room. A washstand for a sink,
a box with oilcloth tacked round for a cupboard, a three-burner gas
plate. Artificial flowers, colorless with dust. Everywhere pictures
foaming: wedding, baby, party, vacation, graduation, family pictures. From the narrow couch under a slit of window, sure enough
the view: lurching rooftops and a scallop of ocean heaving, preen-
ing, twitching under the moon.

"While the water heats. Excuse me . . . down the hall." Ellen
Mays had gone.

"You'll live?" he asks mechanically, sat down to feel his fright;
tried to pull her alongside.

She pushed him away. "For air," she said; stood clinging to the
dresser. Then, in a terrible voice:

After a lifetime of room. Of many rooms.

Shhh

You remember how she lived. Eight children. And now one room
like a coffin

She pays rent!

Shrinking the life of her into one room like a coffin   Rooms and
rooms like this   I lie on a quilt and hear them talk   Once you went
for coffee   I walked   I saw

Shhh Mrs. Orator Without Breath

A Balzac   a Chekhov to write it   Rummage   Alone   On scraps

Better here old than in the old country!

On scraps   And they sanglike . . . like   Wondrous. *Man: one
has to believe.*   So strong.   For what: To rot   not grow?

Your poor lungs beg you. They sob between each word.

Singing! Unused the life in them. She in this poor room with her
pictures. Max   You   The children   Everywhere unused the life

And who has meaning? Century after century still all in man not to grow?

Coffins, rummage, plants: sick woman. O lay down. We will get for you the doctor.

And when will it end. *O, the end.* (*That* nightmare thought, and this time she writhed, crumpled against him, seized his hand— *for a moment again the weight, the soft distant roaring of humanity*) And on the strangled-for breath, begged: "Man . . . will destroy ourselves?"

And looking for answer—in the helpless pity and fear for her (for *her*) that distorted his face—she understood the last months, and knew that she was dying.

IV

"Let us go home," she said after several days.

"You are in training for a cross-country trip? That is why you do not even walk across the room? Here, like a prescription Phil said, till you are stronger from the operation. You want to break doctor's orders?"

She saw the fiction was necessary to him, was silent; then: "At home I will get better. If the doctor here says?"

"And winter? And the visits to Lenny and to Clara? All right," for he saw the tears in her eyes, "I will write Phil, and talk to the doctor."

Days passed. He reported nothing. Jeannie came and took her out for air, past the boarded concessions, the hooded and tented amusement rides, to the end of the pier. They watched the spent waves feeding the new; the gulls in the clouded sky; even up where they sat, the windblown sand stung.

She did not ask to go down the crooked steps to the sea.

Back in her bed, while he was gone to the store, she said: "Jeannie, this doctor, he is not one I can ask questions. Ask him for me, can I go home?"

Jeannie looked at her, said quickly: "Of course, poor Granny, you want your own things around you, don't you? I'll call him to-night . . . Look, I have something to show you," and from her purse unwrapped a large cookie, intricately shaped like a little girl. "Look at the curls—can you hear me well, Granny?—and the darling eye-lashes. I just came from a house where they had finished baking them."

"The dimples," she marveled, "there in the knees," holding it to the better light, turning, studying, "like art. Each singly they cut, or a mold?"

"Singly," said Jeannie, "and if it is a child only the mother can make them. O Granny, it's the likeness of a real little girl who died yesterday—Rosita. She was three years old. *Pan del Muerto*, the Bread of the Dead. It was the custom in the part of Mexico they came from."

Still she turned and inspected. "Look, the hollow in the throat, the little cross necklace . . . I think for the mother it is a good thing to be busy with such bread. You know the family?"

Jeannie nodded. "On my rounds. I nursed . . . O Granny, it is like a party; they play songs she liked to dance to. The coffin is lined with pink velvet and she wears a white dress. There are candles . . ."

"In the house?" Surprised, "They keep her in the house?"

"Yes," said Jeannie, "and it is against the health law. I think she is . . . prepared there. The father said it will be sad to bury her here; in Oaxaca they have a feast night with candles each year; everyone picnics on the graves of those they loved until dawn."

"Yes Jeannie, the living must comfort themselves," and closed her eyes.

"You want to sleep, Granny?"

"Yes, tired from the pleasure of you. I may keep the Rosita? There stand it, on the dresser, where I can see; something of my own around me."

In the kitchenette, helping her grandfather unpack the groceries, Jeannie said in her light voice:

"I'm resigning my job, Granddaddy."

"Ah the lucky young man. Which one is he?"

"Too late. You're spoken for." She made a pyramid of cans, unstacked, and built again.

"Something is wrong with the job?"

"With me. I can't be"—she searched for the word—"professional enough. I let myself feel things. And tomorrow I have to report a family . . ." The cans clicked again. "It's not that, either. I just don't know what I want to do, maybe go back to school, maybe go to art school. I thought if you went to San Francisco I'd come along and talk it over with Mommy and Daddy. But I don't see how you can go. She wants to go home. She asked me to ask the doctor."

The doctor told her himself. "Next week you may travel, when you are a little stronger." But next week there was the fever of an infection, and by the time that was over, she could not leave the bed—a rented hospital bed that stood beside the double bed he slept in alone now.

Outwardly the days repeated themselves. Every other afternoon and evening he went out to his new-found cronies, to talk and play cards. Twice a week, Mrs. Mays came. And the rest of the time, Jeannie was there.

By the sickbed stood Jeannie's FM radio. Often into the room the shapes of music came. She would lie curled on her side, her knees drawn up, intense in listening (Jeannie sketched her so, coiled, convoluted like an ear), then thresh her hand out and abruptly snap the radio mute—still to lie in her attitude of listening, concealing tears.

Once Jeannie brought in a young Marine to visit, a friend from high-school days she had found wandering near the empty pier. Because Jeannie asked him to, gravely, without self-consciousness, he sat himself cross-legged on the floor and performed for them a dance of his native Samoa.

Long after they left, a tiny thrumming sound could be heard where, in her bed, she strove to repeat the beckon, flight, surrender of his hands, the fluttering footbeats, and his low plaintive calls.

Hannah and Phil sent flowers. To deepen her pleasure, he placed one in her hair. "Like a girl," he said and brought the hand mirror so she could see. She looked at the pulsing red flower, the yellow skull face; a desolate, excited laugh shuddered from her, and she pushed the mirror away—but let the flower burn.

The week Lenny and Helen came, the fever returned. With it the excited laugh, and incessant words. She, who in her life had spoken but seldom and then only when necessary (never having learned the easy, social uses of words), now, in dying, spoke incessantly.

In a half whisper: "Like Lisa she is, your Jeannie. Have I told you of Lisa, she who taught me to read? Of the high-born she was, but noble in herself. I was sixteen; they beat me; my father beat me so I would not go to her. It was forbidden, she was a Tolstoyan. At night, past dogs that howled, terrible dogs my son, in the snows of winter to the road, I to ride in her carriage like a lady to books. To her life was holy, knowledge was holy, and she taught me to read. They hung her. Everything that happens one must try to understand why. She killed one who betrayed many. Because of betrayal, betrayed all she lived and believed. In one minute she killed, before my

eyes (there is so much blood in a human being, my son), in prison
with me. All that happens, one must try to understand.

"The name?" Her lips would work. "The name that was their
pole star; the doors of the death houses fixed to open on it; I read of
it my year of penal servitude. Thuban!" very excited, "Thuban, in
ancient Egypt the pole star. Can you see, look out to see it, Jeannie,
if it swings around our pole star that seems to *us* not to move.

"Yes, Jeannie, at your age my mother and grandmother had already buried children; . . . yes, Jeannie, it is more than oceans
between Olshana and you . . . yes Jeannie they danced and for
all the bodies they had they might as well be chickens, and indeed,
they scratched and flapped their arms, and hopped.

"And Andrei Yefimitch, who for twenty years had never known
of it and never wanted to know, said as if he wanted to cry: but
why my dear friend this malicious laughter?" Telling to herself half-
memorized phrases from her few books. "Pain I answer with tears
and cries, baseness with indignation, meanness with repulsion . . .
for life may be hated or wearied of, but never despised."

Delirious: "Tell me, my neighbor, Mrs. Mays, the pictures never
lived, but what of the flowers? Tell them who ask: no rabbis, no
ministers, no priests, no speeches, no ceremonies: ah, false—let the
living please themselves. Tell Sammy's boy, he who flies, tell him to
go to Stuttgart and see where Davy has no grave. And what?" A
conspirator's laugh. "And what? where millions have no graves, save
air."

In delirium or not, wanting the radio on; not seeming to listen,
the words still jetting, wanting the music on. Once, silencing it
abruptly as of old, she began to cry, unconcealed tears this time.
"You have pain, Granny?" Jeannie asked.

"The music," she said, "still it is there and we do not hear; knocks,
and our poor human ears too weak. What else, what else we do not
hear?"

Once she knocked his hand aside as he gave her a pill, swept the
bottles from her bedside table: "no pills, let me feel what I feel," and
laughed as on his hands and knees he groped to pick them up.

Nighttimes her hand reached across the bed to hold his.

A constant retching began. Her breath was too faint for sustained
speech now, but still the lips moved:

When no longer necessary   to injure others
Pick   pick pick   Blind chicken
As a human being   responsibility for action

"David!" imperious, "Basin!" and she would vomit, rinse her mouth, the wasted throat working to swallow, and begin the chant again.

She will be better off in the hospital now, the doctor said.

He sent the telegrams to the children, was packing her suitcase, when her hoarse voice startled. She had roused, was pulling herself to sitting.

"Where now?" she asked. "Where now do you drag me?"

"You do not even have to have a baby to go this time," he soothed, looking for the brush to pack. "Remember, after Davy you told me —worthy to have a baby for the pleasure of the hospital?"

"Where now? Not home yet?" Her voice mourned. "Not home yet? Where *is* my home?"

He rose to ease her back. "The doctor, the hospital," he started to explain, but deftly, like a snake, she had slithered out of bed and stood swaying, propped behind the night table.

"Coward," she hissed, "runner."

"You stand," he said senselessly.

"To take me there and run. Afraid of a little vomit."

He reached her as she fell. She struggled against him, slipped from his arms, pulled herself up again.

"Weakling," she taunted, "to leave me there and run. Betrayer. All your life you have run."

He sobbed, telling Jeannie. "A Marilyn Monroe to run for her virtue. Fifty-nine pounds she weighs, the doctor said, and she beats at me like a Dempsey. Betrayer, she cries, and I running like a dog when she calls; day and night, running to her, her vomit, the bedpan . . ."

"She needs you, Granddaddy," said Jeannie. "Isn't that what they call love? I'll see if she sleeps, and if she does, the poor worn-out darling, we'll have a party, you and I; I brought us rum babas."

They did not move her. By her bed now stood the tall hooked pillar that held the solutions—blood and glucose—to feed her veins. Jeannie moved down the hall to take over the sickroom, her face so radiant, her grandfather asked her once: "You are in love?" (Shameful the joy, the pure overwhelming joy from being with her grandmother; the peace, the serenity that breathed.) "My darling escape," she answered incoherently, "my darling Granny,"—as if that explained.

Now one by one the children came, those that were able. Hannah, Paul, Sammy. Too late to ask: and what did you learn with your living, Mother, and what do we need to know?

Clara, the eldest, clenched:

Pay me back, Mother, pay me back for all you took from me. Those others you crowded into your heart. The hands I needed to be for you, the heaviness, the responsibility.

Is this she? Noises the dying make, the crablike hands crawling over the covers. The ethereal singing.

She hears that music, that singing from childhood; forgotten sound—not heard since, since . . . And the hardness breaks like a cry: Where did we lose each other, first mother, singing mother?

Annulled: the quarrels, the gibing, the harshness between; the fall into silence and the withdrawal.

I do not know you, Mother. Mother, I never knew you.

Lenny, suffering not alone for her who was dying, but for that in her which never lived (for that which in him might never live). From him too, unspoken words: *good-by mother who taught me to mother myself.*

Not Vivi, who must stay with her children; not Davy, but he is already here, having to die again with *her* this time, for the living take their dead with them when they die.

Light she grew, like a bird, and like a bird, sound bubbled in her throat while the body fluttered in agony. Night and day, asleep or awake (though indeed there was no difference now) the songs and the phrases leaping.

And he, who had once dreaded a long dying (from fear of himself, from horror of the dwindling money) now desired her quick death profoundly, for *her* sake. He no longer went out, except when Jeannie forced him; no longer laughed, except when, in the bright kitchenette, Jeannie coaxed his laughter (and she, who seemed to hear nothing else, would laugh too, conspiratorial wisps of laughter).

Light, like a bird, the fluttering body, the little claw hands, the beaked shadow on her face; and the throat, bubbling, straining:

He tried not to listen, as he tried not to look on the face in which only the forehead remained familiar, but trapped with her the long nights in that little room, the sounds worked themselves into his consciousness, with their punctuation of death swallows, whimpers, gurglings.

Even in reality (swallow) *life's lack of it*
The bell Summon what ennobles

78,000 in one minute (whisper of a scream) *78,000 human
beings   destroy ourselves?*

"Ahh Mrs. Miserable," he said, as if she could hear, "all your life
working, and now in bed you lie, servants to tend, you do not even
need to call to be tended, and still you work. Such hard work it is to
die? Such hard work?"

The body threshed, her hand clung in his. A melody, ghost thin,
hovered on her lips, and like a guilty ghost, the vision of her bent in
listening to it, silencing the record instantly he was near. Now, heed-
less of his presence, she floated the melody on and on.

"Hid it from me," he complained, "how many times you listened
to remember it so?" And tried to think when she had first played it,
or first begun to silence her few records when he came near—but
could reconstruct nothing. There was only this room with its tall
hooked pillar and its swarm of sounds.

*An unexamined life   not worth
Strong   with the not yet in the now
Dogma dead   war dead   one country*

"It helps, Mrs. Philosopher, words from books? It helps?" And it
seemed to him that for seventy years she had hidden a tape recorder,
infinitely microscopic, within her, that it had coiled infinite mile on
mile, trapping every song, every melody, every word read, heard
and spoken—and that maliciously she was playing back only what
said nothing of him, of the children, of their intimate life together.

"Let us indeed, Mrs. Babbler," he reproached, "you who called
others babbler and cunningly saved your words. A lifetime you
tended and loved, and now not a word of us, for us. Left us indeed?
Left me."

And he took out his solitaire deck, shuffled the cards loudly,
slapped them down.

Lift high   banner of reason (tatter of an orator's voice) *Justice
freedom and light
Mankind   life worthy   heroic capacities
Seeks* (blur of shudder) *belong   human being*

"Words, words," he accused, "and what human beings did *you*
seek around you, Mrs. Live Alone, and what mankind think
worthy?"

Though even as he spoke, he remembered she had not always
been isolated, had not always wanted to be alone (as he knew there
had been a voice before this gossamer one; before the hoarse voice
that broke from silence to lash, make incidents, shame him—a girl's
voice of eloquence that spoke their highest dreams). But again

he could reconstruct, image nothing of what had been before, or when, or how, it had changed.

Ace, queen, jack. The pillar shadow fell, so, in two tracks; in the mirror depths glistened a moonlike blob, the empty solution bottle. And it worked in him: *of reason and justice and freedom.* *Dogma dead:* he remembered the full quotation, laughed bitterly. "Hah, good you do not know what you say; good Victor Hugo died and did not see it, his twentieth century."

Deuce, ten, five. Dauntlessly she began a song of their youth of belief:

> *These things shall be, a loftier race*
> *than e'er the world hath known shall rise*
> *with flame of freedom in their souls*
> *and light of knowledge in their eyes*

King, four, jack. "In the twentieth century, hah!"

> *They shall be gentle, brave and strong*
> *to spill no drop of blood, but dare*
> *all that may plant man's lordship firm*
> *on earth and fire and sea and air*

"To spill no drop of blood, hah! So, cadaver, and you too, cadaver Hugo, 'in the twentieth century ignorance will be dead, dogma will be dead, war will be dead, and for all mankind one country—of fulfillment.' Hah!"

And every life (long strangling cough) *shall be a   song*
The cards fell from his fingers. Without warning, the bereavement and betrayal he had sheltered—compounded through the years —hidden even from himself—revealed itself,

> uncoiled,
> released,
> *sprung*

and with it the monstrous shapes of what had actually happened in the century.

A ravening hunger or thirst seized him. He groped into the kitchenette, switched on all three lights, piled a tray—"you have finished your night snack, Mrs. Cadaver, now I will have mine." And he was shocked at the tears that splashed on the tray.

"Salt tears. For free. I forgot to shake on salt?"

Whispered: "Lost, how much I lost."

Escaped to the grandchildren whose childhoods were childish, who had never hungered, who lived unravaged by disease in warm houses of many rooms, had all the school for which they cared, could walk on any street, stood a head taller than their grandparents, towered above—beautiful skins, straight backs, clear straightforward eyes. "Yes, you in Olshana," he said to the town of sixty years ago, "they would be nobility to you."

And was this not the dream then, come true in ways undreamed? he asked.

And are there no other children in the world? he answered, as if in her harsh voice.

And the flame of freedom, the light of knowledge?

And to spill no drop of blood?

And he thought that at six Jeannie would get up and it would be his turn to go to her room and sleep, that he could press the buzzer and she would come now; that in the afternoon Ellen Mays was coming, and this time they would play cards and he could marvel at how rouge can stand half an inch on the cheek; that in the evening the doctor would come, and he could beg him to be merciful, to stop the feeding solutions, to let her die.

To let her die, and with her their youth of belief out of which her bright, betrayed words foamed; stained words, that on her working lips came stainless.

Hours yet before Jeannie's turn. He could press the buzzer and wake her to come now; he could take a pill, and with it sleep; he could pour more brandy into his milk glass, though what he had poured was not yet touched.

Instead he went back, checked her pulse, gently tended with his knotty fingers as Jeannie had taught.

She was whimpering; her hand crawled across the covers for his. Compassionately he enfolded it, and with his free hand gathered up the cards again. Still was there thirst or hunger ravening in him.

That world of their youth—dark, ignorant, terrible with hate and disease—how was it that living in it, in the midst of corruption, filth, treachery, degradation, they had not mistrusted man nor themselves; had believed so beautifully, so . . . falsely?

"Aaah children," he said out loud, "how we believed, how we belonged." And he yearned to package for each of the children, the grandchildren, for everyone, *that joyous certainty, that sense of moving and being moved, of being one and indivisible with the great of the past, with all mankind.* Package it, stand on corners, in front of stadiums and on crowded beaches, knock on doors, give it as a fabled gift.

"And why not in cereal boxes, in soap packages?" he mocked himself. "Aah. You have taken my senses, cadaver."

Words foamed, died unsounded. Her body writhed; she made kissing motions with her mouth. (Her lips moving as she read, poring over the Book of the Martyrs, the magnifying glass superimposed over the heavy eyeglasses.) *Still she believed?* "Eva!" he whispered. "Still you believed? You lived by it? These Things Shall Be?"

"One pound soup meat," she answered distinctly, "one soup bone."

"My ears heard you. Ellen Mays was witness: 'Man . . . one has to believe.'" Imploringly: "Eva!"

"Bread, day old." She was mumbling. "Please, in a wooden box . . . for kindling. The thread, hah, the thread breaks. Cheap thread,"—and a gurgling, enormously loud, began in her throat.

"I ask for stone; she gives me bread—day old." He pulled his hand away, shouted: "Who wanted questions? Everything you have to wake?" Then dully, "Ah let me help you turn, poor creature."

Words jumbled, cleared. In a voice of crowded terror:

"Paul, Sammy, don't fight.

"Hannah, have I ten hands?

"How can I give it, Clara, how can I give it if I don't have?"

"You lie," he said sturdily, "there was joy too." Bitterly: "Ah how cheap you speak of us at the last."

As if to rebuke him, as if her voice had no relationship with her flailing body, she sang clearly, beautifully, a school song the children had taught her when they were little; begged:

"Not look   my hair   where they cut . . ."

(The crown of braids shorn.) And instantly he left the mute old woman poring over the Book of the Martyrs; went past the mother treadling at the sewing machine, singing with the children; past the girl in her wrinkled prison dress, hiding her hair with scarred hands, lifting to him her awkward, shamed, imploring eyes of love; and took her in his arms, dear, personal, fleshed, in all the heavy passion he had loved to rouse from her.

"Eva!"

Her little claw hand beat the covers. How much, how much can a man stand? He took up the cards, put them down, circled the beds, walked to the dresser, opened, shut drawers, brushed his hair, moved his hand bit by bit over the mirror to see what of the reflection he could blot out with each move, and felt that at any moment he would

die of what was unendurable. Went to press the buzzer to wake
Jeannie, looked down, saw on Jeannie's sketch pad the hospital bed,
with *her*; the double bed alongside, with him; the tall pillar feeding
into her veins, and their hands, his and hers, clasped, feeding each
other. And as if he had been instructed he went to his bed, lay down,
holding the sketch—as if it could shield against the monstrous shapes
of loss, of betrayal, of death—and with his free hand took hers back
into his.

So Jeannie found them in the morning.

That last day the agony was perpetual. Time after time it lifted
her almost off the bed, so they had to fight to hold her down. He
could not endure and left the room; wept as if there never would
be tears enough.

Jeannie came to comfort him. In her light voice she said: Granddaddy, Granddaddy don't cry. She is not there, she promised me. On
the last day, she said she would go back to when she first heard
music, a little girl on the road of the village where she was born.
She promised me. It is a wedding and they dance, while the flutes so
joyous and vibrant tremble in the air. Leave her there, Granddaddy,
it's all right. She promised me. Come back, come back in and help
her poor body to die.

For two of that generation:

Seevya and Genya
Death deepens the wonder

Big Blonde

Hazel Morse was a large, fair woman of the type that incites some men when they use the word "blonde" to click their tongues and wag their heads roguishly. She prided herself upon her small feet and suffered for her vanity, boxing them in snub-toed, high-heeled slippers of the shortest bearable size. The curious things about her were her hands, strange terminations to the flabby white arms splattered with pale tan spots—long, quivering hands with deep and convex nails. She should not have disfigured them with little jewels.

She was not a woman given to recollections. At her middle thirties, her old days were a blurred and flickering sequence, an imperfect film, dealing with the actions of strangers.

In her twenties, after the deferred death of a hazy widowed mother, she had been employed as a model in a wholesale dress establishment—it was still the day of the big woman, and she was then prettily colored and erect and high-breasted. Her job was not onerous, and she met numbers of men and spent numbers of evenings with them, laughing at their jokes and telling them she loved their neckties. Men liked her, and she took it for granted that the liking of many men was a desirable thing. Popularity seemed to her to be worth all the work that had to be put into its achievement. Men liked you because you were fun, and when they liked you they took you out, and there you were. So, and successfully, she was fun. She was a good sport. Men like a good sport.

No other form of diversion, simpler or more complicated, drew her attention. She never pondered if she might not be better occupied doing something else. Her ideas, or, better, her acceptances, ran right along with those of the other substantially built blondes in whom she found her friends.

When she had been working in the dress establishment some years she met Herbie Morse. He was thin, quick, attractive, with shifting

lines about his shiny, brown eyes and a habit of fiercely biting at the
skin around his finger nails. He drank largely; she found that entertaining. Her habitual greeting to him was an allusion to his state of
the previous night.

"Oh, what a peach you had," she used to say, through her easy
laugh. "I thought I'd die, the way you kept asking the waiter to dance
with you."

She liked him immediately upon their meeting. She was enormously amused at his fast, slurred sentences, his interpolations of apt
phrases from vaudeville acts and comic strips; she thrilled at the feel
of his lean arm tucked firm beneath the sleeve of her coat; she wanted
to touch the wet, flat surface of his hair. He was as promptly drawn
to her. They were married six weeks after they had met.

She was delighted at the idea of being a bride; coquetted with it,
played upon it. Other offers of marriage she had had, and not a few of
them, but it happened that they were all from stout, serious men
who had visited the dress establishment as buyers; men from Des
Moines and Houston and Chicago and, in her phrase, even funnier
places. There was always something immensely comic to her in the
thought of living elsewhere than New York. She could not regard as
serious proposals that she share a Western residence.

She wanted to be married. She was nearing thirty now, and she
did not take the years well. She spread and softened, and her darkening hair turned her to inexpert dabblings with peroxide. There were
times when she had little flashes of fear about her job. And she had
had a couple of thousand evenings of being a good sport among her
male acquaintances. She had come to be more conscientious than
spontaneous about it.

Herbie earned enough, and they took a little apartment far uptown. There was a Mission-furnished dining room with a hanging
central light globed in liver-colored glass; in the living room were an
"overstuffed suite," a Boston fern, and a reproduction of the Henner
Magdalene with the red hair and the blue draperies; the bedroom
was in gray enamel and old rose, with Herbie's photograph on
Hazel's dressing table and Hazel's likeness on Herbie's chest of
drawers.

She cooked—and she was a good cook—and marketed and chatted
with the delivery boys and the colored laundress. She loved the flat,
she loved her life, she loved Herbie. In the first months of their marriage she gave him all the passion she was ever to know.

She had not realized how tired she was. It was a delight, a new
game, a holiday, to give up being a good sport. If her head ached or

her arches throbbed, she complained piteously, babyishly. If her mood was quiet, she did not talk. If tears came to her eyes, she let them fall.

She fell readily into the habit of tears during the first year of her marriage. Even in her good sport days she had been known to weep lavishly and disinterestedly on occasion. Her behavior at the theater was a standing joke. She could weep at anything in a play—tiny garments, love both unrequited and mutual, seduction, purity, faithful servitors, wedlock, the triangle.

"There goes Haze," her friends would say, watching her. "She's off again."

Wedded and relaxed, she poured her tears freely. To her who had laughed so much, crying was delicious. All sorrows became her sorrows; she was Tenderness. She would cry long and softly over newspaper accounts of kidnaped babies, deserted wives, unemployed men, strayed cats, heroic dogs. Even when the paper was no longer before her, her mind revolved upon these things and the drops slipped rhythmically over her plump cheeks.

"Honestly," she would say to Herbie, "all the sadness there is in the world when you stop to think about it!"

"Yeah," Herbie would say.

She missed nobody. The old crowd, the people who had brought her and Herbie together, dropped from their lives, lingeringly at first. When she thought of this at all it was only to consider it fitting. This was marriage. This was peace.

But the thing was that Herbie was not amused.

For a time he had enjoyed being alone with her. He found the voluntary isolation novel and sweet. Then it palled with a ferocious suddenness. It was as if one night, sitting with her in the steam-heated living room, he would ask no more; and the next night he was through and done with the whole thing.

He became annoyed by her misty melancholies. At first, when he came home to find her softly tired and moody, he kissed her neck and patted her shoulder and begged her to tell her Herbie what was wrong. She loved that. But time slid by, and he found that there was never anything really, personally, the matter.

"Ah, for God's sake," he would say. "Crabbing again. All right, sit here and crab your head off. I'm going out."

And he would slam out of the flat and come back late and drunk.

She was completely bewildered by what happened to their marriage. First they were lovers; and then, it seemed without transition, they were enemies. She never understood it.

There were longer and longer intervals between his leaving his
office and his arrival at the apartment. She went through agonies
of picturing him run over and bleeding, dead and covered with a
sheet. Then she lost her fears for his safety and grew sullen and
wounded. When a person wanted to be with a person he came as
soon as possible. She desperately wanted him to want to be with
her; her own hours only marked the time till he would come. It was
often nearly nine o'clock before he came home to dinner. Always he
had had many drinks, and their effect would die in him, leaving him
loud and querulous and bristling for affronts.

He was too nervous, he said, to sit and do nothing for an evening. He boasted, probably not in all truth, that he had never read
a book in his life.

"What am I expected to do—sit around this dump on my tail all
night?" he would ask rhetorically. And again he would slam out.

She did not know what to do. She could not manage him. She
could not meet him.

She fought him furiously. A terrific domesticity had come upon
her, and she would bite and scratch to guard it. She wanted what she
called "a nice home." She wanted a sober, tender husband, prompt
at dinner, punctual at work. She wanted sweet, comforting evenings.
The idea of intimacy with other men was terrible to her; the thought
that Herbie might be seeking entertainment in other women set her
frantic.

It seemed to her that almost everything she read—novels from the
drug-store lending library, magazine stories, women's pages in the
papers—dealt with wives who lost their husbands' love. She could
bear those, at that, better than accounts of neat, companionable marriage and living happily ever after.

She was frightened. Several times when Herbie came home in the
evening he found her determinedly dressed—she had had to alter
those of her clothes that were not new, to make them fasten—and
rouged.

"Let's go wild to-night, what do you say?" she would hail him.
"A person's got lots of time to hang around and do nothing when
they're dead."

So they would go out, to chop houses and the less expensive cab-
arets. But it turned out badly. She could no longer find amusement in
watching Herbie drink. She could not laugh at his whimsicalities,
she was so tensely counting his indulgences. And she was unable to
keep back her remonstrances—"Ah, come on, Herb, you've had
enough, haven't you? You'll feel something terrible in the morning."

He would be immediately enraged. All right, crab; crab, crab, crab, that was all she ever did. What a lousy sport *she* was! There would be scenes, and one or the other of them would rise and stalk out in fury.

She could not recall the definite day that she started drinking, herself. There was nothing separate about her days. Like drops upon a windowpane, they ran together and trickled away. She had been married six months; then a year; then three years.

She had never needed to drink, formerly. She could sit for most of a night at a table where the others were imbibing earnestly and never droop in looks or spirits, nor be bored by the doings of those about her. If she took a cocktail, it was so unusual as to cause twenty minutes or so of jocular comment. But now anguish was in her. Frequently, after a quarrel, Herbie would stay out for the night, and she could not learn from him where the time had been spent. Her heart felt tight and sore in her breast, and her mind turned like an electric fan.

She hated the taste of liquor. Gin, plain or in mixtures, made her promptly sick. After experiment, she found that Scotch whisky was best for her. She took it without water, because that was the quickest way to its effect.

Herbie pressed it on her. He was glad to see her drink. They both felt it might restore her high spirits, and their good times together might again be possible.

" 'Atta girl," he would approve her. "Let's see you get boiled, baby."

But it brought them no nearer. When she drank with him there would be a little while of gayety and then, strangely without beginning, they would be in a wild quarrel. They would wake in the morning not sure what it had all been about, foggy as to what had been said and done, but each deeply injured and bitterly resentful. There would be days of vengeful silence.

There had been a time when they had made up their quarrels, usually in bed. There would be kisses and little names and assurances of fresh starts . . . "Oh, it's going to be great now, Herb. We'll have swell times. I was a crab. I guess I might have been tired. But everything's going to be swell. You'll see."

Now there were no gentle reconciliations. They resumed friendly relations only in the brief magnanimity caused by liquor, before more liquor drew them into new battles. The scenes became more violent. There were shouted invectives and pushes, and sometimes sharp slaps. Once she had a black eye. Herbie was horrified next day at sight of it. He did not go to work; he followed her about, sug-

gesting remedies and heaping dark blame on himself. But after they
had had a few drinks—"to pull themselves together"—she made so
many wistful references to her bruise that he shouted at her, and
rushed out, and was gone for two days.

Each time he left the place in rage he threatened never to come
back. She did not believe him, nor did she consider separation. Somewhere in her head or her heart was the lazy, nebulous hope that
things would change and she and Herbie settle suddenly into soothing married life. Here were her home, her furniture, her husband,
her station. She summoned no alternatives.

She could no longer bustle and potter. She had no more vicarious
tears; the hot drops she shed were for herself. She walked ceaselessly
about the rooms, her thoughts running mechanically round and
round Herbie. In those days began the hatred of being alone that she
was never to overcome. You could be by yourself when things were
all right, but when you were blue you got the howling horrors.

She commenced drinking alone, little, short drinks all through the
day. It was only with Herbie that alcohol made her nervous and
quick in offense. Alone, it blurred sharp things for her. She lived in
a haze of it. Her life took on a dream-like quality. Nothing was
astonishing.

A Mrs. Martin moved into the flat across the hall. She was a great
blonde woman of forty, a promise in looks of what Mrs. Morse was
to be. They made acquaintance, quickly became inseparable. Mrs.
Morse spent her days in the opposite apartment. They drank together, to brace themselves after the drinks of the nights before.

She never confided her troubles about Herbie to Mrs. Martin. The
subject was too bewildering to her to find comfort in talk. She let it
be assumed that her husband's business kept him much away. It was
not regarded as important; husbands, as such, played but shadowy
parts in Mrs. Martin's circle.

Mrs. Martin had no visible spouse; you were left to decide for
yourself whether he was or was not dead. She had an admirer, Joe,
who came to see her almost nightly. Often he brought several friends
with him—"The Boys," they were called. The Boys were big, red,
good-humored men, perhaps forty-five, perhaps fifty. Mrs. Morse was
glad of invitations to join the parties—Herbie was scarcely ever at
home at night now. If he did come home, she did not visit Mrs. Martin. An evening alone with Herbie meant inevitably a quarrel, yet
she would stay with him. There was always her thin and wordless
idea that, maybe, this night, things would begin to be all right.

The boys brought plenty of liquor along with them whenever they came to Mrs. Martin's. Drinking with them, Mrs. Morse became lively and good-natured and audacious. She was quickly popular. When she had drunk enough to cloud her most recent battle with Herbie, she was excited by their approbation. Crab, was she? Rotten sport, was she? Well, there were some that thought different.

Ed was one of The Boys. He lived in Utica—had "his own business" there, was the awed report—but he came to New York almost every week. He was married. He showed Mrs. Morse the then current photographs of Junior and Sister, and she praised them abundantly and sincerely. Soon it was accepted by the others that Ed was her particular friend.

He staked her when they all played poker; sat next her and occasionally rubbed his knee against hers during the game. She was rather lucky. Frequently she went home with a twenty-dollar bill or a ten-dollar bill or a handful of crumpled dollars. She was glad of them. Herbie was getting, in her words, something awful about money. To ask him for it brought an instant row.

"What the hell do you do with it?" he would say. "Shoot it all on Scotch?"

"I try to run this house halfway decent," she would retort. "Never thought of that, did you? Oh, no, his lordship couldn't be bothered with that."

Again, she could not find a definite day to fix the beginning of Ed's proprietorship. It became his custom to kiss her on the mouth when he came in, as well as for farewell, and he gave her little quick kisses of approval all through the evening. She liked this rather more than she disliked it. She never thought of his kisses when she was not with him.

He would run his hand lingeringly over her back and shoulders. "Some dizzy blonde, eh?" he would say. "Some doll."

One afternoon she came home from Mrs. Martin's to find Herbie in the bedroom. He had been away for several nights, evidently on a prolonged drinking bout. His face was gray, his hands jerked as if they were on wires. On the bed were two old suitcases, packed high. Only her photograph remained on his bureau, and the wide doors of his closet disclosed nothing but coat hangers.

"I'm blowing," he said. "I'm through with the whole works. I got a job in Detroit."

She sat down on the edge of the bed. She had drunk much the night before, and the four Scotches she had had with Mrs. Martin had only increased her fogginess.

"Good job?" she said.

"Oh, yeah," he said. "Looks all right."

He closed a suitcase with difficulty, swearing at it in whispers.

"There's some dough in the bank," he said. "The bank book's in your top drawer. You can have the furniture and stuff."

He looked at her, and his forehead twitched.

"God damn it, I'm through, I'm telling you," he cried. "I'm through."

"All right, all right," she said. "I heard you, didn't I?"

She saw him as if he were at one end of a cañon and she at the other. Her head was beginning to ache bumpingly, and her voice had a dreary, tiresome tone. She could not have raised it.

"Like a drink before you go?" she asked.

Again he looked at her, and a corner of his mouth jerked up.

"Cockeyed again for a change, aren't you?" he said. "That's nice. Sure, get a couple of shots, will you?"

She went to the pantry, mixed him a stiff highball, poured herself a couple of inches of whisky, and drank it. Then she gave herself another portion and brought the glasses into the bedroom. He had strapped both suitcases and had put on his hat and overcoat.

He took his highball.

"Well," he said, and he gave a sudden, uncertain laugh. "Here's mud in your eye."

"Mud in your eye," she said.

They drank. He put down his glass and took up the heavy suitcase.

"Got to get a train around six," he said.

She followed him down the hall. There was a song, a song that Mrs. Martin played doggedly on the phonograph, running loudly through her mind. She had never liked the thing.

> Night and daytime,
> Always playtime.
> Ain't we got fun?

At the door he put down the bags and faced her.

"Well," he said. "Well, take care of yourself. You'll be all right, will you?"

"Oh, sure," she said.

He opened the door, then came back to her, holding out his hand.

" 'Bye, Haze," he said. "Good luck to you."

She took his hand and shook it.

"Pardon my wet glove," she said.

When the door had closed behind him she went back to the pantry.

She was flushed and lively when she went into Mrs. Martin's that evening. The Boys were there, Ed among them. He was glad to be in town, frisky and loud and full of jokes. But she spoke quietly to him for a minute.

"Herbie blew to-day," she said. "Going to live out West."

"That so?" he said. He looked at her and played with the fountain pen clipped to his waistcoat pocket.

"Think he's gone for good, do you?" he asked.

"Yeah," she said. "I know he is. I know. Yeah."

"You going to live on across the hall just the same?" he said. "Know what you're going to do?"

"Gee, I don't know," she said. "I don't give much of a damn."

"Oh, come on, that's no way to talk," he told her. "What you need —you need a little snifter. How about it?"

"Yeah," she said. "Just straight."

She won forty-three dollars at poker. When the game broke up Ed took her back to her apartment.

"Got a little kiss for me?" he asked.

He wrapped her in his big arms and kissed her violently. She was entirely passive. He held her away and looked at her.

"Little tight, honey?" he asked anxiously. "Not going to be sick, are you?"

"Me?" she said. "I'm swell."

II

When Ed left in the morning he took her photograph with him. He said he wanted her picture to look at, up in Utica. "You can have that one on the bureau," she said.

She put Herbie's picture in a drawer, out of her sight. When she could look at it she meant to tear it up. She was fairly successful in keeping her mind from racing around him. Whisky slowed it for her. She was almost peaceful, in her mist.

She accepted her relationship with Ed without question or enthusiasm. When he was away she seldom thought definitely of him. He was good to her; he gave her frequent presents and a regular allowance. She was even able to save. She did not plan ahead of any day, but her wants were few, and you might as well put money in the bank as have it lying around.

When the lease of her apartment neared its end it was Ed who suggested moving. His friendship with Mrs. Martin and Joe had become strained over a dispute at poker; a feud was impending.

"Let's get the hell out of here," Ed said. "What I want you to have is a place near the Grand Central. Make it easier for me."

So she took a little flat in the Forties. A colored maid came in every day to clean and to make coffee for her—she was "through with that housekeeping stuff," she said, and Ed, twenty years married to a passionately domestic woman, admired this romantic uselessness and felt doubly a man of the world in abetting it.

The coffee was all she had until she went out to dinner, but alcohol kept her fat. Prohibition she regarded only as a basis for jokes. You could always get all you wanted. She was never noticeably drunk and seldom nearly sober. It required a larger daily allowance to keep her misty-minded. Too little, and she was achingly melancholy.

Ed brought her to Jimmy's. He was proud, with the pride of the transient who would be mistaken for a native, in his knowledge of small, recent restaurants occupying the lower floors of shabby brownstone houses; places where, upon mentioning the name of an habitué friend, might be obtained strange whisky and fresh gin in many of their ramifications. Jimmy's place was the favorite of his acquaintances.

There, through Ed, Mrs. Morse met many men and women, formed quick friendships. The men often took her out when Ed was in Utica. He was proud of her popularity.

She fell into the habit of going to Jimmy's alone when she had no engagement. She was certain to meet some people she knew, and join them. It was a club for her friends, both men and women.

The women at Jimmy's looked remarkably alike, and this was curious, for, through feuds, removals and opportunities of more profitable contacts, the personnel of the group changed constantly. Yet always the newcomers resembled those whom they replaced. They were all big women and stout, broad of shoulder and abundantly breasted, with faces thickly clothed in soft, high-colored flesh. They laughed loud and often, showing opaque and lusterless teeth like squares of crockery. There was about them the health of the big, yet a slight, unwholesome suggestion of stubborn preservation. They might have been thirty-six or forty-five or anywhere between.

They composed their titles of their own first names with their husband's surnames—Mrs. Florence Miller, Mrs. Vera Riley, Mrs. Lilian Block. This gave at the same time the solidity of marriage and the glamour of freedom. Yet only one or two were actually divorced.

Most of them never referred to their dimmed spouses; some, a shorter time separate, described them in terms of great biological interest. Several were mothers, each of an only child—a boy at school somewhere, or a girl being cared for by a grandmother. Often, well on toward morning, there would be displays of kodak portraits and of tears.

They were comfortable women, cordial and friendly and irrepressibly matronly. Theirs was the quality of ease. Become fatalistic, especially about money matters, they were unworried. Whenever their funds dropped alarmingly, a new donor appeared; this had always happened. The aim of each was to have one man, permanently, to pay all her bills, in return for which she would have immediately given up other admirers and probably would have become exceedingly fond of him; for the affections of all of them were, by now, unexacting, tranquil, and easily arranged. This end, however, grew increasingly difficult yearly. Mrs. Morse was regarded as fortunate.

Ed had a good year, increased her allowance and gave her a sealskin coat. But she had to be careful of her moods with him. He insisted upon gayety. He would not listen to admissions of aches or weariness.

"Hey, listen," he would say, "I got worries of my own, and plenty. Nobody wants to hear other people's troubles, sweetie. What you got to do, you got to be a sport and forget it. See? Well, slip us a little smile, then. That's my girl."

She never had enough interest to quarrel with him as she had with Herbie, but she wanted the privilege of occasional admitted sadness. It was strange. The other women she saw did not have to fight their moods. There was Mrs. Florence Miller who got regular crying jags, and the men sought only to cheer and comfort her. The others spent whole evenings in grieved recitals of worries and ills; their escorts paid them deep sympathy. But she was instantly undesirable when she was low in spirits. Once, at Jimmy's, when she could not make herself lively, Ed had walked out and left her.

"Why the hell don't you stay home and not go spoiling everybody's evening?" he had roared.

Even her slightest acquaintance seemed irritated if she were not conspicuously light-hearted.

"What's the matter with you, anyway?" they would say. "Be your age, why don't you? Have a little drink and snap out of it."

When her relationship with Ed had continued nearly three years he moved to Florida to live. He hated leaving her; he gave her a large check and some shares of a sound stock, and his pale eyes were wet when he said good-bye. She did not miss him. He came to New York infrequently, perhaps two or three times a year, and hurried directly from the train to see her. She was always pleased to have him come and never sorry to see him go.

Charley, an acquaintance of Ed's that she had met at Jimmy's, had long admired her. He had always made opportunities of touching her and leaning close to talk to her. He asked repeatedly of all their friends if they had ever heard such a fine laugh as she had. After Ed left Charley became the main figure in her life. She classified him and spoke of him as "not so bad." There was nearly a year of Charley; then she divided her time between him and Sydney, another frequenter of Jimmy's; then Charley slipped away altogether.

Sydney was a little, brightly dressed, clever Jew. She was perhaps nearest contentment with him. He amused her always; her laughter was not forced.

He admired her completely. Her softness and size delighted him. And he thought she was great, he often told her, because she kept gay and lively when she was drunk.

"Once I had a gal," he said, "used to try to throw herself out of the window every time she got a can on. Jee-*zuss*," he added feelingly.

Then Sydney married a rich and watchful bride, and then there was Billy. No—after Sydney came Ferd, then Billy. In her haze she never recalled how men entered her life and left it. There were no surprises. She had no thrill at their advent nor woe at their departure. She seemed to be always able to attract men. There was never another as rich as Ed, but they were all generous to her, in their means.

Once she had news of Herbie. She met Mrs. Martin dining at Jimmy's, and the old friendship was vigorously renewed. The still admiring Joe, while on a business trip, had seen Herbie. He had settled in Chicago, he looked fine, he was living with some woman —seemed to be crazy about her. Mrs. Morse had been drinking vastly that day. She took the news with mild interest, as one hearing of the sex peccadilloes of somebody whose name is, after a moment's groping, familiar.

"Must be damn near seven years since I saw him," she commented. "Gee. Seven years."

More and more her days lost their individuality. She never knew dates, nor was sure of the day of the week.

"My God, was that a year ago!" she would exclaim, when an event was recalled in conversation.

She was tired so much of the time. Tired and blue. Almost everything could give her the blues. Those old horses she saw on Sixth Avenue—struggling and slipping along the car tracks, or standing at the curb, their heads dropped level with their worn knees. The tightly stored tears would squeeze from her eyes as she teetered past on her aching feet in the stubby, champagne-colored slippers.

The thought of death came and stayed with her and lent her a sort of drowsy cheer. It would be nice, nice and restful, to be dead.

There was no settled, shocked moment when she first thought of killing herself; it seemed to her as if the idea had always been with her. She pounced upon all the accounts of suicides in the newspapers. There was an epidemic of self-killings—or maybe it was just that she searched for the stories of them so eagerly that she found many. To read of them roused reassurance in her; she felt a cozy solidarity with the big company of the voluntary dead.

She slept, aided by whisky, till deep into the afternoons, than lay abed, a bottle and glass at her hand, until it was time to dress to go out for dinner. She was beginning to feel toward alcohol a little puzzled distrust, as toward an old friend who has refused a simple favor. Whisky could still soothe her for most of the time, but there were sudden, inexplicable moments when the cloud fell treacherously away from her, and she was sawn by the sorrow and bewilderment and nuisance of all living. She played voluptuously with the thought of cool, sleepy retreat. She had never been troubled by religious belief, and no vision of an after-life intimidated her. She dreamed by day of never again putting on tight shoes, of never having to laugh and listen and admire, of never more being a good sport. Never.

But how would you do it? It made her sick to think of jumping from heights. She could not stand a gun. At the theater, if one of the actors drew a revolver, she crammed her fingers into her ears and could not even look at the stage until after the shot had been fired. There was no gas in her flat. She looked long at the bright blue veins in her slim wrists—a cut with a razor blade, and there you'd be. But it would hurt, hurt like hell, and there would be blood to see. Poison—something tasteless and quick and painless—was the thing. But they wouldn't sell it to you in the drug stores, because of the law.

She had few other thoughts.

There was a new man now—Art. He was short and fat and exacting and hard on her patience when he was drunk. But there had been only occasionals for some time before him, and she was glad of a little stability. Too, Art must be away for weeks at a stretch, selling silks, and that was restful. She was convincingly gay with him, though the effort shook her viciously.

"The best sport in the world," he would murmur, deep in her neck. "The best sport in the world."

One night, when he had taken her to Jimmy's, she went into the dressing room with Mrs. Florence Miller. There, while designing curly mouths on their faces with lip rouge, they compared experiences of insomnia.

"Honestly," Mrs. Morse said, "I wouldn't close an eye if I didn't go to bed full of Scotch. I lie there and toss and turn and toss and turn. Blue! Does a person get blue lying awake that way!"

"Say, listen, Hazel," Mrs. Miller said impressively, "I'm telling you I'd be awake for a year if I didn't take veronal. That stuff makes you sleep like a fool."

"Isn't it poison or something?" Mrs. Morse asked.

"Oh, you take too much and you're out for the count," said Mrs. Miller. "I just take five grains—they come in tablets. I'd be scared to fool around with it. But five grains and you cork off pretty."

"Can you get it anywhere?" Mrs. Morse felt superbly Machiavellian.

"Get all you want in Jersey," said Mrs. Miller. "They won't give it to you here without you have a doctor's prescription. Finished? We'd better go back and see what the boys are doing."

That night Art left Mrs. Morse at the door of her apartment; his mother was in town. Mrs. Morse was still sober, and it happened that there was no whisky left in her cupboard. She lay in bed, looking up at the black ceiling.

She rose early, for her, and went to New Jersey. She had never taken the tube, and did not understand it. So she went to the Pennsylvania Station and bought a railroad ticket to Newark. She thought of nothing in particular on the trip out. She looked at the uninspired hats of the women about her and gazed through the smeared window at the flat, gritty scene.

In Newark, in the first drug store she came to, she asked for a tin of talcum powder, a nail brush, and a box of veronal tablets. The powder and the brush were to make the hypnotic seem also a casual need. The clerk was entirely unconcerned. "We only keep them in bottles," he said, and wrapped up for her a little glass vial containing ten white tablets, stacked one on another.

She went to another drug store and bought a face cloth, an orangewood stick, and a bottle of veronal tablets. The clerk was also uninterested.

"Well, I guess I got enough to kill an ox," she thought, and went back to the station.

At home, she put the little vials in the drawer of her dressing table and stood looking at them with a dreamy tenderness.

"There they are, God bless them," she said, and she kissed her finger tip and touched each bottle.

The colored maid was busy in the living room.

"Hey, Nettie," Mrs. Morse called. "Be an angel, will you? Run around to Jimmy's and get me a quart of Scotch."

She hummed while she awaited the girl's return.

During the next few days, whisky ministered to her as tenderly as it had done when she first turned to its aid. Alone, she was soothed and vague, at Jimmy's she was the gayest of the groups. Art was delighted with her.

Then, one night, she had an appointment to meet Art at Jimmy's for an early dinner. He was to leave afterward on a business excursion, to be away for a week. Mrs. Morse had been drinking all the afternoon; while she dressed to go out she felt herself rising pleasurably from drowsiness to high spirits. But as she came out into the street the effects of the whisky deserted her completely, and she was filled with a slow, grinding wretchedness so horrible that she stood swaying on the pavement, unable for a moment to move forward. It was a gray night with spurts of mean, thin snow, and the streets shone with dark ice. As she slowly crossed Sixth Avenue consciously dragging one foot past the other, a big, scarred horse pulling a rickety express wagon crashed to his knees before her. The driver swore and screamed and lashed the beast insanely, bringing the whip back over his shoulder for every blow, while the horse struggled to get a footing on the slippery asphalt. A group gathered and watched with interest.

Art was waiting, when Mrs. Morse reached Jimmy's.

"What's the matter with you, for God's sake?" was his greeting to her.

"I saw a horse," she said. "Gee, I—a person feels sorry for horses. I—it isn't just horses. Everything's kind of terrible, isn't it? I can't help getting sunk."

"Ah, sunk, me eye," he said. "What's the idea of all the bellyaching? What have you got to be sunk about?"

"I can't help it," she said.

"Ah, help it, me eye," he said. "Pull yourself together, will you? Come on and sit down, and take that face off you."

She drank industriously and she tried hard, but she could not overcome her melancholy. Others joined them and commented on her gloom, and she could do no more for them than smile weakly. She made little dabs at her eyes with her handkerchief, trying to time her movements so they would be unnoticed, but several times Art caught her and scowled and shifted impatiently in his chair.

When it was time for him to go to his train she said she would leave, too, and go home.

"And not a bad idea, either," he said. "See if you can't sleep yourself out of it. I'll see you Thursday. For God's sake, try and cheer up by then, will you?"

"Yeah," she said. "I will."

In her bedroom she undressed with a tense speed wholly unlike her usual slow uncertainty. She put on her nightgown, took off her hair net, and passed the comb quickly through her dry, varicolored hair. Then she took the two little vials from the drawer and carried them into the bathroom. The splintering misery had gone from her, and she felt the quick excitement of one who is about to receive an anticipated gift.

She uncorked the vials, filled a glass with water, and stood before the mirror, a tablet between her fingers. Suddenly she bowed graciously to her reflection and raised the glass to it.

"Well, here's mud in your eye," she said.

The tablets were unpleasant to take, dry and powdery and sticking obstinately halfway down her throat. It took her a long time to swallow all twenty of them. She stood watching her reflection with deep, impersonal interest, studying the movements of the gulping throat. Once more she spoke aloud to it.

"For God's sake, try and cheer up by Thursday, will you?" she said. "Well, you know what he can do. He and the whole lot of them."

She had no idea how quickly to expect effect from the veronal. When she had taken the last tablet she stood uncertainly, wondering, still with a courteous, vicarious interest, if death would strike her down then and there. She felt in no way strange, save for a slight stirring of sickness from the effort of swallowing the tablets, nor did her reflected face look at all different. It would not be immediate, then; it might even take an hour or so.

She stretched her arms high and gave a vast yawn.

"Guess I'll go to bed," she said. "Gee, I'm nearly dead."

That struck her as comic, and she turned out the bathroom light and went in and laid herself down in her bed, chuckling softly all the time.

"Gee, I'm nearly dead," she quoted. "That's a hot one!"

III

Nettie, the colored maid, came in late the next afternoon to clean the apartment and found Mrs. Morse in her bed. But then, that was not unusual. Usually, though, the sounds of cleaning waked her, and she did not like to wake up. Nettie, an agreeable girl, had learned to move softly about her work.

But when she had done the living room and stolen in to tidy the little square bedroom, she could not avoid a tiny clatter as she arranged the objects on the dressing table. Instinctively she glanced over her shoulder at the sleeper, and without warning a sickly uneasiness crept over her. She came to the bed and stared down at the woman lying there.

Mrs. Morse lay on her back, one flabby white arm flung up, the wrist against her forehead. Her stiff hair hung untenderly along her face. The bed covers were pushed down, exposing a deep square of soft neck and a pink nightgown, its fabric worn uneven by many launderings; her great breasts, freed from their tight confiner, sagged beneath her armpits. Now and then she made knotted, snoring sounds, and from the corner of her opened mouth to the blurred turn of her jaw ran a lane of crusted spittle.

"Mis' Morse," Nettie called. "Oh, Mis' Morse! It's terrible late."

Mrs. Morse made no move.

"Mis' Morse," said Nettie. "Look, Mis' Morse. How'm I goin' get this bed made?"

Panic sprang upon the girl. She shook the woman's hot shoulder. "Ah, wake up, will yuh?" she whined. "Ah, please wake up."

Suddenly the girl turned and ran out in the hall to the elevator door, keeping her thumb firm on the black, shiny button until the elderly car and its Negro attendant stood before her. She poured a jumble of words over the boy and led him back to the apartment. He tiptoed creakingly in to the bedside; first gingerly, then so lustily that he left marks in the soft flesh, he prodded the unconscious woman.

"Hey, there!" he cried, and listened intently, as for an echo.

"Jeez. Out like a light," he commented.

At his interest in the spectacle, Nettie's panic left her. Importance was big in both of them. They talked in quick, unfinished whispers, and it was the boy's suggestion that he fetch the young doctor who lived on the ground floor. Nettie hurried along with him. They looked forward to the limelit moment of breaking their news of something

untoward, something pleasurably unpleasant. Mrs. Morse had become the medium of drama. With no ill wish to her, they hoped that
her state was serious, that she would not let them down by being
awake and normal on their return. A little fear of this determined
them to make the most, to the doctor, of her present condition.
"Matter of life and death" returned to Nettie from her thin store of
reading. She considered startling the doctor with the phrase.

The doctor was in and none too pleased at interruption. He wore
a yellow and blue striped dressing gown, and he was lying on his
sofa, laughing, with a dark girl, her face scaly with inexpensive
powder, who perched on the arm. Half-emptied highball glasses
stood beside them, and her coat and hat were neatly hung up with
the comfortable implication of a long stay.

Always something, the doctor grumbled. Couldn't let anybody
alone after a hard day. But he put some bottles and instruments into
a case, changed his dressing gown for his coat, and started out with
the Negroes.

"Snap it up there, big boy," the girl called after him. "Don't be all
night."

The doctor strode loudly into Mrs. Morse's flat and on to the bedroom, Nettie and the boy right behind him. Mrs. Morse had not
moved; her sleep was as deep, but soundless, now. The doctor looked
sharply at her, then plunged his thumbs into the lidded pits above
her eyeballs and threw his weight upon them. A high, sickened cry
broke from Nettie.

"Look like he tryin' to push her right on th'ough the bed," said the
boy. He chuckled.

Mrs. Morse gave no sign under the pressure. Abruptly the doctor
abandoned it, and with one quick movement swept the covers down
to the foot of the bed. With another he flung her nightgown
back and lifted the thick, white legs, crosshatched with blocks of
tiny, iris-colored veins. He pinched them repeatedly, with long, cruel
nips, back of the knees. She did not awaken.

"What's she been drinking?" he asked Nettie, over his shoulder.

With the certain celerity of one who knows just where to lay hands
on a thing, Nettie went into the bathroom, bound for the cupboard
where Mrs. Morse kept her whisky. But she stopped at the sight of
the two vials, with their red and white labels, lying before the mirror.
She brought them to the doctor.

"Oh, for the Lord Almighty's sweet sake!" he said. He dropped Mrs.
Morse's limp legs and pushed them impatiently across the bed. "What
did she want to go taking that tripe for? Rotten yellow trick, that's

what a thing like that is. Now we'll have to pump her out, and all that stuff. Nuisance, a thing like that is; that's what it amounts to. Here, George, take me down in the elevator. You wait here, maid. She won't do anything."

"She won' die on me, will she?" cried Nettie.

"No," said the doctor. "God, no. You couldn't kill her with an ax."

IV

After two days Mrs. Morse came back to consciousness, dazed at first, then with a comprehension that brought with it the slow, saturating wretchedness.

"Oh, Lord, oh, Lord," she moaned, and tears for herself and for life striped her cheeks.

Nettie came in at the sound. For two days she had done the ugly, incessant tasks in the nursing of the unconscious, for two nights she had caught broken bits of sleep on the living room couch. She looked coldly at the big, blown woman in the bed.

"What you been tryin' to do, Mis' Morse?" she said. "What kine o' work is that, takin' all that stuff?"

"Oh, Lord," moaned Mrs. Morse again, and she tried to cover her eyes with her arms. But the joints felt stiff and brittle, and she cried out at their ache.

"Tha's no way to ack, takin' them pills," said Nettie. "You can thank you' stars you heah at all. How you feel now?"

"Oh, I feel great," said Mrs. Morse. "Swell, I feel."

Her hot, painful tears fell as if they would never stop.

"Tha's no way to take on, cryin' like that," Nettie said. "After what you done. The doctor, he says he could have you arrested, doin' a thing like that. He was fit to be tied, here."

"Why couldn't he let me alone?" wailed Mrs. Morse. "Why the hell couldn't he have?"

"Tha's terr'ble, Mis' Morse, swearin' an' talkin' like that," said Nettie, "after what people done for you. Here I ain' had no sleep at all, an' I had to give up goin' out to my other ladies!"

"Oh, I'm sorry, Nettie," she said. "You're a peach. I'm sorry I've given you so much trouble. I couldn't help it. I just got sunk. Didn't you ever feel like doing it? When everything looks just lousy to you?"

"I wouldn't think o' no such thing," declared Nettie. "You got to cheer up. Tha's what you got to do. Everybody's got their troubles."

"Yeah," said Mrs. Morse. "I know."

"Come a pretty picture card for you," Nettie said. "Maybe that will cheer you up."

She handed Mrs. Morse a post card. Mrs. Morse had to cover one eye with her hand, in order to read the message; her eyes were not yet focusing correctly.

It was from Art. On the back of a view of the Detroit Athletic Club he had written:

Greeting and salutations. Hope you have lost that gloom. Cheer up and don't take any rubber nickels. See you on Thursday.

She dropped the card to the floor. Misery crushed her as if she were between great smooth stones. There passed before her a slow, slow pageant of days spent lying in her flat, of evenings at Jimmy's being a good sport, making herself laugh and coo at Art and other Arts; she saw a long parade of weary horses and shivering beggars and all beaten, driven, stumbling things. Her feet throbbed as if she had crammed them into the stubby champagne-colored slippers. Her heart seemed to swell and fester.

"Nettie," she cried, "for heaven's sake, pour me a drink, will you?" The maid looked doubtful.

"Now you know, Mis' Morse," she said, "you been near daid. I don' know if the doctor he let you drink nothin' yet."

"Oh, never mind him," she said. "You get me one and bring in the bottle. Take one yourself."

"Well," said Nettie.

She poured them each a drink, deferentially leaving hers in the bathroom to be taken in solitude, and brought Mrs. Morse's glass in to her.

Mrs. Morse looked into the liquor and shuddered back from its odor. Maybe it would help. Maybe, when you had been knocked cold for a few days, your very first drink would give you a lift. Maybe whisky would be her friend again. She prayed without addressing a God, without knowing a God. Oh, please, please, let her be able to get drunk, please keep her always drunk.

She lifted the glass.

"Thanks, Nettie," she said. "Here's mud in your eye."

The maid giggled. "Tha's the way, Mis' Morse," she said. "You cheer up, now."

"Yeah," said Mrs. Morse. "Sure."

The Downward Path
to Wisdom

In the square bedroom with the big window Mama and Papa were
lolling back on their pillows handing each other things from the
wide black tray on the small table with crossed legs. They were
smiling and they smiled even more when the little boy, with the
feeling of sleep still in his skin and hair, came in and walked up
to the bed. Leaning against it, his bare toes wriggling in the white
fur rug, he went on eating peanuts which he took from his pajama
pocket. He was four years old.

"Here's my baby," said Mama. "Lift him up, will you?"

He went limp as a rag for Papa to take him under the arms and
swing him up over a broad, tough chest. He sank between his parents like a bear cub in a warm litter, and lay there comfortably. He
took another peanut between his teeth, cracked the shell, picked out
the nut whole and ate it.

"Running around without his slippers again," said Mama. "His
feet are like icicles."

"He crunches like a horse," said Papa. "Eating peanuts before
breakfast will ruin his stomach. Where did he get them?"

"You brought them yesterday," said Mama, with exact memory,
"in a grisly little cellophane sack. I have asked you dozens of times
not to bring him things to eat. Put him out, will you? He's spilling
shells all over me."

Almost at once the little boy found himself on the floor again.
He moved around to Mama's side of the bed and leaned confid-
ingly near her and began another peanut. As he chewed he gazed
solemnly in her eyes.

"Bright-looking specimen, isn't he?" asked Papa, stretching his
long legs and reaching for his bathrobe. "I suppose you'll say it's
my fault he's dumb as an ox."

"He's my little baby, my only baby," said Mama richly, hugging him, "and he's a dear lamb." His neck and shoulders were quite boneless in her firm embrace. He stopped chewing long enough to receive a kiss on his crumby chin. "He's sweet as clover," said Mama. The baby went on chewing.

"Look at him staring like an owl," said Papa.

Mama said, "He's an angel and I'll never get used to having him."

"We'd be better off if we never *had* had him," said Papa. He was walking about the room and his back was turned when he said that. There was silence for a moment. The little boy stopped eating, and stared deeply at his mama. She was looking at the back of Papa's head, and her eyes were almost black. "You're going to say that just once too often," she told him in a low voice. "I hate you when you say that."

Papa said, "You spoil him to death. You never correct him for anything. And you don't take care of him. You let him run around eating peanuts before breakfast."

"You gave him the peanuts, remember that," said Mama. She sat up and hugged her only baby once more. He nuzzled softly in the pit of her arm. "Run along, my darling," she told him in her gentlest voice, smiling at him straight in the eyes. "Run along," she said, her arms falling away from him. "Get your breakfast."

The little boy had to pass his father on the way to the door. He shrank into himself when he saw the big hand raised above him. "Yes, get out of here and stay out," said Papa, giving him a little shove toward the door. It was not a hard shove, but it hurt the little boy. He slunk out, and trotted down the hall trying not to look back. He was afraid something was coming after him, he could not imagine what. Something hurt him all over, he did not know why.

He did not want his breakfast; he would not have it. He sat and stirred it round in the yellow bowl, letting it stream off the spoon and spill on the table, on his front, on the chair. He liked seeing it spill. It was hateful stuff, but it looked funny running in white rivulets down his pajamas.

"Now look what you're doing, dirty boy," said Marjory. "You dirty little old boy."

The little boy opened his mouth to speak for the first time. "You're dirty yourself," he told her.

"That's right," said Marjory, leaning over him and speaking so her voice would not carry. "That's right, just like your papa. Mean," she whispered, "mean."

The little boy took up his yellow bowl full of cream and oatmeal and sugar with both hands and brought it down with a crash on the table. It burst and some of the wreck lay in chunks and some of it ran all over everything. He felt better.

"You see?" said Marjory, dragging him out of the chair and scrubbing him with a napkin. She scrubbed him as roughly as she dared until he cried out. "That's just what I said. That's exactly it." Through his tears he saw her face terribly near, red and frowning under a stiff white band, looking like the face of somebody who came at night and stood over him and scolded him when he could not move or get away. "Just like your papa, *mean.*"

The little boy went out into the garden and sat on a green bench dangling his legs. He was clean. His hair was wet and his blue woolly pull-over made his nose itch. His face felt stiff from the soap. He saw Marjory going past a window with the black tray. The curtains were still closed at the window he knew opened into Mama's room. Papa's room. Mommanpoppasroom, the word was pleasant, it made a mumbling snapping noise between his lips; it ran in his mind while his eyes wandered about looking for something to do, something to play with.

Mommanpoppas' voices kept attracting his attention. Mama was being cross with Papa again. He could tell by the sound. That was what Marjory always said when their voices rose and fell and shot up to a point and crashed and rolled like the two tomcats who fought at night. Papa was being cross, too, much crosser than Mama this time. He grew cold and disturbed and sat very still, wanting to go to the bathroom, but it was just next to Mommanpoppasroom; he didn't dare think of it. As the voices grew louder he could hardly hear them any more; he wanted so badly to go to the bathroom. The kitchen door opened suddenly and Marjory ran out, making the motion with her hand that meant he was to come to her. He didn't move. She came to him, her face still red and frowning, but she was not angry; she was scared just as he was. She said, "Come on, honey, we've got to go to your gran'ma's again." She took his hand and pulled him. "Come on quick, your gran'ma is waiting for you." He slid off the bench. His mother's voice rose in a terrible scream, screaming something he could not understand, but she was furious; he had seen her clenching her fists and stamping in one spot, screaming with her eyes shut; he knew how she looked. She was screaming in a tantrum, just as he remembered having heard himself. He stood still, doubled over, and all his body seemed to dissolve, sickly, from the pit of his stomach.

"Oh my God," said Marjory. "Oh my God. Now look at you. Oh my God. I can't stop to clean you up."

He did not know how he got to his grandma's house, but he was there at last, wet and soiled, being handled with disgust in the big bathtub. His grandma was there in long black skirts saying, "Maybe he's sick; maybe we should send for the doctor."

"I don't think so, m'am," said Marjory. "He hasn't et anything; he's just scared."

The little boy couldn't raise his eyes, he was so heavy with shame. "Take this note to his mother," said Grandma.

She sat in a wide chair and ran her hands over his head, combing his hair with her fingers; she lifted his chin and kissed him. "Poor little fellow," she said. "Never you mind. You always have a good time at your grandma's, don't you? You're going to have a nice little visit, just like the last time."

The little boy leaned against the stiff, dry-smelling clothes and felt horribly grieved about something. He began to whimper and said, "I'm hungry. I want something to eat." This reminded him. He began to bellow at the top of his voice; he threw himself upon the carpet and rubbed his nose in a dusty woolly bouquet of roses. "I want my peanuts," he howled. "Somebody took my peanuts."

His grandma knelt beside him and gathered him up so tightly he could hardly move. She called in a calm voice above his howls to Old Janet in the doorway, "Bring me some bread and butter with strawberry jam."

"I want peanuts," yelled the little boy desperately.

"No, you don't, darling," said his grandma. "You don't want horrid old peanuts to make you sick. You're going to have some of grandma's nice fresh bread with good strawberries on it. That's what you're going to have." He sat afterward very quietly and ate and ate. His grandma sat near him and Old Janet stood by, near a tray with a loaf and a glass bowl of jam upon the table at the window. Outside there was a trellis with tube-shaped red flowers clinging all over it, and brown bees singing.

"I hardly know what to do," said Grandma, "it's very . . ."

"Yes, m'am," said Old Janet, "it certainly is . . ."

Grandma said, "I can't possibly see the end of it. It's a terrible . . ."

"It certainly is bad," said Old Janet, "all this upset all the time and him such a baby."

Their voices ran on soothingly. The little boy ate and forgot to listen. He did not know these women, except by name. He could not understand what they were talking about; their hands and their clothes and their voices were dry and far away; they examined him with crinkled eyes without any expression that he could see. He sat there waiting for whatever they would do next with him. He hoped they would let him go out and play in the yard. The room was full of flowers and dark red curtains and big soft chairs, and the windows were open, but it was still dark in there somehow; dark, and a place he did not know, or trust.

"Now drink your milk," said Old Janet, holding out a silver cup.

"I don't want any milk," he said, turning his head away.

"Very well, Janet, he doesn't have to drink it," said Grandma quickly. "Now run out in the garden and play, darling. Janet, get his hoop."

A big strange man came home in the evenings who treated the little boy very confusingly. "Say 'please,' and 'thank you,' young man," he would roar, terrifyingly, when he gave any smallest object to the little boy. "Well, fellow, are you ready for a fight?" he would say, again, doubling up huge, hairy fists and making passes at him. "Come on now, you must learn to box." After the first few times this was fun.

"Don't teach him to be rough," said Grandma. "Time enough for all that."

"Now, Mother, we don't want him to be a sissy," said the big man. "He's got to toughen up early. Come on now, fellow, put up your mitts." The little boy liked this new word for hands. He learned to throw himself upon the strange big man, whose name was Uncle David, and hit him on the chest as hard as he could; the big man would laugh and hit him back with his huge, loose fists. Sometimes, but not often, Uncle David came home in the middle of the day. The little boy missed him on the other days, and would hang on the gate looking down the street for him. One evening he brought a large square package under his arm.

"Come over here, fellow, and see what I've got," he said, pulling off quantities of green paper and string from the box which was full of flat, folded colors. He put something in the little boy's hand. It was limp and silky and bright green with a tube on the end. "Thank you," said the little boy nicely, but not knowing what to do with it.

"Balloons," said Uncle David in triumph. "Now just put your mouth here and blow hard." The little boy blew hard and the green thing began to grow round and thin and silvery.

"Good for your chest," said Uncle David. "Blow some more." The little boy went on blowing and the balloon swelled steadily.

"Stop," said Uncle David, "that's enough." He twisted the tube to keep the air in. "That's the way," he said. "Now I'll blow one, and you blow one, and let's see who can blow up a big balloon the fastest."

They blew and blew, especially Uncle David. He puffed and panted and blew with all his might, but the little boy won. His balloon was perfectly round before Uncle David could even get started. The little boy was so proud he began to dance and shout, "I beat, I beat," and blew in his balloon again. It burst in his face and frightened him so he felt sick. "Ha ha, ho ho ho," whooped Uncle David. "That's the boy. I bet I can't do that. Now let's see." He blew until the beautiful bubble grew and wavered and burst into thin air, and there was only a small colored rag in his hand. This was a fine game. They went on with it until Grandma came in and said, "Time for supper now. No, you can't blow balloons at the table. Tomorrow maybe." And it was all over.

The next day, instead of being given balloons, he was hustled out of bed early, bathed in warm soapy water and given a big breakfast of soft-boiled eggs with toast and jam and milk. His grandma came in to kiss him good morning. "And I hope you'll be a good boy and obey your teacher," she told him.

"What's teacher?" asked the little boy.

"Teacher is at school," said Grandma. "She'll tell you all sorts of things and you must do as she says."

Mama and Papa had talked a great deal about School, and how they must send him there. They had told him it was a fine place with all kinds of toys and other children to play with. He felt he knew about School. "I didn't know it was time, Grandma," he said. "Is it today?"

"It's this very minute," said Grandma. "I told you a week ago."

Old Janet came in with her bonnet on. It was a prickly looking bundle held with a black rubber band under her back hair. "Come on," she said. "This is my busy day." She wore a dead cat slung around her neck, its sharp ears bent over under her baggy chin.

The little boy was excited and wanted to run ahead. "Hold to my hand like I told you," said Old Janet. "Don't go running off like that and get yourself killed."

"I'm going to get killed, I'm going to get killed," sang the little boy, making a tune of his own.

"Don't say that, you give me the creeps," said Old Janet. "Hold to my hand now." She bent over and looked at him, not at his face but at something on his clothes. His eyes followed hers.

"I declare," said Old Janet, "I did forget. I was going to sew it up. I might have known. I *told* your grandma it would be that way from now on."

"What?" asked the little boy.

"Just look at yourself," said Old Janet crossly. He looked at himself. There was a little end of him showing through the slit in his short blue flannel trousers. The trousers came halfway to his knees above, and his socks came halfway to his knees below, and all winter long his knees were cold. He remembered now how cold his knees were in cold weather. And how sometimes he would have to put the part of him that came through the slit back again, because he was cold there too. He saw at once what was wrong, and tried to arrange himself, but his mittens got in the way. Janet said, "Stop that, you bad boy," and with a firm thumb she set him in order, at the same time reaching under his belt to pull down and fold his knit undershirt over his front.

"There now," she said, "try not to disgrace yourself today." He felt guilty and red all over, because he had something that showed when he was dressed that was not supposed to show then. The different women who bathed him always wrapped him quickly in towels and hurried him into his clothes, because they saw something about him he could not see for himself. They hurried him so he never had a chance to see whatever it was they saw, and though he looked at himself when his clothes were off, he could not find out what was wrong with him. Outside, in his clothes, he knew he looked like everybody else, but inside his clothes there was something bad the matter with him. It worried him and confused him and he wondered about it. The only people who never seemed to notice there was something wrong with him were Mommanpoppa. They never called him a bad boy, and all summer long they had taken all his clothes off and let him run in the sand beside a big ocean.

"Look at him, isn't he a love?" Mama would say and Papa would look, and say, "He's got a back like a prize fighter." Uncle David was a prize fighter when he doubled up his mitts and said, "Come on, fellow."

Old Janet held him firmly and took long steps under her big rustling skirts. He did not like Old Janet's smell. It made him a little quivery in the stomach! it was just like wet chicken feathers.

School was easy. Teacher was a square-shaped woman with square short hair and short skirts. She got in the way sometimes, but not often. The people around him were his size; he didn't have always to be stretching his neck up to faces bent over him, and he could sit on the chairs without having to climb. All the children had

names, like Frances and Evelyn and Agatha and Edward and Martin, and his own name was Stephen. He was not Mama's "Baby,"
nor Papa's "Old Man"; he was not Uncle David's "Fellow" or
Grandma's "Darling," or even Old Janet's "Bad Boy." He was Stephen.
He was learning to read, and to sing a tune to some strange-looking
letters or marks written in chalk on a blackboard. You talked one
kind of lettering, and you sang another. All the children talked and
sang in turn, and then all together. Stephen thought it a fine game.
He felt awake and happy. They had soft clay and paper and wires
and squares of colors in tin boxes to play with, colored blocks to
build houses with. Afterward they all danced in a big ring, and then
they danced in pairs, boys with girls. Stephen danced with Frances,
and Frances kept saying, "Now you just follow me." She was a little
taller than he was, and her hair stood up in short, shiny curls, the
color of an ash tray on Papa's desk. She would say, "You can't dance."
"I can dance too," said Stephen, jumping around holding her hands,
"I can, too, dance." He was certain of it. "*You* can't dance," he told
Frances, "you can't dance at all."

Then they had to change partners, and when they came round
again, Frances said, "I don't *like* the way you dance." This was different. He felt uneasy about it. He didn't jump quite so high when
the phonograph record started going dumdiddy dumdiddy again.
"Go ahead, Stephen, you're doing fine," said Teacher, waving her
hands together very fast. The dance ended, and they all played
"relaxing" for five minutes. They relaxed by swinging their arms
back and forth, then rolling their heads round and round. When
Old Janet came for him he didn't want to go home. At lunch his
grandma told him twice to keep his face out of his plate. "Is that
what they teach you at school?" she asked. Uncle David was at
home. "Here you are, fellow," he said and gave Stephen two balloons.
"Thank you," said Stephen. He put the balloons in his pocket and
forgot about them. "I told you that boy could learn something,"
said Uncle David to Grandma. "Hear him say 'thank you'?"

In the afternoon at school Teacher handed out big wads of clay
and told the children to make something out of it. Anything
they liked. Stephen decided to make a cat, like Mama's Meeow at
home. He did not like Meeow, but he thought it would be easy to
make a cat. He could not get the clay to work at all. It simply fell
into one lump after another. So he stopped, wiped his hands on his
pullover, remembered his balloons and began blowing one.

"Look at Stephen's horse," said Frances. "Just look at it."

"It's not a horse, it's a cat," said Stephen. The other children gathered around. "It looks like a horse, a little," said Martin.

"It is a cat," said Stephen, stamping his foot, feeling his face turning hot. The other children all laughed and exclaimed over Stephen's cat that looked like a horse. Teacher came down among them. She sat usually at the top of the room before a big table covered with papers and playthings. She picked up Stephen's lump of clay and turned it round and examined it with her kind eyes. "Now, children," she said, "everybody has the right to make anything the way he pleases. If Stephen says this is a cat, it *is* a cat. Maybe you were thinking about a horse, Stephen?"

"It's a *cat*," said Stephen. He was aching all over. He knew then he should have said at first, "Yes, it's a horse." Then they would have let him alone. They would never have known he was trying to make a cat. "It's Meeow," he said in a trembling voice, "but I forgot how she looks."

His balloon was perfectly flat. He started blowing it up again, trying not to cry. Then it was time to go home, and Old Janet came looking for him. While Teacher was talking to other grown-up people who came to take other children home, Frances said, "Give me your balloon; I haven't got a balloon." Stephen handed it to her. He was happy to give it. He reached in his pocket and took out the other. Happily, he gave her that one too. Frances took it, then handed it back. "Now you blow up one and I'll blow up the other, and let's have a race," she said. When their balloons were only half filled Old Janet took Stephen by the arm and said, "Come on here, this is my busy day."

Frances ran after them, calling, "Stephen, you give me back my balloon," and snatched it away. Stephen did not know whether he was surprised to find himself going away with Frances' balloon, or whether he was surprised to see her snatching it as if it really belonged to her. He was badly mixed up in his mind, and Old Janet was hauling him along. One thing he knew, he liked Frances, he was going to see her again tomorrow, and he was going to bring her more balloons.

That evening Stephen boxed awhile with his uncle David, and Uncle David gave him a beautiful orange. "Eat that," he said, "it's good for your health."

"Uncle David, may I have some more balloons?" asked Stephen.

"Well, what do you say first?" asked Uncle David, reaching for the box on the top bookshelf.

"Please," said Stephen.

"That's the word," said Uncle David. He brought out two balloons, a red and a yellow one. Stephen noticed for the first time they had letters on them, very small letters that grew taller and wider as the balloon grew rounder. "Now that's all, fellow," said Uncle David. "Don't ask for any more because that's all." He put the box back on the bookshelf, but not before Stephen had seen that the box was almost full of balloons. He didn't say a word, but went on blowing, and Uncle David blew also. Stephen thought it was the nicest game he had ever known.

He had only one left, the next day, but he took it to school and gave it to Frances. "There are a lot," he said, feeling very proud and warm; "I'll bring you a lot of them."

Frances blew it up until it made a beautiful bubble, and said, "Look, I want to show you something." She took a sharp-pointed stick they used in working the clay; she poked the balloon, and it exploded. "Look at that," she said.

"That's nothing," said Stephen, "I'll bring you some more."

After school, before Uncle David came home, while Grandma was resting, when Old Janet had given him his milk and told him to run away and not bother her, Stephen dragged a chair to the bookshelf, stood upon it and reached into the box. He did not take three or four as he believed he intended; once his hands were upon them he seized what they could hold and jumped off the chair, hugging them to him. He stuffed them into his reefer pocket where they folded down and hardly made a lump.

He gave them all to Frances. There were so many, Frances gave most of them away to the other children. Stephen, flushed with his new joy, the lavish pleasure of giving presents, found almost at once still another happiness. Suddenly he was popular among the children; they invited him specially to join whatever games were up; they fell in at once with his own notions for play, and asked him what he would like to do next. They had festivals of blowing up the beautiful globes, fuller and rounder and thinner, changing as they went from deep color to lighter, paler tones, growing glassy thin, bubbly thin, then bursting with a thrilling loud noise like a toy pistol.

For the first time in his life Stephen had almost too much of something he wanted, and his head was so turned he forgot how this fullness came about, and no longer thought of it as a secret. The next day was Saturday, and Frances came to visit him with her nurse. The nurse and Old Janet sat in Old Janet's room drinking coffee and gossiping, and the children sat on the side porch blowing balloons.

Stephen chose an apple-colored one and Frances a pale green one. Between them on the bench lay a tumbled heap of delights still to come.

"I once had a silver balloon," said Frances, "a beyootiful silver one, not round like these; it was a long one. But these are even nicer, I think," she added quickly, for she did want to be polite.

"When you get through with that one," said Stephen, gazing at her with the pure bliss of giving added to loving, "you can blow up a blue one and then a pink one and a yellow one and a purple one." He pushed the heap of limp objects toward her. Her clear-looking eyes, with fine little rays of brown in them like the spokes of a wheel, were full of approval for Stephen. "I wouldn't want to be greedy, though, and blow up all your balloons."

"There'll be plenty more left," said Stephen, and his heart rose under his thin ribs. He felt his ribs with his fingers and discovered with some surprise that they stopped somewhere in front, while Frances sat blowing balloons rather halfheartedly. The truth was, she was tired of balloons. After you blow six or seven your chest gets hollow and your lips feel puckery. She had been blowing balloons steadily for three days now. She had begun to hope they were giving out. "There's boxes and boxes more of them, Frances," said Stephen happily. "Millions more. I guess they'd last and last if we didn't blow too many every day."

Frances said somewhat timidly, "I tell you what. Let's rest awhile and fix some liquish water. Do you like liquish?"

"Yes, I do," said Stephen, "but I haven't got any."

"Couldn't we buy some?" asked Frances. "It's only a cent a stick, the nice rubbery, twisty kind. We can put it in a bottle with some water, and shake it and shake it, and it makes foam on top like soda pop and we can drink it. I'm kind of thirsty," she said in a small, weak voice. "Blowing balloons all the time makes you thirsty, I think."

Stephen, in silence, realized a dreadful truth and a numb feeling crept over him. He did not have a cent to buy licorice for Frances and she was tired of his balloons. This was the first real dismay of his whole life, and he aged at least a year in the next minute, huddled, with his deep, serious blue eyes focused down his nose in intense speculation. What could he do to please Frances that would not cost money? Only yesterday Uncle David had given him a nickel, and he had thrown it away on gumdrops. He regretted that nickel so bitterly his neck and forehead were damp. He was thirsty too.

"I tell you what," he said, brightening with a splendid idea, lamely

trailing off on second thought, "I know something we can do, I'll—
I . . ."

"I *am* thirsty," said Frances with gentle persistence. "I think I'm
so thirsty maybe I'll have to go home." She did not leave the bench,
though, but sat, turning her grieved mouth toward Stephen.

Stephen quivered with the terrors of the adventure before him,
but he said boldly, "I'll make some lemonade. I'll get sugar and lemon
and some ice and we'll have lemonade."

"Oh, I love lemonade," cried Frances. "I'd rather have lemonade
than liquish."

"You stay right here," said Stephen, "and I'll get everything."

He ran around the house, and under Old Janet's window he heard
the dry, chattering voices of the two old women whom he must out-
wit. He sneaked on tiptoe to the pantry, took a lemon lying there
by itself, a handful of lump sugar and a china teapot, smooth, round,
with flowers and leaves all over it. These he left on the kitchen
table while he broke a piece of ice with a sharp metal pick he had
been forbidden to touch. He put the ice in the pot, cut the lemon
and squeezed it as well as he could—a lemon was tougher and more
slippery than he had thought—and mixed sugar and water. He decided there was not enough sugar so he sneaked back and took another handful. He was back on the porch in an astonishingly short
time, his face tight, his knees trembling, carrying iced lemonade
to thirsty Frances with both his devoted hands.

A pace distant from her he stopped, literally stabbed through with
a thought. Here he stood in broad daylight carrying a teapot with
lemonade in it, and his grandma or Old Janet might walk through
the door at any moment.

"Come on, Frances," he whispered loudly. "Let's go round to the
back behind the rosebushes where it's shady." Frances leaped up
and ran like a deer beside him, her face wise with knowledge of
why they ran; Stephen ran stiffly, cherishing his teapot with
clenched hands.

It was shady behind the rosebushes, and much safer. They sat
side by side on the dampish ground, legs doubled under, drinking in
turn from the slender spout. Stephen took his just share in large,
cool, delicious swallows. When Frances drank she set her round pink
mouth daintily to the spout and her throat beat steadily as a heart.
Stephen was thinking he had really done something pretty nice for
Frances. He did not know where his own happiness was; it was
mixed with the sweet-sour taste in his mouth and a cool feeling in

his bosom because Frances was there drinking his lemonade which he had got for her with great danger.

Frances said, "My, what big swallows you take," when his turn came next.

"No bigger than yours," he told her downrightly. "You take awfully big swallows."

"Well," said Frances, turning this criticism into an argument for her rightness about things, "that's the way to drink lemonade anyway." She peered into the teapot. There was quite a lot of lemonade left and she was beginning to feel she had enough. "Let's make up a game and see who can take the biggest swallows."

This was such a wonderful notion they grew reckless, tipping the spout into their opened mouths above their heads until lemonade welled up and ran over their chins in rills down their fronts. When they tired of this there was still lemonade left in the pot. They played first at giving the rosebush a drink and ended by baptizing it. "Name father son holygoat," shouted Stephen, pouring. At this sound Old Janet's face appeared over the low hedge, with the tan, disgusted-looking face of Frances' nurse hanging over her shoulder.

"Well, just as I thought," said Old Janet. "Just as I expected." The bag under her chin waggled.

"We were thirsty," he said; "we were awfully thirsty." Frances said nothing, but she gazed steadily at the toes of her shoes.

"Give me that teapot," said Old Janet, taking it with a rude snatch. "Just because you're thirsty is no reason," said Old Janet. "You can ask for things. You don't have to steal."

"We didn't steal," cried Frances suddenly. "We didn't. We didn't!"

"That's enough from you, missy," said her nurse. "Come straight out of there. You have nothing to do with this."

"Oh, I don't know," said Old Janet with a hard stare at Frances' nurse. "He never did such a thing before, by himself."

"Come on," said the nurse to Frances, "this is no place for you." She held Frances by the wrist and started walking away so fast Frances had to run to keep up. "Nobody can call us thieves and get away with it."

"You don't have to steal, even if others do," said Old Janet to Stephen, in a high carrying voice. "If you so much as pick up a lemon in somebody else's house you're a little thief." She lowered her voice then and said, "Now I'm going to tell your grandma and you'll see what you get."

"He went in the icebox and left it open," Janet told Grandma, "and he got into the lump sugar and spilt it all over the floor. Lumps everywhere underfoot. He dribbled water all over the clean kitchen floor, and he baptized the rosebush, blaspheming. And he took your Spode teapot."

"I didn't either," said Stephen loudly, trying to free his hand from Old Janet's big hard fist.

"Don't tell fibs," said Old Janet; "that's the last straw."

"Oh dear," said Grandma. "He's not a baby any more." She shut the book she was reading and pulled the wet front of his pull-over toward her. "What's this sticky stuff on him?" she asked and straightened her glasses.

"Lemonade," said Old Janet. "He took the last lemon."

They were in the big dark room with the red curtains. Uncle David walked in from the room with the bookcases, holding a box in his uplifted hand. "Look here," he said to Stephen. "What's become of all my balloons?"

Stephen knew well that Uncle David was not really asking a question.

Stephen, sitting on a footstool at his grandma's knee, felt sleepy. He leaned heavily and wished he could put his head on her lap, but he might go to sleep, and it would be wrong to go to sleep while Uncle David was still talking. Uncle David walked about the room with his hands in his pockets, talking to Grandma. Now and then he would walk over to a lamp and, leaning, peer into the top of the shade, winking in the light, as if he expected to find something there.

"It's simply in the blood, I told her," said Uncle David. "I told her she would simply have to come and get him, and keep him. She asked me if I meant to call him a thief and I said if she could think of a more exact word I'd be glad to hear it."

"You shouldn't have said that," commented Grandma calmly.

"Why not? She might as well know the facts. . . . I suppose he can't help it," said Uncle David, stopping now in front of Stephen and dropping his chin into his collar, "I shouldn't expect too much of him, but you can't begin too early——"

"The trouble is," said Grandma, and while she spoke she took Stephen by the chin and held it up so that he had to meet her eye; she talked steadily in a mournful tone, but Stephen could not understand. She ended. "It's not just about the balloons, of course."

"It is about the balloons," said Uncle David angrily, "because balloons now mean something worse later. But what can you expect? His father—well, it's in the blood. He——"

"That's your sister's husband you're talking about," said Grandma, "and there is no use making things worse. Besides, you don't really *know*."

"I *do* know," said Uncle David. And he talked again very fast, walking up and down. Stephen tried to understand, but the sounds were strange and floating just over his head. They were talking about his father, and they did not like him. Uncle David came over and stood above Stephen and Grandma. He hunched over them with a frowning face, a long, crooked shadow from him falling across them to the wall. To Stephen he looked like his father, and he shrank against his grandma's skirts.

"The question is, what to do with him now?" asked Uncle David. "If we keep him here, he'd just be a—I won't be bothered with him. Why can't they take care of their own child? That house is crazy. Too far gone already, I'm afraid. No training. No example."

"You're right, they must take him and keep him," said Grandma. She ran her hands over Stephen's head; tenderly she pinched the nape of his neck between thumb and forefinger. "You're your grandma's darling," she told him, "and you've had a nice long visit, and now you're going home. Mama is coming for you in a few minutes. Won't that be nice?"

"I want my mama," said Stephen, whimpering, for his grandma's face frightened hm. There was something wrong with her smile.

Uncle David sat down. "Come over here, fellow," he said, wagging a forefinger at Stephen. Stephen went over slowly, and Uncle David drew him between his wide knees in their loose, rough clothes. "You ought to be ashamed of yourself," he said, "stealing Uncle David's balloons when he had already given you so many."

"It wasn't that," said Grandma quickly. "Don't say that. It will make an impression——"

"I hope it does," said Uncle David in a louder voice; "I hope he remembers it all his life. If he belonged to me I'd give him a good thrashing."

Stephen felt his mouth, his chin, his whole face jerking. He opened his mouth to take a breath, and tears and noise burst from him. "Stop that, fellow, stop that," said Uncle David, shaking him gently by the shoulders, but Stephen could not stop. He drew his breath again and it came back in a howl. Old Janet came to the door.

"Bring me some cold water," called Grandma. There was a flurry, a commotion, a breath of cool air from the hall, the door slammed, and Stephen heard his mother's voice. His howl died away, his breath sobbed and fluttered, he turned his dimmed eyes and saw her standing there. His heart turned over within him and he bleated like a lamb, "Maaaaama," running toward her. Uncle David stood back as Mama swooped in and fell on her knees beside Stephen. She gathered him to her and stood up with him in her arms.

"What are you doing to my baby?" she asked Uncle David in a thickened voice. "I should never have let him come here. I should have known better——"

"You always should know better," said Uncle David, "and you never do. And you never will. You haven't got it here," he told her, tapping his forehead.

"David," said Grandma, "that's your——"

"Yes, I know, she's my sister," said Uncle David. "I know it. But if she must run away and marry a——"

"Shut up," said Mama.

"And bring more like him into the world, let her keep them at home. I say let her keep——"

Mama set Stephen on the floor and, holding him by the hand, she said to Grandma all in a rush as if she were reading something, "Good-by, Mother. This is the last time, really the last. I can't bear it any longer. Say good-by to Stephen; you'll never see him again. You let this happen. It's your fault. You know David was a coward and a bully and a self-righteous little beast all his life and you never crossed him in anything. You let him bully me all my life and you let him slander my husband and call my baby a thief, and now this is the end. . . . He calls my baby a thief over a few horrible little balloons because he doesn't like my husband. . . ."

She was panting and staring about from one to the other. They were all standing. Now Grandma said, "Go home, daughter. Go away, David. I'm sick of your quarreling. I've never had a day's peace or comfort from either of you. I'm sick of you both. Now let me alone and stop this noise. Go away," said Grandma in a wavering voice. She took out her handkerchief and wiped first one eye and then the other and said, "All this hate, hate—what is it for? . . . So this is the way it turns out. Well, let me alone."

"You and your little advertising balloons," said Mama to Uncle David. "The big honest businessman advertises with balloons and if he loses one he'll be ruined. And your beastly little moral notions . . ."

Grandma went to the door to meet Old Janet, who handed her a glass of water. Grandma drank it all, standing there.

"Is your husband coming for you, or are you going home by yourself?" she asked Mama.

"I'm driving myself," said Mama in a far-away voice as if her mind had wandered. "You know he wouldn't set foot in this house."

"I should think not," said Uncle David.

"Come on, Stephen darling," said Mama. "It's far past his bedtime," she said, to no one in particular. "Imagine keeping a baby up to torture him about a few miserable little bits of colored rubber." She smiled at Uncle David with both rows of teeth as she passed him on the way to the door, keeping between him and Stephen. "Ah, where would we be without high moral standards," she said, and then to Grandma, "Good night, Mother," in quite her usual voice. "I'll see you in a day or so."

"Yes indeed," said Grandma cheerfully, coming out into the hall with Stephen and Mama. "Let me hear from you. Ring me up tomorrow. I hope you'll be feeling better."

"I feel very well now," said Mama brightly, laughing. She bent down and kissed Stephen. "Sleepy, darling? Papa's waiting to see you. Don't go to sleep until you've kissed your papa good night."

Stephen woke with a sharp jerk. He raised his head and put out his chin a little. "I don't want to go home," he said; "I want to go to school. I don't want to see Papa, I don't like him."

Mama laid her palm over his mouth softly. "Darling, don't."

Uncle David put his head out with a kind of snort. "There you are," he said. "There you've got a statement from headquarters."

Mama opened the door and ran, almost carrying Stephen. She ran across the sidewalk, jerking open the car door and dragging Stephen in after her. She spun the car around and dashed forward so sharply Stephen was almost flung out of the seat. He sat braced then with all his might, hands digging into the cushions. The car speeded up and the trees and houses whizzed by all flattened out. Stephen began suddenly to sing to himself, a quiet, inside song so Mama would not hear. He sang his new secret; it was a comfortable, sleepy song: "I hate Papa, I hate Mama, I hate Grandma, I hate Uncle David, I hate Old Janet, I hate Marjory, I hate Papa, I hate Mama . . ."

His head bobbed, leaned, came to rest on Mama's knee, eyes closed. Mama drew him closer and slowed down, driving with one hand.

Holiday

At that time I was too young for some of the troubles I was having, and I had not yet learned what to do with them. It no longer can matter what kind of troubles they were, or what finally became of them. It seemed to me then there was nothing to do but run away from them, though all my tradition, background, and training had taught me unanswerably that no one except a coward ever runs away from anything. What nonsense! They should have taught me the difference between courage and foolhardiness, instead of leaving me to find it out for myself. I learned finally that if I still had the sense I was born with, I would take off like a deer at the first warning of certain dangers. But this story I am about to tell you happened before this great truth impressed itself upon me—that we do not run from the troubles and dangers that are truly ours, and it is better to learn what they are earlier than later. And if we don't run from the others, we are fools.

I confided to my friend Louise, a former schoolmate about my own age, not my troubles but my little problem: I wanted to go somewhere for a spring holiday, by myself, to the country, and it should be very simple and nice and, of course, not expensive, and she was not to tell anyone where I had gone; but if she liked, I would send her word now and then, if anything interesting was happening. She said she loved getting letters but hated answering them; and she knew the very place for me, and she would not tell anybody anything. Louise had then—she has it still—something near to genius for making improbable persons, places, and situations sound attractive. She told amusing stories that did not turn grim on you until a little while later, when by chance you saw and heard for yourself. So with this story. Everything was just as Louise had said, if you like, and everything was, at the same time, quite different.

"I know the very place," said Louise. "A family of real old-fashioned

German peasants, in the deep blackland Texas farm country, a household in real patriarchal style—the kind of thing you'd hate to live with but is very nice to visit. Old father, God Almighty himself, with whiskers and all; old mother, matriarch in men's shoes; endless daughters and sons and sons-in-law, and fat babies falling about the place; and fat puppies—my favorite was a darling little black thing named Kuno—cows, calves, and sheep and lambs and goats and turkeys and guineas roaming up and down the shallow green hills, ducks and geese on the ponds. I was there in the summer when the peaches and watermelons were in—"

"This is the end of March," I said, doubtfully.

"Spring comes early there," said Louise. "I'll write to the Müllers about you, you just get ready to go."

"Just where is this paradise?"

"Not far from the Louisiana line," said Louise. "I'll ask them to give you my attic—oh, that was a sweet place! It's a big room, with the roof sloping to the floor on each side, and the roof leaks a little when it rains, so the shingles are all stained in beautiful streaks, all black and gray and mossy green, and in one corner there used to be a stack of dime novels, The Duchess, Ouida, Mrs. E.D.E.N. Southworth, Ella Wheeler Wilcox's poems—one summer they had a lady boarder who was a great reader, and she went off and left her library. I loved it! And everybody was so healthy and goodhearted, and the weather was perfect. . . . How long do you want to stay?"

I hadn't thought of this, so I said at random, "About a month."

A few days later I found myself tossed off like an express package from a dirty little crawling train onto the sodden platform of a country station, where the stationmaster emerged and locked up the waiting room before the train had got round the bend. As he clumped by me he shifted his wad of tobacco to his cheek and asked, "Where you goin'?"

"To the Müller farm," I said, standing beside my small trunk and suitcase with the bitter wind cutting my shoulders through my thin coat.

"Anybody meet you?" he asked, not pausing.

"They *said* so."

"All right," he said, and got into his little ragged buckboard with a sway-backed horse and drove away.

I turned my trunk on its side and sat on it facing the wind and the desolate mud-colored shapeless scene and began making up my first letter to Louise. First I was going to tell her that unless she meant to be a novelist, there was no excuse for her having so much imagination. In daily life, I was going to tell her, there are also such useful things as the plain facts that should be stuck to, through thick and thin. Anything else led to confusion like this. I was beginning to enjoy my letter to Louise when a sturdy boy about twelve years old crossed the platform. As he neared me, he took off his rough cap and bunched it in his thick hand, dirt-stained at the knuckles. His round cheeks, his round nose, his round chin were a cool, healthy red. In the globe of his face, as neatly circular as if drawn in bright crayon, his narrow, long, tip-tilted eyes, clear as pale-blue water, seemed out of place, as if two incompatible strains had collided in making him. They were beautiful eyes, and the rest of the face was not to be taken seriously. A blue woolen blouse buttoned up to his chin ended abruptly at his waist as if he would outgrow it in another half hour, and his blue drill breeches flapped about his ankles. His old clodhopper shoes were several sizes too big for him. Altogether, it was plain he was not the first one to wear his clothes. He was a cheerful, detached, self-possessed apparition against the tumbled brown earth and ragged dark sky, and I smiled at him as well as I could with a face that felt like wet clay.

He smiled back slightly without meeting my eye, motioning for me to take up my suitcase. He swung my trunk to his head and tottered across the uneven platform, down the steps slippery with mud, where I expected to see him crushed beneath his burden like an ant under a stone. He heaved the trunk into the back of his wagon with a fine smash, took my suitcase and tossed it after, then climbed up over one front wheel while I scrambled my way up over the other.

The pony, shaggy as a wintering bear, eased himself into a grudging trot, while the boy, bowed over with his cap pulled down over his ears and eyebrows, held the reins slack and fell into a brown study. I examined the harness, a real mystery. It met and clung in all sorts of unexpected places; it parted company in what appeared to be strategic seats of jointure. It was mended sketchily in risky places with bits of hairy rope. Other seemingly unimportant parts were bound together irrevocably with wire. The bridle was too long for the pony's stocky head, so he had shaken the bit out of his mouth at the start, apparently, and went his own way at his own pace.

Our vehicle was an exhausted specimen of something called a spring wagon, who knows why? There were no springs, and the shallow enclosed platform at the back, suitable for carrying various plunder, was worn away until it barely reached midway of the back wheels, one side of it steadily scraping the iron tire. The wheels themselves spun not dully around and around in the way of common wheels, but elliptically, being loosened at the hubs, so that we proceeded with a drunken, hilarious swagger, like the rolling motion of a small boat on a choppy sea.

The soaked brown fields fell away on either side of the lane, all rough with winter-worn stubble ready to sink and become earth again. The scanty leafless woods ran along an edge of the field nearby. There was nothing beautiful in those woods now except the promise of spring, for I detested bleakness, but it gave me pleasure to think that beyond this there might be something else beautiful in its own being, a river shaped and contained by its banks, or a field stripped down to its true meaning, plowed and ready for the seed. The road turned abruptly and was almost hidden for a moment, and we were going through the woods. Closer sight of the crooked branches assured me that spring was beginning, if sparely, reluctantly; the leaves were budding in tiny cones of watery green besprinkling all the new shoots; a thin sedate rain began again to fall, not so opaque as a fog, but a mist that merely deepened overhead, and lowered, until the clouds became rain in one swathing, delicate gray.

As we emerged from the woods, the boy roused himself and pointed forward, in silence. We were approaching the farm along the skirts of a fine peach orchard, now faintly colored with young buds, but there was nothing to disguise the gaunt and aching ugliness of the farmhouse itself. In this Texas valley, so gently modulated with small crests and shallows, "rolling country" as the famers say, the house was set on the peak of the barest rise of ground, as if the most infertile spot had been thriftily chosen for building a shelter. It stood there staring and naked, an intruding stranger, strange even beside the barns ranged generously along the back, low-eaved and weathered to the color of stone.

The narrow windows and the steeply sloping roof oppressed me; I wished to turn away and go back. I had come a long way to be so disappointed, I thought, and yet I must go on, for there could be nothing here for me more painful than what I had left. But as we drew near the house, now hardly visible except for the yellow lamplight in the back, perhaps in the kitchen, my feelings changed again toward warmth and tenderness, or perhaps just an apprehension that I could feel so, maybe, again.

The wagon drew up before the porch, and I started climbing down. No sooner had my foot touched ground than an enormous black dog of the detestable German shepherd breed leaped silently at me, and as silently I covered my face with my arms and leaped back. "Kuno, down!" shouted the boy, lunging at him. The front door flew open and a young girl with yellow hair ran down the steps and seized the ugly beast by the scruff. "He does not mean anything," she said seriously in English. "He is only a dog."

Just Louise's darling little puppy Kuno, I thought, a year or so older. Kuno whined, apologized by bowing and scraping one front paw on the ground, and the girl holding his scruff said, shyly and proudly, "I teach him that. He has always such bad manners, but I teach him!"

I had arrived, it seemed, at the moment when the evening chores were about to begin. The entire Müller household streamed out of the door, each man and woman going about the affairs of the moment. The young girl walked with me up the porch steps and said, "This is my brother Hans," and a young man paused to shake hands and passed by. "This is my brother Fritz," she said, and Fritz took my hand and dropped it as he went. "My sister Annetje," said the young girl, and a quiet young woman with a baby draped loosely like a scarf over her shoulder smiled and held out her hand. Hand after hand went by, their palms variously younger or older, broad or small, male or female, but all thick hard decent peasant hands, warm and strong. And in every face I saw again the pale, tilted eyes, on every head that taffy-colored hair, as though they might all be brothers and sisters, though Annetje's husband and still another daughter's husband had gone by after greeting me. In the wide hall with a door at front and back, full of cloudy light and the smell of soap, the old mother, also on her way out, stopped to offer her hand. She was a tall strong-looking woman wearing a three-cornered black wool shawl on her head, her skirts looped up over a brown flannel petticoat. Not from her did the young ones get those water-clear eyes. Hers were black and shrewd and searching, a band of hair showed black streaked with gray, her seamed dry face was brown as seasoned bark, and she walked in her rubber boots with the stride of a man. She shook my hand briefly and said in German English that I was welcome, smiling and showing her blackened teeth.

"This is my girl Hatsy," she told me, "and she will show you to your room." Hatsy took my hand as if I were a child needing a guide. I followed her up a flight of steps steep as a ladder, and there we were, in Louise's attic room, with the sloping roof. Yes, the shingles were stained all the colors she had said. There were the dime novels heaped in the corner. For once, Louise had got it straight, and it was homely and familiar, as if I had seen it before. "My mother says we could give you a better place on the downstairs," said Hatsy, in her soft blurred English, "but *she* said in her letter you would like it so." I told her indeed I did like it so. She went down the steep stairs then, and her brother came up as if he were climbing a tree, with the trunk on his head and the suitcase in his right hand, and I could not see what kept the trunk from crashing back to the bottom, as he used the left hand to climb with. He put his burden down and straightened up, wriggling his shoulders and panting only a little. I thanked him and he pushed his cap back and pulled it forward again, which I took for some sort of polite response, and clattered out hugely. Looking out of my window a few minutes later, I saw him setting off across the fields carrying a lighted lantern and a large steel trap.

I began changing my first letter to Louise. "I'm going to like it here. I don't quite know why, but it's going to be all right. Maybe I can tell you later—"

The sound of the German speech in the household below was part of the pleasantness, for they were not talking to me and did not expect me to answer. All the German I understood then was contained in five small deadly sentimental songs of Heine's, learned by heart; and this was a very different tongue, Low German corrupted by three generations in a foreign country. A dozen miles away, where Texas and Louisiana melted together in a rotting swamp whose sluggish undertow of decay nourished the roots of pine and cedar, a colony of French immigrants had lived out two hundred years of exile, not wholly incorruptible, but mystically faithful to the marrow of their bones, obstinately speaking their old French, by then as strange to the French as it was to the English. I had known many of these families during a certain long summer happily remembered, and here, listening to another language nobody could understand except those of this small farming community, I knew that I was again in a house of perpetual exile. These were solid, practical, hard-bitten, land-holding German peasants who stuck their mattocks into the earth deep and held fast wherever they were, because to them life and the land were one indivisible thing; but never in any wise did they confuse nationality with habitation.

I liked the thick warm voices, and it was good not to have to understand what they were saying. I loved that silence which means freedom from the constant pressure of other minds and other opinions and other feelings, that freedom to fold up in quiet and go back to my own center, to find out again, for it is always a rediscovery, what kind of creature it is that rules me finally, makes all the decisions no matter who thinks they make them, even I; who little by little takes everything away except the one thing I cannot live without, and who will one day say, "Now I am all you have left—take me." I paused there a good while listening to this muted unknown language which was silence with music in it; I could be moved and touched but not troubled by it, as by the crying of frogs or the wind in the trees.

The catalpa tree at my window would, I noticed, when it came into leaf, shut off my view of the barns and the fields beyond. When in bloom the branches would almost reach through the window. But now they were a thin screen through which the calves, splotchy red and white, moved prettily against the weathered darkness of the sheds. The brown fields would soon be green again; the sheep would not look then as they did now, merely lumps of moving earth, but would be washed by the rains and become clean gray. All the beauty of the landscape now was in the harmony of the valley rolling fluently away to the wood's edge. It was an inland country, with the forlorn look of all unloved things; winter in this part of the South is a moribund coma, not the Northern death sleep with the sure promise of resurrection. But in my South, my loved and never-forgotten country, after her long sickness, with only a slight stirring, an opening of the eyes between one breath and the next, between night and day, the earth revives and bursts into the plenty of spring with fruit and flowers together, spring and summer at once under the hot shimmering blue sky.

The freshening wind promised another light sedate rain to come at evening. The voices below-stairs dispersed, rose again, separately calling from the yards and barns. The old woman strode down the path toward the cow sheds, Hatsy running behind her. The woman wore her wooden yoke, with the milking pails covered and closed with iron hasps, slung easily across her shoulders, but her daughter carried two tin milking pails on her arm. When they pushed back the bars of cedar which opened onto the fields, the cows came through lowing and crowding, and the calves scampered each to his own dam with reaching, opened mouths. Then there was the battle of separating the hungry children from their mothers when they had taken their scanty share. The old woman slapped their little haunches with her open palm, Hatsy dragged at their halters, her feet slipping wide in the mud, the cows bellowed and brandished their horns, the calves bawled like rebellious babies. Hatsy's long yellow braids whisked round her shoulders, her laughter was a shrill streak of

gaiety above the angry cow voices and the raucous shouting of the
old woman.

From the kitchen porch below came the sound of splashing water,
the creaking of the pump handle, and the stamping boots of men.
I sat in the window watching the darkness come on slowly. All the
sounds of the place gathered under the roof while the lamps were
being lighted. My own small lamp had a handle on the oil bowl,
like a cup's. There was also a lantern with a frosted chimney hanging by a nail on the wall. A voice called to me from the foot of my
stairs and I looked down into the face of a dark-skinned, flaxen-
haired young woman, far advanced in pregnancy, and carrying a
prosperous year-old boy on her hip, one arm clutching him to her,
the other raised above her head so that her lantern shone upon their
heads. "The supper is now ready," she said, and waited for me to
come down before turning away.

In the large square room the whole family was gathering at a
long table covered with a red checkered cotton cloth, heaped-up
platters of steaming food at either end. A crippled and badly deformed servant girl was setting down pitchers of milk. Her head was
so bowed over, her face was almost hidden, and her whole body was
maimed in some painful, mysterious way, probably congenital, I supposed, though she seemed wiry and tough. Her knotted hands shook
continually, her wagging head kept pace with her restless elbows.
She ran unsteadily around the table scattering plates, dodging whoever stood in her way; no one moved aside for her, or spoke to her,
or even glanced after her when she vanished into the kitchen.

The men moved forward to their chairs. Father Müller took his
patriarch's place at the head of the table, Mother Müller looming
behind him like a dark boulder. The young men ranged themselves
about one side, the married ones with their wives standing back of
their chairs to serve them, for three generations in this country had
not made them self-conscious or disturbed their ancient customs. The
two sons-in-law and three sons rolled down their shirt sleeves before
beginning to eat. Their faces were polished with recent scrubbing
and their open collars were damp.

Mother Müller pointed to me, then waved her hand at her household, telling off their names rapidly once more. I was a stranger and
a guest, so was seated on the men's side of the table, and Hatsy, whose
real name turned out to be Huldah, the maiden of the family, was
seated on the children's side of the board, attending to them and
keeping them in order. These infants ranged from two years to ten,
five in number—not counting the one still straddling his mother's

hip behind his father's chair—divided between the two married daughters. The children ravened and gorged and reached their hands into the sugar bowl to sprinkle sugar on everything they ate, solemnly elated over their food and paying no attention to Hatsy, who struggled with them only a little less energetically than she did with the calves, and ate almost nothing. She was about seventeen years old, pale-lipped and too thin, and her sleek fine butter-yellow hair, streaked light and dark, real German peasant hair, gave her an air of fragility. But she shared the big-boned structure, the enormous energy and animal force that was like a bodily presence itself in the room; and seeing Father Müller's pale-gray deep-set choleric eyes and high cheekbones, it was easy to trace the family resemblance around the table: it was plain that poor Mother Müller had never had a child of her own—black-eyed, black-haired South Germany people. True, she had borne them, but that was all; they belonged to their father. Even the tawny Gretchen, expecting another baby, obviously the pet of the family, with the sly smiling manner of a spoiled child, who wore the contented air of a lazy, healthy young animal, seeming always about to yawn, had hair like pulled taffy and those slanted clear eyes. She stood now easing the weight of her little boy on her husband's chair back, reaching with her left arm over his shoulder to refill his plate from time to time.

Annetje's baby drooled comfortably down her back, while she spooned things from platters and bowls for her husband. Whenever their eyes met, they smiled with a gentle, reserved warmth in their eyes, the smile of long and sure friendship.

Father Müller did not in the least believe in his children's marrying and leaving home. Marry, yes, of course; but must that take a son or daughter from him? He always could provide work and a place in the household for his daughters' husbands, and in time he would do the same for his sons' wives. A new room had lately been built on, to the northeast, Annetje explained to me, leaning above her husband's head and talking across the table, for Hatsy to live in when she should be married. Hatsy turned very beautifully pink and ducked her head almost into her plate, then looked up boldly and said, "Jah, jah, I am marrit now soon!" Everybody laughed except Mother Müller, who said in German that girls at home never knew when they were well off—no, they must go bringing in husbands. This remark did not seem to hurt anybody's feelings, and Gretchen said it was nice that I was going to be here for the wedding. This reminded Annetje of something, and she spoke in English to the table at large, saying that the Lutheran pastor had advised her to attend church oftener and

put her young ones in Sunday School, so that God would give her a
blessing with her next child. I counted around again, and sure
enough, with Gretchen's unborn, there were eight children at that
table under the age of ten; somebody was going to need a blessing in
all that crowd, no doubt. Father Müller delivered a short speech to
his daughter in German, then turned to me and said, "What I say
iss, it iss all craziness to go to church and pay a preacher goot money
to talk his nonsense. Say rather that he pay me to come and lissen,
then I vill go!" His eyes glared with sudden fierceness above his
square speckled gray and yellow beard that sprouted directly out
from the high cheekbones. "He thinks, so, that my time maybe costs
nothing? That iss goot! Let him pay me!"

Mother Müller snorted and shuffled her feet. "Ach, you talk, you
talk! Now you vill make the pastor goot and mad if he hears. Vot ve
do, if he vill not chrissen the babies?"

"You give him goot money, he vill chrissen," shouted Father
Müller. "You vait und see!"

"Ah sure, dot iss so," agreed Mother Müller. "Only do not let
him hear!"

There was a gust of excited talk in German, with much rapping
of knife handles on the table. I gave up trying to understand, but
watched their faces. It sounded like a pitched battle, but they were
agreeing about something. They were united in their tribal skepti-
cisms, as in everything else. I got a powerful impression that they
were all, even the sons-in-law, one human being divided into several
separate appearances. The crippled servant girl brought in more
food and gathered up plates and went away in her limping run, and
she seemed to me the only individual in the house. Even I felt divided
into many fragments, having left or lost a part of myself in every place
I had traveled, in every life mine had touched, above all, in every
death of someone near to me that had carried into the grave some
part of my living cells. But the servant, she was whole, and belonged
nowhere.

I settled easily enough into the marginal life of the household ways
and habits. Day began early at the Müllers', and we ate breakfast by
yellow lamplight, with the gray damp winds blowing with spring
softness through the open windows. The men swallowed their last
cups of steaming coffee standing, with their hats on, and went out to
harness the horses to the plows at sunrise. Annetje, with her fat baby
slung over her shoulder, could sweep a room or make a bed with one
hand, all finished before the day was well begun; and she spent the

rest of the day outdoors, caring for the chickens and the pigs. Now and then she came in with a shallow box full of newly hatched chickens, abject dabs of wet fluff, and put them on a table in her bedroom where she might tend them carefully on their first day. Mother Müller strode about hugely, giving orders right and left, while Father Müller, smoothing his whiskers and lighting his pipe, drove away to town with Mother Müller calling out after him final directions and instructions about household needs. He never spoke a word to her or looked at her and appeared not to be listening, but he always returned in a few hours with every commission performed exactly. After I had made my own bed and set my attic in order, there was nothing at all for me to do, and I walked out of this enthusiastic bustle into the lane, feeling extremely useless. But the repose, the almost hysterical inertia of their minds in the midst of this muscular life, communicated itself to me little by little, and I absorbed it gratefully in silence and felt all the hidden knotted painful places in my own mind beginning to loosen. It was easier to breathe, and I might weep, if I pleased. In a very few days I no longer felt like weeping.

One morning I saw Hatsy spading up the kitchen garden plot, and my offer to help, to spread the seeds and cover them, was accepted. We worked at this for several hours each morning, until the warmth of the sun and the stooping posture induced in me a comfortable vertigo. I forgot to count the days, they were one like the other except as the colors of the air changed, deepening and warming to keep step with the advancing season, and the earth grew firmer underfoot with the swelling tangle of crowding roots.

The children, so hungry and noisy at the table, were peaceable little folk who played silent engrossed games in the front yard. They were always kneading mud into loaves and pies and carrying their battered dolls and cotton rag animals through the operations of domestic life. They fed them, put them to bed; they got them up and fed them again, set them to their chores making more mud loaves; or they would harness themselves to their carts and gallop away to a great shady chestnut tree on the opposite side of the house. Here the tree became the *Turnverein*, and they themselves were again human beings, solemnly ambling about in a dance and going through the motions of drinking beer. Miraculously changed once more into horses, they harnessed themselves and galloped home. They came at call to be fed and put to sleep with the docility of their own toys or animal playmates. Their mothers handled them with instinctive, constant gentleness; they never seemed to be troubled by them. They were as devoted and caretaking as a cat with her kittens.

Sometimes I took Annetje's next to youngest child, a baby of two years, in her little wagon, and we would go down through the orchard and into the lane for a short distance. I would turn again into a smaller lane, smoother because less traveled, and we would go slowly between the aisles of mulberry trees where the fruit was beginning to hang and curl like green furry worms. The baby would sit in a compact mound of flannel and calico, her pale-blue eyes tilted and shining under her cap, her little lower teeth showing in a rapt smile. Sometimes several of the other children would follow along quietly. When I turned, they all turned without question, and we would proceed back to the house as sedately as we had set out.

The narrow lane, I discovered, led to the river, and it became my favorite walk. Almost every day I went along the edge of the naked wood, passionately occupied with looking for signs of spring. The changes there were so subtle and gradual, I found one day that branches of willows and sprays of blackberry vine alike were covered with fine points of green; the color had changed overnight, or so it seemed, and I knew that tomorrow the whole valley and wood and edge of the river would be quick and feathery with golden green blowing in the winds.

And it was so. On that day I did not leave the river until after dark and came home through the marsh with the owls and night-jars crying over my head, calling in a strange broken chorus in the woods until the farthest answering cry was a ghostly echo. When I went through the orchard the trees were freshly budded out with pale bloom, the branches were immobile in the thin darkness, but the flower clusters shivered in a soundless dance of delicately woven light, whirling as airily as leaves in a breeze, as rhythmically as water in a fountain. Every tree was budded out with this living, pulsing fire as fragile and cool as bubbles. When I opened the gate their light shone on my hands like fox fire. When I looked back, the shimmer of golden light was there, it was no dream.

Hatsy was on her knees in the dining room, washing the floor with heavy dark rags. She always did this work at night, so the men with their heavy boots would not be tracking it up again and it would be immaculate in the morning. She turned her young face to me in a stupor of fatigue. "Ottilie! Ottilie!" she called loudly, and before I could speak, she said, "Ottilie will give you supper. It is waiting, all ready." I tried to tell her that I was not hungry, but she wished to reassure me. "Look, we all must eat. Now, or then, it's no trouble." She sat back on her heels, and raising her head, looked over the window sill at the orchard. She smiled and paused for a moment and said happily, "Now it is come spring. Every spring we have that." She bent again over the great pail of water with her mops.

The crippled servant came in, stumbling perilously on the slippery floor, and set a dish before me, lentils with sausage and red chopped cabbage. It was hot and savory and I was truly grateful, for I found I was hungry, after all. I looked at her—so her name was Ottilie? —and said, "Thank you." "She can't talk," said Hatsy, simply, stating a fact that need not be emphasized. The blurred, dark face was neither young nor old, but crumpled into crisscross wrinkles, irrelevant either to age or suffering; simply wrinkles, patternless blackened seams as if the perishable flesh had been wrung in a hard cruel fist. Yet in that mutilated face I saw high cheekbones, slanted water-blue eyes, the pupils very large and strained with the anxiety of one peering into a darkness full of danger. She jarred heavily against the table as she turned, her bowed back trembling with the perpetual working of her withered arms, and ran away in aimless, driven haste.

Hatsy sat on her heels again for a moment, tossed her braids back over her shoulder, and said, "That is Ottilie. She is not sick now. She is only like that since she was sick when she was baby. But she can work so well as I can. She cooks. But she cannot talk so you can understand." She went up on her knees, bowed over, and began to scrub again, with new energy. She was really a network of thin taut ligaments and long muscles elastic as woven steel. She would always work too hard, and be tired all her life, and never know that this was anything but perfectly natural; everybody worked all the time, because there was always more work waiting when they had finished what they were doing then. I ate my supper and took my plate to the kitchen and set it on the table. Ottilie was sitting in a kitchen chair with her feet in the open oven, her arms folded, and her head waggling a little. She did not see or hear me.

At home, Hatsy wore an old brown corduroy dress and galoshes without stockings. Her skirts were short enough to show her thin legs, slightly crooked below the knees, as if she had walked too early. "Hatsy, she's a good, quick girl," said Mother Müller, to whom praising anybody or anything did not come easily. On Saturdays, Hatsy took a voluminous bath in a big tub in the closet back of the kitchen, where also were stored the extra chamber pots, slop jars, and water jugs. She then unplaited her yellow hair and bound up the crinkled floss with a wreath of pink cotton rosebuds, put on her pale-blue China silk dress, and went to the *Turnverein* to dance and drink a seidel of dark-brown beer with her devoted suitor, who resembled

her brothers enough to be her brother. On Sundays, the entire family
went to the *Turnverein* after copious washings, getting into starched
dresses and shirts, and getting the baskets of food stored in the wagons.
The servant, Ottilie, would rush out to see them off, standing
with both shaking arms folded over her forehead, shading her troubled
eyes to watch them to the turn of the lane. Her muteness seemed
nearly absolute; she had no coherent language of signs. Yet three
times a day she spread that enormous table with solid food, freshly
baked bread, huge platters of vegetables, immoderate roasts of meat,
extravagant tarts, strudels, pies—enough for twenty people. If neighbors came in for an afternoon on some holiday, Ottilie would stumble
into the big north room, the parlor, with its golden-oak melodeon, a
harsh-green Brussels carpet, Nottingham lace curtains, crocheted
lace antimacassars on the chair backs, to serve them coffee with
cream and sugar and thick slices of yellow cake.

Mother Müller sat but seldom in her parlor, and always with an
air of formal unease, her knotted big fingers cramped in a cluster.
But Father Müller often sat there in the evenings, where no one
ventured to follow him unless commanded; he sometimes played
chess with his elder son-in-law, who had learned a good while ago
that Father Müller was a good player who abhorred an easy victory,
and he dared not do less than put up the best fight he was able, but
even so, if Father Müller felt himself winning too often, he would
roar, "No, you are not trying! You are not doing your best. Now we
stop this nonsense!", and the son-in-law would find himself dismissed
in temporary disgrace.

Most evenings, however, Father Müller sat by himself and read
Das Kapital. He would settle deeply into the red plush base rocker
and spread the volume upon a low table before him. It was an early
edition in blotty black German type, stained and ragged in its leather
cover, the pages falling apart, a very bible. He knew whole chapters
almost by heart, and added nothing to, took nothing from, the canoni-
cal, once-delivered text. I cannot say at that time of my life I had
never heard of *Das Kapital*, but I had certainly never known anyone
who had read it, though if anyone mentioned it, it was always with
profound disapproval. It was not a book one had to read in order to
reject it. And here was this respectable old farmer who accepted its
dogma as a religion—that is to say, its legendary inapplicable precepts
were just, right, proper, one must believe in them, of course; but life,
everyday living, was another and unrelated thing. Father Müller
was the wealthiest man in his community; almost every neighboring
farmer rented land from him, and some of them worked it on the

share system. He explained this to me one evening after he had given up trying to teach me chess. He was not surprised that I could not learn, at least not in one lesson, and he was not surprised either that I knew nothing about *Das Kapital.* He explained his own arrangements to me thus: "These men, they cannot buy their land. The land must be bought, for *Kapital* owns it, and *Kapital* will not give back to the worker the land that is his. Well, somehow, I can always buy land. Why? I do not know. I only know that my first land here I made good crops to buy more land, and so I rent it cheap, more than anybody else I rent it cheap, I lend money so my neighbors do not fall into the hands of the bank, and so I am not *Kapital.* Someday these workers, they can buy land from me, for less than they can get it anywhere else. Well, that is what I can do, that is all." He turned over a page, and his angry gray eyes looked out at me under his shaggy brows. "I buy my land with my hard work, all my life, and I rent it cheap to my neighbors, and then they say they will not elect my son-in-law, my Annetje's husband, to be sheriff because I am atheist. So then I say, all right, but next year you pay more for your land or more shares of your crops. If I am atheist, I will act like one. So, my Annetje's husband is sheriff, that is all."

He had put a stubby forefinger on a line to mark his place, and now he sank himself into his book, and I left quietly without saying good night.

The *Turnverein* was an octagonal pavilion set in a cleared space in a patch of woods belonging to Father Müller. The German colony came here to sit about in the cool shade, while a small brass band played cloppity country dances. The girls danced with energy and direction, their starched petticoats rustling like dry leaves. The boys were more awkward, but willing; they clutched their partners' waists and left crumpled sweaty spots where they clutched. Here Mother Müller took her ease after a hard week. Her gaunt limbs would relax, her knees spread squarely apart, and she would gossip over her beer with the women of her own generation.

On the other side of the pavilion, Father Müller would sit with the sober grandfathers, their long curved pipes wagging on their chests as they discussed local politics with profound gravity, their hard peasant fatalism tempered only a little by a shrewd worldly distrust of all officeholders not personally known to them, all political plans except their own immediate ones. When Father Müller talked, they listened respectfully, with faith in him as a strong man, head of his own house and his community. They nodded slowly whenever he took his pipe from his mouth and gestured, holding it by the bowl as if it were a stone he was getting ready to throw.

On our way back from the *Turnverein* one evening, Mother Müller said to me, "Well, now, by the grace of Gott it is all settled between Hatsy and her man. It is next Sunday by this time they will be marrit."

All the folk who usually went to the *Turnverein* on Sundays came instead to the Müller house for the wedding. They brought useful presents, mostly bed linen, pillow covers, a white counterpane, with a few ornaments for the bridal chamber; and the bridegroom's gift to the bride was a necklace, a double string of red coral twigs. Just before the short ceremony began, he slipped the necklace over her head with trembling hands. She smiled up at him shakily and helped him disentangle her short veil from the coral, then they joined hands and turned their faces to the pastor, not letting go until time for the exchange of rings—the widest, thickest, reddest gold bands to be found, no doubt—and at that moment they both stopped smiling and turned a little pale. The groom recovered first, and bent over—he was considerably taller than she—and kissed her on the forehead. His eyes were a deep blue, and his hair not really Müller taffy color, but a light chestnut; a good-looking, gentle-tempered boy, I decided, and he looked at Hatsy as if he liked what he saw. They knelt and clasped hands again for the final prayer, then stood together and exchanged the bridal kiss, a very chaste reserved one, still not on the lips. Then everybody came to shake hands and the men all kissed the bride and the women all kissed the groom. Some of the women whispered in Hatsy's ear, and all burst out laughing except Hatsy, who turned red from her forehead to her throat. She whispered in turn to her husband, who nodded in agreement. She then tried to slip away quietly, but the watchful young girls were after her, and shortly we saw her running through the blossoming orchard, holding up her white ruffled skirts, with all the girls in pursuit, shrieking and calling like excited hunters, for the first to overtake and touch her would be the next bride. They returned, breathless, dragging the lucky one with them, and held her, against her ecstatic resistance, while all the young boys kissed her.

The guests stayed on for a huge supper, and Ottilie came in, wearing a fresh blue apron, sweat beaded in the wrinkles of her forehead and around her formless mouth, and passed the food around the table. The men ate first, and then Hatsy came in with the women for the first time, still wearing her square little veil of white cotton net bound on her hair with peach blossoms shattered in the bride's race. After supper, one of the girls played waltzes and polkas on the melodeon, and everyone danced. The bridegroom drew gallons of beer from a keg set up in the hall, and at midnight everybody went away, warmly emotional and happy. I went down to the kitchen for a pitcher of hot water. The servant was still setting things to rights, hobbling between table and cupboard. Her face was a brown smudge of anxiety, her eyes were wide and dazed. Her uncertain hands rattled among the pans, but nothing could make her seem real, or in any way connected with the life around her. Yet when I set my pitcher on the stove, she lifted the heavy kettle and poured the scalding water into it without spilling a drop.

The clear honey green of the early morning sky was a mirror of the bright earth. At the edge of the woods there had sprung a reticent blooming of small white and pale-colored flowers. The peach trees were now each a separate nosegay of shell rose and white. I left the house, meaning to take the short path across to the lane of mulberries. The women were deep in the house, the men were away to the fields, the animals were turned into the pastures, and only Ottilie was visible, sitting on the steps of the back porch peeling potatoes. She gazed in my direction with eyes that fell short of me, and seemed to focus on a point midway between us, and gave no sign. Then she dropped her knife and rose, her mouth opened and closed several times, she strained toward me, motioning with her right hand. I went to her, her hands came out and clutched my sleeve, and for a moment I feared to hear her voice. There was no sound from her, but she drew me along after her, full of some mysterious purpose of her own. She opened the door of a dingy, bitter-smelling room, windowless, which opened off the kitchen, beside the closet where Hatsy took her baths. A lumpy narrow cot and a chest of drawers supporting a blistered looking-glass almost filled the space. Ottilie's lips moved, struggling for speech, as she pulled and tumbled over a heap of rubbish in the top drawer. She took out a photograph and put it in my hands. It was in the old style, faded to a dirty yellow, mounted on cardboard elaborately clipped and gilded at the edges. I saw a girl child about five years old, a pretty smiling German baby, looking curiously like a slightly elder sister of Annetje's two-year-old, wearing a frilled frock and a prodigious curl of blonde hair on the crown of her head. The strong legs, round as sausages, were encased in long white ribbed stockings, and the square firm feet were laced into old-fashioned soft-soled black boots. Ottilie peered over the picture, twisted her neck, and looked up into my face. I saw the slanted water-blue eyes and the high cheekbones of the Müllers again, mutilated, almost destroyed, but unmistakable. This child was what she had been, and she was without doubt the elder sister of Annetje and Gretchen and Hatsy; in urgent pantomime she insisted that this was so—she patted the picture and her own face, and strove terribly to speak. She pointed to the name written carefully on the back, Ottilie, and touched her mouth with her bent knuckles. Her head wagged in her perpetual nod; her shaking hand seemed to flap the photograph at me in a roguish humor. The bit of cardboard connected her at once somehow to the world of human beings I knew; for an instant some filament lighter than cobweb spun itself out between that living center in her and in me, a filament from some center that held us all bound to our inescapable common source, so that her life and mine were kin, even a part of each other, and the painfulness and strangeness of her vanished. She knew well that she had been Ottilie, with those steady legs and watching eyes, and she was Ottilie still within herself. For a moment, being alive, she knew she suffered, for she stood and shook with silent crying, smearing away her tears with the open palm of her hand. Even while her cheeks were wet, her face changed. Her eyes cleared and fixed themselves upon that point in space which seemed for her to contain her unaccountable and terrible troubles. She turned her head as if she had heard a voice and disappeared in her staggering run into the kitchen, leaving the drawer open and the photograph face downward on the chest.

At midday meal she came hurrying and splashing coffee on the white floor, restored to her own secret existence of perpetual amazement, and again I had become a stranger to her like all the rest, but she was no stranger to me, and could not be again.

The youngest brother came in, holding up an opossum he had caught in his trap. He swung the furry body from side to side, his eyes fairly narrowed with pride as he showed us the mangled creature. "No, it is cruel, even for the wild animals," said gentle Annetje to me, "but boys love to kill, they love to hurt things. I am always afraid he will trap poor Kuno." I thought privately that Kuno, a wolfish, ungracious beast, might well prove a match for any trap. Annetje was full of silent, tender solicitudes. The kittens, the puppies, the chicks, the lambs and calves were her special care. She was the only one of the women who caressed the weanling calves when she set the pans of milk before them. Her child seemed as much a part of her as if it were not yet born. Still, she seemed to have forgotten that Ottilie was her sister. So had all the others. I remembered how Hatsy had spoken her name but had not said she was her sister. Their silence about her was, I realized, exactly that—simple forgetfulness. She moved among them as invisible to their imaginations as a ghost. Ottilie their sister was something painful that had happened long ago and now was past and done for; they could not live with that memory or its visible reminder—they forgot her in pure self-defense. But I could not forget her. She drifted into my mind like a bit of weed carried in a current and caught there, floating but fixed, refusing to be carried away. I reasoned it out. The Müllers, what else could they have done with Ottilie? By a physical accident in her childhood, she had been stripped of everything but her mere existence. It was not a society or a class that pampered its invalids and the unfit. So long as one lived, one did one's share. This was her place, in this family she had been born and must die; did she suffer? No one asked, no one looked to see. Suffering went with life, suffering and labor. While one lived one worked, that was all, and without complaints, for no one had time to listen, and everybody had his own troubles. So, what else could they have done with Ottilie? As for me, I could do nothing but promise myself that I would forget her, too; and to remember her for the rest of my life.

Sitting at the long table, I would watch Ottilie clattering about in her tormented haste, bringing in that endless food that represented all her life's labors. My mind would follow her into the kitchen, where I could see her peering into the great simmering kettles, the crowded oven, her ruined hands always lifting and stirring, and paring and chopping, her whole body a mere machine of torture. Straight up to the surface of my mind the thought would come urgently, clearly, as if driving time toward the desired event: Let it be now, let it be *now*. Not even tomorrow, no, today. Let her sit down quietly in her rickety chair by the stove and fold those arms, and let us find her there like that, with her head fallen forward on her knees. I would wait, hoping she might not come again, ever again, through that door I gazed at with wincing eyes, as if I might see something unendurable enter. Then she would come, and it was only Ottilie, after all, in the bosom of her family, and one of its most useful and competent members; and they with a deep right instinct had learned to live with her disaster on its own terms, and hers; they had accepted and then made use of what was for them only one more painful event in a world full of troubles, many of them much worse than this. So, a step at a time, I followed the Müllers as nearly as I could in their acceptance of Ottilie and the use they made of her life, for in some way that I could not quite explain to myself, I found great virtue and courage in their steadiness and refusal to feel sorry for anybody, least of all for themselves.

Gretchen bore her child, a son, conveniently between the hours of supper and bedtime, one evening of friendly domestic-sounding rain. The next day brought neighboring women from miles around, and the child was bandied about among them as if he were a new kind of medicine ball. Sedate and shy at dances, emotional at weddings, they were ribald and jocose at births. Over coffee and beer the talk grew broad, the hearty gutturals were swallowed in the belly of laughter; those honest hard-working wives and mothers saw life for a few hours as a hearty low joke, and it did them good. The baby bawled and suckled like a young calf, and the men of the family came in for a look and added their joyful improprieties.

Cloudy weather drove them home earlier than they had meant to go. The whole sky was lined with smoky black and gray vapor hanging in ragged wisps like soot in a chimney. The edges of the woods turned dull purple as the horizon reddened slowly, then faded, and all across the sky ran a deep shuddering mumble of thunder. All the Müllers hurried about getting into rubber boots and oilcloth overalls, shouting to each other, making their plan of action. The youngest boy came over the ridge of the hill with Kuno helping him to drive the sheep into the fold. Kuno was barking, the sheep were baaing and bleating, the horses freed from the plows were excited; they whinnied and trotted at the lengths of their halters, their ears laid back. The cows were bawling in distress and the calves cried back to them. All the men went out among the animals to round them up and quiet them and get them enclosed safely. Even as Mother Müller, her half-dozen petticoats looped about her thighs and tucked into her hip boots, was striding to join them in the barns, the cloud rack was split end to end by a shattering blow of lightning, and the cloudburst struck the house with the impact of a wave against a ship. The wind broke the windowpanes and the floods poured through. The roof beams strained and the walls bent inward, but the house stood to its foundations. The children were huddled into the inner bedroom with Gretchen. "Come and sit on the bed with me now," she told them calmly, "and be still." She sat up with a shawl around her, suckling the baby. Annetje came then and left her baby with Gretchen, too; and standing at the doorstep with one arm caught over the porch rail, reached down into the furious waters which were rising to the very threshold and dragged in a half-drowned lamb. I followed her. We could not make ourselves heard above the cannonade of thunder, but together we carried the creature into the hall under the stairs, where we rubbed the drowned fleece with rags and pressed his stomach to free him from the water and finally got him sitting up with his feet tucked under him. Annetje was merry with triumph and kept saying in delight, "Alive, alive! Look!"

We left him there when we heard the men shouting and beating at the kitchen door and ran to open it for them. They came in, Mother Müller among them, wearing her yoke and milk pails. She stood there with the water pouring from her skirts, the three-cornered piece of black oilcloth on her head dripping, her rubber boots wrinkled down with the weight of her petticoats. She and Father Müller stood near each other, looking like two gnarled lightning-struck old trees, his beard and oilcloth garments streaming, both their faces suddenly dark and old and tired, tired once for all; they would never be rested again in their lives. Father Müller suddenly roared at her, "Go get yourself dry clothes. Do you want to make yourself sick?"

"Ho," she said, taking off her milk yoke and setting the pails on the floor. "Go change yourself. I bring you dry socks." One of the boys told me she had carried a day-old calf on her back up a ladder against the inside wall of the barn and had put it safely in the hay-loft behind a barricade of bales. Then she had lined up the cows in the stable, and sitting on her milking stool in the rising water, she had milked them all. She seemed to think nothing of it.

"Hatsy," she called, "come help with this milk!" Little pale Hatsy came flying, barefoot because she had been called in the midst of taking off her wet shoes. Her new husband followed her, rather shy of his mother-in-law.

"Let me," he said, wishing to spare his dear bride such heavy work, and started to lift the great pails. "No!" shouted Mother Müller, so the poor young man nearly jumped out of his shirt. "Not you. The milk is not business for a man." He fell back and stood there with dark rivulets of mud seeping from his boots, watching Hatsy pour the milk into pans. Mother Müller started to follow her husband to attend him, but said at the door, "Where is Ottilie?", and no one knew, no one had seen her. "Find her," said Mother Müller. "Tell her we want supper, now."

Hatsy motioned to her husband, and together they tiptoed to the door of Ottilie's room and opened it silently. The light from the kitchen showed them Ottilie, sitting by herself, folded up on the edge of the bed. Hatsy threw the door wide open for more light and called in a high penetrating voice as if to a deaf person or one at a great distance, "Ottilie! Suppertime. We are hungry!", and the young pair left the kitchen to look under the stairway to see how Annetje's lamb was getting on. Then Annetje, Hatsy, and I began sweeping the dirty water and broken glass from the floors of the hall and dining room.

The storm lightened gradually, but the flooding rain continued. At supper there was talk about the loss of animals and their replacement. All the crops must be replanted, the season's labor was for nothing. They were all tired and wet, but they ate heartily and calmly, to strengthen themselves against all the labor of repairing and restoring which must begin early tomorrow morning.

By morning the drumming on the roof had almost ceased; from my window I looked upon a sepia-colored plain of water moving slowly to the valley. The roofs of the barns sagged like the ridge-poles of a tent, and a number of drowned animals floated or were caught against the fences. At breakfast, Mother Müller sat groaning over her coffee cup. "Ach," she said, "what it is to have such a pain in the head. Here too." She thumped her chest. "All over. Ach, Gott, I'm sick." She got up sighing hoarsely, her cheeks flushed, calling Hatsy and Annetje to help her in the barn.

They all came back very soon, their skirts draggled to the knees, and the two sisters were supporting their mother, who was speechless and could hardly stand. They put her to bed, where she lay without moving, her face scarlet. Everybody was confused; no one knew what to do. They tucked the quilts about her, and she threw them off. They offered her coffee, cold water, beer, but she turned her head away. The sons came in and stood beside her and joined the cry: "*Mutterchen, Mutti, Mutti,* what can we do? Tell us, what do you need?" But she could not tell them. It was impossible to ride the twelve miles to town for a doctor; fences and bridges were down, the roads were washed out. The family crowded into the room, unnerved, in panic, lost unless the sick woman should come to herself and tell them what to do for her. Father Müller came in, and kneeling beside her, he took hold of her hands and spoke to her most lovingly, and when she did not answer him, he broke out crying openly, in a loud voice, the great tears rolling, "Ach, Gott, Gott. A hundert tousand tollars in the bank"—he glared around at his family and spoke broken English to them, as if he were a stranger to himself and had forgotten his own language—"and tell me, tell, what goot does it?"

This frightened them, and all at once, together, they screamed and called and implored her in a tumult utterly beyond control. The noise of their grief and terror filled the place. In the midst of this, Mother Müller died.

In the midafternoon the rain passed, and the sun was a disk of brass in a cruelly bright sky. The waters flowed thickly down to the river, leaving the hill bald and brown, with the fences lying in a flattened tangle, the young peach trees stripped of bloom and sagging at the roots. In the woods had occurred a violent eruption of ripe foliage of a jungle thickness, glossy and burning, a massing of hot peacock green with cobalt shadows.

The household was in such silence, I had to listen carefully to know that anyone lived there. Everyone, even the younger children, moved on tiptoe and spoke in whispers. All afternoon the thud of hammers and the whine of a saw went on monotonously in the barn loft. At dark, the men brought in a shiny coffin of new yellow pine with rope handles and set it in the hall. It lay there on the floor for an hour or so, where anyone passing had to step over it. Then Annetje and Hatsy, who had been washing and dressing the body, appeared in the doorway and motioned. "You bring it in now."

Mother Müller lay in state in the parlor throughout the night, in her black silk dress with a scrap of white lace at the collar and a small lace cap on her hair. Her husband sat in the plush chair near her, looking at her face, which was very contemplative, gentle, and remote. He wept at intervals, silently, wiping his face with a big handkerchief. His daughters brought him coffee from time to time. He fell asleep there toward morning.

The light burned in the kitchen nearly all night, too, and the sound of Ottilie's heavy boots thumping about unsteadily was accompanied by the locust whirring of the coffee mill and the smell of baking bread. Hatsy came to my room. "There's coffee and cake," she said, "you'd better have some," and turned away crying, crumbling her slice in her hand. We stood about and ate in silence. Ottilie brought in a fresh pot of coffee, her eyes bleared and fixed, her gait as aimless-looking and hurried as ever, and when she spilled some on her own hand, she did not seem to feel it.

For a day longer they waited; then the youngest boy went to fetch the Lutheran pastor, and a few neighbors came back with them. By noon many more had arrived, spattered with mud, the horses heaving and sweating. At every greeting the family gave way and wept afresh, as naturally and openly as children. Their faces were drenched and soft with their tears; there was a comfortable relaxed look in the muscles of their faces. It was good to let go, to have something to weep for that nobody need excuse or explain. Their tears were at once a luxury and a cure of souls. They wept away the hard core of secret trouble that is in the heart of each separate man, secure in a communal grief; in sharing it, they consoled each other. For a while, they would visit the grave and remember, and then life would arrange itself again in another order, yet it would be the same. Already the thoughts of the living were turning to tomorrow, when they would be at the work of rebuilding and replanting and repairing —even now, today, they would hurry back from the burial to milk the cows and feed the chickens, and they might weep again and again for several days, until their tears should heal them at last.

On that day I realized, for the first time, not death, but the terror of dying. When they took the coffin out to the little country hearse and I saw that the procession was about to form, I went to my room and lay down. Staring at the ceiling, I heard and felt the ominous order and purpose in the movements and sounds below—the creaking harness and hoofbeats and grating wheels, the muted grave voices— and it was as if my blood fainted and receded with fright, while my mind stayed wide-awake to receive the awful impress. Yet when I knew they were leaving the yard, the terror began to leave me. As the sounds receded, I lay there not thinking, not feeling, in a mere drowse of relief and weariness.

Through my half-sleep I heard the howling of a dog. It seemed to be in a dream, and I was troubled to awaken. I dreamed that Kuno was caught in the trap; then I thought he was really caught, it was no dream and I must wake, because there was no one but me to let him out. I came broad awake, the cry rushed upon me like a wind, and it was not the howl of a dog. I ran downstairs and looked into Gretchen's room. She was curled up around her baby, and they were both asleep. I ran to the kitchen.

Ottilie was sitting in her broken chair with her feet in the edge of the open oven, where the heat had died away. Her hands hung at her sides, the fingers crooked into the palm; her head lay back on her shoulders, and she howled with a great wrench of her body, an upward reach of the neck, without tears. At sight of me she got up and came over to me and laid her head on my breast, and her hands dangled forward a moment. Shuddering, she babbled and howled and waved her arms in a frenzy through the open window over the stripped branches of the orchard toward the lane where the procession had straightened out into formal order. I took hold of her arms where the unnaturally corded muscles clenched and strained under her coarse sleeves; I led her out to the steps and left her sitting there, her head wagging.

In the barnyard there remained only the broken-down spring wagon and the shaggy pony that had brought me to the farm on the first day. The harness was still a mystery, but somehow I managed to join pony, harness, and wagon not too insecurely, or so I could only hope; and I pushed and hauled and tugged at Ottilie and lifted her until she was in the seat and I had the reins in hand. We careened down the road at a grudging trot, the pony jolting like a churn, the wheels spinning elliptically in a truly broad comedy swagger. I watched the jovial antics of those wheels with attention, hoping for the best. We slithered into round pits of green mud and jogged perilously into culverts where small bridges had been. Once, in what was left of the main road, I stood up to see if I might overtake the funeral train; yes, there it was, going inchmeal up the road over the little hill, a bumbling train of black beetles crawling helter-skelter over clods.

Ottilie, now silent, was doubled upon herself, slipping loosely on the edge of the seat. I caught hold of her stout belt with my free hand, and my fingers slipped between her clothes and bare flesh, ribbed and gaunt and dry against my knuckles. My sense of her realness, her humanity, this shattered being that was a woman, was so shocking to me that a howl as doglike and despairing as her own rose in me unuttered and died again, to be a perpetual ghost. Ottilie slanted her eyes and peered at me, and I gazed back. The knotted wrinkles of her face were grotesquely changed, she gave a choked little whimper, and suddenly she laughed out, a kind of yelp but unmistakably laughter, and clapped her hands for joy, the grinning mouth and suffering eyes turned to the sky. Her head nodded and wagged with the clownish humor of our trundling lurching progress. The feel of the hot sun on her back, the bright air, the jolly senseless staggering of the wheels, the peacock green of the heavens: something of these had reached her. She was happy and gay, and she gurgled and rocked in her seat, leaning upon me and waving loosely around her as if to show me what wonders she saw.

Drawing the pony to a standstill, I studied her face for a while and pondered my ironical mistake. There was nothing I could do for Ottilie, selfishly as I wished to ease my heart of her; she was beyond my reach as well as any other human reach, and yet, had I not come nearer to her than I had to anyone else in my attempt to deny and bridge the distance between us, or rather, her distance from me? Well, we were both equally the fools of life, equally fellow fugitives from death. We had escaped for one day more at least. We would celebrate our good luck, we would have a little stolen holiday, a breath of spring air and freedom on this lovely, festive afternoon.

Ottilie fidgeted, uneasy at our stopping. I flapped the reins, the pony moved on, we turned across the shallow ditch where the small road divided from the main traveled one. I measured the sun westering gently; there would be time enough to drive to the river down the lane of mulberries and to get back to the house before the mourners returned. There would be plenty of time for Ottilie to have supper ready. They need not even know she had been gone.

Lions, Harts, Leaping Does

" 'Thirty-ninth pope. Anastasius, a Roman, appointed that while the Gospel was reading they should stand and not sit. He exempted from the ministry those that were lame, impotent, or diseased persons, and slept with his forefathers in peace, being a confessor.' "

"Anno?"

" 'Anno 404.' "

They sat there in the late afternoon, the two old men grown gray in the brown robes of the order. Angular winter daylight forsook the small room, almost a cell in the primitive sense, and passed through the window into the outside world. The distant horizon, which it sought to join, was still bright and strong against approaching night. The old Franciscans, one priest, one brother, were left among the shadows in the room.

"Can you see to read one more, Titus?" the priest Didymus asked.

"Number fourteen." He did not cease staring out the window at day becoming night on the horizon. The thirty-ninth pope said Titus might not be a priest. Did Titus, reading, understand? He could never really tell about Titus, who said nothing now. There was only silence, then a dry whispering of pages turning. "Number fourteen," Didymus said. "That's Zephyrinus. I always like the old heretic on that one, Titus."

According to one bibliographer, Bishop Bale's *Pageant of Popes Contayninge the Lyves of all the Bishops of Rome, from the Beginninge of them to the Year of Grace 1555* was a denunciation of every pope from Peter to Paul IV. However inviting to readers that might sound, it was in sober fact a lie. The first popes, persecuted and mostly martyred, wholly escaped the author's remarkable spleen and even enjoyed his crusty approbation. Father Didymus, his aged appetite for biography jaded by the orthodox lives, found the work fascinating. He usually referred to it as "Bishop Bale's funny book" and to the bishop as a heretic.

Titus squinted at the yellowed page. He snapped a glance at the light hovering at the window. Then he closed his eyes and with great feeling recited:

"'O how joyous and how delectable is it to see religious men devout and fervent in the love of God, well mannered——'"

"Titus," Didymus interrupted softly.

"'—and well taught in ghostly learning.'"

"Titus, read." Didymus placed the words in their context. The first book of *The Imitation* and Chapter—if he was not mistaken —XXV. The trick was no longer in finding the source of Titus' quotations; it was putting them in their exact context. It had become an unconfessed contest between them, and it gratified Didymus to think he had been able to place the fragment. Titus knew two books by heart: *The Imitation* and *The Little Flowers of St. Francis*. Lately, unfortunately, he had begun to learn another. He was more and more quoting from Bishop Bale. Didymus reminded himself he must not let Titus read past the point where the martyred popes left off. What Bale had to say about Peter's later successors sounded incongruous—"unmete" in the old heretic's own phrase—coming from a Franciscan brother. Two fathers had already inquired of Didymus concerning Titus. One had noted the antique style of his words and had ventured to wonder if Brother Titus, Christ preserve us, might be slightly possessed. He cited the case of the illiterate Missouri farmer who cursed the Church in a forgotten Aramaic tongue.

"Read, Titus."

Titus squinted at the page once more and read in his fine dead voice.

"'Fourteenth pope, Zephyrinus. Zephyrinus was a Roman born, a man as writers do testify, more addicted with all endeavor to the service of God than to the cure of any worldly affairs. Whereas before his time the wine in the celebrating the communion was ministered in a cup of wood, he first did alter that, and instead thereof brought in cups or chalices of glass. And yet he did not this upon any superstition, as thinking wood to be unlawful, or glass to be more holy for that use, but because the one is more comely and seemly, as by experience it appeareth than the other. And yet some wooden dolts do dream that the wooden cups were changed by him because that part of the wine, or as they thought, the royal blood of Christ, did soak into the wood, and so it cannot be in glass. Surely sooner may wine soak into any wood than any wit into those winy heads that thus both deceive themselves and slander this godly martyr.'"

"Anno?"

Titus squinted at the page again. " 'Anno 222,' " he read.

They were quiet for a moment, which ended with the clock in the tower booming once for the half hour. Didymus got up and stood so close to the window his breath became visible. Noticing it, he inhaled deeply and then, exhaling, he sent a gust of smoke churning against the freezing pane, clouding it. Some old unmelted snow in tree crotches lay dirty and white in the gathering dark.

"It's cold out today," Didymus said.

He stepped away from the window and over to Titus, whose face was relaxed in open-eyed sleep. He took Bishop Bale's funny book unnoticed from Titus' hands.

"Thank you, Titus," he said.

Titus blinked his eyes slowly once, then several times quickly. His body gave a shudder, as if coming to life.

"Yes, Father?" he was asking.

"I said thanks for reading. You are a great friend to me."

"Yes, Father."

"I know you'd rather read other authors." Didymus moved to the window, stood there gazing through the tops of trees, their limbs black and bleak against the sky. He rubbed his hands. "I'm going for a walk before vespers. Is it too cold for you, Titus?"

" 'A good religious man that is fervent in his religion taketh all things well, and doth gladly all that he is commanded to do.' "

Didymus, walking across the room, stopped and looked at Titus just in time to see him open his eyes. He was quoting again: *The Imitation* and still in Chapter XXV. Why had he said that? To himself Didymus repeated the words and decided Titus, his mind moving intelligently but so pathetically largo, was documenting the act of reading Bishop Bale when there were other books he preferred.

"I'm going out for a walk," Didymus said.

Titus rose and pulled down the full sleeves of his brown robe in anticipation of the cold.

"I think it is too cold for you, Titus," Didymus said.

Titus faced him undaunted, arms folded and hands muffled in his sleeves, eyes twinkling incredulously. He was ready to go. Didymus got the idea Titus knew himself to be the healthier of the two. Didymus was vaguely annoyed at this manifestation of the truth. *Vanitas.*

"Won't they need you in the kitchen now?" he inquired.

Immediately he regretted having said that. And the way he had said it, with some malice, as though labor *per se* were important and the intention not so. *Vanitas* in a friar, and at his age too. Confronting Titus with a distinction his simple mind could never master and which, if it could, his great soul would never recognize. Titus only knew all that was necessary, that a friar did what he was best at in the community. And no matter the nature of his toil, the variety of the means at hand, the end was the same for all friars. Or indeed for all men, if they cared to know. Titus worked in the kitchen and garden. Was Didymus wrong in teaching geometry out of personal preference and perhaps—if this was so he was—out of pride? Had the spiritual worth of his labor been vitiated because of that? He did not think so, no. No, he taught geometry because it was useful and eternally true, like his theology, and though of a lower order of truth it escaped the common fate of theology and the humanities, perverted through the ages in the mouths of dunderheads and fools. From that point of view his work came to the same thing as Titus'. The vineyard was everywhere, they were in it, and that was essential.

Didymus, consciously humble, held open the door for Titus. Sandals scraping familiarly, they passed through dark corridors until they came to the stairway. Lights from floors above and below spangled through the carved apertures of the winding stair and fell in confusion upon the worn oaken steps.

At the outside door they were ambushed. An old friar stepped out of the shadows to intercept them. Standing with Didymus and Titus, however, made him appear younger. Or possibly it was the tenseness of him.

"Good evening, Father," he said to Didymus. "And Titus."

Didymus nodded in salutation and Titus said deliberately, as though he were the first one ever to put words in such conjunction: "Good evening, Father Rector."

The rector watched Didymus expectantly. Didymus studied the man's face. It told him nothing but curiosity—a luxury which could verge on vice in the cloister. Didymus frowned his incomprehension. He was about to speak. He decided against it, turning to Titus:

"Come on, Titus, we've got a walk to take before vespers."

The rector was left standing.

They began to circle the monastery grounds. Away from the buildings it was brighter. With a sudden shudder Didymus felt the freezing air bite into his body all over. Instinctively he drew up his cowl. That was a little better. Not much. It was too cold for him to relax, breathe deeply, and stride freely. It had not looked this cold from his window. He fell into Titus' gait. The steps were longer, but there was an illusion of warmth about moving in unison. Bit by bit he found himself duplicating every aspect of Titus in motion. Heads down, eyes just ahead of the next step, undeviating, they seemed peripatetic figures in a Gothic frieze. The stones of the walk were trampled over with frozen footsteps. Titus' feet were gray and bare in their open sandals. Pieces of ice, the thin edges of ruts, cracked off underfoot, skittering sharply away. A crystal fragment lit between Titus' toes and did not melt there. He did not seem to notice it. This made Didymus lift his eyes.

A fine Franciscan! Didymus snorted, causing a flurry of vapors. He had the despicable caution of the comfortable who move mountains, if need be, to stay that way. Here he was, cowl up and heavy woolen socks on, and regretting the weather because it exceeded his anticipations. Painfully he stubbed his toe on purpose and at once accused himself of exhibitionism. Then he damned the expression for its modernity. He asked himself: wherein lay the renunciation of the world, the flesh, and the devil, the whole point of following after St. Francis today? Poverty, chastity, obedience, the three vows. There was nothing of suffering in the poverty of the friar nowadays: he was penniless, but materially rich compared to—what was the phrase he used to hear?—"one third of the nation." A beggar, a homeless mendicant by very definition, he knew nothing—except as it affected others "less fortunate"—of the miseries of begging in the streets. Verily, it was no heavy cross, this vow of poverty, so construed and practiced, in the modern world. Begging had become unfashionable. Somewhere along the line the meaning had been lost, they had become too "fortunate." Official agencies, to whom it was a nasty but necessary business, dispensed charity without mercy or grace. He recalled with wry amusement Frederick Barbarossa's appeal to fellow princes when opposed by the might of the medieval Church: "We have a clean conscience, and it tells us that God is with us. Ever have we striven to bring back priests and, in especial, those of the topmost rank, to the condition of the first Christian Church. In those days the clergy raised their eyes to the angels, shone through miracles, made whole the sick, raised the dead, made kings and princes subject to them, not with arms but with their holiness. But now they are smothered in delights. To withdraw from them the harmful riches which burden them to their own undoing is a labor of love in which all princes should eagerly participate."

And chastity, what of that? Well, that was all over for him—a battle he had fought and won many years ago. A sin whose temptations had prevailed undiminished through the centuries, but withal for him, an old man, a dead issue, a young man's trial. Only obedience remained, and that, too, was no longer difficult for him. There was something—much as he disliked the term—to be said for "conditioning." He had to smile at himself: why should he bristle so at using the word? It was only contemporary slang for a theory the Church had always known. "Psychiatry," so called, and all the ghastly superstition that attended its practice, the deification of its high priests in the secular schools, made him ill. But it would pass. Just look how alchemy had flourished, and where was it today?

Clearly an abecedarian observance of the vows did not promise perfection. Stemmed in divine wisdom, they were branches meant to flower forth, but requiring of the friar the water and sunlight of sacrifice. The letter led nowhere. It was the spirit of the vows which opened the way and revealed to the soul, no matter the flux of circumstance, the means of salvation.

He had picked his way through the welter of familiar factors again—again to the same conclusion. The last time when he received the letter from Seraphin asking him to come to St. Louis, saying his years prohibited unnecessary travel and endowed his request with a certain prerogative. No, he had written back, it's simply impossible—not saying why. God help him, as a natural man, he had an inordinate desire to see his brother again. One of them must die soon. But as a friar, he remembered from Titus: "Unless a man be clearly delivered from the love of all creatures he may not fully tend to his Creator." Therein, the keeping of the vows having become an easy habit for him, was his opportunity. It was plain and there was sacrifice and it was hard. And he had not gone.

The flesh just above his knees felt frozen. They were drawing near the entrance again. His face, too, felt the same way, like a slab of pasteboard, stiffest at the tip of his nose. When he wrinkled his brow and puffed out his cheeks to blow hot air up to his nose his skin seemed to crackle like old parchment. His eyes watered from the wind. He pressed a hand, warm from his sleeve, to his exposed neck. Frozen, like his face. It would be chapped tomorrow.

Titus, white hair awry in the wind, looked just the same.

They entered the monastery door. The rector stopped them. It was almost as before, except that Didymus was occupied with feeling his face and patting it back to life.

"Ah, Didymus! It must be cold indeed!" The rector smiled at Titus and returned his gaze to Didymus. He made it appear that they were allied in being amused at Didymus' face. Didymus touched his nose tenderly. Assured it would stand the operation, he blew it lustily. He stuffed the handkerchief up his sleeve. The rector, misinterpreting all this ceremony, obviously was afraid of being ignored.

"The telegram, Didymus. I'm sorry, I thought it might have been important."

"I received no telegram."

They faced each other, waiting, experiencing a hanging moment of uneasiness.

Then, having employed the deductive method, they both looked at Titus. Although he had not been listening, rather had been studying the naked toes in his sandals, he sensed their eyes questioning him.

"Yes, Father Rector?" he answered.

"The telegram for Father Didymus, Titus?" the rector demanded. "Where is it?" Titus started momentarily out of willingness to be of service, but ended, his mind refusing to click, impassive before them. The rector shook his head in faint exasperation and reached his hand down into the folds of Titus' cowl. He brought forth two envelopes. One, the telegram, he gave to Didymus. The other, a letter, he handed back to Titus.

"I gave you this letter this morning, Titus. It's for Father Anthony." Intently Titus stared unremembering at the letter. "I wish you would see that Father Anthony gets it right away, Titus. I think it's a bill."

Titus held the envelope tightly to his breast and said: "Father Anthony."

Then his eyes were attracted by the sound of Didymus tearing open the telegram. While Didymus read the telegram Titus' expression showed he at last understood his failure to deliver it. He was perturbed, mounting inner distress moving his lips silently.

Didymus looked up from the telegram. He saw the grief in Titus' face and said, astonished, "How did you know, Titus?"

Titus' eyes were both fixed and lowered in sorrow. It seemed to Didymus that Titus knew the meaning of the telegram. Didymus was suddenly weak, as before a miracle. His eyes went to the rector to see how he was taking it. Then it occurred to him the rector could not know what had happened.

As though nothing much had, the rector laid an absolving hand lightly upon Titus' shoulder.

"He can't forgive himself for not delivering the telegram now that he remembers it. That's all."

Didymus was relieved. Seeing the telegram in his hand, he folded it quickly and stuffed it back in the envelope. He handed it to the rector. Calmly, in a voice quite drained of feeling, he said, "My brother, Father Seraphin, died last night in St. Louis."

"Father Seraphin *from Rome?*"

"Yes," Didymus said, "in St. Louis. He was my brother. Appointed a confessor in Rome, a privilege for a foreigner. He was ninety-two."

"I know that, Didymus, an honor for the order. I had no idea he was in this country. Ninety-two! God rest his soul!"

"I had a letter from him only recently."

"You did?"

"He wanted me to come to St. Louis. I hadn't seen him for twenty-five years at least."

"Twenty-five years?"

"It was impossible for me to visit him."

"But if he was in this country, Didymus . . ."

The rector waited for Didymus to explain.

Didymus opened his mouth to speak, heard the clock in the tower sound the quarter hour, and said nothing, listening, lips parted, to the last of the three strokes die away.

"Why, Didymus, it could easily have been arranged," the rector persisted.

Didymus turned abruptly to Titus, who, standing in a dream, had been inattentive since the clock struck.

"Come, Titus, we'll be late."

He hastened down the corridor with Titus. "No," he said in agitation, causing Titus to look at him in surprise. "I told him no. It was simply impossible." He was conscious of Titus' attention. "To visit him, Seraphin, who is dead." That had come naturally enough for being the first time in his thoughts that Seraphin was dead. Was there not some merit in his dispassionate acceptance of the fact?

They entered the chapel for vespers and knelt down.

The clock struck. One, two . . . two. Two? No, there must have been one or two strokes before. He had gone to sleep. It was three. At least three, probably four. Or five. He waited. It could not be two: he remembered the brothers filing darkly into the chapel at that hour. Disturbing the shadows for matins and lauds. If it was five—he listened for faint noises in the building—it would only be a few minutes. They would come in, the earliest birds, to say their

masses. There were no noises. He looked toward the windows on
the St. Joseph side of the chapel. He might be able to see a light
from a room across the court. That was not certain even if it was
five. It would have to come through the stained glass. Was that
possible? It was still night. Was there a moon? He looked round
the chapel. If there was, it might shine on a window. There was no
moon. Or it was overhead. Or powerless against the glass. He
yawned. It could not be five. His knees were numb from kneeling.
He shifted on them. His back ached. Straightening it, he gasped
for breath. He saw the sanctuary light. The only light, red. Then
it came back to him. Seraphin was dead. He tried to pray. No
words. Why words? Meditation in the Presence. The perfect prayer.
He fell asleep. . . .

. . . Spiraling brown coil on coil under the golden sun, the river
slithered across the blue and flower-flecked land. On an eminence
they held identical hands over their eyes for visors and mistook it
with pleasure for an endless murmuring serpent. They considered
unafraid the prospect of its turning in its course and standing on
tail to swallow them, gurgling, alive. They sensed it was in them to
command this also by a wish. Their visor hands vanished before
their eyes and became instead the symbol of brotherhood clasped
between them. This they wished. Smiling the same smile back and
forth, they began laughing: "Jonah!" And were walking murkily up
and down the brown belly of the river in mock distress. Above
them, foolishly triumphant, rippling in contentment, mewed the
waves. Below swam an occasional large fish, absorbed in ignoring
them, and the mass of crustacea, eagerly seething, too numerous on
the bottom to pretend exclusiveness. "Jonah indeed!" the brothers
said, surprised to see the bubbles they birthed. They strolled then
for hours this way. The novelty wearing off (without regret, else
they would have wished themselves elsewhere), they began to talk
and say ordinary things. Their mother had died, their father, too,
and how old did that make them? It was the afternoon of the
funerals, which they had managed, transcending time, to have held
jointly. She had seemed older and for some reason he otherwise.
How, they wondered, should it be with them, *memento mori* clicking
simultaneously within them, lackaday. The sound of dirt descending six feet to clatter on the coffins was memorable but unmention-
able. Their own lives, well . . . Only half curious (something to
do), they halted to kick testingly a waterlogged rowboat resting on
the bottom, the crustacea complaining and olive-green silt rising
to speckle the surface with dark stars. . . . Well, what *had* they

been doing? A crayfish pursued them, clad in sable armor, dearly desiring to do battle, brandishing hinged swords. Well, for one thing working for the canonization of Fra Bartolomeo, had got two cardinals interested, was hot after those remaining who were at all possible, a slow business. Yes, one would judge so in the light of past canonizations, though being stationed in Rome had its advantages. Me, the same old grind, teaching, pounding away, giving Pythagoras no rest in his grave . . . They made an irresolute pass at the crayfish, who had caught up with them. More about Fra Bartolomeo; what else is there? Except—you will laugh or have me excommunicated for wanton presumption, though it's only faith in a faithless age—making a vow not to die until he's made a saint, recognized rather—he is one, convinced of it, Didymus (never can get used to calling you that), a saint sure as I'm alive, having known him, no doubt of it. Something wrong with your knee? Knees then! The crayfish, he's got hold of you there, another at your back. If you like we'll leave, only I do like it here. Well, go ahead then; you never did like St. Louis; isn't that what you used to say? Alone, in pain, he rose to the surface, parting the silt stars. The sun like molten gold squirted him in the eye. Numb now, unable to remember and too blind to refurnish his memory by observation, he waited for this limbo to clear away. . . .

Awake now, he was face to face with a flame, blinding him. He avoided it. A dead weight bore him down, his aching back. Slowly, like ink in a blotter, his consciousness spread. The supports beneath him were kneeling limbs, his, the veined hands, bracing him, pressing flat, his own. His body, it seemed, left off there; the rest was something else, floor. He raised his head to the flame again and tried to determine what kept it suspended even with his face. He shook his head, blinking dumbly, a four-legged beast. He could see nothing, only his knees and hands, which he felt rather, and the flame floating unaccountably in the darkness. That part alone was a mystery. And then there came a pressure and pull on his shoulders, urging him up. Fingers, a hand, a rustling related to its action, then the rustling in rhythm with the folds of a brown curtain, a robe naturally, ergo a friar, holding a candle, trying to raise him up, Titus. The clock began striking.

"Put out the candle," Didymus said.

Titus closed his palm slowly around the flame, unflinching, snuffing it. The odor of burning string. Titus pinched the wick deliberately. He waited a moment, the clock falling silent, and said,

"Father Rector expects you will say a mass for the dead at five o'clock."

"Yes, I know." He yawned deliciously. "I told him *that*." He bit his lips at the memory of the disgusting yawn. Titus had found him asleep. Shame overwhelmed him, and he searched his mind for justification. He found none.

"It is five now," Titus said.

It was maddening. "I don't see anyone else if it's five," he snapped. Immediately he was aware of a light burning in the sacristy. He blushed and grew pale. Had someone besides Titus seen him sleeping? But, listening, he heard nothing. No one else was up yet. He was no longer pale and was only blushing now. He saw it all hopefully. He was saved. Titus had gone to the sacristy to prepare for mass. He must have come out to light the candles on the main altar. Then he had seen the bereaved keeping vigil on all fours, asleep, snoring even. What did Titus think of that? It withered him to remember, but he was comforted some that the only witness had been Titus. Had the sleeping apostles in Gethsemane been glad it was Christ?

Wrong! Hopelessly wrong! For there had come a noise after all. Someone else was in the sacristy. He stiffened and walked palely toward it. He must go there and get ready to say his mass. A few steps he took only, his back buckling out, humping, his knees sinking to the floor, his hands last. The floor with fingers smelling of dust and genesis reached up and held him. The fingers were really spikes and they were dusty from holding him this way all his life. For a radiant instant which had something of eternity about it he saw the justice of his position. Then there was nothing.

A little snow had fallen in the night, enough to powder the dead grass and soften the impression the leafless trees etched in the sky. Grayly the sky promised more snow, but now, at the end of the day following his collapse in the chapel, it was melting. Didymus, bundled around by blankets, sat in a wheelchair at the window, unsleepy. Only the landscape wearied him. Dead and unmoving though it must be, of that he was sure, it conspired to make him see everything in it as living, moving, something to be watched, each visible tuft of grass, each cluster of snow. The influence of the snow perhaps? For the ground, ordinarily uniform in texture and drabness, had split up into individual patches. They appeared to be involved in a struggle of some kind, possibly to overlap each other, constantly shifting. But whether it was equally one against one, or one against all, he could not make out. He reminded himself he did not believe it was actually happening. It was confusing and he closed his eyes. After a time this confused and tired him in the same way. The background of darkness became a field of varicolored factions, warring, and, worse than the landscape, things like worms and comets wriggled and exploded before his closed eyes. Finally, as though to orchestrate their motions, they carried with them a bewildering noise or music which grew louder and cacophonous. The effect was cumulative, inevitably unbearable, and Didymus would have to open his eyes again. The intervals of peace became gradually rarer on the landscape. Likewise when he shut his eyes to it the restful darkness dissolved sooner than before into riot.

The door of his room opened, mercifully dispelling his illusions, and that, because no knock, could only be Titus. Unable to move in his chair, Didymus listened to Titus moving about the room at his back. The tinkle of a glass once, the squeak of the bookcase indicating a book taken out or replaced—they were sounds Didymus could recognize. But that first tap-tap and the consequent click of metal on metal, irregular and scarcely audible, was disconcertingly unfamiliar. His curiosity, centering on it, raised it to a delicious mystery. He kept down the urge to shout at Titus. But he attempted to fish from memory the precise character of the corner from which the sound came with harrowing repetition. The sound stopped then, as though to thwart him on the brink of revelation. Titus' footsteps scraped across the room. The door opened and closed. For a few steps Didymus heard Titus going down the corridor. He asked himself not to be moved by idle curiosity, a thing of the senses. He would not be tempted now.

A moment later the keystone of his good intention crumbled, and the whole edifice of his detachment with it. More shakily than quickly, Didymus moved his hands to the wheels of the chair. He would roll over to the corner and investigate the sound. . . . He would? His hands lay limply on the wheels, ready to propel him to his mind's destination, but, weak, white, powerless to grip the wheels or anything. He regarded them with contempt. He had known they would fail him; he had been foolish to give them another chance. Disdainful of his hands, he looked out the window. He could still do that, couldn't he? It was raining some now. The landscape started to move, rearing and reeling crazily, as though drunken with the rain. In horror Didymus damned his eyes. He realized this trouble was probably going to be chronic. He turned his gaze in despair to the trees, to the branches level with his eyes and nearer than the insane ground. Hesitating warily, fearful the gentle boughs under scrutiny would turn into hideous waving tentacles, he looked. With a thrill he knew he was seeing clearly.

Gauzily rain descended in a fine spray, hanging in fat berries from the wet black branches where leaves had been and buds would be, cold crystal drops. They fell now and then ripely of their own weight, or, shaken by the intermittent wind, they spilled before their time. Promptly they appeared again, pendulous.

Watching the raindrops prove gravity, he was grateful for nature's, rather than his, return to reason. Still, though he professed faith in his faculties, he would not look away from the trees and down at the ground, nor close his eyes. Gratefully he savored the cosmic truth in the falling drops and the mildly trembling branches. There was order, he thought, which in justice and science ought to include the treacherous landscape. Risking all, he ventured a glance at the ground. All was still there. He smiled. He was going to close his eyes (to make it universal and conclusive) when the door opened again.

Didymus strained to catch the meaning of Titus' movements. Would the clicking sound begin? Titus did go to that corner of the room again. Then it came, louder than before, but only once this time.

Titus came behind his chair, turned it, and wheeled him over to the corner.

On a hook which Titus had screwed into the wall hung a bird cage covered with black cloth.

"What's all this?" Didymus said.

Titus tapped the covered cage expectantly.

A bird chirped once.

"The bird," Titus explained in excitement, "is inside."

Didymus almost laughed. He sensed in time, however, the necessity of seeming befuddled and severe. Titus expected it.

"I don't believe it," Didymus snapped.

Titus smiled wisely and tapped the cage again.

"There!" he exclaimed when the bird chirped.

Didymus shook his head in mock anger. "You made that beastly noise, Titus, you mountebank!"

Titus, profoundly amused by such skepticism, removed the black cover.

The bird, a canary, flicked its head sidewise in interest, looking them up and down. Then it turned its darting attention to the room. It chirped once in curt acceptance of the new surroundings. Didymus and Titus came under its black dot of an eye once more, this time for closer analysis. The canary chirped twice, perhaps that they were welcome, even pleasing, and stood on one leg to show them what a gay bird it was. It then returned to the business of pecking a piece of apple.

"I see you've given him something to eat," Didymus said, and felt that Titus, though he seemed content to watch the canary, waited for him to say something more. "I am very happy, Titus, to have this canary," he went on. "I suppose he will come in handy now that I must spend my days in this infernal chair."

Titus did not look at him while he said, "He is a good bird, Father. He is one of the saint's own good birds."

Through the window Didymus watched the days and nights come and go. For the first time, though his life as a friar had been copiously annotated with significant references, he got a good idea of eternity. Monotony, of course, was one word for it, but like all the others, as well as the allegories worked up by imaginative retreat masters, it was empty beside the experience itself, untranslatable. He would doze and wonder if by some quirk he had been cast out of the world into eternity, but since it was neither heaven nor exactly purgatory or hell, as he understood them, he concluded it must be an uncharted isle subscribing to the mother forms only in the matter of time. And having thought this, he was faintly annoyed at his ponderous whimsy. Titus, like certain of the hours, came periodically. He would read or simply sit with him in silence. The canary was there always, but except as it showed signs of sleepiness at twilight and spirit at dawn Didymus regarded it as a subtle device, like the days and nights and bells, to give the lie to the vulgar error that time flies. The cage was small and the canary would not sing. Time, hanging in the room like a jealous fog, possessed him and voided everything except it. It seemed impossible each time Titus came that he should be able to escape the room.

"'After him,'" Titus read from Bishop Bale one day, "'came Fabius, a Roman born, who (as Eusebius witnesseth) as he was returning home out of the field, and with his countrymen present to elect a new bishop, there was a pigeon seen standing on his head and suddenly he was created pastor of the Church, which he looked not for.'"

They smiled at having the same thought and both looked up at the canary. Since Didymus sat by the window most of the day now he had asked Titus to put a hook there for the cage. He had to admit to himself he did this to let Titus know he appreciated the canary. Also, as a secondary motive, he reasoned, it enabled the canary to look out the window. What a little yellow bird could see to interest it in the frozen scene was a mystery, but that, Didymus sighed, was a two-edged sword. And he took to watching the canary more.

So far as he was able to detect the moods of the canary he participated in them. In the morning the canary, bright and clownish, flitted back and forth between the two perches in the cage, hanging from the sides and cocking its little tufted head at Didymus querulously. During these acrobatics Didymus would twitch his hands in quick imitation of the canary's stunts. He asked Titus to construct a tiny swing, such as he had seen, which the canary might learn to use, since it appeared to be an intelligent and daring sort. Titus got the swing, the canary did master it, but there seemed to be nothing Didymus could do with his hands that was like swinging. In fact, after watching a while it was as though the canary were fixed to a pendulum, inanimate, a piece of machinery, a yellow blur —ticking, for the swing made a little sound, and Didymus went to sleep and often when he woke the canary was still going, like a clock. Didymus had no idea how long he slept at these times, maybe a minute, maybe hours. Gradually the canary got bored with the swing and used it less and less. In the same way, Didymus suspected, he himself had wearied of looking out the window. The first meager satisfaction had worn off. The dead trees, the sleeping snow, like the swing for the canary, were sources of diversion which soon grew stale. They were captives, he and the canary, and the only thing they craved was escape. Didymus slowly considered the problem. There was nothing, obviously, for him to do. He could pray, which he did, but he was not sure the only thing wrong with him was the fact he could not walk and that to devote his prayer to that end was justifiable. Inevitably it occurred to him his plight might well be an act of God. Why this punishment, though, he asked himself, and immediately supplied the answer. He had, for one thing, gloried too much in having it in him to turn down Seraphin's request to come to St. Louis. The intention, that was all-important, and he, he feared, had done the right thing for the wrong reason. He had noticed something of the faker in himself before. But it was not clear if he had erred. There was a certain consolation, at bottom dismal, in this doubt. It was true there appeared to be a nice justice in being stricken a cripple if he had been wrong in refusing to travel to see Seraphin, if human love was all he was fitted for, if he was incapable of renunciation for the right reason, if the mystic counsels were too strong for him, if he was still too pedestrian after all these years of prayer and contemplation, if . . .

The canary was swinging, the first time in several days.

The reality of his position was insupportable. There were two ways of regarding it and he could not make up his mind. Humbly, he wished to get well and to be able to walk. But if this was a punishment, was not prayer to lift it declining to see the divine point? He did wish to get well; that would settle it. Otherwise his predicament could only be resolved through means more serious than he dared cope with. It would be like refusing to see Seraphin all over again. By some mistake, he protested, he had at last been placed in a position vital with meaning and precedents inescapably Christian. But was he the man for it? Unsure of himself, he was afraid to go on trial. It would be no minor trial, so construed, but one in which the greatest values were involved, a human soul and the means of its salvation or damnation. Not watered-down suburban precautions and routine pious exercises, but faith such as saints and martyrs had, and despair such as only they had been tempted by. No, he was not the man for it. He was unworthy. He simply desired to walk and in a few years to die a normal uninspired death. He did not wish to see (what was apparent) the greatest significance in his affliction. He preferred to think in terms of physical betterment. He was so sure he was not a saint that he did not consider this easier road beneath him, though attracted by the higher one. That was the rub. Humbly, then, he wanted to be able to walk, but he wondered if there was not presumption in such humility.

Thus he decided to pray for health and count the divine hand not there. Decided. A clean decision—not distinction—no mean feat in the light of all the moral theology he had swallowed. The canary, all its rocking come to naught once more, slept motionless in the swing. Despite the manifest prudence of the course he had settled upon Didymus dozed off ill at ease in his wheelchair by the window. Distastefully, the last thing he remembered was that "prudence" is a virtue more celebrated in the modern Church.

At his request in the days following a doctor visited him. The rector came along too. When Didymus tried to find out the nature of his illness the doctor looked solemn and pronounced it to be one of those things. Didymus received this with a look of mystification. So the doctor went on to say there was no telling about it. Time alone would tell. Didymus asked the doctor to recommend some books dealing with cases like his. They might have one of them in the monastery library. Titus could read to him in the meantime.

For, though he disliked being troublesome, "one of those things" as a diagnosis meant very little to an unscientific beggar like him. The phrase had a philosophic ring to it, but to his knowledge neither the Early Fathers nor the Scholastics seemed to have dealt with it. The rector smiled. The doctor, annoyed, replied dryly:

"Is that a fact?"

Impatiently Didymus said, "I know how old I am, if that's it."

Nothing was lost of the communion he kept with the canary. He still watched its antics and his fingers in his lap followed them clumsily. He did not forget about himself, that he must pray for health, that it was best that way—"prudence" dictated it—but he did think more of the canary's share of their captivity. A canary in a cage, he reasoned, is like a bud which never blooms.

He asked Titus to get a book on canaries, but nothing came of it and he did not mention it again.

Some days later Titus read:

"'Twenty-ninth pope, Marcellus, a Roman, was pastor of the Church, feeding it with wisdom and doctrine. And (as I may say with the prophet) a man according to God's heart and full of Christian works. This man admonished Maximianus the Emperor and endeavored to remove him from persecuting the saints——'"

"Stop a moment, Titus," Didymus interrupted.

Steadily since Titus began to read the canary had been jumping from the swing to the bottom of the cage. Now it was quietly standing on one foot in the swing. Suddenly it flew at the side of the cage nearest them and hung there, its ugly little claws, like bent wire, hooked to the slender bars. It observed them intently, first Titus and then Didymus, at whom it continued to stare. Didymus' hands were tense in his lap.

"Go ahead, read," Didymus said, relaxing his hands.

"'But the Emperor, being more hardened, commanded Marcellus to be beaten with cudgels and to be driven out of the city, wherefore he entered into the house of one Lucina, a widow, and there kept the congregation secretly, which the tyrant, hearing, made a stable for cattle of the same house and committed the keeping of it to the Bishop Marcellus. After that he governed the Church by writing epistles, without any other kind of teaching, being condemned to such a vile service. And being thus daily tormented with strife and noisomeness at length gave up the ghost. Anno 308.'"

"Very good, Titus. I wonder how we missed that one before."

The canary, still hanging on the side of the cage, had not moved, its head turned sidewise, its eye as before fixed on Didymus.

"Would you bring me a glass of water, Titus?"

Titus got up and looked in the cage. The canary hung there, as though waiting, not a feather stirring.

"The bird has water here," Titus said, pointing to the small cup fastened to the cage.

"For me, Titus, the water's for me. Don't you think I know you look after the canary? You don't forget us, though I don't see why you don't."

Titus left the room with a glass.

Didymus' hands were tense again. Eyes on the canary's eye, he got up from his wheelchair, his face strained and white with the impossible effort, and, his fingers somehow managing it, he opened the cage. The canary darted out and circled the room chirping. Before it lit, though it seemed about to make its perch triumphantly the top of the cage, Didymus fell over on his face and lay prone on the floor.

In bed that night, unsuffering and barely alive, he saw at will everything revealed in his past. Events long forgotten happened again before his eyes. Clearly, sensitively, he saw Seraphin and himself, just as they had always been—himself, never quite sure. He heard all that he had ever said and that anyone had said to him. He had talked too much too. The past mingled with the present. In the same moment and scene he made his first communion, was ordained, and confessed his sins for the last time.

The canary perched in the dark atop the cage, head warm under wing, already, it seemed to Didymus, without memory of its captivity, dreaming of a former freedom, an ancestral summer day with flowers and trees. Outside it was snowing.

The rector, followed by others, came into the room and administered the last sacrament. Didymus heard them all gathered prayerfully around his bed thinking (they thought) secretly: This sacrament often strengthens the dying, tip-of-the-tongue wisdom indigenous to the priesthood, Henry VIII had six wives. He saw the same hackneyed smile, designed to cheer, pass bravely among them, and marveled at the crudity of it. They went away then, all except Titus, their individual footsteps sounding (for him) the character of each friar. He might have been Francis himself for what he knew then of the little brothers and the cure of souls. He heard them thinking their expectation to be called from bed before daybreak to return to his room and say the office of the dead over his body, become the body, and whispering hopefully to the contrary. Death was now an unwelcome guest in the cloister.

He wanted nothing in the world for himself at last. This may have been the first time he found his will amenable to the divine. He had never been less himself and more the saint. Yet now, so close to sublimity, or perhaps only tempted to believe so (the Devil is most wily at the deathbed), he was beset by the grossest distractions. They were to be expected, he knew, as indelible in the order of things: the bingo game going on under the Cross for the seamless garment of the Son of Man: everywhere the sign of the contradiction, and always. When would he cease to be surprised by it? Incidents repeated themselves, twined, parted, faded away, came back clear, and would not be prayed out of mind. He watched himself mounting the pulpit of a metropolitan church, heralded by the pastor as the renowned Franciscan father sent by God in his goodness to preach this novena —like to say a little prayer to test the microphone, Father?—and later reading through the petitions to Our Blessed Mother, cynically tabulating the pleas for a Catholic boy friend, drunkenness banished, the sale of real estate, and coming furiously upon one: "That I'm not pregnant." And at the same church on Good Friday carrying the crucifix along the communion rail for the people to kiss, giving them the indulgence, and afterwards in the sacristy wiping the lipstick of the faithful from the image of Christ crucified.

"Take down a book, any book, Titus, and read. Begin anywhere."

Roused by his voice, the canary fluttered, looked sharply about, and buried its head once more in the warmth of its wing.

" 'By the lions,' " Titus read, " 'are understood the acrimonies and impetuosities of the irascible faculty, which faculty is as bold and daring in its acts as are the lions. By the harts and the leaping does is understood the other faculty of the soul, which is the concupiscible —that is——' "

"Skip the exegesis," Didymus broke in weakly. "I can do without that now. Read the verse."

Titus read: " 'Birds of swift wing, lions, harts, leaping does, mountains, valleys, banks, waters, breezes, heats, and terrors that keep watch by night, by the pleasant lyres and by the siren's song, I conjure you, cease your wrath and touch not the wall——' "

"Turn off the light, Titus."

Titus went over to the switch. There was a brief period of darkness during which Didymus' eyes became accustomed to a different shade, a glow rather, which possessed the room slowly. Then he saw the full moon had let down a ladder of light through the window. He could see the snow, strangely blue, falling outside. So sensitive were his mind and eye (because his body, now faint, no longer blurred his vision?) he could count the snowflakes, all of them separately, before they drifted, winding, below the sill.

With the same wonderful clarity he saw what he had made of his life. He saw himself tied down, caged, stunted in his apostolate, seeking the crumbs, the little pleasures, neglecting the source, always knowing death changes nothing, only immortalizes . . . and still ever lukewarm. In trivial attachments, in love of things, was death, no matter the appearance of life. In the highest attachment only, no matter the appearance of death, was life. He had always known this truth, but now he was feeling it. Unable to move his hand, only his lips, and hardly breathing, was it too late to act?

"Open the window, Titus," he whispered.

And suddenly he could pray. "Hail Mary . . . Holy Mary, Mother of God, pray for us sinners now and at the hour of our death . . ." Finally the time to say, "pray for *me* now—the hour of *my* death, amen." Lest he deceive himself at the very end that this was the answer to a lifetime of praying for a happy death, happy because painless, he tried to turn his thoughts from himself, to join them to God, thinking how at last he did—didn't he *now?*—prefer God above all else. But ashamedly not sure he did, perhaps only fearing hell, with an uneasy sense of justice he put himself foremost among the wise in their own generation, the perennials seeking after God when doctor, lawyer, and bank fail. If he wronged himself, he did so out of humility, a holy error. He ended, to make certain he had not fallen under the same old presumption disguised as the face of humility, by flooding his mind with maledictions. He suffered the piercing white voice of the Apocalypse to echo in his soul: "But because thou art lukewarm, and neither cold, nor hot, I will begin to vomit thee out of my mouth." And St. Bernard, fiery-eyed in a white habit, thundered at him from the twelfth century: "Hell is paved with the bald pates of priests!"

There was a soft flutter, the canary flew to the window sill, paused, and tilted into the snow. Titus stepped too late to the window and stood gazing dumbly after it. He raised a trembling old hand, fingers bent in awe and sorrow, to his forehead, and turned stealthily to Didymus.

Didymus closed his eyes. He let a long moment pass before he opened them. Titus, seeing him awake then, fussed with the window latch and held a hand down to feel the draft, nodding anxiously as though it were the only evil abroad in the world, all the time straining his old eyes for a glimpse of the canary somewhere in the trees.

Didymus said nothing, letting Titus keep his secret. With his whole will he tried to lose himself in the sight of God, and failed. He was not in the least transported. Even now he could find no divine sign within himself. He knew he still had to look outside, to Titus. God still chose to manifest Himself most in sanctity.

Titus, nervous under his stare, and to account for staying at the window so long, felt for the draft again, frowned, and kept his eye hunting among the trees.

The thought of being the cause of such elaborate dissimulation in so simple a soul made Didymus want to smile—or cry, he did not know which—and could do neither. Titus persisted. How long would it be, Didymus wondered faintly, before Titus ungrievingly gave the canary up for lost in the snowy arms of God? The snowflakes whirled at the window, for a moment for all their bright blue beauty as though struck still by lightning, and Didymus closed his eyes, only to find them there also, but darkly falling.

The Valiant Woman

They had come to the dessert in a dinner that was a shambles. "Well, John," Father Nulty said, turning away from Mrs. Stoner and to Father Firman, long gone silent at his own table. "You've got the bishop coming for confirmations next week."

"Yes," Mrs. Stoner cut in, "and for dinner. And if he don't eat any more than he did last year——"

Father Firman, in a rare moment, faced it. "Mrs. Stoner, the bishop is not well. You know that."

"And after I fixed that fine dinner and all." Mrs. Stoner pouted in Father Nulty's direction.

"I wouldn't feel bad about it, Mrs. Stoner," Father Nulty said. "He never eats much anywhere."

"It's funny. And that new Mrs. Allers said he ate just fine when he was there," Mrs. Stoner argued, and then spit out, "but she's a damned liar!"

Father Nulty, unsettled but trying not to show it, said, "Who's Mrs. Allers?"

"She's at Holy Cross," Mrs. Stoner said.

"She's the housekeeper," Father Firman added, thinking Mrs. Stoner made it sound as though Mrs. Allers were the pastor there.

"I swear I don't know what to do about the dinner this year," Mrs. Stoner said.

Father Firman moaned. "Just do as you've always done, Mrs. Stoner."

"Huh! And have it all to throw out! Is that any way to do?"

"Is there any dessert?" Father Firman asked coldly.

Mrs. Stoner leaped up from the table and bolted into the kitchen, mumbling. She came back with a birthday cake. She plunged it in the center of the table. She found a big wooden match in her apron pocket and thrust it at Father Firman.

"I don't like this bishop," she said. "I never did. And the way he went and cut poor Ellen Kennedy out of Father Doolin's will!"

She went back into the kitchen.

"Didn't they talk a lot of filth about Doolin and the housekeeper?" Father Nulty asked.

"I should think they did," Father Firman said. "All because he took her to the movies on Sunday night. After he died and the bishop cut her out of the will, though I hear he gives her a pension privately, they talked about the bishop."

"I don't like this bishop at all," Mrs. Stoner said, appearing with a cake knife. "Bishop Doran—there was the man!"

"We know," Father Firman said. "All man and all priest."

"He did know real estate," Father Nulty said.

Father Firman struck the match.

"Not on the chair!" Mrs. Stoner cried, too late.

Father Firman set the candle burning—it was suspiciously large and yellow, like a blessed one, but he could not be sure. They watched the fluttering flame.

"I'm forgetting the lights!" Mrs. Stoner said, and got up to turn them off. She went into the kitchen again.

The priests had a moment of silence in the candlelight.

"Happy birthday, John," Father Nulty said softly. "Is it fifty-nine you are?"

"As if you didn't know, Frank," Father Firman said, "and you the same but one."

Father Nulty smiled, the old gold of his incisors shining in the flickering light, his collar whiter in the dark, and raised his glass of water, which would have been wine or better in the bygone days, and toasted Father Firman.

"Many of 'em, John."

"Blow it out," Mrs. Stoner said, returning to the room. She waited by the light switch for Father Firman to blow out the candle.

Mrs. Stoner, who ate no desserts, began to clear the dishes into the kitchen, and the priests, finishing their cake and coffee in a hurry, went to sit in the study.

Father Nulty offered a cigar.

"John?"

"My ulcers, Frank."

"Ah, well, you're better off." Father Nulty lit the cigar and crossed his long black legs. "Fish Frawley has got him a Filipino, John. Did you hear?"

Father Firman leaned forward, interested. "He got rid of the woman he had?"

"He did. It seems she snooped."

"Snooped, eh?"

"She did. And gossiped. Fish introduced two town boys to her, said, 'Would you think these boys were my nephews?' That's all, and the next week the paper had it that his two nephews were visiting him from Erie. After that, he let her believe he was going East to see his parents, though both are dead. The paper carried the story. Fish returned and made a sermon out of it. Then he got the Filipino."

Father Firman squirmed with pleasure in his chair. "That's like Fish, Frank. He can do that." He stared at the tips of his fingers bleakly. "You could never get a Filipino to come to a place like this."

"Probably not," Father Nulty said. "Fish is pretty close to Minneapolis. Ah, say, do you remember the trick he played on us all in Marmion Hall!"

"That I'll not forget!" Father Firman's eyes remembered. "Getting up New Year's morning and finding the toilet seats all painted!"

"*Happy Circumcision!* Hah!" Father Nulty had a coughing fit.

When he had got himself together again, a mosquito came and sat on his wrist. He watched it a moment before bringing his heavy hand down. He raised his hand slowly, viewed the dead mosquito, and sent it spinning with a plunk of his middle finger.

"Only the female bites," he said.

"I didn't know that," Father Firman said.

"Ah, yes . . ."

Mrs. Stoner entered the study and sat down with some sewing—Father Firman's black socks.

She smiled pleasantly at Father Nulty. "And what do you think of the atom bomb, Father?"

"Not much," Father Nulty said.

Mrs. Stoner had stopped smiling. Father Firman yawned.

Mrs. Stoner served up another: "Did you read about this commu nist convert, Father?"

"He's been in the Church before," Father Nulty said, "and so it's not a conversion, Mrs. Stoner."

"No? Well, I already got him down on my list of Monsignor's converts."

"It's better than a conversion, Mrs. Stoner, for there is more rejoicing in heaven over the return of . . . uh, he that was lost, Mrs. Stoner, is found."

"And that congresswoman, Father?"

"Yes. A convert—she."

"And Henry Ford's grandson, Father. I got him down."

"Yes, to be sure."

Father Firman yawned, this time audibly, and held his jaw.

"But he's one only by marriage, Father," Mrs. Stoner said. "I always say you got to watch those kind."

"Indeed you do, but a convert nonetheless, Mrs. Stoner. Remember, Cardinal Newman himself was one."

Mrs. Stoner was unimpressed. "I see where Henry Ford's making steering wheels out of soybeans, Father."

"I didn't see that."

"I read it in the *Reader's Digest* or some place."

"Yes, well . . ." Father Nulty rose and held his hand out to Father Firman. "John," he said. "It's been good."

"I heard Hirohito's next," Mrs. Stoner said, returning to converts.

"Let's wait and see, Mrs. Stoner," Father Nulty said.

The priests walked to the door.

"You know where I live, John."

"Yes. Come again, Frank. Good night."

Father Firman watched Father Nulty go down the walk to his car at the curb. He hooked the screen door and turned off the porch light. He hesitated at the foot of the stairs, suddenly moved to go to bed. But he went back into the study.

"Phew!" Mrs. Stoner said. "I thought he'd never go. Here it is after eight o'clock."

Father Firman sat down in his rocking chair. "I don't see him often," he said.

"I give up!" Mrs. Stoner exclaimed, flinging the holy socks upon the horsehair sofa. "I'd swear you had a nail in your shoe."

"I told you I looked."

"Well, you ought to look again. And cut your toenails, why don't you? Haven't I got enough to do?"

Father Firman scratched in his coat pocket for a pill, found one, swallowed it. He let his head sink back against the chair and closed his eyes. He could hear her moving about the room, making the preparations; and how he knew them—the fumbling in the drawer for a pencil with a point, the rip of page from his daily calendar, and finally the leg of the card table sliding up against his leg.

He opened his eyes. She yanked the floor lamp alongside the table, setting the bead fringe tinkling on the shade, and pulled up her chair on the other side. She sat down and smiled at him for the first time that day. Now she was happy.

She swept up the cards and began to shuffle with the abandoned virtuosity of an old river-boat gambler, standing them on end, fanning them out, whirling them through her fingers, dancing them halfway up her arms, cracking the whip over them. At last they lay before him tamed into a neat deck.

"Cut?"

"Go ahead," he said. She liked to go first.

She gave him her faint, avenging smile and drew a card, cast it aside for another which he thought must be an ace from the way she clutched it face down.

She was getting all the cards, as usual, and would have been invincible if she had possessed his restraint and if her cunning had been of a higher order. He knew a few things about leading and lying back that she would never learn. Her strategy was attack, forever attack, with one baffling departure: she might sacrifice certain tricks as expendable if only she could have the last ones, the heartbreaking ones, if she could slap them down one after another, shatteringly.

She played for blood, no bones about it, but for her there was no other way; it was her nature, as it was the lion's, and for this reason he found her ferocity pardonable, more a defect of the flesh, venial, while his own trouble was all in the will, mortal. He did not sweat and pray over each card as she must, but he did keep an eye out for reneging and demanded a cut now and then just to aggravate her, and he was always secretly hoping for aces.

With one card left in her hand, the telltale trick coming next, she delayed playing it, showing him first the smile, the preview of defeat. She laid it on the table—so! She held one more trump than he had reasoned possible. Had she palmed it from somewhere? No, she would not go that far; that would not be fair, was worse than reneging, which so easily and often happened accidentally, and she believed in being fair. Besides he had been watching her.

God smote the vines with hail, the sycamore trees with frost, and offered up the flocks to the lightning—but Mrs. Stoner! What a cross Father Firman had from God in Mrs. Stoner! There were other housekeepers as bad, no doubt, walking the rectories of the world, yes, but . . . yes. He could name one and maybe two priests who were worse off. One, maybe two. Cronin. His scraggly blonde of sixty— take her, with her everlasting banging on the grand piano, the gift of the pastor; her proud talk about the goiter operation at the Mayo Brothers', also a gift; her honking the parish Buick at passing strange priests because they were all in the game together. She was worse. She was something to keep the home fires burning. Yes sir. And

Cronin said she was not a bad person really, but what was he? He was quite a freak himself.

For that matter, could anyone say that Mrs. Stoner was a bad person? No. He could not say it himself, and he was no freak. She had her points, Mrs. Stoner. She was clean. And though she cooked poorly, could not play the organ, would not take up the collection in an emergency, and went to card parties, and told all—even so, she was clean. She washed everything. Sometimes her underwear hung down beneath her dress like a paratrooper's pants, but it and everything she touched was clean. She washed constantly. She was clean.

She had her other points, to be sure—her faults, you might say. She snooped—no mistake about it—but it was not snooping for snooping's sake; she had a reason. She did other things, always with a reason. She overcharged on rosaries and prayer books, but that was for the sake of the poor. She censored the pamphlet rack, but that was to prevent scandal. She pried into the baptismal and matrimonial records, but there was no other way if Father was out, and in this way she had once uncovered a bastard and flushed him out of the rectory, but that was the perverted decency of the times. She held her nose over bad marriages in the presence of the victims, but that was her sorrow and came from having her husband buried in a mine. And he had caught her telling a bewildered young couple that there was only one good reason for their wanting to enter into a mixed marriage—the child had to have a name, and that—that was what?

She hid his books, kept him from smoking, picked his friends (usually the pastors of her colleagues), bawled out people for calling after dark, had no humor, except at cards, and then it was grim, very grim, and she sat hatchet-faced every morning at Mass. But she went to Mass, which was all that kept the church from being empty some mornings. She did annoying things all day long. She said annoying things into the night. She said she had given him the best years of her life. Had she? Perhaps—for the miner had her only a year. It was too bad, sinfully bad, when he thought of it like that. But all talk of best years and life was nonsense. He had to consider the heart of the matter, the essence. The essence was that housekeepers were hard to get, harder to get than ushers, than willing workers, than organists, than secretaries—yes, harder to get than assistants or vocations.

And she was a *saver*—saved money, saved electricity, saved string, bags, sugar, saved—him. That's what she did. That's what she said she did, and she was right, in a way. In a way, she was usually right. In fact, she was always right—in a way. And you could never get a Filipino to come way out here and live. Not a young one anyway, and he had never seen an old one. Not a Filipino. They liked to dress up and live.

Should he let it drop about Fish having one, just to throw a scare into her, let her know he was doing some thinking? No. It would be a perfect cue for the one about a man needing a woman to look after him. He was not up to that again, not tonight.

Now she was doing what she liked most of all. She was making a grand slam, playing it out card for card, though it was in the bag, prolonging what would have been cut short out of mercy in gentle company. Father Firman knew the agony of losing.

She slashed down the last card, a miserable deuce trump, and did in the hapless king of hearts he had been saving.

"Skunked you!"

She was awful in victory. Here was the bitter end of their long day together, the final murderous hour in which all they wanted to say —all he wouldn't and all she couldn't—came out in the cards. Whoever won at honeymoon won the day, slept on the other's scalp, and God alone had to help the loser.

"We've been at it long enough, Mrs. Stoner," he said, seeing her assembling the cards for another round.

"Had enough, huh!"

Father Firman grumbled something.

"No?"

"Yes."

She pulled the table away and left it against the wall for the next time. She went out of the study carrying the socks, content and clucking. He closed his eyes after her and began to get under way in the rocking chair, the nightly trip to nowhere. He could hear her brewing a cup of tea in the kitchen and conversing with the cat. She made her way up the stairs, carrying the tea, followed by the cat, purring.

He waited, rocking out to sea, until she would be sure to be through in the bathroom. Then he got up and locked the front door (she looked after the back door) and loosened his collar going upstairs.

In the bathroom he mixed a glass of antiseptic, always afraid of pyorrhea, and gargled to ward off pharyngitis.

When he turned on the light in his room, the moths and beetles began to batter against the screens, the lighter insects humming. . . .

Yes, and she had the guest room. How did she come to get that? Why wasn't she in the back room, in her proper place? He knew, if he cared to remember. The screen in the back room—it let in mosquitoes, and if it didn't do that she'd love to sleep back there, Father, looking out at the steeple and the blessed cross on top, Father, if it just weren't for the screen, Father. Very well, Mrs. Stoner, I'll get it fixed or fix it myself. Oh, could you now, Father? I could, Mrs. Stoner, and I will. In the meantime you take the guest room. Yes, Father, and thank you, Father, the house ringing with amenities then. Years ago, all that. She was a pie-faced girl then, not really a girl perhaps, but not too old to marry again. But she never had. In fact, he could not remember that she had even tried for a husband since coming to the rectory, but, of course, he could be wrong, not knowing how they went about it. God! God save us! Had she got her wires crossed and mistaken him all these years for *that*? *That!* Him! Suffering God! No. That was going too far. That was getting morbid. No. He must not think of that again, ever. No.

But just the same she had got the guest room and she had it yet. Well, did it matter? Nobody ever came to see him any more, nobody to stay overnight anyway, nobody to stay very long . . . not any more. He knew how they laughed at him. He had heard Frank humming all right—before he saw how serious and sad the situation was and took pity—humming, "Wedding Bells Are Breaking Up That Old Gang of Mine." But then they'd always laughed at him for something—for not being an athlete, for wearing glasses, for having kidney trouble . . . and mail coming addressed to Rev. and Mrs. Stoner.

Removing his shirt, he bent over the table to read the volume left open from last night. He read, translating easily, "Eisdem licet cum illis . . . Clerics are allowed to reside only with women about whom there can be no suspicion, either because of a natural bond (as mother, sister, aunt) or of advanced age, combined in both cases with good repute."

Last night he had read it, and many nights before, each time as though this time to find what was missing, to find what obviously was not in the paragraph, his problem considered, a way out. She was not mother, not sister, not aunt, and *advanced age* was a relative term (why, she was younger than he was) and so, eureka, she did not meet the letter of the law—but, alas, how she fulfilled the spirit! And besides it would be a slimy way of handling it after all her years of service. He could not afford to pension her off, either.

He slammed the book shut. He slapped himself fiercely on the back, missing the wily mosquito, and whirled to find it. He took a magazine and folded it into a swatter. Then he saw it—oh, the preternatural cunning of it!—poised in the beard of St. Joseph on the bookcase. He could not hit it there. He teased it away, wanting it to light on the wall, but it knew his thoughts and flew high away. He swung wildly, hoping to stun it, missed, swung back, catching St. Joseph across the neck. The statue fell to the floor and broke.

Mrs. Stoner was panting in the hall outside his door.

"What is it!"

"Mosquitoes!"

"What is it, Father? Are you hurt?"

"Mosquitoes—damn it! And only the female bites!"

Mrs. Stoner, after a moment, said, "Shame on you, Father. She needs the blood for her eggs."

He dropped the magazine and lunged at the mosquito with his bare hand.

She went back to her room, saying, "Pshaw, I thought it was burglars murdering you in your bed."

He lunged again.

THOMAS PYNCHON

Under the Rose

As the afternoon progressed, yellow clouds began to gather over Place Mohammed Ali, casting a tendril or two back toward the Libyan desert. A wind from the southwest swept quietly up rue Ibrahim and across the square, bringing the chill of the desert into the city.

Then let it rain, Porpentine thought: rain soon. He sat at a small wrought-iron table in front of a café, smoking Turkish cigarettes with a third cup of coffee, ulster thrown over the back of an adjoining chair. Today he wore light tweeds and a felt hat with muslin tied round it to protect his neck from the sun; he was leery of the sun. Clouds moved in now to dim it out. Porpentine shifted in his seat, took a watch from his waistcoat pocket, consulted it, replaced it. Turned once more to look out at the Europeans milling about the square: some hurrying into the Banque Impériale Ottomane, others lingering by shopwindows, seating themselves at cafés. His face was carefully arranged: nerveless, rakish-expectant; he might have been there to meet a lady.

All for the benefit of anyone who cared. God knew how many there were. In practice it narrowed down to those in the employ of Moldweorp, the veteran spy. One somehow always tacked on "the veteran spy." It might have been a throwback to an earlier time, when such epithets were one reward for any proof of heroism or manhood. Or possibly because now, with a century rushing headlong to its end and with it a tradition in espionage where everything was tacitly on a gentlemanly basis, where the playing-fields of Eton had conditioned (one might say) premilitary conduct as well, the label was a way of fixing identity in this special *haut monde* before death —individual or collective—stung it to stillness forever. Porpentine himself was called *"il semplice inglese"* by those who cared.

Last week in Brindisi their compassion had been relentless as always; it gave them a certain moral advantage, realizing as they did that Porpentine was somehow incapable of returning it. Tender and sheepish, therefore, they wove their paths to cross his own at random. Mirrored, too, his private tactics: living in the most frequented hotels, sitting at the tourist cafés, traveling always by the respectable, public routes. Which surely upset him most; as if, Porpentine once having fashioned such proper innocence, any use of it by others—especially Moldweorp's agents—involved some violation of patent right. They would pirate if they could his child's gaze, his plump angel's smile. For nearly fifteen years he'd fled their sympathy; since the lobby of the Hotel Bristol, Naples, on a winter evening in '83, when everyone you knew in spying's freemasonry seemed to be waiting. For Khartum to fall, for the crisis in Afghanistan to keep growing until it could be given the name of sure apocalypse. There he had come, as he'd known he must at some stage of the game, to face the already aged face of Moldweorp himself, the prizeman or maestro, feel the old man's hand solicitous on his arm and hear the earnest whisper: "Things are reaching a head; we may be for it, all of us. Do be careful." What response? What possible? Only a scrutiny, almost desperate, for any fine trace of insincerity. Of course he'd found none there; and so turned, quickly, flaming, unable to cover a certain helplessness. Hoist thus by his own petard at every subsequent encounter as well, Porpentine by the dog-days of '98 seemed, in contrast, to have grown cold, unkind. They would continue to use so fortunate an engine: would never seek his life, violate The Rules, forbear what had become for them pleasure.

He sat now wondering if either of the two at Brindisi had followed him to Alexandria. Certain he had seen no one on the Venice boat, he reviewed possibilities. An Austrian Lloyd steamer from Trieste also touched at Brindisi; was the only other they would have taken. Today was Monday. Porpentine had left on a Friday. The Trieste boat left on Thursday and arrived late Sunday. So that (a) at second-worst he had six days, or (b) at worst, they knew. In which case they had left the day before Porpentine and were already here.

He watched the sun darken and the wind flutter the leaves of acacias around Place Mohammed Ali. In the distance his name was being called. He turned to watch Goodfellow, blond and jovial, striding toward him down rue Cherif Pacha, wearing a dress suit and a pith helmet two sizes too large. "I say," Goodfellow cried. "Porpentine, I've met a remarkable young lady." Porpentine lit another cigarette and closed his eyes. All of Goodfellow's young ladies were remarkable. After two and a half years as partners one got used to an incidental progress of feminine attachments to Goodfellow's right arm: as if every capital of Europe were Margate and the promenade a continent long. If Goodfellow knew half his salary was sent out every month to a wife in Liverpool he showed none of it, rollicking along unperturbed, cock-a-hoop. Porpentine had seen his running mate's dossier but decided some time ago that the wife at least was none of his affair. He listened now as Goodfellow drew up a chair and summoned a waiter in wretched Arabic: *"Hat fingan kahwa bisukkar, ya weled."*

"Goodfellow," Porpentine said, "you don't have to—"

"Ya weled, ya weled," Goodfellow roared. The waiter was French and did not understand Arabic. "Ah," Goodfellow said, "coffee then. *Café*, you know."

"How are the digs?" asked Porpentine.

"First-rate." Goodfellow was staying at the Hotel Khedival, seven blocks away. There being a temporary hitch in finances, only one could afford the usual accommodations. Porpentine was staying with a friend in the Turkish quarter. "About this girl," Goodfellow said. "Party tonight at the Austrian Consulate. Her escort, Goodfellow: linguist, adventurer, diplomat . . ."

"Name," said Porpentine.

"Victoria Wren. Traveling with family, *videlicet:* Sir Alastair Wren, F.R.C.O., sister Mildred. Mother deceased. Departing for Cairo tomorrow. Cook's tour down the Nile." Porpentine waited. "Lunatic archaeologist," Goodfellow seemed reluctant. "One Bongo-Shaftsbury. Young, addlepated. Harmless."

"Aha."

"Tch-tch. Too highly strung. Should drink less café-fort."

"Possibly," Porpentine said. Goodfellow's coffee arrived. Porpentine continued: "You know we'll end up chancing it anyway. We always do." Goodfellow grinned absently and stirred his coffee.

"I have already taken steps. Bitter rivalry for the young lady's attentions between myself and Bongo-Shaftsbury. Fellow is a perfect ass. Is mad to see the Theban ruins at Luxor."

"Of course," Porpentine said. He arose and tossed the ulster around his shoulders. It had begun to rain. Goodfellow handed him a small white envelope with the Austrian crest on the back.

"Eight, I suppose," said Porpentine.

"Right you are. You must see this girl."

It was then that one of Porpentine's seizures came upon him. The profession was lonely and in constant though not always deadly earnest. At regular intervals he found need to play the buffoon. "A bit of skylarking," he called it. It made him, he believed, more human. "I will be there with false mustaches," he now informed Goodfellow, "impersonating an Italian count." He stood gaily at attention, pressed an imaginary hand: "*Carissima signorina.*" He bowed, kissed the air.

"You're insane," from Goodfellow, amiable.

"*Pazzo son!*" Porpentine began to sing in a wavering tenor. "*Guardate, come io piango ed imploro . . .*" His Italian was not perfect. Cockney inflections danced through. A group of English tourists, hurrying in out of the rain, glanced back at him, curious.

"Enough," Goodfellow winced. "'Twas Turin, I remember. Torino. Was it not? '93. I escorted a marchesina with a mole on her back and Cremonini sang Des Grieux. You, Porpentine, desecrate the memory."

But the antic Porpentine leaped in the air, clicked his heels; stood posturing, fist on chest, the other arm outstretched. "*Come io chiedo pietà!*" The waiter looked on with a pained smile; it began to rain harder. Goodfellow sat in the rain sipping his coffee. Drops of rain rattled on the pith helmet. "The sister isn't bad," he observed as Porpentine frolicked out in the square. "Mildred, you know. Though only eleven." At length it occurred to him that his dress suit was becoming soaked. He arose, left a piastre and a millième on the table and nodded to Porpentine, who now stood watching him. The square was empty except for the equestrian statue of Mohammed Ali. How many times had they faced each other this way, dwarfed horizontal and vertical by any plaza's late-afternoon landscape? Could an argument from design be predicated on that moment only, then the two must have been displaceable, like minor chess-pieces, anywhere across the board of Europe. Both of a color (though one hanging back diagonal in deference to his chief), both scanning any embassy's parquetry for signs of the Opposition, any statue's face for a reassurance of self-agency (perhaps, unhappily, self-humanity), they would try not to remember that every city's square, however you cut it, remains inanimate after all. Soon the two men turned almost formally, to part in opposite directions: Goodfellow back toward the hotel, Porpentine into rue Ras-et-Tin and the Turkish quarter. Until eight he would ponder the Situation.

At the moment it was a bad job all round. Sirdar Kitchener, England's newest colonial hero, recently victorious at Khartum, was just now some four hundred miles farther down the White Nile, foraging about in the jungle. A General Marchand was also rumored to be in the vicinity. Britain wanted no part of France in the Nile Valley.

M. Delcassé, Foreign Minister of a newly formed French cabinet, would as soon go to war as not if there were any trouble when the two detachments met. As meet, everyone realized by now, they would. Kitchener had been instructed not to take any offensive and to avoid all provocation. Russia would support France in case of war, while England had a temporary rapprochement with Germany, which of course meant Italy and Austria as well.

Moldweorp's chief amusement, Porpentine reflected, had always been to harass. All he asked was that eventually there be a war. Not just a small incidental skirmish in the race to carve up Africa, but one pip-pip, jolly-ho, up-goes-the-balloon Armageddon for Europe. Once Porpentine might have been puzzled that his opposite number should desire war so passionately. Now he took it for granted that at some point in these fifteen years of hare-and-hounds he himself had conceived the private mission of keeping off Armageddon. An alignment like this, he felt, could only have taken place in a Western World where spying was becoming less an individual than a group enterprise, where the events of 1848 and the activities of anarchists and radicals all over the Continent seemed to proclaim that history was being made no longer through the *virtù* of single princes but rather by man in the mass; by trends and tendencies and impersonal curves on a lattice of pale blue lines. So it was inevitably single combat between the veteran spy and *il semplice inglese*. They stood alone —God knew where—on deserted lists. Goodfellow knew of the private battle, as doubtless did Moldweorp's subordinates. They all took on the roles of solicitous seconds, attending to the strictly national interests while their chiefs circled and parried above them on some unreachable level. It happened that Porpentine worked nominally for England and Moldweorp for Germany, but this was accident: they would probably have chosen the same sides had their employments been reversed. For he and Moldweorp, Porpentine knew, were cut from the same pattern: comrade Machiavellians, still playing the games of Renaissance Italian politics in a world that had outgrown them. The self-assumed roles became only, then, assertions of a kind of pride, first of all in a profession which still remembered the free-booting agility of Lord Palmerston. Fortunately for Porpentine the Foreign Office had enough of the old spirit left to give him nearly a free hand. Although if they did suspect he'd have no way of knowing. Where his personal mission coincided with diplomatic policy, Porpentine would send back a report to London, and no one ever seemed to complain.

The key man now for Porpentine seemed to be Lord Cromer, the

British Consul-General at Cairo, an extremely able diplomat and cautious enough to avoid any rash impulses: war, for example. Could Moldweorp have an assassination in the works? A trip to Cairo seemed in order. As innocent as possible; that went without saying.

The Austrian Consulate was across the street from the Hotel Khedival, the festivities there unexceptional. Goodfellow sat at the bottom of a wide flight of marble steps with a girl who could not have been more than eighteen and who, like the gown she wore, seemed awkwardly bouffant and provincial. The rain had shrunken Goodfellow's formal attire; his coat looked tight under the armpits and across the stomach; the blond hair had been disarranged by the desert wind, the face was flushed, uncomfortable. Watching him, Porpentine came aware of his own appearance: quaint, anomalous, his evening clothes purchased the same year General Gordon was done in by the Mahdi. Hopelessly passé at gatherings like this, he often played a game in which he was, say, Gordon returned from the dead and headless; that odd, at least, among a resplendent muster of stars, ribbons, and exotic Orders. That out of date, certainly: the Sirdar had retaken Khartum, the outrage was avenged, but people had forgotten. He'd seen the fabled hero of the China wars once, standing on the ramparts at Gravesend. At the time Porpentine had been ten or so and likely to be dazzled; he was. But something had happened between there and the Hotel Bristol. He had thought about Moldweorp that night and about the likelihood of some apocalypse; perhaps a little too on his own sense of estrangement. But not at all about Chinese Gordon, lonely and enigmatic at the mouth of that boyhood Thames; whose hair it was said had turned white in the space of a day as he waited for death in the besieged city of Khartum.

Porpentine looked about the Consulate, checking off diplomatic personnel: Sir Charles Cookson, Mr. Hewat, M. Girard, Hr. von Hartmann, Cav. Romano, Comte de Zogheb, &c., &c. Right ho. All present and accounted for. Except for the Russian Vice-Consul, M. de Villiers. And oddly enough one's host, Count Khevenhüller-Metsch. Could they be together?

He moved over to the steps where Goodfellow sat desperate, yarning about nonexistent adventures in South Africa. The girl regarded him breathless and smiling. Porpentine wondered if he should sing: It isn't the girl I saw you with in Brighton; who, who, who's your lady friend? He said:

"I say." Goodfellow, relieved and more enthusiastic than necessary, introduced them.

"Miss Victoria Wren."

Porpentine smiled, nodded, searched all over for a cigarette. "How do you do, Miss."

"She's been hearing about our show with Dr. Jameson and the Boers," said Goodfellow.

"You were in the Transvaal together," the girl marveled. Porpentine thought: he can do whatever he wants with this one. Whatever he asks her.

"We've been together for some time, Miss." She bloomed, she billowed; Porpentine, shy, withdrew behind pale cheeks, pursed lips. As if her glow were a reminder of any Yorkshire sunset, or at least some vestige of a vision of Home which neither he nor Goodfellow could afford—or when you came down to it, cared—to remember, they did share in her presence this common evasiveness.

A low growl sounded behind Porpentine. Goodfellow cringed, smiled weakly, introduced Sir Alastair Wren, Victoria's father. It became clear almost immediately that he was not fond of Goodfellow. With him was a robust, myopic girl of eleven; the sister. Mildred was in Egypt, she soon informed Porpentine, to gather rock specimens, being daft for rocks in the same way Sir Alastair was for large and ancient pipe-organs. He had toured Germany the previous year, alienating the populations of various cathedral towns by recruiting small boys to toil away half-days at a clip keeping the bellows going: and then underpaying. Frightfully, added Victoria. There was, he continued, no decent pipe-organ anywhere on the African continent (which Porpentine could hardly doubt). Goodfellow mentioned an enthusiasm for the barrel-organ, and had Sir Alastair ever tried his hand at one. The peer growled ominously. Out of the corner of his eye Porpentine saw Count Khevenhüller-Metsch come out of an adjoining room, steering the Russian vice-consul by the arm and talking wistfully; M. de Villiers punctuated the conversation with mirthful little barks. Aha, Porpentine thought. Mildred had produced from her reticule a large rock, which she now held up to Porpentine for inspection. She had found it out near the site of the ancient Pharos, it contained trilobite fossils. Porpentine could not respond; it was his old weakness. A bar was set up on the mezzanine; he loped up the marble stairs after promising to bring punch (lemonade, of course, for Mildred).

Someone touched his arm as he waited at the bar. He turned and saw one of the two from Brindisi, who said: "Lovely girl." It was the first word he could remember any of them speaking to him directly in fifteen years. He only wondered, uneasy, if they reserved such artifice for times of singular crisis. He picked up the drinks, smiled all angelic; turned, started down the stairs. On the second step he tripped and fell: proceeded whirling and bouncing, followed by sounds of glass breaking and a spray of Chablis punch and lemonade, to the bottom. He'd learned in the army how to take falls. He looked up bashful at Sir Alastair Wren, who nodded in approval.

"Saw a fellow do that in a music-hall once," he said. "You're much better, Porpentine. Really."

"Do it again," Mildred said. Porpentine extracted a cigarette, lay there for a bit smoking. "How about late supper at the Fink," Goodfellow suggested. Porpentine got to his feet. "You remember the chaps we met in Brindisi." Goodfellow nodded, impassive, betraying no tics or tightenings; one of the things Porpentine admired him for. But: "Going home," Sir Alastair muttered, yanking fiercely at Mildred's hand. "Behave yourselves." So Porpentine found himself playing chaperon. He proposed another try for punch. When they got to the mezzanine Moldweorp's man had disappeared. Porpentine wedged one foot between the balusters and looked down, surveying rapidly the faces below. "No," he said. Goodfellow handed him a cup of punch.

"I can't wait to see the Nile," Victoria had been saying, "the pyramids, the Sphinx."

"Cairo," Goodfellow added.

"Yes," Porpentine agreed, "Cairo."

Directly across rue de Rosette was the Fink restaurant. They dashed across the street through the rain, Victoria's cloak ballooning about her; she laughed, delighted with the rain. The crowd inside was entirely European. Porpentine recognized a few faces from the Venice boat. After her first glass of white Vöslauer the girl began to talk. Blithe and so green, she pronounced her o's with a sigh, as if fainting from love. She was Catholic; had been to a convent school near her home, a place called Lardwick-in-the-Fen. This was her first trip abroad. She talked a great deal about her religion: had, for a time, considered the son of God as a young lady will consider any eligible bachelor. But had realized eventually that of course he was not but maintained instead an immense harem clad in black, decked with rosaries. She would never stand for such competition, had therefore left the novitiate after a matter of weeks but not the Church: that, with its sad-faced statuary, its odor of candles and incense, formed along with an uncle Evelyn the twin foci of her serene orbit. The uncle, a wild or renegade sundowner, would arrive from Australia once a year bringing no gifts but prepared to weave as many yarns as the sisters could cope with. As far as Victoria remembered, he had never repeated himself. So she was given enough material to evolve between visits a private and imaginary sphere of influence, which she played with and within constantly: developing, exploring, manipulating. Especially during Mass: for here was the stage, the dramatic field already prepared, serviceable to a seedtime fancy. And so it came about that God wore a wide-awake hat and fought skirmishes with an aboriginal Satan out at the antipodes of the firmament, in the name and for the safekeeping of any Victoria.

Now the desire to feel pity can be seductive; it was always so for Porpentine. At this point he could only flick a rapid glance at Good-fellow's face and think with the sort of admiration pity once foundered in makes detestable: a stroke of genius, the Jameson raid. He chose that, he knew. He always knows. So do I.

One had to. He'd realized long before that women had no monopoly on what is called intuition; that in most men the faculty was latent, only becoming developed or painfully heightened at all in professions like this. But men being positivists and women more dreamy, having hunches still remained at base a feminine talent; so that like it or not they all—Moldweorp, Goodfellow, the pair from Brindisi—had to be part woman. Perhaps even in this maintenance of a threshold for compassion one dared not go beneath was some sort of recognition.

But like a Yorkshire sunset, certain things could not be afforded. Porpentine had realized this as a fledgling. You do not feel pity for the men you have to kill or the people you have to hurt. You do not feel any more than a vague *esprit de corps* toward the agents you are working with. Above all, you do not fall in love. Not if you want to succeed in espionage. God knew what preadolescent agonies were responsible; but somehow Porpentine had remained true to that code. He had grown up possessing a sly mind and was too honest not to use it. He stole from street-hawkers, could stack a deck at fifteen, would run away whenever fighting was useless. So that at some point, prowling any mews or alley in midcentury London, the supreme rightness of "the game for its own sake" must have occurred to him, and acted as an irresistible vector aimed toward 1900. Now he would say that any itinerary, with all its doublings-back, emergency stops, and hundred-kilometer feints remained transitory or accidental. Certainly it was convenient, necessary; but never gave an indication of the deeper truth that all of them operated in no conceivable Europe but rather in a zone forsaken by God, between the tropics of diplomacy, lines they were forbidden forever to cross. One had consequently to play that idealized colonial Englishman who, alone in the jungle, shaves every day, dresses for dinner every night, and is committed to St. George and no quarter as an article of love. Curious irony in that, of course. Porpentine grimaced to himself. Because both sides, his and Moldweorp's, had each in a different way done the unforgivable: had gone native. Somehow it had come about that one day neither man cared any longer which government he was working for. As if that prospect of a Final Clash were unable by men like them, through whatever frenzied twists and turns, to be evaded. Something had come to pass: who could guess what, or even when? In the Crimea, at Spicheren, at Khartum; it could make no difference. But so suddenly that there was a finite leap or omission in the maturing process—one fell asleep exhausted among immediacies: F.O. dispatches, Parliamentary resolutions; and awakened to find a tall specter grinning and gibbering over the foot of the bed, know that he was there to stay—hadn't they seen the apocalypse as an excuse for a glorious beano, a grand way to see the old century and their respective careers go out?

"You are so like him," the girl was saying, "my uncle Evelyn: tall, and fair, and oh! not really Lardwick-in-the-Fenish at all."

"Haw, haw," Goodfellow replied.

Hearing the languishment in that voice, Porpentine wondered idly if she were bud or bloom; or perhaps a petal blown off and having nothing to belong to any more. It was difficult to tell—getting more so every year—and he did not know if this were old age beginning to creep up on him at last or some flaw in the generation itself. His own had budded, bloomed, and, sensing some blight in the air, folded its petals up again like certain flowers at sunset. Would it be any use asking her?

"My God," Goodfellow said. They looked up to see an emaciated figure in evening clothes whose head seemed that of a nettled sparrow-hawk. The head guffawed, retaining its fierce expression. Victoria bubbled over in a laugh. "It's Hugh!" she cried, delighted.

"Indeed," echoed a voice inside. "Help me get it off, someone." Porpentine, obliging, stood on a chair to tug off the head.

"Hugh Bongo-Shaftsbury," said Goodfellow, ungracious.

"Harmakhis." Bongo-Shaftsbury indicated the hollow ceramic hawk-head. "God of Heliopolis and chief deity of Lower Egypt. Utterly genuine, this: a mask used in the ancient rituals." He seated himself next to Victoria. Goodfellow scowled. "Literally Horus on the horizon, also represented as a lion with the head of a man. Like the Sphinx."

"Oh," Victoria sighed, "the Sphinx." Enchanted, which did puzzle Porpentine: for this was a violation, was it not, so much rapture over the mongrel gods of Egypt? Her ideal should rightfully have been pure manhood or pure hawkhood; hardly the mixture.

They decided not to have liqueurs but to stay with the Vöslauer, which was off-vintage but only went for ten piastres.

"How far down the Nile do you intend to go?" asked Porpentine. "Mr. Goodfellow has mentioned your interest in Luxor."

"I feel it is fresh territory, sir," replied Bongo-Shaftsbury. "No first-rate work around the area since Grébaut discovered the tomb of the Theban priests back in 'ninety-one. Of course one should have a look round the pyramids at Gizeh, but that is pretty much old hat since Mr. Flinders Petrie's painstaking inspection of sixteen or seventeen years ago."

"I imagine," murmured Porpentine. He could have got the data, of course, from any Baedeker. At least there was a certain intensity or single-minded concern with matters archaeological which Porpentine was sure would drive Sir Alastair to frenzy before the Cook's tour was completed. Unless, like Porpentine and Goodfellow, Bongo-Shaftsbury intended to go no further than Cairo.

Porpentine hummed the aria from *Manon Lescaut* as Victoria poised prettily between the other two, attempting to keep equilibrium. The crowd in the restaurant had thinned out and across the street the Consulate was dark, save two or three lights in the upstairs rooms. Perhaps in a month all the windows would be blazing; perhaps the world would be blazing. Projected, the courses of Marchand and Kitchener would cross near Fashoda, in the district of Behr el-Abyad, some forty miles above the source of the White Nile. Lord Lansdowne, Secretary of State for War, had predicted 25 September as meeting-date in a secret dispatch to Cairo: a message both Porpentine and Moldweorp had seen. All at once a tic came dancing across Bongo-Shaftsbury's face; there was a time-lag of about five seconds before Porpentine—either intuitively or because of his suspicions about the archaeologist—reckoned who it was that stood behind his chair. Goodfellow nodded, sick and timid; said, civilly enough: "Lepsius, I say. Tired of the climate in Brindisi?" Lepsius. Porpentine hadn't even known the name. Goodfellow would have, of course. "Sudden business called me to Egypt," the agent hissed. Goodfellow sniffed at his wine. Soon: "Your traveling companion? I had rather hoped to see him again."

"Gone to Switzerland," Lepsius said. "The mountains, the clean winds. One can have enough, one day, of the sordidness of that South." They never lied. Who was his new partner?

"Unless you go far enough south," Goodfellow said. "I imagine far enough down the Nile one gets back to a kind of primitive cleanness."

Porpentine had been watching Bongo-Shaftsbury closely, since the tic. The face, lean and ravaged like the body, remained expressionless now; but that initial lapse had set Porpentine on his guard.

"Doesn't the law of the wild beast prevail down there?" Lepsius said. "There are no property rights, only fighting; and the victor wins all. Glory, life, power and property, all."

"Perhaps," Goodfellow said. "But in Europe, you know, we are civilized. Fortunately. Jungle-law is inadmissible."

Soon Lepsius took his leave, expressing the hope they would meet again at Cairo. Goodfellow was certain they would. Bongo-Shaftsbury had continued to sit unmoving and unreadable.

"What a queer gentleman," Victoria said.

"Is it queer," Bongo-Shaftsbury said, deliberately reckless, "to favor the clean over the impure?"

So. Porpentine had wearied of self-congratulation ten years ago. Goodfellow looked embarrassed. So: cleanness. After the deluge, the long famine, the earthquake. A desert-region's cleanness: bleached bones, tombs of dead cultures. Armageddon would sweep the house of Europe so. Did that make Porpentine champion only of cobwebs, rubbish, offscourings? He remembered a night-visit in Rome, years ago, to a contact who lived over a bordello near the Pantheon. Moldweorp himself had followed, taking station near a street-lamp to wait. In the middle of the interview Porpentine chanced to look out the window. A streetwalker was propositioning Moldweorp. They could not hear the conversation, only see a slow and unkind fury recast his features to a wrath-mask; only watch him raise his cane and begin to slash methodically at the girl until she lay ragged at his feet. Porpentine was first to break out of that paralysis, open the door, and race down to the street. When he reached her Moldweorp was gone. His comfort was automatic, perhaps out of some abstract sense of duty, while she screamed into the tweed of his coat. *"Mi chiamava sozzura,"* she could say: he called me filth. Porpentine had tried to forget the incident. Not because it was ugly but because it showed his terrible flaw so clear: reminding him it was not Moldweorp he hated so much as a perverse idea of what is clean; not the girl he sympathized with so much as her humanity. Fate, it occurred to him then, chooses weird agents. Moldweorp somehow could love and hate individually. The roles being, it seemed, reversed, Porpentine found it necessary to believe if one appointed oneself savior of humanity that perhaps one must love that humanity only in the abstract. For any descent to the personal level can make a purpose less pure. Whereas a disgust at individual human perversity might as easily avalanche into a rage for apocalypse. He could never bring himself to hate the Moldweorp crew, any more than they could avoid genuine anxiety over his welfare. Worse, Porpentine could never make a try for any of them; would remain instead an inept Cremonini singing Des Grieux, expressing certain passions by calculated musical covenant, would never leave a stage where vehemences and tendresses are merely forte and piano, where the Paris gate at Amiens foreshortens mathematically and is illuminated by the precise glow of calcium light. He remembered his performance in the rain that afternoon: he like Victoria needed the proper setting. Anything intensely European, it seemed, inspired him to heights of inanity.

It got late; only two or three tourists left scattered about the room. Victoria showed no signs of fatigue, Goodfellow and Bongo-Shaftsbury argued politics. A waiter lounged two tables away, impatient. He had the delicate build and high narrow skull of the Copt, and Porpentine realized this had been the only non-European in the place, all along. Any such discord should have been spotted immediately: Porpentine's slip. He had no use for Egypt, had sensitive skin and avoided its sun as if any tinge of it might make part of him the East's own. He cared about regions not on the Continent only so far as they might affect its fortunes and no further; the Fink restaurant could as well have been an inferior Voisin's.

At length the party arose, paid, left. Victoria skipped ahead across rue Cherif Pacha to the hotel. Behind them a closed carriage came rattling out of the drive beside the Austrian Consulate and dashed away hell-for-leather down rue de Rosette, into the wet night.

"Someone is in a hurry," Bongo-Shaftsbury noted.

"Indeed," said Goodfellow. To Porpentine: "At the Gare du Caire. The train leaves at eight." Porpentine gave them all good night and returned to his *pied-à-terre* in the Turkish quarter. Such choice of lodgings violated nothing; for he considered the Porte part of the Western World. He fell asleep reading an old and mutilated edition of *Antony and Cleopatra* and wondering if it were still possible to fall under the spell of Egypt: its tropic unreality, its curious gods.

At 7:40 he stood on the platform of the Gare, watching the porters from Cook's and Gaze's pile boxes and trunks. Across the double line of tracks was a small park, green with palms and acacias.

Porpentine kept to the shadow of the station-house. Soon the others arrived. He noticed the tiniest flicker of communication pass between Bongo-Shaftsbury and Lepsius. The morning express pulled in, amid sudden commotion on the platform. Porpentine turned to see Lepsius in pursuit of an Arab, who had apparently stolen his valise. Goodfellow had already gone into action. Sprinting across the platform, blond mane flapping wild, he cornered the Arab in a doorway, took back the valise and surrendered his quarry to a fat policeman in a pith helmet. Lepsius watched him snake-eyed and silent as he handed back the valise.

Aboard the train they split up into two adjoining compartments, Victoria, her father, and Goodfellow sharing the one next the rear platform. Porpentine felt that Sir Alastair would have been less miserable in his company, but wanted to be sure of Bongo-Shaftsbury. The train pulled out at five past eight, heading into the sun. Porpentine leaned back and let Mildred ramble on about mineralogy. Bongo-Shaftsbury kept silent until the train had passed Sidi Gaber and swung toward the southeast.

He said: "Do you play with dolls, Mildred?" Porpentine gazed out the window. He felt something unpleasant was about to happen. He could see a procession of dark-colored camels with their drivers, moving slowly along the embankments of a canal. Far down the canal were the small white sails of barges.

"When I'm not out after rocks," said Mildred.

Bongo-Shaftsbury said: "I'll wager you do not have any dolls that walk, or speak, or are able to jump rope. Now do you."

Porpentine tried to concentrate on a group of Arabs who lazed about far down the embankment, evaporating part of the water in Lake Mareotis for salt. The train was going at top speed. He soon lost them in the distance.

"No," said Mildred, doubtful.

Bongo-Shaftsbury said: "But have you never seen dolls like that? Such lovely dolls, and clockwork inside. Dolls that do everything perfectly, because of the machinery. Not like real little boys and girls at all. Real children cry, and act sullen, and won't behave. These dolls are much nicer."

On the right now were fallow cotton-fields and mud huts. Occasionally one of the fellahin would be seen going down to the canal for water. Almost out of his field of vision Porpentine saw Bongo-Shaftsbury's hands, long and starved-nervous, lying still, one on each knee.

"They sound quite nice," said Mildred. Though she knew she was being talked down to her voice was unsteady. Possibly something in the archaeologist's face frightened her.

Bongo-Shaftsbury said: "Would you like to see one, Mildred?" It was going too far. For the man had been talking to Porpentine, the girl was being used. For what? Something was wrong.

"Have you one with you?" she wondered, timid. Despite himself Porpentine moved his head away from the window to watch Bongo-Shaftsbury.

Who smiled: "Oh yes." And pushed back the sleeve of his coat to remove a cuff-link. He began to roll back the cuff of his shirt. Then thrust the naked underside of his forearm at the girl. Porpentine recoiled, thinking: Lord love a duck. Bongo-Shaftsbury is insane. Shiny and black against the unsunned flesh was a miniature electric switch, single-pole, double-throw, sewn into the skin. Thin silver wires ran from its terminals up the arm, disappearing under the sleeve.

The young often show a facile acceptance of the horrible. Mildred began to shake. "No," she said, "no: you are not one."

"But I am," protested Bongo-Shaftsbury, smiling, "Mildred. The wires run up into my brain. When the switch is closed like this I act the way I do now. When it is thrown the other—"

The girl shrank away. "Papa," she cried.

"Everything works by electricity," Bongo-Shaftsbury explained, soothing. "And it is simple, and clean."

"Stop it," Porpentine said.

Bongo-Shaftsbury whirled to him. "Why?" he whispered. "Why? For her? Touched by her fright, are you? Or is it for yourself?"

Porpentine retreated, bashful. "One doesn't frighten a child, sir."

"General principles. Damn you." He looked petulant, ready to cry.

There was noise out in the passageway. Goodfellow had been shouting in pain. Porpentine leaped up, shoving Bongo-Shaftsbury aside, and rushed out into the passageway. The door to the rear platform was open: in front of it Goodfellow and an Arab fought, tangled and clawing. Porpentine saw the flash of a pistol-barrel. He moved in cautiously, circling, choosing his point. When the Arab's throat was exposed sufficiently Porpentine kicked, catching him across the windpipe. He collapsed rattling. Goodfellow took the pistol. Pushed back his forelock, sides heaving. "Ta."

"Same one?" Porpentine said.

"No. The railroad police are conscientious. And it is possible, you know, to tell them apart. This is different."

"Cover him, then." To the Arab: "*Auz e. Ma tkhafsh minni.*"

The Arab's head rolled toward Porpentine, he tried to grin but his eyes were sick. A blue mark was appearing on his throat. He could not talk. Sir Alastair and Victoria had appeared, anxious.

"May have been a friend of the fellow I caught back at the Gare," Goodfellow explained easily. Porpentine helped the Arab to his feet. "*Ruh.* Go back. Don't let us see you again." The Arab moved off. "You're not going to let him go?" Sir Alastair rumbled. Goodfellow was magnanimous. He gave a short speech about charity and turning the other cheek which was well received by Victoria but which seemed to nauseate her father. The party resumed their places in the compartments, though Mildred had decided to stay with Sir Alastair.

Half an hour later the train pulled into Damanhur. Porpentine saw Lepsius get off two cars ahead and go inside the station-house. Around them stretched the green country of the Delta. Two minutes later the Arab got off and cut across on a diagonal to the buffet entrance; met Lepsius coming out with a bottle of red wine. He was rubbing the mark on his throat and apparently wanted to speak to Lepsius. The agent glared and cuffed him across the head. "No bakshish," he announced. Porpentine settled back, closed his eyes without looking at Bongo-Shaftsbury. Without even saying aha. The train began to move. So. What did they call clean, then? Not observing The Rules, surely. If so they had reversed course. They'd never played so foul before. Could it mean that this meeting at Fashoda would be important: might even be The One? He opened his eyes to watch Bongo-Shaftsbury, engrossed in a book: Sidney J. Webb's *Industrial Democracy.* Porpentine shrugged. Time was his fellow professionals became adept through practice. Learned ciphers by breaking them, customs officials by evading them, some opponents by killing them. Now the new ones read books: young lads, full of theory and (he'd decided) a faith in nothing but the perfection of their own internal machinery. He flinched, remembering the knife-switch, fastened to Bongo-Shaftsbury's arm like a malignant insect. Moldweorp must have been the oldest spy active but in professional ethics he and Porpentine did belong to the same generation. Porpentine doubted if Moldweorp approved of the young man opposite.

Their silence continued for twenty-five miles. The express passed by farms which began to look more and more prosperous, fellahin who worked in the fields at a faster pace, small factories and heaps of ancient ruin and tall flowering tamarisks. The Nile was in flood: stretching away from them, a glittering network of irrigation canals and small basins caught the water, conducted it through wheat and barley fields which extended to the horizon. The train reached the Rosetta arm of the Nile; crossed high over it by a long, narrow iron bridge, entered the station at Kafr ez-Zaiyat, where it stopped. Bongo-Shaftsbury closed the book, arose and left the compartment. A few moments later Goodfellow entered, holding Mildred by the hand.

"He felt you might want to get some sleep," Goodfellow said. "I should have thought. I was preoccupied with Mildred's sister." Porpentine snorted, shut his eyes and fell asleep before the train started to move. He awoke half an hour out of Cairo. "All secure," Goodfellow said. The outlines of the pyramids were visible off to the west. Closer to the city gardens and villas began to appear. The train reached Cairo's Principal Station about noon.

Somehow, Goodfellow and Victoria managed to be in a phaeton and away before the rest of the party got on the platform. "Damme," Sir Alastair puzzled, "what are they doing, eloping?" Bongo-Shaftsbury looked properly outwitted. Porpentine, having slept, felt rather in a holiday mood. "*Arabiyeh*," he roared, gleeful. A dilapidated pinto-colored barouche came clattering up and Porpentine pointed after the phaeton: "A double piastre if you catch them." The driver grinned; Porpentine hustled everyone into the carriage. Sir Alastair protested, muttering about Mr. Conan Doyle. Bongo-Shaftsbury guffawed and away they galloped, around a sharp curve to the left, over the el-Lemun bridge and pell-mell down Sharia Bab el-Hadid. Mildred made faces at other tourists on foot or riding donkeys, Sir Alastair smiled tentatively. Ahead Porpentine could see Victoria in the phaeton tiny and graceful, holding Goodfellow's arm and leaning back to let the wind blow her hair.

The two carriages arrived at Shepheard's Hotel in a dead heat. All but Porpentine alighted and moved toward the hotel. "Check me in," he called to Goodfellow, "I must see a friend." The friend was a porter at the Hotel Victoria, four blocks south and west. While Porpentine sat in the kitchen discussing game birds with a mad chef he had known at Cannes, the porter crossed the street to the British Consulate, going in by the servants' entrance. He emerged after fifteen minutes and returned to the hotel. Soon an order for lunch was brought in to the kitchen. "*Crème*" had been misspelled to read "*chem.*"; "*Lyonnaise*" was spelled without an *e*. Both were underlined. Porpentine nodded, thanked everyone, and left. He caught a cab and rode up Sharia el-Maghrabi, through the luxurious park at the end; soon arrived at the Crédit Lyonnais.

Nearby was a small pharmacy. He entered and asked about the prescription for laudanum he had brought in to be filled the day before. He was handed an envelope whose contents, once more in the cab, he checked. A raise of £50 for him and Goodfellow: good news. They would both be able to stay at Shepheard's.

Back at the hotel they set about decoding their instructions. F.O. knew nothing about an assassination plot. Of course not. No reason for one, if you were thinking only about the immediate question of who would control the Nile Valley. Porpentine wondered what had happened to diplomacy. He knew people who had worked under Palmerston, a shy, humorous old man for whom the business was a jolly game of blindman's-buff, where every day one reached out and touched, and was touched by, the Specter's cold hand.

"We're on our own, then," Goodfellow pointed out.

"Ah," Porpentine agreed. "Suppose we work it this way: set a thief to catch one. Make plans to do Cromer in ourselves. Go through the motions only, of course. That way whenever they get an opportunity, we can be right on the spot to prevent them."

"Stalk the Consul-General," Goodfellow grew enthusiastic, "like a bloody grouse. Why we haven't done that since—"

"Never mind," Porpentine said.

That night Porpentine commissioned a cab and roved about the city until early morning. The coded instructions had told them nothing more than to bide time: Goodfellow was taking care of that, having escorted Victoria to an Italian summer-theater performance at the Ezbekiyeh Garden. In the course of the night Porpentine visited a girl who lived in the Quartier Rosetti and was the mistress of a junior clerk in the British Consulate; a jewel merchant in the Muski who had lent financial support to the Mahdists and did not wish now that the movement was crushed to have his sympathies known; a minor Esthetic who had fled England on a narcotics charge to the land of no extradition and who was a distant cousin of the valet to Mr. Raphael Borg, the British Consul; and a pimp named Varkumian who claimed to know every assassin in Cairo. From this fine crew Porpentine returned to his room at three in the morning. But hesitated at the door, having heard movement behind it. Only one thing for it: at the end of the corridor was this window with a ledge outside. He grimaced. But then everyone knew that spies were continually crawling about window-ledges, high above the streets of exotic cities. Feeling an utter fool, Porpentine climbed out and got on the ledge. He looked down: there was a drop of about fifteen feet into some bushes. Yawning he made his way quickly but clumsily toward the corner of the building. The ledge became narrower at the corner. As he stood with each foot on a different side and the edge of the building bisecting him from eyebrows to abdomen he lost his balance and fell. On the way down it occurred to him to use an obscene word; he hit the shrubbery with a crash, rolled, and lay there tapping his fingers. After he had smoked half a cigarette he got to his feet and noticed a tree next his own window, easily climbable. He ascended puffing and cursing; crawled out on a limb, straddled it, and peered inside.

Goodfellow and the girl lay on Porpentine's bed, white and exhausted-looking by street-light: her eyes, mouth, and nipples were little dark bruises against the flesh. She cradled Goodfellow's white head in a net or weaving of fingers while he cried, streaking her breasts with tears. "I'm sorry," he was saying, "the Transvaal, a wound. They told me it was not serious." Porpentine, having no idea how this sort of thing worked, fell back on alternatives: (a) Goodfellow was being honorable, (b) was truly impotent and had therefore lied to Porpentine about a long list of conquests, (c) simply had no intention of getting involved with Victoria. Whichever it was, Porpentine felt as always an alien. He swung down by one arm from the limb, nonplused, until the stub of the cigarette burned down to his fingers and made him swear softly; and because he knew it was not really the burn he cursed he began to worry. It was not only seeing Goodfellow weak. He dropped into the bushes and lay there thinking about his own threshold, sustained proudly for twenty years of service. Though it had been hammered at before, he suspected this was the first time it had shown itself truly vulnerable. A pang of superstitious terror caught him flat on his back in the bushes. It seemed he knew, for a space of seconds, that this indeed was The One. Apocalypse would surely begin at Fashoda if for no other reason than that he felt his own so at hand. But soon: gradually, with each lungful of a fresh cigarette's smoke, the old control seeped back to him; and he got at last to his feet, still shaky, walked around to the hotel entrance and up to his room. This time he pretended to've lost his key, making bewildered noises to cover the girl as she gathered her clothing and fled through connecting doors to her own room. All he felt by the time Goodfellow opened was embarrassment, and that he had lived with for a long time.

The theater had presented *Manon Lescaut.* In the shower next morning Goodfellow attempted to sing *"Donna non vidi mai."* "Stop," said Porpentine. "Would you like to hear how it should be done?" Goodfellow howled. "I doubt you could sing Ta-ra-ra-boom-di-ay without mucking it up."

But Porpentine could not resist. He thought it a harmless compromise. "*A dirle io t'amo,*" he caroled, "*a nuova vita l'alma mia si desta.*" It was appalling; one got the impression he had once worked in a music-hall. He was no Des Grieux. Des Grieux knows, soon as he sees that young lady just off the diligence from Arras, what will happen. He does not make false starts or feints, this chevalier, has nothing to decode, no double game to play. Porpentine envied him. As he dressed he whistled the aria. Last night's moment of weakness bloomed again behind his eyes. He thought, if I step below the threshold, you know, I shall never get back again.

At two that afternoon the Consul-General emerged from the front door of the Consulate and entered a carriage. Porpentine watched from a deserted room on the third floor of the Hotel Victoria. Lord Cromer was a perfect target but this vantage at least was unavailable to any hired assassin-in-opposition as long as Porpentine's friends kept on the alert. The archaeologist had taken Victoria and Mildred to tour the bazaars and the Tombs of the Khalifs. Goodfellow was sitting in a closed landau directly under the window. Unobtrusive (as Porpentine watched) he started off behind the carriage, keeping at a safe distance. Porpentine left the hotel, strolled up Sharia el-Maghrabi. At the next corner he noticed a church off to his right; heard loud organ music. On a sudden whim he entered the church. Sure enough, it was Sir Alastair, booming away. It took the unmusical Porpentine some five minutes to come aware of the devastation Sir Alastair was wreaking on the keys and pedals. Music laced the interior of the tiny, Gothic house with certain intricate veinings, weird petal-shapes. But it was violent and somehow Southern foliage. Head and fingers uncontrollable for a neglect of his daughter's or any purity, for the music's own shape, for Bach—was it Bach?—himself? Foreign and a touch shabby, uncomprehending, how could Porpentine say. But was yet unable to pull away until the music stopped abruptly, leaving the church's cavity to reverberate. Only then did he withdraw unseen out into the sun, adjusting his neckcloth as if it were all the difference between wholeness and disintegration.

Lord Cromer was doing nothing to protect himself, Goodfellow reported that night. Porpentine, having rechecked with the valet's cousin, knew the word had gone through. He shrugged, calling the Consul-General a nitwit: tomorrow was 25 September. He left the hotel at eleven and went by carriage to a *Brauhaus* a few blocks north of the Ezbekiyeh Garden. He sat alone at a small table against the wall, listening to maudlin accordion music which must surely have been old as Bach; closed his eyes, letting a cigarette droop from his lips. A waitress brought Munich beer.

"Mr. Porpentine." He looked up. "I followed you." He nodded, waited. Victoria sat down. "Papa would die if he ever found out," gazing at him defiant. The accordion stopped. The waitress left two Krugers.

He pursed his lips, ruthful in that quiet. So she'd sought out and found the woman in him; the very first civilian to do so. He did not go through any routine of asking how she knew. She could not have seen him through the window. He said:

"He was sitting in the German church this afternoon, playing Bach as if it were all he had left. So that he may have guessed."

She hung her head, a mustache of foam on her upper lip. From across the canal came the faint whistle of the express for Alexandria. "You love Goodfellow," he hazarded. Never had he been down so far: he was a tourist here. Could have used, at the moment, any Baedeker of the heart. Almost drowned in a fresh wailing of the accordion her whisper came: yes. Then had Goodfellow told her.
. . . He raised his eyebrows, she shook her head no. Amazing, the knowing of one another, these wordless flickerings. "Whatever I may think I have guessed," she said. "Of course you can't trust me, but I have to say it. It's true." How far down could one go, before
. . . Desperate, Porpentine: "What do you want me to do, then?" She, twisting ringlets round her fingers, would not look at him. Soon: "Nothing. Only understand." If Porpentine had believed in the devil he would have said: you have been sent. Go back and tell him, them, it is no use. The accordionist spotted Porpentine and the girl, recognized them as English. "Had the devil any son," he sang mischievous in German, "it was surely Palmerston." A few Germans laughed, Porpentine winced: the song was fifty years old at least. But a few still remembered.

Varkumian came weaving his way among tables, late. Victoria saw him and excused herself. Varkumian's report was brief: no action. Porpentine sighed. It left only one thing to do. Throw a scare into the Consulate, put them on their guard.

So next day they began "stalking" Cromer in earnest. Porpentine woke up in a foul mood. He donned a red beard and a pearl-gray morning hat and visited the Consulate, posing as an Irish tourist. The staff weren't having any: he got ejected forcibly. Goodfellow had a better idea: "Lob a bomb," he cried. Happily his knowledge of munitions was faulty as his aim. The bomb, instead of falling safely on the lawn, soared in through a window of the Consulate, sending one of the proverbial charwomen into hysterics (though it proved of course to be a dud) and nearly getting Goodfellow arrested.

At noon Porpentine visited the kitchen of the Hotel Victoria to find the place in a turmoil. The meeting at Fashoda had taken place. The Situation had turned to a Crisis. Upset, he dashed out into the street, commandeered a carriage, and tore off in search of Goodfellow. He found him two hours later sleeping in his hotel room where Porpentine had left him. In a rage he emptied a pitcher of ice-water over Goodfellow's head. Bongo-Shaftsbury appeared in the doorway grinning. Porpentine hurled the empty pitcher at him as he vanished down the corridor. "Where's the Consul-General?" Goodfellow inquired, amiable and sleepy. "Get dressed," bellowed Porpentine.

They found the clerk's mistress lying lazy in a patch of sunlight, peeling a mandarin orange. She told them Cromer was planning to attend the opera at eight. Up to then, she could not say. They went to the shop of the chemist, who had nothing for them. Barreling through the Garden Porpentine asked about the Wrens. They were at Heliopolis, as far as Goodfellow knew. "What the bloody hell is wrong with everyone?" Porpentine wanted to know. "Nobody knows anything." They could do nothing till eight; so sat in front of a café in the Garden and drank wine. Egypt's sun beat down, somehow threatening. There was no shade. The fear that had found him night before last now crawled along the flanks of Porpentine's jaw and up his temples. Even Goodfellow seemed nervous.

At a quarter to eight they strolled along the path to the theater, purchased tickets in the orchestra, and settled down to wait. Soon the Consul-General's party arrived and sat near them. Lepsius and Bongo-Shaftsbury drifted in from either side and stationed themselves in boxes; forming, with Lord Cromer as vertex, an angle of 120 degrees. "Bother," said Goodfellow. "We should have got some elevation." Four policemen came marching down the center aisle, glanced up at Bongo-Shaftsbury. He pointed to Porpentine. "My Gawd," Goodfellow moaned. Porpentine closed his eyes. He'd blown it, all right. This was what happened when one blundered right in. The policemen surrounded them, stood at attention. "All right," Porpentine said. He and Goodfellow arose and were escorted out of the theater. "We shall desire your passports," one of them said. Behind them on the breeze came the first sprightly chords of the

opening scene. They marched down a narrow path, two police behind, two in front. Signals had, of course, been arranged years before. "I shall want to see the British Consul," Porpentine said and
spun, drawing an old single-shot pistol. Goodfellow had the other
two covered. The policeman who had asked for their passports
glowered. "No one said they would be armed," another protested.
Methodically, with four raps to the skull, the policemen were neu-
tralized and rolled into the underbrush. "A fool trick," Goodfellow
muttered: "we were lucky." Porpentine was already running back
toward the theater. They took the stairs two at a time and searched
for an empty box. "Here," Goodfellow said. They edged into the box.
It was almost directly across from Bongo-Shaftsbury's. That would
put them next to Lepsius. "Keep down," Porpentine said. They
crouched, peering between small golden balusters. On stage Ed-
mondo and the students chaffed the Romantic, horny Des Grieux.
Bongo-Shaftsbury was checking the action of a small pistol. "Stand
by," Goodfellow whispered. The postilion horn of the diligence was
heard. The coach came rattling and creaking into the inn court-
yard. Bongo-Shaftsbury raised his pistol. Porpentine said: "Lepsius.
Next door." Goodfellow withdrew. The diligence bounced to a halt.
Porpentine centered his sights on Bongo-Shaftsbury, then let the
muzzle drift down and to the right until it pointed at Lord Cromer.
It occurred to him that he could end everything for himself right
now, never have to worry about Europe again. He had a sick moment of uncertainty. Now how serious had anyone ever been? Was
aping Bongo-Shaftsbury's tactics any less real than opposing them?
Like a bloody grouse, Goodfellow had said. Manon was helped
down from the coach. Des Grieux gaped, was transfixed, read his
destiny on her eyes. Someone was standing behind Porpentine. He
glanced back, quickly in that moment of hopeless love, and saw
Moldweorp there looking decayed, incredibly old, face set in a hideous though compassionate smile. Panicking, Porpentine turned
and fired blindly, perhaps at Bongo-Shaftsbury, perhaps at Lord
Cromer. He could not see and would never be sure which one he
had intended as target. Bongo-Shaftsbury shoved the pistol inside
his coat and disappeared. A fight was on out in the corridor. Porpentine pushed the old man aside and ran out in time to see Lepsius
tear away from Goodfellow and flee toward the stairs. "Please, dear
fellow," Moldweorp gasped. "Don't go after them. You are outnum-
bered." Porpentine had reached the top step. "Three to two," he
muttered.
     "More than three. My chief and his, and staff personnel . . ."

Which stopped Porpentine dead. "Your—"

"I have been under orders, you know." The old man sounded apologetic. Then, all in a nostalgic rush: "The Situation, don't you know, it is serious this time, we are all for it—"

Porpentine looked back, exasperated. "Go away," he yelled, "go away and die." And was certain only in a dim way that the interchange of words had now, at last, been decisive.

"The big chief himself," Goodfellow remarked as they ran down the stairs. "Things must be bad." A hundred yards ahead Bongo-Shaftsbury and Lepsius leaped into a carriage. Surprisingly nimble, Moldweorp had taken a short cut. He emerged from an exit to the left of Porpentine and Goodfellow and joined the others. "Let them go," Goodfellow said.

"Are you still taking orders from me?" Without waiting for an answer Porpentine found a phaeton, got in and swung around to pursue. Goodfellow grabbed on and hauled himself up. They galloped down Sharia Kamel Pasha, scattering donkeys, tourists, and dragomans. In front of Shepheard's they nearly ran down Victoria, who had come out into the street. They lost ten seconds while Goodfellow helped her aboard. Porpentine could not protest. Again she had known. Something had passed out of his hands. He was only beginning to recognize, somewhere, a quite enormous betrayal.

It was no longer single combat. Had it ever been? Lepsius, Bongo-Shaftsbury, all the others, had been more than merely tools or physical extensions of Moldweorp. They were all in it; all had a stake, acted as a unit. Under orders. Whose orders? Anything human? He doubted: like a bright hallucination against Cairo's night-sky he saw (it may have been only a line of cloud) a bell-shaped curve, remembered perhaps from some younger F.O. operative's mathematics text. Unlike Constantine on the verge of battle, he could not afford, this late, to be converted at any sign. Only curse himself, silent, for wanting so to believe in a fight according to the duello, even in this period of history. But they—no, it—had not been playing those rules. Only statistical odds. When had he stopped facing an adversary and taken on a Force, a Quantity?

The bell curve is the curve for a normal or Gaussian distribution. An invisible clapper hangs beneath it. Porpentine (though only half-suspecting) was being tolled down.

The carriage ahead took a sharp left, moving toward the canal. There it turned left again, and raced alongside the thin ribbon of water. The moon had risen, half of it, fat and white. "They're going for the Nile Bridge," Goodfellow said. They passed the Khedive's palace and clattered over the bridge. The river flowed dark and viscous under them. On the other side they turned south and sped through moonlight between the Nile and the grounds of the vice-regal palace. Ahead the quarry swung right. "Damned if it isn't the road to the pyramids," Goodfellow said. Porpentine nodded: "About five and a half miles." They made the turn and passed the prison and the village of Gizeh, hit a curve, crossed the railroad tracks and headed due west. "Oh," Victoria said quietly, "we're going to see the Sphinx."

"In the moonlight," Goodfellow added, wry. "Leave her alone," Porpentine said. They were silent for the rest of the way, making little gain. Around them irrigation ditches interlaced and sparkled. The two carriages passed fellahin villages and water-wheels. No sound at all in the night save wheels and hoofbeats. And the wind of their passage. As they neared the edge of the desert Goodfellow said, "We're catching up." The road began to slope upward. Protected from the desert by a wall five feet high, it wound around to the left, ascending. Ahead of them suddenly the other carriage lurched and crashed into the wall. The occupants scrambled out and climbed the rest of the way on foot. Porpentine continued on around the curve, stopping about 100 yards from the great pyramid of Kheops. Moldweorp, Lepsius, and Bongo-Shaftsbury were nowhere in sight.

"Let's have a look about," Porpentine said. They rounded the corner of the pyramid. The Sphinx crouched 600 yards to the south. "Damn," Goodfellow said. Victoria pointed. "There," she cried: "going toward the Sphinx." They moved over the rough ground at a dead run. Moldweorp had apparently twisted his ankle. The other two were helping him. Porpentine drew his pistol. "You are for it, old man," he shouted. Bongo-Shaftsbury turned and fired. Goodfellow said: "What are we going to do with them anyway? Let them go." Porpentine did not answer. A moment or so later they brought the Moldweorp agents to bay against the right flank of the great Sphinx.

"Put it down," Bongo-Shaftsbury wheezed. "That is a single-shot, I have a revolver." Porpentine had not reloaded. He shrugged, grinned, tossed the pistol into the sand. Beside him Victoria looked up rapt at the lion, man, or god towering over them. Bongo-Shaftsbury pushed up his shirt-cuff, opened the switch and closed it the other way. A boyish gesture. Lepsius stood in the shadows, Moldweorp smiled. "Now," Bongo-Shaftsbury said. "Let them go," Porpentine said. Bongo-Shaftsbury nodded. "It is no concern of theirs," he agreed. "This is between you and the Chief, is it not?" Ho, ho, thought Porpentine: couldn't it have been? Like Des Grieux he must have his delusion even now; could never admit himself entirely a gull. Goodfellow took Victoria's hand and they moved away, back toward the carriage, the girl gazing back restless, eyes glowing at the Sphinx.

"You screamed at the Chief," Bongo-Shaftsbury announced. "You said: go away and die."

Porpentine put his hands behind his back. Of course. Had they been waiting for this, then? For fifteen years? He'd crossed some threshold without knowing. Mongrel now, no longer pure. He turned to watch Victoria move away, all tender and winsome for her Sphinx. Mongrel, he supposed, is only another way of saying human. After the final step you could not, nothing could, be clean. It was almost as if they'd tried for Goodfellow because he had stepped below the threshold that morning at the Gare du Caire. Now Porpentine had performed his own fatal act of love or charity by screaming at the Chief. And found out, shortly after, what he'd really screamed at. The two—act and betrayal—canceled out. Canceled to zero. Did they always? Oh God. He turned again to Moldweorp.

His Manon?

"You have been good enemies," he said at last. It sounded wrong to him. Perhaps if there had been more time, time to learn the new role . . .

It was all they needed. Goodfellow heard the shot, turned in time to see Porpentine fall to the sand. He cried out; watched the three turn and move away. Perhaps they would walk straight out into the Libyan desert and keep walking till they reached the shore of some sea. Soon he turned to the girl, shaking his head. He took her hand and they went to find the phaeton. Sixteen years later, of course, he was in Sarajevo, loitering among crowds assembled to greet the Archduke Francis Ferdinand. Rumors of an assassination, a possible spark to apocalypse. He must be there to prevent it if he could. His body had become stooped and much of his hair had fallen out. From time to time he squeezed the hand of his latest conquest, a blond barmaid with a mustache who described him to her friends as a simple-minded Englishman, not much good in bed but liberal with his money.

Gal Young Un

The house was invisible from the road which wound, almost untraveled, through the flat-woods. Once every five days a turpentine
wagon creaked down the ruts, and Negroes moved like shadows
among the pines. A few hunters in season came upon them chipping
boxes, scraping aromatic gum from red pots into encrusted buckets;
inquired the way and whether quail or squirrel or turkey had been
seen. Then hunters and turpentiners moved again along the road,
stepping on violets and yellow pitcher-plants that rimmed the edges.

The Negroes were aware of the house. It stood a few hundred
yards away, hidden behind two live oaks, isolated and remote in a
patch of hammock. It was a tall square two stories. The woman
who gave them water from her well when the nearby branch was
dry looked to them like the house, tall and bare and lonely, weathered gray, like its unpainted cypress. She seemed forgotten.

The two white men, hunting lazily down the road, did not remember—if they had ever known—that a dwelling stood here. Flushing a covey of quail that flung themselves like feathered bronze
discs at the cover of the hammock, their first shots flicked through
the twin oaks. They followed their pointer dog on the trail of single
birds and stopped short in amazement. Entering the north fringe
of the hammock, they had come out on a sandy open yard. A woman
was watching them from the back stoop of an old house.

"Shootin' mighty close, men," she called.

Her voice sounded unused, like a rusty iron hinge.

The older man whistled in the dog, ranging feverishly in the
low palmettos. The younger swaggered to the porch. He pushed
back the black slouch hat from his brazen eyes.

"Never knowed nobody lived in six miles o' here."

His tone was insolent. He drew a flattened package of cigarettes
from his corduroy hunting jacket, lighted one, and waited for her

to begin scolding. Women always quarreled with him. Middle-aged women, like this one, quarreled earnestly; young ones snapped at him playfully.

"It's a long ways from anybody, ain't it?" she agreed.

He stared at her between puffs.

"Jesus, yes."

"I don't keer about you shootin'," she said. "It's purely sociable, hearin' men folks acrost the woods. A shot come thu a winder jest now, that's all the reason I spoke."

The intruders shifted their shotguns uneasily. The older man touched his finger to his cap.

"That's all right, ma'am."

His companion strolled to the stone curbing of an open well. He peered into its depths, shimmering where the sun of high noon struck vertically.

"Good water?"

"The finest ever. Leave me fetch you a clean cup."

She turned into the house for a white china coffee cup. The men wound up a bucket of water on creaking ropes. The older man drank politely from the proffered cup. The other guzzled directly from the bucket. He reared back his head like a satisfied hound, dripping a stream of crystal drops from his red mouth.

"Ain't your dog thirsty? Here—reckon my ol' cat won't fuss if he drinks outen his dish." The woman stroked the animal's flanks as he lapped. "Ain't he a fine feller?"

The hunters began to edge away.

"Men, I jest got common rations, bacon an' biscuit an' coffee, but you're plumb welcome to set down with me."

"No, thank you, ma'am." They looked at the sun. "Got to be moseyin' home."

The younger man was already on his way, sucking a straw. The other fumbled in his game-pocket.

"Sorry we come so clost upon you, lady. How 'bout a bird fer your dinner?"

She reached out a large hand for the quail.

"I'd shore thank you fer it. I'm a good shot on squirrel, an' turkeys when I got 'em roosted. Birds is hard without no dog to point 'em. I gits hungry fer quail . . ."

Her voice trailed off as the hunters walked through the pines toward the road. She waved her hand in case they should turn around. They did not look back.

The man was hunting alone because he had been laughed at. His cronies in the Florida village, to which he had returned after a few years' wandering, knew that he detested solitude. It was alien to him, a silent void into which he sank as into quicksand. He had stopped at the general store to pick up a hunting partner. The men lounging there hours at a time were usually willing to go with him. This time none was ready.

"Come go with me, Willy," he insisted. "I cain't go by myself."

The storekeeper called over his shoulder, weighing out a quarter's worth of water-ground meal for a Negro:

"You'll git ketched out alone in the woods sometime, Trax, an' nobody won't know who 'tis."

The men guffawed.

"Trax always got to git him a buddy."

His smoldering eyes flared at them. He spat furiously across the rough pine floor of the store.

"I ain't got to git me none o' these sorry catbirds."

He had clattered down the wooden steps, spitting angrily every few feet. They were jealous, he thought, because he had been over on the east coast. He had turned instinctively down the south road out of the village. Old man Blaine had brought him this way last week. He hunted carelessly for two or three hours, taking pot shots at several coveys that rose under his feet. His anger made him miss the birds widely. It was poor sport without a companion and a dog.

Now he realized that he was lost. As a boy he had hunted these woods, but always with other boys and men. He had gone through them unseeing, stretching his young muscles luxuriously, absorbing lazily the rich Florida sun, cooling his face at every running branch. His shooting had been careless, avid. He liked to see the brown birds tumble in midair. He liked to hunt with the pack, to gorge on the game dinners they cooked by lake shores under oak trees. When the group turned homeward, he followed, thinking of supper; of the 'shine his old man kept hidden in the smoke-house; of the girls he knew. Someone else knew north and south, and the cross patterns of the piney-woods roads. The lonely region was now as unfamiliar as though he had been a stranger.

It was an hour or two past noon. He leaned his 12-gauge shotgun against a pine and looked about him nervously. He knew by the sun that he had come continuously south. He had crossed and recrossed the road, and could not decide whether it now lay to the right or left. If he missed it to the right, he would come to cypress swamp. He licked his lips. If he picked the wrong road to the left, it would bring him out a couple of miles above the village. That would be better. He could always get a lift back. He picked up his gun and began to walk.

In a few minutes a flat gray surface flashed suddenly from a patch of hammock. He stopped short. Pleasure swept over him, cooling his hot irritation. He recognized the house where he and Blaine had drawn water. He had cursed Blaine for giving a quail to the woman. He wiped the sweat from his face. The woman would feed him and direct him out of the flat-woods. Instinctively he changed his gait from a shuffling drag to his customary swagger.

He rapped loudly on the smooth cypress front door. It had a half-moon fanlight over it. The house was old but it was capacious and good. There was, for all its bareness, an air of prosperity. Clean white curtains hung at the windows. A striped cat startled him by rearing against his legs. He kicked it away. The woman must be gone. A twig cracked in the yard beyond the high piazza. He turned. The woman was stalking around the side of the house to see before she was seen. Her gray face lightened as she recognized him. She laughed.

"Mister, if you knowed how long it's been since I heerd a rap. Don't nobody knock on my front door. The turpentine niggers calls so's I won't shoot, and the hunters comes a-talkin' to the well."

She climbed the front steps with the awkwardness of middle age. She dried a hand on her flour-sacking apron and held it out to him. He took it limply, interrupting the talk that began to flow from her. He was ugly with hunger and fatigue and boredom.

"How 'bout a mess o' them rations you was offerin' me last week?"

His impatience was tempered with the tone of casual intimacy in which he spoke to all women. It bridged time and space. The woman flushed.

"I'd be mighty well pleased——"

She opened the front door. It stuck at the sill, and she threw a strong body against it. He did not offer to help. He strolled in ahead of her. As she apologized for the moments it would take to fry bacon and make coffee, he was already staring about him at the large room. When she came to him from the kitchen half an hour later, her face red with her hurry, the room had made an impress on his mind, as roads and forests could not do. The size of the room, of the clay fireplace, the adequacy of chairs and tables of a frontier period, the luxury of a Brussels carpet, although ancient, over wood, the plenitude of polished, unused kerosene lamps—the details lay snugly in his mind like hoarded money.

Hungry, with the smell of hot food filling his breath, he took time to smooth his sleek black hair at a walnut-framed mirror on the varnished match-board wall. He made his toilet boldly in front of the woman. A close watching of his dark face, of the quickness of his hands moving over his affectation of clipped side-burns, could only show her that he was good to look at. He walked to the kitchen with a roll, sprawling his long legs under the table.

With the first few mouthfuls of food good humor returned to him. He indulged himself in graciousness. The woman served him lavishly with fried cornbread and syrup, coffee, white bacon in thick slices, and fruits and vegetables of her own canning. His gluttony delighted her. His mouth was full, bent low over his heaped plate.

"You live fine, ma'am, for anyone lives plumb alone."

She sat down opposite him, wiping back the wet gray hair from her forehead, and poured herself a convivial cup of coffee.

"Jim—that was my husband—an' Pa always did say if they was good rations in the house they'd orter be on the table. I ain't got over the habit."

"You been livin' alone quite some time?"

"Jim's fifteen year dead. Pa 'bout six."

"Don't you never go nowheres?"

"I got no way to go. I kep' up stock fer two-three year after Pa died, but 'twa'n't wuth the worry. They's a family lives two mile closer to town than me, has a horse an' wagon. I take 'em my list o' things 'bout oncet a month. Seems like . . ."

He scarcely listened.

A change of atmosphere in her narrative indicated suddenly to him that she was asking him about himself.

"You a stranger?"

She was eager, leaning on the table waiting for his answer.

He finished a saucer of preserved figs, scraping at the rich syrup with relish. He tilted back in his chair luxuriously and threw the match from his cigarette in the general direction of the wood stove. He was entirely at home. His belly well filled with good food, his spirit touched with the unfailing intoxication to him of a woman's interest, he teetered and smoked and talked of his life, of his deeds, his dangers.

"You ever heard the name o' Trax Colton?"

She shook her head. He tapped his chest significantly, nodding at her.

"That's me. You've heard tell, if you on'y remembered, o' me leavin' here a few years back on account of a little cuttin' fuss. I

been on the east coast—Daytona, Melbourne, all them places. The
fuss blowed over an' I come back. Fixin' to take up business here."

He frowned importantly. He tapped a fresh cigarette on the table,
as he had learned to do from his companions of the past years. He
thought with pleasure of all that he had learned, of the sophistica-
tion that lay over his Cracker speech and ways like a cheap bright
coat.

"I'm an A-1 bootlegger, ma'am."

For the time being he was a big operator from the east coast. He
told her of small sturdy boats from Cuba, of signal flares on the St.
Augustine beach at midnight, of the stream of swift automobiles
moving in and out just before high tide. Her eyes shone. She
plucked at the throat of her brown-checked gingham dress, breathing quickly. It was fitting that this dark glamorous young man
should belong to the rocket-lit world of danger. It was ecstasy painful
in its sharpness, that he should be tilted back at her table, flicking
his fragrant ashes on her clean, lonely floor.

He was entirely amiable as he left her. Pleased with himself, he
was for a moment pleased with her. She was a good woman. He
laid his hand patronizingly on her shoulder. He stroked the striped
cat on his way down the steps. This time he turned to lift his hand
to her. She waved heartily as long as his lithe body moved in sight
among the pines.

An impulse took her to the mirror where he had smoothed his
hair, as though it would bring him within her vision again. She
saw herself completely for the first time in many years. Isolation
had taken the meaning from age. She had forgotten until this moment that she was no longer young. She turned from the mirror
and washed the dishes soberly. It occurred to her that the young
man had not even asked her name.

The hammock that had been always a friendly curtain about the
old house was suddenly a wall. The flat-woods that had been sunny
and open, populous with birds and the voice of winds, grew dense
and dark. She had been solitary. She had grieved for Jim and for
the old man her father. But solitude had kept her company in a warm
natural way, sitting cozily at her hearth, like the cat. Now loneliness
washed intolerably over her, as though she were drowning in a cold
black pond.

The young man's complacency lasted a mile or two. As his feet
began to drag, fact intruded on the fiction with which he had enraptured the gray-haired woman. Memories seeped back into him
like a poison: memories of the lean years as ignorant hanger-on of

prosperous bootleggers; of his peddling to small garages of lye-cut 'shine in ignominious pints. The world for which he considered himself fitted had evaded him. His condition was desperate. He thought of the woman who had fed him, whom he had entranced with his story. Distaste for her flooded him, as though it was her fault the story was a lie. He lifted his shotgun and blew the head from a red-bird trilling in a wild plum tree.

The storekeeper in the village was the only person who recognized Mattie Syles. The store was packed with the Saturday-night buyers of rations. A layer of whites milled in front of the meat counter; a layer of blacks shifted behind them. At the far grocery counter along a side wall a wedge of Negroes had worked in toward the meal and sugar barrels, where helpers weighed out the dimes' and quarters' worth with deliberately inaccurate haste. Two white women were buying percale of the storekeeper's wife at the dry-goods counter.

The woman came in defiantly, as though the store was a shameful place where she had no business. She looked searchingly from side to side. The storekeeper's wife called, "Evenin', ma'am," and the two white women wheeled to stare and whisper after her. She advanced toward the meat counter. The Negroes parted to let her in. The storekeeper poised his knife over a pork backbone to look at her. He laid it down, wiped his hands with a flourish on his front, and shook hands across the counter.

"If this ain't a surprise! Must be four-five years since you been to town! Meat I been sendin' you by Lantry's been all right? What kin I do fer you? Butchered this mornin'—got fresh beef. How 'bout a nice thin steak?"

She made her purchases slowly and moved to the staples counter. She insisted on being left until the last.

"I ain't in no hurry."

The store was almost empty and ready to close when she gathered her sacks together and climbed into the Lantry's wagon, waiting outside the door. As Lantry clicked to his horse and they moved off she did not notice that the man she had hoped desperately to see was just strolling into the store.

"Gimme a couple o' packs o' Camels to tide me over Sunday."

"Fifteen cents straight now, Trax."

"Jest one, then."

The storekeeper spoke across the vacant store to his wife, rolling up the bolts of cloth.

"Edna, you have better manners with the customers, or we'll be losing 'em. Why'n't you take up some time with Mis' Syles?"

"Who?"

"Mis' Syles—Jim Syles' widder—ol' man Terry's daughter—lives four-five mile south, out beyond Lantry's. You know her, Edna. Lantry's been buyin' fer her."

"I never knowed her. How'd I know her now? Why'n't you call her by name, so's I'd of knowed?"

"Well, you keep better track of her if she's goin' to take to comin' to town agin. She's rich."

Trax turned in the doorway.

"You talkin' about that gank-gutted woman left jest now?"

He had avoided going into the store until she left. He had not intended to bring her volubility upon him in public, have her refer to their meal together. He had half-guessed she had come looking for him. Women did.

"She live alone in a two-story house you cain't see from the road?"

"That's her," the storekeeper agreed. "That's Mis' Syles, a'right."

"She's rich?"

"I mean rich. Got her five dollars a week steady rent-money from turpentine, an' three thousand dollars insurance in the bank her daddy left her. An' then lives 'tother end o' nowhere. Won't leave the old house."

"'Bout time somebody was fixin' to marry all that, goin' to waste."

"She wouldn't suit you, Trax. You didn't git a good look at her. You been used to 'em younger an' purtier."

The man Colton was excited. He walked out of the store without the customary "Well, evenin'" of departure. He hurried to Blaine's, where he was boarding, but did not go in. It was necessary to sit alone on the bench outside and think. His luck had not deserted him. As he leaned his dark head against the wall, the tropical stars glittering over him were the bright lights of city streets. Here and there a fat star flickered. These were the burnished kerosene lamps of the widow Syles. The big room—the fireplace that would heat it on the coolest nights—one by one he drew out the remembered details and tucked them into his plans.

The man courted the woman with the careless impatience of his quail hunting. He intended to be done with it as quickly as possible. There was, astonishingly, a certain pleasure in her infatuation. He responded to any woman's warmth as a hound does to a grate fire, stretching comfortably before it. The maternal lavishness of her emotion for him was satisfying. Younger women, pretty women, expected something of him, coaxed and coquetted.

On his several visits to the widow before he condescended to be married to her, he sprawled in the early spring nights before the big fireplace. He made it plain that he was not one to sit around the kitchen stove. His fastidiousness charmed her. She staggered into the room with her generous arms heaped with wood: live oak and hickory, and some cedar chips, because Trax liked the smell. From his chair he directed the placing of the heavy logs. A fire must crackle constantly to please him. She learned to roll cigarettes for him, bringing them to him to lick flickeringly, like a snake, with his quick tongue. The process stirred her. When she placed the finished cigarette between his lips and lighted it with a blazing lighter'd splinter; when he puffed languidly on it and half-closed his eyes, and laid his fingers perhaps on her large-boned hand, she shivered.

The courting was needlessly protracted because she could not believe that he would have her. It was miracle enough that he should be here at all in these remote flat-woods. It was unbelievable that he should be willing to prolong the favor, to stay with her in this place forever.

She said, "Cain't be you raly wants me."

Yet she drank in his casual insistence.

"Why not? Ain't a thing the matter with you."

She understood sometimes—when she wakened with a clear mind in the middle of the night—that something strange had happened to her. She was moving in a delirium, like the haze of malaria when the fever was on. She solaced herself by thinking that Trax too might be submerged in such a delicious fog.

When he left her one night in the Blaine Ford he had borrowed, the retreating explosions of the car left behind a silence that terrified her. She ran to the beginning of the pines to listen. There was no sound but the breath of the south wind in the needles. There was no light but the endless flickering of stars. She knew that if the man did not come back again she would have to follow him. Solitude she had endured. She could not endure desolation.

When he came the next day she was ready to go to the village with him to the preacher. He laughed easily at her hurry and climbed ahead of her into the borrowed car. He drove zestfully, with abandon, bouncing the woman's big frame over the ruts of the dirt road.

As they approached the village he said casually, "I keep my money in Clark City. We'd orter do our business together. Where's yours?"

"Mine's there too. Some's in the post office an' some in the bank."

"Supposin' we go git married there. An' reckon you kin lend me a hundred till I add up my account?"

She nodded an assent to both questions.

"Don't you go spendin' no money on me, Trax, if you ain't got it real free to spend." She was alarmed for his interests. "You leave me pay fer things a while."

He drew a deep breath of relief. He was tempted for a moment to get her cash and head for the east coast at once. But he had made his plans to stay. He needed the old house in the safe flat-woods to make his start. He could even use the woman.

When they came back through the village from the city she stopped at the store for supplies. The storekeeper leaned across the fresh sausage to whisper confidentially:

"Tain't my business, Mis' Syles, but folks is sayin' Trax Colton is sort o' courtin' you. You come of good stock, an' you'd orter step easy. Trax is purely trash, Mis' Syles."

She looked at him without comprehension.

She said, "Me an' Trax is married."

The gray of the house was overlaid with the tenderness of the April sun. The walls were washed with its thin gold. The ferns and lichens of the shingled roof were shot through with light, and the wren's nest under the eaves was luminous. The striped cat sprawled flattened on the rear stoop, exposing his belly to the soft warmth. The woman moved quietly at her work, for fear of awakening the man. She was washing. When she drew a bucket of water from the well she steadied it with one hand as it swung to the coping, so that there should be no sound.

Near the well stood bamboo and oleander. She left her bucket to draw her fingers along the satin stoutness of the fresh green bamboo shoots, to press apart the new buds of the oleander in search of the pale pinkness of the first blossoms. The sun lay like a friendly arm across her square shoulders. It seemed to her that she had been chilled, year on year, and that now for the first time she was warmed through to her narrow. Spring after the snapping viciousness of February; Trax sleeping in the bed after her solitude. . . . When she finished her washing she slipped in to look at him. A boyish quiet wiped out the nervous shiftiness of his waking expression. She wanted to gather him up, sleeping, in her strong arms and hold him against her capacious breast.

When his breakfast was almost ready, she made a light clatter in the kitchen. It irritated him to be called. He liked to get up of his own accord and find breakfast smoking, waiting for him. He came out gaping, washed his face and hands in the granite basin on the water-shelf, combed his hair leisurely at the kitchen mirror, turning his face this way and that. Matt stood watching him, twisting her apron. When he was quite through, she came to him and laid her cheek against his.

"Mornin', Trax-honey."

Her voice was vibrant.

"Mornin'."

He yawned again as he dropped into his chair. He beat lightly on his down-turned plate with his knife and surveyed the table. He scowled.

"Where's the bacon?"

"Honey, I didn't think you'd want none with the squirrel an' eggs an' fish."

"My God, I cain't eat breakfast without bacon."

"I'm sorry, Trax. 'Twon't take me but a minute now."

She was miserable because she had not fried bacon and he wanted it.

He slid eggs and meat and biscuits to his plate, poured coffee with an angry jerk, so that it spilled on the table, shoveled the food in, chewing with his mouth open. When Matt put the crisp thick slices of white bacon before him, he did not touch them. He lighted a cigarette and strolled to the stoop, pushed off the cat so that he might sit down. He leaned back and absorbed the sun. This was fine.

He had deliberately allowed himself these few idle weeks. He had gone long without comfort. His body needed it. His swaggering spirit needed it. The woman's adoration fed him. He could have had no greater sense of well-being, of affluence if she had been a nigger servant. Now he was ready for business. His weasel mind was gnawing its hole into the world he longed for.

"Matt!"

She left her dishes and came to stand over him.

"Matt, you're goin' in business with me. I want you should git me three hundred dollars. I want to set up a eight-barrel still back o' the house, down by the branch."

Trax had crashed like a meteor into the flat-woods. It had not occurred to her that his world must follow him. That was detached from him, only a strange story that he had told. She had a sensation of dismay that any thing, any person, must intrude on her ecstasy.

She said anxiously, "I got enough to make out on, Trax. You don't need to go startin' up nothin' like that."

"All right—if you want I should put my outfit some'eres else——"

"No, no. Don't you do that. Don't you go 'way. I didn't know you was studyin' on nothin' like that—you jest go ahead an' put it clost as you like."

"Down by the branch, like I said."

He visioned the lay-out for her. She listened, distraught. The platform here, for the barrels of mash. There, the woodpile for the slow fire. Here again, the copper still itself. The cover was dense, utterly concealing. The location was remote.

"The idee, Matt," he was hunched forward, glowing, "is to sell yer own stuff what they call retail, see? It costs you fifty, seventy-five cents a gallon to make. You sell by the five-gallon jug fer seven dollars, like they're doin' now, you don't make nothin'. That's nigger pay. But what do you git fer it by the drink? A quarter. A quarter a drink an' a dollar a pint. You let people know they kin git 'em a drink out here any time to Trax Colton's, you got 'em comin' in from two-three counties fer it. You git twenty gallons ahead an' color some up, cook it a whiles underground to darken it, an' you take it to places like Jacksonville an' Miami—you got you real money."

It was as though thunder and lightning threatened over the flatwoods. The darkness of impending violence filled them. She stared at him.

"'Course, if you don't want to invest in my business with me, I got to be gittin' back where I come from."

The smoke from his cigarette drifted across her.

"No, no! It's all right!"

His glamorousness enfolded her like the April sun.

"Honey, anything you want to do's all right."

Setting up the still was a week's work. Men began to come and go. Where there had been, once in five days, the silent turpentiners, once in a while the winter hunters, there were now Negroes bringing in cut wood; a local mason putting togther brick and mortar; a hack carpenter building a platform with a roof; men in trucks bringing in sacks of meal and sugar, glass demijohns and oak kegs.

The storekeeper brought five hundred pounds of sugar.

"Howdy, Mis' Colton. Reckon you never figgered you'd be 'shinin'."

"No."

"But you couldn't git you no better place fer it."

Her square face brightened.

"That's jest what Trax says."

That night she approached him.

"Trax, all these here men knowin' what you're doin'—reckon it's safe?"

"They got no reason to say nothin'. The only reason anybody'd turn anybody else up was if he'd done somethin' to him. Then they'd git at him that-a-way. Git his still, see? Git him tore up. That way they'd git him."

She made no further comment. Her silence made its way through the wall of his egotism.

"You don't talk as much as you did, Matt. Else I got used to it."

"I was alone so long, honey. Seemed like I had to git caught up."

But the spring warmth was no longer so loosening to the tongue. The alien life the man was bringing in chilled the exuberance that had made her voluble.

"I'm fixin' to learn you to make the whiskey, Matt."

She stared at him.

"Less help we have, knowin' how much I got an' where 'tis, better it suits me, see?"

She said finally, "I kin learn."

The work seemed strange, when all her folk had farmed and timbered. But her closest contact with Trax was over the sour, seething mash. When they walked together back of the house, down to the running branch, their bodies pushing side by side through the low palmettos, they were a unit. Except to curse her briefly when she was clumsy, he was good-natured at his work. Crouching by the fire burning under the copper drum, the slow dripping from the coils, of the distillate, the only sound except for small woods life, she felt themselves man and wife. At other times his lovely body and unlovely spirit both evaded her.

He was ready to sell his wares. He drove to the village and to neighboring towns and cities, inviting friends and acquaintances to have a drink from one of the gallon jugs under the rear seat of the borrowed car. They pronounced it good 'shine. To the favored few financially able to indulge themselves he gave a drink of the "aged" liquor. Accustomed to the water-clear, scalding rawness of fresh 'shine, they agreed gravely that no better whiskey ever came in from Cuba. He let it be known that both brands would be available at any time, day or night, at the old Terry house four miles south of the village. He made a profound impression. Most bootleggers sold stuff whose origin and maker were unknown. Most 'shiners had always made it, or drifted into it aimlessly. Trax brought a pomp and ceremony to the local business.

Men found their way out the deep-rutted road. They left their cars among the pines and stumbled through the hammock to the house. They gathered in the big room Trax had recognized as suitable for his purposes. The long trenchered table old man Terry had sliced from red bay, held the china pitcher of "corn" and the jelly glasses from which they drank. Their bird-dogs and hounds padded across the piazza and lay before the fire. Trax drank with them, keying their gatherings to hilarity. He was a convivial host. Sometimes Blaine brought along his guitar, and Trax clapped his hands and beat his feet on the floor as the old man picked the strings. But he was uneasy when a quarrel developed. Then he moved, white-faced among the men, urging someone else to stop it.

At first the woman tried to meet them hospitably. When, deep in the hammock at the still, she heard the vibration of a motor, she hurried up to the house to greet the guests. She smoothed back the gray hair from her worn face and presented her middle-aged bulk in a clean apron. If there was one man alone, Trax introduced her casually, insolently:

"This is my old woman."

When a group of men came together, he ignored her. She stood in the doorway, smiling vaguely. He continued his talk as though she were not there. Sometimes one of the group, embarrassed, acknowledged her presence.

"How do, ma'am."

For the most part they took their cue from Trax and did not see her. Once, on her withdrawal to the kitchen, a stranger had followed for a match.

"Don't you mind workin' way out here in the woods?"

But she decided that Trax was too delicate to want his wife mixing with men who came to drink. At night he sometimes invited her into the big room with conspicuous courtesy. That was when one or two women had come with the men. Her dignity established the place as one where they might safely come. She sat miserably in their midst while they made banal jokes and drank from the thick glasses. They were intruders. Their laughter was alien among the pine trees. She stayed at the still most of the time. The labor was heavy and exacting. The run must be made when the mash was ready, whether it was day or night. It was better for Trax to stay at the house to take care of the customers.

In the early fall he was ready to expand. Matt was alone, scrubbing the floors between runs of whiskey. She heard a powerful car throbbing down the dirt road. It blew a horn constantly in a minor key. Men usually came into this place silently. She went to the piazza, wet brush in hand. With the autumnal drying of foliage, the road was discernible. The scent of wild vanilla filled the flat-woods. She drew in the sweetness, craning her neck to see.

A large blue sedan of expensive make swerved and rounded into the tracks other cars had made to the house. Trax was driving. He swung past the twin live oaks and into the sandy yard. He slammed the door behind him as he stepped out. He had bought the car with the remainder of Matt's three thousand and most of the summer's profits. He was ready to flash across his old haunts, a big operator from the interior.

"I kin sell that hundred gallons of aged stuff now fer what it's worth."

He nodded widely. He sauntered into the house, humming under his breath.

"Hi-diddy-um-tum——" He was vibrant with an expectancy in which she had no part.

She heard him curse because the floor was wet. The cat crossed his path. He lifted it by the tail and slid it along the slippery boards. The animal came to her on the piazza. She drew it into her lap and sat on her haunches a long time, stroking the smooth hard head.

Life was a bad dream. Trax was away a week at a time. He hired the two Lantry boys to take his place. Matt worked with them, for the boys unwatched would let the mash ferment too long. Trax returned to the flat-woods only for fresh supplies of liquor and of clean clothes. It pleased him to dress in blues that harmonized not too subtly with the blue sedan. He wore light-blue shirts and a red necktie that was a challenging fire under the dark insolent face. Matt spent hours each week washing and ironing the blue shirts. She protested his increasing absences.

"Trax, you jest ain't here at all. I hardly got the heart fer makin' the runs, an' you gone."

He smiled.

"Any time it don't suit you, I kin move my oufit to the east coast."

He laid the threat across her like a whip.

The young Lantrys too saw Trax glamorously. They talked of him to Matt as they mixed the mash, fired, and kept their vigils. This seemed all she had these days of the man: talk of him with the boys beside the still. She was frustrated, filled, not with resentment, but with despair. Yet she could not put her finger on the injustice. She flailed herself with his words, "Any time you don't like it, I kin move."

She waited on Trax's old customers as best she could, running up the slight incline from the still-site to the house when she heard a car. Her strong body was exhausted at the end of the week. Yet when she had finished her elaborate baking on Saturday night she built up a roaring fire in the front room, hung the hot water kettle close to it for his bath, and sat down to wait for him.

Sometimes she sat by the fire almost all night. Sometimes he did not come at all. Men learned they could get a drink at Colton's any hour of the night on Saturday. When the square dance at Trimtree's was done, they came out to the flat-woods at two or three o'clock in the morning. The woman was always awake. They stepped up on the piazza and saw her through the window. She sat brooding by the fire, the striped cat curled in her lap. Around her bony shoulders she hugged the corduroy hunting jacket Trax had worn when he came to her.

She existed for the Saturday nights when the throb of the blue sedan came close; the Sunday mornings when he slept late and arose, sulky, for a lavish breakfast and dinner. Then he was gone again, and she was waving after him down the road. She thought that her love and knowledge of him had been always nothing but this watching through the pine trees as he went away.

The village saw more of him. Occasionally he loitered there a day to show off before he headed for the coast. At times he returned in the middle of the week and picked up fifteen or twenty gallons cached at Blaine's and did not go out to the flat-woods at all. On these occasions he had invariably a girl or woman with him; cheap pretty things whose lightness brought them no more than their shoddy clothes. The storekeeper, delivering meal and sugar to Matt, lingered one day. The still needed her, but she could not with courtesy dismiss him. At last he drew courage.

"Mis' Matt, dogged if I don't hate to complain on Trax to you, but folks thinks you don't know how he's a-doin' you. You're workin' like a dog, an' he ain't never home."

"I know."

"You work at 'shinin', somethin' you nor your folks never done— not that it ain't all right—— An' Trax off in that big fine car spendin' the money fast as he turns it over."

"I know."

"The Klan talks some o' givin' him down the country fer it."

" 'Tain't nobody's business but his an' mine."

"Mis' Matt"—he scuffled in the sand—"I promised I'd speak of it. D'you know Trax has got him women goin' round with him?"

"No. I didn't know that."

"Ev'ybody figgered you didn't know that." He mopped his forehead. "The day you an' Trax was married, I was fixin' to tell you 'twa'n't nothin' but your money an' place he wanted to git him set up."

"That's my business, too," she said stonily.

He dropped his eyes before the cold face and moved to his truck. She called after him defiantly:

"What else did I have he'd want anyway!"

She went into the house. She understood the quality of her betrayal. The injustice was clear. It was only this: Trax had taken what he had not wanted. If he had said, "Give me the money and for the time, the house," it would have been pleasant to give, solely because he wanted. This was the humiliation: that she had been thrown in on the deal, like an old mare traded in with a farm.

The Lantry boys called unanswered from the palmettos.

She had known. There was no need of pretense. There was no difference between to-day and yesterday. There was only the dissipation of a haze, as though a sheet had been lifted from a dead body, so that, instead of knowing, she saw.

The man came home late Saturday afternoon. Startled, Matt heard the purr of the motor and hurried to the house from the still. She thought the woman with him had come for liquor. She came to meet them, wiping her hands on her brown gingham apron. Trax walked ahead of his companion, carrying his own shiny patent leather bag and a smaller shabby one. As they came into the house, she saw that it was not a woman, but a girl.

The girl was close on his heels, like a dog. She was painted crudely, as with a haphazard conception of how it should be done. Stiff blond curls were bunched under a tilted hat. A flimsy silk dress hung loosely on an immature frame. Cheap silk stockings bagged on thin legs. She rocked, rather than walked, on incredibly spiked heels. Her shoes absorbed Matt's attention. They were pumps of blue kid, the precise blue of the sedan.

"I mean, things got hot fer me on the east coast." Trax was voluble. "Used that coastal highway oncet too often. First thing I knowed, down below New Smyrna, I seed a feller at a garage give the high sign, an' I'm lookin' into the end of a .45." He flushed. "I jest did

git away. It'll pay me to work this territory a whiles, till they git
where they don't pay me no mind over there agin."

The girl was watching Matt with solemn blue eyes. Beside the
gray bulk of the older woman, she was like a small gaudy doll. Trax
indicated her to Matt with his thumb.

"Elly here'll be stayin' at the house a while."

He picked up the shabby bag and started up the stairs.

"Long as you an' me is usin' the downstairs, Matt, she kin sleep upstairs in that back room got a bed in it."

She pushed past the girl and caught him by the sleeve.

"Trax! What's this gal?"

"Ain't no harm to her." He laughed comfortably. He tweaked a
wisp of her gray hair.

"She's jest a little gal young un," he said blandly, "'s got no place
to go."

He drew the girl after him. The woman stared at the high-heeled
blue slippers clicking on every step.

II

A warm winter rain thrummed on the roof. The light rush of
water sank muffled into the moss that padded the shingles. The sharp-
est sound was a gurgling in the gutter over the rainbarrel. There had
been no visible rising of the sun. Only the gray daylight had protracted itself, so that it was no longer dawn, but day. Matt sat close
to the kitchen stove, her bulk shadowy in the dimness. Now and
then she opened the door of the fire-box to push in a stick of pine,
and the light of the flames flickered over her drawn face.

She could not tell how much of the night she had sat crouched
by the range. She had lain long hours unsleeping, while Trax
breathed regularly beside her. When the rain began, she left the
bed and dressed by the fresh-kindled fire. Her mouth was dry; yet
every few minutes an uncontrollable chill shook her body. It would
be easy to walk up the unused stairs, down the dusty hall to the
back room with the rough pine bed in it, to open the door and look
in, to see if anyone was there. Yet if she continued to sit by the fire,
moving back the coffee pot when it boiled, surely Trax would come
to the kitchen alone, and she would know that yesterday no woman
had come home with him. Through the long days her distraught mind
had been busy with imaginings. They might easily have material-
ized, for a moment, in a painted girl, small and very young, in blue
kid slippers.

Trax was moving about. She put the frying pan on the stove, sliced bacon into it, stirred up cornmeal into a pone with soda and salt and water. Trax called someone. He came into the kitchen, warmed his hands at the stove. He poured water into the wash basin and soused his face in it. Matt set the coffee pot on the table. The girl pushed open the door a little way and came through. She came to the table uncertainly as though she expected to be ordered away. Matt did not speak.

Trax said, "How's my gal?"

The girl brought her wide eyes to him and took a few steps to his chair.

"Where your shoes, honey?"

She looked down at her stockinged feet.

"I gotta be keerful of 'em."

He laughed indulgently.

"You kin have more when them's gone. Matt, give the young un somethin' to eat."

The thought struck the woman like the warning whir of a rattler that if she looked at the girl in this moment she would be compelled to lift her in her hands and drop her like a scorpion on the hot stove. She thought, "I cain't do sich as that." She kept her back turned until the impulse passed and she could control her trembling. Her body was of metal and wood. It moved of itself, in jerks. A stiff wooden head creaked above a frame so heavy it seemed immovable. Her stomach weighed her down. Her ample breasts hurt her ribs, as though they were of lead. She thought, "I got to settle this now."

She said aloud slowly, "I'll not wait on her, nor no other woman."

The girl twisted one foot over the other.

She said, "I ain't hungry."

Trax stood up. His mouth was thin. He said to Matt, "You'll wait on her, old lady, or you'll git along without my comp'ny."

She thought, "I got to settle it. I got to say it."

But she could not speak.

The girl repeated eagerly, "I ain't a bit hungry."

Trax picked up a plate from the table. He held it out to his wife.

She thought, "Anyway, cornbread an' bacon's got nothin' to do with it."

She dished out meat and bread. Trax held out a cup. She filled it with coffee. The man sat down complacently. The girl sat beside him and pecked at the food. Her eyes were lowered. Between mouthfuls, she twisted her fingers in her lap or leaned over to inspect her unshod feet.

Matt thought. "Remindin' me."

The paint had been rubbed from the round face. The hair was yellow, like allamanda blooms. The artificial curls that had protruded from the pert hat had flattened out during the damp night, and hung in loose waves on the slim neck. She wore the blue silk dress in which she had arrived.

Trax said, "You eat up good, Elly. May be night 'fore we git back to eat agin." He turned to Matt. "Lantry boys been doin' all right?"

"They been doin' all right. Them's good boys. I heerd 'em come in a hour back. But they needs watchin' right on. They'll let the mash go too long, spite of everything, if I ain't right on top of 'em."

She hardened herself.

"You jest as good to stay home an' do the work yourself. I ain't goin' near the outfit."

"They kin make out by theirselves," he said easily.

He rose from the table, picking his teeth.

"Come on, Elly."

The girl turned her large eyes to the older woman, as though she were the logical recipient of her confession.

"I forgot to wash my hands an' face," she said.

Trax spoke curtly.

"Well, do it now, an' be quick."

He poured warm water in the basin for her and stood behind her, waiting. She washed slowly, with neat, small motions, like a cat. Trax handed her the clean end of the towel. They went upstairs together. Trax's voice was low and muffled. It dripped through the ceiling like thick syrup. Suddenly Matt heard the girl laugh.

She thought, "I figgered all thet owl-face didn't let on no more'n she meant it to."

In a few minutes they came down again. Trax called from the front room:

"Best to cook dinner to-night, Matt. We're like not to git back at noon."

They ran from the porch through the rain.

She walked after them. She was in time to see them step in the blue sedan. The high-heeled slippers flickered across the running-board. The car roared through the live oaks, down the tracks among the pines. Matt closed her eyes against the sight ot it.

She thought, "Maybe she takened her satchel an' I jest didn't see it. Maybe she ain't comin' back."

She forced herself to go to the upstairs bedroom. The drumming on the roof sounded close and louder. The bed was awkwardly made. The shabby handbag stood open in a hickory rocker, exposing its sparse contents. A sound startled her. The cat had followed, and was sniffing the unfamiliar garments in the chair. The woman gathered the animal in her arms. They were alone together in the house, desolate and lonely in the rain-drenched flat-woods.

She thought of the Lantry boys under the palmettos. They were careless when they were cold and wet. They might not put the last five hundred pounds of sugar under cover. Shivering in the drizzle, they might use muddy water from the bank of the branch, instead of going a few yards upstream where it ran deep and clear. She threw Trax's corduroy jacket about her and went down the incline behind the house to oversee the work.

She had decided not to cook anything for the evening. But when the mist lifted in late afternoon, and the sun struck slantwise through the wet dark trees, she left the Lantry boys to finish and went to the house. She fried ham and baked soda biscuits and sweet potatoes. The meal was ready and waiting and she stirred up a quick ginger cake and put it in the oven.

She said aloud, desperately, "Might be he'll be back alone."

Yet when the dark gathered the bare house into its loneliness, as she had gathered the cat, and she lighted kerosene lamps in the long front room and a fire, the man and girl came together as she had known they would. Where she had felt only despair, suddenly she was able to hate. She picked up her anger like a stone and hurled it after the blue heels.

"Go eat your dinner."

She spoke to them as she would to Negro field hands. Trax stared at her. He herded Elly nervously ahead of him, as though to protect her from an obscure violence. Matt watched them, standing solidly on big feet. She had not been whole. She had charred herself against the man's youth and beauty. Her hate was healthful. It waked her from a drugged sleep, and she stirred faculties hurt and long unused.

She sat by the clay fireplace in the front room while the pair ate. They spoke in whispers, shot through by the sudden laugh of the girl. It was a single high sound, like the one note of the thrush. Hearing it, Matt twisted her mouth. When the casual clatter of plates subsided, she went to the kitchen and began scraping the dishes to wash them. Trax sat warily in his place. The girl made an effort to hand Matt odds and ends from the table. The woman ignored her.

Trax said to Elly, "Le's go by the fire."

Matt cleaned up the kitchen and fed the cat. She stroked its arching back as it chewed sideways on scraps of meat and potato. She took off her apron, listened at the open door for sounds from the Lantrys, bolted the door, and walked to the front room to sit stiff and defiant by the blazing pine fire. The girl sat with thin legs tucked under her chair. She looked from the man to the woman and back again. Trax stretched and yawned.

He said, "Guess I'll go down back an' give the boys a hand. I ain't any too sure they run one batch soon enough. I got to keep up my stuff. I got high-class trade. Ain't I, Elly?" He touched her face with his finger as he passed her.

The woman and the girl sat silently after his going. The cat padded in and sat between them.

The girl called timidly: "Kitty!"

Matt turned savagely.

"Keep your hands off him."

The girl laced her fingers and studied the animal.

"Do he scratch?"

Matt did not answer. She loosened her gray hair and combed it by the fire with a side-comb, plaiting it into two thin braids over her shoulders. Inside the childish hairdressing her face was bony and haggard. She went into the adjoining bedroom, undressed and got into bed. She lay reared up on one elbow, straining for every sound. The fire popped and crackled. Once the juice oozed from a pine log faster than it could burn. It made a sizzling, like boiling fat. A chair scraped and Elly went up to the back bedroom. Her high heels clicked overhead. Matt thought with satisfaction that the girl had no light. She was floundering around in the dark in the unfamiliar house.

In a little while the front door opened and closed softly. Matt heard Trax creak cautiously up the stairs to the back room.

Trax was sleeping away the bright March morning. Matt made no effort to be silent about her washing. She dipped noisily into the rain barrel. When the soft water was gone she drew from the well, rattling galvanized buckets. Elly sat on the bottom step of the rear stoop, scuffling her bare toes in the sand. She wore the blue silk dress. Beside her was a handful of her own garments in need of washing, a pair of silk stockings and two or three pieces of underwear. Matt passed in front of her to go to the clothes line.

Elly said, "Trax give me this dress."

The woman did not seem to hear her.

Elly continued. "Reckon it'll wash? It's spotted."

Matt did not answer. She hung flour-sacking towels on the line. The girl picked up her small pile, looked uncertainly at the tub of soapsuds, laid down the clothes. She went to the tub and began rubbing on the first garment she drew from the suds. It was one of Matt's gingham aprons. She rubbed with energy, and Matt towered over her before she noticed that the woman had left the line.

"Take your dirty hands out o' my tub."

The girl drew back, dripping suds from her thin arms. She turned her hands back and forth.

"They ain't dirty," she protested.

Matt laughed shortly. "Mighty simple, ain't you?"

An obscure doubt brushed her, like a dove that wavers to a perch and is gone again without lighting.

"Who do you figger I am?"

The girl faced her across the wash-tub. She said gravely, "The lady lives in Trax's house."

"Trax's house? Well, he lives in mine. Never heerd tell o' no sich thing as his wife, eh?"

The girl hesitated. "Trax jest said the old woman."

Matt breathed heavily. The girl took her silence and her questions for a mark of interest.

"Trax said you'd romp on me," she offered confidentially, "but you ain't." She wrapped one bare leg around the other. "I been romped on," she went on brightly. "Pa romped on me reg'lar."

"You got you folks then!"

"Yessum, but I don't know where he is. He run a blacksmith shop an' garage offen the hard road, but he closed up an' goed to Georgia with a lady. Then I lived with another lady down the road a piece. Trax sold her liquor, that's how come him to know me. She moved off, an' he takened me with him from there. Now I'm gonna live with him," she finished, adding with studied tact "—and you."

Trax came yawning to the rear stoop in time to see Matt walk toward the girl. Elly stared uncomprehending. He jumped to the sand and caught the woman's muscular arms from behind.

"Don't you touch her." He cracked his familiar whip over her. "You hurt that gal young un an' you've seed the last o' me."

The woman shook free from him in the strength of her rage.

"You git out o' here before I hurts her an' you, too. You take yer gal young un an' git."

He adjusted his mind slowly. Inconceivably, he had gone too far. Bringing the girl to the flat-woods had been dangerously brazen. It was done now. He understood that his hold on this place had become suddenly precarious. He had the car and he could move the still. Yet the lay-out suited his needs too exactly to be relinquished. He could not give it up. If the gray-headed woman was done with her infatuation, he was in trouble.

He said boldly, "I got no idee o' goin'. Me an' Elly'll be here right on."

She said, "I kin break ary one o' you in two with my hands."

"Not me, you cain't. Leave me tell you, ol' woman, I'm too quick fer you. An' if you hurt Elly"—his dark face nodded at her—"if you crack down on her—with them big hands o' yourn—if you got any notion o' knifin'"—he paused for emphasis—"I'll git you sent to the chair, or up fer life—an' I'll be here in these flat-woods—in this house —right on."

He pushed the girl ahead of him and walked into the house, lighting a cigarette. He said over his shoulder, thickly between puffs, "An' that'd suit me jest fine."

She turned blindly to the wash-tub. She soaped the blue shirts without seeing them, rubbing them up and down automatically. Her life that had run like the flat-woods road, straight and untraveled, was now a maze, doubling back on itself darkly, twisted with confusion. The man stood with his neat trap at the end of every path; the girl with her yellow hair and big eyes, at the beginning.

She thought, "I got to settle it."

Trax and Elly came and went like a pair of bright birds. The blue kid slippers, scuffed by the sand, flashed in and out of the old house. Matt watched the comings and goings heavily, standing solidly on the hand-hewn pine-board floors.

She did not go near the still. Her absence did not make the difference she had imagined. The Lantrys had the work well in hand. Trax paid their wages, and their product was satisfactory. Often she did not hear them come to their work through the pines and past the hammock. A northwest wind sometimes brought the scent of the mash to her nose. The storekeeper brought in sugar and meal by a lower trail, and she seldom saw him. Trax was selling all his liquor at a high urban price, and local patronage dwindled away. The woods were quiet day and night.

Then Trax and Elly were back again, talking of hotels and highways, of new business, the talk pierced through now and again by the girl's single-noted laughter. She eyed Matt gravely, but the woman felt that the girl, oddly, had no fear. Trax was insolent, as always, his eyes narrow and his ways wary. Matt cut down on the table. She cooked scarcely enough for the three to eat. Elly ate with her catlike slowness, taking twice as long at her meager plate as the others. Matt took to rising and clearing the table as soon as she and Trax had finished. She picked up the plates casually, as though unaware that the third one still showed half its food uneaten. Trax did not seem to notice. The girl sometimes looked hungrily after the vanishing portion. She made no protest. Once Matt found her in the kitchen between meals, eating cold cornbread. Trax backed her up in her curt order to Elly to keep out.

It enraged Matt to see Elly feed the cat. Elly saved bits from her sparse helpings and held them under the table when she thought herself unobserved. Occasionally when the girl held the animal in her lap, and Matt ignored it, Trax stroked him too, because it was Elly who held him. Matt knew they sometimes had food in Elly's room at night. She began to hear a soft padding up the stairs and on the bare floor overhead, and knew the cat went up to join them. In the morning he was smug, washing his whiskers enigmatically. His desertion was intolerable. She shut him out at night. He wailed for hours at the door, accustomed to sleeping snugly inside the house.

Suddenly Trax was not taking Elly with him any more. The village had become accustomed to the grave childish face beside him when it disappeared. Casually he left her behind with Matt in the flat-woods. He drove away one morning and did not come back that night or the next.

Matt took it for a taunt. It seemed to her that he was daring her to trap herself. Elly watched the road anxiously the first day. She accepted, hours before Matt, his solitary departure. At their first breakfast alone together, she said hesitantly:

"I had a idee Trax was fixin' to go off alone."

Matt thought, "The fool don't know enough to keep quiet about it."

After the second day, Elly devoted herself to exploring outside the house. Trax had kept her close to him, and the hammock had been only a cluster of shrubs and great trees through which they came and went. The Spanish moss was hazed with green by the early spring, and she discovered that the gray strands were alive with infinitesimal rosy blossoms. Matt saw her sitting at the far edge of the hammock, pulling the stuff apart.

The woman thought, "She better git herself out o' my sight."

Elly roamed, through the pines as far as the road, staring up and down its silent winding, then scampered back toward the house like an alarmed squirrel. She walked stealthily to the palmettos where the Lantrys worked the still, and watched them for hours, unseen. Except when Matt stared directly at her, her round-eyed gravity lifted into a certain lightness, as though she felt newly free to move about in the sunlight. She seemed content.

On a rainy afternoon Matt, ironing in the kitchen, heard a steady snipping from the front room. She stole to the door and peered through a crack. Elly was cutting pictures from an old magazine and making an arrangement of rooms and figures of men and women and children. She was talking to herself and occasionally to them. The cat was curled in her lap, shifting lazily as she moved forward or back.

Their meals together were silent. Matt became aware at dinner one day that the pink oleanders in a jelly glass were not of her picking and placing. She had always a spray of flowers or greenery on the table. Because Elly had brought in the blooms, she snatched them from the water and stuffed them in the stove.

She allowed the girl a minimum of food. Once when she took away the plates before Elly had fairly begun, the girl reached after her desperately and said "Matt!" Again, when Matt moved from the table, leaving a plate of biscuits behind, Elly pounced on the largest and crammed it into her mouth. She began to laugh, poking in the crumbs.

She said, "You ain't romped on me yet."

Matt decided that Trax had put Elly up to goading her. She spoke for the first time in days.

"Don't you let Trax put no notions in yore head. I got no idee o' rompin' on you. That ain't what I'm fixin' to do."

For the most part, the girl was uncomplaining and strangely satisfied. The immature body, however, was becoming rapidly emaciated.

Trax was gone two weeks. He came in for an afternoon and loaded up with twenty gallon-jugs concealed under the large rear seat, and went hurriedly away. He called to the two women who stood watching on the piazza.

"Got a order."

Matt nodded grimly after him. She thought, "You got you one more chance, too, if you on'y knowed it." She turned to observe the girl beside her. There was apparent on the young face a faint wistfulness and no surprise. Matt thought, "She's got her orders jest to set tight."

Trax came home for the following week-end. He slept most of the

time and was sulky. He paid no more attention to Elly than to the
older woman. At no time in the two days or nights did he go to
the upstairs room. When he was about, Elly followed him a few
steps. Then, as he continued to ignore her, she dropped behind and
took up her own simple affairs. Matt told herself that if he left this
time without the girl, she was ready. On Monday morning, after
loading, he went alone to the car.

She said carelessly, "I might take a notion to go some'eres or do
somethin'. When you comin' back this time?"

He laughed insolently. "Steppin' out, Matt?" He was sure of himself. He was too quick for her. Whatever futilities she was planning,
it would surprise her most to return on the day he named.

"Be back Sat'day."

He drove off smiling.

Matt was nervous all week. On Saturday morning she surprised
the Lantry boys by appearing at the still. They had come and gone
without contact with her for some weeks.

She said, "Boys, I jest got word the Pro-hi's is comin' lookin' fer
Trax's outfit. Now I ain't quick as you-all, an' I want each one o' you
should go down the road a good piece an' stay there all day,
watchin', one to the north an' 'tother to the south. I'll tend the outfit,
an' if I hears a whistle I'll know what it means an' it'll give me time
to smash the jugs an' git to the house."

The boys were in instant alarm.

"Must be somebody's turned Trax up," they said.

Matt said, "Mighty likely. Somebody's likely got it in fer him. Trax
hisself done tole me a long ways back, if anybody had it in fer a
man, that was the way they'd git at him."

They nodded in agreement.

"That's about it, Mis' Matt. Git him tore up an' git at him that-a-
way."

They hid several demijohns in near-by cover and hurried anxiously
the two ways of the road. They reported later in the village that they
heard no sound for an hour or so. Toward noon their straining ears
caught the crash of an axe on metal. There was the high thin splin-
tering of glass. The isolated crashes settled into a steady shattering of
wood and iron and copper. A column of smoke began to rise from
the vicinity of the still. The Lantry to the south skirted the road
through the pines and joined his brother. They cut through the woods
to the village and announced that the Pro-hi's had come in from the

west and were tearing up Colton's outfit. The word went out to avoid the flat-woods road.

The Lantrys were waiting for Trax when he came through in late afternoon. They flagged him down. They drove with him as far as their own place, telling him what they knew.

"When we lit out we could hear 'em maulin' on the barrels an' purely see the smoke. Things is tore up an' burnt up all right."

They conjectured who, of his numerous enemies, might have betrayed him. He drove at a spring-breaking clip over the root-filled ruts of the sand road. His face was black and frightened. When he let the boys out of the car he had said nothing about the week's wages. They looked at each other.

One said, "How 'bout us gittin' ten dollars, anyway, Trax?"

"That's it. I ain't got it. I on'y got five myself. I was fixin' to turn over this lot quick."

"We hid out 'bout twenty gallons, if they ain't found it," they informed him eagerly. He listened tensely to a description of the location and was gone.

He drove into the yard and stopped the car in gear with a jerk. No one was in sight. He ran back of the house to the palmettos. A ring of fire had blackened palms and oaks and myrtle for a hundred feet around. A smoldering pile of bricks and barrel hoops and twisted metal in the center marked the site of the still. He began a frenzied search for the hidden jugs.

Matt peered from a window in the front room. She ordered Elly upstairs.

"You stay there till I tell you different."

The woman hurried into the yard with a jug of kerosene and a handful of papers. The sedan was twenty-five feet from the house, but the direction of the wind was safe. She soaked the hood and seats of the car with oil and piled papers on the floor. She tied a bundle of oil-soaked paper on the end of her longest clothes prop; touched a match to it. She lowered the pole to the machine. The oil caught fire. When the blaze reached the gas tank, the explosion disintegrated an already charring mass.

Trax heard the muffled roar up the incline behind him. The demijohns were where the Lantry boys had indicated. They were broken. He left the stench of over-turned mash and spilled alcohol and ran to the house. He could not for a moment comprehend that the twisting mass of metal and flame was the blue sedan.

Matt stood on the rear stoop. He looked at her in bewilderment. His stare dropped from her straggling gray hair down the length of

her frame. Her apron was smudged and torn. Her hands were black
and raw. He came back to her implacable cold eyes. He choked.

"You done it yourself!"

He burst into spasmodic curses, then broke off, overcome by their
futility. The sweat ran into his eyes. He wiped it out and gaped about
him in loose-mouthed confusion. He shuffled a few feet to the stoop
and sank down on the bottom step. The woman looked down at him.

"Better git goin'."

He rose, swaying.

"You ol' . . ."

His obscenities fell away from her as rain washed from the weathered shingles of the old house. She towered over him. The tall house
towered over him. He was as alien as on the bright day when he had
first come hunting here.

He plunged up the steps toward her, his head low between his
shoulders.

"Better git back."

His outstretched fists dropped at his sides. The fingers fell open.
The woman lifted the shotgun.

"Better git——"

He shook his head, unbelieving. His eyes clung to the dark cavities
of the pitted steel. He moved one foot slowly to the next step.

The woman aimed carefully at the shoe, as though it were some
strange reptile creeping into the house. She fired a trifle to the left,
so that the pattern of the double-ought buckshot shell sprayed in a
close mass into the sand. One pellet clipped through the leather, and
a drop of blood sank placidly into the pine step. The man stared
fascinated. His hand jerked to his mouth, like a wooden toy moved
by strings. He stifled a sound, or tried to make one. The woman
could not tell. He lifted a face dry with fear and backed down the
steps.

It was necessary to walk widely to the side to avoid the heat of
the burned car. He threw out his hands hopelessly and hesitated. The
sun slanted orange and gold through the hammock. Beyond, there
were already shadows among the dark pines. It would be twilight
before he could be out of the flat-woods. He found voice.

"Matt," he whined, "how'll I git to town?"

The woman wiped her streaked face with a corner of her apron.

"Reckon you'll have to git there on foot, Mister—the way you come
in the first place."

She turned her back and went into the house. The girl had come
down the stairs and was flattened against a wall. Her face was

brushed with a desperate knowledge. Matt jerked her head at the open front door.

"All right. I'm thu. You kin go on with him now."

"Matt——"

"Go on. Git."

The girl did not move. Matt pushed her headlong to the door. Elly took hold of the big arm with both hands, drawing back, and Matt struck her away. She went confusedly down the steps. Trax was leaving the hammock. He struck wildly through the pines. The girl took a few steps after him, then turned toward the woman watching from the doorway. Matt called loudly:

"Go on. Git."

The man had reached the road and was plunging along it to the north. The girl ran three or four paces in his direction, then stopped again, like a stray dog or cat that would not be driven away. She hesitated at the edge of the hammock. The small uncertain figure was visible between the twin oaks beyond the high porch. Matt turned into the house and closed the door.

She was strong and whole. She was fixed, deep-rooted as the pine trees. They leaned a little, bent by an ancient storm. Nothing more could move them.

The car in the yard had settled into a smoking heap. The acrid smell of burned rubber and paint filled the house. Matt closed the north window to keep out the stench. The glass rattled in its frame. The air was gusty and the spring night would be cold. There were swift movements and rattlings among the oak boughs above the roof, as though small creatures were pattering across the floor of the wind.

Matt shivered and kindled a fire in the front room. She looked about for the cat. The noise and disorder of the day had driven him to distant hunting grounds and he had not yet ventured to return. She drew close to the fire in her rocker and held her smudged hands to the blaze.

She thought, "I've lit a bait o' fires to-day."

That was over and done with. There would be no more 'shining among the palmettos; no more coming and going of folk; no more Trax and his owl-faced girl. She was very tired. Her square frame relaxed in its exhaustion. She leaned back her head and drowsed deeply in her chair.

When she wakened, the fire had burned to ashes. The moon rode high over the flat-woods, with clouds scurrying underneath. The room was silver, then black, as the moonlight came and went. The chill wind sucked through the pines. There was another sound; the sobbing of a lighter breath. Suddenly Matt knew the girl was still there.

She rose in a plunge from the rocker. She wasn't done with them yet. . . . She opened the door a few inches and listened. The muffled sound was unmistakable. It was the choked gasping of a child that has cried itself breathless. It came from the edge of the hammock. Where the pines began she could distinguish a huddle on the ground that was neither stump nor bushes. She closed the door.

Trax was gone—and Elly was here.

He had flung away and left her behind. She was discarded, as Matt had been long discarded. He was through with Elly, too. For the first time the woman was able to conceive of them separately. And the one was gone, and the other was here. She groped her way stupefied to the kitchen, lighted a kerosene lamp, and made a fire in the range. She wanted a scalding pot of tea to stop her shivering. She split a cold biscuit and fried it and sat down with her plate and tea-cup. She breathed hard, and ate and drank mechanically.

"He was done with her a long ways back."

He had driven off alone in the blue sedan, not to infuriate, but because there was nothing else to do with the girl. Matt chewed her biscuit slowly. She laughed grimly.

"I give him too much credit fer smartness."

A flash of anger stirred her, like a spurt of flame from an old fire, that Elly should be now at the edge of the hammock.

"Trax wa'n't man enough to take off his mess with him."

She sipped her cooling tea.

She remembered grudgingly the girl's contentment. The shadow of the man, passing away, left clear the picture of a child, pulling moss apart and cutting paper dolls. Rage at Trax possessed her.

"I'd orter hided him fer takin' sech a young un along his low-down way."

In a burst of fury she conceded the girl's youth. Elly was too young . . .

"I'd orter been hided. Me an' Trax together."

Matt rose from the table and gathered up the few dishes. She stopped in the act. She looked at her hands as though their knotty strength were strange to her.

"Snatchin' off a young un's rations . . ."

She leaned heavily on the table, pondering. Emptiness filled the house—a living presence—appalling—still.

She strode abruptly out the door and through the hammock to the pines. The moon had swung toward its setting and the rays lay long under the trees. The girl lay crouched against a broad mottled trunk.

Matt said, "You kin come on back."

The emaciated figure wavered from the ground on spindling legs. It tried to crowd close to the warmth of the woman's body. As they moved toward the house, the girl stumbled in the run-over slippers.

Matt said, "Here. Gimme them crazy shoes."

Elly stooped and took them from her bare feet. The woman put them in her apron pockets. She went ahead of the girl into the front room and bent down to kindle a fire.

Defender of the Faith

In May of 1945, only a few weeks after the fighting had ended in Europe, I was rotated back to the States, where I spent the remainder of the war with a training company at Camp Crowder, Missouri. Along with the rest of the Ninth Army, I had been racing across Germany so swiftly during the late winter and spring that when I boarded the plane, I couldn't believe its destination lay to the west. My mind might inform me otherwise, but there was an inertia of the spirit that told me we were flying to a new front, where we would disembark and continue our push eastward—eastward until we'd circled the globe, marching through villages along whose twisting, cobbled streets crowds of the enemy would watch us take possession of what, up till then, they'd considered their own. I had changed enough in two years not to mind the trembling of the old people, the crying of the very young, the uncertainty and fear in the eyes of the once arrogant. I had been fortunate enough to develop an infantryman's heart, which, like his feet, at first aches and swells but finally grows horny enough for him to travel the weirdest paths without feeling a thing.

Captain Paul Barrett was my C.O. in Camp Crowder. The day I reported for duty, he came out of his office to shake my hand. He was short, gruff, and fiery, and—indoors or out—he wore his polished helmet liner pulled down to his little eyes. In Europe, he had received a battlefield commission and a serious chest wound, and he'd been returned to the States only a few months before. He spoke easily to me, and at the evening formation he introduced me to the troops. "Gentlemen," he said, "Sergeant Thurston, as you know, is no longer with this company. Your new first sergeant is Sergeant Nathan Marx, here. He is a veteran of the European theatre, and consequently will expect to find a company of soldiers here, and not a company of *boys*."

I sat up late in the orderly room that evening, trying halfheartedly to solve the riddle of duty rosters, personnel forms, and morning reports. The Charge of Quarters slept with his mouth open on a mattress on the floor. A trainee stood reading the next day's duty roster, which was posted on the bulletin board just inside the screen door. It was a warm evening, and I could hear radios playing dance music over in the barracks. The trainee, who had been staring at me whenever he thought I wouldn't notice, finally took a step in my direction.

"Hey, Sarge—we having a G.I. party tomorrow night?" he asked. A G.I. party is a barracks cleaning.

"You usually have them on Friday nights?" I asked him.

"Yes," he said, and then he added, mysteriously, "That's the whole thing."

"Then you'll have a G.I. party."

He turned away, and I heard him mumbling. His shoulders were moving, and I wondered if he was crying.

"What's your name, soldier?" I asked.

He turned, not crying at all. Instead, his green-speckled eyes, long and narrow, flashed like fish in the sun. He walked over to me and sat on the edge of my desk. He reached out a hand. "Sheldon," he said.

"Stand on your feet, Sheldon."

Getting off the desk, he said, "Sheldon Grossbart." He smiled at the familiarity into which he'd led me.

"You against cleaning the barracks Friday night, Grossbart?" I said. "Maybe we shouldn't have G.I. parties. Maybe we should get a maid." My tone startled me. I felt I sounded like every top sergeant I had ever known.

"No, Sergeant." He grew serious, but with a seriousness that seemed to be only the stifling of a smile. "It's just—G.I. parties on Friday night, of all nights."

He slipped up onto the corner of the desk again—not quite sitting, but not quite standing, either. He looked at me with those speckled eyes flashing, and then made a gesture with his hand. It was very slight—no more than a movement back and forth of the wrist—and yet it managed to exclude from our affairs everything else in the orderly room, to make the two of us the center of the world. It seemed, in fact, to exclude everything even about the two of us except our hearts.

"Sergeant Thurston was one thing," he whispered, glancing at the sleeping C.Q., "but we thought that with you here things might be a little different."

"We?"

"The Jewish personnel."

"Why?" I asked, harshly. "What's on your mind?" Whether I was still angry at the "Sheldon" business, or now at something else, I hadn't time to tell, but clearly I was angry.

"We thought you—Marx, you know, like Karl Marx. The Marx Brothers. Those guys are all—M-a-r-x. Isn't that how *you* spell it, Sergeant?"

"M-a-r-x."

"Fishbein said—" He stopped. "What I mean to say, Sergeant—" His face and neck were red, and his mouth moved but no words came out. In a moment, he raised himself to attention, gazing down at me. It was as though he had suddenly decided he could expect no more sympathy from me than from Thurston, the reason being that I was of Thurston's faith, and not his. The young man had managed to confuse himself as to what my faith really was, but I felt no desire to straighten him out. Very simply, I didn't like him.

When I did nothing but return his gaze, he spoke, in an altered tone. "You see, Sergeant," he explained to me, "Friday nights, Jews are supposed to go to services."

"Did Sergeant Thurston tell you you couldn't go to them when there was a G.I. party?"

"No."

"Did he say you had to stay and scrub the floors?"

"No, Sergeant."

"Did the Captain say you had to stay and scrub the floors?"

"That isn't it, Sergeant. It's the other guys in the barracks." He leaned toward me. "They think we're goofing off. But we're not. That's when Jews go to services, Friday night. We have to."

"Then go."

"But the other guys make accusations. They have no right."

"That's not the Army's problem, Grossbart. It's a personal problem you'll have to work out yourself."

"But it's un*fair*."

I got up to leave. "There's nothing I can do about it," I said.

Grossbart stiffened and stood in front of me. "But this is a matter of *religion*, sir."

"Sergeant," I said.

"I mean 'Sergeant,'" he said, almost snarling.

"Look, go see the chaplain. You want to see Captain Barrett, I'll arrange an appointment."

"No, no. I don't want to make trouble, Sergeant. That's the first thing they throw up to you. I just want my rights!"

"Damn it, Grossbart, stop whining. You have your rights. You can stay and scrub floors or you can go to shul—"

The smile swam in again. Spittle gleamed at the corners of his mouth. "You mean church, Sergeant."

"I mean shul, Grossbart!"

I walked past him and went outside. Near me, I heard the scrunching of a guard's boots on the gravel. Beyond the lighted windows of the barracks, young men in T shirts and fatigue pants were sitting on their bunks, polishing their rifles. Suddenly there was a light rustling behind me. I turned and saw Grossbart's dark frame fleeing back to the barracks, racing to tell his Jewish friends that they were right—that, like Karl and Harpo, I was one of them.

The next morning, while chatting with Captain Barrett, I recounted the incident of the previous evening. Somehow, in the telling, it must have seemed to the Captain that I was not so much explaining Grossbart's position as defending it. "Marx, I'd fight side by side with a nigger if a fella proved to me he was a man. I pride myself," he said, looking out the window, "that I've got an open mind. Consequently, Sergeant, nobody gets special treatment here, for the good or bad. All a man's got to do is prove himself. A man fires well on the range, I give him a weekend pass. He scores high in P.T., he gets a weekend pass. He *earns* it." He turned from the window and pointed a finger at me. "You're a Jewish fella, am I right, Marx?"

"Yes, sir."

"And I admire you. I admire you because of the ribbons on your chest. I judge a man by what he shows me on the field of battle, Sergeant. It's what he's got *here*," he said, and then, though I expected he would point to his heart, he jerked a thumb toward the buttons straining to hold his blouse across his belly. "Guts," he said.

"O.K., sir. I only wanted to pass on to you how the men felt."

"Mr. Marx, you're going to be old before your time if you worry about how the men feel. Leave that stuff to the chaplain—that's his business, not yours. Let's us train these fellas to shoot straight. If the Jewish personnel feels the other men are accusing them of goldbricking—well, I just don't know. Seems awful funny that suddenly the Lord is calling so loud in Private Grossman's ear he's just got to run to church."

"Synagogue," I said.

"Synagogue is right, Sergeant. I'll write that down for handy reference. Thank you for stopping by."

That evening, a few minutes before the company gathered outside the orderly room for the chow formation, I called the C.Q., Corporal Robert LaHill, in to see me. LaHill was a dark, burly fellow whose hair curled out of his clothes wherever it could. He had a glaze in his eyes that made one think of caves and dinosaurs. "LaHill," I said, "when you take the formation, remind the men that they're free to attend church services *whenever* they are held, provided they report to the orderly room before they leave the area."

LaHill scratched his wrist, but gave no indication that he'd heard or understood.

"LaHill," I said, "*church*. You remember? Church, priest, Mass, confession."

He curled one lip into a kind of smile; I took it for a signal that for a second he had flickered back up into the human race.

"Jewish personnel who want to attend services this evening are to fall out in front of the orderly room at 1900," I said. Then, as an afterthought, I added, "By order of Captain Barrett."

A little while later, as the day's last light—softer than any I had seen that year—began to drop over Camp Crowder, I heard LaHill's thick, inflectionless voice outside my window: "Give me your ears, troopers. Toppie says for me to tell you that at 1900 hours all Jewish personnel is to fall out in front, here, if they want to attend the Jewish Mass."

At seven o'clock, I looked out the orderly-room window and saw three soldiers in starched khakis standing on the dusty quadrangle. They looked at their watches and fidgeted while they whispered back and forth. It was getting dimmer, and, alone on the otherwise deserted field, they looked tiny. When I opened the door, I heard the noises of the G.I. party coming from the surrounding barracks—bunks being pushed to the walls, faucets pounding water into buckets, brooms whisking at the wooden floors, cleaning the dirt away for Saturday's inspection. Big puffs of cloth moved round and round on the windowpanes. I walked outside, and the moment my foot hit the ground I thought I heard Grossbart call to the others, "'Ten-*hut!*" Or maybe, when they all three jumped to attention, I imagined I heard the command.

Grossbart stepped forward. "Thank you, sir," he said.

"'Sergeant,' Grossbart," I reminded him. "You call officers 'sir.'

I'm not an officer. You've been in the Army three weeks—you know that."

He turned his palms out at his sides to indicate that, in truth, he and I lived beyond convention. "Thank you, anyway," he said.

"Yes," a tall boy behind him said. "Thanks a lot."

And the third boy whispered, "Thank you," but his mouth barely fluttered, so that he did not alter by more than a lip's movement his posture of attention.

"For what?" I asked.

Grossbart snorted happily. "For the announcement. The Corporal's announcement. It helped. It made it—"

"Fancier." The tall boy finished Grossbart's sentence.

Grossbart smiled. "He means formal, sir. Public," he said to me. "Now it won't seem as though we're just taking off—goldbricking because the work has begun."

"It was by order of Captain Barrett," I said.

"Aaah, but you pull a little weight," Grossbart said. "So we thank you." Then he turned to his companions. "Sergeant Marx, I want you to meet Larry Fishbein."

The tall boy stepped forward and extended his hand. I shook it. "You from New York?" he asked.

"Yes."

"Me, too." He had a cadaverous face that collapsed inward from his cheekbone to his jaw, and when he smiled—as he did at the news of our communal attachment—revealed a mouthful of bad teeth. He was blinking his eyes a good deal, as though he were fighting back tears. "What borough?" he asked.

I turned to Grossbart. "It's five after seven. What time are services?"

"Shul," he said, smiling, "is in ten minutes. I want you to meet Mickey Halpern. This is Nathan Marx, our sergeant."

The third boy hopped forward. "Private Michael Halpern." He saluted.

"Salute officers, Halpern," I said. The boy dropped his hand, and, on its way down, in his nervousness, checked to see if his shirt pockets were buttoned.

"Shall I march them over, sir?" Grossbart asked. "Or are you coming along?"

From behind Grossbart, Fishbein piped up. "Afterward, they're having refreshments. A ladies' auxiliary from St. Louis, the rabbi told us last week."

"The chaplain," Halpern whispered.

"You're welcome to come along," Grossbart said.

To avoid his plea, I looked away, and saw, in the windows of the barracks, a cloud of faces staring out at the four of us. "Hurry along, Grossbart," I said.

"O.K., then," he said. He turned to the others. "Double time, *march!*"

They started off, but ten feet away Grossbart spun around and, running backward, called to me, "Good *shabbus*, sir!" And then the three of them were swallowed into the alien Missouri dusk.

Even after they had disappeared over the parade ground, whose green was now a deep blue, I could hear Grossbart singing the double-time cadence, and as it grew dimmer and dimmer, it suddenly touched a deep memory—as did the slant of the light—and I was remembering the shrill sounds of a Bronx playground where, years ago, beside the Grand Concourse, I had played on long spring evenings such as this. It was a pleasant memory for a young man so far from peace and home, and it brought so many recollections with it that I began to grow exceedingly tender about myself. In fact, I indulged myself in a reverie so strong that I felt as though a hand were reaching down inside me. It had to reach so very far to touch me! It had to reach past those days in the forests of Belgium, and past the dying I'd refused to weep over; past the nights in German farmhouses whose books we'd burned to warm us; past endless stretches when I had shut off all softness I might feel for my fellows, and had managed even to deny myself the posture of a conqueror—the swagger that I, as a Jew, might well have worn as my boots whacked against the rubble of Wesel, Münster, and Braunschweig.

But now one night noise, one rumor of home and time past, and memory plunged down through all I had anesthetized, and came to what I suddenly remembered was myself. So it was not altogether curious that, in search of more of me, I found myself following Grossbart's tracks to Chapel No. 3, where the Jewish services were being held.

I took a seat in the last row, which was empty. Two rows in front of me sat Grossbart, Fishbein, and Halpern, holding little white Dixie cups. Each row of seats was raised higher than the one in front of it, and I could see clearly what was going on. Fishbein was pouring the contents of his cup into Grossbart's, and Grossbart looked mirthful as the liquid made a purple arc between Fishbein's hand and his. In the glaring yellow light, I saw the chaplain standing on the platform at the front; he was chanting the first line of the responsive reading. Grossbart's prayer book remained closed on his lap; he was swishing the cup around. Only Halpern responded to the chant by praying. The fingers of his right hand were spread wide across the cover of his open book. His cap was pulled down low onto his brow, which made it round, like a yarmulke. From time to time, Grossbart wet his lips at the cup's edge; Fishbein, his long yellow face a dying light bulb, looked from here to there, craning forward to catch sight of the faces down the row, then of those in front of him, then behind. He saw me, and his eyelids beat a tattoo. His elbow slid into Grossbart's side, his neck inclined toward his friend, he whispered something, and then, when the congregation next responded to the chant, Grossbart's voice was among the others. Fishbein looked into his book now, too; his lips, however, didn't move.

Finally it was time to drink the wine. The chaplain smiled down at them as Grossbart swigged his in one long gulp, Halpern sipped, meditating, and Fishbein faked devotion with an empty cup. "As I look down amongst the congregation"—the chaplain grinned at the word—"this night, I see many new faces, and I want to welcome you to Friday-night services here at Camp Crowder. I am Major Leo Ben Ezra, your chaplain." Though an American, the chaplain spoke deliberately—syllable by syllable, almost—as though to communicate, above all, with the lip readers in his audience. "I have only a few words to say before we adjourn to the refreshment room, where the kind ladies of the Temple Sinai, St. Louis, Missouri, have a nice setting for you."

Applause and whistling broke out. After another momentary grin, the chaplain raised his hands, palms out, his eyes flickering upward a moment, as if to remind the troops where they were and Who Else might be in attendance. In the sudden silence that followed, I thought I heard Grossbart cackle, "Let the goyim clean the floors!" Were those the words? I wasn't sure, but Fishbein, grinning, nudged Halpern. Halpern looked dumbly at him, then went back to his prayer book, which had been occupying him all through the rabbi's talk. One hand tugged at the black kinky hair that stuck out under his cap. His lips moved.

The rabbi continued. "It is about the food that I want to speak to you for a moment. I know, I know, I know," he intoned, wearily, "how in the mouths of most of you the *trafe* food tastes like ashes. I know how you gag, some of you, and how your parents suffer to think of their children eating foods unclean and offensive to the palate. What can I tell you? I can only say, close your eyes and swallow as best you can. Eat what you must to live, and throw away the rest. I wish I could help more. For those of you who find this impossible, may I ask that you try and try, but then come to see me in private. If your revulsion is so great, we will have to seek aid from those higher up."

A round of chatter rose and subsided. Then everyone sang "Ain Kelohainu"; after all those years, I discovered, I still knew the words. Then, suddenly, the service over, Grossbart was upon me. "Higher up? He means the General?"

"Hey, Shelly," Fishbein said, "he means God." He smacked his face and looked at Halpern. "How high can you go!"

"Sh-h-h!" Grossbart said. "What do you think, Sergeant?"

"I don't know," I said. "You better ask the chaplain."

"I'm going to. I'm making an appointment to see him in private. So is Mickey."

Halpern shook his head. "No, no, Sheldon—"

"You have rights, Mickey," Grossbart said. "They can't push us around."

"It's O.K.," said Halpern. "It bothers my mother, not me."

Grossbart looked at me. "Yesterday he threw up. From the hash. It was all ham and God knows what else."

"I have a cold—that was why," Halpern said. He pushed his yarmulke back into a cap.

"What about you, Fishbein?" I asked. "You kosher, too?"

He flushed. "A little. But I'll let it ride. I have a very strong stomach, and I don't eat a lot anyway." I continued to look at him, and he held up his wrist to reinforce what he'd just said; his watch strap was tightened to the last hole, and he pointed that out to me.

"But services are important to you?" I asked him.

He looked at Grossbart. "Sure, sir."

" 'Sergeant.' "

"Not so much at home," said Grossbart, stepping between us, "but away from home it gives one a sense of his Jewishness."

"We have to stick together," Fishbein said.

I started to walk toward the door; Halpern stepped back to make way for me.

"That's what happened in Germany," Grossbart was saying, loud enough for me to hear. "They didn't stick together. They let themselves get pushed around."

I turned. "Look, Grossbart. This is the Army, not summer camp."

He smiled. "So?"

Halpern tried to sneak off, but Grossbart held his arm.

"Grossbart, how old are you?" I asked.

"Nineteen."

"And you?" I said to Fishbein.

"The same. The same month, even."

"And what about him?" I pointed to Halpern, who had by now made it safely to the door.

"Eighteen," Grossbart whispered. "But like he can't tie his shoes or brush his teeth himself. I feel sorry for him."

"I feel sorry for all of us, Grossbart," I said, "but just act like a man. Just don't overdo it."

"Overdo what, sir?"

"The 'sir' business, for one thing. Don't overdo that," I said.

I left him standing there. I passed by Halpern, but he did not look at me. Then I was outside, but, behind, I heard Grossbart call, "Hey, Mickey, my *leben*, come on back. Refreshments!"

"*Leben!*" My grandmother's word for me!

One morning a week later while I was working at my desk, Captain Barrett shouted for me to come into his office. When I entered, he had his helmet liner squashed down so far on his head that I couldn't even see his eyes. He was on the phone, and when he spoke to me, he cupped one hand over the mouthpiece. "Who the hell is Grossbart?"

"Third platoon, Captain," I said. "A trainee."

"What's all this stink about food? His mother called a goddam congressman about the food." He uncovered the mouthpiece and slid his helmet up until I could see his bottom eyelashes. "Yes, sir," he said into the phone. "Yes, sir. I'm still here, sir. I'm asking Marx, here, right now—"

He covered the mouthpiece again and turned his head back toward me. "Lightfoot Harry's on the phone," he said, between his teeth. "This congressman calls General Lyman, who calls Colonel Sousa, who calls the Major, who calls me. They're just dying to stick this thing on me. Whatsa matter?" He shook the phone at me. "I don't feed the troops? What the hell is this?"

"Sir, Grossbart is strange—" Barrett greeted that with a mockingly indulgent smile. I altered my approach. "Captain, he's a very orthodox Jew, and so he's only allowed to eat certain foods."

"He throws up, the congressman said. Every time he eats something, his mother says, he throws up!"

"He's accustomed to observing the dietary laws, Captain."

"So why's his old lady have to call the White House?"

"Jewish parents, sir—they're apt to be more protective than you expect. I mean, Jews have a very close family life. A boy goes away from home, sometimes the mother is liable to get very upset. Probably the boy mentioned something in a letter, and his mother misinterpreted."

"I'd like to punch him one right in the mouth," the Captain said. "There's a goddam war on, and he wants a silver platter!"

"I don't think the boy's to blame, sir. I'm sure we can straighten it out by just asking him. Jewish parents worry—"

"*All* parents worry, for Christ's sake. But they don't get on their high horse and start pulling strings—"

I interrupted, my voice tighter, higher than before. "The home life, Captain, is very important—but you're right, it may sometimes get out of hand. It's a very wonderful thing, Captain, but because it's so close, this kind of thing . . ."

He didn't listen any longer to my attempt to present both myself and Lightfoot Harry with an explanation for the letter. He turned back to the phone. "Sir?" he said. "Sir—Marx, here, tells me Jews have a tendency to be pushy. He says he thinks we can settle it right here in the company. . . . Yes, sir. . . . I *will* call back, sir, soon as I can." He hung up. "Where are the men, Sergeant?"

"On the range."

With a whack on the top of his helmet, he crushed it down over his eyes again, and charged out of his chair. "We're going for a ride," he said.

The Captain drove, and I sat beside him. It was a hot spring day, and under my newly starched fatigues I felt as though my armpits were melting down onto my sides and chest. The roads were dry, and by the time we reached the firing range, my teeth felt gritty with dust, though my mouth had been shut the whole trip. The Captain slammed the brakes on and told me to get the hell out and find Grossbart.

I found him on his belly, firing wildly at the five-hundred-feet target. Waiting their turns behind him were Halpern and Fishbein. Fishbein, wearing a pair of rimless G.I. glasses I hadn't seen on him before, had the appearance of an old peddler who would gladly have sold you his rifle and the cartridges that were slung all over him. I stood back by the ammo boxes, waiting for Grossbart to finish spraying the distant targets. Fishbein straggled back to stand near me.

"Hello, Sergeant Marx," he said.

"How are you?" I mumbled.

"Fine, thank you. Sheldon's really a good shot."

"I didn't notice."

"I'm not so good, but I think I'm getting the hang of it now. Sergeant, I don't mean to, you know, ask what I shouldn't—" The boy stopped. He was trying to speak intimately, but the noise of the shooting forced him to shout at me.

"What is it?" I asked. Down the range, I saw Captain Barrett standing up in the jeep, scanning the line for me and Grossbart.

"My parents keep asking and asking where we're going," Fishbein said. "Everybody says the Pacific. I don't care, but my parents— If I could relieve their minds, I think I could concentrate more on my shooting."

"I don't know where, Fishbein. Try to concentrate anyway."

"Sheldon says you might be able to find out."

"I don't know a thing, Fishbein. You just take it easy, and don't let Sheldon—"

"*I'm* taking it easy, Sergeant. It's at home—"

Grossbart had finished on the line, and was dusting his fatigues with one hand. I called to him. "Grossbart, the Captain wants to see you."

He came toward us. His eyes blazed and twinkled. "Hi!"

"Don't point that goddam rifle!" I said.

"I wouldn't shoot you, Sarge." He gave me a smile as wide as a pumpkin, and turned the barrel aside.

"Damn you, Grossbart, this is no joke! Follow me."

I walked ahead of him, and had the awful suspicion that, behind me, Grossbart was *marching*, his rifle on his shoulder, as though he were a one-man detachment. At the jeep, he gave the Captain a rifle salute. "Private Sheldon Grossbart, sir."

"At ease, Grossman." The Captain sat down, slid over into the empty seat, and, crooking a finger, invited Grossbart closer.

"Bart, sir. Sheldon Gross*bart*. It's a common error." Grossbart nodded at me; *I* understood, he indicated. I looked away just as the mess truck pulled up to the range, disgorging a half-dozen K.P.s with rolled-up sleeves. The mess sergeant screamed at them while they set up the chow-line equipment.

"Grossbart, your mama wrote some congressman that we don't feed you right. Do you know that?" the Captain said.

"It was my father, sir. He wrote to Representative Franconi that my religion forbids me to eat certain foods."

"What religion is that, Grossbart?"

"Jewish."

" 'Jewish, *sir,*' " I said to Grossbart.

"Excuse me, sir. Jewish, sir."

"What have you been living on?" the Captain asked. "You've been in the Army a month already. You don't look to me like you're falling to pieces."

"I eat because I have to, sir. But Sergeant Marx will testify to the fact that I don't eat one mouthful more than I need to in order to survive."

"Is that so, Marx?" Barrett asked.

"I've never seen Grossbart eat, sir," I said.

"But you heard the rabbi," Grossbart said. "He told us what to do, and I listened."

The Captain looked at me. "Well, Marx?"

"I still don't know what he eats and doesn't eat, sir."

Grossbart raised his arms to plead with me, and it looked for a moment as though he were going to hand me his weapon to hold. "But Sergeant—"

"Look, Grossbart, just answer the Captain's questions," I said sharply.

Barrett smiled at me, and I resented it. "All right, Grossbart," he said. "What is it you want? The little piece of paper? You want out?"

"No, sir. Only to be allowed to live as a Jew. And for the others, too."

"What others?"

"Fishbein, sir, and Halpern."

"They don't like the way we serve, either?"

"Halpern throws up, sir. I've seen it."

"I thought *you* throw up."

"Just once, sir. I didn't know the sausage was sausage."

"We'll give menus, Grossbart. We'll show training films about the food, so you can identify when we're trying to poison you."

Grossbart did not answer. The men had been organized into two long chow lines. At the tail end of one, I spotted Fishbein—or, rather, his glasses spotted me. They winked sunlight back at me. Halpern stood next to him, patting the inside of his collar with a khaki handkerchief. They moved with the line as it began to edge up toward the food. The mess sergeant was still screaming at the K.P.s. For a moment, I was actually terrified by the thought that somehow the mess sergeant was going to become involved in Grossbart's problem.

"Marx," the Captain said, "you're a Jewish fella—am I right?"

I played straight man. "Yes, sir."

"How long you been in the Army? Tell this boy."

"Three years and two months."

"A year in combat, Grossbart. Twelve goddam months in combat all through Europe. I admire this man." The Captain snapped a wrist against my chest. "Do you hear him peeping about the food? Do you? I want an answer, Grossbart. Yes or no."

"No, sir."

"And why not? He's a Jewish fella."

"Some things are more important to some Jews than other things to other Jews."

Barrett blew up. "Look, Grossbart. Marx, here, is a good man—a goddam hero. When you were in high school, Sergeant Marx was killing Germans. Who does more for the Jews—you, by throwing up over a lousy piece of sausage, a piece of first-cut meat, or Marx, by killing those Nazi bastards? If I was a Jew, Grossbart, I'd kiss this man's feet. He's a goddam hero, and *he* eats what we give him. Why do you have to cause trouble is what I want to know! What is it you're buckin' for—a discharge?"

"No, sir."

"I'm talking to a wall! Sergeant, get him out of my way." Barrett swung himself back into the driver's seat. "I'm going to see the chaplain." The engine roared, the jeep spun around in a whirl of dust, and the Captain was headed back to camp.

For a moment, Grossbart and I stood side by side, watching the jeep. Then he looked at me and said, "I don't want to start trouble. That's the first thing they toss up to us."

When he spoke, I saw that his teeth were white and straight, and the sight of them suddenly made me understand that Grossbart actually did have parents—that once upon a time someone had taken little Sheldon to the dentist. He was their son. Despite all the talk about his parents, it was hard to believe in Grossbart as a child, an heir—as related by blood to anyone, mother, father, or above all, to me. This realization led me to another.

"What does your father do, Grossbart?" I asked as we started to walk back toward the chow line.

"He's a tailor."

"An American?"

"Now, yes. A son in the Army," he said, jokingly.

"And your mother?" I asked.

He winked. "A *ballabusta*. She practically sleeps with a dustcloth in her hand."

"She's also an immigrant?"

"All she talks is Yiddish, still."

"And your father, too?"

"A little English. 'Clean,' 'Press,' 'Take the pants in.' That's the extent of it. But they're good to me."

"Then, Grossbart—" I reached out and stopped him. He turned toward me, and when our eyes met, his seemed to jump back, to shiver in their sockets. "Grossbart—you were the one who wrote that letter, weren't you?"

It took only a second or two for his eyes to flash happy again. "Yes." He walked on, and I kept pace. "It's what my father *would* have written if he had known how. It was his name, though. *He* signed it. He even mailed it. I sent it home. For the New York postmark."

I was astonished, and he saw it. With complete seriousness, he thrust his right arm in front of me. "Blood is blood, Sergeant," he said, pinching the blue vein in his wrist.

"What the hell *are* you trying to do, Grossbart?" I asked. "I've seen you eat. Do you know that? I told the Captain I don't know what you eat, but I've seen you eat like a hound at chow."

"We work hard, Sergeant. We're in training. For a furnace to work, you've got to feed it coal."

"Why did you say in the letter that you threw up all the time?"

"I was really talking about Mickey there. I was talking *for* him. He would never write, Sergeant, though I pleaded with him. He'll waste away to nothing if I don't help. Sergeant, I used my name—my father's name—but it's Mickey, and Fishbein, too, I'm watching out for."

"You're a regular Messiah, aren't you?"

We were at the chow line now.

"That's a good one, Sergeant," he said, smiling. "But who knows? Who can tell? Maybe you're the Messiah—a little bit. What Mickey says is the Messiah is a collective idea. He went to Yeshiva, Mickey, for a while. He says *together* we're the Messiah. Me a little bit, you a little bit. You should hear that kid talk, Sergeant, when he gets going."

"Me a little bit, you a little bit," I said. "You'd like to believe that, wouldn't you, Grossbart? That would make everything so clean for you."

"It doesn't seem too bad a thing to believe, Sergeant. It only means we should all *give* a little, is all."

I walked off to eat my rations with the other noncoms.

Two days later, a letter addressed to Captain Barrett passed over my desk. It had come through the chain of command—from the office of Congressman Franconi, where it had been received, to General Lyman, to Colonel Sousa, to Major Lamont, now to Captain Barrett.

I read it over twice. It was dated May 14, the day Barrett had spoken with Grossbart on the rifle range.

DEAR CONGRESSMAN:

First let me thank you for your interest in behalf of my son, Private Sheldon Grossbart. Fortunately, I was able to speak with Sheldon on the phone the other night, and I think I've been able to solve our problem. He is, as I mentioned in my last letter, a very religious boy, and it was only with the greatest difficulty that I could persuade him that the religious thing to do—what God Himself would want Sheldon to do—would be to suffer the pangs of religious remorse for the good of his country and all mankind. It took some doing, Congressman, but finally he saw the light. In fact, what he said (and I wrote down the words on a scratch pad so as never to forget), what he said was "I guess you're right, Dad. So many millions of my fellow-Jews gave up their lives to the enemy, the least I can do is live for a while minus a bit of my heritage so as to help end this struggle and regain for all the children of God dignity and humanity." That, Congressman, would make any father proud.

By the way, Sheldon wanted me to know—and to pass on to you —the name of a soldier who helped him reach this decision: SER-GEANT NATHAN MARX. Sergeant Marx is a combat veteran who is Sheldon's first sergeant. This man has helped Sheldon over some of the first hurdles he's had to face in the Army, and is in part responsible for Sheldon's changing his mind about the dietary laws. I know Sheldon would appreciate any recognition Marx could receive.

Thank you and good luck. I look forward to seeing your name on the next election ballot.

Respectfully,
SAMUEL E. GROSSBART

Attached to the Grossbart communiqué was another, addressed to General Marshall Lyman, the post commander, and signed by Representative Charles E. Franconi, of the House of Representatives. The communiqué informed General Lyman that Sergeant Nathan Marx was a credit to the U. S. Army and the Jewish people.

What was Grossbart's motive in recanting? Did he feel he'd gone too far? Was the letter a strategic retreat—a crafty attempt to strengthen what he considered our alliance? Or had he actually changed his mind, via an imaginary dialogue between Grossbart *père* and Grossbart *fils?* I was puzzled, but only for a few days—that is, only until I realized that, whatever his reasons, he had actually decided to disappear from my life; he was going to allow himself to become just another trainee. I saw him at inspection, but he never winked; at chow formations, but he never flashed me a sign. On Sundays, with the other trainees, he would sit around watching the noncoms' softball team, for which I pitched, but not once did he speak an unnecessary word to me. Fishbein and Halpern retreated, too—at Grossbart's command, I was sure. Apparently he had seen that wisdom lay in turning back before he plunged over into the ugliness of privilege undeserved. Our separation allowed me to forgive him our past encounters, and, finally, to admire him for his good sense.

Meanwhile, free of Grossbart, I grew used to my job and my administrative tasks. I stepped on a scale one day, and discovered I had truly become a noncombatant; I had gained seven pounds. I found patience to get past the first three pages of a book. I thought about the future more and more, and wrote letters to girls I'd known before the war. I even got a few answers. I sent away to Columbia for a Law School catalogue. I continued to follow the war in the Pacific, but it was not my war. I thought I could see the end, and sometimes, at night, I dreamed that I was walking on the streets of Manhattan —Broadway, Third Avenue, 116th Street, where I had lived the three years I attended Columbia. I curled myself around these dreams and I began to be happy.

And then, one Saturday, when everybody was away and I was alone in the orderly room reading a month-old copy of the *Sporting News*, Grossbart reappeared.

"You a baseball fan, Sergeant?"

I looked up. "How are you?"

"Fine," Grossbart said. "They're making a soldier out of me."

"How are Fishbein and Halpern?"

"Coming along," he said. "We've got no training this afternoon. They're at the movies."

"How come you're not with them?"

"I wanted to come over and say hello."

He smiled—a shy, regular-guy smile, as though he and I well knew that our friendship drew its sustenance from unexpected visits, remembered birthdays, and borrowed lawnmowers. At first it offended me, and then the feeling was swallowed by the general uneasiness I felt at the thought that everyone on the post was locked away in a dark movie theatre and I was here alone with Grossbart. I folded up my paper.

"Sergeant," he said, "I'd like to ask a favor. It is a favor, and I'm making no bones about it."

He stopped, allowing me to refuse him a hearing—which, of course, forced me into a courtesy I did not intend. "Go ahead."

"Well, actually it's two favors."

I said nothing.

"The first one's about these rumors. Everybody says we're going to the Pacific."

"As I told your friend Fishbein, I don't know," I said. "You'll just have to wait to find out. Like everybody else."

"You think there's a chance of any of us going East?"

"Germany?" I said. "Maybe."

"I meant New York."

"I don't think so, Grossbart. Offhand."

"Thanks for the information, Sergeant," he said.

"It's not information, Grossbart. Just what I surmise."

"It certainly would be good to be near home. My parents—you know." He took a step toward the door and then turned back. "Oh, the other thing. May I ask the other?"

"What is it?"

"The other thing is—I've got relatives in St. Louis, and they say they'll give me a whole Passover dinner if I can get down there. God, Sergeant, that'd mean an awful lot to me."

I stood up. "No passes during basic, Grossbart."

"But we're off from now till Monday morning, Sergeant. I could leave the post and no one would even know."

"I'd know. You'd know."

"But that's all. Just the two of us. Last night, I called my aunt, and you should have heard her. 'Come—come,' she said. 'I got gefilte fish, *chrain*—the works!' Just a day, Sergeant. I'd take the blame if anything happened."

"The Captain isn't here to sign a pass."

"You could sign."

"Look, Grossbart—"

"Sergeant, for two months, practically, I've been eating *trafe* till I want to die."

"I thought you'd made up your mind to live with it. To be minus a little bit of heritage."

He pointed a finger at me. "You!" he said. "That wasn't for you to read."

"I read it. So what?"

"That letter was addressed to a congressman."

"Grossbart, don't feed me any baloney. You *wanted* me to read it."

"Why are you persecuting me, Sergeant?"

"Are you kidding!"

"I've run into this before," he said, "but never from my own!"

"Get out of here, Grossbart! Get the hell out of my sight!"

He did not move. "Ashamed, that's what you are," he said. "So you take it out on the rest of us. They say Hitler himself was half a Jew. Hearing you, I wouldn't doubt it."

"What are you trying to do with me, Grossbart?" I asked him. "What are you after? You want me to give you special privileges, to change the food, to find out about your orders, to give you weekend passes."

"You even talk like a goy!" Grossbart shook his fist. "Is this just a weekend pass I'm asking for? Is a Seder sacred, or not?"

Seder! It suddenly occurred to me that Passover had been cele-brated weeks before. I said so.

"That's right," he replied. "Who says no? A month ago—and I was in the field eating hash! And now all I ask is a simple favor. A Jewish boy I thought would understand. My aunt's willing to go out of her way—to make a Seder a month later. . . ." He turned to go, mumbling.

"Come back here!" I called. He stopped and looked at me. "Gross-bart, why can't you be like the rest? Why do you have to stick out like a sore thumb?"

"Because I'm a Jew, Sergeant. I *am* different. Better, maybe not. But different."

"This is a war, Grossbart. For the time being *be* the same."

"I refuse."

"What?"

"I refuse. I can't stop being me, that's all there is to it." Tears came to his eyes. "It's a hard thing to be a Jew. But now I understand what Mickey says—it's a harder thing to stay one." He raised a hand sadly toward me. "Look at *you*."

"Stop crying!"

"Stop this, stop that, stop the other thing! *You* stop, Sergeant. Stop closing your heart to your own!" And, wiping his face with his sleeve, he ran out the door. "The least we can do for one another—the least . . ."

An hour later, looking out of the window, I saw Grossbart headed across the field. He wore a pair of starched khakis and carried a little leather ditty bag. I went out into the heat of the day. It was quiet; not a soul was in sight except, over by the mess hall, four K.P.s sitting around a pan, sloped forward from their waists, gabbing and peeling potatoes in the sun.

"Grossbart!" I called.

He looked toward me and continued walking.

"Grossbart, get over here!"

He turned and came across the field. Finally, he stood before me.

"Where are you going?" I asked.

"St. Louis. I don't care."

"You'll get caught without a pass."

"So I'll get caught without a pass."

"You'll go to the stockade."

"I'm *in* the stockade." He made an about-face and headed off.

I let him go only a step or two. "Come back here," I said, and he followed me into the office, where I typed out a pass and signed the Captain's name, and my own initials after it.

He took the pass and then, a moment later, reached out and grabbed my hand. "Sergeant, you don't know how much this means to me."

"O.K.," I said. "Don't get in any trouble."

"I wish I could show you how much this means to me."

"Don't do me any favors. Don't write any more congressmen for citations."

He smiled. "You're right. I won't. But let me do something."

"Bring me a piece of that gefilte fish. Just get out of here."

"I will!" he said. "With a slice of carrot and a little horseradish. I won't forget."

"All right. Just show your pass at the gate. And don't tell *anybody*."

"I won't. It's a month late, but a good Yom Tov to you."

"Good Yom Tov, Grossbart," I said.

"You're a good Jew, Sergeant. You like to think you have a hard heart, but underneath, you're a fine, decent man. I mean that."

Those last three words touched me more than any words from Grossbart's mouth had the right to. "All right, Grossbart," I said. "Now call me 'sir,' and get the hell out of here."

He ran out the door and was gone, I felt very pleased with myself; it was a great relief to stop fighting Grossbart, and it had cost me nothing. Barrett would never find out, and if he did, I could manage to invent some excuse. For a while, I sat at my desk, comfortable in my decision. Then the screen door flew back and Grossbart burst in again. "Sergeant!" he said. Behind him I saw Fishbein and Halpern, both in starched khakis, both carrying ditty bags like Grossbart's.

"Sergeant, I caught Mickey and Larry coming out of the movies. I almost missed them."

"Grossbart—did I say tell no one?" I said.

"But my aunt said I could bring friends. That I should, in fact."

"*I'm* the Sergeant, Grossbart—not your aunt!"

Grossbart looked at me in disbelief. He pulled Halpern up by his sleeve. "Mickey, tell the Sergeant what this would mean to you."

Halpern looked at me and, shrugging, said, "A lot."

Fishbein stepped forward without prompting. "This would mean a great deal to me and my parents, Sergeant Marx."

"No!" I shouted.

Grossbart was shaking his head. "Sergeant, I could see you denying me, but how you can deny Mickey, a Yeshiva boy—that's beyond me."

"I'm not denying Mickey anything," I said. "You just pushed a little too hard, Grossbart. *You* denied him."

"I'll give him my pass, then," Grossbart said. "I'll give him my aunt's address and a little note. At least let him go."

In a second, he had crammed the pass into Halpern's pants pocket. Halpern looked at me, and so did Fishbein. Grossbart was at the door, pushing it open. "Mickey, bring me a piece of gefilte fish, at least," he said, and then he was outside again.

The three of us looked at one another, and then I said, "Halpern, hand that pass over."

He took it from his pocket and gave it to me. Fishbein had now moved to the doorway, where he lingered. He stood there for a moment with his mouth slightly open, and then he pointed to himself. "And me?" he asked.

His utter ridiculousness exhausted me. I slumped down in my seat and felt pulses knocking at the back of my eyes. "Fishbein," I said, "you understand I'm not trying to deny you anything, don't you? If it was my Army, I'd serve gefilte fish in the mess hall. I'd sell *kugel* in the PX, honest to God."

Halpern smiled.

"You understand, don't you, Halpern?"

"Yes, Sergeant."

"And you, Fishbein? I don't want enemies. I'm just like you—I want to serve my time and go home. I miss the same things you miss."

"Then, Sergeant," Fishbein said, "why don't you come, too?"

"Where?"

"To St. Louis. To Shelly's aunt. We'll have a regular Seder. Play hide-the-matzo." He gave me a broad, black-toothed smile.

I saw Grossbart again, on the other side of the screen.

"Pst!" He waved a piece of paper. "Mickey, here's the address. Tell her I couldn't get away."

Halpern did not move. He looked at me, and I saw the shrug moving up his arms into his shoulders again. I took the cover off my typewriter and made out passes for him and Fishbein. "Go," I said. "The three of you."

I thought Halpern was going to kiss my hand.

That afternoon, in a bar in Joplin, I drank beer and listened with half an ear to the Cardinal game. I tried to look squarely at what I'd become involved in, and began to wonder if perhaps the struggle with Grossbart wasn't as much my fault as his. What was I that I had to *muster* generous feelings? Who was I to have been feeling so grudging, so tight-hearted? After all, I wasn't being asked to move the world. Had I a right, then, or a reason, to clamp down on Grossbart, when that meant clamping down on Halpern, too? And Fishbein—that ugly, agreeable soul? Out of the many recollections of my childhood that had tumbled over me these past few days, I heard my grandmother's voice: "What are you making a *tsimmes?*" It was what she would ask my mother when, say, I had cut myself while doing something I shouldn't have done, and her daughter was busy bawling me out. I needed a hug and a kiss, and my mother would moralize. But my grandmother knew—mercy overrides justice. I should have known it, too. Who was Nathan Marx to be such a penny pincher with kindness? Surely, I thought, the Messiah himself—if He should ever come—won't niggle over nickels and dimes. God willing, he'll hug and kiss.

The next day, while I was playing softball over on the parade ground, I decided to ask Bob Wright, who was noncom in charge of Classification and Assignment, where he thought our trainees would be sent when their cycle ended, in two weeks. I asked casually, between innings, and he said, "They're pushing them all into the Pacific. Shulman cut the orders on your boys the other day."

The news shocked me, as though I were the father of Halpern, Fishbein, and Grossbart.

That night, I was just sliding into sleep when someone tapped on my door. "Who is it?" I asked.

"Sheldon."

He opened the door and came in. For a moment, I felt his presence without being able to see him. "How was it?" I asked.

He popped into sight in the neardarkness before me. "Great, Sergeant." Then he was sitting on the edge of the bed. I sat up.

"How about you?" he asked. "Have a nice weekend?"

"Yes."

"The others went to sleep." He took a deep, paternal breath. We sat silent for a while, and a homey feeling invaded my ugly little cubicle; the door was locked, the cat was out, the children were safely in bed.

"Sergeant, can I tell you something? Personal?"

I did not answer, and he seemed to know why. "Not about me. About Mickey. Sergeant, I never felt for anybody like I feel for him. Last night I heard Mickey in the bed next to me. He was crying so, it could have broken your heart. Real sobs."

"I'm sorry to hear that."

"I had to talk to him to stop him. He held my hand, Sergeant—he wouldn't let it go. He was almost hysterical. He kept saying if he only knew where we were going. Even if he knew it *was* the Pacific, that would be better than nothing. Just to know."

Long ago, someone had taught Grossbart the sad rule that only lies can get the truth. Not that I couldn't believe in the fact of Halpern's crying; his eyes *always* seemed red-rimmed. But, fact or not, it became a lie when Grossbart uttered it. He was entirely strategic. But then—it came with the force of indictment—so was I! There are strategies of aggression, but there are strategies of retreat as well. And so, recognizing that I myself had not been without craft and guile, I told him what I knew. "It is the Pacific."

He let out a small gasp, which was not a lie. "I'll tell him. I wish it was otherwise."

"So do I."

He jumped on my words. "You mean you think you could do something? A change, maybe?"

"No, I couldn't do a thing."

"Don't you know anybody over at C. and A.?"

"Grossbart, there's nothing I can do," I said. "If your orders are for the Pacific, then it's the Pacific."

"But Mickey—"

"Mickey, you, me—everybody, Grossbart. There's nothing to be done. Maybe the war'll end before you go. Pray for a miracle."

"But—"

"Good night, Grossbart." I settled back, and was relieved to feel the springs unbend as Grossbart rose to leave. I could see him clearly now; his jaw had dropped, and he looked like a dazed prizefighter. I noticed for the first time a little paper bag in his hand.

"Grossbart." I smiled. "My gift?"

"Oh, yes, Sergeant. Here—from all of us." He handed me the bag. "It's egg roll."

"Egg roll?" I accepted the bag and felt a damp grease spot on the bottom. I opened it, sure that Grossbart was joking.

"We thought you'd probably like it. You know—Chinese egg roll. We thought you'd probably have a taste for—"

"Your aunt served egg roll?"

"She wasn't home."

"Grossbart, she invited you. You told me she invited you and your friends."

"I know," he said. "I just reread the letter. *Next* week."

I got out of bed and walked to the window. "Grossbart," I said. But I was not calling to him.

"What?"

"What are you, Grossbart? Honest to God, what are you?"

I think it was the first time I'd asked him a question for which he didn't have an immediate answer.

"How can you do this to people?" I went on.

"Sergeant, the day away did us all a world of good. Fishbein, you should see him, he *loves* Chinese food."

"But the Seder," I said.

"We took second best, Sergeant."

Rage came charging at me. I didn't sidestep. "Grossbart, you're a liar!" I said. "You're a schemer and a crook. You've got no respect for anything. Nothing at all. Not for me, for the truth—not even for poor Halpern! You use us all—"

"Sergeant, Sergeant, I feel for Mickey. Honest to God, I do. I *love* Mickey. I try—"

"You try! You feel!" I lurched toward him and grabbed his shirt front. I shook him furiously. "Grossbart, get out! Get out and stay the hell away from me. Because if I see you, I'll make your life miserable. *You understand that?*"

"Yes."

I let him free, and when he walked from the room, I wanted to spit on the floor where he had stood. I couldn't stop the fury. It engulfed me, owned me, till it seemed I could only rid myself of it with tears or an act of violence. I snatched from the bed the bag Grossbart had given me and, with all my strength, threw it out the window.

And the next morning, as the men policed the area around the barracks, I heard a great cry go up from one of the trainees, who had been anticipating only his morning handful of cigarette butts and candy wrappers. "Egg roll!" he shouted. "Holy Christ, Chinese goddam egg roll!"

A week later, when I read the orders that had come down from C. and A., I couldn't believe my eyes. Every single trainee was to be shipped to Camp Stoneman, California, and from there to the Pacific —every trainee but one. Private Sheldon Grossbart. He was to be sent to Fort Monmouth, New Jersey. I read the mimeographed sheet several times. Dee, Farrell, Fishbein, Fuselli, Fylypowycz, Glinicki, Gromke, Gucwa, Halpern, Hardy, Helebrandt, right down to Anton Zygadlo—all were to be headed West before the month was out. All except Grossbart. He had pulled a string, and I wasn't it.

I lifted the phone and called C. and A.

The voice on the other end said smartly, "Corporal Shulman, sir."

"Let me speak to Sergeant Wright."

"Who is this calling, sir?"

"Sergeant Marx."

And, to my surprise, the voice said, "Oh!" Then, "Just a minute, Sergeant."

Shulman's "Oh!" stayed with me while I waited for Wright to come to the phone. Why "Oh!"? Who was Shulman? And then, so simply, I knew I'd discovered the string that Grossbart had pulled. In fact, I could hear Grossbart the day he'd discovered Shulman in the PX, or in the bowling alley, or maybe even at services. "Glad to meet you. Where you from? Bronx? Me, too. Do you know So-and-So? And So-and-So? Me, too! You work at C. and A.? Really? Hey, how's chances of getting East? Could you do something? Change something? Swindle, cheat, lie? We gotta help each other, you know. If the Jews in Germany . . ."

Bob Wright answered the phone. "How are you, Nate? How's the pitching arm?"

"Good. Bob, I wonder if you could do me a favor." I heard clearly my own words, and they so reminded me of Grossbart that I dropped more easily than I could have imagined into what I had planned. "This may sound crazy, Bob, but I got a kid here on orders to Monmouth who wants them changed. He had a brother killed in Europe, and he's hot to go to the Pacific. Says he'd feel like a coward if he wound up Stateside. I don't know, Bob—can anything be done? Put somebody else in the Monmouth slot?"

"Who?" he asked cagily.

"Anybody. First guy in the alphabet. I don't care. The kid just asked if something could be done."

"What's his name?"

"Grossbart, Sheldon."

Wright didn't answer.

"Yeah," I said. "He's a Jewish kid, so he thought I could help him out. You know."

"I guess I can do something," he finally said. "The Major hasn't been around here for weeks. Temporary duty to the golf course. I'll try, Nate, that's all I can say."

"I'd appreciate it, Bob. See you Sunday." And I hung up, perspiring.

The following day, the corrected orders appeared: Fishbein, Fuselli, Fylypowycz, Glinicki, Gromke, Grossbart, Gucwa, Halpern, Hardy . . . Lucky Private Harley Alton was to go to Fort Monmouth, New Jersey, where, for some reason or other, they wanted an enlisted man with infantry training.

After chow that night, I stopped back at the orderly room to straighten out the guard-duty roster. Grossbart was waiting for me. He spoke first.

"You son of a bitch!"

I sat down at my desk, and while he glared at me, I began to make the necessary alterations in the duty roster.

"What do you have against me?" he cried. "Against my family? Would it kill you for me to be near my father, God knows how many months he has left to him?"

"Why so?"

"His heart," Grossbart said. "He hasn't had enough troubles in a lifetime, you've got to add to them. I curse the day I ever met you, Marx! Shulman told me what happened over there. There's no limit to your anti-Semitism, is there? The damage you've done here isn't enough. You have to make a special phone call! You really want me dead!"

I made the last few notations in the duty roster and got up to leave. "Good night, Grossbart."

"You owe me an explanation!" He stood in my path.

"Sheldon, you're the one who owes explanations."

He scowled. "To *you?*"

"To me, I think so—yes. Mostly to Fishbein and Halpern."

"That's right, twist things around. I owe nobody nothing, I've done all I could do for them. Now I think I've got the right to watch out for myself."

"For each other we have to learn to watch out, Sheldon. You told me yourself."

"You call this watching out for me—what you did?"

"No. For all of us."

I pushed him aside and started for the door. I heard his furious breathing behind me, and it sounded like steam rushing from an engine of terrible strength.

"You'll be all right," I said from the door. And, I thought, so would Fishbein and Halpern be all right, even in the Pacific, if only Grossbart continued to see—in the obsequiousness of the one, the soft spirituality of the other—some profit for himself.

I stood outside the orderly room, and I heard Grossbart weeping behind me. Over in the barracks, in the lighted windows, I could see the boys in their T shirts sitting on their bunks talking about their orders, as they'd been doing for the past two days. With a kind of quiet nervousness, they polished shoes, shined belt buckles, squared away underwear, trying as best they could to accept their fate. Behind me, Grossbart swallowed hard, accepting his. And then, resisting with all my will an impulse to turn and seek pardon for my vindictiveness, I accepted my own.

WILLIAM SAROYAN

The Daring Young Man
on the Flying Trapeze

SLEEP

Horizontally wakeful amid universal widths, practicing laughter and mirth, satire, the end of all, of Rome and yes of Babylon, clenched teeth, remembrance, much warmth volcanic, the streets of Paris, the plains of Jericho, much gliding as of reptile in abstraction, a gallery of watercolors, the sea and the fish with eyes, symphony, a table in the corner of The Eiffel Tower, jazz at the opera house, alarm clock and the tap-dancing of doom, conversation with a tree, the river Nile, Cadillac coupe to Kansas, the roar of Dostoyevsky, and the dark sun.

This earth, the face of one who lived, the form without the weight, weeping upon snow, white music, the magnified flower twice the size of the universe, black clouds, the caged panther staring, deathless space, Mr. Eliot with rolled sleeves baking bread, Flaubert and Guy de Maupassant, a wordless rhyme of early meaning, mathematics highly polished and slick as a green onion to the teeth, Jerusalem, the path to paradox.

The deep song of man, the sly whisper of someone unseen but vaguely known, hurricane in the cornfield, a game of chess, hush the queen, the king, Karl Franz, black Titanic, Mr. Chaplin weeping, Stalin, Hitler, a multitude of Jews, tomorrow is Monday, no dancing in the streets allowed.

O swift moment of life: it is ended, the earth is again now.

II

WAKEFULNESS

He (the living) dressed and shaved, grinning at himself in the mirror. Very unhandsome, he said; where is my tie? (He had but one.) Coffee and a gray sky, Pacific Ocean fog, the drone of a passing streetcar, people going to the city, time again, the day, prose and poetry. He moved swiftly down the stairs to the street and began to walk, thinking suddenly, It is only in sleep that we may know that we live. There only, in that living death, do we meet ourselves and the far earth, God and the saints, the name of our fathers, the substance of remote moments; it is there that the centuries merge in the moment, that the vast becomes the tiny, tangible atom of eternity.

He walked into the day as alertly as might be, making a definite noise with his heels, perceiving with his eyes the superficial truth of streets and structures, the trivial truth of reality. Helplessly his mind sang, He flies through the air with the greatest of ease; the daring young man on the flying trapeze; then laughed with all the might of his being. It was really a splendid morning: gray, cold, and cheerless, a morning for inward vigor; ah Edgar Guest, he said, how I long for your music.

In the gutter he saw a coin which proved to be a penny dated 1923, and placing it in the palm of his hand he examined it closely, remembering that year and thinking of Lincoln whose profile was stamped upon the coin. There was almost nothing a man could do with a penny. I will purchase a motorcar, he thought. I will dress myself in the fashion of a fop, visit the hotel strumpets, drink and dine, and then return to the quiet. Or I will drop the coin into a slot and weigh myself.

It was good to be poor, and the Communists—but it was dreadful to be hungry. What appetites they had, how fond they were of food. Empty stomachs. He remembered how greatly he needed roast turkey, mashed potatoes, cranberry sauce, pumpkin pie, cheese, coffee, walnuts and raisins. Every meal was bread and coffee and cigarettes, and now he had no more bread. Coffee without bread could never honestly serve as supper, and there were really no weeds in the park that could be cooked like spinach.

If the truth were known, he was half starved, and yet there was still no end of books he ought to read before he died. He remembered the young Italian in a Brooklyn hospital, a small sick clerk named Mollica, who had said desperately, I would like to see California once before I die. And he thought earnestly, I ought at least to read Hamlet once again; or perhaps Huckleberry Finn.

It was then that he became thoroughly awake: at the thought of dying. Now wakefulness was a state in the nature of a sustained shock. A young man could perish rather unostentatiously, he thought; and already he was very nearly starved. Water and prose were fine, they filled much inorganic space, but nevertheless they were inadequate. If there were only some work he might do for money, some trivial labor in the name of commerce. If they would only allow him to sit at a desk all day and add trade figures, subtract and multiply and divide, then perhaps he would not die. He would buy food, all sorts of it: untasted delicacies from Norway, Italy, and France; all manner of beef, lamb, fish, cheese; grapes, figs, pears, apples, melons, which he would worship when he had satisfied his hunger. He would place a bunch of red grapes on a dish beside two black figs, a large yellow pear, and a green apple. He would hold a cut melon to his nostrils for hours, meditating. He would buy great brown loaves of French bread, vegetables of all sorts, cases of beer, sacks of nuts, cartons of raisins, pastry, candy, everything.

From a hill he saw the city standing majestically in the east, great towers, dense with his kind, and there he was suddenly outside of it all, almost definitely certain that he should never gain admittance, almost positive that somehow he had ventured upon the wrong earth, or perhaps into the wrong age, and now a young man of twenty-two was to be permanently ejected from it. This thought was not saddening. He said to himself, sometime soon I must write An Application For Permission To Live. He accepted the thought of dying without pity for himself or for man, believing that he would at least sleep another night. His rent for another day was paid; there was yet another tomorrow. And after that he might go where other homeless men went. He might even visit the Salvation Army—sing to God and Jesus (unlover of my soul), be saved, eat and sleep. But he knew that he would not. His life was a private life. He did not wish to destroy this fact. Any other alternative would be better.

Through the air on the flying trapeze, his mind hummed. Amusing it was, astoundingly funny. A trapeze to God, or to nothing, a flying trapeze to some sort of eternity; he prayed objectively for the strength to make the flight with grace.

I have one cent, he said. It is an American coin. In the evening I shall polish it until it glows like a sun and I shall study the words.

He was now walking in the city itself, among living men. There were one or two places to go. He saw his reflection in the plate-glass windows of stores and was disappointed with his appearance. He seemed not at all as strong as he felt; he seemed, in fact, a trifle infirm in every part of his body, in his neck, his shoulders, arms, trunk, and knees. This will never do, he said, and with a brave effort he assembled all his disjointed parts and became tensely, artificially erect and solid.

He passed numerous restaurants with magnificent discipline, refusing even to glance into them, and at last reached a building which he entered. He rose in an elevator to the seventh floor, moved down a hall, and, opening a door, walked into the office of an employment agency. Already there were two dozen young men in the place; he found a corner where he stood waiting his turn to be interviewed. At length he was granted this great privilege and was questioned by a thin, scatterbrained miss of fifty.

Now tell me, she said; what can you do?

He was embarrassed. I can write, he said pathetically.

You mean your penmanship is good? Is that it? said the elderly maiden.

Well, yes, he replied. But I mean that I can write.

Write what? said the miss, almost with anger.

Prose, he said simply.

There was a pause. At last the lady said:

Can you use a typewriter?

Of course, said the young man.

All right, went on the miss, we have your address; we will get in touch with you. There is nothing this morning, nothing at all.

It was much the same at the other agency, except that he was questioned by a conceited young man who closely resembled a pig. From the agencies he went to the large department stores: there was a good deal of pomposity, some humiliation on his part, and then of course the report that work was not available. He did not feel displeased, and strangely did not even feel that he was personally implicated in all the foolishness. He was a living young man who was in need of money with which to go on being one, and there was no way of getting it except by working for it; and there was no work. It was purely an abstract problem which he wished for the last time to attempt to solve. Now he was pleased that the matter was closed.

He began to perceive the definiteness of the course of his life. Except for moments, it had been largely artless, but now at the last minute he was determined that there should be as little imprecision as possible.

He passed countless stores and restaurants on his way to the Y.M.C.A., where he helped himself to paper and ink and began to compose his Application. For an hour he worked on this document, then suddenly, owing to the bad air in the place and to hunger, he became faint. He seemed to be swimming away from himself with great strokes, and hurriedly left the building. In the

Civic Center Park, across from the Public Library Building, he drank almost a quart of water and felt himself refreshed. An old man was standing in the center of the brick boulevard surrounded by sea gulls, pigeons, and robins. He was taking handfuls of bread crumbs from a large paper sack and tossing them to the birds with a gallant gesture.

Dimly he felt impelled to ask the old man for a portion of the crumbs, but he did not allow the thought even nearly to reach consciousness; he entered the Public Library and for an hour read Proust, then, feeling himself to be swimming away again, he rushed outdoors. He drank more water at the fountain in the park and began the long walk to his room.

I'll go and sleep some more, he said; there is nothing else to do. He knew now that he was much too tired and weak to deceive himself about being all right, and yet his mind somehow still seemed lithe and alert. It, as if it were a separate entity, persisted in articulating impertinent pleasantries about his very real physical suffering. He reached his room early in the afternoon and immediately prepared coffee on the small gas range. There was no more milk in the can and the half pound of sugar he had purchased a week before was all gone; he drank a cup of the hot black fluid, sitting on his bed and smiling.

From the Y.M.C.A. he had stolen a dozen sheets of letter paper upon which he hoped to complete his document, but now the very notion of writing was unpleasant to him. There was nothing to say. He began to polish the penny he had found in the morning, and this absurd act somehow afforded him great enjoyment. No American coin can be made to shine so brilliantly as a penny. How many pennies would he need to go on living? Wasn't there something more he might sell? He looked about the bare room. No. His watch was gone; also his books. All those fine books; nine of them for eighty-five cents. He felt ill and ashamed for having parted with his books. His best suit he had sold for two dollars, but that was all right. He didn't mind at all about clothes. But the books. That was different. It made him very angry to think that there was no respect for men who wrote.

He placed the shining penny on the table, looking upon it with the delight of a miser. How prettily it smiles, he said. Without reading them he looked at the words, E Pluribus Unum One Cent United States Of America, and turning the penny over, he saw Lincoln and the words, In God We Trust Liberty 1923. How beautiful it is, he said.

He became drowsy and felt a ghastly illness coming over his blood, a feeling of nausea and disintegration. Bewildered, he stood beside his bed, thinking that there was nothing to do but sleep. Already he felt himself making great strides through the fluid of the earth, swimming away to the beginning. He fell face down upon the bed, saying, I ought first at least to give that coin to some child. A child could buy any number of things with a penny.

Then swiftly, neatly, with the grace of the young man on the trapeze, he was gone from his body. For an eternal moment he was all things at once: the bird, the fish, the rodent, the reptile, and man. An ocean of print undulated endlessly and darkly before him. The city burned. The herded crowd rioted. The earth circled away, and knowing that he did so, he turned his lost face to the empty sky and became dreamless, unalive, perfect.

MARK SCHORER

What We Don't Know Hurts Us

The midafternoon winter sun burned through the high California haze. Charles Dudley, working with a mattock in a thicket of over-growth, felt as steamy and as moldy as the black adobe earth in which his feet kept slipping. Rain had fallen for five days with no glimmer of sunshine, and now it seemed as if the earth, with fetid animation, like heavy breath, were giving all that moisture back to the air. The soil, or the broom which he was struggling to uproot, had a disgusting, acrid odor, as if he were tussling with some ob-scene animal instead of with a lot of neglected vegetation, and sud-denly an overload of irritations—the smell, the stinging sweat in his eyes, his itching skin, his blistering palms—made him throw the mattock down and come diving out of the thicket into the clearing he had already achieved.

"Is it hard?"

He looked up and saw Josephine, his wife, sitting on the railing of the balcony onto which the french doors of their bedroom opened. She was holding a dust mop, and a tea towel was wrapped around her head, and her face seemed pallid and without character, as it always did to Charles when she neglected to wear lipstick.

He snorted instead of replying, and wiped his muddy hands on the seat of his stiff new levis. Then he walked over to the short flight of steps that led up to the balcony from the garden, and lit a cigarette.

"It looks as though the ground levels out up there where you're working," Josephine said.

"Yes, it does. Somebody once had a terrace up there. It's full of overgrown geraniums that are more like snakes, and a lot of damned rose vines."

"You've got the pepper tree almost free. It's going to be very nice, isn't it?"

He looked up at the pepper tree, with its delicate, drooping branches and the long gray tendrils that hung down from the branches to the ground. He had chopped out the broom as far up the incline as the tree, and now he could see that a big branch of the eucalyptus at the very edge of the property had forced the top of the pepper tree to grow out almost horizontally from the main portion of its trunk. "Look at the damned thing!" he said.

"It's charming, like a Japanese print."

"I'm going to hate this house long before it's livable," he said.

"Oh, Charles!"

"I didn't want to buy a house. I never wanted to own any house. I certainly never wanted to own a miserable, half-ruined imitation of a Swiss chalet built on an incline that was meant for goats." Vehemently he flipped his cigarette up into the pile of brush he had accumulated.

Josephine stood up and shook out the dust mop. "Let's not go into all that again. There was no choice. It's no pleasure for me, either, living the way we are, nor is it for the children." She paused, and then she added a cold supplement. "I sometimes think that your disinclination to own anything is a form of irresponsibility." She turned swiftly and went into the house.

He stood staring after her, frowning a little, for it seemed momentarily that with studied intent she had cracked the bland habit of her amiability. But in a minute she reappeared in the doorway and said matter-of-factly, "I heard on the radio that Boston has had eighteen inches of snow." Then she went back inside.

"Are you trying to make me homesick?" he asked of no one as he started back up the incline, and he remembered the frozen river, snow blowing over the Esplanade, and city lights faint in a blizzard.

He began again to chop at the roots of the broom. All right, he told himself, so he was being unpleasant. He did not like the idea of being pinned down by a mortgage to a place his firm had picked for him. He did not even like the idea of being pinned down by a mortgage. To own something was, to that extent, to be owned, and he did not like the feeling. His idea of a good way to live was in a duplex apartment owned by someone else, in Charles River Square, or, better than that but always less likely, in a duplex apartment owned by someone else, on the East River. He connected happiness with a certain luxury, and, probably, sexuality with elegance and freedom. These were not noble associations, he was aware, and he knew that it was foolish to let impossibilities, as they faded, become forms of minor torture. This knowledge made him chop more an-grily than ever at the broom.

It was vegetation with which Charles felt that he had a peculiar intimacy, perhaps the only thing in California which, in the several weeks they had lived there, he had really come to know. And he loathed it with a violence which he recognized as quite undue, and which, now, made him feel childish and curiously guilty. Yet he could not laugh away his loathing. The stuff was ubiquitous, and sprang up anywhere at all the minute the ground was neglected. If it grew up in a patch, it began a foolish competition with itself, and the thin, naked stalks shot ten and twelve and fourteen feet into the air, all stretching up to the sun for the sake of a plume of paltry foliage at the top. Then the foliage tangled together in a thatch, and when you had managed to chop out the shallow roots of the tree, you still had to extricate its trivial but tenacious branches from those of all its neighbors to get it out of the clump. Once it was out, the wood was good for nothing, but dried up into a kind of bamboo stalk so insubstantial that it did not make even decent kindling. As a tree it was a total fraud, and in spite of the nuisance of its num-bers, and of its feminine air of lofty self-importance, it was, with its shallow roots in this loose soil, very vulnerable to attack. Charles beat away at it in an angry frenzy, as if he were overwhelming, after a long struggle, some bitter foe.

He did not hear his son come up the incline behind him, and the boy stood quietly watching until his father turned to toss a stalk up on the pile in the clearing. Then the boy said, "Hi." He said it tentatively, almost shyly, as though his father's responses were un-predictable.

"Hi, Gordon."

"What're you doing?"

"Can't you see? How was school?"

"It stinks," he answered doggedly, his dark eyes half-averted and sorrowful.

Charles felt a twinge of pain for him. "Cheer up. Give it time. You'll get to like it after a while."

"I'll never like it," Gordon said stubbornly.

Charles took up his mattock again. "Sure you will," he said as he began to swing it.

"Nobody likes me."

Charles let the mattock come to rest and, turning once more to the boy, he spoke with an impatient excess of patience. "You say that every day. I've told you it isn't true. You're a new boy in the school, and you came in the middle of the term, and there's never yet been a new boy who entered a school late and made friends right away. You're nearly nine, and you can understand that. Anyway, I'm tired of explaining it to you."

"When can I get a paper route?"

Charles laughed without humor. "My God, boy! Give us a chance to get settled."

"I need money."

"You get an allowance."

"I need more money," the boy insisted. "I want a paper route. How do kids get them?"

"You can work for me. You can get in there with a hedge shears and cut out all those vines."

The boy looked at his father despairingly and shook his head. "No, I need a lot of money."

"You can earn a lot of money working for me," Charles said, swinging his mattock.

"I need a dollar," Gordon said faintly.

His father did not hear him, and he did not turn from his work again until presently he heard his daughter calling him shrilly from the foot of the hill on which the house stood.

"What is it?" he called back. She was climbing the path, and he saw that she had a white envelope in her hand.

Then Gordon broke into rapid, desperate speech. "I need a dollar. I'll pay it back out of my allowance. Remember yesterday I told you about that dollar I found? I have to pay it back."

Charles stared at him. "What dollar?"

Gordon glanced wildly over his shoulder. His sister, holding the menacing white envelope in one hand and her workman's tin lunch box in the other, was halfway up the hill, coming along the side of the house. Pleadingly, Gordon looked back at his father. "The dollar. Remember? I told you I found it. You wanted to know what I did with it."

"What dollar?"

He sighed. "You didn't listen! You never listen!"

Charles patted his shoulder. "Now take it easy. Don't get excited. Tell me again. I don't think you told me anything about a dollar yesterday."

"The dollar I found. You asked me what I did with it, and I told you I gave it to Crow, and you said I should have brought it home to you."

"That Crow! I thought you were joking."

Penelope, the six-year-old, was behind him now, and Gordon's shoulders sagged in despair. "I wasn't joking," he said almost wearily as Penelope handed his father the letter. "You never really listen."

Charles read the precise handwriting on the envelope. "Mr. or Mrs. Dudley," it said, and in the lower left-hand corner, "Courtesy of Penelope." He opened the envelope and read the message:

DEAR MR. AND MRS. DUDLEY,

Gordon became involved in some difficulty about a dollar today, and I wish you would help me. The dollar was lunch money belonging to a girl who says she left it deep in her coat pocket, in the cloakroom, yesterday. When I brought it up with Gordon, he immediately said that he did not steal it. He says that he found it on the floor, and he also says that he told his father about it yesterday and that his father said he should have brought it home to him, and now he is fixed in his confusions. He gave it to an older boy named Will Crow, who spent it, and I have told Gordon that he will have to return a dollar to the girl tomorrow. Gordon is a very worth-while little personality, but I do not think he has been entirely happy here at the Crestview School, and therefore, if you can help me straighten this out to his own best interest, I will be ever so grateful.

Sincerely yours,
GERTRUDE GRANDJENT,
Principal.

Charles groaned in exasperation. "My God, why did you have to drag me into it? What will that woman think?"

Gordon's lips were trembling. "You remember? I did tell you, didn't I?"

"Yes, I remember now. I remember very clearly that you told me you found it on the way to school, and when I asked you what you did with it, and you said you gave it to Crow, naturally I said you should have brought it home. *Listen,* Gordon——" The very simplicity of the boy's strategy infuriated Charles, and it was with an effort that he controlled his temper. He said, "Penny, you go in now and tell your mother you're home."

Penny was staring at her brother. "What did Gordon do?"

"Run along, Penny, as I told you."

She went down the incline reluctantly, staring back over her shoulder, and when she had gone into the house, Charles turned to Gordon again and said, "Sit down."

They sat down side by side on the damp slope. Gordon said, "Will

you lend me a dollar and keep my allowance until it's made up? I
have to take it back tomorrow."

"We'll talk about that later." Charles tapped the letter with his
muddy hand. "Why did you tell me you found it in the street?"

Gordon looked away but answered promptly. "I knew if I told
you I found it in school, you'd have said I should have taken it to
the office."

"So you lied to me instead. That was better?"

Gordon did not answer.

"Answer me."

"Yes."

"Yes, what?"

"I lied."

That was that. Charles started over. "Why did you tell Miss
Grandjent that you did not steal it when she hadn't even said that
you had?"

"I knew that's what she thought."

"How did you know?"

"I just knew."

Charles hesitated. When he spoke again, his voice was warmer,
friendly, almost confidential. "What's the little girl's name, Gordon?"

"She's not little. She's in high fourth."

"What's her name?"

"I don't know. Joan, I guess."

"What color is her coat?"

Gordon glanced at his father sharply. "I don't know. I never
noticed it."

Charles bit his lip in exasperation and stood up. "Let's go inside."
He led the way in.

Josephine was standing on a chair in the middle of the living
room. She was dusting the hideous chandelier of dark metal and
colored glass which hung from the center of the ceiling. It was only
one of many distasteful features in the house which the Dudleys
hoped to rid it of, but it was hard to find men to do all the necessary
work, and none would promise to do it quickly. An electrician had
torn away a good deal of plaster and lathing, and a carpenter had
ripped out some bookshelves and ugly mantels and taken down most
of a wall between the dining room and a useless hallway, but neither
had returned, and painters, plasterers, paper hangers had not yet
come at all. The Dudleys had decided to leave most of their belongings in storage until the work was done, and to bring nothing out
of storage that they cared about. The result was that the house was

almost fantastically disordered and bleak and squalid, and while
Josephine managed to keep an even temper under these conditions,
Charles, who found them very trying, did not.

He stood in the doorway of the living room now and said to her,
"Why do you bother?"

"The light was so dim," she said, and then, seeing his expression,
asked quickly, "What's wrong?"

"Another problem." He came heavily into the living room and
gave her the letter. She read it standing on the chair, her face expressionless. Then she stepped down and went out into the hall
where Gordon was lurking and said, "Come in, dear."

There was one old sofa in the room, and Josephine sat down there
with Gordon. Charles sat facing them on the single straight chair.
Josephine took Gordon's hands and said, "Now tell me everything,
Gordon, just the way it happened."

The boy's face was composed in a kind of stolid determination,
but when he raised his moody eyes from the bare floor to his father,
his chin began to tremble, his eyelids fluttered, and suddenly the
dogged expression broke in despair, his body sagged, his head fell
back against the sofa, and he burst into harsh sobs. Josephine put
her arm around his shoulders and held him close while he cried, and
she shook her head sharply at Charles as he jumped up impatiently.
He sat down again. Finally Gordon stopped crying, almost as
abruptly as he had begun.

"How did it happen, Gordon?" his mother asked.

He straightened up and stared at the floor again. "Nothing happened. I just came in the cloakroom and saw it on the floor. I took
it and put it in my pocket, and at recess I gave it to Crow."

"Didn't anyone see you pick it up?"

"There wasn't anyone else there."

"In the cloakroom? Before school? Why not?"

"I was late."

"Late? But why? You left here in plenty of time."

"I stopped on the way and played with a cat."

Josephine frowned. "So there was no one else there at all to see
you?" she asked meaningfully.

"No."

Josephine glanced at Charles. He drew his lips apart and, with
a heavy satiric edge, said, "Well, Gordon, that's too bad! If there'd
been someone else there, you could prove that you hadn't——"

Josephine broke in. "Tell me just where the dollar was, Gordon," she said softly, and her voice had no relation to the look in her eyes as she glared at Charles.

"On the floor."

"But exactly where? Was it near the little girl's coat?"

"She isn't little."

"Was it near her coat?"

"I don't know which coat is hers."

"Was it near any coat?"

"It was on the floor, near all of them. They hang on a rack, and it was on the floor near them."

Josephine paused, and Gordon wriggled his shoulders out from under her arm and slumped in the corner of the sofa, away from her. "When can I get out of here?" he asked.

"When you start answering our questions," his father said sharply. "You insist that you didn't steal it?"

Gordon raised his lids slowly, as if they were very heavy, and stared out at his father from under his brows. "I found it on the floor."

Josephine spoke brightly. "Very well. We have settled that. But, Gordon, surely you don't think that because you found it on the floor, it belonged to you? Don't you see that it was just as much stealing it as if you had really taken it from the pocket of the person it belonged to?"

"Not as much," Gordon said.

"But it wasn't *yours!* You knew that."

The boy nodded.

"Well, then——"

"Someone else would have found it!"

"But would someone else have kept it?"

"I didn't keep it."

Charles leaped up from his chair. "That's the point! Why in God's name did you give it to that Crow rat?"

"He's my friend," Gordon said with simple defiance, and then he slid off the sofa and lay on the floor.

"Your friend! A fine friend!" Charles shouted in disgust, standing over him. "Get up!"

Gordon did not make any effort to move, and Josephine grasped Charles's arm. "Let me," she said quietly. "Sit down."

"Nonsense!" he cried angrily at her, and pulled his arm free of her touch. "I'll take over now." He seized the boy by the shoulders and pulled him up on the sofa. The jerk which he gave his body made the boy's head bob back and forward like a doll's, and he slumped against the sofa back almost as if he had been injured, dull eyes staring out of his pale face. "Now listen to me, Gordon. I don't know if you took that money out of someone's pocket or not, but it looks, from the way you're behaving, as if you did. Anyway, you took it. It didn't belong to you, you knew that, and yet you took it. Do you see that there is no difference between the floor and the pocket as long as you kept it?"

"I didn't keep it," Gordon repeated, but almost listlessly.

"Oh, my God!" Charles ran his hand through his hair, and the rumpled hair gave him a sudden wild look. "Listen," he said as quietly as he could, "we are all having a very hard time here. We are trying to live in a house that isn't fit to live in. I am trying to get used to a new office. Your mother——"

Josephine said, "Don't bother about me."

"I will bother! We are all having a tough time, and Gordon can't think of anything better to do than to get into this mess at school. Of all the friends you could pick, you pick that nasty Crow brat, who is too old for you by three years and is a snide little——"

"Charles!"

Gordon lay back on the sofa. He looked ill and defeated.

"Will you admit that you stole that dollar? That taking it from the floor was just as much stealing it as if you had taken it from the pocket?"

"Yes," he answered faintly.

"Speak up!"

"Yes, I *do!*" Gordon cried, and turned his face away.

Then the room was very still. Josephine stood stiffly beside the couch, her eyes fixed on Charles with dismay. Charles sagged a little, as if he, too, were defeated. And Gordon might have been asleep or dreaming, so remote had he suddenly become. Then they all heard a sly noise at the door, and Charles and Josephine swung toward it. Penelope stood there, embarrassed to have been caught. She giggled and said, "Why did Gordon steal money?"

"Go away," Charles said.

"Go to your room, dear," Josephine said, "or go outside."

"But why did Gordon steal money?"

Charles walked to the girl, gave her a little push, and closed the door on her face. Then he came back to the sofa. He sat down next to Gordon, and when he spoke, his voice was nearly lifeless. "You want to earn that dollar. All right, you can, Gordon. First go to your room and write your five sentences. Do them quickly for a change, and then go out into that patch of broom with the hedge shears and

cut down all the vines you can find in it. You have an hour left before it gets dark."

Gordon's eyes dreamed over his father's face, and then he slowly
got up and left the room. His parents watched him go, and when
he had closed the door softly behind him, Charles broke out. "What
is it, what stubbornness, that makes that boy so impenetrable? Did
he steal that money or not? I haven't the slightest idea. All I could do
was force him to admit that there was no difference between the
two things."

Josephine was looking a him with studied appraisal.

"Well?" he challenged her.

"You forced his admission. Did that gain anything? And what
did it lose? How much did it hurt him? Is it of very great importance
whether he stole it or not?"

"I don't know what's more important."

"No, I really think you don't."

"Well?"

"What's more important is why he took it, and what he did with
it, and why he did that. What's more important is that he's a miserable little boy, and that you haven't made the slightest effort to understand *that*. All you've done is played the heavy parent, shown
him that you don't trust him or believe him, and left him with a nice
new layer of solidified guilt, and what is he supposed to do with
that?"

"Let's skip the psychology for a change," Charles said. "There is
an old-fashioned principle of honesty and dishonesty."

"There's a more old-fashioned one of simple perception!" Josephine's face was red with anger. She stood in the middle of the bare
room and looked rapidly around her, as if she felt a sudden desperate need, a hunger, for objects. But there was only the sofa, the
chair, and Charles. Her eyes came back to him.

"Have you thought of his difficulties at all? Just the simple matter
of his writing, for example? He came from a school where the children printed, and he printed as well as anyone. He comes here
where the children do cursive writing, and of course he's made to
feel like a fool, and he has to practice at home to learn it when other
boys are playing. Or have you once helped him with that? Have you
even suggested a sentence he might write? No. All you've done is to
give him the extremely comforting bit of information that new boys,
especially if they enter school late, have a hard time making friends!
The one friend he has made you deride. No, don't interrupt. I know
he's a horrid boy. I don't want Gordon playing with him either. But

you haven't the sense to see that what has brought them together is that they are both pariahs. I think Gordon's giving that dollar to that dreadful boy is one of the most touching things I've ever heard of!"

"If what you've told me about Crow is true," Charles said quietly, "I won't have Gordon playing with him, and that's that."

"Because Crow taught him some nasty words and told him some nasty, mistaken things about sex! You're perfectly right. But you can't just stand there and say no to him! If you were half a father, you would have told him yourself. *You* should be his friend! You're the one who should be giving him a decent attitude toward those things. You *are* his father, after all."

"Oh, listen—— He's not even nine!"

"All right. But he's getting it, isn't he? And all wrong?" And then, without warning, she sat down heavily on the single chair and began to sob, her reddened face lifted, her mouth twisted in sorrow, tears streaming down over her cheeks. "All *wrong!*" she wailed.

Charles went to her quickly and, half standing, half kneeling beside the chair, awkwardly put his arms around her. "Josephine, listen——"

"Oh, I know!" she sobbed. "We all get in your way. We're all a nuisance that you're saddled with! We all just *bother* you! I know! It just isn't your idea of the way to live. You really hate it, don't you?"

His arms tightened. "Darling," he said, "don't be a damned fool. Listen, I love you, I love the kids. Why, little Penny, I——"

"Oh, yes. Penny, sure! She's tractable! She doesn't raise any problems. That's different!"

"You're crazy. Gordon, too. You. Maybe I'm not much good with him, but that doesn't mean . . . And listen . . . I'll try. I'll go out there now."

She dug in her pocket for a piece of Kleenex. She blew her nose and wiped her eyes. She pulled the tea towel off her head and shook out her hair. Then she blew her nose again. "I'm all right now," she said, getting up. She picked up the dustcloth which she had flung over the back of the chair, and she said, "It's probably just this awful house, the way we have to camp. I'm going to get cleaned up and dress, and I'm going to find a tablecloth, and we'll have dinner at a table tonight, instead of sitting on the floor with plates in our laps."

He said, "Good girl! I'll go and fix it up with Gordon."

Charles went into Gordon's room. It was empty. He glanced at the table where Gordon worked and saw that there was a sheet of writing there. Then he looked out of the window and saw the boy on his hands and knees in among the remaining broom. He crossed the hall to the bedroom where Josephine was dressing. "I may not be very subtle with him, but I seem to get results," he said. She merely glanced up at him, and as he went out on the balcony, down the steps, and up the slippery incline, he felt no satisfaction whatever in his remark.

"How's it going?" he asked the boy.

Gordon glanced over his shoulder. "All right," he said, and turned at once to his job. The hedge shears made a busy, innocent sound.

Charles found his mattock where he had dropped it, and began to chop at the edge of the overgrowth again. Immediately his nostrils filled with the poisonous smell he had noticed before, his hands began to chafe, and even though the heat of the sun had gone in the late afternoon, sweat broke out with a prickling sensation all over his face and body. Once more he was tense with irritation, and he said, "That awful smell! What is it?"

"I don't know," Gordon replied without looking up.

"Like something decaying."

The boy did not answer, and Charles chopped angrily away at a root. When it came free, he shook the earth off and tossed the slim tree down the slope. "This crazy, piddling stuff!" he shouted, and then reminded himself that it was only a kind of exaggerated weed, a thing that grew everywhere, so futile that it could not even send down a decent root and was hardly designed as a personal affront to him. Or was it? He laughed and started to chop at the next root, but stopped at once. "I'm quitting for today," he said. "Come on, let's go in."

Gordon said, "No, I'll work a while. I want to earn the money."

"Oh, let it go. We'll fix that up."

Gordon stared at him. "I want to earn it," he said, and went on clipping at the rose vines.

"All right," Charles said, "but come in soon. You'll have to wash up thoroughly to get that muck off."

He went back into the house by way of the bedroom, but Josephine was no longer there. He went into Gordon's room, but she was not there, either. On the table lay the white sheet of ruled paper covered with the boy's writing, his five sentences in their hasty, uncertain, and very large cursive characters. Charles picked it up. The first sentence was, "I am going to cut vins." The second was, "I am going to ern mony." The third was, "The sun is shining." The fourth was, "When it rains here it rains hard." The last, which seemed to have been written with greater care, with a kind of precision and flourish which his writing had never shown before, was, "You hate me and I hate you."

Charles took a sharp breath and held it, then sagged. After a moment he walked to the window and put his forehead against the cool glass. He stared out into the desolate garden, at the bare earth and the darkening tangle, and tried to think. When he heard Josephine moving on high heels somewhere in the rugless house, he began to fold the sheet of paper, and he folded it again and again, until it was a small hard square. This he stuffed deep into his pocket.

He came into the hall and saw Josephine standing in the center of the barren living room. She looked tall in an old but still handsome black housecoat, a straight, severe garment which hung from the tightly belted waist in heavy folds, and was without ornament or color anywhere. Her hair was pulled tautly away from her face, and her face was smooth and white, and her mouth was painted dark red.

She was detached from the room, from the house, and utterly from him—remote and beautiful, cold in resolution. Never in the ten years he had known her had she appeared so wonderfully in possession of herself. And, helplessly, Charles turned away.

He went into the boy's room again, and looked out to see the boy. But twilight had obscured the garden now, shadows hung about it like veils, and Charles could hardly see into the trees. Then he thought that he saw Gordon's shape, hunched on the ground among the slim trunks, and he went out quickly to find him. Perhaps, even now, after everything, it was the boy who, somehow, could help.

Gunners' Passage

"In Brazil," Whitejack was saying, "the problem was girls. American girls."

They were lying on the comfortable cots, with the mosquito netting looped gracefully over their heads and the barracks quiet and empty, except for the two of them, and shaded and cool, when you remembered that outside the full sun of Africa stared down.

"Three months in the jungle, on rice and monkey meat." Whitejack lit a large, long, nickel cigar and puffed deeply, squinting up at the tin roof. "When we got to Rio we felt we deserved an American girl. So the lieutenant and Johnny Moffat and myself, we got the telephone directory of the American Embassy and we went down the list, calling up likely names—secretaries, typists, interpreters, filing clerks——" Whitejack grinned up at the ceiling. He had a large, sunburned, rough face that was broken into good looks by his smile, and his speech was Southern, but not the kind of Southern that puts a Northerner's teeth on edge.

"It was the lieutenant's idea, and by the time we got to the Q's, he was ready to give up. But we hit pay dirt on the S's." Slowly he blew out a long column of cigar smoke. "Uh-uh," he said, closing his eyes reflectively. "Two months and eleven days of honey and molasses. Three tender and affectionate American girls, as loving as the day is long, with their own flat. Beer in the icebox from Sunday to Sunday, steaks big enough to saddle a mule with, and nothing to do—just lie on the beach in the afternoon and go swimmin' when the mood seized yuh. On per diem."

"How were the girls?" Stais asked. "Pretty?"

"Well, Sergeant." Whitejack paused thoughtfully and pursed his lips. "To tell you the truth, Sergeant, the girls the lieutenant and Johnny had were as smart and pretty as chipmunks. Mine . . ." Once more he paused. "Ordinarily my girl would find herself hard put to collect a man in the middle of a full division of infantry soldiers. She was small and runty and she had less curves than a rifle barrel and she wore glasses. But from the first time she looked at me I could see she wasn't interested in Johnny or the lieutenant. She looked at me, and behind her glasses her eyes were soft and hopeful and humble and appealing." Whitejack flicked the cigar ash off into a little tin can which was resting on his bare chest. "Sometimes," he said slowly, "a man feels mighty small if he just thinks of himself and turns down an appeal like that. Let me tell you something, Sergeant. I was in Rio two months and eleven days and I didn't look at another woman. All those dark-brown women walkin' along the beach, three quarters out of their bathing suits, just wavin' it in front of your face—I didn't look at them. This runty, skinny little thing with glasses was the most lovin' and satisfactory and decent little person a man could possibly conceive of and a man'd just have to be hog-greedy with sex to have winked an eye at another woman." Whitejack doused his cigar, took the tin can off his chest, and rolled over on his belly. "Now," he said, "I'm going to get myself a little sleep."

In a moment Whitejack was snoring gently, his tough mountaineer's face tucked childishly into the crook of one arm. Outside, on the shady side of the building, a native boy hummed low and wild to himself as he ironed a pair of sun-tan trousers. From the field, two hundred yards away, again and again came the sliding roar of engines climbing or descending the afternoon sky.

Stais closed his eyes wearily. Ever since he'd got into Accra he had done nothing but sleep and lie on his cot daydreaming, listening to Whitejack talk.

"Hi," Whitejack had said as Stais had come slowly into the barracks two days before. "Which way you going?"

"Home," Stais had said, smiling wearily, as he did every time he said it. "Going home. Which way you going?"

"Not home." Whitejack had grinned a little. "Not home at all."

Stais liked to listen to Whitejack. Whitejack talked about America, about the woods of the Blue Ridge Mountains, where he had been in the forestry service, about his mother's cooking and how he had owned great dogs who had been extraordinary at finding a trail and holding it, about how they had tried hunting deer in the hills from the medium bomber (no good because of the swirling winds rising from the gorges), about pleasant, indiscriminate weekend parties in the woods with his friend Johnny Moffat and the girls from the mill in the next town. Stais had been away from

America for nineteen months now, and Whitejack's talk made his native country seem present and pleasantly real to him.

"There was a man in my town by the name of Thomas Wolfe," Whitejack had said irrelevantly that morning. "He was a great big feller and he went away to New York to be an author. Maybe you heard of him?"

"Yes," said Stais. "I read two books of his."

"Well, I read that book of his," said Whitejack, "and the people in town were yellin' to lynch him for a while, but I read that book, and he got that town down fair and proper, and when they brought him back dead I came down from the hills and I went to his funeral. There were a lot of important people from New York and over to Chapel Hill down for the funeral and it was a hot day, too, and I'd never met the feller, but I felt it was only right to go to his funeral after readin' his book. And the whole town was there, very quiet, although just five years before they were yellin' to lynch him, and it was a sad and impressive sight and I'm glad I went."

And another time, the slow, deep voice rolling between sleep and sleep in the shaded heat, "My mother takes a quail and bones it, then she scoops out a great big sweet potato and lays some bacon on it, then she puts the quail in and cooks it slow for three hours, bastin' it with butter all the time. You got to try that sometime."

"Yes," said Stais, "I will."

Stais did not have a high-priority number and there seemed to be a flood of colonels surging toward America, taking all the seats on the C-54s setting out westward, so he'd had to wait. It hadn't been bad. Just to lie down, stretched full out, unbothered, these days, was holiday enough after Greece, and anyway he didn't want to arrive home, in front of his mother, until he'd stopped looking like a tired old man. And the barracks usually were empty and quiet and the chow good at the transient mess and you could get Coca-Cola and chocolate milk at the PX. The rest of the enlisted men in Whitejack's crew were young and ambitious and were out swimming all day and going to the movies or playing poker in another barracks all night, and Whitejack's talk was smooth and amusing in the periods between sleep and dreams. Whitejack was an aerial photographer and gunner in a mapping and survey squadron and he'd been in Alaska and Brazil and back to the States and now was on his way to India, full of conversation. He was in a Mitchell squadron and the whole squadron was supposed to be on its way together, but two of the Mitchells had crashed and burned on the take-off at Natal as Whitejack's plane had circled the field, waiting to form up. The rest of the squadron had been held at Natal and Whitejack's plane had been sent on to Accra, across the ocean, by itself.

Vaguely and slowly, lying on the warm cot, with the wild song of the Negro boy outside the window, Stais thought of the two Mitchells burning between sea and jungle three thousand miles away, and of other planes burning elsewhere, and of what it was going to be like sitting down in the armchair of his own house and looking across the room at his mother, and of the pretty Viennese girl in Jerusalem, and of the DC-3 coming down slowly, like an angel in the dusk, to the rough, secret pasture in the Peloponnesian hills.

He fell asleep. His bones knit gently into dreams on the soft cot, with the sheets, in the quiet barracks, and he was over Athens again, with the ruins pale and shining on the hills, and the fighters boring in, and Lathrop saying, over the intercom, as they persisted into a hundred, fifty yards, twisting, swift and shifty, in the bright Greek sky, "They grounded all the students today. They have the instructors up this afternoon." And, suddenly and wildly, fifty feet over Ploesti, with Liberators going down into the filth in dozens, flaming . . . Then swimming off the white beach at Benghazi, with the dead boys playing in the mild, tideless swell, then the parachute pulling at every muscle in his body, then the green and forest blue of Minnesota woods and his father, fat and small, sleeping on pine needles on his Sunday off, then Athens again, Athens . . .

"I don't know what's come over the lieutenant," a new voice was saying as Stais came out of his dream. "He passes us on the field and he just don't seem to see us."

Stais opened his eyes. Novak, a farm boy from Oklahoma, was sitting on the edge of Whitejack's bed, talking. "It has all the guys real worried." He had a high, shy, rather girlish voice. "I used to think they never came better than the lieutenant. Now . . ." Novak shrugged. "If he does see you, he snaps at you like he was General Ulysses S. Grant."

"Maybe," Whitejack said, "maybe seeing Lieutenant Brogan go down in Natal . . . He and Brogan were friends since they were ten years old. Like as if I saw Johnny Moffat go down."

"It's not that." Novak went over to his own cot and got out his writing pad. "It began back in Miami, four weeks ago. Didn't you notice it?"

"I noticed it," Whitejack said slowly.

"You ought to ask him about it." Novak started writing a letter.

"You and him are good friends. After all, going into combat now, it's bad—the lieutenant just lookin' through us when he passes us on the field. You don't think he's drunk all the time, do you?"

"He's not drunk."

"You ought to ask him."

"Maybe I will." Whitejack sat up. "Maybe I will." He looked forlornly down at his stomach. "Since I got into the Army I've turned pig-fat. On the day I took the oath I was twenty-eight and one half inches around the waist. Today I'm thirty-two and three quarters if I'm an inch. The Army . . . Maybe I shouldn't've joined. I was in a reserved profession, and I was the sole support of an ailing mother."

"Why did you join?" Stais asked.

"Oh." Whitejack smiled at him. "You're awake. Feeling any better, Sergeant?"

"Feeling fine, thanks. Why did you join?"

"Well . . ." Whitejack rubbed the side of his jaw. "Well, I waited and I waited. I sat up in my cabin in the hills and I tried to avoid listenin' to the radio, and I waited and I waited, and finally I went downtown to my mother and I said, 'Ma'am, I just can't wait any longer,' and I joined up."

"When was that?" Stais asked.

"Eight days"—Whitejack lay down again, plumping the pillow under his head—"eight days after Pearl Harbor."

"Sergeant," Novak said, "Sergeant Stais, you don't mind if I tell my girl you're a Greek, do you?"

"No," Stais said gravely. "I don't mind. You know, I was born in Minnesota."

"I know," said Novak, writing industriously. "But your parents came from Greece. My girl'll be very interested, your parents coming from Greece and you bombing Greece and being shot down there."

"What do you mean, your girl?" Whitejack asked. "I thought you said she was going around with a technical sergeant in Flushing, Long Island."

"That's true," Novak said apologetically. "But I still like to think of her as my girl."

"It's the ones that stay at home," said Whitejack darkly, "that get all the stripes and all the girls. My motto is, don't write to a girl once you get out of pillowcase distance from her."

"I like to write to this girl in Flushing, Long Island," Novak said, his voice shy but stubborn. Then to Stais, "How many days were you in the hills before the Greek farmers found you?"

"Fourteen," said Stais.

"And how many of you were wounded?"

"Three. Out of seven. The others were dead."

"Maybe he doesn't like to talk about it, Charlie," Whitejack said.

"Oh, I'm sorry." Novak looked up, his young, unlined face crossed with concern.

"That's all right," Stais said. "I don't mind."

"Did you tell them you were a Greek too?" Novak asked.

"When one finally showed up who could speak English."

"That must be funny," Novak said reflectively. "Being a Greek, bombing Greece, not speaking the language. Can I tell my girl they had a radio and they radioed to Cairo?"

"It's the girl of a technical sergeant in Flushing, Long Island," Whitejack chanted. "Why don't you look facts in the face?"

"I prefer it this way," Novak said with dignity.

"I guess you can tell about the radio," Stais said. "It was pretty long ago. Three days later the DC-3 came down through a break in the clouds. It'd been raining all the time and it just stopped for about thirty minutes at dusk and that plane came down, throwin' water fifteen feet in the air. We cheered, but we couldn't get up from where we were sitting, any of us, because we were too weak to stand."

"I got to write that to my girl," Novak said. "Too weak to stand."

"Then it started to rain again and the field was hip-deep in mud and when we all got into the DC-3 we couldn't get it started." Stais spoke calmly and thoughtfully, as though he were alone, reciting to himself. "We were just bogged down in that Greek mud. Then the pilot got out—he was a captain—and he looked around, with the rain coming down and all those farmers just standing there, sympathizing with him, and nothing anyone could do, and he just cursed for ten minutes. He was from San Francisco and he really knew how to curse. Then everybody started breaking branches off the trees in the woods around that pasture, even those of us who couldn't stand an hour before, and we just covered that big DC-3 complete with branches and waited for the rain to stop. We just sat in the woods and prayed no German patrols would come out in weather like that. In those three days I learned five words of Greek."

"What are they?" Novak asked.

"*Vouno,*" Stais said. That means 'mountain.' *Vrohi*: rain. *Theos*: God. *Avrion*: tomorrow. And *yassou*. That means 'farewell.'"

"*Yassou,*" Novak said. "Farewell."

"Then the sun came out and the field started to steam and nobody said anything. We just sat there, watching the water dry off the grass, then the puddles started to go, here and there, then the mud to cake a little. Then we got into the DC-3 and the Greeks pushed and hauled for a while and we broke loose and got out. And those farmers just standing below waving at us, as though they were seeing us off at Grand Central Station. Ten miles farther on we went right over a German camp. They fired at us a couple of times, but they didn't come anywhere close. The best moment of my whole life was getting into that hospital bed in Cairo. I just stood there and looked at it for a whole minute, looking at the sheets. Then I got in, very slow."

"Did you ever find out what happened to those Greeks?" Novak asked.

"No," said Stais. "I guess they're still there, waiting for us to come back someday."

There was silence, broken only by the slow scratching of Novak's pen. Stais thought of the thin, dark mountain faces of the men he had last seen, fading away, waving, standing in the scrub and short silver grass of the hill pasture near the Aegean Sea. They had been cheerful and anxious to please, and there was a look on their faces that made you feel they expected to die.

"How many missions were you on?" Novak asked.

"Twenty-one and a half," Stais said. He smiled. "I count the last one as half."

"How old are you?" Novak was obviously keeping the technical sergeant's girl carefully posted on all points of interest.

"Nineteen."

"You look older," said Whitejack.

"Yes," said Stais.

"A lot older."

"Yes."

"Did you shoot down any planes?" Novak peered at him shyly, his red face uncertain and embarrassed, like a little boy asking a doubtful question about girls. "Personally?"

"Two," Stais said. "Personally."

"What did you feel?"

"Why don't you leave him alone?" Whitejack said. "He's too tired to keep his eyes open as it is."

"I felt—relieved," Stais said. He tried to think of what he'd really felt when the tracers went in and the Focke-Wulf started to smoke like a crazy smudge pot and the German pilot fought wildly for half a second with the cowling and then didn't fight wildly any more.

There was no way of telling these men, no way of remembering, in words, himself. "You'll find out," he said. "Soon enough. The sky's full of Germans."

"Japs," Whitejack said. "We're going to India."

"The sky's full of Japs."

There was silence once more, with the echo of the word "Japs" rustling thinly in the long, quiet room, over the empty rows of cots. Stais felt the old waving dizziness starting behind his eyes that the doctor in Cairo had said came from shock or starvation or exposure or all of these things, and lay back, still keeping his eyes open, because it became worse and waved more violently when he closed his eyes.

"One more question," Novak said. "Are—are guys afraid?"

"You'll be afraid," Stais said.

"Do you want to send that back to your girl in Flushing?" Whitejack asked sardonically.

"No," said Novak quietly. "I wanted that for myself."

"If you want to sleep," said Whitejack, "I'll shut this farmer up."

"Oh no," said Stais. "I'm pleased to talk."

"If you're not careful," Whitejack said, "he'll talk about his girl in Flushing."

"I'd be pleased to hear it," said Stais.

"It's only natural I should want to talk about her," Novak said. "She was the best girl I ever knew in my whole life. I'd've married her if I could."

"My motto," said Whitejack, "is never marry a girl who goes to bed with you the first time out. The chances are she isn't pure. The second time—that, of course, is different." He winked at Stais.

"I was in Flushing, Long Island, taking a five-week course in aerial cameras," Novak said, "and I was living at the Y.M.C.A."

"This is where I leave." Whitejack got off the bed and put on his pants.

"The Y.M.C.A. was very nice. There were bathrooms for every two rooms, and the food was very good," said Novak, talking earnestly to Stais, "but I must confess, I was lonely in Flushing, Long Island."

"I'll be back"—Whitejack was buttoning up his shirt—"for the ninth installment."

"As long as you're going out," Novak said to him, "I wish you'd talk to the lieutenant. It really makes me feel queer, passing him and him just looking through me like I was a windowpane."

"Maybe I'll talk to the lieutenant," Whitejack said. "And leave the sergeant alone. Remember, he's a tired man who's been to the war and he needs his rest." He went out.

Novak stared after Whitejack. "There's something wrong with him too," he said. "Just lying on his back here for ten days, reading and sleeping. He never did that before. He was the liveliest man in the United States Air Force. Seeing those two planes go down . . . It's a funny thing, you fly with fellers all over the world, over America, Brazil, Alaska, you watch them shoot porpoises and sharks in gunnery practice over the Gulf Stream, you get drunk with them, go to their weddings, talk to them over the radio with their planes maybe a hundred feet away, in the air, and after all that flying, in one minute, for no reason, two planes go down. Fourteen fellers you've been livin' with for over a year." Novak shook his head. "There was a particular friend of Whitejack's in one of those planes. Frank Sloan. Just before we left Miami they had a big fight. Frank went off and married a girl that Whitejack'd been going with off and on for a year, every time we hit Miami. Whitejack told him he was crazy, half the squadron had slept with the lady, and that was true too, and just to teach him a lesson he'd sleep with her himself after they'd been married. And he did, too." Novak sighed. "A lot of funny things happen in the Army when fellers've been together a long time and get to know each other real well. And then one minute the Mitchell goes down. I guess Whitejack must've felt sort of queer, watching Frankie burn." Novak had put his writing pad down and now he screwed the top on his fountain pen. "The truth is," he said, "I don't feel so solid myself. That's why I like to talk. Especially to you. You've been through it. You're young, but you've been through it. But if it's any bother to you I'll keep quiet."

"No," said Stais, still lying back, abstractedly wondering whether the waving would get worse or better, "not at all."

"This girl in Flushing, Long Island," Novak said slowly. "It's easy for Whitejack to make fun of me. The girls fall all over themselves chasing after him. He has no real conception of what it's like to be a man like me. Not very good-looking. Not much money. Not an officer. Not humorous. Shy."

Stais couldn't help grinning. "You're going to have a tough time in India."

"I know," Novak said. "I've resigned myself to not having a girl until the armistice. How did you do with the girls in the Middle East?" he asked politely.

"There was a nice Viennese girl in Jerusalem," Stais said dreamily. "But otherwise zero. You have to be very good, unless you're an officer, in the Middle East."

"That's what I heard," Novak said sorrowfully. "Well, it won't be so different to me from Oklahoma. That was the nice thing about this girl in Flushing, Long Island. She saw me come into the jewelry store where she worked and I was in my fatigues and I was with a very smooth feller who made a date with her for that night. But she smiled at me and I knew if I had the guts I could ask her for a date too. But of course I didn't. But then later that night I was sitting in my room in the Y.M.C.A. and my phone rang. It was this girl. The other feller had stood her up, she said, and would I take her out." Novak smiled dimly, thinking of that tremulous moment of glory in the small Y.M.C.A. room far away. "I got my fatigues off in one minute and shaved and showered and I picked her up. We went to Coney Island. It was the first time in my entire life I had ever seen Coney Island. It took three and a half weeks for me to finish my course and I went out with that girl every single night. Nothing like that ever happened to me before in my life—a girl who just wanted to see me every night of the week. Then, the night before I was due to leave to join my squadron, she told me she had got permission to take the afternoon off and she would like to see me down to the train, if I let her. I called at the jewelry shop at noon and her boss shook my hand and she had a package under her arm and we got into the subway and we rode to New York City. Then we went into a cafeteria and had a wonderful lunch and she saw me off and gave me the package. It was Schrafft's candy, and she was crying at the gate there, crying for me, and she said she would like me to write, no matter what." Novak paused and Stais could tell that the scene at the gate, the hurrying crowds, the package of Schrafft's chocolates, the weeping young girl, were as clear as the afternoon sunlight to Novak, there on the coast of Africa. "So I keep writing," Novak said. "She's written me she has a technical sergeant now, but I keep writing. I haven't seen her in a year and a half and what's a girl to do? Do you blame her?"

"No," said Stais. "I don't blame her."

"I hope I haven't bored you," Novak said.

"Not at all." Stais smiled at him. Suddenly the dizziness had gone and he could close his eyes. As he drifted down into that weird and ever-present pool of sleep in which he half lived these days, he heard Novak say, "Now I have to write my mother."

Outside the Negro boy sang, and the planes grumbled down from the Atlantic and laboriously set out across the Sahara Desert.

Dreams again: Arabs, bundled in rags, driving camels along the perimeter of the field, outlined against the parked Liberators and waiting bombs; two Mitchells still burning on the shores of Brazil and Frank Sloan burning there and, circling above him, Whitejack, who had told him he'd sleep with his wife and had; the hills around Jerusalem, gnarled, rocky, dusty, with the powdered green of olive groves set on slopes here and there, clinging against the desert wind; Mitchells slamming along the gorges of the Blue Ridge Mountains, bucking in the updrafts, their guns going, hunting deer; the Mediterranean, bluer than anything in America, below them on the way home from Italy, coming down below oxygen level, with the boys singing dirty songs over the intercom, and leave in Alexandria ahead of them. The girl from Flushing, Long Island, quietly going hand in hand with Novak to Coney Island on a summer's night.

It was Whitejack who awakened him. He woke slowly. It was dark outside and the electric light was shining in his eyes and Whitejack was standing over him, shaking him gently.

"I thought you'd like to know," Whitejack was saying, "your name's on the bulletin board. You're leaving tonight."

"Thanks," Stais said, dimly grateful at being shaken out of the broken and somehow sorrowful dreams.

"I took the liberty of initialing it for you, opposite your name," Whitejack said. "Save you a trip up to the field."

"Thanks," said Stais. "Very kind of you."

"Also," said Whitejack, "there's fried chicken for chow."

Stais pondered over the fried chicken. He was a little hungry, but the effort of getting up and putting on his shoes and walking the hundred yards to the mess hall had to be weighed in the balance. "Thanks. I'll just lie right here," he said. "Any news of your boys?" he asked.

"Yes," said Whitejack. "The squadron came in."

"That's good."

"All except one plane." Whitejack sat down on the end of Stais's cot. His voice was soft and expressionless. "Johnny Moffat's plane."

In all the months that Stais had been in the Air Force, on fields to which planes had failed to return, he had learned that there was nothing to say. He was only nineteen years old, but he had learned that. So he lay quiet.

"They got separated in clouds on the way out of Ascension, and they never picked them up again. There's still a chance," Whitejack said, "that they'll drop in any minute." He looked at his watch. "Still a chance for another hour and forty minutes."

There was still nothing to say, so Stais lay silent.

"Johnny Moffat," said Whitejack, "at one time looked as though he was going to marry my sister. In a way it's a good thing he didn't. It'd be a little hard, being brothers-in-law, on some of the parties the Air Force goes on in one place and another." Whitejack fell silent and looked down at his belly. Deliberately he let his belt out a notch, then pulled it to, with a severe little click. "That fried chicken was mighty good," he said. "You sure you want to pass it up?"

"I'm saving my appetite for my mother's cooking," Stais said.

"My sister was passing fond of Johnny," said Whitejack, "and I have a feeling when he gets home from the war and settles down she's going to snag him. She came to me right before I left and she asked me if I would let her have ten acres on the north side of my property and three acres of timber to build their house. I said it was okay with me." He was silent again, thinking of the rolling ten acres of upland meadow in North Carolina and the three tall acres of standing timber, oak and pine, from which it would be possible to build a strong country house. "There's nobody in the whole world I'd rather have living on my property than Johnny Moffat. I've known him for twenty years and I've had six fist fights with him and won them all, and been alone with him in the woods for two months at a time, and I still say that." He got up and went over to his own cot, then turned and came back. "By the way," he said softly, "this is between you and me, Sergeant."

"Sure," said Stais.

"My sister said she'd murder me for my hide and taller if I ever let Johnny know what was in store for him." He grinned a little. "Women're very confident in certain fields," he said. "And I never did tell Johnny, not even when I was so drunk I was singing 'Casey Jones' naked in the middle of the city of Tampa at three o'clock in the morning." He went over to his musette bag and got out a cigar and lit it thoughtfully. "You'd be surprised," he said, "how fond you become of nickel cigars in the Army."

"I tried smoking," said Stais. "I think I'll wait until I get a little older."

Whitejack sat heavily on his own cot. "Do you think they'll send you out to fight again?" he asked.

Stais stared up at the ceiling. "I wouldn't be surprised," he said. "There's nothing really wrong with me. I'm just tired."

Whitejack nodded, smoking slowly. "By the way," he said, "you heard us talking about the lieutenant, didn't you?"

"Yes."

"I went out to the field and had a little conversation with him.

He's just been sittin' there all day and most of the night since we got here, outside the operations room, just lookin' and starin' across at the planes comin' in. Him and me, we've been good friends for a long time and I asked him point-blank. I said, 'Freddie,' I said, 'there's a question the boys're askin' themselves these days about you.' And he said, 'What's the matter?' And I said, 'The boys're asking if you've turned bad. You pass 'em and you don't even look at them as though you recognize 'em. What is it, you turn GI after a year?' I said. He looked at me and then he looked at the ground and he didn't say anything for maybe a minute. Then he said, 'I beg your pardon, Arnold. It never occurred to me.' Then he told me what was on his mind." Whitejack looked at his watch, almost automatically, then lifted his head again. "Ever since we got the order to go overseas he's been worrying. You know Simpson, in our crew. Well, he's worrying about him and his navigator."

"What's he worrying about?" For a moment a crazy list of all the thousand things you can worry about in the crew of one airplane flashed through Stais's head.

"They're not fighting men," Whitejack said slowly. "They're both good fellers, you wouldn't want better, but the lieutenant's been watchin' 'em for a long time on the ground, in the air, at their guns, and he's convinced they won't measure. And he feels he's responsible for taking the Mitchell in and getting it out with as many of us alive as possible and he feels Simpson and the navigator're dangerous to have in the plane. And he's makin' up his mind to put in a request for two new men when we get to India, and he can't bear to think of what it'll do to Simpson and the navigator when they find out he's asked to have 'em grounded. That's why he just sits there outside operations, not even seein' us when we go by." Whitejack sighed. "He's twenty-two years old, the lieutenant. It's a strain, something like that, for a man twenty-two years old. If you see Simpson or Novak, you won't tell them anything, will you?"

"No," said Stais.

"I suppose things like this come up all the time in any army."

"All the time," said Stais.

Whitejack looked at his watch. Outside there was the growing and lapsing roar of engines that had been the constant sound of both their lives for so many months.

"Ah," said Whitejack, "they should've put me in the Infantry. I can hit a rabbit at three hundred yards with a rifle. They put me in the Air Force and give me a camera. Well, Sergeant, I think it's about time you were movin'."

Slowly Stais got up. He put on his shoes and put his shaving kit into his musette bag and slung it over one shoulder.

"You ready?" asked Whitejack.

"Yes," said Stais.

"That all the baggage you got, that little musette bag?"

"Yes," said Stais. "I was listed as missing, presumed dead, and they sent all my stuff into the supply room and all my personal belongings home to my mother."

Stais looked around the barracks. They shone in the harsh army light of barracks at night all over the world, by now familiar, homelike, to all the men who passed through them. He had left nothing.

They walked out into the soft, engine-filled night. A beacon flashed nervously across the sky, dimming the enormous pale twinkle of southern stars for a moment.

As they passed the operations room Stais saw a young lieutenant slumped down in a wobbly old wicker chair, staring out across the field.

"They come yet?" Whitejack asked.

"No," said the lieutenant without looking up.

Stais went into the building and into the room where they had the rubber raft and the patented radio and the cloth painted blue on one side and yellow on the other. A fat, middle-aged ATC captain wearily told them about ditching procedure. There were more than thirty people in the room, all passengers on Stais's plane. There were two small, yellow Chinamen and five bouncing fat Red Cross women and three sergeants with a lot of Air Force medals, trying not to seem excited about going home, and two colonels in the Engineers, looking too old for this war. Stais only half listened as the fat captain explained how to inflate the raft, what strings to pull, what levers to move, where to find the waterproofed Bible.

Whitejack was standing outside when Stais started for his plane. He gave Stais a slip of paper. "It's my home address," he said. "After the war, just come down sometime in October and I'll take you hunting."

"Thank you very much," said Stais gravely. Over Whitejack's shoulder he saw the lieutenant, still slumped in the wicker chair, still staring fixedly out across the dark field.

Whitejack walked out to the great plane with Stais, along the oil-spattered concrete of the runway, among the Chinamen and loud Red Cross women and the sergeants. The two men stopped without a word at the steps going up to the doorway of the plane and the other passengers filed past them.

They stood there, silently, with the two days of random conversation behind them, and Brazil and Athens behind them, and five hundred flights behind them, and Jerusalem and Miami behind them, and the girls from Vienna and the American Embassy and Flushing, Long Island, behind them, and the Greek mountaineers behind them, and Thomas Wolfe's funeral, and friends burning like torches, and dogs under treed raccoons in the Blue Ridge Mountains behind them, and a desperate twenty-two-year-old lieutenant painfully staring across a dusty airfield for ten days behind them, and the Mediterranean and the hospital bed in Cairo and Johnny Moffat wandering that night over the southern Atlantic, with ten acres of meadow and three acres of timber for his house and White-jack's sister waiting for him, all behind them. And, ahead of Stais, home, and a mother who had presumed him dead and wept over his personal belongings, and ahead of Whitejack the cold, bitter mountains of India and China, and the tearing dead sound of the fifties and the sky full of Japs.

"All right, Sergeant," the voice of the lieutenant checking the passengers said. "Get on."

Stais waved, a little broken wave, at Whitejack standing there. "See you," he said, "in North Carolina."

"Some October." Whitejack smiled a little, in the light of the flood lamps.

The door closed and Stais sat down in the seat in front of the two Chinamen.

"I think these planes are absolutely charming," one of the Red Cross women was saying loudly. "Don't you?"

The engines started and the big plane began to roll. Stais looked out of the window. A plane was landing. It came slowly into the light of the runway lamps and set down heavily, bumping wearily. Stais stared. It was a Mitchell. Stais sighed. As the big C-54 wheeled at the head of the runway, then started clumsily down, Stais put the slip of paper with "Arnold Whitejack" written on it, and the address, in scrawling, childlike handwriting, into his pocket. And as he saw the Mitchell pull to a stop near the operations room he felt for a moment a little less guilty for going home.

The Everlasting Witness

They three were eating breakfast on the terrace, a thousand and one felicitous birds in the garden trees. The coffee was exactly right, poured from its American electric percolator. In unsullied damp brown circles of soft earth the roses bloomed serenely against the pink Mexican wall. Marian's brother-in-law read the English page, as dedicated as a nice little boy reading the funnies, and Theresa, Marian's sister, chatted softly and merrily about their next Cuernevaca week-end. Theresa's bright smile had always been her mark and now, childless and with a husband beyond war age, and a life both ordered and gay, it looked as if that smile had justified itself.

Marian opened her mouth to tell them what she had done the night before and then she closed it on brioche, no words. What she had done was to try and find the film again, the war news-reel in which she had seen Jerry, her son. Or had she seen him? They ought to be told that the uncertainty had not been removed by this trip to Mexico. If she could explain the plain necessity to them maybe they would help her. But her next and clearer thought, untouched by terrace, food, and birds, was that this matter was all her own and had to be accomplished without help. Evidence of that was her husband's letting her come down alone; the trip to Mexico was for her to find herself, get back on her feet, return to him healed.

Well, she had not expected to look for the film, had not even known she could look with only her smattering of Spanish. But the night before—the first time her sister and brother-in-law had left her alone—she had gone to the dictionary and got the two words *cine* and *guerra,* and combining them with a question mark had asked them over and over on the phone, going down the movie houses in the yellow section of the book. At one of the box offices a golden Mexican voice told her in perfect English that the word she wanted was not *cine* but *noticias,* so she had had to call the first part of the list over again. She now knew, whether correctly or not, that three places had news-reels about the war. Probably she had missed some but she was going to start with these. She had not been able to understand the showing times so she would have to go to the theatre and sit through whatever came. Probably she could only manage one in a day because of Theresa's persistence in helping her towards equanimity; it was doubtful whether more than a few hours' absence would be possible.

The Olimpia, the del Prado, and the Cine Mexico. She found out exactly where each one was on the map in her red guidebook. For that matter she could get into a taxi and say the name of the theatre but she thought she would rather drive herself and keep the whole event within her control. Maybe this was why she had brought her car to Mexico. Her husband had wanted her to fly and she had said no, obstinately and without being able to explain. And he (who was Jerry's stepfather and therefore involved multifoldly in her suffering, not singly as a real father would have been) gently accepted her decision and drove her as far as Memphis. Although they didn't talk about it, she knew he never would have let her go away from him except that her sister was in Mexico, and also because he was pretty sure she wouldn't be able to see the film there. But that part of it had not worked because she hadn't been able to let it work.

Five months ago she had had the notice that Jerry was missing in action. Twenty-and-a-half years old. His father had died early in the other war. Jerry was seven then and she had had to manage him alone, had sometimes failed him, had sometimes been burdened too greatly, but she had always loved him. Maybe that had not been enough. She had married again when he was seventeen but this had not given him a retroactive father for the twelve-thirteen-fourteen-year-old times of crisis. So he was not ready for the army when he had to go. He had been mixed up and scared. And in six months he was missing in action.

She could hardly remember now what happened to her right after the notification. Nightmare rides of balking misery which clattered over wide fields and hills of the rubbled dying. She was looking for him, finding his hand with his father's ring on the little finger, holding the hand to give it warmth, reaching to the wrist; and then the sweat of terror which brought her back to what she supposed must be reality. If this happened at night, her husband was there and his arms came around her, his hand on the side of her head, holding her to his shoulder. But that was also when she reached the ebb of pain because she had comfort and Jerry, wherever he was, had none.

It was like that until she saw the picture the first time. They went to the movies fairly often. Her husband always knew what they were going to see, asked the times carefully, got to the main picture and avoided news-reels. She had hardly noticed this and did not want to. Once two indolent people in the seats next to theirs delayed them, and the news-reel started. From the beginning it was about the war. She sat down again, her hands tight in her lap. Her husband was lost to her. She was alone. They were showing the finest new weapons, grand, shining, and built perfectly for death. Whoever summoned and made palpable all that force and skill knew death was best and would be earless to the little voice of mothers whose sons were their children before they got to be targets or heroes. Her hands and her neck began to sweat. But she knew that no emotion was pertinent.

And then some soldier boys came on the screen. They were prisoners of war. Someone had got a chance to take their pictures at a prison-compound gate. They were thin, young, sick American soldiers moving bemused. She said to herself they don't want to look right at the camera; they are angry or ashamed or both and their guards are saying to them, albeit in a different language, "Smile now so your mother can see you." So they will not smile. Why should they? Who took the picture, she was asking herself, was it an American who got permission or one of their own? Or maybe the boys didn't know the picture was being taken. They lolled against a gate frame and a plank wall. The narrator voice was full of professional pity but it gave no information.

She felt her blood pricking along her temples; now it was pounding, and there was pressure in her chest below the hollow. Jerry could be there. So strong a hope must play delaying games. He was not there.

He was there. One boy stood with his back to the camera, leaning stooped against a gate lintel, and on the finger of the hand that held the post there was a ring she recognised. There wouldn't be another like it. She had had it made for Jerry's father. The boy with his back to the camera began to straighten up; he was turning. But the picture was over.

The next was a roller-skating race. The tailored voice left behind it the sentiment siphoned in for the boys and went with gusto into a wild chant about sports. She got out of the seat still unconscious of her husband, excused herself politely to the people who had held them up, and went to the ladies' room where she vomited and then, immediately, in a renewal of energy, was full of plans.

Her husband went with her three times to see the film, and after that asked her to promise not to go any more. She made the promise but she could not keep it. The first time she saw the picture alone she was sure there was more action, only a flicking motion, but more. That was hope and she had to feed it.

Her husband made inquiries. The War Department answered they had no record of Jerry in a prison camp. Of course the enemy's reports on prisoners of war were not necessarily accurate. And they said they knew about the film. It was taken by American photographers who had been given permission because somehow the enemy thought it was good propaganda, but they had been forced to shoot from outside the gate only what they could catch that way and in a few minutes. The man who wrote said that as far as he had been able to find out nothing had been cut from the film.

But she was sure there was more. She followed the film to every booking in town, second run, in the suburbs, in the drive-ins. Sometimes she stayed afterwards to see the roller-skating queens, Miss Hoboken and Miss Los Angeles. Sometimes she came out quickly, blinking in the light, leaving her boys behind her in the dark. It made her think they were safe there. That was not altogether the point but it was maybe three-quarters of it: that if she saw the picture it meant they were there (and Jerry) not dead on some chewed-up hill. She knew them all and they were Jerry's friends. She thought they were talking to him, "Why don't you turn around, kid? We ain't going to play up to this and grin from ear to ear to make out we're well off, but you better at least turn around. Your mother might be glad to see you." He was obstinate as he always had been, and a little slow, but he had been getting ready to turn. No, she was sure he had turned.

That was the way it was. It had got so that even if she knew the time was past to find it any more, she kept looking and looking as if she had transferred the nightmare battlefield search into this other kind and as if she might have to go back to the first if she stopped this.

And how could she have imagined that Mexico would be any different? The Olimpia, the del Prado, and the Cine Mexico. None of them first run so it was possible. She wanted to ask her brother-in-law behind his newspaper what they did to American news-reels here, cut them more? But the risk was too much. They might lie to her or in some other way keep her from going.

When she arrived a fortnight before she had asked her sister to give her a duty in the house. So Theresa gave her the flowers to arrange. The house was not far from the Dolores market, half a traffic circle of pure flowers. Marian had gone there every few days. Up to now Theresa went with her, or dropped her and picked her up. To-day she would go in her own car, she told them.

"Are you sure you know the way, Marian?"

"Of course, across the park and around that museum the opposite way from the one that looks right, and then the turn and out the gate. I know it perfectly." Her voice was sensible and secure.

But she had dallied, first on the terrace and then on the way across the park. This was the day. But what day?

When she had spent the eighty-four hours alone—from the morning she left her husband in Memphis to the evening she met Theresa, who flew to Monterey to ride into Mexico with her—she had kept hoping that the long flat way would be a highway out of confusion, levelling it, thinning it down to understanding, as if the moving air would whip through the car and dissolve the granulated mass of unanswered worries. She wanted one firm answer: yes, they have a right to take him, no matter what; yes, the clatter and chatter of arms and the frail tremor of boys' fear, lost in a bunker or a new shrapnel-proof vest or wherever however, is a combination of sounds in some way acceptable to a mother. How? But the only thing she discovered on that ride was that there is no firm answer. Some place near Corpus Christi, Texas, she found out that the haze of grey questions was not going to lift.

When Jerry's father had died it was precise: a ring sent back to her; an event reported; sad notes on a gliding trumpet which said that pink gingham, rosebud, golden night love was gone. It broke her heart. After a while that mended in its own way. So if now she could only take her heart in her two hands to break it in a jagged line a little to one side of the middle . . . Was it different for mothers than for wives, this stream of grief muddied by the clay that children are made of? There was no answer for a mother; that was all she found out on the long ride.

She summed it up now on the short ride across the park to the flower market. She did this rather slowly, driving slowly too. And she pulled her car to a curb, because it came to her (like another trumpet call, like a call to duty?) that there was indeed an answer, and that this was why she had followed the movie treadmill around and around. The trouble was that she had never been willing to accept the clear issue of death or life.

Now, stopped by the road in the park, she decided categorically, hitting the back of one hand into the palm of the other over and over, that if she found him, found the picture here and now, maybe even that very day (unreasonably unquestioning that she would see it) then she would know he was alive and she would simply make waiting womanly and rational. And if she did not see it in the del Prado, Olimpia, or Cine Mexico then she would say he was dead. Because war is death or life. The line must be drawn, and if it was on death's side then her heart would have to break and she would have to go on, go back to life, get back to her husband who was waiting for her patiently and with love. It was a decision. The uncertainty was at last behind her.

At the flower market she walked up and down in front of the stalls, and saw more clearly because of her decision, so she thought. First she looked at the flowers: pansies, purple iris, marigolds, and sweet peas—amplitude—some that were like feathers, fluffy and silent, and some like banners, and all marshalled by skilful hands. Behind everything the backdrop of gladioli which because of their colours could be forgiven their pretensions.

She looked at the people. There was a family at the farthest stand. She had just found fresh violets there, and the gladioli were less blatant and unshriven probably because it was a poor stand and a poor family that could not afford the finest and tallest of anything. The woman's face was sad. She was sick. But her hands were beautiful. She was nursing a baby.

Marian wanted no grand flowers, only the soft and touchable. She browsed to other stands and pansies and peonies. She bought a big wheel of red carnations, and some little gentle-petalled primroses with shiny dark green leaves. She was loaded down beyond the vases or even the places for flowers in her sister's house. She turned away at last and ran head on into the man who opened car doors (but he had missed hers when she parked) and who was now tottering out to the curb for someone else.

He had a shaking sickness and his face looked old and bloated under the tremors and jerking muscles. Theresa never seemed to mind him and always gave him two pesos, for nothing, because he shook too much to carry flowers or really even to open car doors. But he was always there, and now Marian, on her own, sincerely hated him. The disgust and horror of him she had suppressed on other visits welled up unchecked.

He seemed to recognise her although he looked all of an idiot. He came back from the curb to her and when she veered away from him he puttered to her car which was parked in front of the stand belonging to the family with the sick mother. He fumbled for her car door.

"No," she said sharply, and shuddered because she could not stand the touch of his hand on her door.

The nursing mother looked up. There was no disapproval in her face but she called to the idiot, "Ven, ven, Pepito."

Marian felt ashamed, only because the other woman had seen her disgust, but she could not have controlled that. Then she turned back, not knowing exactly why—telling herself that it was because to carry that load of flowers and leave them in a parked car for possibly some hours, was absurd. Standing in front of the flower-stand woman she knew she would not have to explain that she wanted to leave them.

The other said, "Si, señora, si," and with lovely gestures asked her husband to take the flowers and put them in the shade behind the stand. The idiot meantime stood to one side awkwardly, and unpleasantly chewed a piece of cocoanut he had picked up in the gutter.

So now she was going to the del Prado. Now she could go, whatever was that need for buying flowers, taken care of. She banged her car door and the idiot trembled but the nursing woman looked up from the baby and smiled.

Down town, she had to park her car in a garage. She would have liked not to go through the grind, clatter, jitter of the narrow entryway. She needed quiet. Everything was getting ready for this moment. She did not carry the flowers in her car but she carried them in her heart. Now she was going to find out whether it was death or life. Either she could tolerate. Again it did not occur to her that the news-reel might not be there.

It was there.

She came in in the middle of a French costume picture about lovemaking in a big bed with a mirror over it. She wondered how they got the fabric sheen that always goes with movie lasciviousness, whether the cloth was really stiff satin or if there was some cheap material which photographed like that? The actress' breasts looked as though they had been gilded to match the gleam of the stuffs around her. The French words were finely enunciated. The audience tittered in Spanish. A young man guffawed over and over on the same pitch. A French gentleman in top hat and cane sang something which ended the picture and tied it all together, judging from the louder laughing and audible translation. Then the theatre was dark. There was the jerking flicker of a reel starting and stopping, conglomerate unhuman figures and motion, whistles from the audience. It started. She saw the word *noticias* and this did not match the way the word had looked in her mind's eye. She corrected the mental image.

She was burning hot from head to foot. The prisoner of war scene opened the news-reel. Here they had omitted the cannons. The boys were before her eyes. She had not doubted she was going to see them but this did not keep her from being frightened.

She had long ago given the boys names. Chris was a slender blond who was whittling away. He stood there all during the picture, the one or two long dear moments. "I love him with all my heart," she whispered to herself, forming the words to make them solid. (She knew she loved Chris that much because of her pent-up love and terror for Jerry.) She looked sideways to the right but without shifting her head. Now it was Walter on the screen, dear Walter with a deep stubble on his face and a scarf wrapped around his neck. "He has a cold," she thought, this time not saying it, and wondering why she had never thought it before. She remembered faster than lightning many and many a cold-remedy including steaming eucalyptus oil. Jerry had always had colds when he was little, and that had worked the best. She smelled eucalyptus. The smell was a barrier she was holding on to, to keep the movie from going ahead. And she managed to keep it back. But all the same it did come to the boy who might be Jerry.

How many times had she thought about that ring: by the law of averages could another wife have designed another exact ring for her husband? Or could it maybe have been that she herself did not design it, but that the drawing she took into the jeweller was skilfully changed and incorporated by him into some ring he had in stock and she had thought it was hers, and so some other person might have had one like it? There was the hand on the gate post, and the ring. The hand looked chapped and wizened, not a boy's.

The boy to whom it belonged began to turn. Her eyes blinked, waiting for the end, anxious now for the roller-skaters that came after and whom she knew almost as well as she knew the boys. He turned farther round. With her eyes riveted on him she could still see that Chris, in the back, looked up for the first time, and that he lifted his hand from whittling, abruptly, as if he were saying, don't do it, don't take the picture. The face of the boy who turned, now filling the camera, unmercifully filling the screen, was Jerry's face, but it was blank, as empty as an idiot's. He grimaced with his mouth and the hand with the ring was lifted to catch the twitching, trying to hold it. His eyes were focused straight out and his mother drowned in those vacant eyes.

There was an indrawn breath of horror from the audience and then the anxious and everlasting titter. And Marian heard everything. She saw everything.

Then a man was talking to her. "May I help you, madam? May I not help you?"

She heard her own breathing which was like someone gasping for the last of life. The man, and then a woman, took her gently arm-in-arm. She had been plucking at her mouth. The helping woman entwined her fingers with hers, and they brought her out into the light.

"Please madam, to where may we take you? Are you in this hotel?" She shook her head, unable yet to speak.

"May I not call a doctor?"

"No, no." She knew now she would be able to take care of herself. She wanted to drive her car, in motion and tension to find rest. She gave them the parking tag. Once she looked at them while they were all waiting for the car and she saw she would always and forever know them and be known by them. Probably there would never be a chance for more than this four minutes in a garage waiting-room, but because of her pain and her trouble they did not try to conceal themselves. She did not have to describe them to herself. She knew them and they her.

"Madam, is it for you to drive all right?" He said the double *l* against the *r* as if it were a caress that one known stranger was permitted to give another.

"Yes," she said, and "Goodbye and thanks." For the first time she felt like crying; it was because she had to say goodbye to them. The man said goodbye and the woman said nothing.

She drove out to the park and around for a while. And then she knew she must go to a place—the flight was ended. She had no place to go except the flower stands. She had marked that for return and she must return to it.

She went around the Dolores traffic circle once not finding any room to park. The second time there was a place; and right in front of it, the opener-and-closer of doors, the idiot, sat on the curb with his knees doubled over into the gutter. He was sleeping, his head thrown back against a telephone pole. His hands were thrown down on the cement of the sidewalk, no longer trembling, but abandoned. Nor was his head trembling and shaking. His face asleep was beautiful. He was not old, no, not old nor bloated as she had thought him, but thin and defenceless as the sleeping young are, beautiful, and an idiot.

JEAN STAFFORD

A Country Love Story

An antique sleigh stood in the yard, snow after snow banked up against its eroded runners. Here and there upon the bleached and splintery seat were wisps of horsehair and scraps of the black leather that had once upholstered it. It bore, with all its jovial curves, an air not so much of desuetude as of slowed-down dash, as if weary horses, unable to go another step, had at last stopped here. The sleigh had come with the house. The former owner, a gifted business-woman from Castine who bought old houses and sold them again with all their pitfalls still intact, had said when she was showing them the place, "A picturesque detail, I think," and, waving it away, had turned to the well, which, with enthusiasm and at considerable length, she said had never gone dry. Actually, May and Daniel had found the detail more distracting than picturesque, so nearly kin was it to outdoor arts and crafts, and when the woman, as they departed in her car, gestured toward it again and said, "Paint that up a bit with something cheery and it will really add no end to your yard," simultaneous shudders coursed them. They had planned to remove the sleigh before they did anything else.

But partly because there were more important things to be done, and partly because they did not know where to put it (a sleigh could not, in the usual sense of the words, be thrown away), and partly because it seemed defiantly a part of the yard, as entitled to be there as permanently as the trees, they did nothing about it. Throughout the summer they saw birds briefly pause on its rakish front and saw the fresh rains wash the runners; in the autumn they watched the golden leaves fill the seat and nestle dryly down; and now, with the snow, they watched this new accumulation.

The sleigh was visible from the windows of the big, bright kitchen where they ate all their meals and, sometimes too bemused with country solitude to talk, they gazed out at it, forgetting their food in speculating on its history. It could have been driven cavalierly by the scion of some sea captain's family, or it could have been used soberly to haul the household's Unitarians to church or to take the womenfolk around the countryside on errands of good will. They did not speak of what its office might have been, and the fact of their silence was often nettlesome to May, for she felt they were silent too much of the time; a little morosely, she thought, if something as absurd and as provocative as this at which we look together—and which is, even though we didn't want it, our own property—cannot bring us to talk, what can? But she did not disturb Daniel in his private musings; she held her tongue, and out of the corner of her eye she watched him watch the winter cloak the sleigh, and, as if she were computing a difficult sum in her head, she tried to puzzle out what it was that had stilled tongues that earlier, before Daniel's illness, had found the days too short to communicate all they were eager to say.

It had been Daniel's doctor's idea, not theirs, that had brought them to the solemn hinterland to stay after all the summer gentry had departed in their beach wagons. The northern sun, the pristine air, the rural walks, and soundless nights, said Dr. Tellenbach, perhaps pining for his native Switzerland, would do more for the "professor's" convalescent lung than all the doctors and clinics in the world. Privately he had added to May that after so long a season in the sanitarium (Daniel had been there a year), where everything was tuned to a low pitch, it would be difficult and it might be shattering for "the boy" (not now the "professor," although Daniel, nearly fifty, was his wife's senior by twenty years and Dr. Tellenbach's by ten) to go back at once to the excitements and the intrigues of the university, to what, with finicking humor, the doctor called "the omnium-gatherum of the schoolmaster's life." The rigors of a country winter would be as nothing, he insisted, when compared to the strain of feuds and cocktail parties. All professors wanted to write books, didn't they? Surely Daniel, a historian with all the material in the world at his fingertips, must have something up his sleeve that could be the *raison d'être* for this year away? May said she supposed he had, she was not sure. She could hear the reluctance in her voice as she escaped the doctor's eyes and gazed through his windows at the mountains behind the sanitarium. In the dragging months Daniel had been gone she had taken solace in imagining the time when they *would* return to just that pandemonium the doctor so deplored, and because it had been pandemonium on the smallest and most discreet scale, she smiled through her disappointment at the little man's Swiss innocence and explained that they had always lived quietly, seldom dining out or entertaining more than twice a week.

"Twice a week!" He was appalled.

"But I'm afraid," she had protested, "that he would find a second year of inactivity intolerable. He does intend to write a book, but he means to write it in England, and we can't go to England now."

"England!" Dr. Tellenbach threw up his hands. "Good *air* is my recommendation for your husband. Good air and little talk."

She said, "It's talk he needs, I should think, after all this time of communing only with himself except when I came to visit."

He had looked at her with exaggerated patience, and then, courtly but authoritative, he said, "I hope you will not think I importune when I tell you that I am very well acquainted with your husband, and, as his physician, I order this retreat. *He* quite agrees."

Stung to see that there was a greater degree of understanding between Daniel and Dr. Tellenbach than between Daniel and herself, May had objected further, citing an occasion when her husband had put his head in his hands and mourned, "I hear talk of nothing but sputum cups and X rays. Aren't people interested in the state of the world any more?"

But Dr. Tellenbach had been adamant, and at the end, when she had risen to go, he said, "You are bound to find him changed a little. A long illness removes a thoughtful man from his fellow beings. It is like living with an exacting mistress who is not content with half a man's attention but must claim it all." She had thought his figure of speech absurd and disdained to ask him what he meant.

Actually, when the time came for them to move into the new house and she found no alterations in her husband but found, on the other hand, much pleasure in their country life, she began to forgive Dr. Tellenbach. In the beginning it was like a second honeymoon, for they had moved to a part of the North where they had never been and they explored it together, sharing its charming sights and sounds. Moreover, they had never owned a house before but had always lived in city apartments, and though the house they bought was old and derelict, its lines and doors and window lights were beautiful, and they were obsessed with it. All through the summer they reiterated, "To think that we own all of this! That it actually belongs to us!" And they wandered from room to room marveling at their windows, from none of which was it possible to see an ugly sight. They looked to the south upon a river, to the north upon a lake; to the west of them were pine woods where the wind forever sighed, voicing a vain entreaty; and to the east a rich man's long meadow that ran down a hill to his old, magisterial house. It was true, even in those bewitched days, that there were times on the lake, when May was gathering water lilies as Daniel slowly rowed, that she had seen on his face a look of abstraction and she had known that he was worlds away, in his memories, perhaps, of his illness and the sanitarium (of which he would never speak) or in the thought of the book he was going to write as soon, he said, as the winter set in and there was nothing to do but work. Momentarily the look frightened her, and she remembered the doctor's words, but then, immediately herself again in the security of married love, she caught at another water lily and pulled at its long stem. Companionably they gardened, taking special pride in the nicotiana that sent its nighttime fragrance into their bedroom. Together, and with fascination, they consulted carpenters, plasterers, and chimney sweeps. In the blue evenings they read at ease, hearing no sound but that of the night birds—the loons on the lake and the owls in the tops of trees. When the days turned cooler and shorter, a cricket came to bless their house, nightly singing behind the kitchen stove. They got two fat and idle tabby cats, who lay insensible beside the fireplace and only stirred themselves to purr perfunctorily.

Because they had not moved in until July and by that time the workmen of the region were already engaged, most of the major repairs of the house were to be postponed until the spring, and in October, when May and Daniel had done all they could by themselves and Daniel had begun his own work, May suddenly found herself without occupation. Whole days might pass when she did nothing more than cook three meals and walk a little in the autumn mist and pet the cats and wait for Daniel to come down from his upstairs study to talk to her. She began to think with longing of the crowded days in Boston before Daniel was sick, and even in the year past, when he had been away and she had gone to concerts and recitals and had done good deeds for crippled children and had endlessly shopped for presents to lighten the tedium of her husband's unwilling exile. And, longing, she was remorseful, as if by desiring another she betrayed this life, and, remorseful, she hid away in sleep. Sometimes she slept for hours in the daytime, imitating the cats, and when at last she got up, she had to push away the dense sleep as if it were a door.

One day at lunch she asked Daniel to take a long walk with her that afternoon to a farm where the owner smoked his own sausages. "You never go outdoors," she said, "and Dr. Tellenbach said you must. Besides, it's a lovely day."

"I can't," he said. "I'd like to, but I can't. I'm busy. You go alone."

Overtaken by a gust of loneliness, she cried, "Oh, Daniel, I have nothing to *do!*"

A moment's silence fell, and then he said, "I'm sorry to put you through this, my dear, but you must surely admit that it's not my fault I got sick."

In her shame, her rapid, overdone apologies, her insistence that nothing mattered in the world except his health and peace of mind, she made everything worse, and at last he said shortly to her, "Stop being a child, May. Let's just leave each other alone."

This outbreak, the very first in their marriage of five years, was the beginning of a series. Hardly a day passed that they did not bicker over something; they might dispute a question of fact, argue a matter of taste, catch each other out in an inaccuracy, and every quarrel ended with Daniel's saying to her, "Why don't you leave me alone?" Once he said, "I've been sick and now I'm busy and I'm no longer young enough to shift the focus of my mind each time it suits your whim." Afterward there were always apologies, and then Daniel went back to his study and did not open the door of it again until the next meal. Finally it seemed to her that love, the very center of their being, was choked off, overgrown, invisible. And silent with hostility or voluble with trivial reproach, they tried to dig it out impulsively and could not—could only maul it in its unkempt grave. Daniel, in his withdrawal from her and from the house, was preoccupied with his research, of which he never spoke except to say that it would bore her, and most of the time, so it appeared to May, he did not worry over what was happening to them. She felt the cold old house somehow enveloping her as if it were their common enemy, maliciously bent on bringing them to disaster. Sunken in faithlessness, they stared, at mealtimes, atrophied within the present hour, at the irrelevant and whimsical sleigh that stood abandoned in the mammoth winter.

May found herself thinking, If we redeemed it and painted it, our house would have something in common with Henry Ford's Wayside Inn. And I might make this very observation to him and he might greet it with disdain and we might once again communicate. Perhaps we could talk of Williamsburg and how we disapproved of it. Her mind went toiling on. Williamsburg was part of our honeymoon trip; somewhere our feet were entangled in suckers as we stood kissing under a willow tree. Soon she found that she did not care for this line of thought, nor did she care what his response to it might be. In her imagined conversations with Daniel she never spoke of the sleigh. To the thin, ill scholar whose scholarship and illness had usurped her place she had gradually taken a weighty but unviolent dislike.

The discovery of this came, not surprising her, on Christmas Day. The knowledge sank like a plummet, and at the same time she was thinking about the sleigh, connecting it with the smell of the barn on damp days, and she thought perhaps it had been drawn by the very animals who had been stabled there and had pervaded the timbers with their odor. There must have been much life within this house once—but long ago. The earth immediately behind the barn was said by everyone to be extremely rich because of the horses, although there had been none there for over fifty years. Thinking of this soil, which earlier she had eagerly sifted through her fingers, May now realized that she had no wish for the spring to come, no wish to plant a garden, and, branching out at random, she found she had no wish to see the sea again, or children, or favorite pictures, or even her own face on a happy day. For a minute or two she was almost enraptured in this state of no desire, but then, purged swiftly of her cynicism, she knew it to be false, knew that actually she did have a desire—the desire for a desire. And now she felt that she was stationary in a whirlpool, and at the very moment she conceived the notion a bit of wind brought to the seat of the sleigh the final leaf from the elm tree that stood beside it. It crossed her mind that she might consider the wood of the sleigh in its juxtaposition to the living tree and to the horses, who, although they were long since dead, reminded her of their passionate, sweating, running life every time she went to the barn for firewood.

They sat this morning in the kitchen full of sun, and, speaking not to him but to the sleigh, to icicles, to the dark, motionless pine woods, she said, "I wonder if on a day like this they used to take the pastor home after lunch." Daniel gazed abstractedly at the bright silver drifts beside the well and said nothing. Presently a wagon went past hauled by two oxen with bells on their yoke. This was the hour they always passed, taking to an unknown destination an aged man in a fur hat and an aged woman in a shawl. May and Daniel listened.

Suddenly, with impromptu anger, Daniel said, "What did you just say?"

"Nothing," she said. And then, after a pause, "It would be lovely at Jamaica Pond today."

He wheeled on her and pounded the table with his fist. "I did not ask for this!" The color rose feverishly to his thin cheeks and his

breath was agitated. "You are trying to make me sick again. It was
wonderful, wasn't it, for you while I was gone?"

"Oh no, no! Oh no, Daniel, it was hell!"

"Then, by the same token, this must be heaven." He smiled, the
professor catching out a student in a fallacy.

"Heaven." She said the word bitterly.

"Then why do you stay here?" he cried.

It was a cheap impasse, desolate, true, unfair. She did not answer
him.

After a while he said, "I almost believe there's something you
haven't told me."

She began to cry at once, blubbering across the table at him: "You
have said that before. What am I to say? What have I done?"

He looked at her, impervious to her tears, without mercy and yet
without contempt. "I don't know. But you've done something."

It was as if she were looking through someone else's scrambled
closets and bureau drawers for an object that had not been named to
her, but nowhere could she find her gross offense.

Domestically she asked him if he would have more coffee, and he
peremptorily refused and demanded, "Will you tell me why it is you
must badger me? Is it a compulsion? Can't you control it? Are you
going mad?"

From that day onward May felt a certain stirring of life within
her solitude, and now and again, looking up from a book to see if
the damper on the stove was right, to listen to a rat renovating its
house-within-a-house, to watch the belled oxen pass, she nursed her
wound, hugged it, repeated his awful words exactly as he had said
them, reproduced the way his wasted lips had looked, and his bright,
far-sighted eyes. She could not read for long at any time, nor could
she sew. She cared little now for planning changes in her house;
she had meant to sand the painted floors to uncover the wood of the
wide boards and she had imagined how the long, paneled windows
of the drawing room would look when yellow velvet curtains hung
there in the spring. Now, schooled by silence and indifference, she
was immune to disrepair and to the damage done by the wind and
snow, and she looked, as Daniel did, without dislike upon the old
and nasty wallpaper and upon the shabby kitchen floor. One day she
knew that the sleigh would stay where it was so long as they stayed
there. From every thought she returned to her deep, bleeding injury.
He had asked her if she were going mad.

She repaid him in the dark afternoons while he was closeted away
in his study, hardly making a sound save when he added wood to his

fire or paced a little, deep in thought. She sat at the kitchen table looking at the sleigh, and she gave Daniel insult for his injury by imagining a lover. She did not imagine his face, but she imagined his clothing, which would be costly and in the best of taste, and his manner, which would be urbane and anticipatory of her least whim, and his clever speech, and his adept courtship that would begin the moment he looked at the sleigh and said, "I must get rid of that for you at once." She might be a widow, she might be divorced, she might be committing adultery. Certainly there was no need to specify in an affair so securely legal. There was no need, that is, up to a point, and then the point came when she took in the fact that she not only believed in this lover but loved him and depended wholly on his companionship. She complained to him of Daniel and he consoled her; she told him stories of her girlhood, when she had gaily gone to parties, squired by boys her own age; she dazzled him sometimes with the wise comments she made on the books she read. It came to be true that if she so much as looked at the sleigh, she was weakened, failing with starvation.

Often, about her daily tasks of cooking food and washing dishes and tending the fires and shopping in the general store of the village, she thought she should watch her step, that it was this sort of thing that *did* make one go mad; for a while, then, she went back to Daniel's question, sharpening its razor edge. But she could not corral her alien thoughts and she trembled as she bought split peas, fearful that the old men loafing by the stove could see the incubus of her sins beside her. She could not avert such thoughts when they rushed upon her sometimes at tea with one of the old religious ladies of the neighborhood, so that, in the middle of a conversation about a deaconess in Bath, she retired from them, seeking her lover, who came, faceless, with his arms outstretched, even as she sat up straight in a Boston rocker, even as she accepted another cup of tea. She lingered over the cake plates and the simple talk, postponing her return to her own house and to Daniel, whom she continually betrayed.

It was not long after she recognized her love that she began to wake up even before the dawn and to be all day quick to everything, observant of all the signs of age and eccentricity in her husband, and she compared him in every particular—to his humiliation, in her eyes —with the man whom now it seemed to her she had always loved at fever pitch.

Once when Daniel, in a rare mood, kissed her, she drew back involuntarily, and he said gently, "I wish I knew what you had done, poor dear." He looked, as if for written words, in her face.

"You said you knew," she said, terrified.

"I do."

"Then why do you wish you knew?" Her baffled voice was high and frantic. "You don't talk sense!"

"I do," he said sedately. "I talk sense always. It is you who are oblique." Her eyes stole like a sneak to the sleigh. "But I wish I knew your motive," he said impartially.

For a minute she felt that they were two maniacs answering each other questions that had not been asked, never touching the matter at hand because they did not know what the matter was. But in the next moment, when he turned back to her spontaneously and clasped her head between his hands and said, like a tolerant father, "I forgive you, darling, because you don't know how you persecute me. No one knows except the sufferer what this sickness is," she knew again, helplessly, that they were not harmonious even in their aberrations.

These days of winter came and went, and on each of them, after breakfast and as the oxen passed, he accused her of her concealed misdeed. She could no longer truthfully deny that she was guilty, for she was in love, and she heard the subterfuge in her own voice and felt the guilty fever in her veins. Daniel knew it, too, and watched her. When she was alone, she felt her lover's presence protecting her —when she walked past the stiff spiraea, with icy cobwebs hung between its twigs, down to the lake, where the black, unmeasured water was hidden beneath a lid of ice; when she walked, instead, to the salt river to see the tar-paper shacks where the men caught smelt through the ice; when she walked in the dead dusk up the hill from the store, catching her breath the moment she saw the sleigh. But sometimes this splendid being mocked her when, freezing with fear of the consequences of her sin, she ran up the stairs to Daniel's room and burrowed her head in his shoulder and cried, "Come downstairs! I'm lonely, please come down!" But he would never come, and at last, bitterly, calmed by his calmly inquisitive regard, she went back alone and stood at the kitchen window, coyly half hidden behind the curtains.

For months she lived with her daily dishonor, rattled, ashamed, stubbornly clinging to her secret. But she grew more and more afraid when, oftener and oftener, Daniel said, "Why do you lie to me? What does this mood of yours mean?" and she could no longer sleep. In the raw nights she lay straight beside him as he slept, and she stared at the ceiling, as bright as the snow it reflected, and tried not to think of the sleigh out there under the elm tree but could think only of it and of the man, her lover, who was connected with it somehow. She said to herself, as she listened to his breathing, "If I confessed to Daniel, he would understand that I was lonely and he would comfort me, saying, 'I am here, May. I shall never let you be lonely again.'" At these times she was so separated from the world, so far removed from his touch and his voice, so solitary, that she would have sued a stranger for companionship. Daniel slept deeply, having no guilt to make him toss. He slept, indeed, so well that he never even heard the ditcher on snowy nights rising with a groan over the hill, flinging the snow from the road and warning of its approach by lights that first flashed red, then blue. As it passed their house, the hurled snow swashed like flames. All night she heard the squirrels adding up their nuts in the walls and heard the spirit of the house creaking and softly clicking upon the stairs and in the attics.

In early spring, when the whippoorwills begged in the cattails and the marsh reeds, and the northern lights patinated the lake and the tidal river, and the stars were large, and the huge vine of Dutchman's-pipe had started to leaf out, May went to bed late. Each night she sat on the back steps waiting, hearing the snuffling of a dog as it hightailed it for home, the single cry of a loon. Night after night she waited for the advent of her rebirth while upstairs Daniel, who had spoken tolerantly of her vigils, slept, keeping his knowledge of her to himself. "A symptom," he had said, scowling in concentration, as he remarked upon her new habit. "Let it run its course. Perhaps when this is over you will know the reason why you torture me with these obsessions and will stop. You know, you may really have a slight disorder of the mind. It would be nothing to be ashamed of; you could go to a sanitarium."

One night, looking out the window, she clearly saw her lover sitting in the sleigh. His hand was over his eyes and his chin was covered by a red silk scarf. He wore no hat and his hair was fair. He was tall, and his long legs stretched indolently along the floorboard. He was younger than she had imagined him to be and he seemed rather frail, for there was a delicate pallor on his high, intelligent forehead and there was an invalid's languor in his whole attitude. He wore a white blazer and gray flannels and there was a yellow rosebud in his lapel. Young as he was, he did not, even so, seem to belong to her generation; rather, he seemed to be the reincarnation of someone's uncle as he had been fifty years before. May did not move until he vanished, and then, even though she knew now that she was truly bedeviled, the only emotion she had was bashfulness mingled with doubt; she was not sure, that is, that he loved her.

That night she slept awhile. She lay near to Daniel, who was smiling in the moonlight. She could tell that the sleep she would have tonight would be as heavy as a coma, and she was aware of the moment she was overtaken.

She was in a canoe in a meadow of water lilies and her lover was tranquilly taking the shell off a hard-boiled egg. "How intimate," he said, "to eat an egg with you." She was nervous lest the canoe tip over, but at the same time she was charmed by his wit and by the way he lightly touched her shoulder with the varnished paddle.

"May? May? I love you, May."

"Oh!" enchanted, she heard her voice replying. "Oh, I love you too!"

"The winter is over, May. You must forgive the hallucinations of a sick man."

She woke to see Daniel's fair, pale head bending toward her. "He is old! He is ill!" she thought, but through her tears, to deceive him one last time, she cried, "Oh, thank God, Daniel!"

He was feeling cold and wakeful and he asked her to make him a cup of tea; before she left the room he kissed her hands and arms and said, "If I am ever sick again, don't leave me, May."

Downstairs, in the kitchen, cold with shadows and with the obtrusion of dawn, she was belabored by a chill. "What time is it?" she said aloud, although she did not care. She remembered, not for any reason, a day when she and Daniel had stood in the yard last October wondering whether they should cover the chimneys that would not be used and he decided that they should not, but he had said, "I hope no birds get trapped." She had replied, "I thought they all left at about this time for the South," and he had answered, with an unintelligible reproach in his voice, "The starlings stay." And she remembered, again for no reason, a day when, in pride and excitement, she had burst into the house crying, "I saw an ermine. It was terribly poised and let me watch it quite a while." He had said categorically, "There are no ermines here."

She had not protested; she had sighed as she sighed now and turned to the window. The sleigh was livid in this light and no one was in it; nor had anyone been in it for many years. But at that moment the blacksmith's cat came guardedly across the dewy field and climbed into it, as if by careful plan, and curled up on the seat. May prodded the clinkers in the stove and started to the barn for kindling. But she thought of the cold and the damp and the smell of the horses, and she did not go but stood there, holding the poker and leaning upon it as if it were an umbrella. There was no place warm to go. "What time is it?" she whimpered, heartbroken, and moved the poker, stroking the lion foot of the fireless stove.

She knew now that no change would come, and that she would never see her lover again. Confounded utterly, like an orphan in solitary confinement, she went outdoors and got into the sleigh. The blacksmith's imperturbable cat stretched and rearranged his position, and May sat beside him with her hands locked tightly in her lap, rapidly wondering over and over again how she would live the rest of her life.

In the Zoo

Keening harshly in his senility, the blind polar bear slowly and ceaselessly shakes his head in the stark heat of the July and mountain noon. His open eyes are blue. No one stops to look at him; an old farmer, in passing, sums up the old bear's situation by observing, with a ruthless chuckle, that he is a "back number." Patient and despairing, he sits on his yellowed haunches on the central rock of his pool, his huge toy paws wearing short boots of mud.

The grizzlies to the right of him, a conventional family of father and mother and two spring cubs, alternately play the clown and sleep. There is a blustery, scoundrelly, half-likable bravado in the manner of the black bear on the polar's left; his name, according to the legend on his cage, is Clancy, and he is a rough-and-tumble, brawling blowhard, thundering continually as he paces back and forth, or pauses to face his audience of children and mothers and release from his great, gray-tongued mouth a perfectly Vesuvian roar. If he were to be reincarnated in human form, he would be a man of action, possibly a football coach, probably a politician. One expects to see his black hat hanging from a branch of one of his trees; at any moment he will light a cigar.

The polar bear's next-door neighbors are not the only ones who offer so sharp and sad a contrast to him. Across a reach of scrappy grass and litter is the convocation of conceited monkeys, burrowing into each other's necks and chests for fleas, picking their noses with their long, black, finicky fingers, swinging by their gifted tails on the flying trapeze, screaming bloody murder. Even when they mourn— one would think the male orangutan was on the very brink of suicide —they are comedians; they only fake depression, for they are firmly secure in their rambunctious tribalism and in their appalling insight and contempt. Their flibbertigibbet gambolling is a sham, and, stealthily and shiftily, they are really watching the pitiful polar bear

("Back number," they quote the farmer. "That's *his* number all right,"
they snigger), and the windy black bear ("Life of the party. Gasbag.
Low I.Q.," they note scornfully on his dossier), and the stupid,
bourgeois grizzlies ("It's feed the face and hit the sack for them," the
monkeys say). And they are watching my sister and me, two middle-
aged women, as we sit on a bench between the exhibits, eating popcorn, growing thirsty. We are thoughtful.

A chance remark of Daisy's a few minutes before has turned us to
memory and meditation. "I don't know why," she said, "but that
poor blind bear reminds me of Mr. Murphy." The name "Mr.
Murphy" at once returned us both to childhood, and we were floated
far and fast, our later lives diminished. So now we eat our popcorn
in silence with the ritualistic appetite of childhood, which has little
to do with hunger; it is not so much food as a sacrament, and in
tribute to our sisterliness and our friendliness I break the silence
to say that this is the best popcorn I have ever eaten in my life. The
extravagance of my statement instantly makes me feel self-indulgent,
and for some time I uneasily avoid looking at the blind bear. My
sister does not agree or disagree; she simply says that popcorn is the
only food she has ever really liked. For a long time, then, we eat
without a word, but I know, because I know her well and know her
similarity to me, that Daisy is thinking what I am thinking; both of
us are mournfully remembering Mr. Murphy, who, at one time in
our lives, was our only friend.

This zoo is in Denver, a city that means nothing to my sister and
me except as a place to take or meet trains. Daisy lives two hundred
miles farther west, and it is her custom, when my every-other-year
visit with her is over, to come across the mountains to see me off on
my eastbound train. We know almost no one here, and because our
stays are short, we have never bothered to learn the town in more
than the most desultory way. We know the Burlington uptown office
and the respectable hotels, a restaurant or two, the Union Station,
and, beginning today, the zoo in the city park.

But since the moment that Daisy named Mr. Murphy by name
our situation in Denver has been only corporeal; our minds and our
hearts are in Adams, fifty miles north, and we are seeing, under the
white sun at its pitiless meridian, the streets of that ugly town, its
parks and trees and bridges, the bandstand in its dreary park, the
roads that lead away from it, west to the mountains and east to the
plains, its mongrel and multitudinous churches, its high school shaped
like a loaf of bread, the campus of its college, an oasis of which we
had no experience except to walk through it now and then, eying

the woodbine on the impressive buildings. These things are engraved forever on our minds with a legibility so insistent that you have only to say the name of the town aloud to us to rip the rinds from our nerves and leave us exposed in terror and humiliation.

We have supposed in later years that Adams was not so bad as all that, and we know that we magnified its ugliness because we looked upon it as the extension of the possessive, unloving, scornful, complacent foster mother, Mrs. Placer, to whom, at the death of our parents within a month of each other, we were sent like Dickensian grotesqueries—cowardly, weak-stomached, given to tears, backward in school. Daisy was ten and I was eight when, unaccompanied, we made the long trip from Marblehead to our benefactress, whom we had never seen and, indeed, never heard of until the pastor of our church came to tell us of the arrangement our father had made on his deathbed, seconded by our mother on hers. This man, whose name and face I have forgotten and whose parting speeches to us I have not forgiven, tried to dry our tears with talk of Indians and of buffaloes; he spoke, however, at much greater length, and in preaching cadences, of the Christian goodness of Mrs. Placer. She was, he said, childless and fond of children, and for many years she had been a widow, after the lingering demise of her tubercular husband, for whose sake she had moved to the Rocky Mountains. For his support and costly medical care, she had run a boarding house, and after his death, since he had left her nothing, she was obliged to continue running it. She had been a girlhood friend of our paternal grandmother, and our father, in the absence of responsible relatives, had made her the beneficiary of his life insurance on the condition that she lodge and rear us. The pastor, with a frankness remarkable considering that he was talking to children, explained to us that our father had left little more than a drop in the bucket for our care, and he enjoined us to give Mrs. Placer, in return for her hospitality and sacrifice, courteous help and eternal thanks. "Sacrifice" was a word we were never allowed to forget.

And thus it was, in grief for our parents, that we came cringing to the dry Western town and to the house where Mrs. Placer lived, a house in which the square, uncushioned furniture was cruel and the pictures on the walls were either dour or dire and the lodgers, who lived in the upper floors among shadowy wardrobes and chiffoniers, had come through the years to resemble their landlady in appearance as well as in deportment.

After their ugly-colored evening meal, Gran—as she bade us call her—and her paying guests would sit, rangy and aquiline, rocking

on the front porch on spring and summer and autumn nights, tasting
their delicious grievances: those slights delivered by ungrateful sons
and daughters, those impudences committed by trolley-car conductors
and uppity salesgirls in the ready-to-wear, all those slurs and calculated elbow-jostlings that were their daily crucifixion and their staff
of life. We little girls, washing the dishes in the cavernous kitchen,
listened to their even, martyred voices, fixed like leeches to their
solitary subject and their solitary creed—that life was essentially a
matter of being done in, let down, and swindled.

At regular intervals, Mrs. Placer, chairwoman of the victims, would
say, "Of course, I don't care; I just have to laugh," and then would
tell a shocking tale of an intricate piece of skulduggery perpetrated
against her by someone she did not even know. Sometimes, with her
avid, partial jury sitting there on the porch behind the bitter hopvines in the heady mountain air, the cases she tried involved Daisy
and me, and, listening, we travailed, hugging each other, whispering,
"I wish she wouldn't! Oh, how did she find out?" How *did* she?
Certainly we never told her when we were snubbed or chosen last
on teams, never admitted to a teacher's scolding or to the hoots of
laughter that greeted us when we bit on silly, unfair jokes. But she
knew. She knew about the slumber parties we were not invited to,
the beefsteak fries at which we were pointedly left out; she knew
that the singing teacher had said in so many words that I could not
carry a tune in a basket and that the sewing superintendent had said
that Daisy's fingers were all thumbs. With our teeth chattering in the
cold of our isolation, we would hear her protestant, litigious voice
defending our right to be orphans, paupers, wholly dependent on
her—except for the really ridiculous pittance from our father's life
insurance—when it was all she could do to make ends meet. She did
not care, but she had to laugh that people in general were so small-
minded that they looked down on fatherless, motherless waifs like
us and, by association, looked down on her. It seemed funny to
her that people gave her no credit for taking on these sickly youngsters who were not even kin but only the grandchildren of a friend.

If a child with braces on her teeth came to play with us, she was,
according to Gran, slyly lording it over us because our teeth were
crooked, but there was no money to have them straightened. And
what could be the meaning of our being asked to come for supper at
the doctor's house? Were the doctor and his la-di-da New York wife
and those pert girls with their solid-gold barrettes and their Shetland
pony going to shame her poor darlings? Or shame their poor Gran

by making them sorry to come home to the plain but honest life that was all she could provide for them?

There was no stratum of society not reeking with the effluvium of fraud and pettifoggery. And the school system was almost the worst of all: if we could not understand fractions, was that not our teacher's fault? And therefore what right had she to give us F? It was as plain as a pikestaff to Gran that the teacher was only covering up her own inability to teach. It was unlikely, too—highly unlikely— that it was by accident that time and time again the free medical clinic was closed for the day just as our names were about to be called out, so that nothing was done about our bad tonsils, which meant that we were repeatedly sick in the winter, with Gran fetching and carrying for us, climbing those stairs a jillion times a day with her game leg and her heart that was none too strong.

Steeped in these mists of accusation and hidden plots and double meanings, Daisy and I grew up like worms. I think no one could have withstood the atmosphere in that house where everyone trod on eggs that a little bird had told them were bad. They spied on one another, whispered behind doors, conjectured, drew parallels beginning "With all due respect . . ." or "It is a matter of indifference to *me* but . . ." The vigilantes patrolled our town by day, and by night returned to lay their goodies at their priestess's feet and wait for her oracular interpretation of the innards of the butcher, the baker, the candlestick maker, the soda jerk's girl, and the barber's unnatural deaf white cat.

Consequently, Daisy and I also became suspicious. But it was suspicion of ourselves that made us mope and weep and grimace with self-judgment. Why were we not happy when Gran had sacrificed herself to the bone for us? Why did we not cut dead the paper boy who had called her a filthy name? Why did we persist in our willful friendliness with the grocer who had tried, unsuccessfully, to overcharge her on a case of pork and beans?

Our friendships were nervous and surreptitious; we sneaked and lied, and as our hungers sharpened, our debasement deepened; we were pitied; we were shifty-eyed, always on the lookout for Mrs. Placer or one of her tattletale lodgers; we were hypocrites.

Nevertheless, one thin filament of instinct survived, and Daisy and I in time found asylum in a small menagerie down by the railroad tracks. It belonged to a gentle alcoholic ne'er-do-well, who did nothing all day long but drink bathtub gin in rickeys and play solitaire and smile to himself and talk to his animals. He had a little, stunted red vixen and a deodorized skunk, a parrot from Tahiti that spoke Parisian French, a woebegone coyote, and two capuchin monkeys, so serious and humanized, so small and sad and sweet, and so religious-looking with their tonsured heads that it was impossible not to think their gibberish was really an ordered language with a grammar that someday some philologist would understand.

Gran knew about our visits to Mr. Murphy and she did not object, for it gave her keen pleasure to excoriate him when we came home. His vice was not a matter of guesswork; it was an established fact that he was half-seas over from dawn till midnight. "With the black Irish," said Gran, "the taste for drink is taken in with the mother's milk and is never mastered. Oh, I know all about those promises to join the temperance movement and not to touch another drop. The way to Hell is paved with good intentions."

We were still little girls when we discovered Mr. Murphy, before the shattering disease of adolescence was to make our bones and brains ache even more painfully than before, and we loved him and we hoped to marry him when we grew up. We loved him, and we loved his monkeys to exactly the same degree and in exactly the same way; they were husbands and fathers and brothers, these three little, ugly, dark, secret men who minded their own business and let us mind ours. If we stuck our fingers through the bars of the cage, the monkeys would sometimes take them in their tight, tiny hands and look into our faces with a tentative, somehow absent-minded sorrow, as if they terribly regretted that they could not place us but were glad to see us all the same. Mr. Murphy, playing a solitaire game of cards called "once in a blue moon" on a kitchen table in his back yard beside the pens, would occasionally look up and blink his beautiful blue eyes and say, "You're peaches to make over my wee friends. I love you for it." There was nothing demanding in his voice, and nothing sticky; on his lips the word "love" was jocose and forthright, it had no strings attached. We would sit on either side of him and watch him regiment his ranks of cards and stop to drink as deeply as if he were dying of thirst and wave to his animals and say to them, "Yes, lads, you're dandies."

Because Mr. Murphy was as reserved with us as the capuchins were, as courteously noncommittal, we were surprised one spring day when he told us that he had a present for us, which he hoped Mrs. Placer would let us keep; it was a puppy, for whom the owner had asked him to find a home—half collie and half Labrador retriever, blue-blooded on both sides.

"You might tell Mrs. Placer—" he said, smiling at the name, for Gran was famous in the town. "You might tell Mrs. Placer," said

Mr. Murphy, "that this lad will make a fine watchdog. She'll never have to fear for her spoons again. Or her honor." The last he said to himself, not laughing but tucking his chin into his collar; lines sprang to the corners of his eyes. He would not let us see the dog, whom we could hear yipping and squealing inside his shanty, for he said that our disappointment would weigh on his conscience if we lost our hearts to the fellow and then could not have him for our own.

That evening at supper, we told Gran about Mr. Murphy's present. A dog? In the first place, why a dog? Was it possible that the news had reached Mr. Murphy's ears that Gran had just this very day finished planting her spring garden, the very thing that a rampageous dog would have in his mind to destroy? What sex was it? A male! Females, she had heard, were more trustworthy; males roved and came home smelling of skunk; such a consideration as this, of course, would not have crossed Mr. Murphy's fuddled mind. Was this young male dog housebroken? We had not asked? That was the limit!

Gran appealed to her followers, too raptly fascinated by Mr. Murphy's machinations to eat their Harvard beets. "Am I being far-fetched or does it strike you as decidedly queer that Mr. Murphy is trying to fob off on my little girls a young cur that has not been trained?" she asked them. "If it were housebroken, he would have said so, so I feel it is safe to assume that it is not. Perhaps cannot *be* housebroken. I've heard of such cases."

The fantasy spun on, richly and rapidly, with all the skilled helping hands at work at once. The dog was tangibly in the room with us, shedding his hair, biting his fleas, shaking rain off himself to splatter the walls, dragging some dreadful carcass across the floor, chewing up slippers, knocking over chairs with his tail, gobbling the chops from the platter, barking, biting, fathering, fighting, smelling to high heaven of carrion, staining the rug with his muddy feet, scratching the floor with his claws. He developed rabies; he bit a child, two children! Three! Everyone in town! And Gran and her poor darlings went to jail for harboring this murderous, odoriferous, drunk, Roman Catholic dog.

And yet, astoundingly enough, she came around to agreeing to let us have the dog. It was, as Mr. Murphy had predicted, the word "watchdog" that deflected the course of the trial. The moment Daisy uttered it, Gran halted, marshalling her reverse march; while she rallied and tacked and reconnoitred, she sent us to the kitchen for the dessert. And by the time this course was under way, the uses of a dog, the enormous potentialities for investigation and law enforcement in a dog trained by Mrs. Placer, were being minutely and passionately scrutinized by the eight upright bloodhounds sitting at the table wolfing their brown Betty as if it were fresh-killed rabbit. The dog now sat at attention beside his mistress, fiercely alert, ears cocked, nose aquiver, the protector of widows, of orphans, of lonely people who had no homes. He made short shrift of burglars, homicidal maniacs, Peeping Toms, gypsies, bogus missionaries, Fuller Brush men with a risqué spiel. He went to the store and brought back groceries, retrieved the evening paper from the awkward place the boy had meanly thrown it, rescued cripples from burning houses, saved children from drowning, heeled at command, begged, lay down, stood up, sat, jumped through a hoop, ratted.

Both times—when he was a ruffian of the blackest delinquency and then a pillar of society—he was full-grown in his prefiguration, and when Laddy appeared on the following day, small, unsteady, and whimpering lonesomely, Gran and her lodgers were taken aback; his infant, clumsy paws embarrassed them, his melting eyes were unapropos. But it could never be said of Mrs. Placer, as Mrs. Placer her own self said, that she was a woman who went back on her word, and her darlings were going to have their dog, soft-headed and feckless as he might be. All the first night, in his carton in the kitchen, he wailed for his mother, and in the morning, it was true, he had made a shambles of the room—fouled the floor, and pulled off the tablecloth together with a ketchup bottle, so that thick gore lay everywhere. At breakfast, the lodgers confessed they had had a most amusing night, for it had actually been funny the way the dog had been determined not to let anyone get a wink of sleep. After that first night, Laddy slept in our room, receiving from us, all through our delighted, sleepless nights, pats and embraces and kisses and whispers. He was our baby, our best friend, the smartest, prettiest, nicest dog in the entire wide world. Our soft and rapid blandishments excited him to yelp at us in pleased bewilderment, and then we would playfully grasp his muzzle, so that he would snarl, deep in his throat like an adult dog, and shake his head violently, and, when we freed him, nip us smartly with great good will.

He was an intelligent and genial dog and we trained him quickly. He steered clear of Gran's radishes and lettuce after she had several times given him a brisk comeuppance with a strap across the rump, and he soon left off chewing shoes and the laundry on the line, and he outgrew his babyish whining. He grew like a weed; he lost his spherical softness, and his coat, which had been sooty fluff, came in stiff and rusty black; his nose grew aristocratically long, and his clever,

pointed ears stood at attention. He was all bronzy, lustrous black
except for an Elizabethan ruff of white and a tip of white at the
end of his perky tail. No one could deny that he was exceptionally
handsome and that he had, as well, great personal charm and style.
He escorted Daisy and me to school in the morning, laughing in-
teriorly out of the enormous pleasure of his life as he gracefully
cantered ahead of us, distracted occasionally by his private interest
in smells or unfamiliar beings in the grass but, on the whole, engrossed in his role of chaperon. He made friends easily with other
dogs, and sometimes he went for a long hunting weekend into the
mountains with a huge and bossy old red hound named Mess, who
had been on the county most of his life and had made a good thing
of it, particularly at the fire station.

It was after one of these three-day excursions into the high country
that Gran took Laddy in hand. He had come back spent and filthy,
his coat a mass of cockleburs and ticks, his eyes bloodshot, loud
râles in his chest; for half a day he lay motionless before the front
door like someone in a hangover, his groaning eyes explicitly saying
"Oh, for God's sake, leave me be" when we offered him food or bowls
of water. Gran was disapproving, then affronted, and finally furious.
Not, of course, with Laddy, since all inmates of her house enjoyed
immunity, but with Mess, whose caddish character, together with
that of his nominal masters, the firemen, she examined closely under
a strong light, with an air of detachment, with her not caring but
her having, all the same, to laugh. A lodger who occupied the back
west room had something to say about the fire chief and his nocturnal
visits to a certain house occupied by a certain group of young women,
too near the same age to be sisters and too old to be the daughters of
the woman who claimed to be their mother. What a story! The ex-
ophthalmic librarian—she lived in one of the front rooms—had some
interesting insinuations to make about the deputy marshal, who had
borrowed, significantly, she thought, a book on hypnotism. She also
knew—she was, of course, in a most useful position in the town, and
from her authoritative pen in the middle of the library her mam-
miform and azure eyes and her eager ears missed nothing—that the
fire chief's wife was not as scrupulous as she might be when she was
keeping score on bridge night at the Sorosis.

There was little at the moment that Mrs. Placer and her disciples
could do to save the souls of the Fire Department and their families,
and therefore save the town from holocaust (a very timid boarder—
a Mr. Beaver, a newcomer who was not to linger long—had sniffed
throughout this recitative as if he were smelling burning flesh), but

at least the unwholesome bond between Mess and Laddy could and
would be severed once and for all. Gran looked across the porch at
Laddy, who lay stretched at full length in the darkest corner, shuddering and baying abortively in his throat as he chased jack rabbits
in his dreams, and she said, "A dog can have morals like a human."
With this declaration Laddy's randy, manly holidays were finished.
It may have been telepathy that woke him; he lifted his heavy head
from his paws, laboriously got up, hesitated for a moment, and then
padded languidly across the porch to Gran. He stood docilely beside
her chair, head down, tail drooping as if to say, "O.K., Mrs. Placer,
show me how and I'll walk the straight and narrow."

The very next day, Gran changed Laddy's name to Caesar, as
being more dignified, and a joke was made at the supper table that
he had come, seen, and conquered Mrs. Placer's heart—for within
her circle, where the magnanimity she lavished upon her orphans
was daily demonstrated, Mrs. Placer's heart was highly thought of.
On that day also, although we did not know it yet, Laddy ceased
to be our dog. Before many weeks passed, indeed, he ceased to be
anyone we had ever known. A week or so after he became Caesar,
he took up residence in her room, sleeping alongside her bed. She
broke him of the habit of taking us to school (temptation to low
living was rife along those streets; there was a chow—well, never
mind) by the simple expedient of chaining him to a tree as soon as
she got up in the morning. This discipline, together with the stamina-
building cuffs she gave his sensitive ears from time to time, gradually
but certainly remade his character. From a sanguine, affectionate,
easygoing Gael (with the fits of melancholy that alternated with the
larkiness), he turned into an overbearing, military, efficient, loud-
voiced Teuton. His bark, once wide of range, narrowed to one dark,
glottal tone.

Soon the paper boy flatly refused to serve our house after Caesar
efficiently removed the bicycle clip from his pants leg; the skin was
not broken, or even bruised, but it was a matter of principle with
the boy. The milkman approached the back door in a seizure of
shakes like St. Vitus's dance. The metermen, the coal men, and the
garbage collector crossed themselves if they were Catholics and,
if they were not, tried whistling in the dark. "Good boy, good Caesar," they carolled, and, unctuously lying, they said they knew his
bark was worse than his bite, knowing full well that it was not, considering the very nasty nip, requiring stitches, he had given a representative of the Olson Rug Company, who had had the folly to pat
him on the head. Caesar did not molest the lodgers, but he disdained

them and he did not brook being personally addressed by anyone except Gran. One night, he wandered into the dining room, appearing to be in search of something he had mislaid, and, for some reason that no one was ever able to divine, suddenly stood stock-still and gave the easily upset Mr. Beaver a long and penetrating look. Mr. Beaver, trembling from head to toe, stammered, "Why—er, hello there, Caesar, old boy, old boy," and Caesar charged. For a moment, it was touch and go, but Gran saved Mr. Beaver, only to lose him an hour later when he departed, bag and baggage, for the Y.M.C.A. This rout and the consequent loss of revenue would more than likely have meant Caesar's downfall and his deportation to the pound if it had not been that a newly widowed druggist, very irascible and very much Gran's style, had applied for a room in her house a week or so before, and now he moved in delightedly, as if he were coming home.

Finally, the police demanded that Caesar be muzzled and they warned that if he committed any major crime again—they cited the case of the Olson man—he would be shot on sight. Mrs. Placer, although she had no respect for the law, knowing as much as she did about its agents, obeyed. She obeyed, that is, in part; she put the muzzle on Caesar for a few hours a day, usually early in the morning when the traffic was light and before the deliveries had started, but the rest of the time his powerful jaws and dazzling white sabre teeth were free and snapping. There was between these two such preternatural rapport, such an impressive conjugation of suspicion, that he, sensing the approach of a policeman, could convey instantly to her the immediate necessity of clapping his nose cage on. And the policeman, sent out on the complaint of a terrorized neighbor, would be greeted by this law-abiding pair at the door.

Daisy and I wished we were dead. We were divided between hating Caesar and loving Laddy, and we could not give up the hope that something, someday, would change him back into the loving animal he had been before he was appointed vice-president of the Placerites. Now at the meetings after supper on the porch he took an active part, standing rigidly at Gran's side except when she sent him on an errand. He carried out these assignments not with the air of a servant but with that of an accomplice. "Get me the paper, Caesar," she would say to him, and he, dismayingly intelligent and a shade smart-alecky, would open the screen door by himself and in a minute come back with the *Bulletin,* from which Mrs. Placer would then read an item, like the Gospel of the day, and then read between the lines of it, scandalized.

In the deepening of our woe and our bereavement and humiliation, we mutely appealed to Mr. Murphy. We did not speak out-
right to him, for Mr. Murphy lived in a state of indirection, and
often when he used the pronoun "I," he seemed to be speaking of
someone standing a little to the left of him, but we went to see him
and his animals each day during the sad summer, taking what comfort we could from the cozy, quiet indolence of his back yard, where
small black eyes encountered ours politely and everyone was half
asleep. When Mr. Murphy inquired about Laddy in his bland, inattentive way, looking for a stratagem whereby to shift the queen
of hearts into position by the king, we would say, "Oh, he's fine,"
or "Laddy is a nifty dog." And Mr. Murphy, reverently slaking the
thirst that was his talent and his concubine, would murmur, "I'm
glad."

We wanted to tell him, we wanted his help, or at least his sympathy, but how could we cloud his sunny world? It was awful to see
Mr. Murphy ruffled. Up in the calm clouds as he generally was, he
could occasionally be brought to earth with a thud, as we had seen
and heard one day. Not far from his house, there lived a bad,
troublemaking boy of twelve, who was forever hanging over the
fence trying to teach the parrot obscene words. He got nowhere,
for she spoke no English and she would flabbergast him with her
cold eye and sneer, "*Tant pis.*" One day, this boorish fellow went
too far; he suddenly shot his head over the fence like a jack-in-the-
box and aimed a water pistol at the skunk's face. Mr. Murphy
leaped to his feet in a scarlet rage; he picked up a stone and threw
it accurately, hitting the boy square in the back, so hard that he fell
right down in a mud puddle and lay there kicking and squalling
and, as it turned out, quite badly hurt. "If you ever come back here
again, I'll kill you!" roared Mr. Murphy. I think he meant it, for I
have seldom seen an anger so resolute, so brilliant, and so voluble.
"How dared he!" he cried, scrambling into Mallow's cage to hug
and pet and soothe her. "He must be absolutely mad! He must be
the Devil!" He did not go back to his game after that but paced the
yard, swearing a blue streak and only pausing to croon to his animals, now as frightened by him as they had been by the intruder,
and to drink straight from the bottle, not bothering with fixings.
We were fascinated by this unfamiliar side of Mr. Murphy, but
we did not want to see it ever again, for his face had grown
so dangerously purple and the veins of his forehead seemed ready
to burst and his eyes looked scorched. He was the closest thing to
a maniac we had ever seen. So we did not tell him about Laddy;

what he did not know would not hurt him, although it was hurting us, throbbing in us like a great, bleating wound.

But eventually Mr. Murphy heard about our dog's conversion, one night at the pool hall, which he visited from time to time when he was seized with a rare but compelling garrulity, and the next afternoon when he asked us how Laddy was and we replied that he was fine, he tranquilly told us, as he deliberated whether to move the jack of clubs now or to bide his time, that we were sweet girls but we were lying in our teeth. He did not seem at all angry but only interested, and all the while he questioned us, he went on about his business with the gin and the hearts and spades and diamonds and clubs. It rarely happened that he won the particular game he was playing, but that day he did, and when he saw all the cards laid out in their ideal pattern, he leaned back, looking disappointed, and he said, "I'm damned." He then scooped up the cards, in a gesture unusually quick and tidy for him, stacked them together, and bound them with a rubber band. Then he began to tell us what he thought of Gran. He grew as loud and apoplectic as he had been that other time, and though he kept repeating that he knew *we* were innocent and he put not a shred of the blame on us, we were afraid he might suddenly change his mind, and, speechless, we cowered against the monkeys' cage. In dread, the monkeys clutched the fingers we offered to them and made soft, protesting noises, as if to say, "Oh, stop it, Murphy! Our nerves!"

As quickly as it had started, the tantrum ended. Mr. Murphy paled to his normal complexion and said calmly that the only practical thing was to go and have it out with Mrs. Placer. "At once," he added, although he said he bitterly feared that it was too late and there would be no exorcising the fiend from Laddy's misused spirit. And because he had given the dog to us and not to her, he required that we go along with him, stick up for our rights, stand on our mettle, get up our Irish, and give the old bitch something to put in her pipe and smoke.

Oh, it was hot that day! We walked in a kind of delirium through the simmer, where only the grasshoppers had the energy to move, and I remember wondering if either smelled like the gin on Mr. Murphy's breath. Daisy and I, in one way or another, were going to have our gizzards cut out along with our hearts and our souls and our pride, and I wished I were as drunk as Mr. Murphy, who swam effortlessly through the heat, his lips parted comfortably, his eyes half closed. When we turned in to the path at Gran's house, my blood began to scald my veins. It was so futile and so dangerous and so absurd. Here we were on a high moral mission, two draggletailed, gumptionless little girls and a toper whom no one could take seriously, partly because he was little more than a gurgling bottle of booze and partly because of the clothes he wore. He was a sight, as he always was when he was out of his own yard. There, somehow, in the carefree disorder, his clothes did not look especially strange, but on the streets of the town, in the barbershop or the post office or on Gran's path, they were fantastic. He wore a pair of hound's-tooth pants, old but maintaining a vehement pattern, and with them he wore a collarless blue flannelette shirt. His hat was the silliest of all, because it was a derby three sizes too big. And as if Shannon, too, was a part of his funny-paper costume, the elder capuchin rode on his shoulder, tightly embracing his thin red neck.

Gran and Caesar were standing side by side behind the screen door, looking as if they had been expecting us all along. For a moment, Gran and Mr. Murphy faced each other across the length of weedy brick between the gate and the front porch, and no one spoke. Gran took no notice at all of Daisy and me. She adjusted her eyeglasses, using both hands, and then looked down at Caesar and matter-of-factly asked, "Do you want out?"

Caesar flung himself full-length upon the screen and it sprang open like a jaw. I ran to meet and head him off, and Daisy threw a library book at his head, but he was on Mr. Murphy in one split second and had his monkey off his shoulder and had broken Shannon's neck in two shakes. He would have gone on nuzzling and mauling and growling over the corpse for hours if Gran had not marched out of the house and down the path and slapped him lightly on the flank and said, in a voice that could not have deceived an idiot, "Why, Caesar, you scamp! You've hurt Mr. Murphy's monkey! Aren't you ashamed!"

Hurt the monkey! In one final, apologetic shudder, the life was extinguished from the little fellow. Bloody and covered with slather, Shannon lay with his arms suppliantly stretched over his head, his leather fingers curled into loose, helpless fists. His hind legs and his tail lay limp and helter-skelter on the path. And Mr. Murphy, all of a sudden reeling drunk, burst into the kind of tears that Daisy and I knew well—the kind that time alone could stop. We stood aghast in the dark-red sunset, killed by our horror and our grief for Shannon and our unforgivable disgrace. We stood upright in a dead faint, and an eon passed before Mr. Murphy picked up Shannon's body and wove away, sobbing, "I don't believe it! I don't *believe* it!"

The very next day, again at morbid, heavy sunset, Caesar died in violent convulsions, knocking down two tall hollyhocks in his throes. Long after his heart had stopped, his right hind leg continued to jerk in aimless reflex. Madly methodical, Mr. Murphy had poisoned some meat for him, had thoroughly envenomed a whole pound of hamburger, and early in the morning, before sunup, when he must have been near collapse with his hangover, he had stolen up to Mrs. Placer's house and put it by the kitchen door. He was so stealthy that Caesar never stirred in his fool's paradise there on the floor by Gran. We knew these to be the facts, for Mr. Murphy made no bones about them. Afterward, he had gone home and said a solemn Requiem for Shannon in so loud a voice that someone sent for the police, and they took him away in the Black Maria to sober him up on strong green tea. By the time he was in the lockup and had confessed what he had done, it was far too late, for Caesar had already gulped down the meat. He suffered an undreamed-of agony in Gran's flower garden, and Daisy and I, unable to bear the sight of it, hiked up to the red rocks and shook there, wretchedly ripping to shreds the sand lilies that grew in the cracks. Flight was the only thing we could think of, but where could we go? We stared west at the mountains and quailed at the look of the stern white glacier; we wildly scanned the prairies for escape. "If only we were something besides kids! Besides girls!" mourned Daisy. I could not speak at all; I huddled in a niche of the rocks and cried.

No one in town, except, of course, her lodgers, had the slightest sympathy for Gran. The townsfolk allowed that Mr. Murphy was a drunk and was fighting Irish, but he had a heart and this was something that could never be said of Mrs. Placer. The neighbor who had called the police when he was chanting the "Dies Irae" before breakfast in that deafening monotone had said, "The poor guy is having some kind of a spell, so don't be rough on him, hear?" Mr. Murphy became, in fact, a kind of hero; some people, stretching a point, said he was a saint for the way that every day and twice on Sunday he sang a memorial Mass over Shannon's grave, now marked with a chipped, cheap plaster figure of Saint Francis. He withdrew from the world more and more, seldom venturing into the streets at all, except when he went to the bootlegger to get a new bottle to snuggle into. All summer, all fall, we saw him as we passed by his yard, sitting at his dilapidated table, enfeebled with gin, graying, withering, turning his head ever and ever more slowly as he maneuvered the protocol of the kings and the queens and the knaves. Daisy and I could never stop to visit him again.

It went on like this, year after year. Daisy and I lived in a mesh of lies and evasions, baffled and mean, like rats in a maze. When we were old enough for beaux, we connived like sluts to see them, but we would never admit to their existence until Gran caught us out by some trick. Like this one, for example: Once, at the end of a long interrogation, she said to me, "I'm more relieved than I can tell you that you *don't* have anything to do with Jimmy Gilmore, because I happen to know that he is after only one thing in a girl," and then, off guard in the loving memory of sitting in the movies the night before with Jimmy, not even holding hands, I defended him and defeated myself, and Gran, smiling with success, said, "I *thought* you knew him. It's a pretty safe rule of thumb that where there's smoke there's fire." That finished Jimmy and me, for afterward I was nervous with him and I confounded and alarmed and finally bored him by trying to convince him, although the subject had not come up, that I did not doubt his good intentions.

Daisy and I would come home from school, or, later, from our jobs, with a small triumph or an interesting piece of news, and if we forgot ourselves and, in our exuberance, told Gran, we were hustled into court at once for cross-examination. Once, I remember, while I was still in high school, I told her about getting a part in a play. How very nice for me, she said, if that kind of make-believe seemed to me worth while. But what was my role? An old woman! A widow woman believed to be a witch? She did not care a red cent, but she did have to laugh in view of the fact that Miss Eccles, in charge of dramatics, had almost run her down in her car. And I would forgive her, would I not, if she did not come to see the play, and would not think her eccentric for not wanting to see herself ridiculed in public?

My pleasure strangled, I crawled, joy-killed, to our third-floor room. The room was small and its monstrous furniture was too big and the rag rugs were repulsive, but it was bright. We would not hang a blind at the window, and on this day I stood there staring into the mountains that burned with the sun. I feared the mountains, but at times like this their massiveness consoled me; they, at least, could not be gossiped about.

Why did we stay until we were grown? Daisy and I ask ourselves this question as we sit here on the bench in the municipal zoo, reminded of Mr. Murphy by the polar bear, reminded by the monkeys not of Shannon but of Mrs. Placer's insatiable gossips at their post-prandial feast.

"But how could we have left?" says Daisy, wringing her buttery hands. "It was the depression. We had no money. We had nowhere to go."

"All the same, we could have gone," I say, resentful still of the waste of all those years. "We could have come here and got jobs as waitresses. Or prostitutes, for that matter."

"I wouldn't have wanted to be a prostitute," says Daisy.

We agree that under the circumstances it would have been impossible for us to run away. The physical act would have been simple, for the city was not far and we could have stolen the bus fare or hitched a ride. Later, when we began to work as salesgirls in Kress's it would have been no trick at all to vanish one Saturday afternoon with our week's pay, without so much as going home to say goodbye. But it had been infinitely harder than that, for Gran, as we now see, held us trapped by our sense of guilt. We were vitiated, and we had no choice but to wait, flaccidly, for her to die.

You may be sure we did not unlearn those years as soon as we put her out of sight in the cemetery and sold her house for a song to the first boob who would buy it. Nor did we forget when we left the town for another one, where we had jobs at a dude camp—the town where Daisy now lives with a happy husband and two happy sons. The succubus did not relent for years, and I can still remember, in the beginning of our days at the Lazy S 3, overhearing an edgy millionaire say to his wife, naming my name, "That girl gives me the cold shivers. One would think she had just seen a murder." Well, I had. For years, whenever I woke in the night in fear or pain or loneliness, I would increase my suffering by the memory of Shannon, and my tears were as bitter as poor Mr. Murphy's.

We have never been back to Adams. But we see that house plainly, with the hopvines straggling over the porch. The windows are hung with the cheapest grade of marquisette, dipped into coffee to impart to it an unwilling color, neither white nor tan but individual and spitefully unattractive. We see the wicker rockers and the swing, and through the screen door we dimly make out the slightly veering corridor, along one wall of which stands a glass-doored bookcase; when we were children, it had contained not books but stale old cardboard boxes filled with such things as W.C.T.U. tracts and anticigarette literature and newspaper clippings related to sexual sin in the Christianized islands of the Pacific.

Even if we were able to close our minds' eyes to the past, Mr. Murphy would still be before us in the apotheosis of the polar bear. My pain becomes intolerable, and I am relieved when Daisy rescues us. "We've got to go," she says in a sudden panic. "I've got asthma coming on." We rush to the nearest exit of the city park and hail a cab, and, once inside it, Daisy gives herself an injection of adrenalin and then leans back. We are heartbroken and infuriated, and we cannot speak.

Two hours later, beside my train, we clutch each other as if we were drowning. We ought to go out to the nearest policeman and say, "We are not responsible women. You will have to take care of us because we cannot take care of ourselves." But gradually the storm begins to lull.

"You're sure you've got your ticket?" says Daisy. "You'll surely be able to get a roomette once you're on."

"I don't know about that," I say. "If there are any V.I.P.s on board, I won't have a chance. 'Spinsters and Orphans Last' is the motto of this line."

Daisy smiles. "I didn't care," she says, "but I had to laugh when I saw that woman nab the redcap you had signalled to. I had a good notion to give her a piece of my mind."

"It will be a miracle if I ever see my bags again," I say, mounting the steps of the train. "Do you suppose that blackguardly porter knows about the twenty-dollar gold piece in my little suitcase?"

"Anything's possible!" cries Daisy, and begins to laugh. She is so pretty, standing there in her bright-red linen suit and her black velvet hat. A solitary ray of sunshine comes through a broken pane in the domed vault of the train shed and lies on her shoulder like a silver arrow.

"So long, Daisy!" I call as the train begins to move.

She walks quickly along beside the train. "Watch out for pickpockets!" she calls.

"You, too!" My voice is thin and lost in the increasing noise of the speeding train wheels. "Goodbye, old dear!"

I go at once to the club car and I appropriate the writing table, to the vexation of a harried priest, who snatches up the telegraph pad and gives me a sharp look. I write Daisy approximately the same letter I always write her under this particular set of circumstances, the burden of which is that nothing for either of us can ever be as bad as the past before Gran mercifully died. In a postscript I add: "There is a Roman Catholic priest (that is to say, he is *dressed* like one) sitting behind me although all the chairs on the opposite side of the car are empty. I can only conclude that he is looking over my shoulder, and while I do not want to cause you any alarm, I think you would be advised to be on the lookout for any appearance of miraculous medals, scapulars, papist booklets, etc., in the shops in your town. It really makes me laugh to see the way he is pretending that all he wants is for me to finish this letter so that he can have the table."

I sign my name and address the envelope, and I give up my place to the priest, who smiles nicely at me, and then I move across the car to watch the fields as they slip by. They are alfalfa fields, but you can bet your bottom dollar that they are chockablock with marijuana.

I begin to laugh. The fit is silent but it is devastating; it surges and rattles in my rib cage, and I turn face to the window to avoid the narrow gaze of the Filipino bar boy. I must think of something sad to stop this unholy giggle, and I think of the polar bear. But even his bleak tragedy does not sober me. Wildly I fling open the newspaper I have brought and I pretend to be reading something screamingly funny. The words I see are in a Hollywood gossip column: "How a well-known starlet can get a divorce in Nevada without her crooner husband's consent, nobody knows. It won't be worth a plugged nickel here."

The Man Who Saw
Through Heaven

People have wondered (there being obviously no question of ro-
mance involved) how I could ever have allowed myself to be let in
for the East African adventure of Mrs. Diana in search of her husband. There were several reasons. To begin with, the time and
effort and money weren't mine; they were the property of the wheel
of which I was but a cog, the Society through which Diana's life
had been insured, along with the rest of that job-lot of missionaries.
The "letting in" was the firm's. In the second place, the wonderers
have not counted on Mrs. Diana's capacity for getting things done
for her. Meek and helpless. Yes, but God was on her side. Too
meek, too helpless to move mountains herself, if those who happened to be handy didn't move them for her then her God would
know the reason why. Having dedicated her all to making straight
the Way, why should her neighbour cavil at giving a little? The
writer for one, a colonial governor general for another, railway mag-
nates, insurance managers, *safari* leaders, the ostrich-farmer of Ndua,
all these and a dozen others in their turns have felt the hundred-ton
weight of her thin-lipped meekness—have seen her in metaphor sitting grimly on the doorsteps of their souls.

A third reason lay in my own troubled conscience. Though I did
it in innocence, I can never forget that it was I who personally conducted Diana's party to the observatory on that fatal night in
Boston before it sailed. Had it not been for that kindly intentioned
"hunch" of mine, the astounded eye of the Reverend Hubert Diana
would never have gazed through the floor of Heaven, and he would
never have undertaken to measure the Infinite with the foot-rule
of his mind.

It all started so simply. My boss at the shipping-and-insurance
office gave me the word in the morning. "Bunch of missionaries for
the *Platonic* to-morrow. They're on our hands in a way. Show 'em

the town." It wasn't so easy when you think of it: one male and seven females on their way to the heathen; though it was easier in Boston than it might have been in some other towns. The evening looked the simplest. My friend Krum was at the Observatory that semester; there at least I was sure their sensibilities would come to no harm.

On the way out in the street car, seated opposite to Diana and having to make conversation, I talked of Krum and of what I knew of his work with the spiral nebulæ. Having to appear to listen, Diana did so (as all day long) with a vaguely indulgent smile. He really hadn't time for me. That night his life was exalted as it had never been, and would perhaps never be again. To-morrow's sailing, the actual fact of leaving all to follow Him, held his imagination in thrall. Moreover, he was a bridegroom of three days with his bride beside him, his nerves at once assuaged and thrilled. No, but more. As if a bride were not enough, arrived in Boston, he had found himself surrounded by a very galaxy of womanhood gathered from the four corners; already within hours one felt the chaste tentacles of their feminine dependence curling about the party's unique man; already their contacts with the world of their new lives began to be made through him; already they saw in part through his eyes. I wonder what he would have said if I had told him he was a little drunk.

In the course of the day I think I had got him fairly well. As concerned his Church he was at once an asset and a liability. He believed its dogma as few still did, with a simplicity, "the old-time religion." He was born that kind. Of the stuff of the fanatic, the reason he was not a fanatic was that, curiously impervious to little questionings, he had never been aware that his faith was anywhere attacked. A self-educated man, he had accepted the necessary smattering facts of science with a serene indulgence, as simply so much further proof of what the Creator could do when He put His Hand to it. Nor was he conscious of any conflict between these facts and the fact that there existed a substantial Heaven, geographically up, and a substantial Hot Place, geographically down.

So, for his Church, he was an asset in these days. And so, and for the same reason, he was a liability. The Church must after all keep abreast of the times. For home consumption, with modern congregations, especially urban ones, a certain streak of "healthy" skepticism is no longer amiss in the pulpit; it makes people who read at all more comfortable in their pews. A man like Hubert Diana is more for the cause than a hundred. But what to do with him? Well, such things arrange themselves. There's the Foreign Field. The blacker the heathen the whiter the light they'll want, and the solider the conception of a God the Father enthroned in a Heaven of which the sky above them is the visible floor.

And that, at bottom, was what Hubert Diana believed. Accept as he would with the top of his brain the fact of a spherical earth zooming through space, deep in his heart he knew that the world lay flat from modern Illinois to ancient Palestine, and that the sky above it, blue by day and by night festooned with guiding stars for wise men, was the nether side of a floor on which the resurrected trod. . . .

I shall never forget the expression of his face when he realized he was looking straight through it that night. In the quiet dark of the dome I saw him remove his eye from the eye-piece of the telescope up there on the staging and turn it in the ray of a hooded bulb on the demon's keeper, Krum.

"What's that, Mr. Krum? I didn't get you!"

"I say, that particular cluster you're looking at——"

"This star, you mean?"

"You'd have to count awhile to count the stars describing their orbits in that 'star,' Mr. Diana. But what I was saying—have you ever had the wish I used to have as a boy—that you could actually look back into the past? With your own two eyes?"

Diana spoke slowly. He didn't know it, but it had already begun to happen; he was already caught. "I have often wished, Mr. Krum, that I might actually look back into the time of our Lord. Actually. Yes."

Krum grunted. He was young. "We'd have to pick a nearer neighbour than *Messier* 79 then. The event you see when you put your eye to that lens is happening much too far in the past. The light-waves thrown off by that particular cluster on the day, say, of the Crucifixion—*you* won't live to see them. They've hardly started yet —a mere twenty centuries on their way—leaving them something like eight hundred and thirty centuries yet to come before they reach the earth."

Diana laughed the queerest catch of a laugh. "And—and there —there won't be any earth here, then, to welcome them."

"*What?*" It was Krum's turn to look startled. So for a moment the two faces remained in confrontation, the one, as I say, startled, the other exuding visibly little sea-green globules of sweat. It was Diana that caved in first, his voice hardly louder than a whisper.

"W-w-will there?"

None of us suspected the enormousness of the thing that had happened in Diana's brain. Krum shrugged his shoulders and snapped his fingers. Deliberately. *Snap!* "What's a thousand centuries or so in the cosmic reckoning?" He chuckled. "We're just beginning to get out among 'em with *Messier,* you know. In the print room, Mr. Diana, I can show you photographs of clusters to which, if you cared to go, travelling at the speed of light——"

The voice ran on; but Diana's eye had gone back to the eye-piece, and his affrighted soul had reëntered the big black tube sticking its snout out of the slit in the iron hemisphere. . . . "At the speed of light!" . . . That unsuspected, that wildly chance-found chink in the armour of his philosophy! The body is resurrected and it ascends to Heaven instantaneously. At what speed must it be borne to reach instantaneously that city beyond the ceiling of the sky? At a speed inconceivable, mystical. At, say (as he had often said to himself), *the speed of light.* . . . And now, hunched there in the trap that had caught him, black rods, infernal levers and wheels, he was aware of his own eye passing vividly through unpartitioned emptiness, *eight hundred and fifty centuries at the speed of light!*

"And still beyond these," Krum was heard, "we begin to come into the regions of the spiral nebulæ. We've some interesting photographs in the print room, if you've the time."

The ladies below were tired of waiting. One had "lots of packing to do." The bride said, "Yes, I do think we should be getting along. Hubert, dear, if you're ready——"

The fellow actually jumped. It's lucky he didn't break anything. His face looked greener and dewier than ever amid the contraptions above. "If you—you and the ladies, Cora—wouldn't mind—if Mr.—Mr.—(he'd mislaid my name) would see you back to the hotel——" Meeting silence, he began to expostulate. "I feel that this is a rich experience. I'll follow shortly; I know the way."

In the car going back into the city Mrs. Diana set at rest the flutterings of six hearts. Being unmarried, they couldn't understand men as she did. When I think of that face of hers, to which I was destined to grow only too accustomed in the weary, itchy days of the trek into Kavirondoland, with its slightly tilted nose, its irregular pigmentation, its easily inflamed lids, and long moist cheeks, like a hunting dog, glorying in weariness, it seems incredible that a light of coyness could have found lodgment there. But that night it did. She sat serene among her virgins.

"You don't know Bert. You wait; he'll get a perfectly wonderful sermon out of all that to-night, Bert will."

Krum was having a grand time with his neophyte. He would have stayed up all night. Immured in the little print room crowded with files and redolent of acids, he conducted his disciple "glassy-eyed" through the dim frontiers of space, holding before him one after another the likenesses of universes sister to our own, islanded in immeasurable vacancy, curled like glimmering crullers on their private Milky Ways, and hiding in their wombs their myriad "coal-pockets," star-dust fœtuses of which—their quadrillion years accomplished—their litters of new suns would be born, to bear their planets, to bear their moons in turn.

"And beyond these?"

Always, after each new feat of distance, it was the same. "And beyond?" Given an ell, Diana surrendered to a pop-eyed lust for nothing less than light-years. "And still beyond?"

"Who knows?"

"The mind quits. For if there's no end to these nebulæ——"

"But supposing there is?"

"An end? But, Mr. Krum, in the very idea of an ending——"

"An end to what we might call this particular category of magnitudes. Eh?"

"I don't get that."

"Well, take this—take the opal in your ring there. The numbers and distances inside that stone may conceivably be to themselves as staggering as ours to us in our own system. Come! that's not so far-fetched. What are we learning about the structure of the atom? A nucleus (call it a sun) revolved about in eternal orbits by electrons (call them planets, worlds). Infinitesimal; but after all, what are bigness and littleness but matters of comparison? To eyes on one of those electrons (don't be too sure there aren't any) its tutelary sun may flame its way across a heaven a comparative ninety million miles away. Impossible for them to conceive of a boundary to their billions of atomic systems, molecular universes. In that category of magnitudes its diameter is infinity; once it has made the leap into our category and become an opal it is merely a quarter of an inch. That's right, Mr. Diana, you may well stare at it: between *now* and *now* ten thousand histories may have come and gone down there. . . . And just so the diameter of our own cluster of universes, going over into another category, may be——"

"May be a—a ring—a little stone—in a—a—a—ring."

Krum was tickled by the way the man's imagination jumped and engulfed it.

"Why not? That's as good a guess as the next. A ring, let's say, worn carelessly on the—well, say the tentacle—of some vast organism—some inchoate creature hobnobbing with its cloudy kind in another system of universes—which in turn——"

It is curious that none of them realized next day that they were dealing with a stranger, a changed man. Why he carried on, why he capped that night of cosmic debauch by shaving, eating an unremarkable breakfast, packing his terrestrial toothbrush and collars, and going up the gangplank in tow of his excited convoy to sail away, is beyond explanation—unless it was simply that he was in a daze.

It wasn't until four years later that I was allowed to know what had happened on that ship, and even then the tale was so disjointed, warped, and opinionated, so darkly seen in the mirror of Mrs. Diana's orthodoxy, that I had almost to guess what it was *really* all about.

"When Hubert turned irreligious. . . ." That phrase, recurrent on her tongue in the meanderings of the East African quest to which we were by then committed, will serve to measure her understanding. Irreligious! Good Lord! But from that sort of thing I had to reconstruct the drama. Evening after evening beside her camp fire (appended to the Mineral Survey Expedition Toward Uganda through the kindness—actually the worn-down surrender—of the Protectorate government) I lingered awhile before joining the merrier engineers, watched with fascination the bumps growing under the mosquitoes on her forehead, and listened to the jargon of her mortified meekness and her scandalized faith.

There had been a fatal circumstance, it seems, at the very outset. If Diana could but have been seasick, as the rest of them were (horribly), all might still have been well. In the misery of desired death, along with the other contents of a heaving midriff, he might have brought up the assorted universes of which he had been led too rashly to partake. But he wasn't. As if his wife's theory was right, as if Satan was looking out for him, he was spared to prowl the swooping decks immune. Four days and nights alone. Time enough to digest and assimilate into his being beyond remedy that lump of whirling magnitudes and to feel himself surrendering with a strange new ecstasy to the drunkenness of liberty.

Such liberty! Given Diana's type, it is hard to imagine it adequately. The abrupt, complete removal of the toils of reward and punishment; the withdrawal of the surveillance of an all-seeing, all-knowing Eye; the windy assurance of being responsible for nothing, important to no one, no longer (as the police say) "wanted"! It must have been beautiful in those few days of its first purity, before it began to be discoloured by his contemptuous pity for others, the mask of his inevitable loneliness and his growing fright.

The first any of them knew of it—even his wife—was in mid-voyage, the day the sea went down and the seven who had been sick came up. There seemed an especial Providence in the calming of the waters; it was Sunday morning and Diana had been asked to conduct the services.

He preached on the text: "For of such is the kingdom of Heaven."

"If our concept of God means anything it means a God *all*-mighty, Creator of *all* that exists, Director of the *infinite*, cherishing in His Heaven the saved souls of *all space and all time*."

Of course; amen. And wasn't it nice to feel like humans again, and real sunshine pouring up through the lounge ports from an ocean suddenly grown kind. . . . But—then—*what* was Diana *saying?*

Mrs. Diana couldn't tell about it coherently even after a lapse of fifty months. Even in a setting as remote from that steamer's lounge as the equatorial bush, the ember-reddened canopy of thorn trees, the meandering camp fires, the chant and tramp somewhere away of Kikuyu porters dancing in honour of an especial largesse of fat zebra meat—even here her memory of that impious outburst was too vivid, too aghast.

"It was Hubert's look! The way he stared at us! As if you'd said he was licking his chops! . . . That 'Heaven' of his!"

It seems they hadn't waked up to what he was about until he had the dimensions of his sardonic Paradise irreparably drawn in. The final haven of all right souls. Not alone the souls released from this our own tiny earth. In the millions of solar systems we see as stars how many millions of satellites must there be upon which at some time in their histories conditions suited to organic life subsist? Uncounted hordes of wheeling populations! Of men? God's creatures at all events, a portion of them reasoning. Weirdly shaped, perhaps, but what of that? And that's only to speak of our own inconsiderable cluster of universes. That's to say nothing of other systems of magnitudes, where God's creatures are to our world what we are to the world's in the atoms in our finger-rings. (He had shaken *his*, here, in their astounded faces.) And all these, all the generations of these enormous and microscopic beings harvested through a time beside which the life-span of our earth is as a second in a million centuries: all these brought to rest for an eternity to which time itself is a watch-tick—all crowded to rest pell-mell, thronged, serried, packed, packed to suffocation in layers unnumbered light-years deep. This must needs be our concept of Heaven if God is the God of the Whole. If, on the other hand——

The other hand was the hand of the second officer, the captain's delegate at divine worship that Sabbath day. He at last had "come to."

I don't know whether it was the same day or the next; Mrs. Diana was too vague. But here's the picture. Seven women huddled in the large stateroom on B-deck, conferring in whispers, aghast, searching one another's eyes obliquely even as they bowed their heads in prayer for some light—and of a sudden the putting back of the door and the in-marching of the Reverend Hubert. . . .

As Mrs. Diana tried to tell me, "You understand, don't you, he had just taken a bath? And he hadn't—he had forgotten to——"

Adam-innocent there he stood. Not a stitch. But I don't believe for a minute it was a matter of forgetting. In the high intoxication of his soul-release, already crossed (by the second officer) and beginning to show his zealot claws, he needed some gesture stunning enough to witness to his separation, his unique rightness, his contempt of match-flare civilizations and infinitesimal taboos.

But I can imagine that stateroom scene: the gasps, the heads colliding in aversion, and Diana's six weedy feet of birthday-suit towering in the shadows, and ready to sink through the deck, I'll warrant, now the act was irrevocable, but still grimly carrying it off.

"And if, on the other hand, you ask me to bow down before a God peculiar to this one earth, this one grain of dust lost among the giants of space, watching its sparrows fall, profoundly interested in a speck called Palestine no bigger than the quadrillionth part of one of the atoms in the ring here on my finger——"

Really scared by this time, one of the virgins shrieked. It was altogether too close quarters with a madman.

Mad? Of course there was the presumption: "Crazy as a loon." Even legally it was so adjudged at the *Platonic's* first port-of-call, Algiers, where, when Diana escaped ashore and wouldn't come back again, he had to be given over to the workings of the French Law. I talked with the magistrate myself some forty months later, when, "let in" for the business as I have told, I stopped there on my way out.

"But what would you?" were his words. "We must live in the world as the world lives, is it not? Sanity? Sanity is what? Is it, for example, an intellectual clarity, a balanced perception of the realities? Naturally, speaking out of court, your friend was of a sanity—of a sanity, sir——" Here the magistrate made with thumb and fingers the gesture only the French can make for a thing that is matchless, a beauty, a transcendent instance of any kind. He himself was Gallic, rational. Then, with a lift of shoulder, "But what would you? We must live in the world that seems."

Diana, impounded in Algiers for deportation, escaped. What, after all, are the locks and keys of this pinchbeck category of magnitudes? More remarkable still, there in Arab Africa, he succeeded in vanishing from the knowledge and pursuit of men. And of women. His bride, now that their particular mission had fallen through, was left to decide whether to return to America or to go on with two of the company, the Misses Brookhart and Smutts, who were bound for a school in Smyrna. In the end she followed the latter course. It was there, nearly four years later, that I was sent to join her by an exasperated and worn-out Firm.

By that time she knew again where her husband-errant was— or where at least, from time to time in his starry dartings over this our mote of dust, he had been heard of, spoken to, seen.

Could we but have a written history of those years of his apostolic vagabondage, a record of the towns in which he was jailed or from which he was kicked out, of the ports in which he starved, of the ships on which he stowed away, presently to reveal himself in proselyting ardour, denouncing the earthlings, the fatelings, the dupes of bugaboo, meeting scoff with scoff, preaching the new revelation red-eyed, like an angry prophet. Or was it, more simply, like a man afraid?

Was that the secret, after all, of his prodigious restlessness? Had it anything in common with the swarming of those pale worms that flee the Eye of the Infinite around the curves of the stone you pick up in a field? Talk of the man without a country! What of the man without a universe?

It is curious that I never suspected his soul's dilemma until I saw the first of his mud-sculptures in the native village of Ndua in the province of Kasuma in British East. Here it was, our objective attained, we parted company with the government *safari* and shifted the burden of Way-straightening to the shoulders of Major Wyeside, the ostrich-farmer of the neighbourhood.

While still on the *safari* I had put to Mrs. Diana a question that had bothered me: "Why on earth should your husband ever have chosen this particular neck of the woods to land up in? Why Kavirondoland?"

"It was here we were coming at the time Hubert turned irreligious, to found a mission. It's a coincidence, isn't it?"

And yet I would have sworn Diana hadn't a sense of humour about him anywhere. But perhaps it *wasn't* an ironic act. Perhaps it was simply that, giving up the struggle with a society blinded by "a little learning" and casting about for a virgin field, he had remembered this.

"I supposed he was a missionary," Major Wyeside told us with a flavour of indignation. "I went on that. I let him live here—six or seven months of it—while he was learning the tongue. I was a bit nonplussed, to put it mildly, when I discovered what he was up to."

What things Diana had been up to the Major showed us in one of the huts in the native kraal—a round dozen of them, modelled in mud and baked. Blackened blobs of mud, that's all. Likenesses of nothing under the sun, fortuitous masses sprouting haphazard tentacles, only two among them showing pustules that might have been experimental heads. . . . The ostrich-farmer saw our faces.

"Rum, eh? Of course I realized the chap was anything but fit. A walking skeleton. Nevertheless, whatever it is about these beasties, there's not a nigger in the village has dared set foot inside this hut since Diana left. You can see for yourselves it's about to crash. There's another like it he left at Suki, above here. Taboo, no end!"

So Diana's "hunch" had been right. He had found his virgin field indeed, fit soil for his cosmic fright. A religion in the making, here before our eyes.

"This was at the very last before he left," Wyeside explained. "He took to making these mud-pies quite of a sudden; the whole lot within a fortnight's time. Before that he had simply talked, harangued. He would sit here in the doorway of an evening with the niggers squatted around and harangue 'em by the hour. I knew something of it through my house-boys. The most amazing rot. All about the stars to begin with, as if these black baboons could half grasp *astronomy!* But that seemed all proper. Then there was talk about a something a hundred times as big and powerful as the world, sun, moon, and stars put together—some perfectly enormous stupendous awful being—but knowing how mixed the boys can get, it still seemed all regular—simply the parson's way of getting at the notion of an Almighty God. But no, they insisted, there wasn't any God. That's the point, they said; there *is no* God. . . . Well, that impressed me as a go. That's when I decided to come down and get the rights of this star-swallowing monstrosity the beggar was feeding my labour on. And here he sat in the doorway with one of these

beasties—here it is, this one—waving it furiously in the niggers' be-
nighted faces. And do you know what he'd done?—you can see the
mark here still on this wabble-leg, this tentacle-business—he had
taken off a ring he had and screwed it on just here. His finger ring,
my word of honour! And still, if you'll believe it, I didn't realize he
was just daft. Not until he spoke to me. 'I find,' he was good enough
to enlighten me, 'I find I have to make it somehow concrete.' . . .
'Make what?' . . . 'Our wearer.' . . . 'Our *what, where?*' . . . 'In
the following category.' . . . His actual words, honour bright. I was
going to have him sent down-country where he could be looked after.
He got ahead of me though. He cleared out. When I heard he'd
turned up at Suki I ought, I suppose, to have attended to it. But I
was having trouble with leopards. And you know how things go."

From there we went to Suki, the Major accompanying. It was as
like Ndua as one flea to its brother, a stockade inclosing round
houses of mud, wattles, and thatch, and full of naked heathen. The
Kavirondo are the nakedest of all African peoples and, it is said,
the most moral. It put a great strain on Mrs. Diana; all that whole
difficult anxious time, as it were detachedly, I could see her itching
to get them into Mother Hubbards and cast-off Iowa pants.

Here, too, as the Major had promised, we found a holy of holies,
rather a dreadful of dreadfuls, "taboo no end," its shadows cluttered
with the hurlothrumbos of Diana's artistry. What puzzled me was
their number. Why this appetite for experimentation? There was an
uncertainty; one would think its effect on potential converts would
be bad. Here, as in Ndua, Diana had contented himself at first with
words and skyward gesticulations. Not for so long, however. Feeling
the need of giving his concept of the cosmic "wearer" a substance
much earlier, he had shut himself in with the work, literally—a fever
of creation. We counted seventeen of the nameless "blobs," all done,
we were told, in the seven days and nights before their maker had
again cleared out. The villagers would hardly speak of him; only
after spitting, their eyes averted, and in an undertone, would they
mention him: "He of the Ring." Thereafter we were to hear of him
only as "He of the Ring."

Leaving Suki, Major Wyeside turned us over (thankfully, I warrant) to a native who told us his name was Charlie Kamba. He had
spent some years in Nairobi, running for an Indian outfitter, and
spoke English remarkably well. It was from him we learned, quite
casually, when our modest eight-load *safari* was some miles on its
way, that the primary object of our coming was non-existent. Hubert
Diana was dead.

Dead nearly five weeks—a moon and a little—and buried in the mission church at Tara Hill.

Mission church! There was a poser for us. *Mission church?*

Well, then, Charlie Kamba gave us to know that he was paraphrasing in a large way suitable to our habits of thought. We shouldn't have understood *his* informant's "wizard house" or "house of the effigy."

I will say for Mrs. Diana that in the course of our halt of lugubrious amazement she shed tears. That some of them were not tears of unrealized relief it would be hardly natural to believe. She had desired loyally to find her husband, but when she should have found him—what? This problem, sturdily ignored so long, was now removed.

Turn back? Never! Now it would seem the necessity for pressing forward was doubled. In the scrub-fringed ravine of our halt the porters resumed their loads, the dust stood up again, the same caravan moved on. But how far it was now from being the same.

From that moment it took on, for me at least, a new character. It wasn't the news especially; the fact that Diana was dead had little to do with it. Perhaps it was simply that the new sense of something aimfully and cumulatively dramatic in our progress had to have a beginning, and that moment would do as well as the next.

Six villages: M'nann, Leika, Leikapo, Shamba, Little Tara, and Tara, culminating in the apotheosis of Tara Hill. Six stops for the night on the road it had cost Diana as many months to cover in his singular pilgrimage to his inevitable goal. Or in his flight to it. Yes, his stampede. Now the pipers at that four-day orgy of liberty on the *Platonic's* decks were at his heels for their pay. Now that his strength was failing, the hosts of loneliness were after him, creeping out of their dreadful magnitudes, the hounds of space. Over all that ground it seemed to me we were following him not by the world of hearsay but, as one follows a wounded animal making for its earth, by the droppings of his blood.

Our progress had taken on a pattern; it built itself with a dramatic artistry; it gathered suspense. As though it were a story at its most breathless places "continued in our next," and I a reader forgetting the road's weariness, the dust, the torment of insects never escaped, the inadequate food, I found myself hardly able to keep from running on ahead to reach the evening's village, to search out the inevitable repository of images left by the white stranger who had come and tarried there awhile and gone again.

More concrete and ever more concrete. The immemorial compromise with the human hunger for a symbol to see with the eyes, touch with the hands. Hierarchy after hierarchy of little mud effigies—one could see the necessity pushing the man. Out of the protoplasmic blobs of Ndua, Suki, even M'nann, at Leikapo Diana's concept of infinity (so pure in that halcyon epoch at sea), of categories nested within categories like Japanese boxes, of an overcreature wearing our cosmos like a trinket, unawares, had become a mass with legs to stand on and a real head. The shards scattered about in the filth of the hut there (as if in violence of despair) were still monstrosities, but with a sudden stride of concession their monstrousness was the monstrousness of lizard and turtle and crocodile. At Shamba there were dozens of huge-footed birds.

It is hard to be sure in retrospect, but I do believe that by the time we reached Little Tara I began to see the thing as a whole—the fœtus, working out slowly, blindly, but surely, its evolution in the womb of fright. At Little Tara there was a change in the character of the exhibits; their numbers had diminished, their size had grown. There was a boar with tusks and a bull the size of a dog with horns, and on a tusk and on a horn an indentation left by a ring.

I don't believe Mrs. Diana got the thing at all. Toward the last she wasn't interested in the huts of relics; at Little Tara she wouldn't go near the place; she was "too tired." It must have been pretty awful, when you think of it, even if all she saw in them was the mud-pie play of a man reverted to a child.

There was another thing at Little Tara quite as momentous as the jump to boar and bull. Here at last a mask had been thrown aside. Here there had been no pretense of proselyting, no astronomical lectures, no doorway harangues. Straightway he had arrived (a fabulous figure already, long heralded), he had commandeered a house and shut himself up in it and there, mysterious, assiduous, he had remained three days and nights, eating nothing, but drinking gallons of the foul water they left in gourds outside his curtain of reeds. No one in the village had ever seen what he had done and left there. Now, candidly, those labours were for himself alone.

Here at last in Tara the moment of that confession had overtaken the fugitive. It was he, ill with fever and dying of nostalgia—not these naked black baboon men seen now as little more than blurs— who had to give the Beast of the Infinite a name and a shape. And more and more, not only a shape, but a *shapeliness*. From the instant when, no longer able to live alone with nothingness, he had given it a likeness in Ndua mud, and perceived that it was intolerable and fled its face, the turtles and distorted crocodiles of Leikapo and the birds of Shamba had become inevitable, and no less inevitable the Little Tara boar and bull. Another thing grows plain in retrospect: the reason why, done to death (as all the way they reported him) he couldn't die. He didn't dare to. Didn't dare to close his eyes.

It was at Little Tara we first heard of him as "Father Witch," a name come back, we were told, from Tara, where he had gone. I had heard it pronounced several times before it suddenly obtruded from the native context as actually two English words. That was what made it queer. It was something they must have picked up by rote, uncomprehending; something then they could have had from no lips but his own. When I repeated it after them with a better accent they pointed up toward the north, saying "Tara! Tara!"—their eagerness mingled with awe.

I shall never forget Tara as we saw it, after our last blistering scramble up a gorge, situated in the clear air on a slope belted with cedars. A mid-African stockade left by some blunder in an honest Colorado landscape, or a newer and bigger Vermont. Here at the top of our journey, black savages, their untidy *shambas*, the very Equator, all these seemed as incongruous as a Gothic cathedral in a Congo marsh. I wonder if Hubert Diana knew whither his instinct was guiding him on the long road of his journey here to die. . . .

He had died and he was buried, not in the village, but about half a mile distant, on the ridge; this we were given to know almost before we had arrived. There was no need to announce ourselves, the word of our coming had outrun us; the populace was at the gates.

"Our Father Witch! Our Father Witch!" They knew what we were after; the funny parrot-wise English stood out from the clack and clatter of their excited speech. "Our Father Witch! Ay! Ay!" With a common eagerness they gesticulated at the hilltop beyond the cedars.

Certainly here was a change. No longer the propitiatory spitting, the averted eyes, the uneasy whispering allusion to him who had passed that way: here in Tara they would shout him from the housetops, with a kind of civic pride.

We learned the reason for this on our way up the hill. It was because they were his chosen, the initiate.

We made the ascent immediately, against the village's advice. It was near evening; the return would be in the dark; it was bad lion country; wouldn't it to-morrow morning do? . . . No, it wouldn't do the widow. Her face was set. . . . And so, since we were resolved to go, the village went with us, armed with spears and rattles and drums. Charlie Kamba walked beside us, sifting the information a hundred were eager to give.

These people were proud, he said, because their wizard was more powerful than all the wizards of all the other villages "in the everywhere together." If he cared to he could easily knock down all the other villages in the "everywhere," destroying all the people and all the cattle. If he cared to he could open his mouth and swallow the sky and the stars. But Tara he had chosen. Tara he would protect. He made their mealies to grow and their cattle to multiply.

I protested, "But he is *dead* now!"

Charlie Kamba made signs of deprecation. I discerned that he was far from clear about the thing himself.

Yes, he temporized, this Father Witch was dead, quite dead. On the other hand, he was up there. On the other hand, he would never die. He was longer than for ever. Yes, quite true, he was dead and buried under the pot.

I gave it up. "How did he die?"

Well, he came to this village of Tara very suffering, very sick. The dead man who walked. His face was very sad. Very eaten. Very frightened. He came to this hill. So he lived here for two full moons, very hot, very eaten, very dead. These men made him a house as he commanded them, also a stockade. In the house he was very quiet, very dead, making magic two full moons. Then he came out and they that were waiting saw him. He had made the magic, and the magic had made him well. His face was kind. He was happy. He was full fed. He was full fed, these men said, without any eating. Yes, they carried up to him very fine food, because they were full of wonder and some fear, but he did not eat any of it. Some water he drank. So, for two days and the night between them, he continued sitting in the gate of the stockade, very happy, very full fed. He told these people very much about their wizard, who is bigger than everywhere and longer than for ever and can, if he cares to, swallow the sky and stars. From time to time, however, ceasing to talk to these people, he got to his knees and talked in his own strange tongue to Our Father Witch, his eyes held shut. When he had done this just at sunset of the second day he fell forward on his face. So he remained that night. The next day these men took him into the house and buried him under the pot. On the other hand, Our Father Witch is longer than for ever. He remains there still. . . .

The first thing I saw in the hut's interior was the earthen pot at the northern end, wrong-side-up on the ground. I was glad I had preceded Mrs. Diana. I walked across and sat down on it carelessly, hoping so that her afflicted curiosity might be led astray. It gave me the oddest feeling, though, to think of what was there beneath my nonchalant sitting-portion—aware as I was of the Kavirondo burial of a great man—up to the neck in mother earth, and the rest of him left out in the dark of the pot for the undertakings of the ants. I hoped his widow wouldn't wonder about that inverted vessel of clay.

I needn't have worried. Her attention was arrested otherwheres. I shall not forget the look of her face, caught above me in the red shaft of sundown entering the western door, as she gazed at the last and the largest of the Reverend Hubert Diana's gods. That long, long cheek of hers, buffeted by sorrow, startled now, and mortified. Not till that moment, I believe, had she comprehended the steps of mud images she had been following for what they were, the steps of idolatry.

For my part, I wasn't startled. Even before we started up the hill, knowing that her husband had dared to die here, I could have told her pretty much what she would find.

This overlord of the cosmic categories that he had fashioned (at last) in his own image sat at the other end of the red-streaked house upon a bench—a throne?—of mud. Diana had been no artist. An ovoid two-eyed head, a cylindrical trunk, two arms, two legs, that's all. But indubitably man, man-size. Only one finger of one of the hands had been done with much care. It wore an opal, a two-dollar stone from Mexico, set in a silver ring. This was the hand that was lifted, and over it the head was bent.

I've said Diana was no artist. I'll take back the words. The figure was crudeness itself, but in the relation between that bent head and that lifted hand there was something which was something else. A sense of scrutiny one would have said no genius of mud could ever have conveyed. An attitude of interest centred in that bauble, intense and static, breathless and eternal all in one—penetrating to its bottom atom, to the last electron, to a hill upon it, and to a two-legged mite about to die. Marking (yes, I'll swear to the incredible) the sparrow's fall.

The magic was made. The road that had commenced with the blobs of Ndua—the same that commenced with our hairy ancestors listening to the night wind in their caves—was run.

And from here Diana, of a sudden happy, of a sudden looked after, "full fed," had walked out——

But no; I couldn't stand that mortified sorrow on the widow's face any longer. She had to be made to see. I said it aloud:

"From here, Mrs. Diana, your husband walked out——"

"He had sunk to idolatry. *Idolatry!*"

"To the bottom, yes. And come up its whole history again. And from here he walked out into the sunshine to kneel and talk with 'Our Father Which——'"

She got it. She caught it. I wish you could have seen the light going up those long, long cheeks as she got it:

"Our Father which art in Heaven, Hallowed be Thy Name!"

We went down hill in the darkness, convoyed by a vast rattling of gourds and beating of goat-hide drums.

Beyond the Glass Mountain

Someone had left a funny paper in the booth, and while he waited
with his ear intent on the regular buzzing rings, Mark let his eye
follow the pictured squares. I know somebody that likes your new
hat, Emmy, Kayo's balloon said, and Emmy's pleased balloon said,
Well, for thirty-nine fifty they ought to, who is he? and Kayo's balloon
said, It's Beefy McGuire, he'd like it for his bird's-nest collection,
and on the fourth ring the line clicked and Mel's inquiring voice
said, "Hello?"

The voice was as familiar as yesterday, a voice whose wire-filtered
flatness Mark had heard over telephones ten thousand times. The
rising hairs prickled on the back of his neck; he felt as he might
have felt if a door had opened and the face of someone long dead
had looked casually out.

And he noted instantly, in refutation of his fears, that the voice
was sober. He found himself leaning forward, grinning into the
mouthpiece.

"Hello, you poop out," he said. "This is Canby."

The old password came naturally, as if he were back seventeen
years. In their college crowd everybody had called everybody else
Canby, for no reason except that someone, probably Mel, had begun
it and everyone else had followed suit. There had been a real Canby,
a sort of goof. Now he was a CPA in Denver and the usurpers of
his name were scattered from coast to coast.

"Well, Canby!" the filtered voice said heartily. "How's the boy?"

There was a pause. Then Mel's voice, more distorted now, beginning to be his clowning voice, said suspiciously, "What was that
name again?"

"Canby," Mark said. "Cornelius C. Canby." He raised his head,
grinning and waiting for the real recognition.

"Cornelius C. Canby?" Mel's thickening, burbling voice said. "I didn't get the name."

"It's a hell of a note," Mark said. "Your old friend Canby was here, and you didn't even get the name."

Mel's voice was thick as glue now, like something mired down, except that on occasional syllables it fluttered upward like a mud-heavy bird. It was a maudlin, wandering, caressing voice, very convincing to strangers and drunks, and it always made any drunk his instant pal. "*Canby?*" it said. "D'you say *Canby*? Cornelius Canby? Well, my God. Wonnersnevercease. *Canby*, after all these years! Come on over here and shake my hand. Where are you? Hire a car. Wait a minute, I'll come and get you myself."

"Don't bother," Mark said. "I can walk over in five minutes." He grinned again into the mouthpiece. "Are you at home or out at some bar?"

"Just down at the corner pub having little drink," Mel said. "But I'll be home in minute, home quick as you are. Not far away." There was another pause. "What was z'name?"

Mark was beginning to feel a shade uncomfortable. The clowning was routine, but there was a point where it should have stopped. It left things uncertain. "You stinker," he said, "this is Aker. Remember me?"

The drunken voice was an amazed buzz in the earpiece. Out of the buzz words formed. "You mean Belly Aker, the basketball player, erstwhile holder of the Big Ten scoring record?"

"The same."

"Not Mark Aker, the eminent penicillinologist?"

"It is he."

"Well, my God," Mel said. "I remember you. Seen your name in the Alumni Magazine."

The words degenerated into a buzz, then became articulate again. "You old spore-picker. How's boy?" Then in a moment the earphone bellowed, "What the hell you standing around there for?"

"Hold it," Mark said. "I'm on my way."

He hung up and stepped out of the booth self-consciously, looking around to see if anyone had been close enough to hear the nonsense he had been talking. As he walked through the drugstore and out into the street he found himself explaining as if to some critical stranger. Just to listen to Cottam, you'd think he was a maudlin sot, but that's just a manner he wears. He pus it on for the same reason some people put on dark glasses. . . .

He found himself at the corner of College and Dubuque streets in Iowa City, at a little past ten on a Sunday morning in May, and as he stopped on the corner to let a car pass, the utter and passionate familiarity of everything smote him like a wind. Mel's voice on the wire had prepared him for nostalgia. Now the past moved up on him in a wave; it was as if he had never left here, or had just awakened from a long confused dream and found the solid and reassuring edge of reality again.

The brick street ran warm and empty down across the powerhouse bridge and up the other side, curving under big elms and hickories. On the crown of the hill across the river the Quadrangle's squat ivied towers barely topped the trees, and over on the other hill to the right the stone lace of the hospital tower rose above the massive rectangularity of the medical buildings. The lawns below Old Capitol were almost deserted, and the locusts were shrilling in the streetside trees.

Odd compulsions moved him. He found himself reciting the names of all the main university buildings. Crossing the river, he ran his hand along the cool cement rail as if establishing a contact, and halfway across he looked back to see how the union and the reserve library strung out along the riverbank and the footbridge arched across to the experimental theater. The banks of the river had been landscaped since his time, but otherwise he saw no change. The highway traffic west poured across the Iowa Avenue bridge, and the law commons clung to the limestone bluffs. Mark looked curiously at the few students he met, wondering if they felt as he felt the charm and warmth that lay in the brick streets and the sleepy river and the sun-warmed brick and stone of the university. Probably no one appreciated things like that until they were gone and lost and irretrievable.

On his left as he stepped off the bridge he saw the little eating shack where he and Mel had had long johns and coffee practically every morning for four years. The mere look of its outside, patched with coke signs and Baby Ruth signs and Chesterfield signs, filled his nostrils with the peculiar and unique odors of the place: coffee and smoke and slightly rancid fat, oily-sweet doughnuts and baked paint and the reek of the bug spray they used on the cockroaches, and under all the watery, tarry, wet-mud smells of the river.

The metal rasping of the seventeen-year-locusts rose loud as a crescendo in a symphonic poem as he climbed the hill, and it struck him as amusing that he too should return here at the end of exactly seventeen years. He couldn't quite imagine where those years had gone; it did not seem that either he or the town had changed a particle. The tennis courts he passed reflected hundreds of remembered mornings like this, and in the field house beyond them were whole lifetimes of recollection.

He would have liked to go in under the big round roof just to soak himself in the sensations he remembered: smell of lockers opened on stale gym clothes and stiff sweated socks; steam and thumping radiators and liquid-soap smell; sweat and medicated foot baths and the chlorine smell and the jiggly reflecting chemical blue of the pool; splat of naked feet on concrete, pink of bare flesh, lean bellies and tiptoe-bunching calves, the bulging triceps of the gymnastics team working out on the horses. Most of all, the barnlike cold of the basketball floor, and the tiny brittle feeling of coming out before a game to warm up in front of that crowd-faced emptiness, and the clubbing roar of crowd-sound as you drove in for a setup. It was the same roar whether you made it or missed it.

All of it was still there—unimaginably varied smells and sounds and sights that together made up the way he had once lived, the thing he had once been, perhaps the thing he still was. He was in all of it, and Mel with him. It came to him like a pang that never since the days when he and Mel used to fool around after lunch in the Quad cafeteria, throwing rolled-up paper napkins at water tumblers, had he had a completely relaxed and comfortable ability to enjoy himself. They had made games out of everything; whole Sunday mornings they had spent throwing curves with pot covers in Mel's mother's kitchen. In those Damon-and-Pythias days there had been a sharp and tingling sense of identity and one intense and constant comradeship, and those were the best days of his life. Passing the field house, he passed himself and Mel as they had used to be, and the feeling that he had not merely lived this but was somehow contained in it was as pervasive as the mild spring morning, as insistent as the skirring of the locusts. It was like skywriting on the big warm sky.

The light over the whole hill was pure, pale, of an exaggerated clarity, as if all the good days of his youth had been distilled down into this one day, and the whole coltish ascendant time when he was eighteen, nineteen, twenty, had been handed back to him briefly, intact and precious. That was the time when there had been more hours in the day, and every hour precious enough so that it could be fooled away. By the time a man got into the high thirties the hours became more frantic and less precious, more needed and more carefully hoarded and more fully used, but less loved and less enjoyed.

Then he was pushing the doorbell button, bracing himself ob-

scurely for something—for joy? for recognition? for a renewed flood
of this potent and unexpected nostalgia?—and the door opened. Mel
stood there in his shirt sleeves, a little mussy as usual, still decep-
tively round-armed and round-faced, with his beaked nose and his
tender child's mouth.

He was either drunk or playing drunk. He smirked, and his eyes
blinked in owlish amazement. "Let me shake your hand!" he said,
and hauled Mark inside.

Tamsen got up off the couch where she had been sitting with a
highball in her hand. As she came forward, smiling, transferring
the glass to her left hand, Mark noted how she adjusted her face
for greeting. She was probably prettier than she had ever been, her
hair in a long bob with sun-bleached streaks in it, her face smoothly
tanned, her eyes candid, her smile white and frank. Presumably
the two of them had been drinking together, but where Mel was
frowzy and blinking, with red-streaked eyeballs, she was smooth
and sober and impeccable.

"Of all the unexpected people!" she said, and gave him a firm hand.
She left him in no doubt who was in command in this familiar house,
who had established dominance.

Mel's hand pulled him around. "Canby, you old snake in the grass,
where you been? I've tried to call you up every night for ten years."

"You did," Mark said. "Twice. Once in New Haven and once in
New York. Both times at two in the morning."

Tamsen laughed. "Old Melly," she said, almost as if affectionately.
"Every time he gets tight he wants to call somebody up. The further
away they are, the more he wants to call."

Mel was standing spraddling, a little flickering smile on his mouth.
One hand was on Mark's shoulder. With the other he captured
Mark's right hand again and shook it slowly. His breath was heavy
with whisky, and Mark felt dismayed and half sick. He had been so
sure at first that the thickening voice had been put on as part of the
old clowning act. Now he was bothered precisely as he had been
bothered by those telephone calls. Even while he laughed at the ponderous solemnity, the incoherent, bumbling, repetitive nonsense, the
marvelously accurate imitation of a soggy drunk, Mark backed away,
because he couldn't be quite sure that the act was conscious any
more. The act had become the man, and he went around living and
acting out a grotesque parody of himself; or if it hadn't become the
man, then it had been put on defensively so much that communication was no longer possible. Nothing had come of those telephone
calls except a mumble of double talk and affectionate profanity, and

yet Mark felt that there had been in each instance a need, a lone-liness, a reaching out. He felt that there was the same thing now, if Mel would let it show. The old comradeship was there; this drunken parody was embarrassment as much as anything, the defense of a thin-skinned organism.

"Been peeking down those microscopes," Mel said solemnly, pump-ing Mark's hand. "You biological old pot-licker. D'you invent pen-icillin?"

"I'm a modest man," Mark said. "Two or three other people helped."

He got his hand free, and as his eyes crossed Mel's there was al-most communication between them, a flash of perfectly sober un-derstanding and warmth. Mel's delicate, bruised-looking lips pursed, but then the look slipped and was gone, and he was pawing for Mark's hand again, saying, "Canby, you old Rhodes scholar, slip me the grip."

Tamsen was amused. "You should charge him. Remember when he paid a barfly a dollar an hour to shake his hand down at Frank's?"

"Kept me poor," Mel said, with a sweet imbecilic grin. "Lose all your friends, got to buy more." He smiled into Mark's face, hang-ing to hand and shoulder, and Mark looked deep behind that idiot alcoholic smile trying to compel expression of what he knew was there: the recognition and the pain. Mel beamed at him.

Tamsen too was staring, tipping her head sideways. "I can't get over how much you've changed," she said. "You used to be such a string bean."

"Cheer up," Mark said. "I'm still a string bean at heart."

"No fooling," Mel said. He plucked the cloth of Mark's sleeve, sniffed his fingers. "Where'd you get that jacket?"

"Montreal," Mark said, and immediately felt an obscure guilty shame, as if he had been betrayed into boasting, rubbing in the fact that he had gone up and out in the world and Mel had been ma-rooned behind. "I was up there a couple weeks ago at a genetics conference," he said lamely, in extenuation.

For an instant he was furious at Mel, so furious he shook. In college it had been Mel who had everything—money enough, and clothes, and a car, and a home where starveling students could come like grateful sidling dogs off the street. And he had been brought up well, he had good parents, his home was full of music and books and a certain sense of social grace and personal responsibility. Mel had taught the whole unlicked lot of them something, how to win and how to lose, how to live with people and like them and forgive them. He had never owned a dime's worth of anything that he wasn't glad to share. Now the shoe was on the other foot. Now Mark had gone higher and farther than any of them had ever aimed, and it embarrassed and enraged him to know that he could give lessons to Mel. And it was unjust that having shared everything for four years in college, they couldn't share this trouble that Mel was in now.

Tamsen's level blue eyes were inspecting him, and it struck him that here at least was something they had never shared. He had always known more about Tamsen than Mel had. When he stood up as Mel's best man he could have told the bridegroom the names of four people who had slept with the bride. He wished now that he had; he had wished it a hundred times. And catching Tamsen's eyes, twinkling with a little spark of malice, he knew she understood precisely what he was thinking. She had always been shrewd, and she had been all her life one of the world's most accomplished and convincing liars. When she went after Mel she had fooled even the people who knew her best, made them believe she was infatuated. . . .

"I tell you for sure," she said, "if you'd been as good-looking then as you are now I'd never have let old Melly take me in to church."

"Maybe there's still time," Mark said.

Mel's tugging hand hauled him around. "You've *changed*, you know that, you damn Yale professor?"

"So have you," Mark said, but his attempt to hold Mel's eye was unsuccessful, and he added, "I stay in nights, now. Once I got free of your influence I steadied right down."

"That's fact," Mel said. "Terrible influence. Half stiff ten-thirty Sunday morning. Blame that boy of mine. Got his old man out playing baseball with a hangover before breakfast. You ever meet that boy?"

"Never did."

"Where is he, Tam?"

"He's around," Tamsen said. "How about me getting you two a drink?"

Mark let her go. It was a way of getting Mel alone. It seemed to him that some of the drunken pose fell away from Mel as soon as his wife left the room. He looked into the streaked eyes and shook his head and grinned. "How are things going, anyway?"

The eyes were round and innocent. "Things going wonderful. I run the business now, since my dad died. My dad was a good businessman, you know that, Canby?"

"I know that," Mark said. "It wasn't business I was thinking about."

With a quick estimate that he might have only two minutes more before Tamsen returned, he opened his mouth to say what he had come to say and found that his tongue wouldn't go around it. In that instant it was clear that you did not come in on an old friend and say, "I hear your wife's been playing around with a golf pro. I could have warned you about her that way. Probably I should have. But I hear you found out all right, and were all set to get a divorce. Bailey told me that much, a year ago. Then I heard that instead of getting a divorce you went down to St. Louis, you and Tamsen and the boy, and stayed six months, and came back home and no more said about any divorce. Get rid of her. She'll cheat on you all her life, and break you in the process. If she's pulled some lie out of the bag and convinced you that you were mistaken, don't believe it, she could lie her way out of hell. For the love of God, get that divorce, for the sake of the boy and for your own sake. She'll suck you dry like an old orange skin. You're already so far gone I could cry—soggy with alcohol and with that comedy-routine front on all the time. Come and stay with me, I'll line you up with Alcoholics Anonymous if you want. Give me a chance to pay some of what I owe you."

You simply did not say things like that. Even thinking about them made them sound self-righteous and prying. Instead, you looked uneasily at your oldest and closest friend, trying to surprise in his eyes the things you knew were there, pain and shame and bitterness and defeat. But there was too thick an insulating layer between. Seventeen years were too many. Mel was like the elk in Jim Bridger's Yellowstone story. He grazed on the other side of the glass mountain, clear and undistorted, looking only a hundred yards away. The hunter's gun went off, and the elk didn't even raise his head, didn't even hear the report. He just went on grazing, with blankness like a membrane over his eyeballs and an unpierceable transparent wall between him and the world.

Mel's lips twitched. He lurched forward, looking puzzled and solicitous. "Whazza name?" he said, besotted and polite, and turned his ear sideward like a deaf man.

Mark pushed him away angrily just as Tamsen came in with glasses. Mel took two and handed one to Mark with a crooked grin. "Here, rinse your mouth," he said.

Tamsen raised her glass. "Here's to the local boy who made good." They clicked glasses elaborately all around. Irritated, baffled, frustrated, gnawed by that odd obscure shame, Mark drank with them to himself.

"I was thinking about you the other day," Tamsen was saying.

"We were down watching the spring canoe race and two kids went over the falls by the power plant just the way you and Mel did once."

"I hope they didn't swallow as much water as I did," Mark said.

"Yeah, but this the other day was an accident," Mel said. "You, you pot-licker, you put us over there just to duck me."

"I was along," Mark said. "I went over too. Remember?"

Tamsen shook her head. "You were a pair," she said. "I guess I'd forgotten what a pair you were."

They sat nursing their drinks, the door open upon the street and the locust noise, and groped carefully backward for the things to remember and laugh about, gleaning the safe nostalgic past. But it was not the canoes over waterfalls, the times Jay Straup tried to climb Old Capitol steps in his old Model T, the picnics on Signal Hill when all the farmer kids used to creep up and spy on the college kids necking, that Mark wanted to remember. People who recalled such things and shook their heads over them bored him. He kept looking at Mel in search of that spark of understanding, and he kept wanting to say——

Remember the times we used to go out on dates and come in late in your old Ford, and stop down along one of the river joints for a pork tenderloin and a ginger beer, two or three o'clock in the morning, only a truck driver or two on the stools? How good sandwiches tasted at that hour, and how late the moon would be over the bluffs when we came out yawning and started up to your house? Remember the mornings we woke up in this house, this very house seventeen or eighteen or twenty years ago, and found the sun scrambled in the bedclothes, and had a shower and breakfast and went out onto the sidewalk, not for anything especially, but just to be outdoors, and walked under those trees out there up to the corner and back again, loafing, alive to the finger tips, talking about anything, nothing, girls, games, profundities? Remember? It isn't what we did, but what we were, that I remember, and I know that what we were is still here, if we'd peel off the defenses and the gag lines and the double-talk routines and the Montreal jackets.

The porch thudded with feet and a chubby boy of twelve came in with a bat in his hand. He stood forward gravely when Mel introduced him, shook hands with polite indifference, coasted into the kitchen, and came back gnawing on a cookie.

"Canby, my friend," Mel said to him, "you'll be as fat as your old man."

The child was a curious blend of his parents, with Tamsen's de-

ceptively clear eyes and Mel's twisting delicate mouth. He looked at
his father over the cookie, grinning.

"Stay away from Pappy," Tamsen said. "Pappy started out to cure
a hangover and behold he's swizzled again."

A grunt that sounded almost like an angry outburst escaped Mel.
He lunged for the boy. "Come here!" he said, as the boy eluded him.
"Come here and I'll knock your two heads together."

Still grinning, the boy banged out onto the porch. "How about
another drink for the two old grads?" Tamsen said.

"Why not?" Mel said, but Mark rose.

"I've got to catch a train at twelve-thirty."

"You don't have to go," Mel said. "You just came, Canby."

Mark put out his hand to Tamsen. "Good-by," he said. "If you ever
come East don't forget me."

He was trying to decide whether the look in her clear eyes had
been triumphant or whether there had actually been any look at all,
as he and Mel went out the sidewalk and down to the corner. They
did not speak on the way down, but on the corner, under the warm
shade, their voices almost lost in the incessant shrilling of the locusts,
they shook hands again. Mark knew there was no use in trying to
say any of what it had been in his mind to say. But even so he
gripped Mel's hand and held his eyes.

"I wish you the best, you bum," he said, and his throat tightened
up as it sometimes tightened at an emotional crisis in a play. "If
you're not so stiff you can't listen straight, listen to this. I wish you
the best, and if there's ever a time I can——"

He stopped. Mel was looking at him without any of the sodden
fuzziness that had marked him for the past hour. His eyes were
pained, intent, sad. On his delicate bruised lips there was a flicker
of derision.

The Promise

In a midafternoon of spring the little boy Jody walked martially along the brush-lined road toward his home ranch. Banging his knee against the golden lard bucket he used for school lunch, he contrived a good bass drum, while his tongue fluttered sharply against his teeth to fill in snare drums and occasional trumpets. Some time before, the other members of the squad that walked so smartly from the school had turned into the various little canyons and taken the wagon roads to their own home ranches. Now Jody marched seemingly alone, with high-lifted knees and pounding feet; but behind him there was a phantom army with great flags and swords, silent but deadly.

The afternoon was green and gold with spring. Underneath the spread branches of the oaks the plants grew pale and tall, and on the hills the feed was smooth and thick. The sage bushes shone with new silver leaves and the oaks wore hoods of golden green. Over the hills there hung such a green odor that the horses on the flats galloped madly and then stopped, wondering; lambs and even old sheep jumped in the air unexpectedly and landed on stiff legs, and went on eating; young clumsy calves butted their heads together and drew back and butted again.

As the gray and silent army marched past, led by Jody, the animals stopped their feeding and their play and watched it go by.

Suddenly Jody stopped. The gray army halted, bewildered and nervous. Jody went down on his knees. The army stood in long uneasy ranks for a moment, and then, with a soft sigh of sorrow, rose up in a faint gray mist and disappeared. Jody had seen the thorny crown of a horny toad moving under the dust of the road. His grimy hand went out and grasped the spiked halo and held firmly while the little beast struggled. Then Jody turned the horny toad over, exposing its pale gold stomach. With a gentle forefinger he stroked the throat and chest until the horny toad relaxed, until its eyes closed and it lay languorous and asleep.

Jody opened his lunch pail and deposited the first game inside. He moved on now, his knees bent slightly, his shoulders crouched; his bare feet were wise and silent. In his right hand there was a long gray rifle. The brush along the road stirred restively under a new and unexpected population of gray tigers and gray bears. The hunting was very good, for by the time Jody reached the fork of the road where the mailbox stood on a post he had captured two more horny toads, four little grass lizards, a blue snake, sixteen yellow-winged grasshoppers and a brown damp newt from under a rock. This assortment scrabbled unhappily against the tin of the lunch bucket.

At the road fork the rifle evaporated and the tigers and bears melted from the hillsides. Even the moist and uncomfortable creatures in the lunch pail ceased to exist, for the little red metal flag was up on the mailbox, signifying that some postal matter was inside. Jody set his pail on the ground and opened the letter box. There was a Montgomery Ward catalogue and a copy of the Salinas *Weekly Journal*. He slammed the box, picked up his lunch pail and trotted over the ridge and down into the cup of the ranch. Past the barn he ran, and the bunkhouse and the cypress tree. He banged through the front screen door of the ranch house calling, "Ma'am, ma'am, there's a catalogue."

Mrs Tiflin was in the kitchen spooning clabbered milk into a cotton bag. She put down her work and rinsed her hands under the tap. "Here in the kitchen, Jody. Here I am."

He ran in and clattered his lunch pail on the sink. "Here it is. Can I open the catalogue, ma'am?"

Mrs Tiflin took up the spoon again and went back to her cottage cheese. "Don't lose it, Jody. Your father will want to see it." She scraped the last of the milk into the bag. "Oh, Jody, your father wants to see you before you go to your chores." She waved a cruising fly from the cheese bag.

Jody closed the new catalogue in alarm. "Ma'am?"

"Why don't you ever listen? I say your father wants to see you."

The boy laid the catalogue gently on the sink board. "Do you— is it something I did?"

Mrs Tiflin laughed. "Always a bad conscience. What did you do?"

"Nothing, ma'am," he said lamely. But he couldn't remember, and besides it was impossible to know what action might later be construed as a crime.

His mother hung the full bag on a nail where it could drip into the sink. "He just said he wanted to see you when you got home. He's somewhere down by the barn."

Jody turned and went out the back door. Hearing his mother open the lunch pail and then gasp with rage, a memory stabbed him and he trotted away toward the barn, conscientiously not hearing the angry voice that called him from the house.

Carl Tiflin and Billy Buck, the ranch hand, stood against the lower pasture fence. Each man rested one foot on the lowest bar and both elbows on the top bar. They were talking slowly and aimlessly. In the pasture half-a-dozen horses nibbled contentedly at the sweet grass. The mare, Nellie, stood backed up against the gate, rubbing her buttocks on the heavy post.

Jody sidled uneasily near. He dragged one foot to give an impression of great innocence and nonchalance. When he arrived beside the men he put one foot on the lowest fence rail, rested his elbows on the second bar and looked into the pasture too. The two men glanced sideways at him.

"I wanted to see you," Carl said in the stern tone he reserved for children and animals.

"Yes sir," said Jody guiltily.

"Billy, here, says you took good care of the pony before it died." No punishment was in the air. Jody grew bolder. "Yes sir, I did."

"Billy says you have a good patient hand with horses."

Jody felt a sudden warm friendliness for the ranch hand.

Billy put in, "He trained that pony as good as anybody I ever seen."

Then Carl Tiflin came gradually to the point. "If you could have another horse would you work for it?"

Jody shivered. "Yes sir."

"Well, look here then. Billy says the best way for you to be a good hand with horses is to raise a colt."

"It's the *only* good way," Billy interrupted.

"Now, look here, Jody," continued Carl. "Jess Taylor, up to the ridge ranch, has a fair stallion, but it 'll cost five dollars. I'll put up the money, but you'll have to work it out all summer. Will you do that?"

Jody felt that his insides were shriveling. "Yes sir," he said softly.

"And no complaining? And no forgetting when you're told to do something?"

"Yes sir."

"Well, all right then. Tomorrow morning you take Nellie up to the ridge ranch and get her bred. You'll have to take care of her too till she throws the colt."

"Yes sir."

"You better get to the chickens and the wood now."

Jody slid away. In passing behind Billy Buck he very nearly put out his hand to touch the blue-jeaned legs. His shoulders swayed a little with maturity and importance.

He went to his work with unprecedented seriousness. This night he did not dump the can of grain to the chickens so that they had to leap over one another and struggle to get it. No, he spread the wheat so far and so carefully that the hens couldn't find some of it at all. And in the house, after listening to his mother's despair over boys who filled their lunch pails with slimy, suffocated reptiles and bugs, he promised never to do it again. Indeed, Jody felt that all such foolishness was lost in the past. He was far too grown up ever to put horny toads in his lunch pail any more. He carried in so much wood and built such a high structure with it that his mother walked in fear of an avalanche of oak. When he was done, when he had gathered eggs that had remained hidden for weeks, Jody walked down again past the cypress tree and past the bunkhouse toward the pasture. A fat warty toad that looked out at him from under the watering trough had no emotional effect on him at all.

Carl Tiflin and Billy Buck were not in sight, but from a metallic ringing on the other side of the barn Jody knew that Billy Buck was just starting to milk a cow.

The other horses were eating toward the upper end of the pasture, but Nellie continued to rub herself nervously against the post. Jody walked slowly near, saying, "So, girl, so-o, Nellie." The mare's ears went back naughtily and her lips drew away from her yellow teeth. She turned her head round; her eyes were glazed and mad. Jody climbed to the top of the fence and hung his feet over and looked paternally down on the mare.

The evening hovered while he sat there. Bats and night hawks flicked about. Billy Buck, walking toward the house carrying a full milk bucket, saw Jody and stopped. "It's a long time to wait," he said gently. "You'll get awful tired waiting."

"No, I won't, Billy. How long will it be?"

"Nearly a year."

"Well, I won't get tired."

The triangle at the house rang stridently. Jody climbed down from the fence and walked to supper beside Billy Buck. He even put out his hand and took hold of the milk-bucket bail to help carry it.

The next morning after breakfast Carl Tiflin folded a five-dollar bill in a piece of newspaper and pinned the package in the bib pocket of Jody's overalls. Billy Buck haltered the Nellie mare and led her out of the pasture.

"Be careful now," he warned. "Hold her up short here so she can't bite you. She's crazy as a coot."

Jody took hold of the halter leather itself and started up the hill toward the ridge ranch with Nellie skittering and jerking behind him. In the pasturage along the road the wild oat heads were just clearing their scabbards. The warm morning sun shone on Jody's back so sweetly that he was forced to take a serious, stiff-legged hop now and then in spite of his maturity. On the fences the shiny black-birds with red epaulets clicked their dry call. The meadow larks sang like water, and the wild doves, concealed among the bursting leaves of the oaks, made a sound of restrained grieving. In the fields the rabbits sat sunning themselves with only their forked ears show-ing above the grass heads.

After an hour of steady uphill walking Jody turned into a narrow road that led up a steeper hill to the ridge ranch. He could see the red roof of the barn sticking up above the oak trees, and he could hear a dog barking unemotionally near the house.

Suddenly Nellie jerked back and nearly freed herself. From the direction of the barn Jody heard a shrill whistling scream and a splin-tering of wood, and then a man's voice shouting. Nellie reared and whinnied. When Jody held to the halter rope she ran at him with bared teeth. He dropped his hold and scuttled out of the way into the brush. The high scream came from the oaks again, and Nellie answered it. With hoofs battering the ground, the stallion appeared and charged down the hill trailing a broken halter rope. His eyes glittered feverishly. His stiff erected nostrils were as red as flame. His black sleek hide shone in the sunlight. The stallion came on so fast that he couldn't stop when he reached the mare. Nellie's ears went back; she whirled and kicked at him as he went by. The stallion spun round and reared. He struck the mare with his front hoof, and while she staggered under the blow, his teeth raked her neck and drew a thread of blood.

Instantly Nellie's mood changed. She became coquettishly femi-nine. She nibbled his arched neck with her lips. She edged round and rubbed her shoulder against his shoulder.

Jody stood half hidden in the brush and watched. He heard the step of a horse behind him, but before he could turn, a hand caught him by the overall straps and lifted him off the ground. Jess Taylor sat the boy behind him on the horse.

"You might have got killed," he said. "Sundog's a mean devil sometimes. He busted his rope and went right through a gate."

Jody sat quietly, but in a moment he cried, "He'll hurt her, he'll
kill her. Get him away!"

Jess chuckled. "She'll be all right. Maybe you'd better climb
off and go up to the house for a little. You could get maybe a piece
of pie up there."

But Jody shook his head. "She's mine, and the colt's going to be
mine. I'm going to raise it up."

Jess nodded. "Yes, that's a good thing. Carl has good sense sometimes."

In a little while the danger was over. Jess lifted Jody down and
then caught the stallion by its broken halter rope. And he rode ahead,
while Jody followed, leading Nellie.

It was only after he had unpinned and handed over the five dollars
and after he had eaten two pieces of pie that Jody started for home
again. And Nellie followed docilely after him. She was so quiet that
Jody climbed on a stump and rode her most of the way home.

The five dollars his father had advanced reduced Jody to peonage
for the whole late spring and summer. When the hay was cut he
drove a rake. He led the horse that pulled on the Jackson-fork tackle,
and when the baler came he drove the circling horse that put pressure
on the bales. In addition Carl Tiflin taught him to milk and put a cow
under his care, so that a new chore was added night and morning.

The bay mare, Nellie, quickly grew complacent. As she walked
about the yellowing hillsides or worked at easy tasks her lips were
curled in a perpetual fatuous smile. She moved slowly, with the
calm importance of an empress. When she was put to a team she
pulled steadily and unemotionally. Jody went to see her every day.
He studied her with critical eyes and saw no change whatever.

One afternoon Billy Buck leaned the many-tined manure fork
against the barn wall. He loosened his belt and tucked in his shirt-
tail and tightened the belt again. He picked one of the little straws
from his hatband and put it in the corner of his mouth. Jody, who
was helping Doubletree Mutt, the big serious dog, to dig out a gopher,
straightened up as the ranch hand sauntered out of the barn.

"Let's go up and have a look at Nellie," Billy suggested.

Instantly Jody fell into step with him. Doubletree Mutt watched
them over his shoulder; then he dug furiously, growled, sounded
little sharp yelps to indicate that the gopher was practically caught.
When he looked over his shoulder again and saw that neither Jody

nor Billy was interested, he climbed reluctantly out of the hole and
followed them up the hill.

The wild oats were ripening. Every head bent sharply under its
load of grain, and the grass was dry enough so that it made a swishing sound as Jody and Billy stepped through it. Halfway up the hill
they could see Nellie and the iron-gray gelding Pete nibbling the
heads from the wild oats. When they approached, Nellie looked at
them and backed her ears and bobbed her head up and down rebel-
liously. Billy walked over to her, put his hand under her mane and
patted her neck, until her ears came forward again and she nibbled
delicately at his shirt.

Jody asked, "Do you think she's really going to have a colt?"

Billy rolled the lids back from the mare's eyes with his thumb and
forefinger. He felt her lower lip and fingered the black, leathery
teats. "I wouldn't be surprised," he said.

"Well, she isn't changed at all. It's three months gone."

Billy rubbed the mare's flat forehead with his knuckle while she
grunted with pleasure. "I told you you'd get tired waiting. It 'll be
five months more before you can even see a sign, and it 'll be at least
eight months before she throws the colt, about next January."

Jody sighed deeply. "It's a long time, isn't it?"

"And then it 'll be about two years more before you can ride."

Jody cried out in despair, "I'll be grown up."

"Yep, you'll be an old man," said Billy.

"What color do you think the colt 'll be?"

"Why, you can't ever tell. The stud is black and the dam is bay.
Colt might be black or bay or gray or dappled. You can't tell. Sometimes a black dam might have a white colt."

"Well, I hope it's black and a stallion."

"If it's a stallion we'll have to geld it. Your father wouldn't let
you have a stallion."

"Maybe he would," Jody said. "I could train him not to be mean."

Billy pursed his lips, and the little straw that had been in the
corner of his mouth rolled down to the center. "You can't ever trust
a stallion," he said critically. "They're mostly always fighting and
making trouble. Sometimes when they're feeling funny they won't
work. They make the mares uneasy and kick hell out of the geldings.
Your father wouldn't let you keep a stallion."

Nellie sauntered away, nibbling the drying grass. Jody skinned
the grain from a grass stem and threw the handful into the air, so
that each pointed, feathered seed sailed out like a dart. "Tell me how
it 'll be, Billy. Is it like when the cows have calves?"

"Just about. Mares are a little more sensitive. Sometimes you have to be there to help the mare. And sometimes, if it's wrong, you have to . . ." He paused.

"Have to what, Billy?"

"Have to tear the colt apart to get it out, or the mare 'll die."

"But it won't be that way this time, will it, Billy?"

"Oh no. Nellie's thrown good colts."

"Can I be there, Billy? Will you be certain to call me? It's my colt."

"Sure, I'll call you. Of course I will."

"Tell me how it 'll be."

"Why, you've seen the cows calving. It's almost the same. The mare starts groaning and stretching, and then, if it's a good right birth, the head and forefeet come out and the front hoofs kick a hole just the way the calves do. And the colt starts to breathe. It's good to be there, 'cause if its feet aren't right maybe he can't break the sack, and then he might smother."

Jody whipped his leg with a bunch of grass. "We'll have to be there then, won't we?"

"Oh, we'll be there all right."

They turned and walked slowly down the hill toward the barn. Jody was tortured with a thing he had to say, although he didn't want to. "Billy," he began miserably. "Billy, you won't let anything happen to the colt, will you?"

And Billy knew he was thinking of the red pony Gabilan, and of how it died of strangles. Billy knew he had been infallible before that, and now he was capable of failure. This knowledge made Billy much less sure of himself than he had been. "I can't tell," he said roughly. "All sorts of things might happen, and they wouldn't be my fault. I can't do everything." He felt badly about his lost prestige, and so he said meanly, "I'll do everything I know, but I won't promise anything. Nellie's a good mare. She's thrown good colts before. She ought to this time." And he walked away from Jody and went into the saddle room beside the barn, for his feelings were hurt.

Jody traveled often to the brush line behind the house. A rusty iron pipe ran a thin stream of spring water into an old green tub. Where the water spilled over and sank into the ground there was a patch of perpetually green grass. Even when the hills were brown and baked in the summer that little patch was green. The water whined softly into the trough all the year round. This place had grown to be a center point for Jody. When he had been punished the cool green grass and the singing water soothed him. When he had been mean the biting acid of meanness left him at the brush line. When he sat in the grass and listened to the puling stream the barriers set up in his mind by the stern day went down to ruin.

On the other hand, the black cypress tree by the bunkhouse was as repulsive as the water tub was dear; for to this tree all the pigs came, sooner or later, to be slaughtered. Pig killing was fascinating, with the screaming and the blood; but it made Jody's heart beat so fast that it hurt him. After the pigs were scalded in the big iron tripod kettle and their skins were scraped and white, Jody had to go to the water tub to sit in the grass until his heart grew quiet. The water tub and the black cypress were opposites and enemies.

When Billy left him and walked angrily away, Jody turned up toward the house. He thought of Nellie as he walked and of the little colt. Then suddenly he saw that he was under the black cypress, under the very single tree where the pigs were hung. He brushed his dry-grass hair off his forehead and hurried on. It seemed to him an unlucky thing to be thinking of his colt in the very slaughter place, especially after what Billy had said. To counteract any evil result of that bad conjunction he walked quickly past the ranch house, through the chicken yard, through the vegetable patch, until he came at last to the brush line.

He sat down in the green grass. The trilling water sounded in his ears. He looked over the farm buildings and across at the round hills, rich and yellow with grain. He could see Nellie feeding on the slope. As usual the water place eliminated time and distance. Jody saw a black long-legged colt, butting against Nellie's flanks, demanding milk. And then he saw himself breaking a large colt to halter. All in a few moments the colt grew to be a magnificent animal, deep of chest, with a neck as high and arched as a sea horse's neck, with a tail that tongued and rippled like black flame. This horse was terrible to everyone but Jody. In the school yard the boys begged rides, and Jody smilingly agreed. But no sooner were they mounted than the black demon pitched them off. Why, that was his name, Black Demon! For a moment the trilling water and the grass and the sunshine came back, and then . . .

Sometimes in the night the ranch people, safe in their beds, heard a roar of hoofs go by. They said, "It's Jody, on Demon. He's helping out the sheriff again." And then . . .

The golden dust filled the air in the arena at the Salinas Rodeo. The announcer called the roping contests. When Jody rode the black horse to the starting chute the other contestants shrugged their shoulders and gave up first place; for it was well known that Jody and Demon could rope and throw and tie a steer a great deal quicker than any roping team of two men could. Jody was not a boy any more, and Demon was not a horse. The two together were one glorious individual. And then . . .

The President wrote a letter and asked them to help catch a bandit in Washington. Jody settled himself comfortably in the grass. The little stream of water whined into the mossy tub.

The year passed slowly on. Time after time Jody gave up his colt for lost. No change had taken place in Nellie. Carl Tiflin still drove her to a light cart, and she pulled on a hay rake and worked the Jackson-fork tackle when the hay was being put into the barn.

The summer passed and the warm bright autumn. And then the frantic morning winds began to twist along the ground and a chill came into the air and the poison oak turned red. One morning in September when he had finished his breakfast Jody's mother called him into the kitchen. She was pouring boiling water into a bucket full of dry middlings and stirring the materials to a steaming paste.

"Yes ma'am?" Jody asked.

"Watch how I do it. You'll have to do it after this every morning."

"Well, what is it?"

"Why, it's warm mash for Nellie. It 'll keep her in good shape."

Jody rubbed his forehead with a knuckle. "Is she all right?" he asked timidly.

Mrs Tiflin put down the kettle and stirred the mash with a wooden paddle. "Of course she's all right, only you've got to take better care of her from now on. Here, take this breakfast out to her!"

Jody seized the bucket and ran, down past the bunkhouse, past the barn, with the heavy bucket banging against his knees. He found Nellie playing with the water in the trough, pushing waves and tossing her head so that the water slopped out on the ground.

Jody climbed the fence and set the bucket of steaming mash beside her. Then he stepped back to look at her. And she was changed. Her stomach was swollen. When she moved, her feet touched the ground gently. She buried her nose in the bucket and gobbled the hot breakfast. And when she had finished and had pushed the bucket round the ground with her nose a little, she stepped quietly over to Jody and rubbed her cheek against him.

Billy Buck came out of the saddle room and walked over. "Starts fast when it starts, doesn't it"

"Did it come all at once?"

"Oh no, you just stopped looking for a while." He pulled her head round toward Jody. "She's goin' to be nice too. See how nice her eyes are! Some mares get mean, but when they turn nice they just love everything." Nellie slipped her head under Billy's arm and rubbed her neck up and down between his arm and his side. "You better treat her awful nice now," Billy said.

"How long will it be?" Jody demanded breathlessly.

The man counted in whispers on his fingers. "About three months," he said aloud. "You can't tell exactly. Sometimes it's eleven months to the day, but it might be two weeks early or a month late without hurting anything."

Jody looked hard at the ground. "Billy," he began nervously, "Billy, you'll call me when it's getting born, won't you? You'll let me be there, won't you?"

Billy bit the tip of Nellie's ear with his front teeth. "Carl says he wants you to start right at the start. That's the only way to learn. Nobody can tell you anything. Like my old man did with me about the saddle blanket. He was a government packer when I was your size, and I helped him some. One day I left a wrinkle in my saddle blanket and made a saddle sore. My old man didn't give me hell at all. But the next morning he saddled me up with a forty-pound stock saddle. I had to lead my horse and carry that saddle over a whole damn mountain in the sun. It darn near killed me, but I never left no wrinkles in a blanket again. I couldn't. I never in my life since then put on a blanket but I felt that saddle on my back."

Jody reached up a hand and took hold of Nellie's mane. "You'll tell me what to do about everything, won't you? I guess you know everything about horses, don't you?"

Billy laughed. "Why I'm half horse myself, you see," he said. "My ma died when I was born, and being my old man was a government packer in the mountains, and no cows around most of the time, why he just gave me mostly mare's milk." He continued seriously, "And horses know that. Don't you know it, Nellie?"

The mare turned her head and looked full into his eyes for a moment, and this is a thing horses practically never do. Billy was proud and sure of himself now. He boasted a little. "I'll see you get a good colt. I'll start you right. And if you do like I say you'll have the best horse in the county."

That made Jody feel warm and proud too, so proud that when he went back to the house he bowed his legs and swayed his shoulders as horsemen do. And he whispered, "Whoa, you Black Demon, you! Steady down there and keep your feet on the ground."

The winter fell sharply. A few preliminary gusty showers, and then a strong steady rain. The hills lost their straw color and blackened under the water, and the winter streams scrambled noisily down the canyons. The mushrooms and puffballs popped up and the new grass started before Christmas.

But this year Christmas was not the central day to Jody. Some undetermined time in January had become the axis day around which the months swung. When the rains fell he put Nellie in a box stall and fed her warm food every morning and curried her and brushed her.

The mare was swelling so greatly that Jody became alarmed. "She'll pop wide open," he said to Billy.

Billy laid his strong square hand against Nellie's swollen abdomen. "Feel here," he said quietly. "You can feel it move. I guess it would surprise you if there was twin colts."

"You don't think so?" Jody cried. "You don't think it will be twins, do you, Billy?"

"No, I don't, but it does happen sometimes."

During the first two weeks of January it rained steadily. Jody spent most of his time when he wasn't in school in the box stall with Nellie. Twenty times a day he put his hand on her stomach to feel the colt move. Nellie became more and more gentle and friendly to him. She rubbed her nose on him. She whinnied softly when he walked into the barn.

Carl Tiflin came to the barn with Jody one day. He looked admiringly at the groomed bay coat, and he felt the firm flesh over ribs and shoulders. "You've done a good job," he said to Jody. And this was the greatest praise he knew how to give. Jody was tight with pride for hours afterward.

The fifteenth of January came, and the colt was not born. And the twentieth came; a lump of fear began to form in Jody's stomach. "Is it all right?" he demanded of Billy.

"Oh, sure."

And again, "Are you sure it's going to be all right?"

Billy stroked the mare's neck. She swayed her head uneasily. "I told you it wasn't always the same time, Jody. You just have to wait."

When the end of the month arrived with no birth, Jody grew frantic. Nellie was so big that her breath came heavily, and her ears were close together and straight up, as though her head ached. Jody's sleep grew restless, and his dreams confused.

On the night of the second of February he awakened crying. His mother called in to him, "Jody, you're dreaming. Wake up and start over again."

But Jody was filled with terror and desolation. He lay quietly a few moments, waiting for his mother to go back to sleep, and then he slipped his clothes on and crept out in his bare feet.

The night was black and thick. A little misting rain fell. The cypress tree and the bunkhouse loomed and then dropped back into the mist. The barn door screeched as he opened it, a thing it never did in the daytime. Jody went to the rack and found a lantern and a tin box of matches. He lighted the wick and walked down the long straw-covered aisle to Nellie's stall. She was standing up. Her whole body weaved from side to side. Jody called to her, "So, Nellie, so-o, Nellie," but she did not stop her swaying nor look round. When he stepped into the stall and touched her on the shoulder she shivered under his hand. Then Billy Buck's voice came from the hay loft right above the stall.

"Jody, what are you doing?"

Jody started back and turned miserable eyes up toward the nest where Billy was lying in the hay. "Is she all right, do you think?"

"Why sure, I think so."

"You won't let anything happen, Billy, you're sure you won't?"

Billy growled down at him, "I told you I'd call you, and I will. Now you get back to bed and stop worrying that mare. She's got enough to do without you worrying her."

Jody cringed, for he had never heard Billy speak in such a tone. "I only thought I'd come and see," he said. "I woke up."

Billy softened a little then. "Well, you get to bed. I don't want you bothering her. I told you I'd get you a good colt. Get along now."

Jody walked slowly out of the barn. He blew out the lantern and set it in the rack. The blackness of the night and the chilled mist struck him and enfolded him. He wished he believed everything Billy said as he had before the pony died. It was a moment before his eyes, blinded by the feeble lantern flame, could make any form of the darkness. The damp ground chilled his bare feet. At the cypress tree the roosting turkeys chattered a little in alarm, and the two good dogs responded to their duty and came charging out, barking to frighten away the coyotes they thought were prowling under the tree.

As he crept through the kitchen Jody stumbled over a chair. Carl called from his bedroom, "Who's there? What's the matter there?"

And Mrs Tiflin said sleepily, "What's the matter, Carl?"

The next second Carl came out of the bedroom carrying a candle, and found Jody before he could get into bed. "What are you doing out?"

Jody turned shyly away. "I was down to see the mare."

For a moment anger at being awakened fought with approval in Jody's father. "Listen," he said finally, "there's not a man in this country that knows more about colts than Billy. You leave it to him."

Words burst out of Jody's mouth. "But the pony died——"

"Don't you go blaming that on him," Carl said sternly. "If Billy can't save a horse it can't be saved."

Mrs Tiflin called, "Make him clean his feet and go to bed, Carl. He'll be sleepy all day tomorrow."

It semed to Jody that he had just closed his eyes to try to go to sleep when he was shaken violently by the shoulder. Billy Buck stood beside him, holding a lantern in his hand. "Get up," he said. "Hurry up." He turned and walked quickly out of the room.

Mrs Tiflin called, "What's the matter? Is that you, Billy?"

"Yes ma'am."

"Is Nellie ready?"

"Yes ma'am."

"All right, I'll get up and heat some water in case you need it."

Jody jumped into his clothes so quickly that he was out the back door before Billy's swinging lantern was halfway to the barn. There was a rim of dawn on the mountaintops, but no light had penetrated into the cup of the ranch yet. Jody ran frantically after the lantern and caught up to Billy just as he reached the barn. Billy hung the lantern to a nail on the stallside and took off his blue denim coat. Jody saw that he wore only a sleeveless shirt under it.

Nellie was standing rigid and stiff. While they watched she crouched. Her whole body was wrung with a spasm. The spasm passed. But in a few moments it started over again, and passed.

Billy muttered nervously, "There's something wrong." His bare hand disappeared. "Oh, Jesus," he said. "It's wrong."

The spasm came again, and this time Billy strained, and the muscles stood out on his arm and shoulder. He heaved strongly, his forehead beaded with perspiration. Nellie cried with pain. Billy was muttering, "It's wrong. I can't turn it. It's way wrong. It's turned all around wrong."

He glared wildly toward Jody. And then his fingers made a careful diagnosis. His cheeks were growing tight and gray. He looked for a long questioning minute at Jody standing back of the stall. Then Billy stepped to the rack under the manure window and picked up a horseshoe hammer with his wet right hand.

"Go outside, Jody," he said.

The boy stared dully at him.

"Go outside, I tell you. It 'll be too late."

Jody didn't move.

Then Billy walked quickly to Nellie's head. He cried, "Turn your face away, damn you, turn your face."

This time Jody obeyed. His head turned sideways. He heard Billy whispering hoarsely in the stall. And then he heard a hollow crunch of bone. Nellie chuckled shrilly. Jody looked back in time to see the hammer rise and fall again on the flat forehead. Then Nellie fell heavily to her side and quivered for a moment.

Billy jumped to her, his big pocket knife in his hand. . . .

For a moment after he had finished, he held the little black colt in his arms and looked at it. And then he walked slowly over and laid it in the straw at Jody's feet.

Billy's body shivered and his teeth chattered. His voice was gone; he spoke in a throaty whisper. "There's your colt. I promised. And there it is. I had to do it—had to." He stopped and looked over his shoulder into the box stall. "Go get hot water and a sponge," he whispered. "Wash him and dry him the way his mother would. You'll have to feed him by hand. But there's your colt, the way I promised."

Jody stared stupidly at the wet panting foal. It stretched out its chin and tried to raise its head. Its blank eyes were navy blue.

"God damn you," Billy shouted, "will you go now for the water? *Will you go?*"

Then Jody turned and trotted out of the barn into the dawn. He ached from his throat to his stomach. His legs were stiff and heavy. He tried to be glad because of the colt, but the haunted, tired eyes of Billy Buck hung in the air ahead of him.

Venus, Cupid, Folly and Time

Their house alone would not have made you think there was anything so awfully wrong with Mr. Dorset or his old maid sister. But
certain things about the way both of them dressed had, for a long
time, annoyed and disturbed everyone. We used to see them together
at the grocery store, for instance, or even in one of the big department stores downtown, wearing their bedroom slippers. Looking
more closely we would sometimes see the cuff of a pyjama top or the
hem of a hitched up nightgown showing from underneath their
ordinary daytime clothes. Such slovenliness in one's neighbors is so
unpleasant that even husbands and wives in West Vesey Place,
which was the street where the Dorsets lived, had got so they didn't
like to joke about it with each other. Were the Dorsets, poor old
things, losing their minds? If so, what was to be done about it? Some
neighbors got so they would not even admit to themselves what they
saw. And a child coming home with an ugly report on the Dorsets
was apt to be told that it was time he learned to curb his imagination.

Mr. Dorset wore tweed caps and sleeveless sweaters. Usually he
had his sweater stuffed down inside his trousers with his shirt tails.
To the women and young girls in West Vesey Place this was extremely distasteful. It made them feel as though Mr. Dorset had just
come from the bathroom and had got his sweater inside his trousers
by mistake. There was, in fact, nothing about Mr. Dorset that was
not offensive to the women. Even the old touring car he drove was
regarded by most of them as a disgrace to the neighborhood. Parked
out in front of his house, as it usually was, it seemed a worse violation of West Vesey's zoning than the house itself. And worst of all
was seeing Mr. Dorset wash the car.

Mr. Dorset washed his own car! He washed it not back in the
alley or in his driveway but out there in the street of West Vesey
Place. This would usually be on the day of one of the parties which

he and his sister liked to give for young people or on a day when they were going to make deliveries of the paper flowers or the home grown figs which they sold to their friends. Mr. Dorset would appear in the street carrying two buckets of warm water and wearing a pair of skin-tight coveralls. The skin-tight coveralls, of khaki material but faded almost to flesh color, were still more offensive to the women and young girls than his way of wearing his sweaters. With sponges and chamois cloths and a large scrub brush (for use on the canvas top) the old fellow would fall to and scrub away, gently at first on the canvas top and more vigorously as he progressed to the hood and body, just as though the car were something alive. Neighbor children felt that he went after the headlights exactly as if he were scrubbing the poor car's ears. There was an element of brutality in the way he did it and yet an element of tenderness too. An old lady visiting in the neighborhood once said that it was like the cleansing of a sacrificial animal. I suppose it was some such feeling as this that made all women want to turn away their eyes whenever the spectacle of Mr. Dorset washing his car presented itself.

As for Mr. Dorset's sister, her behavior was in its way just as offensive as his. To the men and boys in the neighborhood it was she who seemed quite beyond the pale. She would come out on her front terrace at mid-day clad in a faded flannel bathrobe and with her dyed black hair all undone and hanging down her back like the hair of an Indian squaw. To us whose wives and mothers did not even come downstairs in their negligees, this was very unsettling. It was hard to excuse it even on the grounds that the Dorsets were too old and lonely and hard-pressed to care about appearances any more.

Moreover, there was a boy who had gone to Miss Dorset's house one morning in the early fall to collect for his paper route and saw this very Miss Louisa Dorset pushing a carpet sweeper about one of the downstairs rooms without a stitch of clothes on. He saw her through one of the little lancet windows that opened on the front loggia of the house, and he watched her for quite a long while. She was cleaning the house in preparation for a party they were giving for young people that night, and the boy said that when she finally got hot and tired she dropped down in an easy chair and crossed her spindly, blue veined, old legs and sat there completely naked, with her legs crossed and shaking one scrawny little foot, just as unconcerned as if she didn't care that somebody was likely to walk in on her at any moment. After a little bit the boy saw her get up again and go and lean across a table to arrange some paper flowers in a vase. Fortunately he was a nice boy, though he lived only on the edge of the West Vesey Place neighborhood, and he went away without ringing the doorbell or collecting for his paper that week. But he could not resist telling his friends about what he had seen. He said it was a sight he would never forget! And she an old lady more than sixty years old who, had she not been so foolish and self-willed, might have had a house full of servants to push the carpet sweeper for her!

This foolish pair of old people had given up almost everything in life for each other's sake. And it was not at all necessary. When they were young they could have come into a decent inheritance, or now that they were old they might have been provided for by a host of rich relatives. It was only a matter of their being a little tolerant —or even civil—toward their kinspeople. But this was something that old Mr. Dorset and his sister could never consent to do. Almost all their lives they had spoken of their father's kin as "Mama's in-laws" and of their mother's kin as "Papa's in-laws." Their family name was Dorset, not on one side but on both sides. Their parents had been distant cousins. As a matter of fact, the Dorset family in the city of Mero had once been so large and was so long established there that it would have been hard to estimate how distant the kin-ship might be. But still it was something that the old couple never like to have mentioned. Most of their mother's close kin had, by the time I am speaking of, moved off to California, and most of their father's people lived somewhere up east. But Miss Dorset and her old bachelor brother found any contact, correspondence, even an exchange of Christmas cards with these in-laws intolerable. It was a case, so they said, of the in-laws respecting the value of the dollar above all else, whereas they, Miss Louisa and Mr. Alfred Dorset, placed importance on other things.

They lived in a dilapidated and curiously mutilated house on a street which, except for their own house, was the most splendid street in the entire city. Their house was one that you or I would have been ashamed to live in—even in the lean years of the early thirties. In order to reduce taxes the Dorsets had had the third story of the house torn away, leaving an ugly, flat-topped effect without any trim or ornamentation. Also they had had the south wing pulled down and had sealed the scars not with matching brick but with a speckled stucco that looked raw and naked. All this the old couple did in violation of the strict zoning laws of West Vesey Place, and for doing so they would most certainly have been prose-cuted except that they were the Dorsets and except that this was during the depression when zoning laws weren't easy to enforce in a city like Mero.

To the young people whom she and her brother entertained at their house once each year Miss Louisa Dorset liked to say: "We have given up everything for each other. Our only income is from our paper flowers and our figs." The old lady, though without showing any great skill or talent for it, made paper flowers. During the winter months her brother took her in that fifteen-year-old touring car of theirs, with its steering wheel on the wrong side and with isinglass side-curtains that were never taken down, to deliver these flowers to her customers. The flowers looked more like sprays of tinted potato-chips than like any real flowers. Nobody could possibly have wanted to buy them except that she charged next to nothing for them and except that to people with children it seemed important to be on the Dorsets' list of worthwhile people. Nobody could really have wanted Mr. Dorset's figs either. He cultivated a dozen little bushes along the back wall of their house, covering them in the wintertime with some odd looking boxes which he had had constructed for the purpose. The bushes were very productive, but the figs they produced were dried up little things without much taste. During the summer months he and his sister went about in their car, with the side-curtains still up, delivering the figs to the same customers who bought the paper flowers. The money they made could hardly have paid for the gas it took to run the car. It was a great waste and it was very foolish of them.

And yet, despite everything, this foolish pair of old people, this same Miss Louisa and Mr. Alfred Dorset, had become social arbiters of a kind in our city. They had attained this position entirely through their fondness for giving an annual dancing party for young people. To *young* people—to *very* young people—the Dorsets' hearts went out. I don't mean to suggest that their hearts went out to orphans or to the children of the poor, for they were not foolish in that way. The guests at their little dancing parties were the thirteen and fourteen year-olds from families like the one they had long ago set themselves against, young people from the very houses to which, in season, they delivered their figs and their paper flowers. And when the night of one of their parties came round, it was in fact the custom for Mr. Alfred to go in the same old car and fetch all the invited guests to his house. His sister might explain to reluctant parents that this saved the children the embarrassment of being taken to their first dance by mommy and daddy. But the parents knew well enough that for twenty years the Dorsets had permitted no adult person, besides themselves, to put foot inside their house.

At those little dancing parties which the Dorsets gave, peculiar things went on—unsettling things to the boys and girls who had been fetched round in the old car. Sensible parents wished to keep their children away. Yet what could they do? For a Mero girl to have to explain, a few years later, why she never went to a party at the Dorsets' was like having to explain why she had never been a debutante. For a boy it was like having to explain why he had not gone up East to school or even why his father hadn't belonged to the Mero Racquet Club. If when you were thirteen or fourteen you got invited to the Dorsets' house, you went; it was the way of letting people know from the outset who you were. In a busy, modern city like Mero you cannot afford to let people forget who you are—not for a moment, not at any age. Even the Dorsets knew that.

Many a little girl, after one of those evenings at the Dorsets', was heard to cry out in her sleep. When waked, or half waked, her only explanation might be: "It was just the fragrance from the paper flowers." Or: "I dreamed I could really smell the paper flowers." Many a boy was observed by his parents to seem "different" afterward. He became "secretive." The parents of the generation that had to attend those parties never pretended to understand what went on at the Dorsets' house. And even to those of us who were in that unlucky generation it seemed we were half a lifetime learning what really took place during our one evening under the Dorsets' roof. Before our turn to go ever came round we had for years been hearing about what it was like from older boys and girls. Afterward, we continued to hear about it from those who followed us. And, looking back on it, nothing about the one evening when you were actually there ever seemed quite so real as the glimpses and snatches which you got from those people before and after you—the second-hand impressions of the Dorsets' behavior, of things they said, of looks that passed between them.

Since Miss Dorset kept no servants she always opened her own door. I suspect that for the guests at her parties the sight of her opening her door, in her astonishing attire, came as the most violent shock of the whole evening. On these occasions she and her brother got themselves up as we had never seen them before and never would again. The old lady invariably wore a modish white evening gown, a garment perfectly fitted to her spare and scrawny figure and cut in such high fashion that it must necessarily have been new that year. And never to be worn but that one night! Her hair, long and thick and newly dyed for the occasion, would be swept upward and forward in a billowy mass which was topped by a corsage of yellow and coral paper flowers. Her cheeks and lips would be darkly rouged. On her long bony arms and her bare shoulders she would have applied some kind of sun-tan powder. Whatever else you had been led to expect of the evening, no one had warned you sufficiently about the radical change to be noted in her appearance—or in that of her brother, either. By the end of the party Miss Louisa might look as dowdy as ever, and Mr. Alfred a little worse than usual. But at the outset, when the party was assembling in their drawing room, even Mr. Alfred appeared resplendent in a nattily tailored tuxedo, with exactly the shirt, the collar, and the tie which fashion prescribed that year. His grey hair was nicely trimmed, his puffy old face freshly shaven. He was powdered with the same dark powder that his sister used. One felt even that his cheeks had been lightly touched with rouge.

A strange perfume pervaded the atmosphere of the house. The moment you set foot inside, this awful fragrance engulfed you. It was like a mixture of spicy incense and sweet attar of roses. And always, too, there was the profusion of paper flowers. The flowers were everywhere—on every cabinet and console, every inlaid table and carved chest, on every high, marble mantel piece, on the book shelves. In the entrance hall special tiers must have been set up to hold the flowers, because they were there in overpowering masses. They were in such abundance that it seemed hardly possible that Miss Dorset could have made them all. She must have spent weeks and weeks preparing them, even months, perhaps even the whole year between parties. When she went about delivering them to her customers, in the months following, they were apt to be somewhat faded and dusty; but on the night of the party the colors of the flowers seemed even more impressive and more unlikely than their number. They were fuchsia, they were chartreuse, they were coral, aquamarine, brown, they were even black.

Everywhere in the Dorsets' house too were certain curious illuminations and lighting effects. The source of the light was usually hidden and its purpose was never obvious at once. The lighting was a subtler element than either the perfume or the paper flowers, and ultimately it was more disconcerting. A shaft of lavender light would catch a young visitor's eye and lead it, seemingly without purpose, in among the flowers. Then just beyond the point where the strength of the light would begin to diminish, the eye would discover something. In a small aperture in the mass of flowers, or sometimes in a larger grotto-like opening, there would be a piece of sculpture—in the hall a plaster replica of Rodin's *The Kiss,* in the library an antique plaque of Leda and the Swan. Or just above the flowers would be hung a picture, usually a black and white print but sometimes a reproduction in color. On the landing of the stairway leading down to the basement ballroom was the only picture that one was likely to learn the title of at the time. It was a tiny color print of Bronzino's *Venus, Cupid, Folly and Time.* This picture was not even framed. It was simply tacked on the wall, and it had obviously been torn—rather carelessly, perhaps hurriedly—from a book or magazine. The title and the name of the painter were printed in the white margin underneath.

About these works of art most of us had been warned by older boys and girls; and we stood in painful dread of that moment when Miss Dorset or her brother might catch us staring at any one of their pictures or sculptures. We had been warned, time and again, that during the course of the evening moments would come when she or he would reach out and touch the other's elbow and indicate, with a nod or just the trace of a smile, some guest whose glance had strayed among the flowers.

To some extent the dread which all of us felt of that evening at the Dorsets' cast a shadow over the whole of our childhood. Yet for nearly twenty years the Dorsets continued to give their annual party. And even the most sensible of parents were not willing to keep their children away.

But a thing happened finally which could almost have been predicted. Young people, even in West Vesey Place, will not submit forever to the prudent counsel of their parents. Or some of them won't. There was a boy named Ned Meriwether and his sister Emily Meriwether, who lived with their parents in West Vesey Place just one block away from the Dorsets' house. In November Ned and Emily were invited to the Dorsets' party, and because they dreaded it they decided to play a trick on everyone concerned—even on themselves, as it turned out. . . . They got up a plan for smuggling an uninvited guest into the Dorsets' party.

The parents of this Emily and Ned sensed that their children were concealing something from them and suspected that the two were up to mischief of some kind. But they managed to deceive themselves with the thought that it was only natural for young people—"mere children"—to be nervous about going to the Dorsets' house. And so instead of questioning them during the last hour before they left for the party, these sensible parents tried to do everything in their power to calm their two children. The boy and the girl, seeing that this was the case, took advantage of it.

"You must not go down to the front door with us when we leave," the daughter insisted to her mother. And she persuaded both Mr. and Mrs. Meriwether that after she and her brother were dressed for the party they should all wait together in the upstairs sitting room until Mr. Dorset came to fetch the two young people in his car.

When, at eight o'clock, the lights of the automobile appeared in the street below, the brother and sister were still upstairs—watching from the bay window of the family sitting room. They kissed Mother and Daddy goodbye and then they flew down the stairs and across the wide, carpeted entrance hall to a certain dark recess where a boy named Tom Bascomb was hidden. This boy was the uninvited guest whom Ned and Emily were going to smuggle into the party. They had left the front door unlatched for Tom, and from the upstairs window just a few minutes ago they had watched him come across their front lawn. Now in the little recess of the hall there was a quick exchange of overcoats and hats between Ned Meriwether and Tom Bascomb; for it was a feature of the plan that Tom should attend the party as Ned and that Ned should go as the uninvited guest.

In the darkness of the recess Ned fidgeted and dropped Tom Bascomb's coat on the floor. But the boy, Tom Bascomb, did not fidget. He stepped out into the light of the hall and began methodically getting into the overcoat which he would wear tonight. He was not a boy who lived in the West Vesey Place neighborhood (he was in fact the very boy who had once watched Miss Dorset cleaning house without any clothes on), and he did not share Emily's and Ned's nervous excitement about the evening. The sound of Mr. Dorset's footsteps outside did not disturb him. When both Ned and Emily stood frozen by that sound, he continued buttoning the unfamiliar coat and even amused himself by stretching forth one arm to observe how high the sleeve came on his wrist.

The doorbell rang, and from his dark corner Ned Meriwether whispered to his sister and to Tom: "Don't worry. I'll be at the Dorsets' in plenty of time."

Tom Bascomb only shrugged his shoulders at this reassurance. Presently when he looked at Emily's flushed face and saw her batting her eyes like a nervous monkey, a crooked smile played upon his lips. Then, at a sign from Emily, Tom followed her to the entrance door and permitted her to introduce him to old Mr. Dorset as her brother.

From the window of the upstairs sitting room the Meriwether parents watched Mr. Dorset and this boy and this girl walking across the lawn toward Mr. Dorset's peculiar looking car. A light shone bravely and protectively from above the entrance of the house, and in its rays the parents were able to detect the strange angle at which Brother was carrying his head tonight and how his new fedora already seemed too small for him. They even noticed that he seemed a bit taller tonight.

"I hope it's all right," said the mother.

"What do you mean 'all right'?" the father asked petulantly.

"I mean—," the mother began, and then she hesitated. She did not want to mention that the boy out there did not look like their own Ned. It would have seemed to give away her feelings too much. "I mean that I wonder if I should have put Sister in that long dress at this age and let her wear my cape. I'm afraid the cape is really inappropriate. She's still young for that sort of thing."

"Oh," said the father, "I thought you meant something else."

"Whatever else did you think I meant, Edwin?" the mother said, suddenly breathless.

"I thought you meant the business we've discussed before," he said although this was of course not what he had thought she meant. He had thought she meant that the boy out there did not look like their Ned. To him it had seemed even that the boy's step was different from Ned's. "The Dorsets' parties," he said, "are not very nice affairs to be sending your children off to, Muriel. That's all I thought you meant."

"But we *can't* keep them away," the mother said defensively.

"Oh, it's just that they are growing up faster than we realize," said the father, glancing at his wife out of the corner of his eye.

By this time Mr. Dorset's car had pulled out of sight, and from downstairs Muriel Meriwether thought she heard another door closing. "What was that?" she said, putting one hand on her husband's.

"Don't be so jumpy," her husband said irritably, snatching away his hand. "It's the servants closing up in the kitchen."

Both of them knew that the servants had closed up in the kitchen long before this. Both of them had heard quite distinctly the sound of the side door closing as Ned went out. But they went on talking and deceiving themselves in this fashion during most of that evening.

Even before she opened the door to Mr. Dorset, little Emily Meriwether had known that there would be no difficulty about passing Tom Bascomb off as her brother. In the first place, she knew that

without his spectacles Mr. Dorset could hardly see his hand before
his face and knew that due to some silly pride he had never put on
his spectacles except when he was behind the wheel of his automobile. This much was common knowledge. In the second place,
Emily knew from experience that neither he nor his sister ever made
any real pretense of knowing one child in their general acquaintance
from another. And so, standing in the doorway and speaking almost
in a whisper, Emily had merely to introduce first herself and then
her pretended brother to Mr. Dorset. After that the three of them
walked in silence from her father's house to the waiting car.

Emily was wearing her mother's second best evening wrap, a white
lapin cape which, on Emily, swept the ground. As she walked between the boy and the man, the touch of the cape's soft silk lining
on her bare arms and on her shoulders spoke to her silently of
a strange girl she had seen in her looking glass upstairs tonight. And
with her every step toward the car the skirt of her long taffeta gown
whispered her own name to her: *Emily . . . Emily*. She heard it
distinctly, and yet the name sounded unfamilar. Once during this
unreal walk from house to car she glanced at the mysterious boy,
Tom Bascomb, longing to ask him—if only with her eyes—for some
reassurance that she was really she. But Tom Bascomb was absorbed
in his own irrelevant observations. With his head tilted back he was
gazing upward at the nondescript winter sky where, among drifting
clouds, a few pale stars were shedding their dull light alike on West
Vesey Place and on the rest of the world. Emily drew her wrap
tightly about her, and when presently Mr. Dorset held open the
door to the back seat of his car she shut her eyes and plunged into
the pitch-blackness of the car's interior.

Tom Bascomb was a year older than Ned Meriwether and he was
nearly two years older than Emily. He had been Ned's friend first.
He and Ned had played baseball together on Saturdays before
Emily ever set eyes on him. Yet according to Tom Bascomb himself, with whom several of us older boys talked just a few weeks
after the night he went to the Dorsets, Emily always insisted that
it was she who had known him first. On what she based this false
claim Tom could not say. And on the two or three other occasions
when we got Tom to talk about that night, he kept saying that he
didn't understand what it was that had made Emily and Ned quarrel
over which of them knew him first and knew him better.

We could have told him what it was, I think. But we didn't. It
would have been too hard to say to him that at one time or another
all of us in West Vesey had had our Tom Bascombs. Tom lived with

his parents in an apartment house on a wide thoroughfare known as
Division Boulevard, and his only real connection with West Vesey
Place was that that street was included in his paper route. During
the early morning hours he rode his bicycle along West Vesey and
along other quiet streets like it, carefully aiming a neatly rolled paper
at the dark loggia, at the colonnaded porch, or at the ornamented
doorway of each of the palazzos and chateaux and manor houses that
glowered at him in the dawn. He was well thought of as a paper boy.
If by mistake one of his papers went astray and lit on an upstairs
balcony or on the roof of a porch, Tom would always take more careful aim and throw another. Even if the paper only went into the
shrubbery, Tom got off his bicycle and fished it out. He wasn't the
kind of boy to whom it would have occurred that the old fogies and
the rich kids in West Vesey could very well get out and scramble for
their own papers.

Actually a party at the Dorsets' house was more a grand tour of
the house than a real party. There was a half hour spent over very
light refreshments (fruit Jell-o, English tea biscuits, lime punch).
There was another half hour ostensibly given to general dancing in
the basement ballroom (to the accompaniment of victrola music).
But mainly there was the tour. As the party passed through the house,
stopping sometimes to sit down in the principal rooms, the host and
hostess provided entertainment in the form of an almost continuous
dialogue between themselves. This dialogue was famous and was
full of interest, being all about how much the Dorsets had given up
for each other's sake and about how much higher the tone of Mero
society used to be than it was nowadays. They would invariably speak
of their parents, who had died within a year of each other when Miss
Louisa and Mr. Alfred were still in their teens; they even spoke of
their wicked in-laws. When their parents died, the wicked in-laws
had first tried to make them sell the house, then had tried to separate
them and send them away to boarding schools, and had ended by
trying to marry them off to "just anyone." Their two grandfathers
had still been alive in those days and each had had a hand in the
machinations, after the failure of which each grandfather had disin-
herited them. Mr. Alfred and Miss Louisa spoke also of how, a few
years later, a procession of "young nobodies" had come of their own
accord trying to steal the two of them away from each other. Both
he and she would scowl at the very recollection of those "just any-
bodies" and those "nobodies," those "would-be suitors" who always

turned out to be misguided fortune-hunters and had to be driven away.

The Dorsets' dialogue usually began in the living room the moment Mr. Dorset returned with his last collection of guests. (He sometimes had to make five or six trips in the car.) There, as in other rooms afterward, they were likely to begin with a reference to the room itself or perhaps to some piece of furniture in the room. For instance, the extraordinary length of the drawing room—or reception room, as the Dorsets called it—would lead them to speak of an even longer room which they had had torn away from the house. "It grieved us, we wept," Miss Dorset would say, "to have Mama's French drawing room torn away from us."

"But we tore it away from ourselves," her brother would add, "as we tore away our in-laws—because we could not afford them." Both of them spoke in a fine declamatory style, but they frequently interrupted themselves with a sad little laugh which expressed something quite different from what they were saying and which seemed to serve them as an aside not meant for our ears.

"That was one of our greatest sacrifices," Miss Dorset would say, referring still to her mother's French drawing room.

And her brother would say: "But we knew the day had passed in Mero for entertainments worthy of that room."

"It was the room which Mama and Papa loved best, but we gave it up because we knew, from our upbringing, which things to give up."

From this they might go on to anecdotes about their childhood. Sometimes their parents had left them for months or even a whole year at a time with only the housekeeper or with trusted servants to see after them. "You could trust servants then," they explained. And: "In those days parents could do that sort of thing, because in those days there was a responsible body of people within which your young people could always find proper companionship."

In the library, to which the party always moved from the drawing room, Mr. Dorset was fond of exhibiting snapshots of the house taken before the south wing was pulled down. As the pictures were passed around, the dialogue continued. It was often there that they told the story of how the in-laws had tried to force them to sell the house. "For the sake of economy!" Mr. Dorset would exclaim, adding an ironic, "Ha ha!"

His sister would repeat the exclamation, "For the sake of economy!" and also the ironic "Ha ha!"

"As though money——" he would begin.

"As though money ever took the place," his sister would come in, "of living with your own kind."

"Or of being well born," said Mr. Dorset.

After the billiard room, where everyone who wanted it was permitted one turn with the only cue that there seemed to be in the house, and after the dining room, where it was promised refreshments would be served later, the guests would be taken down to the ballroom—purportedly for dancing. Instead of everyone's being urged to dance, however, once they were assembled in the ballroom, Miss Dorset would announce that she and her brother understood the timidity which young people felt about dancing and that all that she and he intended to do was to set the party a good example. . . . It was only Miss Louisa and Mr. Alfred who danced. For perhaps thirty minutes, in a room without light excepting that from a few weak bulbs concealed among the flowers, the old couple danced; and they danced with such grace and there was such perfect harmony in all their movements that the guests stood about in stunned silence, as if hypnotized. The Dorsets waltzed, they two-stepped, they even fox-trotted, stopping only long enough between dances for Mr. Dorset, amid general applause, to change the victrola record.

But it was when their dance was ended that all the effects of the Dorsets' careful grooming that night would have vanished. And, alas, they made no effort to restore themselves. During the remainder of the evening Mr. Dorset went about with his bow tie hanging limply on his damp shirtfront, a gold collar button shining above it. A strand of grey hair, which normally covered his bald spot on top, now would have fallen on the wrong side of his part and hung like fringe about his ear. On his face and neck the thick layer of powder was streaked with perspiration. Miss Dorset was usually in an even more dishevelled state, depending somewhat upon the fashion of her dress that year. But always her powder was streaked, her lipstick entirely gone, her hair falling down on all sides, and her corsage dangling somewhere about the nape of her neck. In this condition they led the party upstairs again, not stopping until they had reached the second floor of the house.

On the second floor we—the guests—were shown the rooms which the Dorsets' parents had once occupied (the Dorsets' own rooms were never shown). We saw, in glass museum cases along the hallway, the dresses and suits and hats and even the shoes which Miss Louisa and Mr. Alfred had worn to parties when they were very young. And now the dialogue, which had been left off while the Dorsets danced, was resumed. "Ah, the happy time," one of them would say, "was when we were *your* age!" And then, exhorting us to be happy and gay while we were still safe in the bosom of our own kind and before the world came crowding in on us with its ugly demands, the Dorsets would recall the happiness they had known when they were very young. This was their *pièce de résistance*. With many a wink and blush and giggle and shake of the forefinger— and of course standing before the whole party—they each would remind the other of his or her naughty behavior in some old-fashioned parlor game or of certain silly little flirtations which they had long ago caught each other in.

They were on their way downstairs again now, and by the time they had finished with this favorite subject they would be downstairs. They would be in the dark, flower bedecked downstairs hall and just before entering the dining room for the promised refreshments: the fruit Jell-o, the English tea biscuits, the lime punch.

And now for a moment Mr. Dorset bars the way to the dining room and prevents his sister from opening the closed door. "Now, my good friends," he says, "let us eat, drink and be merry!"

"For the night is yet young," says his sister.

"Tonight you must be gay and carefree," Mr. Dorset enjoins.

"Because in this house we are all friends," Miss Dorset says. "We are all young, we all love one another."

"And love can make us all young forever," her brother says.

"Remember!"

"Remember this evening always, sweet young people!"

"Remember!"

"Remember what our life is like here!"

And now Miss Dorset, with one hand on the knob of the great door which she is about to throw open, leans a little toward the guests and whispers hoarsely: "This is what it is like to be young forever!"

Ned Meriwether was waiting behind a big japonica shrub near the sidewalk when, about twenty minutes after he had last seen Emily, the queer old touring car drew up in front of the Dorsets' house. During the interval, the car had gone from the Meriwether house to gather a number of other guests, and so it was not only Emily and Tom who alighted on the sidewalk before the Dorsets' house. The group was just large enough to make it easy for Ned to slip out from his dark hiding place and join them without being noticed by Mr. Dorset. And now the group was escorted rather unceremoniously up to the door of the house, and Mr. Dorset departed to fetch more guests.

They were received at the door by Miss Dorset. Her eyesight was no doubt better than her brother's, but still there was really no danger of her detecting an uninvited guest. Those of us who had gone to that house in the years just before Ned and Emily came along, could remember that during a whole evening, when their house was full of young people, the Dorsets made no introductions and made no effort to distinguish which of their guests was which. They did not even make a count of heads. Perhaps they did vaguely recognize some of the faces, because sometimes when they had come delivering figs or paper flowers to a house they had of necessity encountered a young child there, and always they smiled sweetly at it, asked its age, and calculated on their old fingers how many years must pass before the child would be eligible for an invitation. Yet at those moments something in the way they had held up their fingers and in the way they had gazed *at* the little face instead of into it had revealed their lack of interest in the individual child. And later when the child was finally old enough to receive their invitation he found it was still no different with the Dorsets. Even in their own house it was evidently to the young people as a group that the Dorsets' hearts went out; while they had the boys and girls under their roof they herded them about like so many little thoroughbred calves. Even when Miss Dorset opened the front door she did so exactly as though she were opening a gate. She pulled it open very slowly, standing half behind it to keep out of harm's way. And the children, all huddled together, surged in.

How meticulously this Ned and Emily Meriwether must have laid their plans for that evening! And the whole business might have come out all right if only they could have foreseen the effect which one part of their plan—rather a last minute embellishment of it—would produce upon Ned himself. Barely ten minutes after they entered the house Ned was watching Tom as he took his seat on the piano bench beside Emily. Ned probably watched Tom closely, because certainly he knew what the next move was going to be. The moment Miss Louisa Dorset's back was turned Tom Bascomb slipped his arm gently about Emily's little waist and commenced kissing her all over her pretty face. It was almost as if he were kissing away tears.

This spectacle on the piano bench, and others like it which followed, had been an inspiration of the last day or so before the party. Or so Ned and Emily maintained afterward when defending themselves to their parents. But no matter when it was conceived, a part of their plan it was, and Ned must have believed himself fully prepared for it. Probably he expected to join in the round of giggling which it produced from the other guests. But now that the time had come—it is easy to imagine—the boy Ned Meriwether found himself not quite able to join in the fun. He watched with the others, but he was not quite infected by their laughter. He stood a little apart, and possibly he was hoping that Emily and Tom would not notice his failure to appreciate the success of their comedy. He was no doubt baffled by his own feelings, by the failure of his own enthusiasm, and by a growing desire to withdraw himself from the plot and from the party itself.

It is easy to imagine Ned's uneasiness and confusion that night. And I believe the account which I have given of Emily's impressions and her delicate little sensations while on the way to the party has the ring of truth about it, though actually the account was supplied by girls who knew her only slightly, who were not at the party, who could not possibly have seen her afterward. It may, after all, represent only what other girls imagined she would have felt. As for the account of how Mr. and Mrs. Meriwether spent the evening, it is their very own. And they did not hesitate to give it to anyone who would listen.

It was a long time, though, before many of us had a clear picture of the main events of the evening. We heard very soon that the parties for young people were to be no more, that there had been a wild scramble and chase through the Dorsets' house, and that it had ended by the Dorsets locking some boy—whether Ned or Tom was not easy to determine at first—in a queer sort of bathroom in which the plumbing had been disconnected, and even the fixtures removed, I believe. (Later I learned that there was nothing literally sinister about the bathroom itself. By having the pipes disconnected to this, and perhaps other bathrooms, the Dorsets had obtained further reductions in their taxes.) But a clear picture of the whole evening wasn't to be had—not without considerable searching. For one thing, the Meriwether parents immediately, within a week after the party, packed their son and daughter off to boarding schools. Accounts from the other children were contradictory and vague—perversely so, it seemed. Parents reported to each other that the little girls had nightmares which were worse even than those which their older sisters had had. And the boys were secretive and elusive, even with us older boys when we questioned them about what had gone on.

One sketchy account of events leading up to the chase, however, did go the rounds almost at once. Ned must have written it back to some older boy in a letter, because it contained information which no one but Ned could have had. The account went like this: When Mr. Dorset returned from his last round-up of guests, he came hurrying into the drawing room where the others were waiting and said in a voice trembling with excitement: "Now, let us all be seated, my young friends, and let us warm ourselves with some good talk."

At that moment everyone who was not already seated made a dash for a place on one of the divans or love seats or even in one of the broad window seats. (There were no individual chairs in the room.) Everyone made a dash, that is, except Ned. Ned did not move. He remained standing beside a little table rubbing his fingers over its polished surface. And from this moment he was clearly an object of suspicion in the eyes of his host and hostess. Soon the party moved from the drawing room to the library, but in whatever room they stopped Ned managed to isolate himself from the rest. He would sit or stand looking down at his hands until once again an explosion of giggles filled the room. Then he would look up just in time to see Tom Bascomb's cheek against Emily's or his arm about her waist.

For nearly two hours Ned didn't speak a word to anyone. He endured the Dorsets' dialogue, the paper flowers, the perfumed air, the works of art. Whenever a burst of giggling forced him to raise his eyes he would look up at Tom and Emily and then turn his eyes away. Before looking down at his hands again he would let his eyes travel slowly about the room until they came to rest on the figures of the two Dorsets. That, it seems, was how he happened to discover that the Dorsets understood, or thought they understood, what the giggles meant. In the great mirror mounted over the library mantel he saw them exchanging half suppressed smiles. Their smiles lasted precisely as long as the giggling continued, and then, in the mirror, Ned saw their faces change and grow solemn when their eyes—their identical, tiny, dull, amber colored eyes—focussed upon himself.

From the library the party continued on the regular tour of the house. At last when they had been to the ballroom and watched the Dorsets dance, had been upstairs to gaze upon the faded party clothes in the museum cases, they descended into the downstairs hall and were just before being turned into the dining room. The guests had already heard the Dorsets teasing each other about the silly little flirtations and about their naughtiness in parlor games when they were young and had listened to their exhortations to be gay and happy and carefree. Then just when Miss Dorset leaned toward them and whispered, "This is what it is like to be young forever," there rose a chorus of laughter, breathless and shrill, yet loud and intensely penetrating.

Ned Meriwether, standing on the bottom step of the stairway, lifted his eyes and looked over the heads of the party to see Tom and Emily half hidden in a bower of paper flowers and caught directly in a ray of mauve light. The two had squeezed themselves into a little niche there and stood squarely in front of the Rodin statuary. Tom had one arm placed about Emily's shoulders and he was kissing her lightly first on the lobe of one ear and then on the tip of her nose. Emily stood as rigid and pale as the plaster sculpture behind her and with just the faintest smile on her lips. Ned looked at the two of them and then turned his glance at once on the Dorsets.

He found Miss Louisa and Mr. Alfred gazing quite openly at Tom and Emily and frankly grinning at the spectacle. It was more than Ned could endure. "Don't you *know*?" he fairly wailed, as if in great physical pain. "Can't you *tell*? Can't you see who they *are*? They're *brother* and *sister!*"

From the other guests came one concerted gasp. And then an instant later, mistaking Ned's outcry to be something he had planned all along and probably intended—as they imagined—for the very cream of the jest, the whole company burst once again into laughter —not a chorus of laughter this time but a volley of loud guffaws from the boys, and from the girls a cacophony of separately articulated shrieks and trills.

None of the guests present that night could—or would—give a satisfactory account of what happened next. Everyone insisted that he had not even looked at the Dorsets, that he, or she, didn't know how Miss Louisa and Mr. Alfred reacted at first. Yet this was precisely what those of us who had gone there in the past *had* to know. And when finally we did manage to get an account of it, we knew that it was a very truthful and accurate one. Because we got it, of course, from Tom Bascomb.

Since Ned's outburst came after the dancing exhibition, the Dorsets were in their most dishevelled state. Miss Louisa's hair was fallen half over her face, and that long, limp strand of Mr. Alfred's was dangling about his left ear. Like that, they stood at the doorway to the dining room grinning at Tom Bascomb's antics. And when Tom Bascomb, hearing Ned's wail, whirled about, the grins were still on the Dorsets' faces even though the guffaws and the shrieks of laughter were now silenced. Tom said that for several moments they continued to wear their grins like masks and that you couldn't really tell how they were taking it all until presently Miss Louisa's face, still wearing the grin, began turning all the queer colors of her paper flowers. Then the grin vanished from her lips and her mouth fell open and every bit of color went out of her face. She took a step backward and leaned against the doorjamb with her mouth still open and her eyes closed. If she hadn't been on her feet, Tom said he would have thought she was dead. Her brother didn't look at her, but his own grin had vanished just as hers did, and his face, all drawn and wrinkled, momentarily turned a dull copperish green.

Presently, though, he too went white, not white in faintness but in anger. His little brown eyes now shone like rosin. And he took several steps toward Ned Meriwether. "What we know is that you are not one of us," he croaked. "We have perceived that from the beginning! We don't know how you got here or who you are. But the important question is, What are you doing here among these nice children?"

The question seemed to restore life to Miss Louisa. Her amber eyes popped wide open. She stepped away from the door and began pinning up her hair which had fallen down on her shoulders, and at the same time addressing the guests who were huddled together in the center of the hall. "Who is he, children? He is an intruder, that we know. If you know who he is, you must tell us."

"Who *am* I? Why, I am Tom Bascomb!" shouted Ned, still from the bottom step of the stairway. "I am Tom Bascomb, your paper boy!"

Then he turned and fled up the stairs toward the second floor. In a moment Mr. Dorset was after him.

To the real Tom Bascomb it had seemed that Ned honestly believed what he had been saying; and his own first impulse was to shout a denial. But being a levelheaded boy and seeing how bad things were, Tom went instead to Miss Dorset and whispered to her that Tom Bascomb was a pretty tough guy and that she had better let *him* call the police for her. She told him where the telephone was in the side hall, and he started away.

But Miss Dorset changed her mind. She ran after Tom telling him not to call. Some of the guests mistook this for the beginning of another chase. Before the old lady could overtake Tom, however, Ned himself had appeared in the doorway toward which she and Tom were moving. He had come down the back stairway and he was calling out to Emily, "We're going *home*, Sis!"

A cheer went up from the whole party. Maybe it was this that caused Ned to lose his head, or maybe it was simply the sight of Miss Dorset rushing at him that did it. At any rate, the next moment he was running up the front stairs again, this time with Miss Dorset in pursuit.

When Tom returned from the telephone, all was quiet in the hall. The guests—everybody except Emily—had moved to the foot of the stairs and they were looking up and listening. From upstairs Tom could hear Ned saying, "All right. All right. All right." The old couple had cornered him.

Emily was still standing in the little niche among the flowers. And it is the image of Emily Meriwether standing among the paper flowers that tantalizes me whenever I think or hear someone speak of that evening. That, more than anything else, can make me wish that I had been there. I shall never cease to wonder what kind of thoughts were in her head to make her seem so oblivious to all that was going on while she stood there, and, for that matter, what had been in her mind all evening while she endured Tom Bascomb's caresses. When, in years since, I have had reason to wonder what some girl or woman is thinking—some Emily grown older—my mind nearly always returns to the image of that girl among the paper flowers. Tom said that when he returned from the telephone she looked very solemn and pale still but that her mind didn't seem to be on any of the present excitement. Immediately he went to her and said, "Your dad is on his way over, Emily." For it was the Meriwether parents he had telephoned, of course, and not the police.

It seemed to Tom that so far as he was concerned the party was now over. There was nothing more he could do. Mr. Dorset was upstairs guarding the door to the strange little room in which Ned was locked up. Miss Dorset was serving lime punch to the other guests in the dining room, all the while listening with one ear for the arrival of the police whom Tom pretended he had called. When the doorbell finally rang and Miss Dorset hurried to answer it, Tom slipped quietly out through the pantry and through the kitchen and left the house by the back door as the Meriwether parents entered by the front.

There was no difficulty in getting Edwin and Muriel Meriwether, the children's parents, to talk about what happened after they arrived that night. Both of them were sensible and clearheaded people, and they were not so conservative as some of our other neighbors in West Vesey. Being fond of gossip of any kind and fond of reasonably funny stories on themselves, they told how their children had deceived them earlier in the evening and how they had deceived themselves later. They tended to blame themselves more than the children for what had happened. They tried to protect the children from any harm or embarrassment that might result from it by sending them off to boarding school. In their talk they never referred directly to Tom's reprehensible conduct or to the possible motives that the children might have had for getting up their plan. They tried to spare their children and they tried to spare Tom, but fortunately it didn't occur to them to try to spare the poor old Dorsets.

When Miss Louisa opened the door, Mr. Meriwether said, "I'm Edwin Meriwether, Miss Dorset. I've come for my son, Ned."

"And for your daughter Emily, I hope," his wife whispered to him.

"And for my daughter Emily."

Before Miss Dorset could answer him Edwin Meriwether spied Mr. Dorset descending the stairs. With his wife, Muriel, sticking close to his side Edwin now strode over to the foot of the stairs. "Mr. Dorset," he began, "my son Ned——"

From behind them, Edwin and Muriel now heard Miss Dorset saying, "All the invited guests are gathered in the dining room." From where they were standing the two parents could see into the dining room. Suddenly they turned and hurried in there. Mr. Dorset and his sister of course followed them.

Muriel Meriwether went directly to Emily, who was standing in a group of girls. "Emily, where is your brother?"

Emily said nothing, but one of the boys answered: "I think they've got him locked up upstairs somewhere."

"Oh, no!" said Miss Louisa, a hairpin in her mouth—for she was still rather absent-mindedly working at her hair. "It is an intruder that my brother has upstairs."

Mr. Dorset began speaking in a confidential tone to Edwin. "My dear neighbor," he said, "our paper boy saw fit to intrude himself upon our company tonight. But we recognized him as an outsider from the start."

Muriel Meriwether asked: "Where *is* the paper boy? Where is the paper boy, Emily?"

Again one of the boys volunteered: "He went out through the back door, Mrs. Meriwether."

The eyes of Mr. Alfred and Miss Louisa searched the room for Tom. Finally their eyes met and they smiled coyly. "*All* the children are being mischievous tonight," said Miss Louisa, and it was quite as though she had said, "all *we* children." Then, still smiling, she said, "Your tie has come undone, Brother. Mr. and Mrs. Meriwether will hardly know what to think."

Mr. Alfred fumbled for a moment with his tie but soon gave it up. Now with a bashful glance at the Meriwether parents, and giving a nod in the direction of the children, he actually said, "I'm afraid we've all decided to play a trick on Mr. and Mrs. Meriwether."

Miss Louisa said to Emily: "We've hidden our brother somewhere, haven't we?"

Emily's mother said firmly: "Emily, tell me where Ned is."

"He's upstairs, Mother," said Emily in a whisper.

Emily's father said: "I wish you to take me to the boy upstairs, Mr. Dorset."

The coy, bashful expressions vanished from the two Dorsets' faces. Their eyes were little dark pools of incredulity, growing narrower by the second. And both of them were now trying to put their hair in order. "Why, *we* know nice children when we see them," Miss Louisa said peevishly. There was a pleading quality in her voice, too. "We knew from the beginning that that boy upstairs didn't belong amongst us," she said. "Dear neighbors, it isn't just the money, you know." All at once she sounded like a little girl about to burst into tears.

"It isn't just the money?" Edwin Meriwether repeated.

"Miss Dorset," said Muriel with new gentleness in her tone, as though she had just sensed that she was talking to a little girl, "there has been some kind of mistake—a misunderstanding."

Mr. Alfred Dorset said: "Oh, we wouldn't make a mistake of that kind! People *are* different. It isn't something you can put your finger on, but it isn't the money."

"I don't know what you're talking about," Edwin said, exasperated. "But I'm going upstairs and find that boy." He left the room with Mr. Dorset following him with quick little steps—steps like those of a small boy trying to keep up with a man.

Miss Louisa now sat down in one of the high-backed dining chairs which were lined up along the oak wainscot. She was trembling, and Muriel came and stood beside her. Neither of them spoke, and in almost no time Edwin Meriwether came downstairs again with Ned. Miss Louisa looked at Ned, and tears came into her eyes. "Where is my brother?" she asked accusingly, as though she thought possibly Ned and his father had locked Mr. Dorset in the bathroom.

"I believe he has retired," said Edwin. "He left us and disappeared into one of the rooms upstairs."

"Then I must go up to him," said Miss Louisa. For a moment she seemed unable to rise. At last she pushed herself up from the chair and walked from the room with the slow, steady gait of a somnambulist. Muriel Meriwether followed her into the hall and as she watched the old woman ascending the steps, leaning heavily on the rail, her impulse was to go and offer to assist her. But something made her turn back into the dining room. Perhaps she imagined that her daughter, Emily, might need her now.

The Dorsets did not reappear that night. After Miss Louisa went upstairs, Muriel promptly got on the telephone and called the parents of some of the other boys and girls. Within a quarter of an hour a dozen parents had arrived. It was the first time in many years that any adult had set foot inside the Dorset house. It was the first time that any parent had ever inhaled the perfumed air or seen the masses of paper flowers and the illuminations and the statuary. In the guise of holding consultations over whether or not they should put out the lights and lock up the house the parents lingered much longer than was necessary before taking the young people home. Some of them even tasted the lime punch. But in the presence of their children they made no comment on what had happened and gave no indication of what their own impressions were—not even their impressions of the punch. At last it was decided that two of the men should see to putting out the lights everywhere on the first floor and down in the ballroom. They were a long time in finding the switches for the indirect lighting. In most cases they simply resorted to unscrewing the bulbs. Meanwhile the children went to the large cloak closet behind the stairway and got their wraps. When Ned and Emily Meriwether rejoined their parents at the front door to leave the house, Ned was wearing his own overcoat and held his own fedora in his hand.

Miss Louisa and Mr. Alfred Dorset lived on for nearly ten years after that night, but they gave up selling their figs and paper flowers and of course they never entertained young people again. I often wonder if growing up in Mero can ever have seemed quite the same since. Some of the terror must have gone out of it. Half the dread of coming of age must have vanished with the dread of the Dorsets' parties.

After that night, their old car would sometimes be observed creeping about town, but it was never parked in front of their house any more. It stood usually at the side entrance where the Dorsets could climb in and out of it without being seen. They began keeping a servant too—mainly to run their errands for them, I imagine. Sometimes it would be a man, sometimes a woman, never the same one for more than a few months at a time. Both of the Dorsets died during the Second World War while many of us who had gone to their parties were away from Mero. But the story went round—and I am inclined to believe it—that after they were dead and the house was sold, Tom Bascomb's coat and hat were found still hanging in the cloak closet behind the stairs.

Tom himself was a pilot in the War and was a considerable hero. He was such a success and made such a name for himself that he never came back to Mero to live. He found bigger opportunities elsewhere I suppose, and I don't suppose he ever felt the ties to Mero that people with Ned's kind of upbringing do. Ned was in the War too, of course. He was in the navy and after the War he did return to Mero to live, though actually it was not until then that he had spent much time here since his parents bundled him off to boarding school. Emily came home and made her debut just two or three years before the War, but she was already engaged to some boy in the East; she never comes back any more except to bring her children to see their grandparents for a few days during Christmas or at Easter.

I understand that Emily and Ned are pretty indifferent to each other's existence nowadays. I have been told this by Ned Meriwether's own wife. Ned's wife maintains that the night Ned and Emily went to the Dorsets' party marked the beginning of this indifference, that it marked the end of their childhood intimacy and the beginning of a shyness, a reserve, even an animosity between them that was destined to be a sorrow forever to the two sensible parents who had sat in the upstairs sitting room that night waiting until the telephone call came from Tom Bascomb.

Ned's wife is a girl he met while he was in the navy. She was a Wave, and her background isn't the same as his. Apparently she isn't too happy with life in what she refers to as "Mero proper." She and Ned have recently moved out into a suburban development, which she doesn't like either and which she refers to as "greater Mero." She asked me at a party one night how Mero ever got its absurd name, and when I told her that it was named for the last Spanish governor of Louisiana she burst out laughing. I don't know why exactly. But what interests me most about her is that after a few drinks she likes to talk about Ned and Emily and Tom Bascomb and the Dorsets. Tom Bascomb has become a kind of hero—and I don't mean a wartime hero—in her eyes, though of course not having grown up in Mero she has never seen him in her life. But she is a clever girl, and there are times when she will say to me, "Tell me about Mero. Tell me about the Dorsets." And I try to tell her. I tell her to remember that Mero looks upon itself as a rather old city. I tell her to remember that it was one of the first English-speaking settlements west of the Alleghenies and that by the end of the American Revolution, when veterans began pouring westward over the Wilderness Road or down

the Ohio River, Mero was often referred to as a thriving village. Then
she tells me that I am being dull, because it is hard for her to concentrate on any aspect of the story that doesn't center around Tom
Bascomb and that night at the Dorsets'.

But I make her listen. Or at least one time I did. The Dorset family,
I insisted on saying, was in Mero even in those earliest times right
after the Revolution, but they had come here under somewhat different circumstances from those of the other early settlers. How could
that really matter, Ned's wife asked, after a hundred and fifty years?
How could distinctions between the first settlers matter after the
Irish had come to Mero, after the Germans, after the Italians? Well,
in West Vesey Place it could matter. It had to. If the distinction was
false, it mattered all the more and it was all the more necessary to
make it.

But let me interject here that Mero is located in a state about
whose history most Mero citizens—not newcomers like Ned's wife,
but old timers—have little interest and less knowledge. Most of us,
for instance, are never even quite sure whether during the 1860's
our state did secede or didn't secede. As for the city itself, some of
us hold that it is geographically Northern and culturally Southern.
Others say the reverse is true. We are all apt to want to feel misplaced
in Mero, and so we are not content merely to say that it is a border
city. How you stand on this important question is apt to depend entirely on whether your family is one of those with a good Southern
name or one that had its origin in New England, because those are
the two main categories of old society families in Mero.

But truly—I told Ned's wife—the Dorset family was never in either
of those categories. The first Dorset had come, with his family and his
possessions and even a little capital, direct from a city in the English
Midlands to Mero. The Dorsets came not as pioneers but paying their
way all the way. They had not bothered to stop for a generation or
two to put down roots in Pennsylvania or Virginia or Massachusetts.
And this was the distinction which some people wished always to
make. Apparently those early Dorsets had cared no more for putting
down roots in the soil of the New World than they had cared for
whatever they had left behind in the Old. They were an obscure
mercantile family who came to invest in a new western city. Within
two generations the business—no, the industry!—which they established made them rich beyond any dreams they could have had in the
beginning. For half a century they were looked upon, if any family
ever was, as our first family.

And then the Dorsets left Mero—practically all of them except the one old bachelor and the one old maid—left it just as they had come, not caring much about what they were leaving or where they were going. They were city people, and they were Americans. They knew that what they had in Mero they could buy more of in other places. For them Mero was an investment that had paid off. They went to live in Santa Barbara and Laguna Beach, in Newport and on Long Island. And the truth which it was so hard for the rest of us to admit was that, despite our family memories of Massachusetts and Virginia, we were all more like the Dorsets—those Dorsets who left Mero— than we were *un*like them. Their spirit was just a little closer to being the very essence of Mero than ours was. The obvious difference was that we had to stay on here and pretend that our life had a meaning which it did not. And if it was only by a sort of chance that Miss Louisa and Mr. Alfred played the role of social arbiters among the young people for a number of years, still no one could honestly question their divine right to do so.

"It may have been their right," Ned's wife said at this point, "but just think what might have happened."

"It's not a matter of what might have happened," I said. "It is a matter of what did happen. Otherwise, what have you and I been talking about?"

"Otherwise," she said with an irrepressible shudder, "I would not be forever getting you off in a corner at these parties to talk about my husband and my husband's sister and how it is they care so little for each other's company nowadays."

And I could think of nothing to say to that except that probably we had now pretty well exhausted our subject.

The Doctor's Wife

"Sharks?" The tip of the doctor's wife's freckled nose seemed to sharpen in the sparkling air. Her eyes, momentarily rendered colorless by thought, took up the green of the Caribbean; the plane of the water intersected her throat. "Yes, we have some. Big dark fellows, too."

Ralph, hanging beside her, squatting on buoyance, straightened up, splashing, and tried to survey the beryl depths around him. His sudden movements rendered even the immediate water opaque. The doctor's wife's surprisingly young laughter rang out.

"You Americans," she said, "so nervy," and with complacence pushed a little deeper into the sea, floating backward while the water gently bubbled around her mouth. She had a small face, gone freckled and rosy in this climate; her stringy auburn hair had been dulled by daily sea-bathing. "They rarely come in this far," she said, tilting her face upward and speaking to the sky. "Only in the turtle-killing season, when the blood draws them in. We're fortunate. Our beaches go out shallowly. Over in St. Martin, now, the offshore water is deep, and they must be careful."

She turned and, with the casual paddling stroke of a plump woman who floats easily, swam smiling toward him. "A shame," she said, her voice strained by the effort of curving her throat to keep her lips free, "Vic Johnson is gone. He was a dear soul. The old Anglican vicar." She pronounced "vicar" rather harshly, perhaps humorously. She stood up beside Ralph and pointed to the horizon. "Now *he*," she said, "used to swim far out into the bay, he and his great black dog Hooker. Vic would swim straight out, until he couldn't move a muscle, and then he would float, and grab Hooker's tail, and the dog would pull him in. Honestly, it was a sight, this fat old English gentleman, his white hair streaming, coming in on the tail of a dog. He never gave a thought to sharks. Oh, he'd swim *way* out, until he was just a dot."

They were waist-deep in the sea, and at a motion from Ralph they walked toward shore together. The calm warm water leaped from their strides. She was small beside him, and her voice piped at his shoulder. "I'm sorry he's gone," she said. "He was a lovely old gentleman. He had been here forty years. He loved the island."

"I can see why he would," Ralph said. He turned his head to review the crescent of landscape around the beach, as if through his fresh eyes the doctor's wife could renew—what obscurely seemed to him to need renewing—her sense of the island's beauty. The white beach was empty. The natives used it only as a path. Their homes were set behind the ragged hedge of sea grape that rimmed the sand. Bits of tarpaper, pink-painted cement, corrugated roofing reddened by rust, wooden walls weathered to silver and patched by flattened kerosene tins, shacks on stilts, and unfinished cinder-block shells peeped above the dull, low foliage. There were few flowers. This was January. But the clusters of coconuts nested under the shuffling branches of the palms, and the high, small, soft clouds, like the quick clouds of spring in his own climate, suggested that here the season of bloom and the season of harvest were parallel and perpetual: germination and fruition ceaselessly intertwined. There were no mountains in the view. The island was low; when they came in on the airplane, it seemed a two-dimensional twin, or sketch, of St. Martin, which thrust from the sea like a set of Vermont mountaintops. There the beaches were steep and dangerous, here, they were safe. There, Dutchmen and Frenchmen built bustling hotels and restaurants to entice American dollars; here, strangers rarely came. Here, even the place names were bestowed without enterprise or effort. East End, West End, The Road, The Forest—thus the island was geographically divided. The uninhabited ridge of scrub and coral rubble that formed one side of the bay was named High Hill. The village was called The Bay. The orange cliffs on the other side of the bay were called The Cliffs. During these short winter days the sun set on a diagonal above them and, between six and seven o'clock, touched the sea at the fingertips of the most distant arm of land. Yet after the sun had drowned, light, itself lazy, lingered among the huts and the oleander bushes. Now it was late afternoon; the tiny tropical sun, not yet swollen to red, patiently poured white brilliance down through the hushed air. The air was as soft, as kind, as the water; there was no hostility in either. The two elements, as Ralph came out of one into the other, seemed tints of a single enveloping benevolence.

"Oh, yes, but not merely that," the doctor's wife said. "He loved the people. He built them three churches and, oh, did all manner of good works. We're talking of Reverend Johnson," she explained to Eve, who had remained on the beach with the children. "The Anglican padre. He retired last year and went back to England. Sussex, I think."

"He loved the people?" Eve asked. She had heard. Voices carried well in the air, disturbed, during the day, by only the whispering beat of the surf and infrequent voices calling in English made musical by an unintelligible lilt.

The doctor's wife dropped down on the sand. "These are my children," she intoned gruffly. She chased the abrupt parody away with her sharp laughter. "Oh, yes, he loved them. He gave his life to them." The youthful excitement of her voice and the innocent clarity of her eyes went queerly with her body, which was middle-aged. Her plump legs had gone lumpy and sodden, and her small face was finely wrinkled, each wrinkle accented by a line of white where the pinched skin had evaded the sun. "He didn't have any children of his own," she thought to add. "Just this dreadful dog Hooker. Such a funny old man. You might have liked him. I'm sure you never see his kind in America."

"I know we would have liked him," Eve said. "Hannah often mentions Reverend Johnson." Hannah was their cook, a woman of over thirty yet as shy and subtle as a girl. Her skin was always shining as if in embarrassment, but she had a jaunty way of crooning hymns to herself in the kitchen. The children, at first timid of her color, adored her, and listened with eyes rounded by delight when she held up a two-tone forefinger and told them to be good. Goodness had never before been presented to them seriously. Ralph and Eve had not expected a servant. They had picked the most obscure island they could find. But Hannah came with the house; the owner, a svelte widow who had children in Florida, Peru, and Antigua, assumed they would need her. As it turned out, they did. They could never have unravelled alone all the riddles of this novel world. Eve could never have managed the shopping, which was carried on by gossip—invisible voices as liquid as the wind, telling who had just slaughtered a pig, and whose fishing boat had come in with a catch. The village was full of stores; almost every shack at least sold—for disturbingly discrepant prices—American cigarettes smuggled from St. Martin. But even the business hours of the most official store, a cement corridor of shelves attached to the customs office, had proved a mystery the Americans were unable to crack. They always found barred the large green door bearing in wobbly chalk script the ancient announcement, "Attention Members! Attention Friends! This Store will be CLOSED Thursday afternoon."

"Oh, Hannah. She's a good girl," the doctor's wife said, and rolled over on her stomach. The corrugated backs of her thighs were frosted with sand like wet sugar.

"She *is*, you know," Eve said. "She's lovely. I think they're all lovely. They've all been lovely to us." Such insistence was unlike his wife. Ralph wondered what was between the two women, who had just met a day ago. "I can see why Reverend Johnson loved the people," Eve added in a deliberate, though cautiously soft, voice. "The people" were all around them; their huts came down to the edge of the sand, and, windows shuttered, the patched walls seemed to be listening raptly.

The doctor's wife rolled over again and returned to a sitting position. What was making her so restless?

"Yes," she said, and an especially heavy curl of surf foamed up the white slope and soaked in just short of their feet. The sand was porous; innumerable punctures dotted it, the breathing holes of crabs. The doctor's wife's eyes fixed on the horizon and became, from the side, colorless lenses. Her nose in profile turned acute. "They're simple souls," she said.

The doctor's wife was a queen here. She was the only fully white woman resident on the island. When the rare British official and the rare, fantastically minor member of royalty came to grace this most remote and docile scrap of empire with a visit, she was the hostess. When she roared along the dirt roads in her spattered English Ford —its muffler had long ago rotted away—the older natives touched their foreheads ironically and the children flapped their arms in her wake of dust. When she and the doctor condescended to call upon the American family staying three weeks in The Bay, Hannah had trembled with pride and broken a cup in the kitchen. The doctor was a slight, rapid-voiced man with a witty air of failure. His fingertips were dyed deep yellow by smuggled cigarettes. He preferred Camels, but Chesterfields were all that were coming through now. He had never seen a filtered cigarette. He and his wife had been ten years in the tropics—B.G., Trinidad, Barbados, now this. He had some vague scheme of getting to America and making a fortune and retiring to a Yorkshire village. He was off for the day to St. Martin.

"In America, now," the doctor's wife said, vehemently brushing sand from her knees, "are the coloreds well cared for?"

"How do you mean?" Eve asked.

"Are they well off?"

"Not really," Ralph said, because he sensed that it would be better if he, rather than Eve, answered. "In some parts better than others. In the South, of course, they're openly discriminated against; in the North they by and large have to live in the city slums but at least they have full legal rights."

"Oh dear," the doctor's wife said. "It is a problem, isn't it?"

Eve's face flashed up from studying a shell. "Whose problem?" she asked. She was a graduate of one of those female colleges where only a member of a racial minority or a cripple can be elected class president. News from South Africa made her voice thrash, and she was for anyone—Castro, Ben-Gurion, Martin Luther King—who in her mind represented an oppressed race. That such automatic sympathy was itself condescending had not occurred to her. Of English blood, enriched by remote and aristocratic injections of French and Russian, she denied the less favored even the compliment of fearing them.

The doctor's wife returned her gaze to the horizon, and Ralph wondered if they had been rude. In the woman's pointed profile there was a certain perhaps deliberately noble thrust. But, the hostess, she relented and tried to make the conversation go again. She turned her head, shading her eyes with a quick hand and exposing her neat white teeth in a tense smile. "The schools," she said. "Can they go to your schools?"

"Of course," Ralph said swiftly, at the same time realizing that for her there was no "of course" to it. She knew nothing about his country. He felt firmer, having gauged her ignorance, and having moved to the hard ground of information. "Nobody denies them schools. In the South the schools are segregated. But in the North, and the West, and so on, there's no problem." He hunched his shoulders, feeling at his back Eve's disapproval of his saying "problem."

"But"—the doctor's wife's freckles gathered under her eyes as she squinted into the focus of the issue—"would *your* children go to school with them?"

"Sure. Good heavens. Why not?" He was relieved to clear this up, to lock this door. He hoped the doctor's wife would now turn away and talk of something else.

She sighed. "Of course, you in America have lived with the problem so long. In England, now, they're just waking up; the blacks are *pouring* into London."

A wave, pushed by one behind it, slid so far up the slant of sand their feet were delicately shocked and soaked. For a few seconds their ankles glittered in rippling sleeves of retreating water. Eve said slowly, "You talk as if they had asked to be made slaves and brought here."

"Mommy, look! Mommy, look!" Kate's voice, mingling with Larry's babyish yips of excitement, came from far down the beach. Their little silhouettes were jiggling around something dark at their feet, and out of the sea grape an old woman in a kerchief and a young sailor with a naked chest had emerged to watch them, amused to see what amused these strange children. Eve rose, casting down, for Ralph to see, a startled and indignant look at the doctor's wife's body, as if it were an offensive piece of rubbish washed up on the pure sands of her mind.

As Eve walked away, the doctor's wife said, "Doesn't she take a tan beautifully?"

"Yes, she always does. She's part French." With his wife out of earshot, Ralph relaxed into the sand. Mediating between the two women had demanded an exhausting equilibrium. He resigned himself to listening; he knew the doctor's wife's tongue would be loosened. The presence of another white queen inhibited her, diluted her authority.

"Do you want to hear a frightening story?"

"Sure." He acquiesced uneasily. The attention of the houses behind them seemed to grow more intense. He felt that he and his family were liked in the village; the doctor's wife, driving down from the center of the island to enjoy their beach, assumed an incriminating alliance which he did not wish to exist. For when the sun went down, she would go home, leaving them alone in the village with the night and its noises.

"When Vic Johnson left," she said, lowering her voice and sinking back on her elbow, to bring her face closer to his, "they had a party to greet the new parson, a very nice young colored boy from St. Kitts. *Very* nice, I must say, and they say very intelligent, though I haven't heard him preach. Well, the Warden—you haven't met him, and I daresay you won't, a big smooth Jamaican, takes himself oh *ever* so seriously—the Warden makes this little speech. He of course mentions Vic, forty years and so on, but right at the end he says that he knows we will not miss Reverend Johnson, because the new vicar is such a fine young man, comes to us with such an excellent record of study, and the rest of it, and furthermore, *furthermore*, what makes us especially happy and proud, he is one of us. Imagine! One of us! Of course, the young parson was embarrassed to death. It made me so mad I would have jumped up and left if the doctor hadn't held my hand. *One of us!* Vic had given his life to these people."

Her voice had become shrill; Ralph spoke in the hope of restraining it. "It seems unnecessary; but natural," he said.

"I don't see anything natural about it. *Un*natural, in my book. Unnatural, childish ingratitude. You just don't know how unnatural these people are. If you could see one-tenth of the antics, and then the selfishness, the doctor puts up with. At two in the morning, 'Doctor, Doctor, come save my child,' and then a week later, when he tries to collect his poor little dollar or two, they don't *remember*. They don't remember at all. And if he insists—'The white people are stealing our money.' Oh. I hate them. God forgive me, I've come to hate them. They're *not* natural. They're not fully human." Seeing his hand begin a protesting movement, she added, "And for that matter, do you know what they say about you and your wife?" It was as if a shadow cruising through her words now made its lunge.

"No. Do they say something?"

"This is just to show how malicious they are. They say your wife has a touch of the brush." It took Ralph a moment to expand "brush" into "tarbrush." He laughed; what else?

The doctor's wife laughed, too; but under the blond eyebrows her blue eyes, the pupils pinpricks in the sun, were fixed on his face. She expected his face to crack and the truth to escape. "You see how dark she is," she explained. "How tan." He watched her tongue tick as she suspensefully pronounced the last two words. Girlish curiosity gave a taut surface to her mature malice.

Blood rushed through his body; the wound was confused; his anger entangled him with his attacker. He was supplying an absurd assault with teeth out of himself. "She just naturally gets that brown."

"And you see," the doctor's wife went on, still not unpinning her eyes from his face, "that's why they say you came here. No tourists come here, least of all with children. They say your wife's being part Negro has kept you out of the hotels on the better islands."

He felt certain that this ingenious argument was wholly her own. "We came here because it was cheap," he said.

"Of *course*," she said, "of *course*," and giggled, sensing that she had exposed herself to his defense. "But they can't believe that. They believe, you see, that all Americans are *rich*." Which was just what, Ralph knew, she and the doctor believed.

He stood up, wet sand collapsing from his legs. In an effort to rein his excitement, he threw several unrelated laughs, as if out of a renewed realization of absurdity, outward into the air. He looked down at the woman and said, "Well, that explains why they seem to like her better than me."

The doctor's wife, having strained her neck to squint up at him, collapsed the rest of the way. She pillowed her head with one arm and threw the other over her eyes. Without her eyes her lips seemed vague and numb. "Oh, no," she said. "They hate her for getting away with it."

His laughter this time was totally vacant; it humiliated him. "I think I'll go in again," he said. "Before the sun fades."

"It won't fade," was the faint answer.

From the safety of the water he watched his dark wife herd two pale, burned children up the beach. The distance between her and the doctor's wife's inert body diminished; he had an urge to shout a warning, then smiled, picturing the laughter that would greet this story when they were home, at a cocktail party, secure among their own. Abruptly he felt guilty in relation to his wife. He had betrayed her. His seriousness had been unworthy of her. She would have wanted him to say yes, her grandfather picked cotton in Alabama, in America these things are taken for granted, we have no problem. But he saw, like a movement glimpsed in a liquid volume, that the comedy of this response depended upon, could only live within, a vast and unconscious pride of race. That since this medium was poisoned all its creatures must be evil. That he and the doctor's wife were immersed together; he hated her blue eyes because they were pinned to his face, hated the taste of her because—could it be? —she was dying. His guilt could not be mapped. Its intricacy was as dense as a simple mass. He moved backward in the ocean, touching the ribbed bottom with his toes, until the water wrapped around his throat. Something—seaweed or the pulse of a current—touched his calf. He thrashed, and peered down, but saw nothing. He was afraid of the sharks, and he was afraid of the doctor's wife, so he hung there between them, bleeding shame, while the water forgave him.

The Bulgarian Poetess

"Your poems. Are they difficult?"

She smiled and, unaccustomed to speaking English, answered carefully, drawing a line in the air with two delicately pinched fingers holding an imaginary pen. "They are difficult—to write."

He laughed, startled and charmed. "But not to read?"

She seemed puzzled by his laugh, but did not withdraw her smile, though its corners deepened in a defensive, feminine way. "I think," she said, "not so very."

"Good." Brainlessly he repeated "Good," disarmed by her unexpected quality of truth. He was, himself, a writer, this fortyish young man, Henry Bech, with his thinning curly hair and melancholy Jewish nose, the author of one good book and three others, the good one having come first. By a kind of oversight, he had never married. His reputation had grown while his powers declined. As he felt himself sink, in his fiction, deeper and deeper into eclectic sexuality and bravura narcissism, as his search for plain truth carried him further and further into treacherous realms of fantasy and, lately, of silence, he was more and more thickly hounded by homage, by flat-footed exegetes, by arrogantly worshipful undergraduates who had hitchhiked a thousand miles to touch his hand, by querulous translators, by election to honorary societies, by invitations to lecture, to "speak," to "read," to participate in symposia trumped up by ambitious girlie magazines in shameless conjunction with venerable universities. His very government, in airily unstamped envelopes from Washington, invited him to travel, as an ambassador of the arts, to the other half of the world, the hostile, mysterious half. Rather automatically, but with some faint hope of shaking himself loose from the burden of himself, he consented, and found himself floating, with a passport so stapled with visas it fluttered when pulled from his pocket, down into the dim airports of Communist cities.

He arrived in Sofia the day after a mixture of Bulgarian and African students had smashed the windows of the American Legation and ignited an overturned Chevrolet. The cultural officer, pale from a sleepless night of guard duty, tamping his pipe with trembling fingers, advised Bech to stay out of crowds and escorted him to his hotel. The lobby was swarming with Negroes in black wool fezzes and pointed European shoes. Insecurely disguised, he felt, by an astrakhan hat purchased in Moscow, Bech passed through to the elevator, whose operator addressed him in German. *"Ja, vier,"* Bech answered, *"danke,"* and telephoned, in his bad French, for dinner to be brought up to his room. He remained there all night, behind a locked door, reading Hawthorne. He had lifted a paperback collection of short stories from a Legation window sill littered with broken glass. A few curved bright crumbs fell from between the pages onto his blanket. The image of Roger Malvin lying alone, dying, in the forest—"Death would come like the slow approach of a corpse, stealing gradually towards him through the forest, and showing its ghastly and motionless features from behind a nearer and yet a nearer tree"—frightened him. Bech fell asleep early and suffered from swollen, homesick dreams. It had been Thanksgiving Day.

In the morning, venturing downstairs for breakfast, he was surprised to find the restaurant open, the waiters affable, the eggs actual, the coffee hot, though syrupy. Outside, Sofia was sunny and (except for a few dark glances at his big American shoes) amenable to his passage along the streets. Lozenge-patterns of pansies, looking flat and brittle as pressed flowers, had been set in the public beds. Women with a touch of Western chic walked hatless in the park behind the mausoleum of Georgi Dimitrov. There was a mosque, and an assortment of trolley cars salvaged from the remotest corner of Bech's childhood in the nineteen-twenties, and a tree that talked —that is, it was so full of birds that it swayed under their weight and emitted volumes of chirping sound like a great leafy loudspeaker. It was the inverse of his hotel, whose silent walls presumably contained listening microphones. Electricity was somewhat enchanted in the Socialist world. Lights flickered off untouched and radios turned themselves on. Telephones rang in the dead of the night and breathed wordlessly in his ear. Six weeks ago, flying from New York, Bech had expected Moscow to be a blazing counterpart and instead saw, through the plane window, a skein of hoarded lights no brighter, on that vast black plain, than a girl's body in a dark room.

Past the talking tree was the American Legation. The sidewalk,

heaped with broken glass, was roped off, so pedestrians had to de-
tour into the gutter. Bech detached himself from the stream, crossed
the little barren of pavement, smiled at the Bulgarian militiamen
who were sullenly guarding the greenish heaps of shards, and
pulled open the bronze door. The cultural officer was crisper after a
normal night's sleep. He clenched his pipe in his teeth and handed
Bech a small list. "You're to meet with the Writer's Union at eleven.
These are writers you might ask to see. As far as we can tell, they're
among the more progressive."

Words like "progressive" and "liberal" had a somewhat reversed
sense in this world. At times, indeed, Bech felt he had passed through
a mirror, a dingy flecked mirror that reflected feebly the capitalist
world; in its dim depths everything was similar but left-handed.
One of the names ended in "-ova." Bech said, "A woman."

"A poetess," the cultural officer said, sucking and tamping in a
fury of bogus efficiency. "Very popular, apparently. Her books are
impossible to buy."

"Have you read anything by these people?"

"I'll be frank with you. I can just about make my way through a
newspaper."

"But you always know what a newspaper will say anyway."

"I'm sorry. I don't get your meaning."

"There isn't any." Bech didn't quite know why the Americans he
met irritated him, whether because they garishly refused to blend
into this shadow-world or because they were always solemnly sending him on ridiculous errands.

At the Writer's Union, he handed the secretary the list as it had
been handed to him, on U.S. Legation stationery. The secretary, a
large stooped man with the hands of a stonemason, grimaced and
shook his head but obligingly reached for the telephone. Bech's
meeting was already waiting in another room. It was the usual one,
the one that, with small differences, he had already attended in
Moscow and Kiev, Yerevan and Alma-Ata, Bucharest and Prague:
the polished oval table, the bowl of fruit, the morning light, the
gleaming glasses of brandy and mineral water, the lurking portrait
of Lenin, the six or eight patiently sitting men who would leap to
their feet with quick blank smiles. These men would include a few
literary officials, termed "critics," high in the Party, loquacious and
witty and destined to propose a toast to international understanding;
a few selected novelists and poets, mustachioed, smoking, sulking at
this invasion of their time; a university professor, the head of the

Anglo-American Literature department, speaking in a beautiful withered English of Mark Twain and Sinclair Lewis; a young interpreter with a moist handshake; a shaggy old journalist obsequiously scribbling notes; and, on the rim of the group, in chairs placed to suggest that they had invited themselves, one or two gentlemen of ill-defined status, fidgety and tieless, maverick translators who would turn out to be the only ones present who had ever read a word by Henry Bech.

Here this type was represented by a stout man in a tweed coat leather-patched at the elbows in the British style. The whites of his eyes were distinctly red. He shook Bech's hand eagerly, made of it almost an embrace of reunion, bending his face so close Bech could distinguish the smells of tobacco, garlic, cheese, and alcohol. Even as they were seating themselves around the table, and the Writer's Union chairman, a man elegantly bald, with very pale eyelashes, was touching his brandy glass as if to lift it, this anxious red-eyed interloper blurted at Bech, "Your 'Travel Light' was so marvellous a book. The motels, the highways, the young girls with their lovers who were motorcyclists, so marvellous, so American, the youth, the adoration for space and speed, the barbarity of the advertisements in neon lighting, the very poetry. It takes us truly into another dimension."

"Travel Light" was the first novel, the famous one. Bech disliked discussing it. "At home," he said, "it was criticized as despairing."

The man's hands, stained orange with tobacco, lifted in amazement and plopped noisily to his knees. "No, no a thousand times. Truth, wonder, terror even, vulgarity, yes. But despair, no, not at all, not one iota. Your critics are dead wrong."

"Thank you."

The chairman softly cleared his throat and lifted his glass an inch from the table, so that it formed with its reflection a kind of playing card.

Bech's admirer excitedly persisted. "You are not a *wet* writer, no. You are a dry writer, yes? You have the expressions, am I wrong in English, dry, hard?"

"More or less."

"I want to translate you!"

It was the agonized cry of a condemned man, for the chairman coldly lifted his glass to the height of his eyes, and like a firing squad the others followed suit. Blinking his white lashes, the chairman gazed mistily in the direction of the sudden silence, and spoke in Bulgarian.

The young interpreter murmured in Bech's ear. "I wish to propose now, ah, a very brief toast. I know it will seem doubly brief to our honored American guest, who has so recently enjoyed the, ah, hospitality of our Soviet comrades." There must have been a joke here, for the rest of the table laughed. "But in seriousness permit me to say that in our country we have seen in years past too few Americans, ah, of Mr. Bech's progressive and sympathetic stripe. We hope in the next hour to learn from him much that is interesting and, ah, socially useful about the literature of his large country, and perhaps we may in turn inform him of our own proud literature, of which perhaps he knows regrettably little. Ah, so let me finally, then, since there is a saying that too long a courtship spoils the marriage, offer to drink, in our native plum brandy *slivovica,* ah, firstly to the success of his visit and, in the second place, to the mutual increase of international understanding."

"Thank you," Bech said and, as a courtesy, drained his glass. It was wrong; the others, having merely sipped, stared. The purple burning revolved in Bech's stomach and a severe distaste for himself, for his role, for this entire artificial and futile process, focussed into a small brown spot on a pear in the bowl so shiningly posed before his eyes.

The red-eyed fool smelling of cheese was ornamenting the toast. "It is a personal honor for me to meet the man who, in 'Travel Light,' truly added a new dimension to American prose."

"The book was written," Bech said, "twelve years ago."

"And since?" A slumping, mustachioed man sat up and sprang into English. "Since, you have written what?"

Bech had been asked that question often in these weeks and his answer had grown curt. "A second novel called 'Brother Pig,' which is St. Bernard's expression for the body."

"Good. Yes, and?"

"A collection of essays and sketches called 'When the Saints.' "

"I like the title less well."

"It's the beginning of a famous Negro song."

"We know the song," another man said, a smaller man, with the tense, dented mouth of a hare. He lightly sang, "Lordy, I just want to be in that number."

"And the last book," Bech said, "was a long novel called 'The Chosen' that it took six years to write and that nobody liked."

"I have read reviews," the red-eyed man said. "I have not read the book. Copies are difficult here."

"I'll give you one," Bech said.

The promise seemed, somehow, to make the recipient unfortunately conspicuous; wringing his stained hands, he appeared to swell in size, to intrude grotesquely upon the inner ring, so that the interpreter took it upon himself to whisper, with the haste of an apology, into Bech's ear, "This gentleman is well known as the translator into our language of 'Erewhon.'"

"A marvellous book," the translator said, deflating in relief, pulling at his pockets for a cigarette. "It truly takes us into another dimension. Something that must be done. We live in a new cosmos."

The chairman spoke in Bulgarian, musically, at length. There was polite laughter. Nobody translated for Bech. The professorial type, his hair like a flaxen toupee, jerked forward. "Tell me, is it true, as I have read"—his phrases whistled slightly, like rusty machinery—"that the stock of Sinclair Lewis has plummeted under the Salinger wave?"

And so it went, here as in Kiev, Prague, and Alma-Ata, the same questions, more or less predictable, and his own answers, terribly familiar to him by now, mechanical, stale, irrelevant, untrue, claustrophobic. The door opened. In came, with the rosy air of a woman fresh from a bath, a little breathless, having hurried, hatless, a woman in a blond coat, her hair also blond. The secretary, entering behind her, seemed to make a cherishing space around her with his large curved hands. He introduced her to Bech as Vera Something-ova, the poetess he had asked to meet. None of the others on the list, he explained, answered their telephones.

"Aren't you kind to come?" As Bech asked it, it was a genuine question, to which he expected some sort of an answer.

She spoke to the interpreter in Bulgarian. "She says," the interpreter told Bech, "she is sorry she is so late."

"But she was just called!" In the warmth of his confusion and pleasure Bech turned to speak directly to her, forgetting he would not be understood. "I'm terribly sorry to have interrupted your morning."

"I am pleased," she said, "to meet you. I heard of you spoken in France."

"You speak English!"

"No. Very little amount."

"But you *do*."

A chair was brought for her from a corner of the room. She yielded her coat, revealing herself in a suit also blond, as if her clothes were an aspect of a total consistency. She sat down opposite Bech, crossing her legs. Her legs were very good; her face was perceptibly broad. Lowering her lids, she tugged her skirt to the curve of her knee. It was his sense of her having hurried, hurried to him, and of being, still, graciously flustered, that most touched him.

He spoke to her very clearly, across the fruit, fearful of abusing and breaking the fragile bridge of her English. "You are a poetess. When I was young, I also wrote poems."

She was silent so long he thought she would never answer; but then she smiled and pronounced, "You are not old now."

"Your poems. Are they difficult?"

"They are difficult—to write."

"But not to read?"

"I think—not so very."

"Good. Good."

Despite the decay of his career, Bech had retained an absolute faith in his instincts; he never doubted that somewhere an ideal course was open to him and that his intuitions were pre-dealt clues to his destiny. He had loved, briefly or long, with or without consummation, perhaps a dozen women; yet all of them, he now saw, shared the trait of approximation, of narrowly missing an undisclosed prototype. The surprise he felt did not have to do with the appearance, at last, of this central woman; he had always expected her to appear. What he had not expected was her appearance here, in this remote and abused nation, in this room of morning light, where he discovered a small knife in his fingers and on the table before him, golden and moist, a precisely divided pear.

Men travelling alone develop a romantic vertigo. Bech had already fallen in love with a freckled Embassy wife in Prague, a buck-toothed chanteuse in Rumania, a stolid Mongolian sculptress in Kazakstan. In the Tretyakov Gallery he had fallen in love with a recumbent statue, and at the Moscow Ballet School with an entire roomful of girls. Entering the room, he had been struck by the aroma, tenderly acrid, of young female sweat. Sixteen and seventeen, wearing patchy practice suits, the girls were twirling so strenuously their slippers were unravelling. Demure student faces crowned the unconscious insolence of their bodies. The room was doubled in depth by a floor-to-ceiling mirror. Bech was seated on a bench at its base. Staring above his head, each girl watched herself with frowning eyes frozen, for an instant in the turn, by the imperious delay and snap of her head. Bech tried to remember the lines of Rilke that expressed it, this snap and delay: *did not the drawing remain/that the dark stroke of your eyebrow/swiftly wrote on the wall of its own turning?* At one point the teacher, a shapeless old Ukrainian lady with gold canines, a *prima* of the thirties, had arisen; cried something translated to Bech as "No, no, the arms free, *free;*" and in demonstration executed a rapid series of pirouettes with such proud effortlessness that all the girls, standing this way and that like deer along the wall, had applauded. Bech had loved them for that. In all his loves, there was an urge to rescue—to rescue the girls from the slavery of their exertions, the statue from the cold grip of its own marble, the Embassy wife from her boring and unctuous husband, the chanteuse from her nightly humiliation (she could not sing), the Mongolian from her stolid race. But the Bulgarian poetess presented herself to him as needing nothing, as being complete, poised, satisfied, achieved. He was aroused and curious and, the next day, inquired about her of the man with the vaguely contemptuous mouth of a hare—a novelist turned playwright and scenarist, who accompanied him to the Rila Monastery. "She lives to write," the playwright said. "I do not think it is healthy."

Bech said, "But she seems so healthy." They stood beside a small church with whitewashed walls. From the outside it looked like a hovel, a shelter for pigs or chickens. For five centuries the Turks had ruled Bulgaria, and the Christian churches, however richly adorned within, had humble exteriors. A peasant woman with wildly snarled hair unlocked the door for them. Though the church could hardly ever have held more than thirty worshippers, it was divided into three parts, and every inch of wall was covered with eighteenth-century frescoes. Those in the narthex depicted a Hell where the devils wielded scimitars. Passing through the tiny nave, Bech peeked through the iconostas into the screened area that, in the symbolism of Orthodox architecture, represented the next, the hidden world —Paradise—and glimpsed a row of books, an easy chair, a pair of ancient oval spectacles. Outdoors again, he felt released from the unpleasantly tight atmosphere of a children's book. They were on the side of a hill. Above them was a stand of pines whose trunks glistened with ice. Below them sprawled the monastery, a citadel of Bulgarian national feeling during the years of the Turkish Yoke. The last monks had been moved out in 1961. An aimless soft rain was falling in these mountains, and there were not many German tourists today. Across the valley, whose little silver river still turned a water wheel, a motionless white horse stood silhouetted against a green meadow, pinned there like a brooch.

"I am an old friend of hers," the playwright said. "I worry about her."

"Are the poems good?"

"It is difficult for me to judge. They are very feminine. Perhaps shallow."

"Shallowness can be a kind of honesty."

"Yes. She is very honest in her work."

"And in her life?"

"As well."

"What does her husband do?"

The other man looked at him with parted lips and touched his arm, a strange Slavic gesture, communicating an underlying racial urgency, that Bech no longer shied from. "But she has no husband. As I say, she is too much for poetry to have married."

"But her name ends in '-ova.'"

"I see. You are mistaken. It is not a matter of marriage; I am Petrov, my unmarried sister is Petrova. All females."

"How stupid of me. But I think it's such a pity, she's so charming."

"In America, only the uncharming fail to marry?"

"Yes, you must be very uncharming not to marry."

"It is not so here. The government indeed is alarmed; our birth rate is one of the lowest in Europe. It is a problem for economists."

Bech gestured at the monastery. "Too many monks?"

"Not enough, perhaps. With too few of monks, something of the monk enters everybody."

The peasant woman, who seemed older to Bech than he was but who was probably under thirty, saw them to the edge of her domain. She huskily chattered in what Petrov said was very amusing rural slang. Behind her, now hiding in her skirts and now darting away, was her child, a boy not more than three. He was faithfully chased, back and forth, by a small white pig, who moved, as pigs do, on tiptoe, with remarkably abrupt changes of direction. Something in the scene, in the open glee of the woman's parting smile and the unselfconscious way her hair thrust out from her head, something in the mountain mist and spongy rutted turf into which frost had begun to break at night, evoked for Bech a nameless absence to which was attached, like a horse to a meadow, the image of the poetess, with her broad face, her good legs, her Parisian clothes, and her sleekly brushed hair. Petrov, in whom he was beginning to sense, through the wraps of foreignness, a clever and kindred mind, seemed to have overheard his thoughts, for he said, "If you would like, we could have dinner. It would be easy for me to arrange."

"With her?"

"Yes, she is my friend, she would be glad."

"But I have nothing to say to her. I'm just curious about such an intense conjunction of good looks and brains. I mean, what does a soul do with it all?"

"You may ask her. Tomorrow night?"

"I'm sorry, I can't. I'm scheduled to go to the ballet, and the next night the Legation is giving a cocktail party for me, and then I fly home."

"Home? So soon?"

"It does not feel soon to me. I must try to work again."

"A drink, then. Tomorrow evening before the ballet? It is possible? It is not possible."

Petrov looked puzzled, and Bech realized that it was his fault, for he was nodding to say Yes, but in Bulgaria nodding meant No, and a shake of the head meant Yes. "Yes," he said. "Gladly."

The ballet was entitled "Silver Slippers." As Bech watched it, the word "ethnic" kept coming to his mind. He had grown accustomed, during his trip, to this sort of artistic evasion, the retreat from the difficult and disappointing present into folk dance, folk tale, folk song, with always the implication that, beneath the embroidered peasant costume, the folk was really one's heart's own darling, the proletariat.

"Do you like fairy tales?" It was the moist-palmed interpreter who accompanied him to the theatre.

"I *love* them," Bech said, with a fervor and gaiety lingering from the previous hour. The interpreter looked at him anxiously, as when Bech had swallowed the brandy in one swig, and throughout the ballet kept murmuring explanations of self-evident events on the stage. Each night, a princess would put on silver slippers and dance through her mirror to tryst with a wizard, who possessed a magic stick that she coveted, for with it the world could be ruled. The wizard, as a dancer, was inept, and once almost dropped her, so that anger flashed from her eyes. She was, the princess, a little redhead with a high round bottom and a frozen pout and beautiful free arm motions, and Bech found it oddly ecstatic when, preparatory to her leap, she would dance toward the mirror, an empty oval, and another girl, identically dressed in pink, would emerge from the wings and perform as her reflection. And when the princess, haughtily adjusting her cape of invisibility, leaped through the oval of gold wire, Bech's heart leaped backward into the enchanted hour he had spent with the poetess.

Though the appointment had been established, she came into the restaurant as if, again, she had been suddenly summoned and had hurried. She sat down between Bech and Petrov slightly breathless and fussed, but exuding, again, that impalpable warmth of intelligence and virtue.

"Vera, Vera," Petrov said.

"You hurry too much," Bech told her.

"Not so very much," she said.

Petrov ordered her a cognac and continued with Bech their discussion of the newer French novelists. "It is tricks," Petrov said. "Good tricks, but tricks. It does not have enough to do with life, it is too much verbal nervousness. Is that sense?"

"It's an epigram," Bech said.

"There are just two of their number with whom I do not feel this: Claude Simon and Samuel Beckett. You have no relation, Bech, Beckett?"

"None."

Vera said, "Nathalie Sarraute is a very modest woman. She felt motherly to me."

"You have met her?"

"In Paris I heard her speak. Afterward there was the coffee. I liked her theories, of the, oh, *what?* Of the *little* movements within the heart." She delicately measured a pinch of space and smiled, through Bech, back at herself.

"Tricks," Petrov said. "I do not feel this with Beckett; there, in a low form, believe it or not, one has human content."

Bech felt duty-bound to pursue this, to ask about the theatre of the absurd in Bulgaria, about abstract painting (these were the touchstones of "progressiveness;" Russia had none, Rumania some, Czechoslovakia plenty), to subvert Petrov. Instead, he asked the poetess, "Motherly?"

Vera explained, her hands delicately modelling the air, rounding into nuance, as it were, the square corners of her words. "After her talk, we—talked."

"In French?"

"And in Russian."

"She knows Russian?"

"She was born Russian."

"How is her Russian?"

"Very pure but—old-fashioned. Like a book. As she talked, I felt in a book, safe."

"You do not always feel safe?"

"Not always."

"Do you find it difficult to be a woman poet?"

"We have a tradition of woman poets. We have Elisaveta Bagriana, who is very great."

Petrov leaned toward Bech as if to nibble him. "Your own works? Are they influenced by the *nouvelle vague*? Do you consider yourself to write anti-*romans*?"

Bech kept himself turned toward the woman. "Do you want to hear about how I write? You don't, do you?"

"Very much yes," she said.

He told them, told them shamelessly, in a voice that surprised him with its steadiness, its limpid urgency, how once he had written, how in "Travel Light" he had sought to show people skimming the surface of things with their lives, taking tints from things the way that objects in a still-life color one another, and how later he had attempted to place beneath the melody of plot a counter-melody of imagery, interlocking images which had risen to the top and drowned his story, and how in "The Chosen" he had sought to make of this confusion the theme itself, an epic theme, by showing a population of characters whose actions were all determined, at the deepest level, by nostalgia, by a desire to get back, to dive, each, into the springs of their private imagery. The book probably failed; at least, it was badly received. Bech apologized for telling all this. His voice tasted flat in his mouth; he felt a secret intoxication and a secret guilt, for he had contrived to give a grand air, as of an impossibly noble and quixotically complex experiment, to his failure when at bottom, he suspected, a certain simple laziness was the cause.

Petrov said, "Fiction so formally sentimental could not be composed in Bulgaria. We do not have a happy history."

It was the first time Petrov had sounded like a Communist. If there was one thing that irked Bech about these people behind the mirror, it was their assumption that, however second-rate elsewhere, in suffering they were supreme. He said, "Believe it or not, neither do we."

Vera calmly intruded. "Your personae are not moved by love?"

"Yes, very much. But as a form of nostalgia. We fall in love, I tried to say in the book, with women who remind us of our first landscape. A silly idea. I used to be interested in love. I once wrote an essay on the orgasm—you know the word?—"

She shook her head. He remembered that it meant Yes.

"—on the orgasm as perfect memory. The one mystery is, what are we remembering?"

She shook her head again, and he noticed that her eyes were gray, and that in their depths his image (which he could not see) was searching for the thing remembered. She composed her fingertips around the brandy glass and said, "There is a French poet, a young one, who has written of this. He says that never else do we, do we so gather up, collect into ourselves, *oh—*" Vexed, she spoke to Petrov in rapid Bulgarian.

He shrugged, and said, "Concentrate our attention."

"—concentrate our attention," she repeated to Bech, as if the words, to be believed, had to come from her. "I say it foolish—foolishly —but in French it is very well put and—*correct.*"

Petrov smiled neatly and said, "This is an enjoyable subject for discussion, love."

"It remains," Bech said, picking his words as if the language were not native even to him, "one of the few things that still deserve meditation."

"I think it is good," she said.

"Love?" he asked, startled.

She shook her head and tapped the stem of her glass with a fingernail, so that Bech had an inaudible sense of ringing, and she bent as if to study the liquor, so that her entire body borrowed a rosiness from the brandy and burned itself into Bech's memory—the silver gloss of her nail, the sheen of her hair, the symmetry of her arms relaxed on the white tablecloth, everything except the expression on her face.

Petrov asked aloud Bech's opinion of Dürrenmatt.

Actuality is a running impoverishment of possibility. Though he had looked forward to seeing her again at the cocktail party and had made sure that she was invited, when it occurred, though she came, he could not get to her. He saw her enter, with Petrov, but he was fenced in by an attaché of the Yugoslav Embassy and his burnished Tunisian wife; and, later, when he was worming his way toward her diagonally, a steely hand closed on his arm and a rasping American female told him that her fifteen-year-old nephew had decided to be a writer and desperately needed advice. Not the standard crap, but real brass-knuckles advice. Bech found himself balked. He was surrounded by America: the voices, the narrow suits, the watery drinks, the clatter, the glitter. The mirror had gone opaque and gave him back only himself. He managed, in the end, as the officials were thinning out, to break through and confront her in a corner. Her coat, blond, with a rabbit collar, was already on; from its side pocket she pulled a pale volume of poems in the Cyrillic alphabet. "Please," she said. On the flyleaf she had written, "to H. Beck, sincerelly, with bad spellings but much"—the last word looked like "leave" but must have been "love."

"Wait," he begged, and went back to where his ravaged pile of presentation books had been and, unable to find the one he wanted, stole the Legation library's jacketless copy of "The Chosen." Placing it in her expectant hands, he told her, "Don't look," for inside he had written, with a drunk's stylistic confidence,

Dear Vera Glavanakova—
    It is a matter of earnest regret for me that you and I must live on opposite sides of the world.

Livvie Is Back

Solomon carried Livvie twenty-one miles away from her home when he married her. He carried her away up on the Old Natchez Trace into the deep country to live in his house. She was sixteen then. People said he thought nobody would ever come along there. It had been a long time, and a day she did not know about, he told her himself, since that road was a traveled road with *people* coming and going. He was good to her, but he kept her in the house. She had not thought that she could not get back. Where she came from, people said an old man did not want anybody in the world to find his wife, for fear they would steal her back from him. Solomon had asked her before he took her, "Would she be happy?"—very dignified, for he was a colored man that owned his land and had it written down in the courthouse; and she said, "Yes sir," since he was an old man then and she was young, and just listened and answered. He asked her, if she was choosing winter, would she pine for spring, and she said, "No indeed." Whatever she said, always, was because he was an old man, while nine years went by. All the time he got old, and he got so old he gave out. At last he slept the whole day in bed, and she was young still.

It was a nice house, inside and outside both. In the first place, it had three rooms. The front room was papered in holly paper, with green palmettos from the swamp spaced at careful intervals over the walls. There was fresh newspaper cut with fancy borders on the mantelshelf, on which were propped straight-up photographs of old or very young men printed in faint yellow—Solomon's people. Solomon had a houseful of furniture. There was a double settee, a tall scrolled rocker, and an organ in the front room, all around a three-legged table with a pink marble top, on which was set a lamp with three gold feet, besides a jelly glass with pretty hen feathers in it.

The room behind the front room had a bright iron bed with

polished knobs like a throne, in which Solomon slept all day. There
were snow-white curtains of wiry lace at the window, and a lace bed-
spread belonged on the bed. But what old Solomon slept so sound
under was a big featherstitched piece quilt in the pattern Trip
Around the World, which had twenty-one different colors, four
hundred and forty pieces, and a thousand yards of thread; and that
was what Solomon's mother made in her life and old age. There was
a table holding the Bible, and a trunk with a key. On the wall were
two calendars and a diploma from somewhere in Solomon's family,
and under that Livvie's one possession was nailed, a picture of the
little white baby of the family she worked for, back in Natchez before she was married.

In the kitchen beyond there were a big wood stove and a big round
table always with a wet top and with the knives and forks in one
jelly glass and the spoons in another, and a cut-glass vinegar bottle
between, and going out from those, many shallow dishes of pickled
peaches, fig preserves, watermelon pickles, and blackberry jam always sitting there. The churn sat in the sun, the doors of the safe
were always both shut, and there were four baited mousetraps in the
kitchen, one in every corner.

The outside of Solomon's house looked nice. It was not painted,
but across the porch was an even balance. On each side there was
one easy chair with high springs, looking out, and a fern basket
hanging over it from the ceiling, and a dishpan of zinnia seedlings
growing at its foot on the floor. By the door there was a plow wheel,
just a pretty iron circle nailed up on one wall, and a square mirror
on the other, a turquoise-blue comb stuck up in the frame, with the
washstand beneath it. On the door was a wooden knob with a pearl
in the end, and Solomon's black hat hung on that, if he was in the
house.

Out front was a clean dirt yard with every vestige of grass patiently uprooted and the ground scarred in deep whorls from the
strike of Livvie's broom. Rosebushes with tiny blood-red roses blooming every month grew in threes on either side of the steps. On one
side was a peach tree, on the other a pomegranate. Then coming
around up the path from the deep cut of the Natchez Trace below
was a line of bare crape-myrtle trees with every branch of them ending in a colored bottle, green or blue. There was no word that fell
from Solomon's lips to say what they were for, but Livvie knew that
there could be a spell put in trees, and she was familiar from the time
she was born with the way bottle trees keep evil spirits from coming
into the house—by luring them inside the colored bottles, where they

cannot get out again. Solomon had made the bottle trees with his own hands over the nine years, in labor amounting to about a tree a year, and without a sign that he had any uneasiness in his heart, for he took as much pride in his precautions against spirits coming in the house as he took in the house, and sometimes in the sun the bottle trees looked prettier than the house did.

But there was nobody, nobody at all, not even a white person. And if there had been anybody, Solomon would not have let Livvie look at them, just as he would not let her look at a field hand, or a field hand look at her. There was no house near, except for the cabins of the tenants that were forbidden to her, and there was no house as far as she had been, stealing away down the still, deep trace. She felt as if she waded a river when she went, for the dead leaves on the ground reached as high as her knees, and when she was all scratched and bleeding she said it was not like a road that went anywhere. One day, climbing up the high bank, she had found a graveyard without a church, with ribbon grass growing about the foot of an angel (she had climbed up because she thought she saw angel wings), and in the sun, trees shining like burning flames through the great caterpillar nets which enclosed them. Scarey thistles stood looking like the prophets in the Bible in Solomon's house. Indian paintbrushes grew over her head, and the mourning dove made the only sound in the world. Oh, for a stirring of the leaves, and a breaking of the nets! But not by a ghost, prayed Livvie, jumping down the bank. After Solomon took to his bed she never went out, except one more time.

Livvie knew she made a nice girl to wait on anybody. She fixed things to eat on a tray like a surprise. She could keep from singing when she ironed; and to sit by a bed and fan away the flies, she could be so still she could not hear herself breathe. She could clean up the house and never drop a thing, and wash the dishes without a sound, and she would step outside to churn, for churning sounded too sad to her, like sobbing, and if it made her homesick and not Solomon, she did not think of that.

But Solomon scarcely opened his eyes to see her, and scarcely tasted his food. He was not sick or paralyzed or in any pain that he mentioned, but he was surely wearing out in the body, and no matter what nice hot thing Livvie would bring him to taste, he would only look at it now, as if he were past seeing how he could add anything more to himself. Before she could beg him, he would go fast asleep. She could not surprise him any more if he would not taste, and she was afraid he was never in the world going to taste another thing she brought him—and so how could he last?

But one morning it was breakfast time, and she cooked his eggs and grits, carried them in on the tray, and called his name. He was sound asleep. He lay in a dignified way with his watch beside him, on his back in the middle of the bed. One hand drew the quilt up high, though it was the first day of spring. Through the white lace curtains a little puffy wind was blowing in as if it came from round cheeks. All night the frogs had sung out in the swamp like a commotion in the room, and he had not stirred, though she lay wide awake and saying, "Shh, frogs!" for fear he would mind them.

He looked as if he would like to sleep a little longer, and so she put back the tray and waited a little. When she tiptoed and stayed so quiet she surrounded herself with a little reverie, and sometimes it seemed to her, when she was so stealthy, that the quiet she kept was for a sleeping baby, and that she had a baby and was its mother. When she stood at Solomon's bed and looked down at him she would be thinking, "He sleeps so well," and she would hate to wake him up. And in some other way, too, she was afraid to wake him up because even in his sleep he seemed to be such a strict man.

Of course, nailed to the wall over the bed—only she would forget who it was—there was a picture of him when he was young. Then he had a fan of hair over his forehead like a king's crown. Now his hair lay down on his head; the spring had gone out of it. Solomon had a lightish face, with eyebrows scattered but rugged, the way privet grows, strong eyes, with second sight, a strict mouth, and a little gold smile. This was the way he looked in his clothes, but in bed in the daytime he looked like a different and smaller man, even when he was wide awake and holding the Bible. He looked like somebody kin to himself. And then sometimes when he lay in sleep and she stood fanning the flies away, and the light came in, his face was like new, so smooth and clear that it was like a glass of jelly held to the window, and she could almost look through his forehead and see what he thought.

She fanned him, and at length he opened his eyes and spoke her name, but he would not taste the nice eggs she had kept warm under a pan.

Back in the kitchen she ate heartily, his breakfast and hers, and looked out the open door at what went on. The whole day, and the whole night before, she had felt the stir of spring close to her. It was as present in the house as a young man would be. The moon was in

the last quarter, and outside they were turning the sod and planting
peas and beans. Up and down the red fields, over which smoke from
the brush burning hung, showing like a little skirt of sky, a white
horse and a white mule pulled the plow.

At intervals hoarse shouts came through the air and roused her as
if she dozed neglectfully in the shade, and they were telling her,
"Jump up!" She could see how over each ribbon of field were moving
men and girls, on foot and mounted on mules, with hats set on their
heads, and bright with tall hoes and forks as if they carried streamers
on them and were going to some place on a journey—and how as if at
a signal now and then they would all start at once shouting, hollering, cajoling, calling and answering back, running, being leaped on,
and breaking away, flinging to the earth with a shout and lying motionless in the trance of noon. The old women came out of the cabins
and brought them the food they had ready for them, and then all
worked together, spread evenly out. The little children came too, like
a bouncing stream overflowing the fields, and set upon the men, the
women, the dogs, the rushing birds, and the wavelike rows of earth,
their little voices almost too high to be heard. In the middle distance
like some white and gold towers were the haystacks, with black cows
coming around to eat their edges. High above everything—the wheel
of fields, house, and cabins, and the deep road surrounding like a
moat to keep them in—was the turning sky, blue with long, far-flung
white mare's-tail clouds, serene and still as high flames. And sound
asleep while all this went around him that was his, Solomon was like
a little still spot in the middle.

Even in the house the earth was sweet to breathe. Solomon had
never let Livvie go any farther than the chicken house and the well.
But what if she would walk now into the heart of the fields and take
a hoe and work until she fell stretched out and drenched with her
efforts, like other girls, and laid her cheek against the laid-open
earth, and shamed the old man with her humbleness and delight?
To shame him! A cruel wish could come in uninvited and so fast
while she looked out the back door. She washed the dishes and
scrubbed the table. She could hear the cries of the little lambs. Her
mother, whom she had not seen since her wedding day, had said one
time, "I rather a man be anything than a woman be mean."

So all morning she kept tasting the chicken broth on the stove,
and when it was right she poured off a nice cupful. She carried it
in to Solomon, and there he lay having a dream. Now what did he
dream about? For she saw him sigh gently as if not to disturb some
whole thing he held round in his mind, like a fresh egg. So even an

old man dreamed about something pretty. Did he dream of her, while his eyes were shut and sunken, and his small hand with the wedding ring curled close in sleep around the quilt? He might be dreaming of what time it was, for even through his sleep he kept track of it like a clock, and knew how much of it went by, and waked up knowing where the hands were, even before he consulted the silver watch that he never let go. He would sleep with the watch in his palm, and even holding it to his cheek like a child that loves a plaything. Or he might dream of journeys and travels on a steamboat to Natchez. Yet she thought he dreamed of her; but even while she scrutinized him the rods of the foot of the bed seemed to rise up like a rail fence between them, and she could see that people never could be sure of anything as long as one of them was asleep and the other awake. To look at him dreaming of her when he might be going to die frightened her a little, as if he might carry her with him that way, and she wanted to run out of the room. She took hold of the bed and held on, and Solomon opened his eyes and called her name, but he did not want anything. He would not taste the good broth.

Just a little after that, as she was taking up the ashes in the front room for the last time in the year, she heard a sound. It was somebody coming. She pulled the curtains together and looked through the slit.

Coming up the path under the bottle trees was a white lady. At first she looked young, but then she looked old. Marvelous to see, a little car stood steaming like a kettle out in the field track—it had come without a road.

Livvie stood listening to the long, repeated knockings at the door, and then she opened it just a little. The lady came in through the crack, though she was more than middlesized and wore a big hat.

"My name is Miss Baby Marie," she said.

Livvie gazed respectfully at the lady and at the little suitcase she was holding close to her by the handle until the proper moment. The lady's eyes were running over the room, from palmetto to palmetto, but she was saying, "I live at home . . . out from Natchez . . . and get out and show these pretty cosmetic things to the white people and the colored people both . . . all around . . . years and years . . . both shades of powder and rouge . . . it's the kind of work a girl can do and not go clear 'way from home. . . ." And the harder she looked, the faster she talked. Suddenly she turned up her nose and said, "It is not Christian or sanitary to put feathers in a vase," and then she took a gold key out of the front of her dress and began unlocking the locks on her suitcase. Her face drew the light, the way it was covered with intense white and red, with a little patty-cake of white between the wrinkles by her upper lip. Little red tassels of hair bobbed under the rusty wires of her picture hat, as with an air of triumph and secrecy she now drew open her little suitcase and brought out bottle after bottle and jar after jar, which she put down on the table, the mantelpiece, the settee, and the organ.

"Did you ever see so many cosmetics in your life?" asked Miss Baby Marie.

"No'm," Livvie tried to say, but the cat had her tongue.

"Have you ever applied cosmetics?" asked Miss Baby Marie next. "No'm."

"Then look!" she said, and pulling out the last thing of all, "Try this!" she said. And in her hand was unclenched a golden lipstick which popped open like magic. A fragrance came out of it like incense, and Livvie cried out suddenly, "Chinaberry flowers!"

Her hand took the lipstick, and in an instant she was carried away in the air through the spring; and looking down with a half-drowsy smile from a purple cloud which floated above a chinaberry tree, dark and smooth and neatly leaved, neat as a guinea hen in the door-yard, she saw again her home that she had left. On one side of the tree was her mama holding up her heavy apron, and she could see it was loaded with ripe figs; and on the other side was her papa holding a fish pole over the pond, and she could see it transparently, the little clear fishes swimming up to the brim.

"Oh no, not chinaberry flowers—secret ingredients," said Miss Baby Marie. "My cosmetics have secret ingredients—not chinaberry flowers."

"It's purple," Livvie breathed, and Miss Baby Marie said, "Use it freely. Rub it on."

Livvie tiptoed out to the washstand on the front porch and, before the mirror, put the paint on her mouth. In the wavery surface her face danced before her like a flame. Miss Baby Marie followed her out, took a look at what she had done, and said, "That's it."

Livvie tried to say "Thank you" without moving her parted lips where the paint lay so new.

By now Miss Baby Marie stood behind Livvie and looked in the mirror over her shoulder, twisting up the tassels of her hair. "The lipstick I can let you have for only two dollars," she said, close to her neck.

"Lady, but I don't have no money, never did have," said Livvie.

"Oh, but you don't pay the first time. I make another trip, that's the way I do. I come back again—later."

"Oh—*then.*"

"But if you don't take it now, this may be the last time I'll call at your house," said Miss Baby Marie sharply. "It's far away from any-where, I'll tell you that. You don't live close to anywhere."

"Yes'm. My husband, he keep the *money,*" said Livvie, trembling. "He is strict as he can be. He don't know *you* walk in here—Miss Baby Marie!"

"Where is he?"

"In yonder, sound asleep, an old man. I wouldn't ever ask him for anything."

Miss Baby Marie took back the lipstick and packed it up. She gathered up her jars and got them all inside the suitcase, with the same little fuss of triumph with which she had brought them out. She started away.

"Good-by," she said, making herself look grand from the back, but she could not help turning around in the door. Her old hat wobbled as she whispered, "Let me see your husband."

Livvie obediently went on tiptoe and opened the door to the other room. Miss Baby Marie came behind her and rose on her toes and looked in.

"My, what a little tiny old, old man!" she whispered, clasping her hands and shaking her head over them. "What a beautiful quilt! What a tiny old, old man!"

"He can sleep like that all day," whispered Livvie proudly.

They looked at him awhile so fast asleep, and then they looked at each other. Somehow that was as if they had a secret, for he had never stirred. Livvie then politely, but all at once, closed the door.

"Well! I'd certainly like to leave you with a lipstick!" said Miss Baby Marie vivaciously. She smiled in the door.

"Lady, I told you I don't have no money and never did have."

"And never will?" In the air and all around, like a bright halo around the white lady's nodding head, it was a true spring day.

"Would you take eggs, lady?" asked Livvie softly.

"No, eggs I have plenty of," said Miss Baby Marie.

"I still don't have no money," said Livvie, and Miss Baby Marie took her suitcase and went on somewhere else.

Livvie stood watching her go, and all the time she felt her heart beating in her left side. She touched the place with her hand. It seemed as if her heart beat and her whole face flamed from the puls-ing color of her lips. She went in to sit by Solomon, and when he opened his eyes he could not see a change in her. "He's fixin' to die," she said inside. That was the secret. That was when she went out of the house for a little breath of air.

She went down the path and down the Natchez Trace a way, and she did not know how far she had gone, but it was not far, when she saw a sight. It was a man, looking like a vision—she standing on one side of the Old Natchez Trace and he standing on the other.

As soon as this man caught sight of her, he began to look himself over. Starting at the bottom with his pointed shoes, he began to look up, lifting his peg-top pants the higher to see fully his bright socks. His coat, long and wide and leaf-green, he opened like doors to see his high-up tawny pants, and his pants he smoothed downward from the points of his collar, and he wore a luminous baby-pink satin shirt. At the end he reached gently above his wide platter-shaped round hat, the color of a plum, and one finger touched at the feather, emerald green, blowing in the spring winds.

No matter how she looked, she could never look so fine as he did, and she was not sorry for that, she was pleased.

He took three jumps, one down and two up, and was by her side. "My name is Cash," he said.

He had a guinea pig in his pocket. They began to walk along. She stared on and on at him, as if he were doing some daring spectacular thing, instead of just walking beside her. It was not simply the city way he was dressed that made her look at him and see hope in its insolence looking back. It was not only the way he moved along, kicking the flowers as if he could break through everything in the way and destroy anything in the world, that made her eyes grow bright. It might be, if he had not appeared the way he did appear that day, she would never have looked so closely at him, but the time people come makes a difference.

They walked through the still leaves of the Natchez Trace, the light and the dark falling through trees about them, the white irises shining like candles on the banks and the new ferns shining like green stars up in the oak branches. They came out at Solomon's house, bottle trees and all. Livvie stopped and hung her head.

Cash began whistling a little tune. She did not know what it was, but she had heard it before from a distance, and she had a revelation. Cash was a field hand. He was a transformed field hand. Cash belonged to Solomon. But he had stepped out of his overalls into this. There in front of Solomon's house he laughed. He had a round head, a round face; all of him was young, and he flung his head up, rolled it against the mare's-tail sky in his round hat, and he could laugh just to see Solomon's house sitting there. Livvie looked at it, and there was Solomon's black hat hanging on the peg on the front door, the blackest thing in the world.

"I been to Natchez," Cash said, wagging his head around against the blue sky. "I taken a trip, I been to Natchez, I been today. I am ready for Easter!"

How was it possible to look so fine before the harvest? Cash must have stolen the money. He stood in the path and lifted his spread hand high and brought it down again and again in his laughter. He kicked up his heels. A chill went through her. It was as if Cash were bringing that strong hand down to beat a drum or to rain blows upon a man, such an abandon and menace were in his laugh. Frowning, she went closer to him, and his swinging arm drew her in at once and the fright was crushed from her body, as a little match flame might be smothered out by what it lighted. She gathered the folds of his coat behind him and fastened her red lips to his mouth, and she was dazzled at herself then, the way he had been dazzled at himself to begin with.

In that instant she felt something that could not be told—that Solomon's death was at hand, that he was the same to her as if he were dead now. She cried out and, uttering little cries, turned and ran for the house.

At once Cash was coming, following after; he was running behind her. He came close, and halfway up the path he laughed and passed her. He even picked up a stone and sailed it into the bottle trees. She put her hands over her head, and sounds clattered through the bottle trees like cries of outrage. Cash stamped and plunged zigzag up the front steps and in at the door.

When she got there he had stuck his hands in his pockets and was turning slowly about in the front room. The little guinea pig peeped out. Around Cash the pinned-up palmettos looked as if a lazy green monkey had walked up and down and around the walls leaving green prints of his hands and feet.

She got through the room, and his hands were still in his pockets, and fell upon the closed door to the other room and pushed it open. She ran to Solomon's bed, calling "Solomon! Solomon!" The little shape of the old man never moved at all, wrapped under the quilt as if it were winter still.

"Solomon!" She pulled the quilt away, but there was another one under that, and she fell on her knees beside him. He made no sound except a sigh, and then she could hear in the silence the light springy steps of Cash walking and walking in the front room, and the ticking of Solomon's silver watch, which came from the bed. Old Solomon was far away in his sleep; his face looked small, relentless, and devout, as if he were walking somewhere where she could imagine the snow falling.

Then there was a noise like a hoof pawing the floor, and the door gave a creak, and Cash appeared beside her. When she looked up Cash's face was so black it was bright, and so bright and bare of pity that it looked sweet to her. She stood up and held up her head. Cash was so powerful that his presence gave her strength even when she did not need any.

Under their eyes Solomon slept. People's faces tell of things and places not known to the one who looks at them while they sleep, and while Solomon slept under the eyes of Livvie and Cash his face told them like a mythical story how all his life he had built, little scrap by little scrap, respect. A beetle could not have been more laborious or more ingenious in the task of its destiny. When Solomon was young, as he was in his picture overhead, it was the infinite thing with him, and he could see no end to the respect he would contrive and keep in a house. He had built a lonely house, the way he would make a cage, but it grew to be the same with him as a great monumental pyramid, and sometimes in his absorption of getting it erected he was like the builder slaves of Egypt who forgot or never knew the origin and meaning of the thing to which they gave all the strength of their bodies and used up all their days. Livvie and Cash could see that as a man might rest from a life labor he lay in his bed, and they could hear how, wrapped in his quilt, he sighed to himself comfortably in sleep, while in his dream he might have been an ant, a beetle, a bird, an Egyptian, assembling and carrying on his back and building with his hands, or he might have been an old man of India or a swaddled baby about to smile and brush all away.

Then without warning old Solomon's eyes flew wide open under the hedgelike brows. He was wide awake.

And instantly Cash raised his quick arm. A radiant sweat stood on his temples. But he did not bring his arm down—it stayed in the air, as if something might have taken hold.

It was not Livvie—she did not move. As if something said "Wait," she stood waiting. Even while her eyes burned under motionless lids, her lips parted in a stiff grimace, and with her arms stiff at her sides she stood above the prone old man and the panting young one, erect and apart.

Movement, when it came, came in Solomon's face. It was an old and strict face, a frail face, but behind it, like a covered light, came an animation that could play hide-and-seek, that would dart and escape—had always escaped. The mystery flickered in him and invited from his eyes. It was that very mystery that Cash with his quick arm would have to strike, and that Livvie could not weep for. But Cash only stood holding his arm in the air, when the gentlest flick of his great strength, almost a puff of his breath, would have been enough, if he had known how to give it, to send the old man over the obstruction that kept him away from death. If it could not be that the tiny illumination in the fragile and ancient face caused a crisis, a mystery in the room that would not permit a blow to fall, at least it was certain that Cash, throbbing in his Easter clothes, felt a pang of shame that the vigor of a man would come to such an end that he could not be struck without warning. He took down his hand and stepped back behind Livvie, like a round-eyed schoolboy on whose unsuspecting head the dunce cap has been placed.

"Young ones can't wait," said Solomon.

Livvie shuddered violently, and then in a gush of tears she stooped for a glass of water and handed it to him, but he did not see her.

"So here come the young man Livvie wait for. There was no prevention. No prevention. Now I lay eyes on him and it come to be somebody I know all the time, and been knowing since he were born in a cotton patch, and watched grow up year to year, Cash McCord, growed to size, growed to come in my house in the end—ragged and barefoot."

Solomon gave a cough of distaste. Then he shut his eyes vigorously, and his lips began to move like a chanter's.

"When Livvie married, her husband were already somebody. He had paid great cost for his land. He spread sycamore leaves over the ground from wagon to door, day he brought her home, so her foot would not have to touch ground. He carried her through his door. Then he growed old and could not lift her, and she were still young."

Livvie's sobs followed his words like a soft melody repeating each thing as he stated it. His lips moved for a little without sound, or she cried too fervently, and unheard he might have been telling his whole life, and then he said, "God forgive Solomon for sins great and small. God forgive Solomon for carrying away too young a wife and keeping her away from her people and from young people who would want her back."

Then he lifted up his right hand toward Livvie where she stood by the bed, and offered her his silver watch. He dangled it before her eyes, and she hushed crying; her tears stopped. For a moment the watch could be heard ticking precisely in his proud hand. She lifted it away. Then he took hold of the quilt; then he was dead.

Livvie left Solomon dead and went out of the room. Stealthily, nearly without noise, Cash went beside her. He was like a shadow, but his shiny shoes moved over the floor in spangles, and the green downy feather shone like a light in his hat. As they reached the front room he seized her deftly as a long black cat and dragged her hanging by the waist round and round him, while he turned in a circle, his face bent down to hers. The first moment she kept one arm and its hand stiff and still, the one that held Solomon's watch. Then the fingers softly let go, all of her was limp, and the watch fell somewhere on the floor. It ticked away in the still room, and all at once there began outside the full song of a bird.

They moved around and around the room and into the brightness of the open door, then he stopped and shook her once. She rested in silence in his trembling arms, unprotesting as a bird on a nest. Outside the redbirds were flying and crisscrossing, the sun was in all the bottles on the prisoned trees, and the young peach was shining in the middle of them with the bursting light of spring.

The Demonstrators

Near eleven o'clock that Saturday night the doctor stopped again by his office. He had recently got into playing a weekly bridge game at the club, but tonight it had been interrupted for the third time, and he'd just come from attending to Miss Marcia Pope. Now bedridden, scorning all medication and in particular tranquillizers, she had a seizure every morning before breakfast and often on Saturday night for some reason, but had retained her memory; she could amuse herself by giving out great wads of Shakespeare and *Arma virumque cano,*" or the like. The more forcefully Miss Marcia Pope declaimed, the more innocent grew her old face—the lines went right out.

"She'll sleep naturally now, I think," he'd told the companion, still in her rocker.

Mrs. Warrum did well, perhaps hadn't hit yet on an excuse to quit that suited her. She failed to be alarmed by Miss Marcia Pope, either in convulsions or in recitation. From where she lived, she'd never gone to school to this lady, who had taught three generations of Holden, Mississippi, its Latin, civics, and English, and who had carried, for forty years, a leather satchel bigger than the doctor's bag.

As he'd snapped his bag shut tonight, Miss Marcia had opened her eyes and spoken distinctly: "Richard Strickland? I have it on my report that Irene Roberts is not where she belongs. Now which of you wants the whipping?"

"It's all right, Miss Marcia. She's still my wife," he'd said, but could not be sure the answer got by her.

In the office, he picked up the city newspaper he subscribed to —seeing as he did so the picture on the front of a young man burning his draft card before a camera—and locked up, ready to face home. As he came down the stairway onto the street, his sleeve was plucked.

It was a Negro child. "We got to hurry," she said.

His bag was still in the car. She climbed into the back and stood there behind his ear as he drove down the hill. He met the marshal's car as both bounced over the railroad track—no passenger rode with the marshal that he could see—and the doctor asked the child, "Who got hurt? Whose house?" But she could only tell him how to get there, an alley at a time, till they got around the cottonseed mill.

Down here, the street lights were out tonight. The last electric light of any kind appeared to be the one burning in the vast shrouded cavern of the gin. His car lights threw into relief the dead goldenrod that stood along the road and made it look heavier than the bridge across the creek.

As soon as the child leaned on his shoulder and he had stopped the car, he heard men's voices; but at first his eyes could make out little but an assembly of white forms spaced in the air near a low roof—chickens roosting in a tree. Then he saw the reds of cigarettes. A dooryard was as packed with a standing crowd as if it were funeral time. They were all men. Still more people seemed to be moving from the nearby churchyard and joining onto the crowd in front of the house.

The men parted before them as he went following the child up broken steps and across a porch. A kerosene lamp was being held for him in the doorway. He stepped into a roomful of women. The child kept going, went to the foot of an iron bed and stopped. The lamp came up closer behind him and he followed a path of newspapers laid down on the floor from the doorway to the bed.

A dark quilt was pulled up to the throat of a girl alive on the bed. A pillow raised her at the shoulders. The dome of her forehead looked thick as a battering ram, because of the rolling of her eyes.

Dr. Strickland turned back the quilt. The young, very black-skinned woman lay in a white dress with her shoes on. A maid? Then he saw that of course the white was not the starched material of a uniform but shiny, clinging stuff, and there was a banner of some kind crossing it in a crumpled red line from the shoulder. He unfastened the knot at the waist and got the banner out of the way. The skintight satin had been undone at the neck already; as he parted it farther, the girl kicked at the foot of the bed. He exposed the breast and then, before her hand had pounced on his, the wound below the breast. There was a small puncture with little evidence of external bleeding. He had seen splashes of blood on the dress, now almost dry.

"Go boil me some water. Too much excitement to send for the doctor a little earlier?"

The girl clawed at his hand with her sticky nails.

"Have you touched her?" he asked.

"See there? And she don't want you trying it, either," said a voice in the room.

A necklace like sharp and pearly teeth was fastened around her throat. It was when he took that off that the little girl who had been sent for him cried out. "I bid that!" she said, but without coming nearer. He found no other wounds.

"Does it hurt you to breathe?" He spoke almost absently as he addressed the girl.

The nipples of her breasts cast shadows that looked like figs; she would not take a deep breath when he used the stethoscope. Sweat in the airless room, in the bed, rose and seemed to weaken and unstick the newspapered walls like steam from a kettle already boiling; it glazed his own white hand, his tapping fingers. It was the stench of sensation. The women's faces coming nearer were streaked in the hot lamplight. Somewhere close to the side of his head something glittered; hung over the knob of the bedpost, where a boy would have tossed his cap, was a tambourine. He let the stethoscope fall, and heard women's sighs travel around the room, domestic sounds like a broom being flirted about, women getting ready for company.

"Stand back," he said. "You got a fire on in here?" Warm as it was, crowded as it was in here, he looked behind him and saw the gas heater burning, half the radiants burning blue. The girl, with lips turned down, lay pulling away while he took her pulse.

The child who had been sent for him and then had been sent to heat the water brought the kettle in from the kitchen too soon and had to be sent back to make it boil. When it was ready and in the pan, the lamp was held closer; it was beside his elbow as if to singe his arm.

"Stand back," he said. Again and again the girl's hand had to be forced away from her breast. The wound quickened spasmodically as if it responded to light.

"Icepick?"

"You right this time," said voices in the room.

"Who did this to her?"

The room went quiet; he only heard the men in the yard laughing together. "How long ago?" He looked at the path of newspapers spread on the floor. "Where? Where did it happen? How did she get here?"

He had an odd feeling that somewhere in the room somebody was sending out beckoning smiles in his direction. He lifted, half turned his head. The elevated coal that glowed at regular intervals was the pipe of an old woman in a boiled white apron standing near the door.

He persisted. "Has she coughed up anything yet?"

"Don't you know her?" they cried, as if he never was going to hit on the right question.

He let go the girl's arm, and her hand started its way back again to her wound. Sending one glowing look at him, she covered it again. As if she had spoken, he recognized her.

"Why, it's Ruby," he said.

Ruby Gaddy *was* the maid. Five days a week she cleaned up on the second floor of the bank building where he kept his office and consulting rooms.

He said to her, "Ruby, this is Dr. Strickland. What have you been up to?"

"*Nothin'!*" everybody cried for her.

The girl's eyes stopped rolling and rested themselves on the expressionless face of the little girl, who again stood at the foot of the bed watching from this restful distance. Look equalled look: sisters.

"Am I supposed to just know?" The doctor looked all around him. An infant was sitting up on the splintery floor near his feet, he now saw, on a clean newspaper, a spoon stuck pipelike in its mouth. From out in the yard at that moment came a regular guffaw, not much different from the one that followed the telling of a dirty story or a race story by one of the clowns in the Elks' Club. He frowned at the baby; and the baby, a boy, looked back over his upside down spoon and gave it a long audible suck.

"She married? Where's her husband? That where the trouble was?"

Now, while the women in the room, too, broke out in sounds of amusement, the doctor stumbled where he stood. "What the devil's running in here? Rats?"

"You wrong there."

Guinea pigs were running underfoot, not only in this room but on the other side of the wall, in the kitchen where the water had finally got boiled. Somebody's head turned toward the leaf end of a stalk of celery wilting on top of the Bible on the table.

"Catch those things!" he exclaimed.

The baby laughed; the rest copied the baby.

"They lightning. Get away from you so fast!" said a voice.

"Them guinea pigs ain't been caught since they was born. Let you try."

"Know why? 'Cause they's Dove's. Dove left 'em here when he move out, just to be in the way."

The doctor felt the weight recede from Ruby's fingers, and saw it flatten her arm where it lay on the bed. Her eyes had closed. A little boy with a sanctimonious face had taken the bit of celery and knelt down on the floor; there was scrambling about and increasing laughter until Dr. Strickland made himself heard in the room.

"All right. I heard you. Is Dove who did it? Go on. Say."

He heard somebody spit on the stove. Then:

"It's Dove."

"Dove."

"Dove."

"Dove."

"You got it right that time."

While the name went around, passed from one mouth to the other, the doctor drew a deep breath. But the sigh that filled the room was the girl's own, luxuriously uncontained.

"Dove Collins? I believe you. I've had to sew him up enough times on Sunday morning, you all know that," said the doctor. "I know Ruby, I know Dove, and if the lights would come back on I can tell you the names of the rest of you and you know it." While he was speaking, his eyes fell on Oree, a figure of the Holden square for twenty years, whom he had inherited—sitting here in the room in her express wagon, the flowered skirt spread down from her lap and tucked in over the stumps of her knees.

While he was preparing the hypodermic, he was aware that more watchers, a row of them dressed in white with red banners like Ruby's, were coming in to fill up the corners. The lamp was lifted— higher than the dipping shadows of their heads, a valentine tacked on the wall radiated color—and then, as he leaned over the bed, the lamp was brought down closer and closer to the girl, like something that would devour her.

"Now I can't see what I'm doing," the doctor said sharply, and as the light jumped and swung behind him he thought he recognized the anger as a mother's.

"Look to me like the fight's starting to go out of Ruby mighty early," said a voice.

Still her eyes stayed closed. He gave the shot.

"Where'd he get to—Dove? Is the marshal out looking for him?" he asked.

The sister moved along the bed and put the baby down on it close to Ruby's face.

"Remove him," said the doctor.

"She don't even study him," said the sister. "Poke her," she told the baby.

"Take him out of here," ordered Dr. Strickland.

The baby opened one of his mother's eyes with his fingers. When she shut it on him he cried, as if he knew it to be deliberate of her.

"Get that baby out of here and all the kids, I tell you," Dr. Strickland said into the room. "This ain't going to be pretty."

"Carry him next door, Twosie," said a voice.

"I ain't. You all promised me if I leave long enough to get the doctor I could stand right here until." The child's voice was loud.

"O.K. Then you got to hold Roger."

The baby made a final reach for his mother's face, putting out a hand with its untrimmed nails, gray as the claw of a squirrel. The woman who had held the lamp set that down and grabbed the baby out of the bed herself. His legs began churning even before she struck him a blow on the side of the head.

"You trying to raise him an idiot?" the doctor flung out.

"I ain't going to raise him," the mother said toward the girl on the bed.

The deliberation had gone out of her face. She was drifting into unconsciousness. Setting her hand to one side, the doctor inspected the puncture once more. It was clean as the eye of a needle. While he stood there watching her, he lifted her hand and washed it—the wrist, horny palm, blood-caked fingers one by one.

But as he again found her pulse, he saw her eyes opening. As long as he counted he was aware of those eyes as if they loomed larger than the watch face. They were filled with the unresponding gaze of ownership. She knew what she had. Memory did not make the further effort to close the lids when he replaced her hand, or when he took her shoes off and set them on the floor, or when he stepped away from the bed and again the full lamplight struck her face.

The twelve-year-old stared on, over the buttress of the baby she held to her chest.

"Can you ever hush that baby?"

A satisfied voice said, "He going to keep-a-noise till he learn better."

"Well, I'd like a little peace and consideration to be shown!" the doctor said. "Try to remember there's somebody in here with you that's going to be pumping mighty hard to breathe." He raised a finger and pointed it at the old woman in the boiled apron whose pipe had continued to glow with regularity by the door. "You stay. You sit here and watch Ruby," he called. "The rest of you clear out of here."

He closed his bag and straightened up. The woman stuck the lamp hot into his own face.

"Remember Lucille? I'm Lucille. I was washing for your mother when you was born. Let me see you do something," she said with fury. "You ain't even tied her up! You sure ain't your daddy!"

"Why, she's bleeding inside," he retorted. "What do you think *she's* doing?"

They hushed. For a minute all he heard was the guinea pigs racing. He looked back at the girl; her eyes were fixed with possession. "I gave her a shot. She'll just go to sleep. If she doesn't, call me and I'll come back and give her another one. One of you kindly bring me a drink of water," the doctor continued in the same tone.

With a crash, hushed off like cymbals struck by mistake, something was moved on the kitchen side of the wall. The little boy who had held the celery to catch the guinea pigs came in carrying a teacup. He passed through the room and out onto the porch, where he could be heard splashing fresh water from a pump. He came back inside and at arm's length held the cup out to the doctor.

Dr. Strickland drank with a thirst they all could and did follow. The cup, though it held the whole smell of this house in it, was of thin china, was an old one.

Then he stepped across the gaze of the girl on the bed as he would have had to step over a crack yawning in the floor.

"Fixing to leave?" asked the old woman in the boiled white apron, who still stood up by the door, the pipe gone from her lips. He then remembered her. In the days when he travelled East to medical school, she used to be the sole factotum at the Holden depot when the passenger train came through sometime between two and three in the morning. It was always late. Circling the pewlike benches of the waiting rooms, she carried around coffee which she poured boiling hot into paper cups out of a white-enamelled pot that looked as long as her arm. She wore then, in addition to the apron, a white and flaring head covering—something between a chef's cap and a sunbonnet. As the train at last steamed in, she called the stations. She didn't use a loudspeaker but just the power of her lungs. In all the natural volume of her baritone voice she thundered them out to the scattered and few who had waited under lights too poor to read by—first in the colored waiting room, then in the white waiting room, to echo both times from the vault of the roof: ". . . Meridian. Birmingham. Chattanooga. Bristol. Lynchburg. Washington. Baltimore. Philadelphia. And New York." Seizing all the bags, two by two, in her own hands, walking slowly in front of the passengers, she saw to it that they left.

He said to her, "I'm going, but you're not. You're keeping a watch on Ruby. Don't let her slide down in the bed. Call me if you need me." As a boy, had he never even wondered what her name was—this tyrant? He didn't know it now. He put the cup into her reaching hand. "Aren't you ready to leave?" he asked Oree, the legless woman. She still lived by the tracks where the train had cut off her legs.

"I ain't in no hurry," she replied and as he passed her she called her usual "Take it easy, Doc."

When he stepped outside onto the porch, he saw that there was moonlight everywhere. Uninterrupted by any lights from Holden, it filled the whole country lying out there in the haze of the long rainless fall. He himself stood on the edge of Holden. Just one house and one church farther, the Delta began, and the cotton fields ran into the scattered paleness of a dimmed-out Milky Way.

Nobody called him back, yet he turned his head and got a sideways glimpse all at once of a row of dresses hung up across the front of the house, starched until they could have stood alone (as his mother complained), and in an instant had recognized his mother's gardening dress, his sister Annie's golf dress, his wife's favorite duster that she liked to wear to the breakfast table, and more dresses, less substantial. Elevated across the front of the porch, they were hung again between him and the road. With sleeves spread wide, trying to scratch his forehead with the tails of their skirts, they were flying around this house in the moonlight.

The moment of vertigo passed, as a small black man came up the steps and across the porch wearing heeltaps on his shoes.

"Sister Gaddy entered yet into the gates of joy?"

"No, Preacher, you're in time," said the doctor.

As soon as he left the house, he heard it become as noisy as the yard had been, and the men in the yard went quiet to let him through. From the road, he saw the moon itself. It was above the tree with the chickens in it; it might have been one of the chickens flown loose. He scraped children off the hood of his car, pulled another from position at the wheel, and climbed inside. He turned the car around in the churchyard. There was a flickering light inside the church. Flat-roofed as a warehouse, it had its shades pulled down like a bedroom. This was the church where the sounds of music and dancing came from habitually on many another night besides Sunday, clearly to be heard on top of the hill.

He drove back along the road, across the creek, its banks glittering now with the narrow bottles, the size of harmonicas, in which paregoric was persistently sold under the name of Mother's Helper. The telephone wires along the road were hung with shreds of cotton, the sides of the road were strewn with them too, as if the doctor were out on a paper chase.

He passed the throbbing mill, working on its own generator. No lights ever shone through the windowless and now moonlit sheet iron, but the smell came out freely and spread over the town at large —a cooking smell, like a dish ordered by a man with an endless appetite. Pipes hung with streamers of lint fed into the moonlit gin, and wagons and trucks heaped up round as the gypsy caravans or circus wagons of his father's, or even his grandfather's, stories, stood this way and that, waiting in the yard outside.

Far down the railroad track, beyond the unlighted town, rose the pillowshaped glow of a grass fire. It was gaseous, unveined, unblotted by smoke, a cloud with the November flush of the sedge grass by day, sparkless and nerveless, not to be confused with a burning church, but like anesthetic made visible.

Then a long beam of electric light came solid as a board from behind him to move forward along the long loading platform, to some bales of cotton standing on it, some of them tumbled one against the others as if pushed by the light; then it ran up the wall of the dark station so you could read the name, "Holden." The hooter sounded. This was a grade crossing with a bad record, and it seemed to the doctor that he had never started over it in his life that something was not bearing down. He stopped the car, and as the train in its heat began to pass in front of him he saw it to be a doubleheader, a loaded freight this time. It was going right on through Holden.

He cut off his motor. One of the sleepers rocked and complained with every set of wheels that rolled over it. Presently the regular, slow creaking reminded the doctor of an old-fashioned porch swing holding lovers in the dark.

He had been carried a cup tonight that might have been his own mother's china or his wife's mother's—the rim not a perfect round, a thin, porcelain cup his lips and his fingers had recognized. In that house of murder, comfort had been brought to him at his request. After drinking from it he had all but reeled into a flock of dresses stretched wide-sleeved across the porch of that house like a child's drawing of angels.

Faintly rocked by the passing train, he sat bent at the wheel of the car, and the feeling of well-being persisted. It increased, until he had come to the point of tears.

The doctor was the son of a doctor, practicing in his father's office; all the older patients, like Miss Marcia Pope—and like Lucille and Oree—spoke of his father, and some confused the young doctor with the old; but not they. The watch he carried was the gold one that had belonged to his father. Richard had grown up in Holden, married "the prettiest girl in the Delta." Except for his years at the university and then at medical school and during his interneship, he had lived here at home and had carried on the practice—the only practice in town. Now his father and his mother both were dead, his sister had married and moved away, a year ago his child had died. Then, back in the summer, he and his wife had separated, by her wish.

Sylvia had been their only child. Until her death from pneumonia last Christmas, at the age of thirteen, she had never sat up or spoken. He had loved her and mourned her all her life; she had been injured at birth. But Irene had done more; she had dedicated her life to Sylvia, sparing herself nothing, tending her, lifting her, feeding her, everything. What do you do after giving all your devotion to something that cannot be helped, and that has been taken away? You give all your devotion to something else that cannot be helped. But you shun all the terrible reminders, and turn not to a human being but to an idea.

Last June, there had come along a student, one of the civil-rights workers, calling at his office with a letter of introduction. For the sake of an old friend, the doctor had taken him home to dinner. (He had been reminded of him once tonight, already, by a photograph in the city paper.) He remembered that the young man had already finished talking about his work. They had just laughed around the table after Irene had quoted the classic question the governor-before-this-one had asked, after a prison break: "If you can't trust a trusty, who can you trust?" Then the doctor had remarked, "Speaking of who can you trust, what's this I read in your own paper, Philip? It said some of your outfit over in the next county were forced at gun-point to go into the fields at hundred-degree temperature and pick cotton. Well, that didn't happen—there isn't any cotton in June."

"I asked myself the same question you do. But I told myself, 'Well, they won't know the difference where the paper is read,'" said the young man.

"It's lying, though."

"We are dramatizing your hostility," the young bearded man had corrected him. "It's a way of reaching people. Don't forget—what they *might* have done to us is even worse."

"Still—you're not justified in putting a false front on things, in my opinion," Dr. Strickland had said. "Even for a good cause."

"*You* won't tell Herman Fairbrothers what's the matter with him," said his wife, and she jumped up from the table.

Later, as a result of this entertainment, he supposed, broken glass had been spread the length and breadth of his driveway. He hadn't seen in time what it wouldn't have occurred to him to look for, and Irene, standing in the door, had suddenly broken into laughter. . . .

He had eventually agreed that she have her wish and withdraw herself for as long as she liked. She was back now where she came from, where, he'd heard, they were all giving parties for her. He had offered to be the one to leave. "Leave Holden without its Dr. Strickland? You wouldn't to save your soul, would you?" she had replied. But as yet it was not divorce.

He thought he had been patient, but patience had made him tired. He was so increasingly tired, so sick and even bored with the bitterness, intractability that divided everybody and everything.

And suddenly, tonight, things had seemed just the way they used to seem. He had felt as though someone had stopped him on the street and offered to carry his load for a while—had insisted on it— some old, trusted, half-forgotten family friend that he has lost sight of since youth. Was it the sensation, now returning, that there was still allowed to everybody on earth a *self*—savage, death-defying, private? The pounding of his heart was like the assault of hope, throwing itself against him without a stop, merciless.

It seemed a long time that he had sat there, but the cars were still going by. Here came the caboose. He had counted them without knowing it—seventy-two cars. The grass fire at the edge of town came back in sight.

The doctor's feeling gradually ebbed away, like nausea put down. He started up the car and drove across the track and on up the hill.

Candles, some of them in dining-room candelabra, burned clear across the upstairs windows in the Fairbrothers' house. His own house, next door, was of course dark, and while he was wondering where Irene kept candles for emergencies he had driven on past his driveway for the second time that night. But the last place he wanted to go now was back to the club. He'd only tried it anyway to please his sister Annie. Now that he'd got by Miss Marcia Pope's dark window, he smelled her sweet-olive tree, solid as the bank building.

Here stood the bank, with its doorway onto the stairs to Drs.

Strickland & Strickland, their names in black and gilt on three windows. He passed it. The haze and the moonlight were one over the square, over the row of storefronts opposite with the line of poles thin as matchsticks rising to prop the one long strip of tin over the sidewalk, the drygoods store with its ornamental top that looked like opened paper fans held up by acrobats. He slowly started around the square. Behind its iron railings, the courthouse-and-jail stood barely emerging from its black cave of trees and only the slicked iron steps of the stile caught the moon. He drove on, past the shut-down movie house with all the light bulbs unscrewed from the sign that spelled out in empty sockets "BROADWAY." In front of the new post office the flagpole looked feathery, like the track of a jet that is already gone from the sky. From in front of the fire station, the fire chief's old Buick had gone home.

What was there, who was there, to keep him from going home? The doctor drove on slowly around. From the center of the deserted pavement, where cars and wagons stood parked helter-skelter by day, rose the water tank, pale as a balloon that might be only tethered here. A clanking came out of it, for the water supply too had been a source of trouble this summer—a hollow, irregular knocking now and then from inside, but the doctor no longer heard it. In turning his car, he saw a man lying prone and colorless in the arena of moonlight.

The lights of the car fastened on him and his clothes turned golden yellow. The man looked as if he had been sleeping all day in a bed of flowers and rolled in their pollen and were sleeping there still, with his face buried. He was covered his length in cottonseed meal.

Dr. Strickland stopped the car short and got out. His footsteps made the only sound in town. The man raised up on his hands and looked at him like a seal. Blood laced his head like a net through which he had broken. His wide tongue hung down out of his mouth. But the doctor knew the face.

"So you're alive, Dove, you're still alive?"

Slowly, hardly moving his tongue, Dove said: "Hide me." Then he hemorrhaged through the mouth.

Through the other half of the night, the doctor's calls came to him over the telephone—all chronic cases. Eva Duckett Fairbrothers telephoned at daylight.

"Feels low in his mind? Of course he feels low in his mind," he had finally shouted at her. "If I had what Herman has, I'd go down in the back yard and shoot myself!"

The *Sentinel,* owned and edited by Horatio Duckett, came out on Tuesdays. The next week's back-page headline read, "TWO DEAD, ONE ICEPICK. FREAK EPISODE AT NEGRO CHURCH." The subhead read, "No Racial Content Espied."

The doctor sat at the table in his dining room, finishing breakfast as he looked it over.

An employee of the Fairbrothers Cotton Seed Oil Mill and a Holden maid, both Negroes, were stabbed with a sharp instrument judged to be an icepick in a crowded churchyard here Saturday night. Both later expired. The incident was not believed by Mayor Herman Fairbrothers to carry racial significance.

"It warrants no stir," the Mayor declared.

The mishap boosted Holden's weekend death toll to 3. Billy Lee Warrum Jr. died Sunday before reaching a hospital in Jackson where he was rushed after being thrown from his new motorcycle while on his way there. He was the oldest son of Mrs. Billy Lee Warrum, Rt. 1. Reputedly en route to see his fiance he was pronounced dead on arrival. Multiple injuries was listed as the cause, the motorcycle having speeded into an interstate truck loaded to capacity with holiday turkeys. (See eye-witness account, page 1.)

As Holden marshal Curtis "Cowboy" Stubblefield reconstructed the earlier mishap, Ruby Gaddy, 21, was stabbed in full view of the departing congregation of the Holy Gospel Tabernacle as she attempted to leave the church when services were concluded at approximately 9:30 P.M. Saturday.

Witnesses said Dove Collins, 25, appeared outside the church as early as 9:15 P.M. having come directly from his shift at the mill where he had been employed since 1959. On being invited to come in and be seated he joked and said he preferred to wait outdoors as he was only wearing work clothes until the Gaddy woman, said to be his common-law wife, came outside the frame structure.

In the ensuing struggle at the conclusion of the services, the woman, who was a member of the choir, is believed to have received fatal ice-pick injuries to a vital organ, then to have wrested the weapon from her assailant and paid him back in kind. The Gaddy woman then walked to her mother's house but later collapsed.

Members of the congregation said they chased Collins 13 or 14 yds. in the direction of Snake Creek on the South side of the church then he fell to the ground and rolled approximately ten feet down the bank, rolling over six or seven times. Those present believed him to have succumbed since it was said the pick while in the woman's hand had been seen to drive in and pierce either his ear or his eye, either of which, is in close approximation to the brain. However, Collins later managed to crawl unseen from the creek and to make his way undetected up Railroad Avenue and to the Main St. door of an office occupied by Richard Strickland, M.D., above the Citizens Bank & Trust.

Witnesses were divided on which of the Negroes struck the first blow. Percy McAtee, pastor of the church, would not take sides but declared on being questioned by Marshal Stubblefield he was satisfied no outside agitators were involved and no arrests were made.

Collins was discovered on his own doorstep by Dr. Strickland who had been spending the evening at the Country Club. Collins is reported by Dr. Strickland to have expired shortly following his discovery, alleging his death to chest wounds.

"He offered no statement," Dr. Strickland said in response to a query.

Interviewed at home where he is recuperating from an ailment, Mayor Fairbrothers stated that he had not heard of there being trouble of any description at the Mill. "We are not trying to ruin our good reputation by inviting any, either," he said. "If the weatherman stays on our side we expect to attain capacity production in the latter part of next month," he stated. Saturday had been pay day as usual.

When Collins' body was searched by officers the pockets were empty however.

An icepick, reportedly the property of the Holy Gospel Tabernacle, was later found by Deacon Gaddy, 8, brother of Ruby Gaddy, covered with blood and carried it to Marshal Stubblefield. Stubblefield said it had been found in the grounds of the new $100,000.00 Negro school. It is believed to have served as the instrument in the twin slayings, the victims thus virtually succeeding in killing each other.

"Well, I'm surprised didn't more of them get hurt," said Rev. Alonzo Duckett, pastor of the Holden First Baptist Church. "And yet they expect to be seated in our churches." County Sheriff Vince Lasseter, reached fishing at Lake Bourne, said: "That's one they can't pin the blame on us for. That's how they treat their own kind. Please take note our conscience is clear."

Members of the Negro congregation said they could not account for Collins having left Snake Creek at the unspecified time. "We stood there a while and flipped some bottle caps down at him and threw his cap down after him right over his face and didn't get a stir out of him," stated an official of the congregation. "The way he acted, we figured he was dead. We would not have gone off and left him if we had known he was able to subsequently crawl up the hill." They stated Collins was not in the habit of worshipping at Holy Gospel Tabernacle.

The Gaddy woman died later this morning, also from chest wounds. No cause was cited for the fracas.

The cook had refilled his cup without his noticing. The doctor dropped the paper and carried his coffee out onto the little porch; it was still his morning habit.

The porch was at the back of the house, screened on three sides. Sylvia's daybed used to stand here; it put her in the garden. No other houses were in sight; the gin could not be heard or even the traffic whining on the highway up off the bypass.

The roses were done for, the perennials too. But the surrounding crape-myrtle tree, the redbud, the dogwood, the Chinese tallow tree, and the pomegranate bush were bright as toys. The ailing pear tree had shed its leaves ahead of the rest. Past a falling wall of Michaelmas daisies that had not been tied up, a pair of flickers were rifling the grass, the cock in one part of the garden, the hen in another, picking at the devastation right through the bright leaves that appeared to have been left lying there just for them, probing and feeding. They stayed year round, he supposed, but it was only in the fall of the year that he ever noticed them. He was pretty sure that Sylvia had known the birds were there. Her eyes would follow birds when they flew across the garden. As he watched, the cock spread one wing, showy as a zebra's hide, and with a turn of his head showed his red seal.

Dr. Strickland swallowed the coffee and picked up his bag. It was all going to be just about as hard as seeing Herman and Eva Fairbrothers through. He thought that in all Holden, as of now, only Miss Marcia Pope was still quite able to take care of herself—or such was her own opinion.

Prohibition

Old Riley lay, without hands or feet, on a red tapestry couch in the dirty sitting room and blinked happily at the sunshine and at a bottle which stood in it beside him. An exceptionally hairy white dog crouched under his outstretched arm. All around him there were geraniums and begonias in rusty tin pails on dry-goods boxes. Through the window one could see little slatternly groves here and there, and a hill hollowed out on one side by a gravel pit like a great empty grave. Though no one asked him to, Old Riley sang a song. A child, standing as near the door as he could without being asked where he was going, stared reverently at the little drunkard, now crippled and famous and apparently happier than ever before.

Though the temperance movement had gained strength in that part of the country long before drink was prohibited by law, Old Riley was not the only notorious drunkard in the township. There was a farmer named Theodore Osten who was said to have broken off a bull's horns with his bare hands. He often pounded on the district schoolhouse door in the afternoon, demanded as many of his six children as were there, and took them whimpering home with him. Once he came back from the village with a butcher's knife in his hand. His wife escaped through the back yard, leaving her sixth baby behind. When she brought a crowd of the neighbours to rescue the child, he stuck somebody's hired man in the leg and, bursting into gloomy laughter, threw the knife at them all. But his wife would not be separated from him or let the neighbours have him sent to jail, and complained bitterly about the fines he was obliged to pay.

There was also the sickly old bachelor, Charlie Fox, who got drunk only in bad weather. He began to complain whenever clouds came up, but after five or six bottles of beer ceased to mind the elements. He would wander up and down in the worst blizzards, murmuring to anyone he met, "Hell of a storm we're having—suits me!" Or he would sit down in the mud outside a saloon window, his arms folded, his eyes shut, the rain streaming over his cheeks and under his wet wing collar, the lamplight shining on his white, serene, weak face.

Even before the accident which had confined him to his bed Old Riley had never been melancholy or dangerous. At his very worst he amused himself by letting young cattle out of pasture, by pushing over shocks of grain, chicken coops, and beehives until he got tired. In spite of his practical jokes and his bad example to the young, the sober, God-fearing farmers and their wives could not hate him; neither could they pity him at any time. The mingling of joy and catastrophe in his life confused even the most opinionated among them. They regarded him as something less than a man, an irresponsible animal in human form.

To their children, on the other hand, he always seemed more than human, and began to charm and frighten them even before he came into sight. Through the harvest fields at dusk they would hear a song coming toward them as if it were stumbling over the fields without a singer. Out of hollows or from the far side of hills there would come the revolving thunder of his lumber-wagon wheels, the hiss and crack of the whip which he flourished like a long leather snake, and strangely melodious shouts—the shouts of a hunter or a jockey, the cries of a drunken hunter or a jockey on a wild horse. "Holy this" or "Holy that," he cried—this or that being one of those short words which mean more in sound to children than in sense to their elders. Children never had the courage to inquire about anything he did or said.

Dissipated happiness and a tragic accident. . . . His happiness, while it lasted, was injurious to others and furnished the community with a token of its inner desperation, the inarticulate fields and farmhouses with an appalling voice. Disaster, when it overtook him, made him a symbol of every abnormal delight, of the durability of character, of contentment with catastrophe, and saved his family from the consequences of his pleasures. Roistering joy on summer afternoons and evenings, a terrible event among deep snowdrifts, in the starlight. . . . It is no wonder that the neighbours made no attempt to explain the meaning of Old Riley's story to their children, for a tragedy was its happy ending.

He usually went to a saloon in one of the adjacent villages about four o'clock in the afternoon. Sawing on the mouths of his nervous mares, he brought them to a standstill, clambered down from the high seat, gathered some flowers along the fence, tearing them up by the root, pinned them to the lid of his lamentable greasy cap with a nail, clambered back up, and started his team again with a good deal of shouting.

Some children on their way home from school, undaunted by his curses and his wild driving, climbed into the back of the lumber wagon. Old Riley turned about and shouted, "Open yer mouths and shut yer eyes," and amused himself greatly by dropping pennies, nickels, and dimes into their mouths with one hand, cracking the whip over their heads with the other. When he missed his aim one youngster or another dropped to the ground instantaneously, like a little warrior picked off a vehicle by a sharpshooter, to spend the rest of the afternoon hunting the coins in the dust and gravel and among the nettles by the side of the road.

A few hours later, drunk enough and ready to go home, his pockets were empty. "I must 'a' gave it all to the brats on the way," he explained to the bartender. "What a blasted fool I am! Now, wouldn't ye know I'd do that? Ye know me anyway, Bill."

The bartender did know him: the next day or the day after he would deny his indebtedness; but his boys also knew their father and could be made to pay what was due—secretly, lest he give them a beating.

In his boyhood the eldest son, who was called Young Riley, had indeed followed his father into saloons in hope of getting him home sober. During this period the incorrigible man lost less of his money and did somewhat less damage to other people's property, but otherwise the youngster's presence put no restraint on him. And he was fonder of his boys than of other men and liked to drink with them; so little by little, Young Riley, and eventually the other son, Terrie, adopted the old man's ways. But Young Riley had some principles, and would not leave the farm in the afternoon or permit his brother to do so; together they pretended to do the work in the fields which their father optimistically neglected.

All alone, therefore, in the early evening, Old Riley started home, too drunk to care when he arrived. He saw the open gate of a neighbour's barnyard and swung through it, shouting and flourishing his black-snake whip. He tied the team to a heavy pig trough, but they pulled it along the ground until they could eat from a haystack.

As he entered the warm stable where men were milking, boys and little girls throwing down corn fodder and feeding the calves, Old Riley swayed and bowed ceremoniously. In his hand he was carrying a length of wild grapevine in blossom, and he knotted it under his chin like a necktie. "Gad," he said, "wild grapes smell like a snake."

A small boy who heard him say this spent much of his time in hunting the delicate brilliant grass snakes, and resolved to kill another to-morrow to find out how it smelled.

Then Old Riley sat down on a milkstool and gave an account of what had happened to him lately, boasting and putting on airs, and reciting in conclusion a long list of curse words, softly, rather mechanically, like a priest telling his beads. He nodded his head as old hens do when they have a certain sickness and kept on shaking his fist in the air while his tired body sagged lower and lower, lurching a little from side to side. He fell off the milkstool; and there at last he lay, on a pile of clean straw for bedding the animals, taking a short nap, the one belligerent arm still raised above him.

The farmer and his young hired men, laughing uneasily, went on with their work. They also might have taken to drink; this was the moral lesson of the ridiculous. The youngsters were enchanted, as if the old fellow were a small dancing bear or the monkey of an invisible organ grinder whose music only they could hear; and they gazed at him with starry, disgusted, incredulous eyes—the admirable eyes of children born and bred in the country.

He was tolerated thus in the evening in the barns even of his most self-respecting neighbours because, when all was said and done, he did no harm. Not, at least, to anyone but his own flesh and blood, wife and children, and that was the sort of harm which seemed appropriate to them, or which they deserved. The worst gossips in the community said "They're all kind o' heartless, those Rileys. Heaven knows what could happen to make such as them unhappy"; and their faces lighted up as if they had discovered a recipe for simplifying life; some people have no hearts to break. . . . Perhaps they found Old Riley sympathetic because he had as little patience with human disappointments as they.

So when he had rested and cheered himself by the seeming benevolence of some neighbour or another, he would set out again, disputing with himself as he untied his horses whether he was hungrier than he was thirsty; his thirst was never altogether quenched, but it was always hunger which brought him home. He remembered that he had forgotten the groceries he had promised his wife to buy, and the money she had given him was gone. She would upbraid him; he would probably have to beat her to put her in the wrong.

May Riley was a pleasant, shiftless woman who had been frightened for so many years that she had begun to seem a little weak in her mind. People believed that he did not actually hurt her; at any rate, she hid her face in her skirts without crying out, and never whimpered or showed any bruises after it was over. But she gave her entire time to shivering anticipation of his next drunken return from the village, and so neglected her housework, cooked badly, and wore her dresses, petticoats, and shawls in mere tatters wound around her loose-jointed body. Sometimes it was because she cooked badly that he abused her, or because she was not as pretty as she had been on their wedding day.

In those days, years before, she had looked like their daughter Angeline. Her brothers called her Candy on account of her hair, which hung in curls the colour of taffy all around her pretty, pale face.

Driving home through the bland summer evening Old Riley meditated on the weather or the landscape or the poor farms he passed. The weather was an entertainment, the landscape never seemed tedious, the farmhouses never mean and melancholy—because he was always drunk. Alcohol saved him from the mediocrity of the world.

His younger son, Terence or Terrie, the lovable Riley, was like him in this respect. He also drank for fun, and being drunk was an enchantment; then even the banal saloons, the poor farmers' women with dirty hair and sagging bodies who knew only too well how to take care of themselves, the lonely sheds and stables took on a bright and distorted appearance. But, unlike his father, he could not be drunk all the time. His brother, for the pleasure of governing him, allowed him little money to spend, little time to make love to such women as there were; and he dreamed of a life which would have that shining, deformed appearance even in broad daylight when he was sober. He wanted to join the navy, talking to others and even to himself about the places where the battleship would probably stop —the shore of the sea covered with odd buildings, the hundreds of sailors as good as but no better than he, the welcoming women crying out and agitating their shawls. . . . What a wild life he would lead in those places, buying what he liked, fed and clothed like a child by the government! He thought it would be the most agreeable thing in the world, and perhaps he was not wrong.

Driving home, sitting up very straight and gesturing with the whip or the long reins as if the road were lined with people with their eyes fixed on him, Old Riley thought of a quarrel he had been engaged in. A great anger arose in his heart and, forgetting the quarrel in the storm of his emotion, he searched his mind for another pretext, an object or person upon whom it might be spent. If his sons were arguing about the navy when he got home, he would thrash them and they would see.

For Young Riley would not let his brother enlist, indeed, threatened to kill him if he did—perhaps out of jealous affection, perhaps in dread of the tedium of his own experience if he were left alone. Nor would he go away with the boy, somehow unwilling to leave the scene of an honest, laborious life, though not leading it or likely to. He was ashamed of keeping Terrie back, but as long as he suffered from alcoholic stomach trouble he could make no sacrifices; blamed everything, including his own selfishness, on their father; and turned for forgetfulness to the very cup which he wanted to forget. Then, drunk or sober, his anger arose and confused him about everything.

It wore itself out like any other forbidden passion, and was succeeded by a heavy anxiety and a sense of guilt. He had no right to blame his father and brother; he was equally good for nothing; but he had too much common sense to be so cheerful about the results of their dissipation. The farm had been mortgaged twice; no one knew what would happen to the old people if it came to a foreclosure; and Young Riley, especially in the early morning after a night's drinking, thought desperately about the future.

Old Riley did not. Driving home he brooded upon a stupendous lie that he was preparing to tell, a song that he might sing or was singing. Though to his regret he had no bottle in his pocket, he seemed to be getting more and more drunk and was not sure that he knew his way home; it did not matter, his horses knew. And in a vague way he foresaw that he would be surprised to find his wife and children in the house that could scarcely be called his home, though he had been born in it, and looked forward with vague pleasure to falling upon them in instantaneous fury and chasing one or another outdoors or indoors, and spoiling all their plans.

In and about that house there was an atmosphere of slatternly grace and peace until he came. Neglect had contributed to the ordinary building and the barn and sheds its ramshackle beauty, the great comfort of idle men. The gables were sway-backed, the weathervane twisted; the barn doors hung from one hinge apiece; the half-wild fowls had learned to fly up on the rotten branches; and two or three sheep that were left of a large flock lay at the doorstep with the dogs. The moon was coming up and filled the yard with liquid brightness and clean shadows tossed about by the weeds and the grass. All about stood slim poplars whose little branches hung down in rows of curls as perfect as Angeline's. The soft moon rose higher, stirred up new odours, warmed the dew. The balm, the dust, the summer, drifting down, clouded the faces of May Riley and her children.

The old woman crouched on the doorstep, asleep, with her fists full of goose feathers she was sorting to put in a pillow. A little way away, on a dry-goods box, her sons sat close together, with a whisky bottle on the ground within reach. They had a large accordion which each played in turn, the other singing, or even, with a good deal of laughter, both playing at once—one large ruddy hand fingering the keys, one manipulating the bellows out of which some of the air escaped with a sigh.

Angeline was hiding in the haymow with her beau. It had always been the same one, a young man named Andie Roy. He had been going with her less of late, or seemed, at least, to be less serious in his intentions. Angeline blamed her father and brothers and determined to have him, in spite of their bad reputation, in spite of his scruples. They hid in the haymow now because Andie was pretending to be afraid of Young Riley, who knew, of course, that he was there— actually because he was trying to be there without thinking of it himself, having made up his mind not to come.

At a pause in the music the brothers, hearing their whispers and laughter, shook their fists in that direction and winked at each other. Then the throbbing of music ran out again in the blood heat of the air, far out, their unskilled, heavy, palpitating voices joining it now and then. Over the drowsy countryside these sounds troubled young girls lying ill at ease, and reawakened the ambitions, the shames and grievances, the homesickness for places unseen, of boys more finely bred than the Rileys, and set overworked mothers weeping for dead children. But in the Irish yard there was no sadness in the music nor in anything else: Terrie had forgotten the navy for the moment; his brother had forgotten the mortgages, was neither drunk nor sober, and did not care; the mother was asleep; Angeline was in her young man's arms; and they all enjoyed the music and the time of night as if there were no past or future.

Then the lumber wagon rolled into the yard. Old Riley clambered down, threw the reins on the ground, shouted a few curses, picked up a good-sized stick, and strode into the midst of his family. He made a lunge at the boys with the stick. They took refuge in the wagon shed, knowing that their father, in his condition, would not be able to find his way in the dark among the wheels and thills and harness lying about. The accordion sank to the ground and cried one hopeless note like a dying swan's as the breath went out of it and it collapsed. The whisky bottle tipped over, the whisky gurgled out— the dry earth drank it up.

Then the old man turned his attention to his wife, shaking out the bag of goose feathers in her face. She woke in a sort of little winter of its contents, and at first did not know where she was. Just as he was about to strike her for her complaints, his sons, from the shadow of the house, jumped on his back and tied his hands and feet with some pieces of rope. He roared and his wife wept, and then he began to sing a song. The boys squatted at his feet in menacing attitudes, but they listened to the song, and it was evident that they loved him.

Angeline came out of the barn into the moonlight, rubbing her forehead where the curls caressed it. Terrie shouted, "Where's your beau, Candy?"

"He ain't been here, has he?" she answered craftily. "I been asleep. What's the matter with Pa?"

"You're a liar," the boys said, "but wha' do we care?"

Andie Roy was not there then. At the first of her father's shouts the girl had whispered to him, "You better skip, there's trouble." He had slid down out of the haymow, mistaken a trapdoor for the ladder into the stable, and landed heavily on a pile of hay in the bull's manger. The little old bull, which smelled like a lion, had snuffled him, and he got up and hurried out through the barnyard.

Andie Roy was so much excited and so much in love that he wondered if he were going to die, and there was pain in several parts of his body. So he lay down by the side of the road and, for a while, cried like a small boy, pressing his mouth against the knuckles of his fists. It seemed to be one of the greatest sorrows in the world that night. The night grew more and more fair. The tree over his head dropped now and then a burned or withered leaf. The lovelier the weather the more the boy suffered from his feelings about Angeline, which seemed to lead nowhere.

His widowed mother and the Catholic priest, Father Hoyle, had encouraged his determination not to marry her. Father Hoyle said over and again that Andie was one of the most superior boys in his parish, so he ought not to mix with disobedient riffraff like the Rileys. He was particularly anxious that his young men should not drink, since the Protestants favoured prohibition and made of the excesses of the Irish Catholics both a political and a doctrinal issue. Andie knew that he was inclined to liquor and that Terrie and Young Riley had too much power over him.

During the spring of that year, having loitered in a saloon with those two, he had been going down a lane which led through one corner of a woods. And a voice had said to him, "Andrew, Andrew— get you!" He had been infinitely moved and frightened, not so much

by the sound of the voice which had been no more alarming than
that of a tomcat or a hoot owl or anything else one may hear when
one has had too much to drink, as by the meaning of what it said in
relation to the bad company he had been keeping, his temptations,
his mother's grievances.

He had told Father Hoyle about it, and the superstitious old man,
not knowing what to believe himself and hoping for a matter-of-fact
explanation, had repeated the story to a number of his parishioners.
Thereafter when Andie saw the two Rileys, out with girls or in a
saloon, they had shouted at him, "Andrew, Andrew—get you!" If they
got him he would be as bad as they were. His mother had assured
him that if he did not reform their little farm would have to be
mortgaged before long, and he would probably beat her, and they
would be looked down upon by everybody. So Andie had told Father
Hoyle that he meant to give no more thought to Angeline Riley.

The old priest had said, "Now if ye don't mean to marry the girl,
keep away from there. I know what you young Irish are. There's the
old Nick in yuh."

Andie had tried to keep away, but a sort of fixed idea of Candy's
pale yellow curls and her eyes of a melted, diluted blue tempted him
back in the evening very often. He had tried to persuade himself that
he was getting over it by degrees, but he was not. Instead, his disapproval of her family was wearing away; he was beginning to enjoy
their kind of happiness. But for his mother he would not have
hesitated to drive the girl into another township and get married before another priest. He did not dare to try to seduce her, and she
would not let him go any farther than so far, fearing that he would
cease to care for her as soon as he had had his own way. That was a
good thing, for he knew that he would care all the more and cared
too much as it was.

So as he went back home from her house he shed tears, gnawed
at the back of his hand, and even cursed a little.

He stopped his sniffling just in time, for his mother was leaning
over the garden fence in the moonlight, and like an echo she began
to cry where he had left off. "You don't look at things right. You been
off havin' a good time with those wild Rileys, and little you care
whether I've been here cryin' my eyes out or not."

Before he went to bed Andie spent an hour defending the Rileys
and trying to prove that he had a right to marry whomever he liked,
though he realized that there was not a particle of honesty in what
he said, for at bottom his mother and he were always of the same
opinion. Since he could not free his heart or change his mind, matters

went from bad to worse for him the rest of the summer and all fall.

The Rileys also began to look at the seamy side of things. The man who held the mortgages would give them only until spring, and obviously money could not be raised during the winter. May began to fail in health. Terrie told his sister, "I guess Bud is getting funny in his head"; by which he meant that Young Riley was growing infinitely sad and bad tempered. Terrie himself grew more and more sullen about the navy; on one occasion he struck his mother, and his father and brother took turns punishing him. Angeline lost hope of getting Andie to marry her. They all grew older and looked faded. Only Old Riley never changed in appearance or behaviour—he seemed immortal.

The winter set in early, frosting the corn before it was ripe and spoiling good pasture, as if to make sure that they should be unable to meet the mortgage. Old Riley had to begin to sell the pigs and cows, as money was needed for food and drink.

There was a heavy fall of snow just before Christmas, and at that time a special election was held in Belleville. Riley left home with his boys right after the noonday meal, Young Riley and Terrie with the bobsleigh and the team, he himself following alone in the cutter. They always made of any political occasion a carnival of drinking.

Under the sleigh runners the crisp snow made a loud chirruping; the sleigh bells left behind them in the air their flurry of jangling notes. Around the muzzles of the horses and the mouths of the men the breath floated like visible souls about to vanish. Where there had been masses of living flowers, there lay a vast garden of dead-white and blue-white—the wind having twisted the tops of all the snow banks into bloom.

In Belleville the Rileys established themselves at Schimmel's saloon, the one nearest the town hall. The boys began by playing cards, and earned a good many drinks. The men of the country came in before or after voting; since it was bitterly cold, all drank more than usual for the warmth. Old Riley wedged himself between a barrel and the bar so that he did not have to depend entirely on his legs, and there made eloquent speeches for all the factions in turn, tossing off the rewards of his eloquence.

Smoke, hanging in warm layers, blotted out the eyes or hands or mouths of men on the other side of the room, and mixed in a vague sparkle the shining of varnished wood, glasses, lighted matches. Outside the temperature fell below zero. Men shuddered when it came time to go; the Rileys felt fortunate to be too drunk to have to think of it. They ate some sausages from the bar and let the time pass. At last they were alone in the foul, clouded, warm place amid the débris of refreshment, fatigue, argument; and the barkeeper wanted to go to bed.

So, cursing and stumbling about in their sheepskin coats, they went down to the stables over the crunching snow, over the frosted filth, and through the stiff, echoing cold. The boys were engaged in another argument about the navy and hitched up their horses without paying any attention to the old man, expecting him to follow them with his cutter. But instead he rolled into the back of their bobsleigh and fell asleep there before they drove out of the yard.

There were dazzling stars. The snowdrifts over the land looked like innumerable ghosts lying side by side. Terrie and Young Riley were angry with each other; but after all, it was an arctic night and they were young and warm, so they drew close together under the blankets and ceased to argue.

Behind them their father did not snore, because he was lying face down in the straw, and they did not discover him. The road rose in a hump over every drift that had been blown up; the sleigh lifted on the crest, lurched into the trough of wave after wave of snow.

About halfway home, Old Riley rolled out in the road. Perhaps he did not wake up; at least he was not sufficiently sobered by the fall to shout or to rise and follow his boys on foot.

The next day at dawn the first farmer on that road to go to the cheese factory found him there and brought him home. The doctor who was called in found it necessary to remove his feet at the ankles and his hands at the wrists.

In due time it became evident that it was a happy ending for them all. His wife was no longer afraid of him and became quite a capable woman. The effort of ministering to his pain until the amputations healed, of clothing and feeding him and giving him drink, roused her from her apathy of years—years of waiting at home to be abused.

Shaken to the bottom of his sluggish heart, Young Riley had no difficulty now in ceasing to drink. He went to a Ladies' Aid supper at the Methodist Church, stole a temperance pledge, signed it without telling anyone, and kept it hidden in his bedroom. Refreshed by disaster, his fleshy face, once inanimate and middle-aged with gloom, lighted up. To all intents and purposes he had inherited the farm and he would make it profitable. The banker who owned the mortgages was persuaded to give them another year to begin paying their debts.

Young Riley was glad to let his brother go away somewhere to make a fresh start in life. So Terrie joined the navy in the spring, and sent home picture postal cards from Villefranche, Cardiff, and Kiel.

Since the Rileys were a changed family, there was nothing to keep Angeline and Andie apart. They were married and were happy in the most ordinary way in the world. In a little less than due time a child was born; they named it after Old Riley, whose given name had been forgotten for years.

The prohibition law was passed. Some of Old Riley's temperance neighbours, greatly elated, wanted to ask him what he thought of that. They found the little mutilated man who had been the terror of the community lying in a bay window, and forgot what they had come for. The room was filled with an atmosphere of patience, indolence, and lawlessness. Sword ferns, begonias, and radiant geraniums stood all about his couch. Over his head one could see out over the countryside, and there was a hill hollowed out like the grave of a giant who has come to life, dug himself up, and wandered away. A child who had come in with the neighbours shrank in terror toward the door, shrank from the little man's air of happiness. For he was drunk, though he had been punished by a divine law against it and though a law on earth had been passed. His arms came to an end inside his sleeves, his legs inside his tattered trouser legs. He seemed to enjoy the scrutiny due him as an object lesson and not to care what the lesson was. His smiling wife went on giving him whisky, setting the glass with a straw in it on a chair within reach of his mouth.

Fire and Cloud

"A naughts a naught . . ."

As he walked his eyes looked vacantly on the dusty road, and the words rolled without movement from his lips, each syllable floating softly up out of the depth of his body.

"N fives a figger . . ."

He pulled out his pocket handkerchief and mopped his brow without lessening his pace.

"All fer the white man . . ."

He reached the top of the slope and paused, head down.

"N none fer the nigger. . . ."

His shoulders shook in half laugh and half shudder. He finished mopping his brow and spat, as though to rid himself of some bitter thing. He thought, Thas the way its awways been! Wistfully he turned and looked back at the dim buildings of the town lying sprawled mistily on the crest of a far hill. Seems like the white folks jus erbout own this whole worl! Looks like they done conquered *everthing*. We black folks is jus los in one big white fog. . . . With his eyes still on the hazy buildings, he flexed his lips slowly and spoke under his breath:

"They could do something! They could do *something*, awright! Mabbe ef five er six thousan of us marched downtown we could *scare* em inter doin something! Lawd knows, mabbe them Reds *is* right!"

He walked again and tucked his handkerchief back into his pocket. He could feel the heat of the evening over all his body, not strongly, but closely and persistently, as though he were holding his face over a tub of steaming suds. Far below him, at the bottom of the valley, lay a cluster of bleak huts with windowpanes red-lit from dying sunlight. Those huts were as familiar to his eyes as a nest is to the eyes of a bird, for he had lived among them all his life. He knew by sight or sound every black man, woman and child living within those huddled walls. For a moment an array of soft black faces hovered before his eyes. N whut kin Ah tell em? Whut kin Ah say t em? He stopped, looked at the ground and sighed. And then he saw himself as he had stood but a few minutes ago, facing the white woman who sat behind the brown, gleaming desk: her arms had been round, slender, snow-white, like cold marble; her hair had been the color of flowing gold and had glinted in the sunlight; her eyes had been wide and gray behind icily white spectacles. It seemed he could hear her saying in her dry, metallic voice: I'm sorry, Taylor. You'll just have to do the best you can. Explain it to them, make them understand that we cant do anything. Everybodys hongry, and after all, its no harder on your people than it is on ours. Tell them theyll just have to wait. . . .

He wagged his head and his lips broke in a slow sick smile. Whut she know erbout bein hongry? Whut she know erbout it? He walked again, thinking, Here Ah is a man called by Gawd t preach n whut kin Ah do? Hongry folks lookin t me fer hep n whut kin Ah do? Ah done tried everything n cant do *nuthin!* Shucks, mabbe Hadley n Greens right? They *might* be right. Gawd knows, they *might* be right.

He lifted his head and saw the wide fields plunging before him, down the hillside. The grass was dark and green. All this, he thought. All *this* n folks hongry! Good Gawd, whuts *wrong!* He saw the road running before him, winding, vanishing, the soft yellow dust filled with the ruts of wagon wheels and tiny threads of auto tires. He threw back his head and spoke out loud:

"The good Lawds gonna clean up this ol worl someday! Hes gonna make a new Heaven n a new Earth! N Hes gonna do it in a eye-twinkle change! Hes gotta do it! Things cant go on like this ferever! Gawd knows they cant!" He pulled off his coat and slung it under his left arm. "Waal, there ain nothin t do but go back n tell em. . . . Tell em the white folks wont let em eat. . . ."

The road curved, descending among the green fields that tumbled to a red sky. This was the land on which the Great God Almighty had first let him see the light of His blessed day. This was the land on which he had first taken unto himself a wife, leaving his mother and father to cleave to her. And it was on the green slopes of these struggling hills that his first-born son, Jimmy, had romped and played, growing to a strong, upright manhood. He wagged his head, musing, Lawd, them wuz the good ol days. . . . There had been plenty to eat; the blessings of God had been overflowing. He had toiled from sunup to sundown, and in the cool of the evenings his wife, May, had taught him to read and write. Then God had spoken to him, a quiet, deep voice coming out of the black night; God had called him to preach His word, to spread it to the four corners of the earth, to save His black people. And he had obeyed God and had built a church on a rock which the very gates of Hell could not prevail against. Yes, he had been like Moses, leading his people out of the wilderness into the Promised Land. He sighed, walking and taking his coat from his left arm and tucking it under his right. Yes, things had been clear-cut then. In those days there had stretched before his eyes a straight and narrow path and he had walked in it, with the help of a Gracious God. On Sundays he had preached God's Word, and on Mondays and Tuesdays and Wednesdays and Thursdays and Fridays and Saturdays he had taken old Bess, his mule, and his plow and had broke God's ground. For a moment while walking through the dust and remembering his hopes of those early years he seemed to feel again the plow handles trembling in his calloused hands and hear the earth cracking and breaking open, black, rich and damp; it seemed he could see old Bess straining forward with the plow, swishing her tail and tossing her head and snorting now and then. Yes, there had been something in those good old days when he had walked behind his plow, between the broad green earth and a blue sweep of sunlit sky; there had been in it all a surge of will, clean, full, joyful; the earth was his and he was the earth's; they were one; and it was that joy and will and oneness in him that God had spoken to when He had called him to preach His Word, to save His black people, to lead them, to guide them, to be a shepherd to His flock. But now the whole thing was giving way, crumbling in his hands, right before his eyes. And every time he tried to think of some way out, of some way to stop it, he saw wide gray eyes behind icily white spectacles. He mopped his brow again. Mabbe Hadley n Greens right. . . . Lawd, Ah don know what t do! Ef Ah fight fer things the white folk say Ahma bad nigger stirrin up trouble. N ef Ah don do nothin, we starve. . . . But somethings *gotta* be done! Mabbe ef we hada demonstration like Hadley n Green said, we could *scare* them white folks inter doin something. . . .

He looked at the fields again, half wistfully, half curiously. Lawd, we could make them ol fiels bloom ergin. We could make em feed us. Thas whut Gawd put em there fer. Plows could break and hoes could chop and hands could pick and arms could carry. . . . On and on that could happen and people could eat and feel as he had

felt with the plow handles trembling in his hands, following old
Bess, hearing the earth cracking and breaking because he wanted
it to crack and break; because he willed it, because the earth was
his. And they could sing as he had sung when he and May were
first married; sing about picking cotton, fishing, hunting, about sun
and rain. They could . . . But whuts the usa thinkin erbout stuff
like this? Its all gone now. . . . And he had to go and tell his congregation, the folks the Great God Almighty had called him to lead
to the Promised Land—he had to tell them that relief would give
them no food.

That morning he had sent a committee of ten men and a woman
from his congregation to see the mayor. Wondah how they come
out? The mayor tol em something, sho! So fer hes been pretty wid
me even ef he is a white man. As his feet sank softly into the dust
he saw Mayor Bolton; he saw the red chin that always had a short,
black stubble of beard; he saw the cigar glowing red in front of a
pink, fat face. But he needs something t scare im now, he thought.
Hes been running over us too long. . . .

He reached the bottom of the slope, turned into a cinder path
and approached the huts. N Lawd, when Ah do try t do somethin
mah own folks wont stan by me, wont stick wid me. Theres ol
Deacon Smith a-schemin n a-plottin, jus a-watchin me like a hawk,
jus a-waitin fer me t take mah eyes off the groun sos he kin trip me
up, sos he kin run t the white folks n tell em Ahm doin somethin
wrong! A black snake in the grass! A black Judas! Thas all he is!
Lawd, the Devils sho busy in this worl. . . .

He was walking among the crowded huts now.

hello, reveren

"How yuh tonight, sonny!" Let ol Deacon Smith tell it, no mattah
whut Ah do Ahm wrong. . . .

good evenin, reveren

"Good evenin, Sistah!" Hes been a-tryin t cheat me outta mah
church ever since hes been erroun here. . . .

how yuh tonight, reveren taylor?

"Jus fine. N how yuh tonight, Brother?" Hes awways a-whisperin
berhin mah back, a-tryin t take mah congregation erway from me.
. . . N when he ain doin tha hes a-tryin his bes t give me wrong
advice, jus like the Devil a-tryin t tempt Jesus. But Ahm gonna
march on wida hepa Gawd. . . . Yeah, Ah might preach a sermon
erbout tha nex Sunday.

As he turned into the street leading to his home and church, he saw a tall brown-skinned boy hurrying toward him. Here comes Jimmy! Ah bet hes lookin fer me. . . . Lawd, Ah hope ain nothin wrong. . . .

II

"Pa!" said Jimmy breathlessly when he was some twenty feet away. Taylor stopped.

"Whuts the mattah, son?"

Jimmy came close.

"The mayors at home, waitin t see yuh," he whispered.

"The *mayor?*"

"Yeah, n two mo white men. One of em is the chiefa police."

"They there *now?*"

"Yeah; in the parlor."

"How long they been there?"

"Bout two-three minutes, Ah reckon. N lissen, Pa . . . Sam wuz by jus now. He say the white folks is ridin up n down the streets in their cars warnin all the black folks t stay off the streets cause theres gonna be trouble. . . ."

"Sam say tha?"

"Thas whut he tol me. N lissen, Pa . . . Ahma git Sam n Pete n Bob n Jack n some mo boys together sos ef anything happens . . ."

Taylor gripped Jimmy's shoulders.

"Naw, son! Yuh fixin t git us *all* inter trouble now! Yuh cant do nothin like tha! Yuh gotta be careful! Ef them white folks jus *thought* we wuz doin something like tha theyd crack down on us! Wed hava riot!"

"But we cant let em ride erroun n talk big n we do nothin!"

"Lissen here, son! Yuh do whut Ah tell you t do!" He shook Jimmy's shoulders and his voice was husky. "Yuh go tell them boys t do *nuthin* till Ah see em, yuh hear me? Yuh young fools fixin t git us *all* murdered!"

"We just as waal git killed fightin as t git killed doin nothin," said Jimmy sullenly.

"Yuh go n do whut Ah tol yuh, *hear* me? Ah gotta go n see tha mayor. . . ."

"Hes here t see yuh erbout tha demonstration," said Jimmy.

"How yuh know?"

"Cause thas whut everbodys sayin."

"Who yuh hear say tha?"

"Deacon Smiths spreadin the word."

Taylor winced as though struck by a blow and looked at the dust.

"Hes tellin alla deacons n the church membahs tha the mayors here t stop yuh," said Jimmy. "Hes tellin em yuhs mixed up wid the Reds."

"Deacon Smith there now *too?*"

"Yeah; hes in the basement wida other deacons. Theys waitin t see yuh."

"How long they been there?"

"Bout hafa hour. N Hadley n Greens in the Bible Room, waitin t talk wid yuh too. . . ."

Fear gripped Taylor and he stammered:

"Ddddid the mmmmayor sssee em?"

"Naw, ain nobody seen em yit. Ah brought em in thu the back do and tol em t wait fer yuh. Ahm mighty scared wid them Reds waitin fer yuh in the Bible Room and tha chiefa police waitin fer yuh in the parlor. Ef ol Deacon Smith knowed tha he sho would make a lotta trouble. . . ."

"Where yo ma?"

"She upstairs, sewin."

"She know whuts happenin?"

"Naw, Pa."

Taylor stood still, barely breathing.

"Whut yuh gonna do, Pa?" asked Jimmy.

"Yuh go n tell them boys not t do nothin wrong, son. Go on n tell em now! Ah got too much on mah hans now widout yuh boys stirrin up mo trouble!"

"Yessuh."

"Yuh bettah go n do it *now!*"

"Yessuh."

He watched Jimmy hurry down the street. Lawd, Ah hope tha boy don go n git inter trouble. . . .

"Yuh do whut Ah tol you, Jimmy!" he yelled.

"Yessuh!" Jimmy hollered back.

He saw Jimmy turn a dusty corner and go out of sight. Hadley n Greens there in the Bible Room n the chiefa police is waitin in the parlor! Ah cant let them white folks see them Reds! N ef Deacon Smith tells on me theyll lynch me. . . . Ah gotta git em out of tha church widout em seein each other. . . . Good Gawd, whut a mess!

III

No sooner had he opened the door of his church than he heard a crescendo of voices. They back awready! Tha committees back! Aw, Ah bet the mayor followed em here. . . . He walked down the hall, turned into the church's waiting room and saw a roomful of black faces.

"Reveren Taylor! The mayor run us out!"

"He put the police on us!"

The black brothers and sisters ran to Taylor and surrounded him.

"The mayor tol us t git out n don come back no mo!"

A thin black woman swung onto Taylor's arm, crying:

"Whut Ahm gonna do? Ah ain gotta mouthful bread at home!"

"Sistahs n Brothers, jusa minute," said Taylor. "Firs, tell me whut the mayor said. . . ."

"He say he cant do *nuthin!* N say fer us not t come back t his office no *mo!* N say ef we do hes gonna put us in jail!"

"In *jail?*" asked Taylor.

"Thas whut he said."

"N he tol us not t march, Reveren. He said ef we demonstrated hed put us *all* in jail."

"Who tol em yuh wuz gonna march?" asked Taylor.

"Ah bet it wuz the ol Deacon Smith," said Sister Harris.

"The Bible says testify whut yuh see n speak whut yuh know," said Sister Davis to Sister Harris.

"Ah knows whut Ahm talkin erbout!" blazed Sister Harris.

"Sistahs n Brothers, les don start no fuss," said Taylor, sighing and dropping his shoulders.

"Whut they tell yuh at the relief station, Reveren Taylor?" asked Sister James.

"They say they cant do nothin," said Taylor.

The thin black woman came and knelt at Taylor's feet, her face in her hands.

"Reveren Taylor, it ain fer me Ahm astin! Its fer ma chillun! Theys hongry! It ain fer me, its fer them! Gawd, have mercy, theys hongry. . . ."

Taylor stepped back, ran his hand into his pocket and pulled out a palmful of loose coins.

"Here, Sistahs n Brothers, split this up between yuh all. Its ever cent Ah got in this worl, so hep me Gawd!"

He laid the coins on a small table. Brother Booker divided them as far as they would go. Then they swarmed around him again.

"Reveren, whut we gonna do?"

"Cant we make the white folks do something fer us?"

"Ahm tireda bein hongry!"

"Reveren, mah babys sick n Ah cant git her no milk!"

"Reveren, whut kin Ah tell mah wife?"

"Lawd knows, Ahm just erbout sick of this!"

"Whut kin we do, Reveren?"

Taylor looked at them and was ashamed of his own helplessness and theirs.

"Sistahs n Brothers, les call on the great Gawd who made us n put us in this worl. . . ."

He clasped his hands in front of him, closed his eyes and bowed his head. The room grew still and silent.

"Lawd Gawd Awmighty, Yuh made the sun n the moon n the stars n the earth n the seas n mankind n the beasts of the fiels!"

yes jesus

"Yuh made em all, Lawd, n Yuh tol em whut t do!"

yuh made em lawd

"Yuhs strong n powerful n Yo will rules this worl!"

yuh rules it lawd

"Yuh brought the chillun of Israel outta the lan of Egypt!"

yuh sho did

"Yuh made the dry bones rise up outta the valley of death n live!"

yuh made em live lawd

"Yuh saved the Hebrew chillun in the fiery furnace!"

yes jesus

"Yuh stopped the storm n yuh made the sun stan still!"

yuh stopped it lawd

"Yuh knocked down the walls of Jericho n Yuh kept Jona in the belly of the whale!"

yuh kept im lawd

"Yuh let Yo son Jesus walk on watah n Yuh brought Im back from the dead!"

have mercy jesus

"Yuh made the lame walk!"

yuh did it lawd

"Yuh made the blin see!"

hep us now lawd

"Yuh made the deaf hear!"

glory t the mos high

"Lawd, Yuhs a rock in the tima trouble n Yuhs a shelter in the tima storm!"

he is he is

"Lawd, Yuh said Yuhd strike down the wicked men who plagued yo chillun!"

glory t gawd

"Yuh said Yuhd destroy this ol worl n create a new Heaven n a new Earth!"

wes waitin on yuh jesus

"Lawd, Yuh said call on Yo name n Yuhd answer!"

yuh said it lawd n now wes callin

"Yuh made us n put the breatha life in us!"

yuh did lawd

"Now look down on us, Lawd! Speak t our hearts n let us know whut Yo will is! Speak t us like Yuh spoke t Jacob!"

speak lawd n our souls will be clay in yo hans

"Lawd, ack in us n well obey! Try us, lawd, try us n watch us move t Yo will! Wes helpless at Yo feet a-waitin fer Yo sign!"

send it lawd

"The white folks say we cant raise nothin on Yo earth! They done put the lans of the worl in their pockets! They done fenced em off n nailed em down! Theys a-tryin t take Yo place, Lawd!"

speak t em lawd

"Yuh put us in this worl n said we could live in it! Yuh said this worl wuz Yo own! Now show us the sign like Yuh showed Saul! Show us the sign n well ack! We ast this in the name of Yo son Jesus who died tha we might live! Amen!"

amen amen

Taylor stopped and opened his eyes. The room was quiet; he could hear the clock ticking softly above his head, and from the rear came the sound of children playing back of the church. The sisters and brothers rose from their knees and began talking in subdued tones.

"But, Reveren, whut kin we *do?*"

"The issues wid Gawd now, Sistahs n Brothers."

"Is we gonna march?"

"Is yuh goin wid us t the mayor?"

"Have faith, Sistahs n Brothers. Gawd takes care of His own."

"But Ahm hongry, Reveren. . . ."

"Now, Sistahs n Brothers, Ah got t go. Ah got business t tend t. . . ."

He pushed ahead of the black hands that clung to his sleeve.

"Reveren Taylor. . . ."

The thin black woman wailed, kneeling:

"Please, Reveren, cant yuh do *somethin.* . . ."

He pushed through the door, closed it and stood for a moment with his eyes shut and with his fingers slowly loosening on the knob, his ears filled with the sound of wailing voices.

IV

How come all this gotta happen at *once?* Folks a-beggin fer bread n the mayor here t see me n them Reds a-waitin in the Bible Room. . . . Ef Deacon Smith knowed tha hed ruin me sho! Ah cant let the mayor see them Reds. . . . Naw, Gawd! He looked at a door at the far end of the room, then hurried to it and opened it softly.

"May!" he called in a hoarse whisper.

"Hunh?"

"C mere, quick!"

"Whutcha wan, Dan?"

"C mon in the *room,* May!"

She edged through the half-opened door and stood in front of him, wide-eyed.

"Whutcha wan, Dan?"

"Now, lissen. . . ."

"Ain nothin wrong, is it, Dan? Ain nothin happened, is it?"

He grabbed her arm.

"Naw, n don git scared!"

"Ah ain scared!"

"Yuh cant do whut Ah wan yuh t do ef yuhs scared!"

"Ah *ain* scared, Dan!"

"Lissen. . . ."

"Yeah?"

"The mayors here, in the parlor. N the chiefa police. . . ."

She stood stock still and seemed not to breathe.

"The *mayor?*"

"Yeah. . . ."

"*Ain* nothin wrong, is it, Dan?"

"There wont be ef yuh lissen n try t do right."

"Be careful, Dan!"

"Yeah," he said, his voice low and husky. "Go in and tell them white folks Ahm sick, hear?"

She stepped back from him and shook her head.

"Gawd *ain* wid yuh when yuh lie, Dan!"

"We *gotta* lie t white folks! Theys on our necks! They *make* us lie t them! Whut kin we do but lie?"

"*Dan!*"

"Lissen t whut Ahm tellin yuh, May! Tell the mayor Ahm gittin outta bed t see im. Tell im Ahm dressin, see? Tell im t wait a few minutes."

"Yeah?"

"Then go t the basement n tell Deacon Smith Ahm wid the mayor. Tell im n the other deacons t wait."

"Now?"

"Yeah; but Ah ain thu yit. Yuh know Hadley n Green?"

"Them *Reds?*"

"Yeah. . . ."

"Dan!" said May, her lungs suspiring in one gasp of amazed helplessness.

"May, fer Chrissakes!"

She began to cry.

"Don do nothin wrong, Dan, please! Don fergit Jimmy! Hes jus a young boy n hes gotta grow up in this town wid these white folks. Don go n do nothin n fix it so he wont hava chance. . . . Me n yuh don mattah, but thinka him, Dan, please. . . ."

Taylor swallowed and looked hard at her.

"May, yuh do whut *Ah* tell yuh t do! Ah know whut Ahm doin. Hadley n Greens downstairs, in the Bible Room. Tell em so nobody kin hear yuh, hear?—tell em aftah yuh done tol the others—tell em t come in here. Let em in thu *yo* room. . . ."

"Naw!"

She tried to get through the door. He ran to her and caught her hand again.

"Yuh do whut Ah tell yuh, May!"

"Ah ain gonna have them Reds in *here* wid the mayor n chiefa police out *there!* Ah *ain!*"

"Go on n do whut Ah tell yuh, May!"

"Dan!"

"Go *erhead,* May!"

He pushed her. She went through the door, slowly, looking back at him. When the door was closed he rammed his hands deep into his pants pockets, turned to the open window and looked out into the street. It was profoundly quiet, save for the silvery sound of children's voices back of the church. The air was soft, warm and full of the scent of magnolias and violets. Windowpanes across the street were blood-red from dying sunlight. A car sped past, lifting a great cloud of yellow-brown dust. He went to the center of the room and stood over a table littered with papers. He cocked his head, listening. He heard a door slam; footsteps echoed and ceased. A big eight-day clock above his head boomed six times; he looked and his eyes strayed up and rested on a gleaming brass cross. Gawd, hep me now! Jus hep me t go thu wid this! Again he heard a door slam. Lawd,

Ah hope May do right now. . . . N Ah hope Jimmy don go n ack a fool. . . . He crossed the floor on tiptoe, opened the door and peeped into May's room. It was empty. A slender prism of dust-filled sunlight cut across the air. He closed the door, turned, pulled off his coat and threw it across the table. Then he loosened his collar and tie. He went to the window again and leaned with his back against the ledge, watching the door of May's room. He heard a hoarse voice rise and die. Footsteps again sounded and ceased. He frowned, listening. How come its takin May so long? He started when a timid knock came. He hurried to the door and cracked it.

v

"Hello, Reverend Taylor!" said Hadley, a white man.

"How yuh, Brother Hadley?"

"N how yuh, Reveren?" asked Green, a black man.

"Ahm fine, Brother Green. C mon in, yuh all."

Hadley and Green edged through the door.

"Say, whuts alla mystery?" asked Green.

"Ssssh! Don talk so loud," cautioned Taylor. "The mayor n the chiefa police is out there."

The Negro and the white man stood stone still.

"Do they know wes here?" asked Green.

"Naw, n don git scared. They done come t see me erbout tha demonstration. . . ."

Hadley and Green looked at each other.

"Pull down tha shade," whispered Green, pointing a shaking black finger.

Quickly Hadley moved to one side, out of range of the window. His cheeks flushed pink. Taylor lowered the shade and faced them in the semidarkness. The eyes of the white man and the black man were upon him steadily.

"Waal?" said Green.

"Ah spose yuh know whuts up," said Taylor.

"Theyre here to scare you," said Hadley.

"Ahm trustin Gawd," sighed Taylor.

"Whut yuh gonna tell em?" asked Green.

"Thas whut Ah wanna see yuh all erbout," said Taylor.

"O.K. Whut kin we do?" asked Green.

Taylor looked around and motioned toward two chairs.

"Set down, Brothers."

"Naw, this is awright," said Green, still standing.

"Come on," said Hadley. "What's on your mind?"

Taylor folded his arms and half sat and half leaned on the edge of the table.

"Yuh all think wes gonna have many folks out in the mawnin fer the demonstration?"

"Whut yuh mean?" asked Green.

"When Ahm talkin wid the mayor and chiefa police Ah wanna know how many folks Ahm talkin fer. There ain no use in us havin a demonstration ef ain but a few of us is gonna be out there. The police will try t kill us then. . . ."

"How many folks we can get out tomorrow depends a great deal on you, Reverend," said Hadley.

"Hows tha?" asked Taylor.

"If you had let us use your name on those handbills, we could say five thousand easily. . . ."

Taylor turned sharply to Hadley.

"Lissen, Brother, Ah done tol yuh Ah cant do tha! N there ain no use in us talkin erbout it no mo! Ah done tol yuh Ah cant let them white folks know Ahm callin folks t demonstrate. After all, Ahma preacher. . . ."

"Its yo duty, Reveren," said Green. "We owes it our black folks."

"Ahm doin mah duty as Gawd lets me see it," said Taylor.

"All right, Reverend," said Hadley. "Heres what happened: Weve covered the city with fifteen thousand leaflets. Weve contacted every organization we could think of, black and white. In other words, weve done all *we* could. The rest depends on the leaders of each group. If we had their active endorsement, none of us would have to worry about a crowd tomorrow. And if we had a crowd we would not have to worry about the police. If they see the whole town turning out, theyll not start any trouble. Now, youre known. White and black in this town respect you. If you let us send out another leaflet with your name on it, calling for . . ."

Taylor turned from them and drew his hand nervously across his face. Hadley and Green were silent, watching him. Taylor went to the window and pulled back the curtain slightly and peeped out. Without turning he said softly:

"Ah done tol yuh all Ah ain scareda lettin yuh use mah name."

"We don mean *tha*," said Green hastily.

"Ef it wuz jus me who wuz takin the chance," said Taylor, "Ah wouldn't care none. But Gawd knows it ain right fer me to send them po folks out inter the streets in fronta police. Gawd knows, Ah cant do tha!"

"Honest, Reveren," said Green touching Taylor's arm, "Ah don understan. Yuh done been thu harder things than this befo."

"N Ahll go thu wid em ergin," said Taylor proudly.

"All right!" said Hadley. "You can say the word that can make this thing a success. If you dont and we have no crowd, then youre to blame. . . ."

Taylor's eyes narrowed and when he spoke there was a note of anger in his voice.

"Gawd hep yuh ef yuhs a-tryin t say yuh gonna blame me ef things don go right!"

"Naw, Reveren!" said Green, coming hurriedly forward and spreading his black palms softly upon the air. "Don feel tha way! Wes all jus in a jam. We got t do either two things: Call off this demonstration and let the folks stay hongry, er git as many as we kin together n go downtown in the mawnin. Ef we git five thousan down there the police wont bother us. Ef yuh let us send out yo name tellin the black folks . . ."

"Naw, Brother!" said Taylor emphatically.

"Then the demonstrations going to be smashed," said Hadley. "*You* can stop it! You have the responsibility and the blame!"

Taylor sighed.

"Gawd knows Ah ain t blame. Ahm doin whut mah heart tells me t do. . . ."

"Then whats keeping you from working with us?" asked Hadley. "Im a white man and Im here willing to fight for your peoples rights!"

"Ahm wid yuh, Brother!" said Taylor in a voice which carried a deep note of pleading. "Ahm wid yuh no matter whut yuh *think!* But yuh *cant* use mah name! Ef them white folks knowed Ah wuz callin mah folks in the streets t demonstrate, they wouldnt never gimme a chance t git something fer mah folks ergin. . . ."

"Thats just it, Reverend," said Hadley. "Don't be afraid of their turning you down because youre fighting for your people. If they knew youd really fight, theyd dislike you; yes? But you can *make* them give something to *all* of your people, not just to *you*. Don't you see, Taylor, youre standing *between* your people and the white folks. You can make them give something to *all* of them. And the poor, hungry white folks will be with you."

"Ah can't lead mah folks t go ergin them white folks like tha," said Taylor. "Thas *war!*"

Hadley came close to Taylor.

"Reverend, cant you see thats just the way the white folks *want* you to feel? Are you leading your folks just because the white folks *say* you should, or are you leading them because you *want* to? Dont you believe in what youre doing? What kind of leaders are black people to have if the white folks pick them and tell them what to do?"

"Brothers, Ahma Christian, n whut yuhs astin fer is something tha makes blood!" thundered Taylor.

Hadley and Green looked at each other.

"Waal, whut yuh gonna tell the mayor?" asked Green.

Taylor stood in the center of the room with his hands in his pockets, looking down at his feet. His voice came low, as though he were talking to himself, trying to convince himself.

"Ahma tell em mah folks is hongry. Ahma tell em they wanna march. Ahma tell em ef they march Ahma march wid em. Ahma tell em they wan bread. . . ."

"Reverend," asked Hadley, "why do you feel that this is so different from all the other times youve gone straight to the white folks and *demanded* things for your people?"

"It is different!" said Taylor.

"You didnt say that when you saved Scott from that *mob!*"

"Tha wuz different, Brother Hadley."

"I dont see it."

Taylor's voice came low.

"Ah feels differently erbout it, Brothers."

"You saved Scotts life. All right, youre saving the lives of your congregation now. Scott was one man, but there are five hundred starving people in your church."

"We ain facin no mob now, Brother Hadley."

"Then what in Gods name are we facing, Reverend? If those police wholl be out there in the morning with their guns and clubs arent a *legal* mob, then what . . ."

"It more than a mob, Brother Hadley."

Hadley and Green shook their heads.

"Ah don understan yuh, Reveren," said Green.

"When Ah saved Scott from tha mob, Ah wuz going erginst *some* of the white folks. But this thing is going ergin em *all!* This is too much like war!"

"You mean youre going against the ones with *money* now!" said Hadley. "Over three thousand of the poor white folks will be with *us.* . . ."

"But, Brother Hadley, the white folks whos got moneys got *everything!* This is jus like civil war!"

"Reverend," said Hadley, "cant you see that if they were not afraid they wouldn't be here asking to *talk* with you? Go in and talk with them, speak to them in the name of five thousand hungry people. Tell the mayor and the chief of police that if they dont give the relief back we will demonstrate."

"Ah cant do tha, Brothers. Ah cant let these white folks think Ahm leadin mah folks tha way. Ah tol yuh brothers when Ah ergreed t work wid yuh Ahd go as fer as Ah could. Waal, Ah done done tha. Now yuh here astin me t threaten this whole town n Ah ain gonna do tha!" said Taylor.

"Yuh astin fer bread, Reveren," said Green.

"Its threatenin, Brothers," said Taylor. "N tha ain Gawds way!"

"So youll let your folks starve before youll stand up and talk to those white folks?" asked Hadley.

"Ahm ackin as Gawd gives me the light t see," said Taylor.

There was silence. Then Hadley laughed, noiselessly.

"Well," he said. "I didnt know you felt this way, Reverend. I thought we could count on you. You know the Party will stand behind you no matter what happens."

"Ahm sorry, Brother Hadley," said Taylor.

"When kin we see yuh t fin out whut the mayor n chiefa police say?" asked Green.

Taylor looked at his watch.

"Its a little aftah six now. Make it haf-pas six. Thall gimme time t see the Deacon Board."

Green sighed.

"O.K."

"O.K."

Taylor held the door for them. Then he stood in the center of the room and looked miles through the floor. Lawd, Ah hope Ahm doin right. N they think Ahm scared. . . . He flushed hot with shame and anger. He sat in a chair for a moment, then got right up. He drummed his fingers on the corner of the table. Shucks, Ah jus as waal see them white folks now n git it over wid. Ah knowed this wuz comin up! Ah knowed it! He went through May's room, walking slowly, softly, seeing in his mind the picture of the fat, pink face of Mayor Bolton and the lean, red face of Chief of Police Bruden. As he turned into the narrow hall that led to the parlor he heard children yelling in the playground. He went down a stairway, opened a door and walked through his hushed, dim-lit church. Pale rose light fell slantwise through stained windows and glinted on mahogany pews. He lifted his eyes and saw the figure of Christ on a huge snow-white cross. Gawd, hep me now! Lemme do the right thing! He followed a red carpet to a door that opened into the parlor. He paused and passed his tongue over his dry lips. He could feel his heart beating. Ahll let them do all the talkin. Ahll jus tell em mah folks is hongry. Thas all Ah kin do. Slowly he turned the knob, his lips half parted in dread.

VI

"Why, hello, Dan!"

"Good evenin, Mistah Mayor."

"Howve you been, Dan?"

"Fairly well, wid the hepa Gawd, suh."

Taylor shook hands with a tall, fat white man in a blue serge suit.

"Its been a long time since Ive seen you, Dan."

"Yessuh. It sho has, yo honah."

"Hows Jimmy?"

"Jus fine, suh."

"Thats a fine boy youve got, Dan."

"Ahm sho glad yuh think so, suh."

"If you raise that boy right he will be a leader of his people someday, Dan."

"Thas the one hope of mah life, suh," said Taylor with deep emotion.

"May was tellin me youre sick," said the mayor.

"Aw, it ain nothin, suh. Jusa summer col, suh."

"I didnt mean to bother you if youre sick, Dan."

"Thas awright, suh. Ahm feelin much bettah now, suh."

"Oh, youll pull through all right; itll take a lot more than a summer cold to kill old war horses like you and me, eh, Dan?"

The mayor laughed and winked.

"Ahm hopin Gawd spares me a few mo years, suh," said Taylor.

"But at least you look all right now," said the mayor. "Say, Dan, I want you to meet Chief Bruden. This is Dan, Chief, the boy I was telling you about."

"How yuh, Mistah Chief?" asked Taylor.

A black cigar burned red in Bruden's mouth. He shifted his thin body and growled:

"Hello, boy."

"And, Dan, this is Mr Lowe, head of our fine Industrial Squad."

"How yuh, suh?" asked Taylor.

Lowe nodded with half-closed eyes.

"Sit down, Dan," said the mayor.

"Yessuh."

Taylor sat on the edge of a chair and rested his palms lightly on his knees.

"Maybe our little visit is a surprise, hunh?" asked the mayor.

"Yessuh. It is. But Ahm glad to be of any hep Ah kin, suh."

"Good! I knew youd talk that way. Now, Dan, we want you to help us. Youre a responsible man in this community; thats why we are here."

"Ah tries t do mah duty as Gawd shows it t me, suh."

"Thats the spirit, Dan!" The mayor patted Taylor's knee. "Now Im going to be perfectly frank with you, Dan." The mayor peeled a wrapper from a black cigar. "Here, have one."

"Thank yuh, suh." Taylor put the cigar into his vest pocket. "Ahll smoke it aftah dinner, suh."

There was a silence during which the three white men looked at Taylor.

"Dan," began the mayor, "its not every nigger Id come to and talk this way. Its not every nigger Id trust as Im about to trust you." The mayor looked straight at Taylor. "Im doing this because Ive faith in you. Ive known you for twenty-five years, Dan. During that time I think Ive played pretty fair with you, havent I?"

Taylor swallowed.

"Ahll have t say yuh have, yo honah."

"Mister Lowe and the chief here had another plan," said the mayor. "But I wouldnt hear of it. I told them Id work this thing *my* way. I thought *my* way would be much better. After all, Dan, you and I have worked together in the past and I dont see why we cant work together now. Ive backed you up in a lot of things, Dan. Ive backed you even when other white folks said you were wrong. But I believe in doing the right thing. After all, we are human beings, arent we?"

"Yessuh."

"What Ive done for you in the past Im willing to do again. You remember Scott, dont you?"

"Yessuh. Yuhs been a big hep t me n mah folks, suh."

"Well, Dan, my office is always open to you when you want to see me about any of your problems or the problems of your people," said the mayor.

"N Gawd knows Ah sho thanks yuh, suh!"

The mayor bit off the tip of his cigar and spat it into a brass spittoon.

"Im not going to beat about the bush, Dan."

The mayor paused again. There was silence. Taylor felt called upon to say something.

"Yessuh. Ah sho preciates tha, suh."

"You know these Goddam Reds are organizing a demonstration for tomorrow, dont you?" asked the mayor.

Taylor licked his lips before he answered.

"Yessuh. Ah done heard a lotta folks talkin erbout it, suh."

"Thats too bad, Dan," said the mayor.

"Folks is talking erbout it everwhere . . ." began Taylor.

"What *folks?*" interjected Bruden.

"Waal, mos everbody, suh."

Bruden leaned forward and shook his finger in Taylor's face.

"Listen, boy! I want you to get this straight! Reds aint *folks!* Theyre Goddam sonofabitching lousy bastard rats trying to wreck our country, see? Theyre stirring up race hate! Youre old enough to understand that!"

"Hes telling you straight, boy," said Lowe. "And furthermore . . ."

"Say, whats all this?" demanded the mayor, turning to Lowe and Bruden. "Wait a minute! Whats the big idea of talking to Dan like that? Hes not mixed up in anything like that. Save that kind of talk for bad niggers. . . ."

"The quicker all you niggers get sense enough in your Goddam thick skulls to keep away from them Reds the better off youll be!" said Bruden, ignoring the mayor.

"Aw, c mon," said the mayor. "Dans all right. Aint that right, Dan?"

Taylor looked down and saw at his feet a sharp jutting angle of sunshine falling obliquely through a window. His neck felt hot. This is the showdown, he thought. Theys tryin t trap me. . . . He cleared his throat and looked up slowly and saw the mayor gazing at him with cold gray eyes. He shifted his body slightly and saw the glint of Chief Bruden's police star; he saw Lowe's red lips twisted in half smile and half leer.

"Isnt that right, Dan?" the mayor asked again.

"Yessuh. Whut yuh white folks say is right. N Ah ergrees wid yuh. But Ah ain foolin wid nobody thas tryin t stir up race hate; naw *suh!* Ah ain never done nothin like tha n Ah never will, so hep me Gawd! Now erbout this demonstration: Yessuh, Ah heard erbout it. Thas all everbodys been talkin erbout erroun here fer a week, yo honah. Waal, suh, Ahll tell yuh. Theys jus hongry! Theys marchin cause they don know whut else t do, n thas the truth from here t

Heaven! Mistah Mayor, theys hongry! Just plain *hongry!* Ah give mah las dime today t a woman wid eight chillun. . . ."

"We know all about that, Dan," said the mayor.

"Everybodys hungry," said Bruden.

"Boy, cant you see we are all in the *same* boat?" asked Lowe.

"Waal . . ." drawled Taylor.

"Thingsll be straightened out soon, Dan," interjected the mayor soothingly. "We will see that nobody starves."

"Ah beg yo pardon, suh. A man died jus the other day from starvation. . . ."

Taylor's voice died in his throat and he looked at the floor. He knew that he had said too much.

"I reckon that makes you out a liar, dont it?" Bruden asked the mayor.

"Aw, naw suh!" said Taylor eagerly. "Ah ain disputin nobodys word, suh. Ah jus thought yuh hadnt heard erbout it. . . ."

"We know all about it," said Bruden, turning his head away and looking out of the window; as though he was through with the conversation, as though his mind was made up.

"What do they think theyre going to get by marching?" asked Lowe.

"They think they kin git some bread," said Taylor.

"It wont get em a Goddam crumb!" said Lowe.

There was silence. Taylor looked again at the jutting angle of sunshine and heard the mayor's shoes shifting uneasily on the brown carpet. A match struck; he heard it drop with an angry hiss into the spittoon.

"I dont see why we cant get along, Dan," drawled the mayor.

"Ahm willin t git erlong, Mistah Mayor!" protested Taylor.

"Dan, here we all are, living in good old Dixie. There are twenty-five thousand people in this town. Ten thousand of those people are black, Dan. Theyre your people. Now its our job to keep order among the whites, and we would like to think of you as being a responsible man to keep order among the blacks. Lets get together, Dan. You know these black people better than we do. We want to feel we can depend on you. Why dont you look at this thing the right way? You know Ill never turn you down if you do the right thing. . . ."

"Mistah Mayor, as Gawds mah judge, Ahm doin right when Ah tell you mah folks is hongry. . . ."

"Youre not doing right when you act like a Goddam Red!" said Lowe.

"These niggers around here trust you, Dan," said the mayor. "Theyll do what you tell them to do."

"Speak to them," urged Lowe. "Tell them whats right."

"Mistah Mayor, Gawd in Heaven knows mah people is hongry," said Taylor humbly.

The mayor threw his body forward in the chair and rested his hands on his knees.

"Listen, Dan. I know just how you feel. We *all* feel that way. White people are hungry too. But weve got to be prudent and do this thing right. Dan, youre a leader and youve got great influence over your congregation here." The mayor paused to let the weight of his words sink in. "Dan, I helped you to get that influence by doing your people a lot of favors through *you* when you came into my office a number of times." The mayor looked at Taylor solemnly. "Im asking you now to use that influence and tell your people to stay *off* the streets tomorrow!"

When Taylor spoke he seemed to be outside of himself, listening to his own words, aghast and fearful.

"Ahm sho thankful as Gawd knows fer all yuh done done fer me n mah people, suh. But mah word don go so fer in times like these, yo honah. These folks is lookin t me fer bread n Ah cant give it t em. They hongry n Ah cant tell em where t eat. Theys gonna march no mattah whut Ah say. . . ."

"Youve got influence here, Dan, and you can use it!"

"They wouldnt be marchin ef they wuznt hongry, yo honah!"

"Thats Red talk, nigger!" said Lowe, standing.

"Aw, thats all right, Lowe," said the mayor placatingly.

"Im not going to sit here and let this Goddam nigger insult me to my face!" said Lowe.

Taylor stood up.

"Ahm sorry, suh!"

"You *will* be sorry when you find a Goddam rope around your neck!" said Lowe.

"Now, now," said the mayor, laying his hand on Lowe's arm. He turned to Taylor. "You dont mean you wont speak to em, do you, Dan?"

"There ain nothin Ah kin say t em, Mistah Mayor. . . ."

"Youre doing the wrong thing, Dan!"

"Ahm lettin Gawd be mah judge, suh!"

"If you dont do the right thing *we* will be your judges!" said Lowe.

"Ahm trustin Gawd, suh."

"Well, Goddammit, you better let Him guide you right!" said Bruden, jumping to his feet.

"But, white folks!" pleaded Taylor. "Mah folks cant plant nothin! Its erginst the law! They cant git no work! Whut they gonna do? They don want no trouble. . . ."

"Youre heading for aplenty right now!" said Bruden.

The mayor spoke and his voice was low and resigned.

"Ive done all I could, Dan. You wouldnt follow my advice, now the rest is up to Mister Lowe and Chief Bruden here."

Bruden's voice came with a shout:

"A niggers a nigger! I was against coming here talking to this nigger like he was a white man in the first place. He needs his teeth kicked down his throat!" Bruden poked the red tip of his cigar at Taylor's face. "Im the chief of police of this town, and Im here to see that orders kept! The Chamber of Commerce says therell be no demonstration tomorrow. Therell be three hundred police downtown in the morning to see that thats done! If you send them niggers down there, or if you let these Goddam Reds fool you into it, Ill not be responsible for whatll happen! Weve never had a riot in this town, but youre plotting one right now when you act like this! And you know wholl get the worst of it!"

"Cant yuh do something, Mistah Mayor? Cant yuh fix it sos we kin git some relief?"

The mayor did not answer; Lowe came close to him.

"We know youve been seeing Hadley and Green! We know whats going on! So watch yourself, nigger!"

"Suh?"

They went out. Taylor stood at the window and saw them get into their car and disappear in a cloud of dust around a corner. He sat down, feeling sweat over all his body. Gawd knows whut t do. . . . He brought Lowe n Bruden here t threaten me. . . . N they know erbout Hadley n Green. . . . Somebody tol. . . . He looked up, hearing the soft boom of a clock. Hadley n Greens comin back here at six-thirty. . . . He went down the hall, thinking, Lawd, ef Ah only knowed whut t do. . . .

VII

May met him in the hall.

"Whut they say, Dan?" she asked with suppressed hysteria.

"Don bother me now, May!"

"There wont be no trouble, will it, Dan?"

"Naw, May! Now please! Yuh worryin me!"

"Yuhll spoil things fer Jimmy, Dan! Don do nothin wrong! Its fer Jimmy Ahm astin!"

"Itll be awright! Now lemme go!"

He hurried down the hallway, leaving her crying. Good Gawd! How come she wont leave me erlone? Firs its Jimmy; then its her. . . . Ef it ain one its the other. . . . He went to the end of the hall, down the steps, turned and came to the door of the Deacon Room. He heard subdued voices. He knew that the deacons were waiting for him, waiting for some definite word. Shucks, Ahm willin t go thu wid tha march ef they is. Them white folks cant kill us *all*. . . . He pushed the door in. The voices ceased. He saw a dense cloud of tobacco smoke and a circle of black faces. He forced a wan smile.

"Good evenin, Brothers!" he said.

"How yuh, Reveren?" asked Deacon Bonds.

"Ahm sorry Ahm late," said Taylor.

"Wuz tha the mayor out there?" asked Deacon Williams.

Taylor paused and pulled out his handkerchief.

"Yeah, Brothers, it wuz the mayor. N the chiefa police n tha man Lowe from the Red Squad. . . ."

"RED SQUAD!" shouted Deacon Smith, jumping to his feet with an outraged look.

"Whut they say, Reveren?" asked Deacon Williams quietly, ignoring Deacon Smith.

Taylor sighed and looked at the floor. For a moment he loathed them because he knew they were expecting an answer to their questions. They were expecting him to speak now as he had always spoken, to the point, confidently, and finally. He had wanted them to do the talking, and now they were silent, waiting for him to speak. Lawd, Ah hope Ahm doin right. Ah don wanna lead these folks wrong. . . .

"They know all erbout tha demonstration," he said.

"But whut they *say?*" asked Deacon Bonds.

"Shucks, man! Yuh *know* whut they said!" said Deacon Smith. "Yuh *know* how them white folks feel erbout this thing!"

"They don wan us t march," said Taylor. "They said ef we march theyll put the police on us. . . ."

Deacon Smith leveled his forefinger at Taylor and intoned:

"AH TOL YUH SO!"

"They said therell be a riot," Taylor went on stubbornly.

"Yessuh! Brothers, wes gotta do *right!*" said Deacon Smith, banging his open palm down on the table. "Ah awways said wes gotta do *right*, Reveren!"

"Ahm prayin t Gawd t guide us right," said Taylor.

"Yuh sho don ack like it!" said Deacon Smith.

"Let the Reveren finish, will yuh?" asked Deacon Bonds.

"Wes gotta do right!" said Deacon Smith again, sitting down, folding his arms, crossing his legs and turning his face sternly away.

"Whut else they say, Reveren?" asked Deacon Bonds.

Taylor sighed.

"They say wes mixed up wid the Reds. . . ."

"N by Gawd we *is!*" bawled Deacon Smith. "At least *yuh* is! Ah tol yuh t leave them Reds erlone! They don mean *no*body *no* good! When men starts t deny Gawd, nothin good kin come from em!"

"Brother Smith, let the Reveren talk, will yuh?" asked Deacon Williams.

"He ain talkin *sense!*" said Deacon Smith.

"They say therell be three hundred police downtown in the mawnin," said Taylor, ignoring Smith. "They say only Washington kin do something erbout relief, n tha we must wait. . . ."

"N Gawd Awmighty knows thas all we kin do: wait!" said Deacon Smith.

"Fer Chrissakes, Brother Smith, let im talk!" said Deacon Williams. "We all knows *yuhs* scared!"

"Ah ain scared! Ah got sense! Ah . . ."

"Yuh sho don ack like it, the way yuh shoot off yo mouth!" said Deacon Williams.

Deacon Smith stood up.

"Yuh cant talk tha way t me!"

"Then keep yo big mouth shut!" said Deacon Williams.

"Whos gonna make me?"

"Brothers, please!" begged Taylor.

"A fool kin see tha the white folks is scared!" said Deacon Williams.

"N jus cause theys *scared*, theyll kill *any*body whuts fool ernuff t go downtown in the mawnin," said Deacon Smith.

"Shucks, Ahm willin t taka chance," said Deacon Hilton.

"Me too!"

"We ain got nothin t lose!"

"Any *fool* kin git his head busted!" said Deacon Smith.

"Brothers, fer the lova Gawd, quit fussin!" said Taylor.

They were silent. Taylor looked at them, letting his eyes rove from face to face.

"Brothers, this is the case," he said finally. "They threatenin us not t march, but they ain sayin our folks kin git no relief. Now Ah figgers ef we hada big crowd downtown in the mawnin they wont bother us. . . ."

"Thas whut *yuh* think," sneered Deacon Smith.

"N ef we don hava big crowd, theyll smash us. Now its up t us . . ."

"Reveren, do the *po* white folks say they gonna be *wid* us?" asked Deacon Jones.

"Brother Hadley tol me theys gonna be wid us," said Taylor.

"Tha Hadley is a lie n the trutha Gawd ain in im!" shouted Deacon Smith. "Tha white man is jus tryin t trick yuh, Ahm tellin yuh!"

"Waal, we kin never know less we try n see," said Deacon Bonds.

"Yeah, they ain gonna let yuh try but *once*," said Deacon Smith.

"Waal, Ah ain got but *one* time t die!" said Deacon Bonds.

"Ah think the white folksll be there," said Taylor. "Theys hongry too. . . ."

"Yuhll wake up *some* day!" said Deacon Smith.

"Whut yuh gonna do, Reveren?" asked Deacon Williams.

"Do the congregation wanna march?" asked Taylor.

"They say theys *gonna* march!"

"Waal, Ahll march wid em," said Taylor quietly. "They wont march erlone. . . ."

Deacon Smith waved his arms and screamed:

"Yeah, yuhll march! But yuhs scared t let me use yo name! Whut kinda leader *is* yuh? If yuhs gonna ack a fool n be a *Red*, then how come yuh wont come on out n say so sos we kin all hear it? Naw, yuh ain man ernuff t say whut yuh is! Yuh wanna stan in wid the white folks! Yuh wanna stan in wid the Reds! Yuh wanna stan in wid the congregation! Yuh wanna stan in wid the Deacon Board! Yuh wanna stan in wid *ever*body n yuh stan in wid *no*body!"

"Ahm ackin accordin t mah lights!" said Taylor.

"Waal, they ain lettin yuh see fer!" said Deacon Smith.

"Ef yuh gotta plan bettah than mine, Brother Smith, tell us erbout it!"

"AH SAY WE OUGHTNT MARCH!"

"Then whut we gonna do?"

"Wait n see how things come out!"

"Ahm tireda waitin," said Taylor.

"How come yuh didnt send yo name out on them leaflets?" demanded Deacon Smith. Without waiting for Taylor to answer, he flared: "Ahll tell yuh why yuh didnt! Yuh *scared!* Yuh didnt wan

them white folks t know yuhs mixed up in this demonstration. Yuh
wanted em t think yuh wuz being pushed erlong by other folks n
yuh couldnt hep whut wuz happenin! But, Reveren, as sho as theres
a Gawd in Heaven yuh ain foolin nobody!"

Taylor stood up.

"Brother Smith, Ah knows whut yuhs up t! Yuh tryin t run me
outta mah church, but yuh cant! Gawd Awmighty Himself put me
here n Ahm stayin till He says fer me t go! Yuh been schemin t git
me out, but yuh cant do it this way! It ain right n Gawd knows it
ain! Yeah; ef mah folks marches in the mawnin Ahm marchin wid
em!"

"Thas the time, Reveren!"

"We kin show tha ol mayor something!"

"N therell be white folks wid us too!"

"Ahll go wid the Reveren n the congregation!"

"Ahll go!"

"N me too!"

"Gawd ain wid yuh when yuh ain in the right!" said Deacon
Smith.

"Gawd didnt mean fer folks t be hongry!" said Deacon Bonds.

"But He ain wid yuh when yuh stirrin up trouble, makin blood
n riots!" said Deacon Smith. "N any man whut sets here n calls himself a leader called by Gawd t preach n leads his folks the wrong way
is a fool n the spirita Gawd ain in im!"

"Now wait a minute there, Brother Smith!" said Taylor. "Yuhs
talkin *dangerous!*"

"Ah say any man whut leads his folks inter guns n police . . ."

"Ain nobody leadin us *nowhere!*" said Deacon Bonds.

"We gwine *ourselves!*" said Deacon Williams.

"Ah ain in this!" said Deacon Smith, jumping again to his feet.
"Ah ain in this n Ahm gonna do whut Ah kin t hep mah people!"

The room grew quiet.

"Whut yuh mean, Brother Smith?" asked Taylor.

"Ah say Ahm gonna hep mah people!" said Deacon Smith again.

Taylor walked over to him.

"Is yuh gonna tell the white folks on us?"

Deacon Smith did not answer.

"Talk, Brother Smith!" said Taylor. "Tell us whut yuh mean!"

"Ah means whut Ah means!" said Deacon Smith; and he clamped
his teeth tight, sat again, crossed his legs, folded his arms and stared
at the blank wall.

Taylor swallowed and looked at the floor. Lawd, Ah don know

whut t do! Ah wish this wuz over. . . . This niggers gonna tell on us! Hes gonna tell the white folks sos he kin stan in wid em. . . .

"Brother Smith . . ." began Taylor.

The door opened and Jimmy stepped into the room.

"Say, Pa!"

"Whut yuh wan, son?"

"Somebodys out front t see yuh. Theys in a car. Theys white folks."

"Scuse me, Brothers," said Taylor. "Ahll be right back."

"Wes gonna set right here till yuh git back," said Deacon Smith. When outside the door, Taylor turned to Jimmy.

"Who is they, Jimmy? How come they wouldnt come in?"

"Ah dunno, Pa. The car drove up jus as Ah wuz comin thu the gate. They white men. They said fer yuh t come right out."

"Awright. N, son, yuh bettah go see bout yo ma."

"Whuts the mattah?"

"Shes jus upset erbout the demonstration."

"Is they gonna march, Pa?"

"Ah reckon so."

"Is many gonna be out?"

"Ah dunno, son. Ah hope so. Yuh bettah go see erbout yo ma now."

"Yessuh."

"Yuh tell them boys whut Ah tol yuh?"

"Yessuh."

Taylor paused at the front door and peeped out from behind a curtain. In front of his gate was a long black car. Who kin tha be? For a moment he thought the mayor had come back. But his cars gray. . . . He opened the door and walked slowly down the steps. Lawd, mabbe we oughtnt go thu wid this demonstration aftah all? We might all be sorry ef somebodys killed in the mawnin. . . . He walked along a flower-bordered path that smelt of violets and magnolias. Dust rested filmily on tree leaves. The sun was almost gone. As he came to the car a white face looked out.

"You Taylor?"

"Yessuh," answered Taylor, smiling.

The rear door of the car opened and the white man stepped to the ground.

"So youre Taylor, hunh?"

"Yessuh," said Taylor again, still smiling, but puzzled. "Kin Ah be of service t yuh, suh?"

Taylor saw it coming, but could do nothing. He remembered

afterward that he had wanted to ask, Whut yuh doin? The blow caught him flush on the point of the jaw, sending him flying backward. His head struck the edge of the running board; a flash of red shot before his eyes. He rolled, face downward, into a bed of thick violets. Dazed, he turned his head, trying to speak. He felt a hand grab the back of his collar and jerk him up.

"Get in the car, nigger!"

"Say, whut yuh . . ."

"Shut up and get in the car, Goddam you!"

A blow came to his right eye. There were three white men now. They lifted him and rammed him down on the floor in the back of the car.

"Say, you cant do this!"

"Get your Goddam mouth shut, you bastard!"

A hard palm slapped him straight across his face. He struggled up, protesting.

"You . . ."

The heel of a shoe came hard into his solar plexus. He doubled up like a jackknife. His breath left, and he was rigid, half paralyzed.

"You think you can run this whole Goddam town, don't you? You think a nigger can run over white folks and get away with it?"

He lay still, barely breathing, looking at blurred white faces in the semidarkness of the roaring car.

VIII

The moment he tried to tell the direction in which the car was moving he knew he had waited too long. He remembered dimly that they had turned corners at least three times. He lay with closed eyes and wondered what they were going to do with him. She gonna be worried t death, he thought, thinking of May. And then he thought of Jimmy and said to himself, Ah hope he don go n ack a fool now. . . . The numbness which had deadened most of his stomach and chest was leaving. He felt sweat on his back and forehead. The car slowed, turned; then it ran fast again. He knew by the way the rocks crunched beneath the humming rubber tires that they were speeding over gravel. Whut roads this? He could not tell. There were so many gravel roads leading out of town. He tried to recall how long he had lain there half paralyzed from that kick in the solar plexus. He was confused; it might have been five minutes or it might have been an hour. The car slowed again, turning. He smelt the strong scent of a burning cigarette and heard the toll of a far-off church bell. The car stopped; he heard the sound of other cars, gears shifting and motors throbbing. We mus be at some cross-roads. But he could not guess which one. He had an impulse to call for help. But there would not be any use in his doing that now. Mabbe they white folks anyhow. He would be better off as he was; even six white men were better than a mob of white men. The car was speeding again, lurching. He smelt dust, clay dust. Then he heard a hard, rasping voice:

"How is he?"

"O.K."

"Keep im quiet!"

"O.K."

He said nothing. He began to wonder how many of them were in the car. Yes, he should have been watching for something like this. They been threatenin me fer a long time. Now this is it. The car was gradually slowing with that long slow slowing preceding a final stop. He felt the rubber tires turning over rough ground; his head rocked from side to side, hitting against the lower back of the front seat. Then the car stopped; the motor stopped; for a moment there was complete silence. Then he heard wind sighing in trees. Wes out in the country somewhere. In the woods, he thought.

"O.K.?"

"O.K.!"

He heard a door open.

"C mon, nigger! Get up and watch yourself!"

He pulled up and caught a glimpse of starry sky. As his feet hit the ground his head began to ache. He had lain cramped so long the blood had left his limbs; he took a step, kicking out his legs to restore circulation. His arms were grabbed from behind and he felt the pressure of a kneecap in the center of his spine. He gasped and reeled backward.

"Where you think youre going?"

He rested on his knees, his body full of pain. He heard a car door slam.

"Awright, nigger! Lets go! Straight ahead!"

He got up and twisted his head about to see who had spoken. He saw four blurred white faces and then they were blotted out. He reeled backward again, his head striking the ground. A pain knotted in his temple.

"Get up, nigger! Keep your eyes in front, and walk, Goddammit!"

He pulled up and limped off, his head down. Mabbe they gonna shoot me? His feet and the feet behind him made a soft *cush-cush* in the dew-wet grass and leaves.

"All right, nigger!"

He stopped. Slowly he raised his eyes; he saw a tall white man holding a platted leather whip in his hand, hitting it gently against his trousers leg.

"You know what this is, nigger?"

He said nothing.

"Wont talk, hunh? Well, this is a nigger lesson!"

The whip flashed in faint starlight. The blow numbed his lips. He tasted blood.

"You know what this is? Im asking you again, nigger?"

"Nawsuh," he whispered.

"This is a nigger whip!"

The leather whacked across his shoulders.

"Mistah, Ah ain done nothin!"

"Aw, naw! You aint done nothing! You aint never done a God-dam thing, have you?" White men were standing close around him now. "All you ever do is play around with Reds, dont you? All you ever do is get crowds of niggers together to threaten white folks, dont you? When we get through with you tonight youll know how to stay in a niggers place! C mon! Get that Goddam vest off!"

He did not move. The whip wrapped itself around his neck, leaving a ring of fire.

"You want me to *beat* it off you?"

He pulled off the vest and held it in his hands.

"C mon! Get that shirt and undershirt off!"

He stripped to his waist. A night wind cooled his sweaty body; he was conscious of his back as he had never been before, conscious of every square inch of black skin there. One of the white men walked off a few paces and stopped.

"Bring im over here!"

"O.K.!"

They guided him with prods and kicks.

"On your knees, nigger!"

He did not move. Again his arms were caught from behind and a kneecap came into the center of his back. Breathless, he dropped, his hands and knees cooling in the wet grass. He lifted his fingers to feel his swelling lips; he felt his wrists being grabbed and carried around the trunk of a tree. He held stiffly and struggled against a rope.

"Let go!"

His arms went limp. He rested his face against a cold tree trunk. A rope cut into his wrists. They tied his feet together, drawing the rope tight about his ankles. He looked around; they stood watching.

"Well, nigger, what do you know?"

"Nothin, suh."

"Youre a preacher, aint you?"

"Yessuh."

"Well, lets hear you pray some!"

He said nothing. The whip lashed across his bare back, *whick!* He flinched and struggled against the rope that cut his wrists to the bone. The leather thong hummed again, *whick!* and his spine arched inward, like a taut bow.

"Goddam your black soul, pray!"

He twisted his face around, pleading:

"Please, mistah! Don whip me! Ah ain done nothin. . . ."

Another lash came across his half-turned cheek, *whick!* He jerked around and sheltered his face against the tree trunk. The lash hit his back, *whick!*

"*Hit* that black bastard, Bob!"

"Let me have that whip!"

"Naw, wait a minute!"

He said nothing. He clenched his teeth, his whole body quivering and waiting. A split second after each blow his body would lurch, as though absorbing the shock.

"You going to pray? You want me to beat you till you *cant* pray?"

He said nothing. He was expecting each blow now; he could almost feel them before they came, stinging, burning. Each flick came straight on his back and left a streak of fire, a streak that merged with the last streak, making his whole back a sheet of living flame. He felt his strength ebbing; he could not clench his teeth any more. His mouth hung open.

"Let me have it, Bob?"

"Naw, its my turn!"

There was a pause. Then the blows came again; the pain burned its way into his body, wave upon wave. It seemed that when he held his muscles taut the blows hurt less; but he could not hold taut long. Each blow weakened him; each blow told him that soon he would give out. Warm blood seeped into his trousers, ran down his thighs. He felt he could not stand it any longer; he held his breath, his lungs swelling. Then he sagged, his back a leaping agony of fire; leaping as of itself, as though it were his but he could not control it any longer. The weight of his body rested on his arms; his head dropped to one side.

"Ahhlll ppppprray," he sobbed.

"Pray, then! Goddam you, pray!"

He tried to get his breath, tried to form words, hearing trees sighing somewhere. The thong flicked again, *whick!*

"Aint you going to pray?"

"Yyyyyessuh. . . ."

He struggled to draw enough air into his lungs to make his words sound.

"Ooour ffather . . ."

The whip cut hard, *whick!* pouring fire and fire again.

"Have mercy, Lawd!" he screamed.

"Pray, nigger! Pray like you *mean* it!"

". . . wwwhich aaaaart in Hheaven . . . hhhallowed bbe Tttthy nname. . . ." The whip struck, *whick!* "Ahm prayin, mmmmistah!"

"Goddam your black heart, *pray!*"

". . . Ttthy kkkindom ccome . . . Ttthy wwwill bbe ddd-done. . . ."

He sobbed, his breath leaving his lungs, going out from him, not wanting to stay to give sound to his words. The whip brought more fire and he could not stand it any longer; his heart seemed about to burst. He screamed, stretched his knees out and twisted his arms till he lay sideways, half on his stomach. The whip came into his stomach, *whick!* He turned over; it came on his back again, *whick!* He stopped struggling and hung limply, his weight suspended on arms he could not feel. Then fire flamed over all his body; he stiffened, glaring upward, wild-eyed.

"Whats the matter, nigger? You hurt?"

"Awright, kill me! Tie me n kill me! Yuh white-trash cowards, kill me!"

"Youre tough, aint you? Just wait! We'll kill you, you black sonofabitch!"

"Lemme have that whip!"

"C mon, now! Its my turn!"

"Give me that whip, Ellis!"

He was taut, but not feeling the effort to be taut.

"Well git yuh white trash someday! So hep me Gawd, well git yuh!"

The whip stopped.

"Say that again, Goddam you!"

The whip lashed, *whick!* but there was no streak of fire now;

there was only one sheet of pain stretching all over his body, leaping, jumping, blazing in his flesh.

"Say it!"

He relaxed and closed his eyes. He stretched his legs out, slowly, not listening, not waiting for the whip to fall. *say it whick! say it whick! say it whick!* He groaned. Then he dropped his head and could not feel any more.

IX

Moonlight pained his eyeballs and the rustle of tree leaves thundered in his ears. He seemed to have only a head that hurt, a back that blazed and eyes that ached. In him was a feeling that some power had sucked him deep down into the black earth, had drained all strength from him. He was waiting for that power to go away so he could come back to life, to light. His eyes were half open, but his lids did not move. He was thirsty; he licked his lips, wanting water. Then the thunder in his ears died, rolling away. He moved his hand and touched his forehead; his arm fell limply in the wet grass and he lay waiting to feel that he wanted to move. As his blood began to flow swiftly again he felt sweat breaking out over his body. It seemed he could hear a tiny, faraway sound whispering over and over like a voice in an empty room: Ah got fever. . . . His back rested on a bed of fire, the imprint of leaves and grass searing him with a scalding persistence. He turned over on his stomach and groaned. Then he jerked up, half sitting. He was fully conscious now, fighting for his strength, remembering the curses, the prayer and the whip. The voice whispered again, this time louder: Ah gotta git home. . . . With fumbling fingers he untied the rope from his wrists and ankles. They didnt kill me, he thought. He stood up and the dark earth swayed and the stars blurred. Lawd, have mercy! He found himself on his knees; he had not known when he had started falling; he just found himself on his knees. Lawd, Ahm weak! He stood up again, more slowly this time, holding onto a tree. He would have to get his shirt; he could not go through the streets with a naked and bleeding back. He put one foot in front of the other with conscious effort, holding his body stiffly. Each slight twist of his shoulders sent a wave of liquid metal over him. In the grass at his feet his shirt was smeared like a white blur. He touched it; it was wet. He held it, instinctively fearing to put it on. When it did touch, his whole back blazed with a pain so intense that it seemed to glow white hot. No, he could not put it on now. Stiffly he went among the trees, holding the shirt in his hands, looking at the ground.

He stopped at the edge of a dirt road, conscious of the cool steady stars and the fire that smoldered in his back. Whut roads this? He could not tell. Then he heard a clock striking so faintly that it seemed to be tolling in his own mind. He counted, Wun, tuh. . . . Its tuh erclock, he thought. He could not stay here all night; he had to go in one direction or another. He watched the brown dusty road winding away in the darkness, like a twisting ribbon. Then he ducked his head, being seared again with fire and feeling a slight rush of air brush across his face. A small bird wheeled past his eyes and fluttered dizzily in the starlight. He watched it veer and dip, then crash softly into a tree limb. It fell to the ground, flapping tiny wings blindly. Then the bird twittered in fright and sailed straight upward into the starlight, vanishing. He walked northward, not going anywhere in particular, but walked northward because the bird had darted in the direction.

The road curved, turned to gravel, crunching under his shoes. This mus be the way, he thought. There were fences along the sides of the road now. He went faster, holding his legs stiffly to avoid pulling the muscles in his back. A church steeple loomed in the starlight, slender and faint. Yeah, thas Houstons church. N Ah gotta go thu a white neighborhood, he thought with despair. He saw houses, white, serene and cool in the night. Spose Ah go to Houston? Naw, hes white. *White*. . . . Even tho he preaches the gospel Ah preaches, he might not take me in. . . . He passed a small graveyard surrounded by a high iron picket fence. A *white* graveyard, he thought and snickered bitterly. Lawd Gawd in Heaven, even the dead cant be together! He stopped and held his shirt in his hands. He dreaded trying to put it on, but he had to. Ah cant go thu the streets like this. Gingerly he draped the shirt over his shoulders; the whole mass of bruised and mangled flesh flamed, glowed white. With a convulsive movement he rammed his arms into the sleeves, thinking that the faster he did it the less pain there would be. The fire raged so he had a wild impulse to run, feeling that he would have no time then to suffer. But he could not run in a white neighborhood. To run would mean to be shot, for a burglar, or anything. Stiff-legged, he went down a road that turned from brown dust to black asphalt. Ahead street lamps glowed in round, rosy hazes.

Far down the shadow-dappled pavement he heard the sound of feet. He walked past a white man, then he listened to the white man's footsteps dying away behind him. He stopped at a corner and held onto a telephone pole. It would be better to keep in the residential district than to go through town. He would be stopped and questioned in town surely. And jailed maybe. Three blocks later on a white boy came upon him so softly and suddenly that he started in panic. After the boy had gone he turned to look; he saw the boy turning, looking at him. He walked on hurriedly. A block later a white woman appeared. When she was some fifty feet away she crossed to the other side of the street. Hate tightened his throat, then he emptied his lungs in a short, silent, bitter laugh. Ah ain gonna bother yuh, white lady. Ah only wan t git home. . . .

Like a pillar of fire he went through the white neighborhood. Someday theys gonna burn! Someday theys gonna burn in Gawds Awmighty fire! How come they make us suffer so? The worls got too mucha everthing! Yit they bleed us! They fatten on us like leeches! There ain no groun yuh kin walk on tha they don own! N Gawd knows tha ain right! He made the earth fer us all! He ain tol no lie when He put us in this worl n said be fruitful n multiply. . . . Fire fanned his hate; he stopped and looked at the burning stars. "Gawd, ef Yuh gimme the strength Ahll tear this ol buildin down! Tear it down, Lawd! Tear it down like ol Samson tore the temple down!" He walked again, mumbling. "Lawd, tell me whut t do! Speak t me, Lawd!" He caught his breath; a dark figure came out of the shadows in front of him. He saw a glint of metal; it was a policeman. He held erect and walked rapidly. Ahll stop, he thought. He wont have t ast me t stop. . . . He saw the white face drawing closer. He stopped and waited.

"Put your hands up, nigger!"

"Yessuh."

He lifted his arms. The policeman patted his hips, his sides. His back blazed, but he bit his lips and held still.

"Who you work for?"

"Ahma preacher, suh."

"A *preacher?*"

"Yessuh."

"What you doing out here this time of night?"

"Ah wuz visitin a sick man, a janitah, suh, whut comes t mah church. He works fer Miz Harvey. . . ."

"Who?"

"Miz Harvey, suh."

"Never heard of her, and Ive been on this beat for ten years."

"She lives right back there, suh," he said, half turning and pointing.

"Well, you look all right. You can go on. But keep out of here at night."

"Yessuh."

He was near his own people now. Across a grassy square he could see the top of the roundhouse glinting dully in the moonlight. The black asphalt turned to cinders and the houses were low, close together, squatting on the ground as though hiding in fear. He saw his church and relaxed. He came to the steps, caught hold of a banister and rested a moment.

When inside he went quietly down a hall, mounted the stairs and came to the door of his room. He groped in the dark and felt the bed. He tried to pull off the shirt. It had stuck. He peeled it. Then he eased onto the bed and lay on his stomach. In the darkness his back seemed to take new fire. He went to the kitchen and wet a cloth with cold water. He lay down again with the cloth spread over him. That helped some. Then he began to shake. He was crying.

x

The door creaked.

"Tha yuh, Pa?"

"Son?"

"Good Gawd, wes been lookin all over fer yuh! Where yuh been? Mas worried t death!"

"C mon in, son, n close the do."

"Don yuh wanna light?"

"Naw; close the do."

There was a short silence.

"Whuts the mattah, Pa? Yuh sick?"

"Close the do n set down, son!"

Taylor could hear Jimmy's breathing, then a chair scraping over the floor and the soft rustle of Jimmy's clothes as he sat.

"Whuts the mattah, Pa? What happened?"

Taylor stared in the darkness and slowly licked his swollen lips. He wanted to speak, but somehow could not. Then he stiffened, hearing Jimmy rise.

"Set *down*, son!"

"But, Pa . . ."

Fire seethed not only in Taylor's back, but all over, inside and out. It was the fire of shame. The questions that fell from Jimmy's lips burned as much as the whip had. There rose in him a memory of all the times he had given advice, counsel and guidance to Jimmy. And he wanted to talk to him now as he had in the past. But his impulses were deadlocked. Then suddenly he heard himself speaking, hoarsely, faintly. His voice was like a whisper rising from his whole body.

"They whipped me, son. . . ."

"Whipped yuh? Who?"

Jimmy ran to the bed and touched him.

"Son, set *down!*"

Taylor's voice was filled with a sort of tense despair. He felt Jimmy's fingers leaving him slowly. There was a silence in which he could hear only his own breath struggling in his throat.

"Yuh mean the *white* folks?"

Taylor buried his face in his pillow and tried to still the heaving in his chest.

"They beat me, son. . . ."

"Ahll git a doctah!"

"Naw!"

"But yuhs hurt!"

"Naw; lock the do! Don let May in here. . . ."

"Goddam them white bastards!"

"Set down, son!"

"Who wuz they, Pa?"

"Yuh cant do nothin, son. Yuhll have t wait. . . ."

"Wes been waitin too long! All we do is wait, *wait!*"

Jimmy's footsteps scuffed across the floor. Taylor sat up.

"Son?"

"Ahma git mah gun n git Pete n Bob n Joe n Sam! Theyll see they cant do this t us!"

Taylor groped in the darkness; he found Jimmy's shoulders.

"C mon, son! Ahm awright. . . ."

"Thas the reason why they kill us! We take everthing they put on us! We take everthing! *Everthing!*"

"Yuh cant do nothin *erlone,* Jimmy!"

Jimmy's voice was tense, almost hysterical.

"But we kin *make* em know they cant do this t us widout us doin *something!* Aw, hell, Pa! Is we gonna be dogs *all* the time?"

"But theyll kill yuh, son!"

"Somebody *has* t die!"

Taylor wanted to tell Jimmy something, but he could not find the words. What he wanted to say boiled in him, but it seemed too big to come out. He flinched from pain, pressing his fingers to his mouth, holding his breath.

"Pa?"

"Yeah, son?"

"Hadley n Green wuz here t see yuh three-fo times."

"Yeah?"

Jimmy said nothing. Taylor twisted around, trying to see his son's face in the darkness.

"Whut they say, son?"

"Aw, hell! It don mattah. . . ."

"Tell me whut they *said!*"

"Ttthey ssaid . . . Aw, Pa, they didn't know!"

"Whut they *say?*"

"They said yuh had done run out on em. . . ."

"Run *out?*"

"Everbody wuz astin where yuh wuz," said Jimmy. "Nobody knowed. So they tol em yuh run out. N Brother Smith had the Deacon Board t vote yuh outta the church. . . ."

"Vote me *out?*"

"They said they didn't wan yuh fer pastah no mo. It wuz Smith who made em do it. He tol em yuh had planned a demonstration n lef em holdin the bag. He fussed n stormed at em. They thought they wuz doin right. . . ."

Taylor lay on his bed of fire in the darkness and cried. He felt Jimmy's fingers again on his face.

"Its awright, Pa. Well git erlong somehow. . . ."

"Seems like Gawds done lef me! Ahd die fer mah people ef Ah only knowed how. . . ."

"Pa . . ."

"How come Ah cant never do nothin? All mah life Ah done tried n cant do nothin! *Nothin!*"

"Its awright, Pa!"

"Ah done lived all mah life on mah knees, a-beggin n a-pleadin wid the white folks. N all they gimme wuz crumbs! All they did wuz kick me! N then they come wida gun n ast me t give mah own soul! N ef Ah so much as talk lika man they try t kill me. . . ."

He buried his face in the pillow, trying to sink himself into something so deeply that he could never feel again. He heard Jimmy turning the key in the lock.

"Son!"

Again he ran to Jimmy and held him.

"Don do tha, son!"

"Thingsll awways be like this less we *fight!*"

"Set down, son! Yo po ol pas a-*beggin* yuh to set down!"

He pulled Jimmy back to the bed. But even then it did not seem he could speak as he wanted to. He felt what he wanted to say, but it was elusive and hard to formulate.

"Son . . ."

"Ah ain gonna live this way, Pa!"

He groped for Jimmy's shoulders in the darkness and squeezed them till the joints of his fingers cracked. And when words came they seemed to be tearing themselves from him, as though they were being pushed upward like hot lava out of a mountain from deep down.

"Don be a fool, son! Don thow yo life erway! We cant do nothin erlone."

"But theys gonna treat us this way as long as we *let* em!"

He had to make Jimmy understand; for it seemed that in making him understand, in telling him, he, too, would understand.

"We gotta git wid the *people,* son. Too long we done tried t do this thing our way n when we failed we wanted t run out n pay off the white folks. Then they kill us up like flies. Its the *people,* son! Wes too much erlone this way! Wes los when wes erlone! Wes gotta be wid our folks. . . ."

"But theys killin us!"

"N theyll keep on killin us less we learn how t fight! Son, its the people we mus git wid us! Wes empty n weak this way! The reason we cant do nothin is cause wes so much erlone. . . ."

"Them Reds wuz right," said Jimmy.

"Ah dunno," said Taylor. "But let nothin come tween yuh n *yo* people. Even the Reds cant do nothin ef yuh lose yo people. . . ." Fire burned him as he talked, and he talked as though trying to escape it. "Membah whut Ah told yuh prayer wuz, son?"

There was silence, then Jimmy answered slowly:

"Yuh mean lettin Gawd be so real in yo life tha everthing yuh do is cause of Im?"

"Yeah, but its different now, son. Its the *people!* Theys the ones whut mus be real t us! Gawds wid the people! N the peoples gotta be real as Gawd t us! We cant hep ourselves er the people when wes erlone. Ah been wrong erbout a lotta things Ah tol yuh, son. Ah tol yuh them things cause Ah thought they wuz right. Ah tol yuh t work hard n climb t the top. Ah tol yuh folks would lissen t yuh then. But they wont, son! All the will, all the strength, all the power, all the numbahs is in the people! Yuh cant live by yoself! When they beat

me tonight, they beat *me*. . . . There wuznt nothing Ah could do
but lay there n hate n pray n cry. . . . Ah couldnt *feel* mah people,
Ah couldnt *see* mah people, Ah couldnt *hear* mah people. . . . All
Ah could feel wuz tha whip cuttin mah blood out. . . ."

In the darkness he imagined he could see Jimmy's face as he had
seen it a thousand times, looking eagerly, his eyes staring before
him, fashioning his words into images, into life. He hoped Jimmy
was doing that now.

"Ahll awways hate them bastards! Ahll *aw*ways hate em!"

"Theres other ways, son."

"Yuhs sick, Pa. . . ."

"Wes all sick, son. Wes gotta think erbout the people, night n day,
think erbout em so hard tha our po selves is fergotten. . . . Whut
they suffer is whut Ah suffered las night when they whipped me.
Wes gotta keep the people wid us."

Jimmy was silent. A soft knock came at the door.

XI

"Dan!"

"Thas Ma," said Jimmy.

Taylor heard Jimmy rise to his feet; he gripped Jimmy's hands.

"Please, Pa! Let her come in n hep yuh!"

"Naw."

"Dan!"

Jimmy broke from him; he heard the key turn in the lock. The
door opened.

"Dan! Fer Gawds sake, whuts the mattah?"

Jimmy switched on the light. Taylor lay blinking at May's anxious
face. He felt shame again, knowing that he should not feel it, but
feeling it anyway. He turned over and buried his face in his hands.

"Dan!"

She ran and knelt at the side of the bed.

"They tried t kill im, Ma! They beat im!" said Jimmy.

"Ah knowed them white folks wuz gonna do something like this!
Ah knowed it," sobbed May.

Taylor sat up.

"Yuh be still! Lay down!" said May. She pushed him back onto the
bed.

"Cant yuh do something fer im, Ma? Hes sufferin tha way."

Taylor heard May leave the room and come back.

"Hol still, Dan. This ain gonna hurt yuh. . . ."

He felt warm water laving him, then something cool that smelled of oil. He heard Jimmy moving to and fro, getting things for May. When his back was dressed he felt the bed sink as May sat on the edge of it. The heavy odors of violets and magnolias came to him; he was slowly coming back to the world again. He was the same man, but he was coming back somehow changed. He wondered at the strange peace that seeped into his mind and body there in the room with May and Jimmy, with the white folks far off in the darkness.

"Feel bettah, Dan?"

"Ahm awright."

"Yuh hongry?"

"Naw."

He wanted to talk to Jimmy again, to tell him about the black people. But he could not think of words that would say what he wanted to say. He would tell it somehow later on. He began to toss, moving jerkily, more now from restlessness of mind than from the dying fire that still lingered in his body.

XII

Suddenly the doorbell pealed. Taylor turned and saw May and Jimmy looking at each other.

"Somebody at the do," said Jimmy in a tense voice.

"Yuh reckon they white folks?" asked May.

"Yuh bettah go down, Jimmy," said Taylor.

"Ef its any white folks tell em Dans out," said May.

Jimmy's footsteps died away on the stairs. A door slammed. There were faint sounds of voices. Footsteps echoed, came on the stairs, grew loud. Taylor knew that more than one person was coming up. He lifted himself and sat on the edge of the bed.

"Dan, yuh cant git up! Yuhll make yoself sick!"

He ignored her. The door opened and Jimmy ran in.

"Its Brother Bonds, Pa!"

Bonds stood in the doorway with his head wrapped in blood-stained bandages. His face twitched and his eyes stared at something beyond the walls of the room, as though his attention had been riveted once and for always upon one fixed spot.

"Whut happened, Brother?" asked Taylor.

Bonds stared, dazed, with hunched and beaten shoulders. Then he sank to the floor, sobbing softly:

"They beat me! They beat mah chillun! They beat mah wife! They beat us all cause Ah tol em t git outta mah house! Lawd, how long

Yuh gonna let em treat us this way? How long Yuh gonna let em make us suffer?"

May sobbed. Jimmy ran out of the room. Taylor caught him on the stairs.

"Don be a fool, boy! Yuh c mon back here, *now!*"

Jimmy flopped on the edge of a chair and mumbled to himself. The room was quiet save for the rustle of tree leaves that drifted in from the outside and the sound of Bonds sobbing on the floor. As Taylor stood his own suffering was drowned in a sense of widening horror. There was in his mind a vivid picture of all the little dingy huts where black men and women were crouched, afraid to stir out of doors. Bonds stopped crying and looked at Taylor; again that sense of shame spread over Taylor, inside and out. It stirred him to speech.

"Who else they beat, Brother?"

"Seem like everybody, Reveren! Them two Commoonists got beat something terrible n they put em in jail. N Ah heard they kilt one black man whut tried t fight back. They ketchin everbody they kin on the streets n lettin em have it. They ridin up n down in cars. . . ."

Jimmy cursed. The doorbell pealed again.

"Git me a shirt, May!"

"Dan, yuh ain able t do nothin!"

The doorbell pealed again, then again. Taylor started toward the dresser; but May got there before he did and gave him a shirt.

"Dan, be careful!"

"C mon downstairs, Brother Bonds. N yuh, too, Jimmy," said Taylor.

XIII

The church's waiting room was full. Black men and women sat and stood, saying nothing, waiting. Arms were in slings; necks were wrapped in white cloth; legs were bound in bloodstained rags.

"LOOK AT WHUT YUH DONE DONE!" a voice bawled.

It was Deacon Smith. Taylor's eyes went from face to face; he knew them all. Every Sunday they sat in the pews of his church, praying, singing and trusting the God he gave them. The mute eyes and silent lips pinned him to a fiery spot of loneliness. He wanted to protest that loneliness, wanted to break it down; but he did not know how. No parables sprang to his lips now to give form and meaning to his words; alone and naked, he stood ashamed. Jimmy came through the door and placed his hand on his shoulder.

"Its daylight, Pa. The folks is gatherin in the playgroun; theys waitin fer yuh. . . ."

Taylor went into the yard with the crowd at his heels. It was broad daylight and the sun shone. The men in their overalls and the women with children stood about him on all sides, silent. A fat black woman elbowed her way in and faced him.

"Well, Reveren, we done got beat up. Now is we gonna march?"

"Yuh wanna march?" asked Taylor.

"It don make no difference wid me," she said. "Them white folks cant do no mo than theys awready done."

The crowd chimed in.

"N Gawd knows they cant!"

"Ahll go ef the nex one goes!"

"Ah gotta die sometime, so Ah jus as waal die now!"

"They cant kill us but once!"

"Ahm tired anyhow! Ah don care!"

"The white folks says theys gonna meet us at the park!"

Taylor turned to Jimmy.

"Son, git yo boys together n tell em t roun up everbody!"

"Yessuh!"

May was pulling at his sleeve.

"Dan, yuh *cant* do this. . . ."

Deacon Smith pushed his way in and faced him.

"Yuhll never set foot in a church ergin ef yuh lead them po black folks downtown t be killed!"

The crowd surged.

"Ain nobody leadin us nowhere!"

"We goin ourselves!"

"Is we gonna march, Reveren?"

"Yeah; soon as the crowd gits together," said Taylor.

"Ain nobody t blame but yuh ef yuh carry em t their *death!*" warned Deacon Smith.

"How come yuh don shut yo ol big mouth n let the Reveren talk?" asked the fat woman.

"Sistah, Ah got as much right t speak as yuh!"

"Well, don speak to me, yuh hear!"

"Somebody has t say something when ain *nobody* got no sense!"

"Man, don yuh tell me Ah ain got no sense!"

"Yuh sho don ack like it!"

"Ah got as much sense as yuh got!"

"How come yuh don use it?"

The fat sister slapped Deacon Smith straight across his face. Taylor

ran between them and pried them apart. The crowd surged and
screamed.

"Ef he touches Sistah Henry ergin Ahll kill im!"

"He ain got no bisness talkin tha way t a woman!"

Taylor dragged the fat woman toward the gate. The crowd followed, yelling. He stopped and faced them. They circled around,
tightly, asking questions. May had hold of his sleeve. Jimmy came to
him.

"Pa, theys comin!"

Taylor turned and walked across the yard with the crowd following. He took two planks and laid them upon the ends of two saw-
horses and made a solid platform. He climbed up and stood in the
quiet sunshine. He did not know exactly what it was he wanted to
say, but whatever it was he would say it when they were quiet. He
felt neither fear nor joy, just a humble confidence in himself, as
though he were standing before his mirror in his room. Then he was
conscious that they were quiet; he took one swift look over their
heads, heads that stretched away to the street and beyond, a solid
block of black, silent faces; then he looked down, not to the dust,
but just a slight lowering of eyes, as though he were no longer looking at them, but at something within himself.

"Sistahs n Brothers, they tell me the Deacon Boards done voted
me outta the church. Ef thas awright wid yuh, its awright wid me.
The white folks says Ahma bad nigger n they don wanna have nothin
else t do wid me. N thas awright, too. But theres one thing
Ah wanna say. Ah knows how yuh feel erbout bein hongry. N how
yuh feel is no different from how Ah feel. Yuh been waitin a week
fer me t say whut yuh ought t do. Yuh been wonderin how come Ah
didnt tell yuh whut yuh oughta do. Waal . . ."

He paused and looked over the silent crowd; then again his eyes,
his gaze, went inward.

"Sistahs n Brothers, the reason Ah didnt say nothin is cause Ah
didnt know *whut* t say. N the only reason Ahm speakin now is cause
Ah *do* know. Ah know whut t do. . . ."

He paused again, swallowing. The same feeling which had
gripped him so hard last night when he had been talking to Jimmy
seized him. He opened his mouth to continue; his lips moved several
times before words came; and when they did come they fell with a
light and hoarse whisper.

"Sistahs n Brothers, las night the white folks took me out t the
woods. They took me out cause Ah tol em yuh wuz hongry. They
ast me t tell yuh not t march, n Ah tol em Ah wouldnt. Then they

beat me. They tied me t a tree n beat me till Ah couldnt feel no mo. They beat me cause Ah wouldnt tell yuh not t ast fer bread. They said yuhd blieve everthing Ah said. All the time they wuz hepin me, all the time they been givin me favors, they wuz doin it sos *they* could tell *me* t tell *yuh* how t ack! Sistahs n Brothers, as Gawds mah judge, Ah thought Ah wuz doin right when Ah did tha. Ah thought Ah wuz doin right when Ah tol yuh t do the things they said. N cause Ah wouldnt do it this time, they tied me t a tree n beat me till mah blood run. . . ."

Mist covered his eyes. He heard the crowd murmuring; but he did not care if they were murmuring for or against him; he wanted to finish, to say what he had been trying so hard to say for many long hours.

"Sistahs n Brothers, they whipped me n made me take the name of *Gawd* in vain! They made me say mah prayers n beat me n laughed! They beat me till Ah couldnt membah nothin! All las night Ah wuz lyin stretched out on the groun wid mah back burnin. . . . All this mawnin befo day Ah wuz limpin thu white folks streets. Sistahs n Brothers, Ah *know* now! Ah done seen the *sign!* Wes gotta git together. Ah know whut yo life is! Ah done felt it! Its *fire!* Its like the fire tha burned me las night! Its sufferin! Its hell! Ah cant bear this fire erlone! Ah know now whut t do! Wes gotta git close t one ernother! Gawds done spoke! Gawds done sent His sign. Now its fer us t *ack.* . . ."

The crowd started yelling:

"Well go ef yuh go!"

"Wes ready!"

"The white folks says theyll meet us at the park!"

The fat black woman started singing:

"So the sign of the fire by night
"N the sign of the cloud by day
"A-hoverin oer
"Jus befo
"As we journey on our way. . . ."

Taylor got down. He moved with the crowd slowly toward the street. May went with him, looking, wondering, saying nothing. Jimmy was at his side. They sang as they marched. More joined along the way. When they reached the park that separated the white district from the black, the poor whites were waiting. Taylor trembled when he saw them join, swelling the mass that moved toward the town. He looked ahead and saw black and white marching; he

looked behind and saw black and white marching. And still they
sang:

"*So the sign of the fire by night. . .*"

They turned into the street that led to town.

"*N the sign of the cloud by day . . .*"

Taylor saw blue-coated policemen standing lined along the curb.

"*A-hoverin oer . . .*"

Taylor felt himself moving between the silent lines of blue-coated
white men, moving with a sea of placards and banners, moving under
the sun like a pregnant cloud. He said to himself, They ain gonna
bother us! They bettah *not* bother us. . . .

"*Jus befo . . .*"

Across a valley, in front of him, he could see the buildings of the
town sprawled on a hill.

"*As we journey on our way. . . .*"

They were tramping on pavement now. And the blue-coated men
stood still and silent. Taylor saw Deacon Smith standing on the curb,
and Smith's face merged with the faces of the others, meaningless,
lost. Ahead was the City Hall, white and clean in the sunshine. The
autos stopped at the street corners while the crowd passed; and as
they entered the downtown section people massed quietly on the
sidewalks. Then the crowd began to slow, barely moving. Taylor
looked ahead and wondered what was about to happen; he wondered
without fear; as though whatever would or could happen could not
hurt this many-limbed, many-legged, many-handed crowd that was
he. He felt May clinging to his sleeve. Jimmy was peering ahead.
A policeman came running up to him.

"You Taylor?"

"Yessuh," he said quietly, his gaze straight and steady.

"The mayors down front; he wants to see you!"

"Tell im Ahm back here," said Taylor.

"But he wants to see the leader up front!"

"Tell im Ahm back here," said Taylor again.

The man hesitated, then left; they waited, quiet, still. Then the
crowd parted. Taylor saw Mayor Bolton hurrying toward him, his
face beet-red.

"Dan, tell your people not to make any trouble! We dont want
any trouble, Dan. . . ."

"There ain gonna be no trouble, yo honah!"

"Well, tell them they can get food if they go back home peace-
fully. . . ."

"Yuh tell em, yo honah!"

They looked at each other for a moment. Then the mayor turned and walked back. Taylor saw him mount the rear seat of an auto and lift his trembling hands high above the crowd, asking for silence, his face a pasty white.

A baptism of clean joy swept over Taylor. He kept his eyes on the sea of black and white faces. The song swelled louder and vibrated through him. This is the way! he thought. Gawd ain no lie! He ain no lie! His eyes grew wet with tears, blurring his vision: the sky trembled; the buildings wavered as if about to topple; and the earth shook. . . . He mumbled out loud, exultingly:

"Freedom belongs t the strong!"

Index